THE SHO~~
PROUST

An abridged edition of

Remembrance
Of
Things past

Translated by
C.K. Scott Moncrieff

Edited by
Jim Putz

The final section Time Regained
is a new translation by the editor

Copyright © 2021 Jim Putz

All rights reserved. No part of this publication may be reproduced or transmitted in any form or by any means, electronic or mechanical including photocopying, recording or any information storage or retrieval system, without prior permission in writing from the publishers.

The right of Jim Putz to be identified as the editor of this work has been asserted by him in accordance with the Copyright, Designs and Patents Act 1988

First published in the United Kingdom in 2021 by The Cloister House Press

ISBN 978-1-913460-40-2

Cover image: Zipporah, the wife of Moses taken from *The Youth of Moses* by Sandro Botticelli. Swann compares the beauty of Zipporah with Odette. *See pp 79-80.*

CONTENTS

Editor's Introduction	iv
SWANNS WAY	
Overture	1
Combray	19
Swann in Love	59
Place Names: The Name	123
WITHIN A BUDDING GROVE	
Madam Swann at Home	137
Place Names: The Place	182
Seascape, with Frieze of Girls	224
THE GUERMANTES WAY	
Chapter 1	263
Chapter 2	340
CITIES OF THE PLAIN	
Part I	392
Part II	
Chapter 1	403
The Heart's Intermissions	438
Chapter 2	449
Chapter 3	502
Chapter 4	517
THE CAPTIVE	
Chapter 1	521
Chapter II	534
Chapter III	555
THE SWEET CHEAT GONE	
Chapter 1 Grief and Oblivion	561
Chapter 2 Mlle. De Forcheville	574
Chapter 3 Venice	588
Chapter 4 A Fresh Light on Robert De Saint-Loup	597
TIME REGAINED	
Chapter 1 Tansonville	602
Chapter 2 M. de Charlus	608
Chapter 3 Afternoon Party	626

Editor's Introduction

'A la Recherche du Temps Perdu' by Marcel Proust is a magnificent and towering achievement of French literature published in eight volumes between 1913 and 1927 and totalling nearly one and a half million words.

I am not alone in having found it difficult to find the time and concentration needed to be able to read and absorb the rich detail which the books contain but when I eventually succeeded in reading continuously through the whole work, I realised what a powerful structure underlies it and how important the cumulative details of the characters and the events are in understanding the revelation of the narrator's theme at the end of the novel.

In this version I have selected those elements which build up the essential structure and show all the crucial characters, places and themes and omitted everything else. I have not attempted to improve the work by editing, quite the reverse as I have omitted many wonderful passages and descriptions.

The style of the book in its vocabulary and sentence structure is unaltered. Nothing is paraphrased or condensed. Sentences are not cut except very occasionally at the beginning of a new section where there may be some trivial alterations such as substituting a name for a pronoun or omitting a conjunction so that the narrative flows naturally. To assist this, the points at which cuts have been made are not indicated as they are so numerous and hopefully not too self evident.

Proust himself encouraged wide publication of excerpts of his work and approved what he described as " a montage of selected passages to show a coherent whole, which is not diffused and will make one want to read the whole book" which is what this book aims to be.

My hope is that the reader, having read this edition which is less than a quarter of the original in length, will feel inspired to go to the full text, be able to enjoy individual sections in the knowledge of where they fit into the whole and to understand any passing references to Proust's work.

Jim Putz

SWANN'S WAY

OVERTURE

For a long time I used to go to bed early. Sometimes, when I had put out my candle, my eyes would close so quickly that I had not even time to say "I'm going to sleep." And half an hour later the thought that it was time to go to sleep would awaken me; I would try to put away the book which I imagined was still in my hands, and to blow out the light; I had been thinking all the time, while I was asleep, of what I had just been reading, but my thoughts had run into a channel of their own, until I myself seemed actually to have become the subject of my book: a church, a quartet, the rivalry between François 1 and Charles V. This impression would persist for some moments after I was awake; it did not disturb my mind, but it lay like scales upon my eyes and prevented them from registering the fact that the candle was no longer burning. Then it would begin to seem intelligible, as the thoughts of a former existence must be to a reincarnate spirit; the subject of my book would separate itself from me, leaving me free to choose whether I would form part of it or no; and at the same time my sight would return and I would be astonished to find myself in a state of darkness, pleasant and restful enough for the eyes, and even more, perhaps, for my mind.

I would lay my cheeks gently against the comfortable cheeks of my pillow, as plump and blooming as the cheeks of babyhood. Or I would strike a match to look at my watch. Nearly midnight. The hour when an invalid, who has been obliged to start on a journey and to sleep in a strange hotel, awakens in a moment of illness and sees with glad relief a streak of daylight showing under his bedroom door. Oh, joy of joys it is morning. The servants will be about in a minute, he can ring, and someone will come to look after him. The thought of being made comfortable gives him strength to endure his pain. He is certain he heard footsteps: they come nearer, and then die away. The ray of light beneath his door is extinguished. It is midnight; someone has turned out the gas; the last servant has gone to bed, and he must lie all night in agony with no one to bring him any help.

At Combray, as every afternoon ended, long before the time when I should have to go up to bed, and to lie there, unsleeping, far from my mother and grandmother, my bedroom became the fixed point on which my melancholy and anxious thoughts were centred. Someone had had the happy idea of giving me, to distract me on evenings when I seemed abnormally wretched, a magic lantern, which used to be set on top of my lamp while we waited for dinnertime to come: in the manner of the master-builders and glasspainters of gothic days it substituted for the opaqueness of my walls an impalpable iridescence, supernatural phenomena of many colours, in which legends were depicted, as on a shifting and transitory window. But my sorrows were only increased, because this change of lighting destroyed, as nothing else could have done, the customary impression I had formed of my room, thanks to which the room itself, but for the torture of having to go to bed in it, had become quite endurable. For now I no longer recognised it, and I became uneasy, as though I were in a room in some hotel or furnished lodging, in a place where I had just arrived, by train, for the first time.

Riding at a jerky trot, Golo, his mind filled with an infamous design, issued from the little three-cornered forest which dyed dark green the slope of a convenient hill, and advanced by leaps and bounds towards the castle of poor Geneviève de Brabant. This castle was cut off short by a curved line which was in fact the circumference of one of the transparent ovals in the slides which were pushed into position through a slot in the lantern. It was only the wing of a castle, and in front of it stretched a moor on which Geneviève stood, lost in contemplation, wearing a blue girdle. The castle and the moor were yellow, but I could tell their colour without waiting to see them, for before the slides made their appearance the old-gold sonorous name of Brabant had given me an unmistakable clue. Golo stopped for a moment and listened sadly to the little speech read aloud by my great-aunt, which he seemed perfectly to understand, for he modified his attitude with a docility not devoid of a degree of majesty, so as to conform to the indications given in the text; then he rode away at the same jerky trot. And nothing could arrest his slow progress. If the lantern were moved I could still distinguish Golo's horse advancing across the window curtains, swelling out with their curves and diving into their folds. The body of Golo himself, being of the same supernatural substance as his steed's, overcame all material obstacles— everything that seemed to bar his way—by taking each as it might be a skeleton and embodying it in himself: the doorhandle, for instance, over which, adapting itself at once, would float invincibly his red cloak or his pale face, never losing its nobility or its melancholy, never showing any sign of trouble at such a transubstantiation.

As soon as the dinner-bell rang I would run down to the diningroom, where the big hanging lamp, ignorant of Golo and Bluebeard but well acquainted with my family and the dish of stewed beef, shed the same light as on every other evening; and I would fall into the arms of my mother, whom the misfortunes of Genevière de Brabant had made all the dearer to me, just as the crimes of Golo had driven me to a more than ordinarily scrupulous examination of my own conscience.

But after dinner, alas, I was soon obliged to leave Mamma, who stayed talking with the others, in the garden if it was fine, or in the little parlour where everyone took shelter when it was wet. Everyone except my grandmother, who held that "It is a pity to shut oneself indoors in the country," and used to carry on endless discussions with my father on the very wettest days, because he would send me up to my room with a book instead of letting me stay out of doors. "That is not the way to make him strong and active," she would say sadly, "especially this little man, who needs all the strength and character that he can get." My father would shrug his shoulders and study the barometer, for he took an interest in meteorology, while my mother, keeping very quiet so as not to disturb him, looked at him with tender respect, but not too hard, not wishing to penetrate the mysteries of his superior mind. But my grandmother, in all weathers, even when the rain was coming down in torrents and Françoise had rushed indoors with the precious wicker armchairs, so that they should not get soaked, you would see my grandmother pacing the deserted garden, lashed by the storm, pushing back her grey hair in disorder so that her brows might be more free to imbibe the life-giving draughts of wind and rain. She would say, "At last one can breathe!" and would run up and down the soaking paths—too straight and symmetrical for her liking, owing to the want of any feeling for nature in the new gardener, whom my father had been asking all morning if the weather were going to improve—with her keen, jerky little step regulated by the various effects wrought upon her soul by the intoxication of the storm, the force of hygiene, the stupidity of my education and of symmetry in gardens, rather than by any anxiety (for that was quite unknown to her) to save her plum-coloured skirt from the spots of mud under which it would gradually disappear to a depth which always provided her maid with a fresh problem and filled her with fresh despair.

My sole consolation when I went upstairs for the night was that Mamma would come in and kiss me after I was in bed. But this good night lasted for so short a time: she went down again so soon that the moment in which I heard her climb the stairs, and then caught the sound of her garden dress of blue muslin, from which hung little tassels of plaited straw, rustling along the double-doored corridor, was for me a moment of the keenest sorrow. So much did I love that good night that I reached the stage of hoping that it would come as late as possible, so as to prolong the time of respite during which Mamma would not yet have appeared. Sometimes when, after kissing me, she opened the door to go, I longed to call her back, to say to her "Kiss me just once again," but I knew that then she would at once look displeased, for the concession which she made to my wretchedness and agitation in coming up to me with this kiss of peace always annoyed my father, who thought such ceremonies absurd, and she would have liked to try to induce me to outgrow the need, the custom of having her there at all, which was a very different thing from letting the custom grow up of my asking her for an additional kiss when she was already crossing the threshold. And to see her look displeased destroyed all the sense of tranquility she had brought me a moment before, when she bent her loving face down over my bed, and held it out to me like a Host, for an act of Communion in which my lips might drink deeply the sense of her real presence, and with it the power to sleep. But those evenings on which Mamma stayed so short a time in my room were sweet indeed compared to those on which we had guests to dinner, and therefore she did not come at all. Our 'guests' were practically limited to M. Swann, who, apart from a few passing strangers, was almost the only person who ever came to the house at Combray, sometimes to a neighbourly dinner (but less frequently since his unfortunate marriage, as my family did not care to receive his wife) and sometimes after dinner, uninvited. On those evenings when, as we sat in front of the house beneath the big chestnut-tree and round the iron table, we heard, from the far end of the garden, not the large and noisy rattle which heralded and deafened as he approached with its ferruginous, interminable, frozen sound any member of the household who had put it out of action by coming in 'without ringing', but the double peal—timid, oval, gilded—of the visitors' bell, everyone would at once exclaim "A visitor! Who in the world can it be?" but they knew quite well that it could only be M. Swann. My great-aunt, speaking in a loud voice, to set an example, in a tone which she endeavoured to make sound natural, would tell the others not to whisper so; that nothing could be more unpleasant for a stranger coming in, who would be led to think that people were saying things about him which he was not meant to hear; and then my grandmother would be sent out as a scout, always happy to find an excuse for an additional turn in the garden, which she would utilise to remove surreptitiously, as she passed, the stakes of a rose-tree or two, so as to make the roses look a little more natural, as a mother might run her hand through her boy's hair, after the barber had smoothed it down, to make it stick out properly round his head.

For many years, especially before his marriage—M. Swann the younger came often to see them at Combray; my great-aunt and grandparents never suspected that he had entirely ceased to live in the kind of society which his family had frequented, or that, under the sort of incognito which the name of Swann gave him among us, they were harbouring—with the complete innocence of a family of honest innkeepers who have in their midst some distinguished highwayman and never know it—one of the smartest members of the Jockey Club, a particular friend of the Comte de Paris and of the Prince of Wales, and one of the men most sought after in the aristocratic world of the Faubourg Saint-Germain.

Our utter ignorance of the brilliant part which Swann was playing in the world of fashion was, of course, due in part to his own reserve and discretion, but also to the fact that middle-class people in those days took what was almost a Hindu view of society, which they held to consist of sharply defined castes, so that everyone at his birth found himself called to that station in life which his parents already occupied, and nothing, except the chance of a brilliant career or of a 'good' marriage, could extract you from that station or admit you to a superior caste. M. Swann, the father, had been a stockbroker; and so 'young Swann' found himself immured for life in a caste where one's fortune, as in a list of taxpayers, varied between such and such limits of income. We knew the people with whom his father had associated, and so we knew his own associates, the people with whom he was 'in a position to mix'. If he knew other people besides, those were youthful acquaintances on whom the old friends of the family, like my relatives, shut their eyes all the more good-naturedly that Swann himself, after he was left an orphan, still came most faithfully to see us; but we would have been ready to wager that the people outside our acquaintance whom Swann knew were of the sort to whom he would not have dared to raise his hat, had he met them while he was walking with ourselves. Had there been such a thing as a determination to apply to Swann a social coefficient peculiar to himself, as distinct from all the other sons of other stockbrokers in his father's position, his coefficient would have been rather lower than theirs, because, leading a very simple life, and having always had a craze for 'antiques' and pictures, he now lived and piled up his collections in an old house which my grandmother longed to visit, but which stood on the Quai d'Orléans, a neighbourhood in which my great-aunt thought it most degrading to be quartered

But if anyone had suggested to my aunt that this Swann, who, in his capacity as the son of old M. Swann, was fully qualified to be received by any of the 'upper middle class', the most respected barristers and solicitors of Paris (though he was perhaps a trifle inclined to let this hereditary privilege go into abeyance), had another almost secret existence of a wholly different kind: that when he left our house in Paris, saying that he must go home to bed, he would no sooner have turned the corner than he would stop, retrace his steps, and be off to some drawing-room on whose like no stockbroker or associate of stockbrokers had ever set eyes—that would have seemed to my aunt as extraordinary as, to a woman of wider reading, the thought of being herself on terms of intimacy with Aristaeus, of knowing that he would, when he had finished his conversation with her, plunge deep into the realms of Thetis, into an empire veiled from mortal eyes, in which Virgil depicts him as being received with open arms; or—to be content with an image more likely to have occurred to her, for she had seen it painted on the plates we used for biscuits at Combray—as the thought of having had to dinner Ali Baba, who, as soon as he found himself alone and unobserved, would make his way into the cave, resplendent with its unsuspected treasures.

One day when he had come to see us after dinner in Paris, and had begged pardon for being in evening clothes, Françoise, when he had gone, told us that she had got it from his coachman that he had been dining "with a princess." "A pretty sort of princess," drawled my aunt; "I know them," and she shrugged her shoulders without raising her eyes from her knitting, serenely ironical.

Altogether, my aunt used to treat him with scant ceremony. Since she was of the opinion that he ought to feel flattered by our invitations, she thought it only right and proper that he should never come to see us in summer without a basket of peaches or raspberries from his garden, and that from each of his visits to Italy he should bring back some photographs of old masters for me.

And yet one day, when my grandmother had gone to ask some favour of a lady whom she had known at the Sacré Coeur (and with whom, because of our caste theory, she had not cared to keep up any degree of intimacy in spite of several common interests), the Marquise de Villeparisis, of the famous house of Bouillon, this lady had said to her: "I think you know M. Swann very well; he is a great friend of my nephews, the des Laumes.

Now, the effect of that remark about Swann had been, not to raise him in my great-aunt's estimation, but to lower Mme de Villeparisis. It appeared that the deference which, on my grandmother's authority, we owed to Mme. de Villeparisis imposed on her the reciprocal obligation to do nothing that would render her less worthy of our regard and that she had failed in her duty in becoming aware of Swann's existence and in allowing members of her family to associate with him. "How should she know Swann? A lady who, you always made out, was related to Marshal MacMahon!" This view of Swann's social atmosphere which prevailed in my family seemed to be confirmed later on by his marriage with a woman of the worst class, you might almost say a 'fast' woman, whom, to do him justice he never attempted to introduce to us, for he continued to come to us alone though he came more and more seldom; but from whom they thought they could establish, on the assumption that he had found her there, the circle, unknown to them, in which he ordinarily moved.

But the only one of us in whom the prospect of Swann's arrival gave rise to an unhappy foreboding was myself . And that was because on the evenings when there were visitors, or just M. Swann in the house, Mamma did not come up to my room. I did not, at that time, have dinner with the family: I came out to the garden after dinner, and at nine I said good night and went to bed. But on these evenings I used to dine earlier than the others, and to come in afterwards and sit at table until eight o'clock, when it was understood that I must go upstairs; that frail and precious kiss which Mamma used always to leave upon my lips when I was in bed and just going to sleep, I had to take with me from the dining-room to my own, and to keep inviolate all the time that it took me to undress, without letting its sweet charm be broken, without letting its volatile essence diffuse itself and evaporate. I never took my eyes off my mother. I knew that when they were at table I should not be permitted to stay there for the whole of dinner-time, and that Mamma, for fear of annoying my father, would not allow me to give her in public the series of kisses that she would have had in my room. And so I promised myself that in the dining-room, as they began to eat and drink and as I felt the hour approach, I would put beforehand into this kiss, which was bound to be so brief and stealthy in execution, everything that my own efforts could put into it: would look out very carefully first the exact spot on her cheek where I would imprint it, and would so prepare my thoughts that I might be able, thanks to these mental preliminaries, to consecrate the whole of the minute Mamma would allow me, to the sensation of her cheek against my lips, as a painter who can have his subject for short sittings only, prepares his palette, and from what he remembers and from rough notes does in advance everything which he possibly can do in the sitter's absence. But to-night, before the dinner-bell had sounded, my grandfather said with unconscious cruelty: "The little man looks tired; he'd better go up to bed. Besides, we are dining late to-night."

And my father, who was less scrupulous than my grandmother or mother in observing the letter of a treaty, went on: "Yes; run along; to bed with you." I would have kissed Mamma then and there, but at that moment the dinner-bell rang. "No, no, leave your mother alone. You've said good night quite enough. These exhibitions are absurd. Go on upstairs."

Once in my room I had to stop every loophole, to close the shutters, to dig my own grave as I turned down the bedclothes, to wrap myself in the shroud of my nightshirt. But before burying myself in the iron bed which had been placed there because, on summer nights, I was too hot among the rep curtains of the four-poster, I was stirred to revolt, and attempted the desperate stratagem of a condemned prisoner. I wrote to my mother begging her to come upstairs for an important reason which I could not put in writing. My fear was that Françoise, my aunt's cook who used to be put in charge of me when I was at Combray, might refuse to take my note. I had a suspicion that, in her eyes, to carry a message to my mother when there was a stranger in the room would appear flatly inconceivable, just as it would be for the door-keeper of a theatre to hand a letter to an actor upon the stage. But to give myself one chance of success I lied without hesitation, telling her that it was not in the least myself who had wanted to write to Mamma, but Mamma who, on saying good night to me, had begged me not to forget to send her an answer about something she had asked me to find, and that she would certainly be very angry if this note were not taken to her. I think that Françoise disbelieved me, for, like those primitive men whose senses were so much keener than our own, she could immediately detect, by signs imperceptible by the rest of us, the truth or falsehood of anything that we might wish to conceal from her. She studied the envelope for five minutes as though an examination of the paper itself and the look of my handwriting could enlighten her as to the nature of the contents, or tell her to which article of her code she ought to refer the matter. Then she went out with an air of resignation which seemed to imply : "What a dreadful thing for parents to have a child like this!"

A moment later she returned to say that they were still at the ice stage and that it was impossible for the butler to deliver the note at once, in front of everybody; but that when the finger-bowls were put round he would find a way of slipping it into Mamma's hand. At once my anxiety subsided; it was now no longer (as it had been a moment ago) until to-morrow that I had lost my mother, for my little line was going to annoy her, no doubt, and doubly so because this contrivance would make me ridiculous in Swann's eyes—but was going all the same to admit me, invisibly and by stealth, into the same room as herself, was going to whisper from me into her ear; for that forbidden and unfriendly dining-room, where but a moment ago the ice itself—with burned nuts in it—and the finger-bowls seemed to me to be concealing pleasures that were mischievous and of a mortal sadness because Mamma was tasting of them and I was far away, had opened its doors to me and, like a ripe fruit which bursts through its skin, was going to pour out into my intoxicated heart the gushing sweetness of Mamma's attention while she was reading what I had written. Now I was no longer separated from her; the barriers were down; an exquisite thread was binding us. Besides, that was not all, for surely Mamma would come.

My mother did not appear, but with no attempt to safeguard my self-respect (which depended upon her keeping up the fiction that she had asked me to let her know the result of my search for something or other) made Françoise tell me, in so many words : "There is no answer"—words I have so often, since then, heard the hall-porters in 'mansions' and the flunkeys in gambling-clubs and the like, repeat to some poor girl, who replies in bewilderment "What! he's said nothing? It's not possible. You did give him my letter, didn't you ? Very well, I shall wait a little longer." And just as she invariably protests that she does not need the extra gas which the porter offers to light for her, and sits on there, hearing nothing further, except an occasional remark on the weather which the porter exchanges with a messenger whom he will send off suddenly, when he notices the time, to put some customer`s wine on the ice; so, having declined Françoise's offer to make me some tea or to stay beside me, I let her go off again to the servants' hall, and lay down and shut my eyes, and tried not to hear the voices of my family who were drinking their coffee in the garden.

But after a few seconds I realised that, by writing that line to Mamma, by approaching ---at the risk of making her angry—so near to her that I felt I could reach out and grasp the moment in which I should see her again, I had cut myself off from the possibility of going to sleep until I actually had seen her, and my heart began to beat more and more painfully as I increased my agitation by ordering myself to keep calm and to acquiesce in my ill-fortune. Then, suddenly, my anxiety subsided, a feeling of intense happiness coursed through me, as when a strong medicine begins to take effect and one's pain vanishes: I had formed a resolution to abandon all attempts to go to sleep without seeing Mamma, and had decided to kiss her at all costs, even with the certainty of being in disgrace with her for long afterwards, when she herself came up to bed.

If I went out to meet my mother as she herself came up to bed, and when she saw that I had remained up so as to say good night to her again in the passage, I should not be allowed to stay in the house a day longer, I should be packed off to school next morning; so much was certain. Very good, had I been obliged, the next moment, to hurl myself out of the window, I should still have preferred such a fate. For what I wanted now was Mamma, and to say good night to her. I had gone too far along the road which led to the realisation of this desire to be able to retrace my steps.

I could hear my parents' footsteps as they went with Swann; and, when the rattle of the gate assured me that he had really gone, I crept to the window. Mamma was asking my father if he had thought the lobster good, and whether M. Swann had had some more of the coffee-and-pistachio ice. "I thought it rather so-so," she was saying; "next time we shall have to try another flavour."

My father and mother were left alone and sat down for a moment; then my father said: "Well, shall we go up to bed?"

"As you wish, dear, though I don't feel in the least like sleeping. I don't know why; it can't be the coffee-ice—it wasn't strong enough to keep me awake like this. But I see a light in the servants' hall: poor Françoise has been sitting up for me, so I will get her to unhook me while you go and undress."

My mother opened the latticed door which led from the hall to the staircase. Presently I heard her coming upstairs to close her window. I went quietly into the passage; my heart was beating so violently that I could hardly move, but at least it was throbbing no longer with anxiety, but with terror and with joy. I saw in the well of the stair a light coming upwards, from Mamma's candle. Then I saw Mamma herself: I threw myself upon her. For an instant she looked at me in astonishment, not realising what could have happened. Then her face assumed an expression of anger. She said not a single word to me; and, for that matter, I used to go for days on end without being spoken to, for far less offences than this. A single word from Mamma would have been an admission that further intercourse with me was within the bounds of possibility, and that might perhaps have appeared to me more terrible still, as indicating that, with such a punishment as was in store for me, mere silence, and even anger, were relatively puerile.

A word from her then would have implied the false calm in which one converses with a servant to whom one has just decided to give notice; the kiss one bestows on a son who is being packed off to enlist, which would have been denied him if it had merely been a matter of being angry with him for a few days. But she heard my father coming from the dressing-room, where he had gone to take off his clothes, and, to avoid the 'scene' which he would make if he saw me, she said, in a voice half-stifled by her anger "Run away at once. Don't let your father see you standing there like a crazy jane!"

But I begged her again to "Come and say good night to me!" terrified as I saw the light from my father's candle already creeping up the wall, but also making use of his approach as a means of blackmail, in the hope that my mother, not wishing him to find me there, as find me he must if she continued to hold out, would give in to me, and say: "Go back to your room. I will come."

Too late: my father was upon us. Instinctively I murmured, though no one heard me, "I am done for!"

I was not, however. My father used constantly to refuse to let me do things which were quite clearly allowed by the more liberal charters granted me by my mother and grandmother, because he paid no heed to 'Principles', and because in his sight there were no such things as 'Rights of Man'. For some quite irrelevant reason, or for no reason at all, he would at the last moment prevent me from taking some particular walk, one so regular and so consecrated to my use that to deprive me of it was a clear breach of faith; or again, as he had done this evening, long before the appointed hour he would snap out: "Run along up to bed now; no excuses!" But then again, simply because he was devoid of principles (in my grandmother's sense), he could not, properly speaking, be called inexorable. He looked at me for a moment with an air of annoyance and surprise, and then when Mamma had told him, not without some embarrassment, what had happened, said to her: "Go along with him, then; you said just now that you didn't feel like sleep, so stay in his room for a little. I don't need anything."

"But, dear," my mother answered timidly, "whether or not I feel like sleep is not the point; we must not make the child accustomed ...."

"There's no question of making him accustomed," said my father, with a shrug of the shoulders; "you can see quite well that the child is unhappy. After all, we aren't gaolers. You'll end by making him ill, and a lot of good that will do. There are two beds in his room; tell Françoise to make up the big one for you, and stay beside him for the rest of the night. I'm off to bed, anyhow; I'm not nervous like you. Good night."

It was impossible for me to thank my father; what he called my sentimentality would have exasperated him. I stood there, not daring to move; he was still confronting us, an immense figure in his white nightshirt, crowned with the pink and violet scarf of Indian cashmere in which, since he had begun to suffer from neuralgia, he used to tie up his head, standing like Abraham in the engraving after Benozzo Gozzoli which M. Swann had given me, telling Sarah that she must tear herself away from Isaac. Many years have passed since that night. The wall of the staircase, up which I had watched the light of his candle gradually climb, was long ago demolished. And in myself, too, many things have perished which, I imagined, would last for ever, and new structures have arisen, giving birth to new sorrows and new joys which in those days I could not have foreseen, just as now the old are difficult of comprehension. It is a long time, too, since my father has been able to tell Mamma to "Go with the child." Never again will such hours be possible for me. But of late I have been increasingly able to catch, if I listen attentively, the sound of the sobs which I had the strength to control in my father's presence, and which broke out only when I found myself alone with Mamma. Actually, their echo has never ceased: it is only because life is now growing more and more quiet round about me that I hear them afresh, like those convent bells which are so effectively drowned during the day by the noises of the streets that one would suppose them to have been stopped for ever, until the sound out again through the silent evening air.

Mamma spent that night in my room: when I had just committed a sin so deadly that I was waiting to be banished from the household, my parents gave me a far greater concession than I should ever have won as the reward of a good action. Even at the moment when it manifested itself in this crowning mercy, my father's conduct towards me was still somewhat arbitrary, and regardless of my deserts, as was characteristic of him and due to the fact that his actions were generally dictated by chance expediencies rather than based on any formal plan. And perhaps even what I called his strictness, when he sent me off to bed, deserved that title less, really, than my mother's or grandmother's attitude, for his nature, which in some respects differed more than theirs from my own, had probably prevented him from guessing, until then, how wretched I was every evening, a thing which my mother and grandmother knew well; but they loved me enough to be unwilling to spare me that suffering, which they hoped to teach me to overcome, so as to reduce my nervous sensibility and to strengthen my will. As for my father, whose affection for me was of another kind, I doubt if he would have shewn so much courage, for as soon as he had grasped the fact that I was unhappy he had said to my mother: "Go and comfort him."

Mamma stayed all night in my room, and it seemed that she did not wish to mar by recrimination those hours, so different from anything that I had had a right to expect; for when Françoise (who guessed that something extraordinary must have happened when she saw Mamma sitting by my side, holding my hand and letting me cry unchecked) said to her: "But, Madame, what is little Master crying for?" she replied : "Why, Françoise, he doesn't know himself: it is his nerves. Make up the big bed for me quickly and then go off to your own." And thus for the first time my unhappiness was regarded no longer as a fault for which I must be punished, but as an involuntary evil which had been officially recognised, a nervous condition for which I was in no way responsible: I had the consolation that I need no longer mingle apprehensive scruples with the bitterness of my tears; I could weep henceforward without sin. I felt no small degree of pride, either, in Françoise's presence at this return to humane conditions which, not an hour after Mamma had refused to come up to my room and had sent the snubbing message that I was to go to sleep, raised me to the dignity of a grown-up person, brought me of a sudden to a sort of puberty of sorrow, to emancipation from tears. I ought then to have been happy; I was not. It struck me that my mother had just made a first concession which must have been painful to her, that it was a first step down from the ideal she had formed for me, and that for the first time she, with all her courage, had to confess herself beaten. It struck me that if I had just scored a victory it was over her; that I had succeeded, as sickness or sorrow or age might have succeeded, in relaxing her will, in altering her judgment that this evening opened a new era, must remain a black date in the calendar. And if I had dared now, I should have said to Mamma: "No, I don't want you; you mustn't sleep here." But I was conscious of the practical wisdom, of what would be called nowadays the realism with which she tempered the ardent idealism of my grandmother's nature, and I knew that now the mischief was done she would prefer to let me enjoy the soothing pleasure of her company, and not to disturb father again. Certainly my mother's beautiful features seemed to shine again with youth that evening, as she sat gently holding my hands and trying to check my tears; but, just for that reason, it seemed to me that this should not have happened; her anger would have been less difficult to endure than this new kindness which my childhood had not known; I felt that I had with an impious and secret finger traced a first wrinkle upon her soul and made the first white hair shew upon her head. This thought redoubled my sobs, and then I saw that Mamma, who had never allowed herself to go to any length of tenderness with me, was suddenly overcome by my tears and had to struggle to keep back her own. Then, as she saw that I had noticed this, she said to me, with a smile "Why, my little buttercup, my little canary-boy he's going to make Mamma as silly as himself if this goes on. Look, since you can't sleep, and Mamma can't either, we mustn't go on in this stupid way; we must do something; I'll get one of your books." But I had none there. "Would you like me to get out the books now that your grandmother is going to give you for your birthday? Just think it over first, and don't be disappointed if there is nothing new for you then."

I was only too delighted, and Mamma went to find a parcel of books in which I could not distinguish, through the paper in which it was wrapped, any more than its squareness and size, but which, even at this first glimpse, brief and obscure as it was, bade fair to eclipse already the paintbox of last New Year's Day and the silkworms of the year before. It contained *La Mare au Diable, François le Champi, La Petite Fadette*, and *Les Maitres Sonneurs*. My grandmother, as I learned afterwards, had at first chosen Musset's poems, a volume of Rousseau, and *Indiana;* for while she considered light reading as unwholesome as sweets and cakes, she did not reflect that the strong breath of genius must have upon the very soul of a child an influence at once more dangerous and less quickening than those of fresh air and country breezes upon his body. But when my father had seemed almost to regard her as insane on learning the names of the books she proposed to give me, she had journeyed back by herself to Jouy-le-Vicomte to the bookseller's, so that there should be no fear of my not having my present in time (it was a burning hot day, and she had come home so unwell that the doctor had warned my mother not to allow her again to tire herself in that way), and had there fallen back upon the four pastoral novels of George Sand.

"My dear," she had said to Mamma, "I could not allow myself to give the child anything that was not well written." The truth was that she could never make up her mind to purchase anything from which no intellectual profit was to be derived, and, above all, that profit which good things bestowed on us by teaching us to seek our pleasures elsewhere than in the barren satisfaction of worldly wealth. Even when she had to make someone a present of the kind called 'useful', when she had to give an armchair or some table-silver or a walking-stick, she would choose 'antiques,' as though their long desuetude had effaced from them any semblance of utility and fitted them rather to instruct us in the lives of the men of other days than to serve the common requirements of our own.

In precisely the same way the pastoral novels of George Sand, which she was giving me for my birthday, were regular lumber-rooms of antique furniture, full of expressions that have fallen out of use and returned as imagery, such as one finds now only in country dialects. And my grandmother had bought them in preference to other books, just as she would have preferred to take a house that had a gothic dovecot, or some other such piece of antiquity as would have a pleasant effect on the mind, filling it with a nostalgic longing for impossible journeys through the realms of time.

Mamma sat down by my bed; she had chosen *François le Champi*, whose reddish cover and incomprehensible title gave it a distinct personality in my eyes and a mysterious attraction. I had not then read any real novels. I had heard it said that George Sand was a typical novelist.

My agony was soothed; I let myself be borne upon the current of this gentle night on which I had my mother by my side. I knew that such a night could not be repeated; that the strongest desire I had in the world, namely, to keep my mother in my room through the sad hours of darkness, ran too much counter to general requirements and to the wishes of others for such a concession as had been granted me this evening to be anything but a rare and casual exception. To-morrow night I should again be the victim of anguish and Mamma would not stay by my side. But when these storms of anguish grew calm I could no longer realise their existence; besides, to-morrow evening was still a long way off; I reminded myself that I should still have time to think about things, albeit that remission of time could bring me no access of power, albeit the coming event was in no way dependent upon the exercise of my will, and seemed not quite inevitable only because it was still separated from me by this short interval.

And so it was that, for a long time afterwards, when I lay awake at night and revived old memories of Combray, I saw no more of it than this sort of luminous panel, sharply defined against a vague and shadowy background, like the panels which a Bengal fire or some electric sign will illuminate and dissect from the front of a building the other parts of which remain plunged in darkness: broad enough at its base, the little parlour, the dining-room, the alluring shadows of the path along which would come M. Swann, the unconscious author of my sufferings, the hall through which I would journey to the first step of that staircase, so hard to climb, which constituted, all by itself, the tapering elevation of an irregular pyramid; and, at the summit, my bedroom, with the little passage through whose glazed door Mamma would enter; in a word, seen always at the same evening hour, isolated from all its possible surroundings, detached and solitary against its shadowy background, the bare minimum of scenery necessary (like the setting one sees printed at the head of an old play, for its performance in the provinces) to the drama of my undressing, as though all Combray had consisted of but two floors joined by a slender staircase, and as though there had been no time there but seven o'clock at night. I must own that I could have assured any questioner that Combray did include other scenes and did exist at other hours than these. But since the facts which I should then have recalled would have been prompted only by an exercise of the will, by my intellectual memory, and since the pictures which that kind of memory shews us of the past preserve nothing of the past itself, I should never have had any wish to ponder over this residue of Combray. To me it was in reality all dead.

Permanently dead? Very possibly.

There is a large element of hazard in these matters, and a second hazard, that of our own death, often prevents us from awaiting for any length of time the favours of the first.

I feel that there is much to be said for the Celtic belief that the souls of those whom we have lost are held captive in some inferior being, in an animal, in a plant, in some inanimate object, and so effectively lost to us until the day (which to many never comes) when we happen to pass by the tree or to obtain possession of the object which forms their prison. Then they start and tremble, they call us by our name, and as soon as we have recognised their voice the spell is broken. We have delivered them: they have overcome death and return to share our life.

And so it is with our own past. It is a labour in vain to attempt to recapture it: all the efforts of our intellect must prove futile. The past is hidden somewhere outside the realm, beyond the reach of intellect, in some material object (in the sensation which that material object will give us) which we do not suspect. And as for that object, it depends on chance whether we come upon it or not before we ourselves must die.

Many years had elapsed during which nothing of Combray, save what was comprised in the theatre and the drama of my going to bed there, had any existence for me, when one day in winter, as I came home, my mother, seeing that I was cold, offered me some tea, a thing I did not ordinarily take. I declined at first, and then, for no particular reason, changed my mind. She sent out for one of those short, plump little cakes called 'petites madeleines', which look as though they had been moulded in the fluted scallop of a pilgrim's shell. And soon, mechanically, weary after a dull day with the prospect of a depressing morrow, I raised to my lips a spoonful of the tea in which I had soaked a morsel of the cake. No sooner had the warm liquid, and the crumbs with it, touched my palate than a shudder ran through my whole body, and I stopped, intent upon the extraordinary changes that were taking place. An exquisite pleasure had invaded my senses, but individual, detached, with no suggestion of its origin. And at once the vicissitudes of life had become indifferent to me, its disasters innocuous, its brevity illusory—this new sensation having had on me the effect which love has of filling me with a precious essence; or rather this essence was not in me, it was myself. I had ceased now to feel mediocre, accidental, mortal. Whence could it have come to me, this allpowerful joy? I was conscious that it was connected with the taste of tea and cake, but that it infinitely transcended those savours, could not, indeed, be of the same nature as theirs. Whence did it come? What did it signify? How could I seize upon and define it?

I drink a second mouthful, in which I find nothing more than in the first, a third, which gives me rather less than the second. It is time to stop; the potion is losing its magic. It is plain that the object of my quest, the truth, lies not in the cup but in myself. The tea has called up in me, but does not itself understand, and can only repeat indefinitely, with a gradual loss of strength, the same testimony; which I, too, cannot interpret, though I hope at least to be able to call upon the tea for it again and to find it there presently, intact and at my disposal, for my final enlightenment. I put down my cup and examine my own mind. It is for it to discover the truth. But how? What an abyss of uncertainty whenever the mind feels that some part of it has strayed beyond its own borders; when it, the seeker, is at once the dark region through which it must go seeking, where all its equipment will avail it nothing. Seek? More than that: create. It is face to face with something which does not so far exist, to which it alone can give reality and substance, which it alone can bring into the light of day.

And I begin again to ask myself what it could have been, this unremembered state which brought with it no logical proof of its existence, but only the sense that it was a happy, that it was a real state in whose presence other states of consciousness melted and vanished. I decide to attempt to make it reappear. I retrace my thoughts to the moment at which I drank the first spoonful of tea. I find again the same state; illumined by no fresh light. I compel my mind to make one further effort, to follow and recapture once again the fleeting sensation. And that nothing may interrupt it in its course I shut out every obstacle, every extraneous idea, I stop my ears and inhibit all attention to the sounds which come from the next room. And then, feeling that my mind is growing fatigued without having any success to report, I compel it for a change to enjoy that distraction which I have just denied it, to think of other things, to rest and refresh itself before the supreme attempt. And then for the second time I clear an empty space in front of it. I place in position before my mind's eye the still recent taste of that first mouthful, and I feel something start within me, something that leaves its resting place and attempts to rise, something that has been embedded like an anchor at a great depth; I do not know yet what it is, but I can feel it mounting slowly; I can measure the resistance, I can hear the echo of great spaces traversed.

Undoubtedly what is thus palpitating in the depths of my being must be the image, the visual memory which, being linked to that taste, has tried to follow it into my conscious mind. But its struggles are too far off, too much confused; scarcely can I perceive the colourless reflection in which are blended the uncapturable whirling medley of radiant hues, and I cannot distinguish its form, cannot invite it, as the one possible interpreter, to translate to me the evidence of its contemporary, its inseparable paramour, the taste of cake soaked in tea; cannot ask it to inform me what special circumstance is in question, of what period in my past life.

And suddenly the memory returns. The taste was that of the little crumb of madeleine which on Sunday mornings at Combray (because on those mornings I did not go out before church time), when I went to say good day to her in her bed-room, my aunt Léonie used to give me, dipping it first in her own cup of real or of lime-flower tea. The sight of the little madeleine had recalled nothing to my mind before I tasted it; perhaps because I had so often seen such things in the interval, without tasting them, on the trays in pastry-cooks' windows, that their image had dissociated itself from those Combray days to take its place among others more recent; perhaps because of those memories, so long abandoned and put out of mind, nothing now survived, everything was scattered; the forms of things, including that of the little scallop-shell of pastry, so richly sensual under its severe, religious folds, were either obliterated or had been so long dormant as to have lost the power of expansion which would have allowed them to resume their place in my consciousness. And once I had recognised the taste of the crumb of madeleine soaked in her decoction of lime-flowers which my aunt used to give me (although I did not yet know and must long postpone the discovery of why this memory made me so happy) immediately the old grey house upon the street, where her room was, rose up like the scenery of a theatre to attach itself to the little pavilion, opening on to the garden, which had been built out behind it for my parents (the isolated panel which until that moment had been all that I could see); and with the house the town, from morning to night and in all weathers, the Square where I was sent before luncheon, the streets along which I used to run errands, the country roads we took when it was fine. And just as the Japanese amuse themselves by filling a porcelain bowl with water and steeping in it little crumbs of paper which until then are without character or form, but, the moment they become wet, stretch themselves and bend, take on colour and distinctive shape, become flowers or houses or people, permanent and recognisable, so in that moment all the flowers in our garden and in M. Swann's park, and the water-lilies on the Vivonne and the good folk of the village and their little dwellings and the parish church and the whole of Combray and of its surroundings, taking their proper shapes and growing solid, sprang into being, town and gardens alike, from my cup of tea.

COMBRAY

COMBRAY at a distance, from a twenty-mile radius, as we used to see it from the railway when we arrived there every year in Holy Week, was no more than a church epitomising the town, representing it, speaking of it and for it to the horizon, and as one drew near, gathering close about its long, dark cloak, sheltering from the wind, on the open plain, as a shepherd gathers his sheep, the woolly grey backs of its flocking houses, which a fragment of its mediaeval ramparts enclosed, here and there, in an outline as scrupulously circular as that of a little town in a primitive painting. To live in, Combray was a trifle depressing, like its streets, whose houses, built of the blackened stone of the country, fronted with outside steps, capped with gables which projected long shadows downwards, were so dark that one had, as soon as the sun began to go down, to draw back the curtains in the sitting-room windows; streets with the solemn names of Saints, not a few of whom figured in the history of the early lords of Combray, such as the Rue Saint-Hilaire, the Rue Saint-Jacques, in which my aunt's house stood, the Rue Sainte-Hildegarde, which ran past her railings, and the Rue du Saint-Esprit; on to which the little garden gate opened; and these Combray streets exist in so remote a quarter of my memory, painted in colours so different from those in which the world is decked for me today, that in fact one and all of them, and the church which towered above them in the Square, seem to me now more unsubstantial than the projections of my magic-lantern while at times I feel that to be able to cross the Rue Saint-Hilaire again, to engage a room in the Rue de l'Oiseau, in the old hostelry of the Oiseau Flesché, from whose windows in the pavement used to rise a smell of cooking which rises still in my mind, now and then, in the same warm gusts of comfort, would be to secure a contact with the unseen world more marvellously supernatural than it would be to make Golo's acquaintance and to chat with Geneviève de Brabant.

My grandfather's cousin—by courtesy my great-aunt— with whom we used to stay, was the mother of that aunt Léonie who, since her husband's (my uncle Octave's) death, had gradually declined to leave, first Combray, then her house in Combray, then her bedroom, and finally her bed; and who now never 'came down', but lay perpetually in an indefinite condition of grief, physical exhaustion, illness, obsessions, and religious observances. Her own room looked out over the Rue Saint-Jacques, which ran a long way further to end in the Grand-Pré (as distinct from the Petit-Pré, a green space in the centre of the town where three streets met) and which, monotonous and grey, with the three high steps of stone before almost every one of its doors, seemed like a deep furrow cut by some sculptor of gothic images in the very block of stone out of which he had fashioned a Calvary or a Crib. My aunt's life was now practically confined to two adjoining rooms, in one of which she would rest in the afternoon while they aired the other.

The air of those rooms was saturated with the fine bouquet of a silence so nourishing, so succulent that I could not enter them without a sort of greedy enjoyment, particularly on those first mornings, chilly still, of the Easter holidays, when I could taste it more fully, because I had just arrived then at Combray: before I went in to wish my aunt good day, I would be kept waiting a little time in the outer room.

In the next room I could hear my aunt talking quietly to herself. She never spoke save in low tones, because she believed that there was something broken in her head and floating loose there, which she might displace by talking too loud; but she never remained for long, even when alone, without saying something, because she believed that it was good for her throat, and that by keeping the blood there in circulation it would make less frequent the chokings and other pains to which she was liable; besides, in the life of complete inertia which she led, she attached to the least of her sensations an extraordinary importance, endowed them with a Protean ubiquity which made it difficult for her to keep them secret, and, failing a confidant to whom she might communicate them, she used to promulgate them to herself in an unceasing monologue which was her sole form of activity. Unfortunately, having formed the habit of thinking aloud, she did not always take care to see that there was no one in the adjoining room, and I would often hear her saying to herself: " I must not forget that I never slept a wink" for "never sleeping a wink" was her great claim to distinction, and one admitted and respected in our household vocabulary; in the morning Françoise would not 'call' her, but would simply 'come to' her; during the day, when my aunt wished to take a nap, we used to say just that she wished to 'be quiet' or to 'rest'; and when in conversation she so far forgot herself as to say "what made me wake up," or " I dreamed that," she would flush and at once correct herself. After waiting a minute, I would go in and kiss her; Françoise would be making her tea; or, if my aunt were feeling 'upset', she would ask instead for her 'tisane', and it would be my duty to shake out of the chemist's little package on to a plate the amount of lime-blossom required for infusion in boiling water. Presently my aunt was able to dip in the boiling infusion, in which she would relish the savour of dead or faded blossom, a little madeleine, of which she would hold out a piece to me when it was sufficiently soft.

At one side of her bed stood a big yellow chest-of-drawers of lemon-wood, and a table which served at once as pharmacy and as high altar, on which, beneath a statue of Our Lady and a bottle of Vichy-Célestins, might be found her service-books and her medical prescriptions, everything that she needed for the performance, in bed, of her duties to soul and body, to keep the proper times for pepsin and for vespers. On the other side her bed was bounded by the window: she had the street beneath her eyes, and would read in it from morning to night to divert the tedium of her life, like a Persian prince, the daily but immemorial chronicles of Combray, which she would discuss in detail afterwards with Françoise.

I would not have been five minutes with my aunt before she would send me away in case I made her tired. She would hold out for me to kiss her sad brow, pale and lifeless, on which at this early hour she would not yet have arranged the false hair and through which the bones shone like the points of a crown of thorns or the beads of a rosary, and she would say to me: "Now, my poor child, you must go away; go and get ready for mass; and if you see Françoise downstairs, tell her not to stay too long amusing herself with you; she must come up soon to see if I want anything."

Françoise, who had been for many years in my aunt's service and did not at that time suspect that she would one day be transferred entirely to ours, was a little inclined to desert my aunt during the months which we spent in her house. There had been in my infancy, before we first went to Combray, and when my aunt Léonie used still to spend the winter in Paris with her mother, a time when I knew Françoise so little that on New Year's Day, before going into my great-aunt's house, my mother put a five-franc piece in my hand and said "Now, be careful. Don't make any mistake. Wait until you hear me say 'Good morning, Françoise,' and I touch your arm, before you give it to her." No sooner had we arrived in my aunt's dark hall than we saw in the gloom, beneath the frills of a snowy cap as stiff and fragile as if it had been made of spun sugar, the concentric waves of a smile of anticipatory gratitude. It was Françoise, motionless and erect, framed in the small doorway of the corridor like the statue of a saint in its niche. When we had grown more accustomed to this religious darkness we could discern, in her features a disinterested love of all humanity, blended with a tender respect for the 'upper classes' which raised to the most honourable quarter of her heart the hope of receiving her due reward. Mamma pinched my arm sharply and said in a loud voice "Good morning, Françoise." At this signal my fingers parted and I let fall the coin, which found a receptacle in a confused but outstretched hand. But since we had begun to go to Combray there was no one I knew better than François. We were her favourites, and in the first years at least, while she showed the same consideration for us as for my aunt, she enjoyed us with a keener relish, because we had, in addition to our dignity as part of 'the family' (for she had for those invisible bonds by which community of blood unites the members of a family as much respect as any Greek tragedian), the fresh charm of not being her customary employers. And so with what joy would she welcome us, with what sorrow complain that the weather was still so bad for us, on the day of our arrival, just before Easter, when there was often an icy wind; while Mamma inquired after her daughter and her nephews, and if her grandson was goodlooking, and, what they were going to make of him, and whether he took after his granny.

Later, when no one else was in the room, Mamma, who knew that Françoise was still mourning for her parents, who had been dead for years, would speak of them kindly, asking her endless little questions about them and their lives. She had guessed that Françoise was not over-fond of her son-in-law, and that he spoiled the pleasure she found in visiting her daughter, as the two could not talk so freely when he was there. And so one day, when Françoise was going to their house, some miles from Combray, Mamma said to her, with a smile : "Tell me, Françoise, if Julien has had to go away, and you have Marguerite to yourself all day, you will be very sorry, but you will make the best of it, won't you?"

And Françoise answered, laughing: "Madame knows everything; Madame is worse than the X-rays" (she pronounced 'x' with an affectation of difficulty and with a smile in deprecation of her, an unlettered woman daring to employ a scientific term) "they brought here for Mme. Octave, which see what is in your heart" —and she went off, disturbed that anyone should be caring about her, perhaps anxious that we should not see her in tears: Mamma was the first person who had given her the pleasure of feeling that her peasant existence, with its simple joys and sorrows, might offer some interest, might be a source of grief or pleasure to some one other than herself.

My aunt resigned herself to doing without Françoise to some extent during our visits, knowing how much my mother appreciated the services of so active and intelligent a maid, one who looked as smart at five o'clock in the morning in her kitchen, under a cap whose stiff and dazzling frills seemed to be made of porcelain, as when dressed for churchgoing; who did everything in the right way, who toiled like a horse, whether she was well or ill, but without noise, without the appearance of doing anything; the only one of my aunt's maids who when Mamma asked for hot water or black coffee would bring them actually boiling; she was one of those servants who in a household seem least satisfactory, at first, to a stranger, doubtless because they take no pains to make a conquest of him and show him no special attention, knowing very well that they have no real need of him, that he will cease to be invited to the house sooner than they will be dismissed from it; who, on the other hand, cling with most fidelity to those masters and mistresses who have tested and proved their real capacity, and do not look for that superficial responsiveness, that slavish affability, which may impress a stranger favourably, but often conceals an utter barrenness of spirit in which no amount of training can produce the least trace of individuality.

It was the steeple of Saint-Hilaire which shaped and crowned and consecrated every occupation, every hour of the day, every point of view in the town. From my bedroom window I could discern no more than its base, which had been freshly covered with slates; but when on Sundays I saw these, in the hot light of a summer morning, blaze like a black sun I would say to myself: "Good heavens! Nine o'clock! I must get ready for mass at once if I am to have time to go in and kiss aunt Léonie first," and I would know exactly what was the colour of the sunlight upon the Square, I could feel the heat and dust of the market, the shade behind the blinds of the shop into which Mamma would perhaps go on her way to mass, penetrating its odour of unbleached calico to purchase a handkerchief or something, of which the draper himself would let her see what he had, bowing from the waist: who, having made everything ready for shutting up, had just gone into the back shop to put on his Sunday coat and to wash his hands, which it was his habit, every few minutes and even on the saddest occasions, to rub one against the other with an air of enterprise, cunning, and success.

On our way home from mass we would often meet M. Legrandin, who, detained in Paris by his professional duties as an engineer, could only (except in the regular holiday seasons) visit his home at Combray between Saturday evenings and Monday mornings. He was one of that class of men who, apart from a scientific career in which they may well have proved brilliantly successful, have acquired an entirely different kind of culture, literary or artistic, of which they make no use in the specialised work of their profession, but by which their conversation profits. Tall, with a good figure, a fine, thoughtful face, drooping fair moustaches, a look of disillusionment in his blue eyes, an almost exaggerated refinement of courtesy; a talker such as we had never heard; he was in the sight of my family, who never ceased to quote him as an example, the very pattern of a gentleman, who took life in the noblest and most delicate manner. My grandmother alone found fault with him for speaking a little too well, a little too much like a book, for not using a vocabulary as natural as his loosely knotted Lavallière neckties, his short, straight, almost schoolboyish coat. She was astonished, too, at the furious invective which he was always launching at the aristocracy, at fashionable life, and 'snobbishness'; "undoubtedly," he would say, "the sin of which Saint Paul is thinking when he speaks of the sin for which there is no forgiveness."

Worldly ambition was a thing which my grandmother was so little capable of feeling, or indeed of understanding, that it seemed to her futile to apply so much heat to its condemnation. Besides, she thought it in not very good taste that M. Legrandin, whose sister was married to a country gentleman of Lower Normandy, near Balbec, should deliver himself of such violent attacks upon the nobles, going so far as to blame the Revolution for not having guillotined them all.

In earlier days, before going upstairs to read, I would steal into the little sitting-room which my uncle Adolphe, a brother of my grandfather and an old soldier who had retired from the service as a major, used to occupy on the ground floor, a room which, even when its opened windows let in the heat, if not actually the rays of the sun which seldom penetrated so far, would never fail to emit that vague and yet fresh odour, suggesting at once an open-air and an old-fashioned kind of existence, which sets and keeps the nostrils dreaming when one goes into a disused gun-room.
For some years now I had not gone into my uncle Adolphe's room, since he no longer came to Combray on account of a quarrel which had arisen between him and my family, by my fault, and in the following circumstances:
Once or twice every month, in Paris, I used to be sent to pay him a visit, as he was finishing his luncheon, wearing a plain alpaca coat, and waited upon by his servant in a working-jacket of striped linen, purple and white. He would complain that I had not been to see him for a long time; that he was being neglected; he would offer me a marchpane or a tangerine, and we would cross a room in which no one ever sat, whose fire was never lighted, whose walls were picked out with gilded mouldings, its ceiling painted blue in imitation of the sky, and its furniture upholstered in satin, as at my grandparents', only yellow; then we would enter what he called his 'study', a room whose walls were hung with prints which shewed, against a dark background, a plump and rosy goddess driving a car, or standing upon a globe, or wearing a star on her brow; pictures which were popular under the Second Empire because there was thought to be something about them that suggested Pompeii, which were then generally despised, and which now people are beginning to collect again for one single and consistent reason (despite any others which they may advance), namely, that they suggest the Second Empire. And there I would stay with my uncle until his man came, with a message from the coachman, to ask him at what time he would like the carriage. My uncle would

then be lost in meditation, while his astonished servant stood there, not daring to disturb him by the least movement, wondering and waiting for his answer, which never varied. For in the end, after a supreme crisis of hesitation, my uncle would utter, infallibly, the words: "A quarter past two" which the servant would echo with amazement, but without disputing them : "A quarter past two! Very good, sir . . .. I will go and tell him. . ."

Now my uncle knew many actresses personally, and also ladies of another class, not clearly distinguished from actresses in my mind. He used to entertain them at his house. And if we went to see him on certain days only, that was because on the other days ladies might come whom his family could not very well have met. So we at least thought; as for my uncle, his fatal readiness to pay pretty widows (who had perhaps never been married) and countesses (whose high-sounding titles were probably no more than *noms de guerre*) the compliment of presenting them to my grandmother, or even of presenting to them some of our family jewels, had already embroiled him more than once with my grandfather. Often, if the name of some actress were mentioned. in conversation, I would hear my father say, with a smile, to my mother "One of your uncle's friends," and I would think of the weary novitiate through which, perhaps for years on end, a grown man, even a man of real importance, might have to pass, waiting on the doorstep of some such lady, while she refused to answer his letters and made her hall-porter drive him away; and imagine that my uncle was able to dispense a little jackanapes like myself from all these sufferings by introducing me in his own home to the actress, unapproachable by all the world, but for him an intimate friend.

And so—on the pretext that some lesson, the hour of which had been altered, now came at such an awkward time that it had already more than once prevented me, and would continue to prevent me, from seeing my uncle—one day, not one of the days which he set apart for our visits, I took advantage of the fact that my parents had had luncheon earlier than usual; I slipped out and, instead of going to read the playbills on their column, for which purpose I was allowed to go out unaccompanied, I ran all the way to his house. I noticed before his door a carriage and pair, with red carnations on the horses' blinkers and in the coachman's buttonhole. As I climbed the staircase I could hear laughter and a woman's voice, and, as soon as I had rung, silence and the sound of shutting doors. The man-servant who let me in appeared embarrassed, and said that my uncle was extremely busy and probably could not see me; he went in, however, to announce my arrival; and the same voice I had heard before said: "Oh, yes! Do let him come in; just for a moment; it will be so amusing. Is that his photograph there, on your desk? And his mother (your niece, isn't she?) beside it? The image of her, isn't he? I should so like to see the little chap, just for a second."

I could hear my uncle grumbling and growing angry; finally the man-servant told me to come in. On the table was the same plate of marchpanes that was always there; my uncle wore the same alpaca coat as on other days; but opposite to him, in a pink silk dress with a great necklace of pearls about her throat, sat a young woman who was just finishing a tangerine. My uncertainty whether I ought to address her as Madame or Mademoiselle made me blush, and not daring to look too much in her direction, in case I should be obliged to speak to her, I hurried across to kiss my uncle. She looked at me and smiled; my uncle said "My nephew!" without telling her my name or telling me hers, doubtless because, since his difficulties with my grandfather, he had endeavoured as far as possible to avoid any association of his family with this other class of acquaintance.

"How like his mother he is," said the lady.

"But you have never seen my niece, except in photographs," my uncle broke in quickly, with a note of anger.

"I beg your pardon, dear friend, I passed her on the staircase last year when you were so ill. It is true I only saw her for a moment, and your staircase is rather dark; but I saw well enough to see how lovely she was. This young gentleman has her beautiful eyes, and also *this*," she went on, tracing a line with one finger across the lower part of her forehead. "Tell me," she asked my uncle, "is your niece Mme. —; is her name the same as yours?"

"He takes most after his father," muttered my uncle, who was no more anxious to effect an introduction by proxy, in repeating Mamma's name aloud, than to bring the two together in the flesh. He's his father all over, and also like my poor mother."

"I have not met his father, dear," said the lady in pink, bowing her head slightly, "and I never saw your poor mother. You will remember it was just after your great sorrow that we got to know one another."

I felt somewhat disillusioned, for this young lady was in no way different from other pretty women whom I had seen from time to time at home, especially the daughter of one of our cousins, to whose house I went every New Year's Day. Only better dressed; otherwise my uncle's friend had the same quick and kindly glance, the same frank and friendly manner. I could find no trace in her of the theatrical appearance which I admired in photographs of actresses, nothing of the diabolical expression which would have been in keeping with the life she must lead. I had difficulty in believing that this was one of 'those women', and certainly I should never have believed her one of the 'smart ones' had I not seen the carriage and pair, the pink dress, the pearl necklace, had I not been aware, too, that my uncle knew only the very best of them. But I asked myself how the millionaire who gave her her carriage and her flat and her jewels could find any pleasure in flinging his money away upon a woman who had so simple and respectable an appearance. And yet, when I thought of what her life must be like, its immorality disturbed me more, perhaps, than if it had stood before me in some concrete and recognisable form, by its secrecy and invisibility, like the plot of a novel, the hidden truth of a scandal which had driven out of the home of her middle-class parents and dedicated to the service of all mankind, which had brought to the flowering-point of her beauty, had raised to fame or notoriety this woman, the play of whose features, the intonations of whose voice, like so many others I already knew, made me regard her, in spite of myself, as a young lady of good family; her who was no longer of a family at all.

We had gone by this time into the 'study,' and my uncle, who seemed a trifle embarrassed by my presence, offered her a cigarette.

"No, thank you, dear friend," she said. "You know I only smoke the ones the Grand Duke sends me. I tell him that they make you jealous." And she drew from a case cigarettes covered with inscriptions in gold, in a foreign language. "Why, yes," she began again suddenly. "Of course I have met this young man's father with you. Isn't he your nephew? How on earth could I have forgotten? He was so nice, so charming to me," she went on, modestly and with feeling. But when I thought to myself what must actually have been the rude greeting (which, she made out, had been so charming), I, who knew my father's coldness and reserve, was shocked, as though at some indelicacy on his part, at the contrast between the excessive recognition bestowed on it and his never adequate geniality.

"Look here, my boy, it is time you went away," said my uncle.

I rose; I could scarcely resist a desire to kiss the hand of the lady in pink, but I felt that to do so would require as much audacity as a forcible abduction of her. My heart beat loud while I counted out to myself "Shall I do it, shall I not?" and then I ceased to ask myself what I ought to do so as at least to do something. Blindly, hotly, madly, flinging aside all the reasons I had just found to support such action, I seized and raised to my lips the hand she held out to me.

"Isn't he delicious! Quite a ladies' man already; he takes after his uncle. He'll be a perfect gentleman," she went on, setting her teeth so as to give the word a kind of English accentuation. "Couldn't he come to me some day for 'a cup of tea', as our friends across the channel say he need only send me a 'blue' in the morning?"

I had not the least idea of what a 'blue' might be. I did not understand half the words which the lady used, but my fear lest there should be concealed in them some question which it would be impolite in me not to answer kept me from withdrawing my close attention from them, and I was beginning to feel extremely tired.

My uncle, said nothing, and ushered me out into the hall. Madly in love with the lady in pink, I covered my old uncle's tobacco-stained cheeks with passionate kisses, and while he, awkwardly enough, gave me to understand (without actually saying) that he would rather I did not tell my parents about this visit, I assured him, with tears in my eyes, that his kindness had made so strong an impression upon me that some day I would most certainly find a way of expressing my gratitude. So strong an impression had it made upon me that two hours later, after a string of mysterious utterances which did not strike me as giving my parents a sufficiently clear idea of the new importance with which I had been invested, I found it simpler to let them have a full account, omitting no detail, of the visit I had paid that afternoon. In doing this I had no thought of causing my uncle any unpleasantness. How could I have thought such a thing, since I did not wish it? And I could not suppose that my parents would see any harm in a visit in which I myself saw none. Unfortunately my parents had recourse to principles entirely different from those which I suggested they should adopt when they came to form their estimate of my uncle's conduct. My father and grandfather had 'words' with him, of a violent order; as I learned indirectly. A few days later, passing my uncle in the street as he drove by in an open carriage, I felt at once all the grief, the gratitude, the remorse which I should have liked to convey to him. Beside the immensity of these emotions I considered that merely to raise my hat to him would be incongruous and petty, and might make him think that I regarded myself as bound to show him no more than the commonest form of courtesy. I decided to abstain from so inadequate a gesture, and turned my head away. My uncle thought that, in doing so, I was obeying my parents' orders; he never forgave them; and though he did not die until many years later, not one of us ever set eyes on him again.

And so I no longer used to go into the little sitting-room (now kept shut) of my uncle Adolphe; instead, after hanging about on the outskirts of the back-kitchen until Françoise appeared on its threshold and announced: "I am going to let the kitchen-maid serve the coffee and take up the hot water; it is time I went off to Mme. Octave," I would then decide to go indoors, and would go straight upstairs to my room to read.

I had heard Bergotte spoken of, for the first time, by a friend older than myself, for whom I had a strong admiration, a precious youth of the name of Bloch. One Sunday, while I was reading in the garden, I was interrupted by Swann, who had come to call upon my parents. "What are you reading? May I look? Why, it's Bergotte! Who has been telling you about him?" I replied that Bloch was responsible.

"Oh, yes, that boy I saw here once, who looks so like the Bellini portrait of Mahomet II. It's an astonishing likeness; he has the same arched eyebrows and hooked nose and prominent cheekbones. When his beard comes he'll be Mahomet himself. Anyhow, he has good taste, for Bergotte is a charming creature." And seeing how much I seemed to admire Bergotte, Swann, who never spoke at all about the people he knew, made an exception in my favour and said:

"I know him well; if you would like him to write a few words on the title-page of your book I could ask him for you."

I dared not accept such an offer, but bombarded Swann with questions about his friend. "Can you tell me, please, who is his favourite actor?"

"Actor? No, I can't say. But I do know this: there's not a man on the stage whom he thinks equal to Berma; he puts her above everyone. Have you seen her?"

"No, sir, my parents do not allow me to go to the theatre."

"That is a pity. You should insist. Berma in *Phèdre*, in the *Cid*; well, she's only an actress, if you like, but you know that I don't believe very much in the 'hierarchy' of the arts."

"Are there any books in which Bergotte has written about Berma," I asked M. Swann.

"I think he has, in that little essay on Racine, but it must be out of print. Still, there has perhaps been a second impression. I will find out. Anyhow, I can ask Bergotte himself all that you want to know next time he comes to dine with us. He never misses a week, from one year's end to another. He is my daughter's greatest friend. They go about together, and look at old towns and cathedrals and castles."

As I was still completely ignorant of the different grades in the social hierarchy, the fact that my father found it impossible for us to see anything of Swann's wife and daughter had, for a long time, had the contrary effect of making me imagine them as separated from us by an enormous gulf, which greatly enhanced their dignity and importance in my eyes. I was sorry that my mother did not dye her hair and redden her lips, as I had heard our neighbour, Mme. Sazerat, say that Mme. Swann did, to gratify not her husband but M. de Charlus; and I felt that, to her, we must be an object of scorn, which distressed me particularly on account of the daughter, such a pretty little girl, as I had heard, and one of whom I used often to dream, always imagining her with the same features and appearance, which I bestowed upon her quite arbitrarily, but with a charming effect. But from this afternoon, when I had learned that Mlle. Swann was a creature living in such rare and fortunate circumstances, bathed, as in her natural element, in such a sea of privilege that, if she should ask her parents whether anyone were coming to dinner, she would be answered in those two syllables, radiant with celestial light, would hear the name of that golden guest who was to her no more than an old friend of her family, Bergotte; that for her the intimate conversation at table, corresponding to what my great-aunt's conversation was for me, would be the words of Bergotte upon all those subjects which he had not been able to take up in his writings, and on which I would fain have heard him utter oracles; and that, above all, when she went to visit other towns, he would be walking by her side, unrecognised and glorious, like the gods who came down, of old, from heaven to dwell among mortal men then I realised both the rare worth of a creature such as Mlle. Swann, and, at the same time, how coarse and ignorant I should appear to her; and I felt so keenly how pleasant and yet how impossible it would be for me to become her friend that I was filled at once with longing and with despair.

During May we used to go out on Saturday evenings after dinner to the 'Month of Mary' devotions. As we were liable, there, to meet M. Vinteuil, who held very strict views on "the deplorable untidiness of young people, which seems to be encouraged in these days," my mother would first see that there was nothing out of order in my appearance, and then we would set out for the church. It was in these 'Month of Mary' services that I can remember having first fallen in love with hawthorn-blossom. The hawthorn was not merely in the church, for there, holy ground as it was, we had all of us a right of entry; but, arranged upon the altar itself inseparable from the mysteries in whose celebration it was playing a part, it thrust in among the tapers and the sacred vessels its rows of branches, tied to one another horizontally in a stiff, festal scheme of decoration; and they were made more lovely still by the scalloped outline of the dark leaves, over which were scattered in profusion, as over a bridal train, little clusters of buds of a dazzling whiteness.

M.Vinteuil had come in with his daughter and had sat down beside us. He belonged to a good family, and had once been music-master to my grandmother's sisters so that when, after losing his wife and inheriting some property, he had retired to the neighbourhood of Combray, we used often to invite him to our house. But with his intense prudishness he had given up coming, so as not to be obliged to meet Swann, who had made what he called "a most unsuitable marriage, as seems to be the fashion in these days." My mother, on hearing that he 'composed,' told him by way of a compliment that, when she came to see him, he must play her something of his own. M. Vinteuil would have liked nothing better, but he carried politeness and consideration for others to so fine a point, always putting himself in their place, that he was afraid of boring them, or of appearing egotistical, if he carried out, or even allowed them to suspect what were his own desires. On the day when my parents had gone to pay him a visit, I had accompanied them, but they had allowed me to remain outside, and as M. Vinteuil's house, Montjouvain, stood on a site actually hollowed out from a steep hill covered with shrubs, among which I took cover, I had found myself on a level with his drawing-room, upstairs, and only a few feet away from its window. When a servant came in to tell him that my parents had arrived, I had seen M. Vinteuil run to the piano and lay out a sheet of music so as to catch the eye. But as soon as they entered the room he had snatched it away and hidden it in a corner. He was afraid, no doubt, of letting them suppose that he was glad to see them only because it gave him a chance of playing them some of his compositions. And every time that my mother, in the course of her visit, had returned to the subject of his playing, he had hurriedly protested: "I cannot think who put that on the piano it is not the proper place for it at all," and had turned the conversation aside to other topics simply because those were of less interest to himself.

His one and only passion was for his daughter, and she, with her somewhat boyish appearance, looked so robust that it was hard to restrain a smile when one saw the precautions her father used to take for her health, with spare shawls always in readiness to wrap round her shoulders. My grandmother had drawn our attention to the gentle, delicate, almost timid expression which might often be caught flitting across the face, dusted all over with freckles, of this otherwise stolid child. When she had spoken, she would at once take her own words in the sense in which her audience must have heard them, she would be alarmed at the possibility of a misunderstanding, and one would see, in clear outline, as though in a transparency, beneath the mannish face of the 'good sort' that she was, the finer features of a young woman in tears.

One Sunday, when my aunt had received simultaneous visits from the Curé and from Eulalie, and had been left alone, afterwards, to rest, the whole family went upstairs to bid her good night, and Mamma ventured to console with her on the unlucky coincidence that always brought both visitors to her door at the same time.

"I hear that things went wrong again to-day, Léonie," she said kindly, "you have had all your friends here at once." And my great-aunt interrupted with: "Too many good things . . ." for, since her daughter's illness, she felt herself in duty bound to revive her as far as possible by always drawing her attention to the brighter side of things. But my father had begun to speak.

"I should like to take advantage," he said, "of the whole family's being here together, to tell you a story, so as not to have to begin all over again to each of you separately. I am afraid we are in M. Legrandin's bad books; he would hardly say 'How d'ye do' to me this morning."

I did not wait to hear the end of my father's story, for I had been with him myself after mass when we had passed M. Legrandin; instead, I went downstairs to the kitchen to ask for the bill of fare for our dinner, which was of fresh interest to me daily, like the news in a paper, and excited me as might the programme of a coming festivity.

As M. Legrandin had passed close by us on our way from church, walking by the side of a lady, the owner of a country house in the neighbourhood, whom we knew only by sight, my father had saluted him in a manner at once friendly and reserved, without stopping in his walk; M Legrandin had barely acknowledged the courtesy, and with an air of surprise, as though he had not recognised us, and with that distant look characteristic of people who do not wish to be agreeable, and who from the suddenly receding depths of their eyes seem to have caught sight of you at the far end of an interminably straight road, and at so great a distance that they content themselves with directing towards you an almost imperceptible movement of the head, in proportion to your doll-like dimensions.

Now, the lady who was walking with Legrandin was a model of virtue, known and highly respected; there could be no question of his being out for amorous adventure, and annoyed at being detected; and my father asked himself how he could possibly have displeased our friend.

"I should be all the more sorry to feel that he was angry with us," he said, "because among all those people in their Sunday clothes there is something about him, with his little cut-away coat and his soft neckties, so little 'dressed-up', so genuinely simple; an air of innocence, almost, which is really attractive."

But the vote of the family council was unanimous, that my father had imagined the whole thing, or that Legrandin, at the moment in question, had been preoccupied in thinking about something else. Anyhow, my father's fears were dissipated no later than the following evening. As we returned from a long walk we saw, near the Pont-Vieux, Legrandin himself, who, on account of the holidays, was spending a few days more in Combray and he came up to us with outstretched hand.

Alas we had definitely to alter our opinion of M. Legrandin. On one of the Sundays following our meeting with him on the Pont-Vieux, after which my father had been forced to confess himself mistaken, as mass drew to an end, and, with the sunshine and the noise of the outer world, something else invaded the church, an atmosphere so far from sacred that Mme. Goupil, Mme. Percepied (everyone, in fact, who a moment ago, when I arrived a little late, had been sitting motionless, their eyes fixed on their prayer-books; who, I might even have thought, had not seen me come in, had not their feet moved slightly to push away the little kneeling-desk which was preventing me from getting to my chair) began in loud voices to discuss with us all manner of utterly mundane topics, as though we were already outside in the Square, we saw, standing on the sun-baked steps of the porch, dominating the many-coloured tumult of the market, Legrandin himself, whom the husband of the lady we had seen with him, on the previous occasion, was just going to introduce to the wife of another large landed proprietor of the district. Legrandin's face shewed an extraordinary zeal and animation; he made a profound bow, with a subsidiary backward movement which brought his spine sharply up into a position behind its starting-point, a gesture in which he must have been trained by the husband of his sister, Mme. de Cambremer. This rapid recovery caused a sort of tense muscular wave to ripple over Legrandin's hips, which I had not supposed to be so fleshy; I cannot say why, but this undulation of pure matter, this wholly carnal fluency, with not the least hint in it of spiritual significance, this wave lashed to a fury by the wind of an assiduity, an obsequiousness of the basest sort, awoke my mind suddenly to the possibility of a Legrandin altogether different from the one whom we knew. The lady gave him some message for her coachman, and while he was stepping down to her carriage the impression of joy, timid and devout, which the introduction had stamped there, still lingered on his face. Carried away in a sort of dream, he smiled, then he began to hurry back towards the lady; he was walking faster than usual, and his shoulders swayed backwards and forwards, right and left, in the most absurd fashion; altogether he looked, so utterly had he abandoned himself to it, ignoring all other considerations, as though he were the lifeless and wire-pulled puppet of his own happiness. Meanwhile we were coming out through the porch; we were passing close beside him; he was too well bred to turn his head away; but he fixed his eyes, which had suddenly changed to those of a seer, lost in the profundity of his vision, on so distant a point of the horizon that he could not see us, and so had not to acknowledge our presence. His face emerged, still with an air of innocence, from his straight and pliant coat, which looked as though conscious of having been led astray, in spite of itself, and plunged into surroundings of a detested splendour. And a spotted necktie, stirred by the breezes of the Square, continued to float in front of Legrandin, like the standard of his proud isolation, of his noble independence. Just as we reached the house my mother discovered that we had forgotten the 'Saint-Honoré', and asked my father to go back with me and tell them to send it up at once. Near the church we met Legrandin, coming towards us with the same lady whom he was escorting to her carriage. He brushed past us and did not interrupt what he was saying to her, but gave us, out of the corner of his blue eye, a little sign, which began and ended, so to speak, inside his eyelids, and as it did not involve the least movement of his facial muscles, managed to pass quite unperceived by the lady; but, striving to compensate by the intensity of his feelings for the somewhat restricted field in which they had to find expression, he made that blue chink, which was set apart for us, sparkle with all the animation of cordiality, which went far beyond mere playfulness, and almost touched the border-line of roguery; he subtilised the refinements of good-fellowship into a wink of connivance, a hint, a hidden meaning, a secret understanding, all the mysteries of cornplicity in a plot, and finally exalted his assurances of friendship to the level of protestations of affection, even of a declaration of love, lighting up for us, and for us alone, with a secret and languid flame invisible by the great lady upon his other side, an enamoured pupil in a countenance of ice.

Only the day before he had asked my parents to send me to dine with him on this same Sunday evening. The question was raised at home whether, all things considered, I ought still to be sent to dine with M. Legrandin. But my grandmother refused to believe that he could have been impolite. "You admit yourself that he appears at church there, quite simply dressed, and all that; he hardly looks like a man of fashion." She added that, in any event, even if, at the worst, he had been intentionally rude, it was far better for us to pretend we had noticed nothing.

I dined with Legrandin on the terrace of his house, by moonlight. "There is a charming quality, is there not," he said to me, "in this silence; for hearts that are wounded, as mine is, a novelist, whom you will read in time to come, claims that there is no remedy but silence and shadow. And see you this, my boy, there comes in all lives a time, towards which you still have far to go, when the weary eyes can endure but one kind of light, the light which a fine evening like this prepares for us in the stillroom of darkness, when the ears can listen to no music save what the moonlight breathes through the flute of silence."

I could hear what M. Legrandin was saying; like everything that he said, it sounded attractive; but I was disturbed by the memory of a lady whom I had seen recently for the first time; and thinking, now that I knew that Legrandin was on friendly terms with several of the local aristocracy, that perhaps she also was among his acquaintance, I summoned up all my courage and said to him: "Tell me, sir, do you, by any chance, know the lady—the ladies of Guermantes" and I felt glad because, in pronouncing the name, I had secured a sort of power over it, by the mere act of drawing it up out of my dreams and giving it an objective existence in the world of spoken things.

But, at the sound of the word Guermantes, I saw in the middle of each of our friend's blue eyes a little brown dimple appear, as though they had been stabbed by some invisible pin-point, while the rest of his pupils, reacting from the shock, received and secreted the azure overflow. His fringed eyelids darkened, and drooped. His mouth, which had been stiffened and seared with bitter lines, was the first to recover, and smiled, while his eyes still seemed full of pain, like the eyes of a good-looking martyr whose body bristles with arrows.

"No, I do not know them," he said, but instead of uttering so simple a piece of information, a reply in which there was so little that could astonish me, in the natural and conversational tone which would have befitted it; he recited it with a separate stress upon each word, leaning forward, bowing his head, with at once the vehemence which a man gives, so as to be believed, to a highly improbable statement (as though the fact that he did not know the Guermantes could be due only to some strange accident of fortune) and with the emphasis of a man who, finding himself unable to keep silence about what is to him a painful situation, chooses to proclaim it aloud, so as to convince his hearers that the confession he is making is one that causes him no embarrassment, but is easy, agreeable, spontaneous, that the situation in question, in this case the absence of relations with the Guermantes family, might very well have been not forced upon but actually designed by Legrandin himself, might arise from some family tradition, some moral principle or mystical vow which expressly forbade his seeking their society. "No," he resumed, explaining by his words the tone in which they were uttered. "No, I do not know them; I have never wished to know them; I have always made a point of preserving complete independence; at heart, as you know, I am a bit of a Radical. People are always coming to me about it, telling me I am mistaken in not going to Guermantes, that I make myself seem ill-bred, uncivilised, an old bear. But that's not the sort of reputation that can frighten me; it's too true! In my heart of hearts I care for nothing in the world now but a few churches, books—two or three, pictures—rather more, perhaps, and the light of the moon when the fresh breeze of youth (such as yours) wafts to my nostrils the scent of gardens whose flowers my old eyes are not sharp enough, now, to distinguish."

I did not understand very clearly why, in order to refrain from going to the houses of people whom one did not know, it should be necessary to cling to one's independence, nor how that could give one the appearance of a savage or a bear. But what I did understand was this, that Legrandin was not altogether truthful when he said that he cared only for churches, moonlight, and youth; he cared also, he cared a very great deal for people who lived in country houses, and would be so much afraid, when in their company, of incurring their displeasure that he would never dare to let them see that he numbered, as well, among his friends middle-class people, the families of solicitors and stockbrokers, preferring, if the truth must be known, that it should be revealed in his absence, when he was out of earshot, that judgment should go against him (if so it must) by default: in a word, he was a snob.

At home, meanwhile, we had no longer any illusions as to M.

Legrandin, and our relations with him had become much more distant. Mamma would be greatly delighted whenever she caught him red-handed in what he continued to call the unpardonable sin of snobbery. As for my father, he found it difficult to take Legrandin's airs in so light, in so detached a spirit; and when there was some talk, one year, of sending me to spend the long summer holidays at Balbec with my grandmother, he said "I must, most certainly, tell Legrandin that you are going to Balbec, to see whether he will offer you an introduction to his sister. He probably doesn't remember telling us that she lived within a mile of the place."

My grandmother, who held that, when one went to the seaside, one ought to be on the beach from morning to night, to taste the sea breezes, that one should not know anyone in the place, because calls and parties and excursions were so much time stolen from what belonged, by rights, to the sea-air, begged him on no account to speak to Legrandin of our plans; for already, in her mind's eye, she could see his sister, Mme. de Cambremer, alighting from her carriage at the door of our hotel just as we were on the point of going out fishing, and obliging us to remain indoors all afternoon to entertain her. But Mamma laughed her fears to scorn, for she herself felt that the danger was not so threatening, and that Legrandin would show no undue anxiety to make us acquainted with his sister. And, as it happened, there was no need for any of us to introduce the subject of Balbec, for it was Legrandin himself who, without the least suspicion that we had ever had any intention of visiting those parts, walked into the trap uninvited one evening; when we met him strolling on the banks of the Vivonne.

"There are tints in the clouds this evening, violets and blues, which are very beautiful, are they not, my friend?" he said to my father, "especially a blue which is far more floral than atmospheric, a cineraria blue, which it is surprising to see in the sky. And that little pink cloud there, has it not just the tint of some flower, a carnation or hydrangea? Nowhere, perhaps, except on the shores of the English Channel, where Normandy merges into Brittany, have I been able to find such copious examples of what you might call a vegetable kingdom in the clouds. Down there, close to Balbec, among all those places which are still so uncivilised, there is a little bay, charmingly quiet, where the sunsets of the Auge Valley, those red-and-gold sunsets (which, all the same, I am very far from despising) seem commonplace and insignificant; for in that moist and gentle atmosphere these heavenly flower-beds will break into blossom, in a few moments, in the evenings, incomparably lovely, and often lasting for hours before they fade. Others shed their leaves at once, and then it is more beautiful still to see the sky strewn with the scattering of their innumerable petals, sulphurous yellow and rosy red. Balbec; yes they are building hotels there now, superimposing them upon its ancient and charming soil, which they are powerless to alter; how delightful it is, down there, to be able to step out at once into regions so primitive and so entrancing."

"Indeed! And do you know anyone at Balbec?" inquired my father. "This young man is just going to spend a couple of months there with his grandmother, and my wife too, perhaps."

Legrandin, taken unawares by the question at a moment when he was looking directly at my father, was unable to turn aside his gaze, and so concentrated it with steadily increasing intensity—smiling mournfully the while—upon the eyes of his questioner, with an air of friendliness and frankness and of not being afraid to look him in the face, until he seemed to have penetrated my father's skull, as it had been a ball of glass, and to be seeing, at the moment, a long way beyond and behind it, a brightly coloured cloud, which provided him with a mental alibi, and would enable him to establish the theory that, just when he was being asked whether he knew anyone at Balbec, he had been thinking of something else, and so had not heard the question. As a rule these tactics make the questioner proceed to ask, "Why, what are you thinking about?" But my father, inquisitive, annoyed, and cruel, repeated: "Have you friends, then, in that neighbourhood, that you know Balbec so well."

In a final and desperate effort the smiling gaze of Legrandin struggled to the extreme limits of its tenderness, vagueness, candour, and distraction; then feeling, no doubt, that there was nothing left for it now but to answer, he said to us: "I have friends all the world over, wherever there are companies of trees, stricken but not defeated, which have come together to offer a common supplication, with pathetic obstinacy, to an inclement sky which has no mercy upon them."

"That is not quite what I meant," interrupted my father, obstinate as a tree and merciless as the sky. "I asked you, in case anything should happen to my mother-in-law and she wanted to feel that she was not all alone down there, at the ends of the earth, whether you knew any of the people."

"There as elsewhere, I know everyone and I know no one," replied Legrandin, who was by no means ready yet to surrender; "places I know well, people very slightly. But, down there, the places themselves seem to me just like people, rare and wonderful people, of a delicate quality which would have been corrupted and ruined by the gift of life.

Perhaps it is a castle which you encounter upon the cliff's edge; standing there by the roadside, where it has halted to contemplate its sorrows before an evening sky, still rosy, through which a golden moon is climbing; while the fishing-boats, homeward bound, creasing the watered silk of the Channel, hoist its pennant at their mastheads and carry its colours. Or perhaps it is a simple dwelling-house that stands alone, ugly, if anything, timid-seeming but full of romance, hiding from every eye some imperishable secret of happiness and disenchantment. That land which knows not truth," he continued with 'Machiavellian' subtlety, "that land of infinite fiction makes bad reading for any boy; and is certainly not what I should choose or recommend for my young friend here, who is already so much inclined to melancholy, for a heart already predisposed to receive its impressions. Climates that breathe amorous secrets and futile regrets may agree with an old and disillusioned man like myself; but they must always prove fatal to a temperament which is still unformed. Believe me," he went on with emphasis, "the waters of that bay—more Breton than Norman—may exert a sedative influence, though even that is of questionable value, upon a heart which, like mine, is no longer unbroken, a heart for whose wounds there is no longer anything to compensate. But at your age, my boy, those waters are contra-indicated.. . . Good night to you, neighbours," he added, moving away from us with that evasive abruptness to which we were accustomed; and then, turning towards us, with a physicianly finger raised in warning, he resumed the consultation: "No Balbec before you are *fifty!*" he called out to me, "and even then it must depend on the state of the heart."

My father spoke to him of it again, as often as we met him, and tortured him with questions, but it was labour in vain: like that scholarly swindler who devoted to the fabrication of forged palimpsests a wealth of skill and knowledge and industry the hundredth part of which would have sufficed to establish him in a more lucrative—but an honourable occupation, M. Legrandin, had we insisted further, would in the end have constructed a whole system of ethics, and a celestial geography of Lower Normandy, sooner than admit to us that, within a mile of Balbec, his own sister was living in her own house; sooner than find himself obliged to offer us a letter of introduction, the prospect of which would never have inspired him with such terror had he been absolutely certain—as, from his knowledge of my grandmother's character, he really ought to have been certain—that in no circumstances whatsoever would we have dreamed of making use of it.

There were, in the environs of Combray, two ways which we used to take for our walks, and so diametrically opposed that we would actually leave the house by a different door, according to the way we had chosen: the way towards Méséglise-la-Vineuse, which we called also 'Swann's way', because, to get there, one had to pass along the boundary of M. Swann's estate, and the 'Guermantes way'. Of Méséglise-la-Vineuse, to tell the truth, I never knew anything more than the way there, and the strange people who would come over on Sundays to take the air in Combray, people whom, this time, neither my aunt nor any of us would 'know at all', and whom we would therefore assume to be people who must have come over from Méséglise. As for Guermantes, I was to know it well enough one day, but that day had still to come; and, during the whole of my boyhood, if Méséglise was to me something as inaccessible as the horizon, which remained hidden from sight, however far one went, by the folds of a country which no longer bore the least resemblance to the country round Combray; Guermantes, on the other hand, meant no more than the ultimate goal, ideal rather than real, of the 'Guermantes way', a sort of abstract geographical term like the North Pole or the Equator.

When we had decided to go the 'Méséglise way' we would start (without undue haste, and even if the sky were clouded over, since the walk was not very long, and did not take us too far from home) as though we were not going anywhere in particular, by the front-door of my aunt's house, which opened on to the Rue du Saint-Esprit. We would be greeted by the gunsmith, we would drop our letters into the box, we would tell Theodore, from Françoise, as we passed, that she had run out of oil or coffee, and we would leave the town by the road which ran along the white fence of M. Swann's park. Before reaching it we would be met on our way by the scent of his lilac-trees, come out to welcome strangers. Out of the fresh little green hearts of their foliage the lilacs raised inquisitively over the fence of the park their plumes of white or purple blossom, which glowed, even in the shade, with the sunlight in which they had been bathed. Some of them, half-concealed by the little tiled house, called the Archers' Lodge, in which Swann's keeper lived, overtopped its gothic gable with their rosy minaret. The nymphs of spring would have seemed coarse and vulgar in comparison with these young houris, who retained, in this French garden, the pure and vivid colouring of a Persian miniature. Despite my desire to throw my arms about their pliant forms and to draw down towards me the starry locks that crowned their fragrant heads, we would pass them by without stopping, for my parents had ceased to visit Tansonville since

Swann's marriage, and, so as not to appear to be looking into his park, we would, instead of taking the road which ran beside its boundary and then climbed straight up to the open fields, choose another way, which led in the same direction, but circuitously, and brought us out rather too far from home. One day my grandfather said to my father: "Don't you remember Swann's telling us yesterday that his wife and daughter had gone off to Rheims and that he was taking the opportunity of spending a day or two in Paris? We might go along by the park, since the ladies are not at home; that will make it a little shorter.

The absence of Mlle. Swann, which—since it preserved me from the terrible risk of seeing her appear on one of the paths, and of being identified and scorned by this so privileged little girl who had Bergotte for a friend and used to go with him to visit cathedrals—made the exploration of Tansonville, now for the first time permitted me, a matter of indifference to myself, seemed however to invest the property, in my grandfather's and father's eyes, with a fresh and transient charm, and (like an entirely cloudless sky when one is going mountaineering) to make the day extraordinarily propitious for a walk in this direction; I should have liked to see their reckoning proved false to see, by a miracle, Mlle. Swann appear, with her father, so close to us that we should not have time to escape and should therefore be obliged to make her acquaintance.

The hedge allowed us a glimpse, inside the park, of an alley bordered with jasmine, pansies, and verbenas, among which the stocks held open their fresh plump purses, of a pink as fragrant and as faded as old Spanish leather, while on the gravel-path a long watering-pipe, painted green, coiling across the ground, poured, where its holes were, over the flowers whose perfume those holes inhaled, a vertical and prismatic fan of infinitesimal, rainbow coloured drops. Suddenly I stood still, unable to move, as happens when something appears that requires not only our eyes to take it in, but involves a deeper kind of perception and takes possession of the whole of our being. A little girl, with fair, reddish hair, who appeared to be returning from a walk, and held a trowel in her hand, was looking at us, raising towards us a face powdered with pinkish freckles. Her black eyes gleamed, and as I did not at that time know, and indeed have never since learned how to reduce to its objective elements any strong impression, since I had not, as they say, enough 'power of observation' to isolate the sense of their colour, for a long time afterwards, whenever I thought of her, the memory of those bright eyes would at once present itself to me as a vivid azure, since her complexion was fair; so much so that, perhaps, if her eyes had not been quite so black—which was what struck one most forcibly on first meeting her—I should not have been, as I was, especially enamoured of their imagined blue.

I gazed at her, at first with that gaze which is not merely a messenger from the eyes, but in whose window all the senses assemble and lean out, petrified and anxious, that gaze which would fain reach, touch, capture, bear off in triumph the body at which it is aimed, and the soul with the body; then (so frightened was I lest at any moment my grandfather and father, catching sight of the girl, might tear me away from her, by making me run on in front of them) with another, an unconsciously appealing look, whose object was to force her to pay attention to me, to see, to know me. She cast a glance forwards and sideways, so as to take stock of my grandfather and father, and doubtless the impression she formed of them was that we were all absurd people, for she turned away with an indifferent and contemptuous air, withdrew herself so as to spare her face the indignity of remaining within their field of vision; and while they, continuing to walk on without noticing her, had overtaken and passed me, she allowed her eyes to wander, over the space that lay between us, in my direction, without any particular expression, without appearing to have seen me, but with an intensity, a half-hidden smile which I was unable to interpret, according to the instruction I had received in the ways of good breeding, save as a mark of infinite disgust; and her hand, at the same time, sketched in the air an indelicate gesture, for which, when it was addressed in public to a person whom one did not know, the little dictionary of manners which I carried in my mind supplied only one meaning, namely, a deliberate insult.

"Gilberte, come along, what are you doing?" called out in a piercing tone of authority a lady in white, whom I had not seen until that moment, while, a little way beyond her, a gentleman in a suit of linen 'ducks', whom I did not know either, stared at me with eyes which seemed to be starting from his head; the little girl's smile abruptly faded, and, seizing her trowel, she made off without turning to look again in my direction, with an air of obedience, inscrutable and sly.

And so was wafted to my ears the name of Gilberte, bestowed on me like a talisman which might, perhaps, enable me some day to rediscover her whom its syllables had just endowed with a definite personality, whereas, a moment earlier, she had been only something vaguely seen. So it came to me, uttered across the heads of the stocks and jasmines, pungent and cool as the drops which fell from the green watering-pipe; impregnating and irradiating the zone of pure air through which it had passed, which it set apart and isolated from all other air, with the mystery of the life of her whom its syllables designated to the happy creatures that lived and walked and travelled in her company; unfolding through the arch of the pink hawthorn, which opened at the height of my shoulder, the quintessence of their familiarity— so exquisitely painful to myself—within her, and with all that unknown world of her existence, into which I should never penetrate.

For a moment (while we moved away, and my grandfather murmured: "Poor Swann, what a life they are leading him; fancy sending him away so that she can be left alone with her Charlus—for that was Charlus: I recognised him at once and the child too; at her age, to be mixed up in all that!") the impression left on me by the despotic tone in which Gilberte's mother had spoken to her, without her replying, by exhibiting her to me as being obliged to yield obedience to some one else, as not being indeed superior to the whole world, calmed my sufferings somewhat, revived some hope in me, and cooled the ardour of my love but very soon that love surged up again in me like a reaction by which my humiliated heart was endeavouring to rise to Gilberte's level, or to draw her down to its own. I loved her; I was sorry not to have had the time and the inspiration to insult her, to do her some injury, to force her to keep some memory of me. I knew her to be so beautiful that I should have liked to be able to retrace my steps so as to shake my fist at her and shout, "I think you are hideous, grotesque; you are utterly disgusting!" However, I walked away, carrying with me, then and for ever afterwards, as the first illustration of a type of happiness rendered inaccessible to a little boy of my kind by certain laws of nature which it was impossible to transgress, the picture of a little girl with reddish hair, and a skin freckled with tiny pink marks, who held a trowel in her hand, and smiled as she directed towards me a long and subtle and inexpressive stare.

It was along the 'Méséglise way,' at Montjouvain, a house built on the edge of a large pond, and overlooked by a steep, shrub-grown hill, that M. Vinteuil lived. And so we used often to meet his daughter driving her dogcart at full speed along the road. After a certain year we never saw her alone, but always accompanied by a friend, a girl older than herself, with an evil reputation in the neighbourhood, who in the end installed herself permanently, one day, at Montjouvain. People said: "That poor M. Vinteuil must be blinded by love not to see what everyone is talking about, and to let his daughter—a man who is horrified if you use a word in the wrong sense—bring a woman like that to live under his roof. He says that she is a most superior woman, with a heart of gold, and that she would have shewn extraordinary musical talent if she had only been trained. He may be sure it is not music that she is teaching his daughter."

Anyone who, like ourselves, had seen M. Vinteuil, about this time, avoiding people whom he knew, and turning away as soon as he caught sight of them, changed in a few months into an old man, engulfed in a sea of sorrows, incapable of any effort not directly aimed at promoting his daughter's happiness, spending whole days beside his wife's grave, could hardly have failed to realise that he was gradually dying of a broken heart, could hardly have supposed that he paid no attention to the rumours which were going about. He knew, perhaps he even believed, what his neighbours were saying.

One day, when we were walking with Swann in one of the streets of Combray, M. Vinteuil, turning out of another street, found himself so suddenly face to face with us all that he had not time to escape and Swann, with that almost arrogant charity of a man of the world who, amid the dissolution of all his own moral prejudices, finds in another's shame merely a reason for treating him with a friendly benevolence, the outward signs of which serve to enhance and gratify the self-esteem of the bestower because he feels that they are all the more precious to him upon whom they are bestowed, conversed at great length with M. Vinteuil, with whom for a long time he had been barely on speaking terms, and invited him, before leaving us, to send his daughter over, one day, to play at Tansonville. It was an invitation, which, two years earlier, would have enraged M. Vinteuil, but which now filled him with so much gratitude that he felt himself obliged to refrain from the indiscretion of accepting. Swann's friendly regard for his daughter seemed to him to be in itself so honourable, so precious a support for his cause that he felt it would perhaps be better to make no use of it, so as to have the wholly Platonic satisfaction of keeping it in reserve.

"What a charming man!" he said to us, after Swann had gone, with the same enthusiasm and veneration which make clever and pretty women of the middle classes fall victims to the physical and intellectual charms of a duchess, even though she be ugly and a fool. "What a charming man! What a pity that he should have made such a deplorable marriage!"

If the weather was bad all morning, my family would abandon the idea of a walk, and I would remain at home. But, later on, I formed the habit of going out by myself on such days, and walking towards

Méséglise-la-Vineuse, during that autumn when we had to come to Combray to settle the division of my aunt Léonie's estate; for she had died at last, leaving both parties among her neighbours triumphant in the fact of her demise—those who had insisted that her mode of life was enfeebling and must ultimately kill her, and, equally, those who had always maintained that she suffered from some disease not imaginary, but organic, by the visible proof of which the most sceptical would be obliged to own themselves convinced, once she had succumbed to it; causing no intense grief to any save one of her survivors, but to that one a grief savage in its violence. During the long fortnight of my aunt's last illness Françoise never went out of her room for an instant, never took off her clothes, allowed no one else to do anything for my aunt, and did not leave her body until it was actually in its grave. Then, at last, we understood that the sort of terror in which Françoise had lived of my aunt's harsh words, her suspicions and her anger, had developed in her a sentiment which we had mistaken for hatred, and which was really veneration and love. Her true mistress, whose decisions it had been impossible to foresee, from whose stratagems it had been so hard to escape, of whose good nature it had been so easy to take advantage, her sovereign, her mysterious and omnipotent monarch was no more. Compared with such a mistress we counted for very little. The time had long passed when, on our first coming to spend our holidays at Combray, we had been of equal importance, in Françoise's eyes, with my aunt.

During that autumn my parents, finding the days so fully occupied with the legal formalities that had to be gone through, and discussions with solicitors and farmers, that they had little time for walks which, as it happened, the weather made precarious, began to let me go, without them, along the 'Méséglise way', wrapped up in a huge Highland plaid which protected me from the rain, and which I was all the more ready to throw over my shoulders because I felt that the stripes of its gaudy tartan scandalised Françoise, whom it was impossible to convince that the colour of one's clothes had nothing whatever to do with one's mourning for the dead, and to whom the grief which we had shewn on my aunt's death was wholly unsatisfactory, since we had not entertained the neighbours to a great funeral banquet, and did not adopt a special tone when we spoke of her, while I at times might be heard humming a tune.

And it is perhaps from another impression which I received at Montjouvain, some years later, an impression which at that time was without meaning, that there arose, long afterwards, my idea of that cruel side of human passion called 'sadism'. We shall see, in due course, that for quite another reason the memory of this impression was to play an important part in my life. It was during a spell of very hot weather; my parents, who had been obliged to go away for the whole day, had told me that I might stay out as late as I pleased; and having gone as far as the Montjouvain pond, where I enjoyed seeing again the reflection of the tiled roof of the hut, I had lain down in the shade and gone to sleep among the bushes on the steep slope that rose up behind the house, just where I had waited for my parents, years before, one day when they had gone to call on M. Vinteuil. It was almost dark when I awoke, and I wished to rise and go away, but I saw Mlle. Vinteuil (or thought, at least, that I recognised her, for I had not seen her often at Combray, and then only when she was still a child, whereas she was now growing into a young woman), who probably had just come in, standing in front of me, and only a few feet away from me, in that room in which her father had entertained mine, and which she had now made into a little sitting-room for herself. The window was partly open, the lamp was lighted, I could watch her every movement without her being able to see me; but, had I gone away, I must have made a rustling sound among the bushes, she would have heard me, and might have thought that I had been hiding there in order to spy upon her.

She was in deep mourning, for her father had but lately died. We had not gone to see her; my mother had not cared to go, on account of that virtue which alone in her fixed any bounds to her benevolence—namely, modesty; but she pitied the girl from the depths of her heart. My mother had not forgotten the sad end of M. Vinteuil's life, his complete absorption, first in having to play both mother and nursery-maid to his daughter, and, later, in the suffering which she had caused him; she could see the tortured expression which was never absent from the old man's face in those terrible last years; she knew that he had definitely abandoned the task of transcribing in fair copies the whole of his later work, the poor little pieces, we imagined, of an old music-master, a retired, village organist, which, we assumed, were of little or no value in themselves, though we did not despise them, because they were of such great value to him and had been the chief motive of his life before he sacrificed them to his daughter; pieces which, being mostly not even written down, but recorded only in his memory, while the rest were scribbled on loose sheets of paper, and quite illegible, must now remain unknown for ever; my mother thought, also, of that other and still more cruel renunciation to which M. Vinteuil had been driven, that of seeing the girl happily settled, with an honest and respectable future; when she called to mind all this utter and crushing misery that had come upon my aunts' old music-master, she was moved to very real grief, and shuddered to think of that other grief, so different in its bitterness, which Mlle. Vinteuil must now be feeling, tinged with remorse at having virtually killed her father. "Poor M. Vinteuil," my mother would say, "he lived for his daughter, and now he has died for her, without getting his reward. Will he get it now, I wonder, and in what form? It can only come to him from her." At the far end of Mle. Vinteuil's sitting~room, on the mantelpiece, stood a small photograph of her father which she went briskly to fetch, just as the sound of carriage wheels was heard from the road outside, then flung herself down on a sofa and drew close beside her a little table on which she placed the photograph, just as, long ago, M. Vinteuil had 'placed' beside him the piece of music which he would have liked to play over to my parents. And then her friend came in. Mlle. Vinteuil greeted her without rising, clasping her hands behind her head, and drew her body to one side of the sofa, as though to 'make room'. But no sooner had she done this than she appeared to feel that she was perhaps suggesting a particular position to her friend, with an emphasis which might well be regarded as importunate. She thought that her friend would prefer, no doubt, to sit down at some distance from her, upon a chair; she felt that she had been indiscreet; her sensitive heart took fright; stretching herself out again over the whole of the sofa, she closed her eyes and began to yawn, so as to indicate that it was a desire to sleep, and that alone, which had made her lie down there. Despite the rude and hectoring familiarity with which she treated her companion I could recognise in her the obsequious and reticent advances, the abrupt scruples and restraints which had characterised her father. Presently she rose and came to the window, where she pretended to be trying to close the shutters and not succeeding "Leave them open," said her friend "I am hot." "But it's too dreadful! People will see us," Mlle. Vinteuil answered. And then she guessed, probably, that her friend would think that she had uttered these words simply in order to provoke a reply in certain other words, which she seemed, indeed, to wish to hear spoken, but, from, prudence, would let her friend be the first to speak. And so, although I could not see her face clearly enough, I am sure that the expression must have appeared on it which my grandmother had once found so delightful, when she hastily went on: "When I say see us, I mean, of course, see us reading. It's so dreadful to think that in every trivial little thing you do some one may be overlooking you."

"Oh, yes, it is so extremely likely that people are looking at us at this time of night in this densely populated district!" said her friend, with bitter irony. "And what if they are?" she went on, feeling bound to annotate with a malicious yet affectionate wink these words which she was repeating, out of good nature, like a lesson prepared beforehand which, she knew, it would please Mlle. Vinteuil to hear. "And what if they are? All the better that they should see us."

Mlle. Vinteuil shuddered and rose to her feet. In her sensitive and scrupulous heart she was ignorant what words ought to flow, spontaneously, from her lips, so as to produce the scene for which her eager senses clamoured. She reached out as far as she could across the limitations of her true character to find the language appropriate to a vicious young woman such as she longed to be thought, but the words which, she imagined, such a young woman might have uttered with sincerity sounded unreal in her own mouth. And what little she allowed herself to say was said in a strained tone, in which her ingrained timidity paralysed her tendency to freedom and audacity of speech; while she kept on interrupting herself with "You're sure you aren't cold ? You aren't too hot? You don't want to sit and read by yourself?........"

"Your ladyship's thoughts seem to be rather `warm` this evening," she concluded, doubtless repeating a phrase which she had heard used, on some earlier occasion, by her friend.

In the V-shaped opening of her crepe bodice Mlle. Vinteuil felt the sting of her friend's sudden kiss; she gave a little scream and ran away; and then they began to chase one another about the room, scrambling over the furniture, their wide sleeves fluttering like wings, clucking and crowing like a pair of amorous fowls. At last Mlle. Vinteuil fell down exhausted upon the sofa, where she was screened from me by the stooping body of her friend. But the latter now had her back turned to the little table on which the old music-master's portrait had been arranged. Mlle. Vinteuil realised that her friend would not see it unless her attention were drawn to it, and so exclaimed, as if she herself had just noticed it for the first time "Oh! There's my father's picture looking at us, I can't think who can have put it there; I'm sure I've told them twenty times, that is not the proper place for it."

I remembered the words that M. Vinteuil had used to my parents in apologising for an obtrusive sheet of music. This photograph was, of course, in common use in their ritual observances, was subjected to daily profanation, for the friend replied in words which were evidently a liturgical response "Let him stay there. He can't trouble us any longer.

D'you think he'd start whining, d'you think he'd pack you out of the house if he could see you now, with the window open, the ugly old monkey?"

To which Mlle. Vinteuil replied, "Oh, please!"—a gentle reproach which testified to the genuine goodness of her nature, not that it was prompted by any resentment at hearing her father spoken of in this fashion (for that was evidently a feeling which she had trained herself, by a long course of sophistries, to keep in close subjection at such moments), but rather because it was the bridle which, so as to avoid all appearance of egotism, she herself used to curb the gratification which her friend was attempting to procure for her. It may well have been, too, that the smiling moderation with which she faced and answered these blasphemies, that this tender and hypocritical rebuke appeared to her frank and generous nature as a particularly shameful and seductive form of that criminal attitude towards life which she was endeavouring to adopt. But she could not resist the attraction of being treated with affection by a woman who had just shewn herself so implacable towards the defenceless dead; she sprang on to the knees of her friend and held out a chaste brow to be kissed; precisely as a daughter would have done to her mother, feeling with exquisite joy that they would thus, between them, inflict the last turn of the screw of cruelty, in robbing M. Vinteuil, as though they were actually rifling his tomb, of the sacred rights of fatherhood. Her friend took the girl's head in her hands and placed a kiss on her brow with a docility prompted by the real affection she had for Mlle. Vinteuil, as well as by the desire to bring what distraction she could into the dull and melancholy life of an orphan.

"Do you know what I should like to do to that old horror?" she said, taking up the photograph. She murmured in Mlle. Vinteuil's ear something that I could not distinguish.

"Oh! You would never dare."

"Not dare to spit on it? On that?" shouted the friend with deliberate brutality.

I heard no more, for Mlle. Vinteuil, who now seemed weary, awkward, preoccupied, sincere, and rather sad, came back to the window and drew the shutters close; but I knew now what was the reward that M Vinteuil, in return for all the suffering that he had endured in his lifetime, on account of his daughter, had received from her after his death.

If the 'Méséglise way' was so easy, it was a very different matter when we took the 'Guermantes way', for that meant a long walk, and we must make sure, first, of the weather. When we seemed to have entered upon a spell of fine days, when Françoise, in desperation that not a drop was falling upon the 'poor crops', gazing up at the sky and seeing there only a little white cloud floating here and there upon its calm, azure surface, groaned aloud and exclaimed-: "You would say they were nothing more nor less than a lot of dogfish swimming about and sticking up their snouts! Ah, they never think of making it rain a little for the poor labourers! And then when the corn is all ripe, down it will come, rattling all over the place, and think no more of where it is falling than if it was on the sea!"—when my father's appeals to the gardener had met with the same encouraging answer several times in succession, then some one would say, at dinner: "Tomorrow, if the weather holds, we might go the Guermantes way." And off we would set, immediately after luncheon, through the little garden gate which dropped us into the Rue des Perchamps, narrow and bent at a sharp angle, dotted with grass-plots over which two or three wasps would spend the day botanising, a street as quaint as its name, from which its odd characteristics and its personality were, I felt, derived; a street for which one might search in vain through the Combray of to-day, for the public school now rises upon its site. But in my dreams of Combray (like those architects, pupils of Viollet-le-Duc, who, fancying that they can detect, beneath a Renaissance rood-loft and an eighteenth-century altar, traces of a Norman choir, restore the whole church to the state in which it probably was in the twelfth century and leave not a stone of the modern edifice standing,) pierce through it and 'restore' the Rue des Perchamps.

The great charm of the ' Guermantes way' was that we had beside us, almost all the time, the course of the Vivonne. We crossed it first, ten minutes after leaving the house, by a footbridge called the Pont-Vieux. We would follow the towpath, which ran along the top of a steep bank several feet above the stream. The ground on the other side was lower, and stretched in a series of broad meadows as far as the village and even to the distant railway station. Over these were strewn the remains, half-buried in the long grass, of the castle of the old Counts of Combray, who, during the Middle Ages, had had on this side the course of the Vivonne as a barrier and defence against attack from the Lords of Guermantes and Abbots of Martinville.

Never, in the course of our walks along the Guermantes way, might we penetrate as far as the source of the Vivonne, nor could we ever reach that other goal, to which I longed so much to attain; Guermantes itself. I knew that it was the residence of its proprietors, the Duc and Duchesse de Guermantes, I knew that they were real personages who did actually exist, but whenever I thought about them I pictured them to myself either in tapestry, as was the 'Coronation of Esther' which hung in our church or, else in changing, rainbow colours, as was Gilbert the Bad in his window, where he passed from cabbage green, when I was dipping my fingers in the holy water stoup, to plum blue when I had reached our row of chairs, or, again altogether impalpable, like the image of Geneviève de Brabant, ancestress of the Guermantes family, which the magic lantern sent wandering over the curtains of my room or flung aloft upon the ceiling in short, always wrapped in the mystery of the Merovingian age, and bathed, as in a sunset, in the orange light which glowed from the resounding syllable 'antes'. And if, in spite of that, they were for me, in their capacity as a duke and a duchess, real people, though of an unfamiliar kind, this ducal personality was in its turn enormously, distended, immatenialised, so as to encircle and contain that Guermantes of which they were duke and duchess, all that sunlit 'Guermantes way' of our walks, the course of the Vivonne, its water-lilies and its overshadowing trees, and an endless series of hot summer afternoons. And I knew that they bore not only the titles of Duc and Duchesse de Guermantes, but that since the fourteenth century, when, after vain attempts to conquer its earlier lords in battle, they had allied themselves by marriage, and so become Counts of Combray, the first citizens, consequently, of the place, and yet the only ones among its citizens who did not reside in it—Comtes de Combray, possessing Combray, threading it on their string of names and titles, absorbing it in their personalities, and illustrating, no doubt, in themselves that strange and pious melancholy which was peculiar to Combray; proprietors of the town, though not of any particular house there; dwelling, presumably, out of doors, in the street, between heaven and earth, like that Gilbert de Guermantes, of whom I could see, in the stained glass of the apse of Saint-Hilaire, only the 'other side' in dull black lacquer, if I raised my eyes to look for him, when I was going to Camus's for a packet of salt.

And then it happened that, going the Guermantes way, I passed occasionally by a row of well-watered little gardens, over whose hedges rose clusters of dark blossom. I would stop before them, hoping to gain some precious addition to my experience, for I seemed to have before my eyes a fragment of that riverside country which I had longed so much to see and know since coming upon a description of it by one of my favourite authors. And it was with that storybook land, with its imagined soil intersected by a hundred bubbling water-courses, that Guermantes, changing its form in my mind, became identified, after I heard Dr. Percepied speak of the flowers and the charming rivulets and fountains that were to be seen there in the ducal park. I used to dream that Mme. de Guermantes, taking a sudden capricious fancy for myself, invited me there, that all day long she stood fishing for trout by my side. And when evening came, holding my hand in her own, as we passed by the little gardens of her vassals, she would point out to me the flowers that leaned their red and purple spikes along the tops of the low walls, and would teach me all their names. She would make me tell her, too, all about the poems that I meant to compose. And these dreams reminded me that, since I wished, some day, to become a writer, it was high time to decide what sort of books I was going to write. But as soon as I asked myself the question, and tried to discover some subject to which I could impart a philosophical significance of infinite value, my mind would stop like a clock, I would see before me vacuity, nothing, would feel either that I was wholly devoid of talent, or that, perhaps, a malady of the brain was hindering its development.. And so, utterly despondent, I renounced literature for ever, despite the encouragements that had been given me by Bloch.

One day my mother said: "You are always talking about Mme. de Guermantes. Well, Dr. Percepied did a great deal for her when she was ill, four years ago, and so she is coming to Combray for his daughter's wedding. You will be able to see her in church." It was from Dr. Percepied, as it happened, that I had heard most about Mme. de Guermantes, and he had even shewn us the number of an illustrated paper in which she was depicted in the costume which she had worn at a fancy dress ball given by the Princesse de Léon.

Suddenly, during the nuptial mass, the beadle, by moving to one side, enabled me to see, sitting in a chapel, a lady with fair hair and a large nose, piercing blue eyes, a billowy scarf of mauve silk, glossy and new and brilliant, and a little spot at the corner of her nose. And because on the surface of her face which was red, as though she had been very warm, I could make out, diluted and barely perceptible, details which resembled the portrait that had been shewn to me; because, more especially, the particular features which I remarked in this lady, if I attempted to catalogue them, formulated themselves in precisely the same terms:— a *large nose, blue eyes,* as Dr. Percepied had used when describing in my presence the Duchesse de Guermantes, I said to myself: "This lady is like the Duchesse de Guermantes." Now the chapel from which she was following the service was that of Gilbert the Bad; beneath its flat tombstones, yellowed and bulging like cells of honey in a comb, rested the bones of the old Counts of Brabant; and I remembered having heard it said that this chapel was reserved for the Guermantes family, whenever any of its members came to attend a ceremony at Combray; there was, indeed, but one woman resembling the portrait of Mme. de Guermantes who on that day, the very day on which she was expected to come there, could be sitting in that chapel: it was she! My disappointment was immense. It arose from my not having borne in mind, when I thought of Mme. de Guermantes, that I was picturing her to myself in the colours of a tapestry or a painted window, as living in another century, as being of another substance than the rest of the human race. Never had I taken into account that she might have a red face, a mauve scarf like Mme. Sazerat and the oval curve of her cheeks reminded me so strongly of people whom I had seen at home that the suspicion brushed against my mind (though it was immediately banished) that this lady in her creative principle, in the molecules of her physical composition, was perhaps not substantially the Duchesse de Guermantes, but that her body, in ignorance of the name that people had given it, belonged to a certain type of femininity which induded, also, the wives of doctors and tradesmen "It is, it must be Mme. de Guermantes and no one else!" were the words underlying the attentive and astonished expression with which I was gazing upon this image, which, naturally enough, bore no resemblance to those that had so often, under the same title of 'Mme. de Guermantes', appeared to me in dreams, since this one had not been, like the others, formed arbitrarily by myself, but had sprung into sight for the first time, only a moment ago, here in church; an image which was not of the same nature, was not colourable at will, like those others that allowed themselves to imbibe the orange tint of a sonorous syllable, but which was so real that everything, even to the fiery little spot at the corner of her nose, gave an assurance of her subjection to the laws of life, as in a transformation scene on the stage a crease in the dress of a fairy, a quivering of her tiny finger, indicate the material presence of a living actress before our eyes, whereas we were uncertain, till then, whether we were not looking merely at a projection of limelight from a lantern.

And then—oh, marvellous independence of the human gaze, tied to the human face by a cord so loose, so long, so elastic that it can stray, alone, as far as it may choose—while Mme. de Guermantes sat in the chapel above the tombs of her dead ancestors, her gaze lingered here and wandered there, rose to the capitals of the pillars, and even rested upon myself, like a ray of sunlight straying down the nave, but a ray of sunlight which, at the moment when I received its caress, appeared conscious of where it fell. As for Mme. de Guermantes herself, since she remained there motionless, sitting like a mother who affects not to notice the rude or awkward conduct of her children who, in the course of their play, are speaking to people whom she does not know, it was impossible for me to determine whether she approved or condemned the vagrancy of her eyes in the careless detachment of her heart.

I felt it to be important that she should not leave the church before I had been able to look long enough upon her, reminding myself that for years past I had regarded the sight of her as a thing eminently to be desired, and I kept my eyes fixed on her, as though by gazing at her I should be able to carry away and incorporate, to store up, for later reference, in myself the memory of that prominent nose, those red cheeks, of all those details which struck me as so much precious, authentic, unparalleled information with regard to her face. And my gaze resting upon her fair hair, her blue eyes, the lines of her neck, and overlooking the features which might have reminded me of the faces of other women, I cried out within myself, as I admired this deliberately unfinished sketch: "How lovely she is! What true nobility. It is indeed a proud Guermantes, the descendant of Geneviève de Brabant, that I have before me." And the care which I took to focus all my attention upon her face succeeded in isolating it so completely that to-day, when I call that marriage ceremony to mind, I find it impossible to visualise any single person who was present except her, and the beadle who answered me in the affirmative when I inquired whether the lady was, indeed, Mme. de Guermantes. But her, I can see her still quite clearly, especially at the moment when the procession filed into the sacristy, lighted by the intermittent, hot sunshine of a windy and rainy day, where Mme.de Guermantes found herself in the midst of all those Combray people whose names, even, she did not know, but whose inferiority proclaimed her own supremacy so loud that she must, in return, feel for them a genuine, pitying sympathy, and whom she might count on impressing even more forcibly by virtue of her simplicity and natural charm. I can see again to-day, above her mauve scarf, silky and buoyant, the gentle astonishment in her eyes, to which she had added, without daring to address it to anyone in particular, but so that everyone might enjoy his share of it, the almost timid smile of a sovereign lady who seems to be making an apology for her presence among the vassals whom she loves. This smile rested upon myself, who had never ceased to follow her with my eyes. And I, remembering the glance which she had let fall upon me during the service, blue as a ray of sunlight that had penetrated the window of Gilbert the Bad, said to myself "Of course, she is thinking about me." I fancied that I had found favour in her sight, that she would continue to think of me after she had left the church, and would, perhaps, grow pensive again, that evening, at Guermantes, on my account. And at once I fell in love with her, for if it is sometimes enough to make us love a woman that she looks on us with contempt, as I supposed Mlle. Swann to have done, while we imagine that she cannot ever be ours it is enough, also, sometimes that she looks on us kindly, as Mme. de Guermantes did then, while we think of her as almost ours already.

Once, however, when we had prolonged our walk far beyond its ordinary limits, and so had been very glad to encounter, half way home, as afternoon darkened into evening, Dr. Percepied, who drove past us at full speed in his carriage, saw and recognised us, stopped, and made us jump in beside him, I received an impression of this sort which I did not abandon without having first subjected it to an examination a little more thorough. I had been set on the box beside the coachman, we were going like the wind because the Doctor had still, before returning to Combray, to call at Martinville-le-Sec, at the house of a patient, at whose door he asked us to wait for him. At a bend in the road I experienced, suddenly, that special pleasure, which bore no resemblance to any other, when I caught sight of the twin steeples of Martinville, on which the setting sun was playing, while the movement of the carriage and the windings of the road seemed to keep them continually changing their position; and then of a third steeple, that of Vieuxvicq, which, although separated from them by a hill and a valley, and rising from rather higher ground in the distance, appeared none the less to be standing by their side.

In ascertaining and noting the shape of their spires, the changes of aspect, the sunny warmth of their surfaces, I felt that I was not penetrating to the full depth of my impression, that something more lay behind that mobility, that luminosity, something which they seemed at once to contain and to conceal. The steeples appeared so distant, and we ourselves seemed to come so little nearer them, that I was astonished when, a few minutes later, we drew up outside the church of Martinville. I did not know the reason for the pleasure which I had found in seeing them upon the horizon, and the business of trying to find out what that reason was seemed to me irksome; I wished only to keep in reserve in my brain those converging lines, moving in the sunshine, and, for the time being, to think of them no more. And it is probable that, had I done so, those two steeples would have vanished for ever, in a great medley of trees and roofs and scents and sounds which I had noticed and set apart on account of the obscure sense of pleasure which they gave me, but without ever exploring them more fully. I got down from the box to talk to my parents while we were waiting for the Doctor to reappear. Then it was time to start; I climbed up again to my place, turning my head to look back, once more, at my steeples, of which, a little later, I caught a farewell glimpse at a turn in the road. The coachman, who seemed little inclined for conversation, having barely acknowledged my remarks, I was obliged, in default of other society, to fall back on my own, and to attempt to recapture the vision of my steeples. And presently their outlines and their sunlit surface, as though they had been a sort of rind, were stripped apart ; a little of what they had concealed from me became apparent; an idea came into my mind which had not existed for me a moment earlier, framed itself in words in my head; and the pleasure with which the first sight of them, just now, had filled me was so much enhanced that, overpowered by a sort of intoxication, I could no longer think of anything but them. At this point, although we had now travelled a long way from Martinville, I turned my head and caught sight of them again, quite black this time, for the sun had meanwhile set. Every few minutes a turn in the road would sweep them out of sight; then they shewed themselves for the last time, and so I saw them no more.

Without admitting to myself that what lay buried within the steeples of Martinville must be something analogous to a charming phrase, since it was in the form of words which gave me pleasure that it had appeared to me, I borrowed a pencil and some paper from the Doctor, and composed, in spite of the jolting of the carriage, to appease my conscience and to satisfy my enthusiasm, the following little fragment, which I have since discovered, and now reproduce, with only a slight revision here and there.

Alone, rising from the level of the plain, and seemingly lost in that expanse of open country, climbed to the sky the twin steeples of Martinville. Presently we saw three springing into position, confronting them by a daring vault, a third, a dilatory steeple, that of Vieuxvicq, was come to join them. The minutes passed, we were moving rapidly, and yet the three steeples were always a long way ahead of us, like three birds perched upon the plain, motionless and conspicuous in the sunlight. Then the steeple of Vieuxvicq withdrew, took its proper distance, and the steeples of Martinville remained alone, gilded by the light of the setting sun, which, even at that distance, I could see playing and smiling upon their sloped sides. We had been so long in approaching them that I was thinking of the time that must still elapse before we could reach them when, of a sudden, the carriage, having turned a corner, set us down at their feet; and they had flung themselves so abruptly in our path that we had barely time to stop before being dashed against the porch of the church.

We resumed our course; we had left Martinville some little time, and the village, after accompanying us for a few seconds, had already disappeared, when, lingering alone on the horizon to watch our flight, its steeples and that of Vieuxvicq waved once again, in token of farewell, their sun-bathed pinnacles. Sometimes one would withdraw, so that the other two might watch us for a moment still; then the road changed direction, they veered in the light like three golden pivots, and vanished from my gaze. But, a little later, when we were already close to Combray, the sun having set meanwhile, I caught sight of them for the last time, far away, and seeming no more now than three flowers painted upon the sky above the low line of fields. They made me think, too, of three maidens in a legend, abandoned in a solitary place over which night had begun to fall; and while we drew away from them at a gallop, I could see them timidly seeking their way, and, after some awkward, stumbling movements of their noble silhouettes, drawing close to one another, slipping one behind another, shewing nothing more, now, against the still rosy sky than a single dusky form, charming and resigned, and so vanishing in the night.

I never thought again of this page, but at the moment when, on my corner of the box-seat, where the Doctor's coachman was in the habit of placing, in a hamper, the fowls which he had bought at Martinville market, I had finished writing it, I found such a sense of happiness, felt that it had so entirely relieved my mind of the obsession of the steeples, and of the mystery which they concealed, that, as though I myself were a hen and had just laid an egg, I began to sing at the top of my voice.

And so I would often lie until morning, dreaming of the old days at Combray, of my melancholy and wakeful evenings there; of other days besides, the memory of which had been more lately restored to me by the taste—by what would have been called at Combray the 'perfume'— of a cup of tea and, by an association of memories, of a story which, many years after I had left the little place, had been told me of a love affair in which Swann had been involved before I was born; with that accuracy of detail which it is easier, often, to obtain when we are studying the lives of people who have been dead for centuries.

SWANN IN LOVE

To admit you to the 'little nucleus', the 'little group', the 'little clan', at the Verdurins', one condition sufficed, but that one was indispensable; you must give tacit adherence to a Creed one of whose articles was that the young pianist, whom Mme. Verdurin had taken under her patronage that year, and of whom she said, "Really, it oughtn't to be allowed, to play Wagner as well as that! Left both Planté and Rubinstein 'sitting'." Each 'new recruit' whom the Verdurins failed to persuade that the evenings spent by other people, in other houses than theirs, were as dull as ditch-water, saw himself banished forthwith. Women being in this respect more rebellious than men, more reluctant to lay aside all worldly curiosity and the desire to find out for themselves whether other drawing-rooms might not sometimes be as entertaining, and the Verdurins feeling, moreover, that this critical spirit and this demon of frivolity might, by their contagion, prove fatal to the orthodoxy of the little church, they had been obliged to expel, one after another, all those of the 'faithful' who were of the female sex. Apart from the doctor's young wife, they were reduced almost exclusively that season (for all that Mme. Verdurin herself was a thoroughly 'good' woman, and came of a respectable middle-class family, excessively rich and wholly undistinguished, with which she had gradually and of her own accord severed all connection) to a young woman almost of a 'certain class', a Mme. de Crécy, whom Mme. Verdurin called by her Christian name, Odette, and pronounced a 'love', and to the pianist's aunt, who looked as though she had, at one period, 'answered the bell': ladies quite ignorant of the world, who in their social simplicity were so easily led to believe that the Princesse de Sagan and the Duchesse de Guermantes were obliged to pay large sums of money to other poor wretches, in order to have anyone at their dinner-parties, that if somebody had offered to procure them an invitation to the house of either of those great dames, the old doorkeeper and the woman of 'easy virtue' would have contemptuously declined.

The Verdurins never invited you to dinner; you had your 'place laid' there. There was never any programme for the evening's entertainment. The young pianist would play, but only if he felt inclined, for no one was forced to do anything, and, as M. Verdurin used to say: "We're all friends here. Liberty Hall, you know!" If the pianist suggested playing the Ride of the Valkyries, or the Prelude to Tristan, Mme. Verdurin would protest, not that the music was displeasing to her, but, on the contrary, that it made too violent an impression. "Then you want me to have one of my headaches? You know quite well, it's the same every time he plays that. I know what I'm in for. To-morrow, when I want to get up—nothing doing!" If he was not going to play they talked, and one of the friends—usually the painter who was in favour there that year— would "spin," as M. Verdurin put it, "a damned funny yarn that made 'em all split with laughter," and especially Mme. Verdurin, for whom—so strong was her habit of taking literally the figurative accounts of her emotions—Dr. Cottard, who was then just starting in general practice, would "really have to come one day and set her jaw, which she had dislocated with laughing too much."

Evening dress was barred, because you were all 'good pals', and didn't want to look like the 'boring people' who were to be avoided like the plague, and only asked to the big evenings, which were given as seldom as possible, and then only if it would amuse the painter or make the musician better known. The rest of the time you were quite happy playing charades and having supper in fancy dress, and there was no need to mingle any strange element with the 'little clan'.

And so, too, if one of the 'faithful' had a friend, or one of the ladies a young man, who was liable, now and then, to make them miss an evening, the Verdurins, who were not in the least afraid of a woman's having a lover, provided that she had him in their company, loved him in their company and did not prefer him to their company, would say : "Very well, then, bring your friend along." And he would be put to the test, to see whether he was willing to have no secrets from Mme. Verdurin, whether he was susceptible of being enrolled in the 'little clan'. If he failed to pass, the faithful one who had introduced him would be taken on one side, and would be tactfully assisted to quarrel with the friend or mistress. But if the test proved satisfactory, the newcomer would in turn be numbered among the 'faithful'. And so when, in the course of this same year, the courtesan told M. Verdurin that she had made the acquaintance of such a charming gentleman, M. Swann, and hinted that he would very much like to be allowed to come,

M. Verdurin carried the request at once to his wife. He never formed an opinion on any subject until she had formed hers, his special duty being to carry out her wishes and those of the 'faithful' generally, which he did with boundless ingenuity.

"My dear, Mme. de Crécy has something to say to you. She would like to bring one of her friends here, a M. Swann. What do you say?"

"Why, as if anybody could refuse anything to a little piece of perfection like that. Be quiet; no one asked your opinion. I tell you that you are a piece of perfection."

"Just as you like," replied Odette, in an affected tone, and then went on: "You know I'm not fishing for compliments."

"Very well; bring your friend, if he's nice."

Now there was no connection whatsoever between the 'little nucleus' and the society which Swann frequented, and a purely worldly man would have thought it hardly worth his while, when occupying so exceptional a position in the world, to seek an introduction to the Verdurins. But Swann was so ardent a lover that, once he had got to know almost all the women of the aristocracy, once they had taught him all that there was to learn, he had ceased to regard those naturalisation papers, almost a patent of nobility, which the Faubourg Saint-Germain had bestowed upon him, save as a sort of negotiable bond, a letter of credit with no intrinsic value, which allowed him to improvise a status for himself in some little hole in the country, or in some obscure quarter of Paris, where the good-looking daughter of a local squire or solicitor had taken his fancy. For at such times desire, or love itself, would revive in him a feeling a vanity from which he was now quite free in his everyday life, although it was, no doubt, the same feeling which had originally prompted him towards that career as a man of fashion in which he had squandered his intellectual gifts upon frivolous amusements, and had made use of his erudition in matters of art only to advise society ladies what pictures to buy and how to decorate their houses; and this vanity it was which made him eager to shine, in the sight of any fair unknown who had captivated him for the moment, with a brilliance which the name of Swann by itself did not emit. And he was most eager when the fair unknown was in humble circumstances. Just as it is not by other men of intelligence that an intelligent man is afraid of being thought a fool, so it is not by the great gentleman but by boors and 'bounders' that a man of fashion is afraid of finding his social value underrated. Three-fourths of the mental ingenuity displayed, of the social falsehoods scattered broadcast ever since the world began by people whose importance they have served only to diminish, have been aimed at inferiors. And Swann, who behaved quite simply and was at his ease when with a duchess, would tremble, for fear of being despised, and would instantly begin to pose, were he to meet her grace's maid. He belonged to that class of intelligent men who have led a life of idleness, and who seek consolation and, perhaps, an excuse in the idea, which their idleness offers to their intelligence, of objects as worthy of their interest as any that could be attained by art or learning, the idea that 'Life' contains situations more interesting and more romantic than all the romances ever written. So, at least, he would assure and had no difficulty in persuading the more subtle among his friends in the fashionable world, notably the Baron de Charlus, whom he liked to amuse with stories of the startling adventures that had befallen him, such as when he had met a woman in the train, and had taken her home with him, before discovering that she was the sister of a reigning monarch, in whose hands were gathered, at that moment, all the threads of European politics, of which he found himself kept informed in the most delightful fashion, or when, in the complexity of circumstances, it depended upon the choice which the Conclave was about to make whether he might or might not become the lover of somebody's cook.

It was not only the brilliant phalanx of virtuous dowagers, generals and academicians, to whom he was bound by such close ties, that Swann compelled with so much cynicism to serve him as panders. All his friends were accustomed to receive, from time to time, letters which called on them for a word of recommendation or introduction, with a diplomatic adroitness which, persisting throughout all his successive affairs and using different pretexts, revealed more glaringly than the clumsiest indiscretion, a permanent trait in his character and an unvarying quest. I used often to recall to myself when, many years later, I began to take an interest in his character because of the similarities which, in wholly different respects, it offered to my own, how, when he used to write to my grandfather (though not at the time we are now considering, for it was about the date of my own birth that Swann's great 'affair' began, and made a long interruption in his amatory practices) the latter, recognising his friend's handwriting on the envelope, would exclaim: 'Here is Swann asking for something; on guard!" And, either from distrust or from the unconscious spirit of devilry which urges us to offer a thing only to those who do not want it, my grandparents would meet with an obstinate refusal the most easily satisfied of his prayers, as when he begged them for an introduction to a girl who dined with us every Sunday, and whom they were obliged, whenever Swann mentioned her, to pretend that they no longer saw, although they would be wondering, all through the week, whom they could invite to meet her, and often failed, in the end, to find anyone, sooner than make a sign to him who would so gladly have accepted.

But while each of these attachments, each of these flirtations had been the realisation, more or less complete, of a dream born of the sight of a face or a form which Swann had spontaneously, and without effort on his part, found charming, it was quite another matter when, one day at the theatre, he was introduced to Odette de Crécy by an old friend of his own, who had spoken of her to him as a ravishing creature with whom he might very possibly come to an understanding but had made her out to be harder of conquest than she actually was, so as to appear to be conferring a special favour by the introduction. She had struck Swann not, certainly, as being devoid of beauty, but as endowed with a style of beauty which left him indifferent, which aroused in him no desire, which gave him, indeed, a sort of physical repulsion; as one of those women of whom every man can name some, and each will name different examples, who are the converse of the type which our senses demand. To give him any pleasure, her profile was too sharp, her skin too delicate, her cheek-bones too prominent, her features too tightly drawn. Her eyes were fine, but so large that they seemed to be bending beneath their own weight, strained the rest of her face and always made her appear unwell or in an ill humour. Some time after this introduction at the theatre she had written to ask Swann whether she might see his collections, which would interest her so much, she, "an ignorant woman with a taste for beautiful things," saying that she would know him better when once she had seen him in his home, where she imagined him to be "so comfortable with his tea and his books"; although she had not concealed her surprise at his being in that part of the town, which must be so depressing, and was "not nearly smart enough for such a very smart man." And when he allowed her to come she had said to him as she left how sorry she was to have stayed so short a time in a house into which she was so glad to have found her way at last, speaking of him as though he had meant something more to her than the rest of the people she knew, and appearing to unite their two selves with a kind of romantic bond which had made him smile.

Odette de Crécy came again to see Swann; her visits grew more frequent, and doubtless each visit revived the sense of disappointment which he felt at the sight of a face whose details he had somewhat forgotten in the interval, not remembering it as either so expressive or, in spite of her youth, so faded; he used to regret, while she was talking to him, that her really considerable beauty was not of the kind which he spontaneously admired. It must be remarked that Odette's face appeared thinner and more prominent than it actually was, because her forehead and the upper part of her cheeks, a single and almost plane surface, were covered by the masses of hair which women wore at that period, drawn forward in a fringe, raised in crimped waves and falling in stray locks over her ears; while as for her figure, and she was admirably built, it was impossible to make out its continuity (on account of the fashion then prevailing, and in spite of her being one of the best dressed women in Paris) for the corset, jutting forwards in an arch, as though over an imaginary stomach, and ending in a sharp point, beneath which bulged out the balloon of her double skirts, gave a woman, that year, the appearance of being composed of different sections badly fitted together; to such an extent did the frills, the flounces, the inner bodice follow, in complete independence, controlled only by the fancy of their designer or the rigidity of their material, the line which led them to the knots of ribbon, falls of lace, fringes of vertically hanging jet, or carried them along the bust, but nowhere attached themselves to the living creature, who, according as the architecture of their fripperies drew them towards or away from her own, found herself either strait-laced to suffocation or else completely buried.

But, after Odette had left him, Swann would think with a smile of her telling him how the time would drag until he allowed her to come again; he remembered the anxious, timid way in which she had once begged him that it might not be very long, and the way in which she had looked at him then, fixing upon him her fearful and imploring gaze, which gave her a touching air beneath the bunches of artificial pansies fastened in the front of her round bonnet of white straw, tied with strings of black velvet. "And won't you," she had ventured, "come just once and take tea with me?" He had pleaded pressure of work, an essay—which, in reality, he had abandoned years ago—on Vermeer of Delft. "I know that I am quite useless," she had replied, "a little wild thing like me beside a learned great man like you. I should be like the frog in the fable! And yet I should so much like to learn, to know things, to be initiated. What fun it would be to become a regular bookworm, to bury my nose in a lot of old papers!" she had gone on, with that self-satisfied air which a smart woman adopts when she insists that her one desire is to give herself up, without fear of soiling her fingers, to some unclean task, such as cooking the dinner, with her " hands right in the dish itself." "You will only laugh at me, but this painter who stops you from seeing me," she meant Vermeer, "I have never even heard of him; is he alive still? Can I see any of his things in Paris, so as to have some idea of what is going on behind that great brow which works so hard, that head which I feel sure is always puzzling away about things; just to be able to say 'There, that's what he's thinking about!' What a dream it would be to be able to help you with your work."

He had sought an excuse in his fear of forming new friendships, which he gallantly described as his fear of a hopeless passion. "You are afraid of falling in love? How funny that is, when I go about seeking nothing else, and would give my soul just to find a little love somewhere!" she had said, so naturally and with such an air of conviction that he had been genuinely touched. "Some woman must have made you suffer. And you think that the rest are all like her. She can't have understood you: you are so utterly different from ordinary men. That's what I liked about you when I first saw you; I felt at once that you weren't like everybody else."

"And then, besides, there's yourself—" he had continued, "I know what women are; you must have a whole heap of things to do, and never any time to spare." "I ? Why, I have never anything to do. I am always free, and I always will be free if you want me. At whatever hour of the day or night it may suit you to see me, just send for me, and I shall be only too delighted to come. Will you do that? Do you know what I should really like—to introduce you to Mme. Verdurin, where I go every evening. Just fancy my finding you there, and thinking that it was a little for my sake that you had gone."

It so happened that my grandfather had known—which was more than could be said of any of their actual acquaintance—the family of these Verdurins. But he had entirely severed his connection with what he called "young Verdurin," taking a general view of him as one who had fallen— though without losing hold of his millions—among the riffraff of Bohemia. One day he received a letter from Swann asking whether my grandfather could put him in touch with the Verdurins : "On guard! On guard !" he exclaimed as he read it, "I am not at all surprised; Swann was bound to finish up like this. A nice lot of people! I cannot do what he asks, because, in the first place, I no longer know the gentleman in question. Besides, there must be a woman in it somewhere, and I don't mix myself up in such matters, Ah, well, we shall see some fun if Swann begins running after the little Verdurins."

And on my grandfather's refusal to act as sponsor, it was Odette herself who had taken Swann to the house. The Verdurins had had dining with them, on the day when Swann made his first appearance, Dr. and Mme. Cottard, the young pianist and his aunt, and the painter then in favour, while these were joined, in the course of the evening, by several more of the 'faithful'. Dr. Cottard was never quite certain of the tone in which he ought to reply to any observation, or whether the speaker was jesting or in earnest. And so in any event he would embellish all his facial expressions with the offer of a conditional, a provisional smile whose expectant subtlety would exonerate him from the charge of being a simpleton, if the remark addressed to him should turn out to have been facetious. But as he must also be prepared to face the alternative, he never dared to allow this smile a definite expression on his features, and you would see there a perpetually flickering uncertainty, in which you might decipher the question that he never dared to ask: "Do you really mean that?" He was no more confident of the manner in which he ought to conduct himself in the street, or indeed in life generally, than he was in a drawing-room; and he might be seen greeting passers-by, carriages, and anything that occurred with a malicious smile which absolved his subsequent behaviour of all impropriety, since it proved, if it should turn out unsuited to the occasion, that he was well aware of that, and that if he had assumed a smile, the jest was a secret of his own.

When Mme. Verdurin had announced that they were to see M. Swann that evening, "Swann!" the Doctor had exclaimed in a tone rendered brutal by his astonishment, for the smallest piece of news would always take utterly unawares this man who imagined himself to be perpetually in readiness for anything. And seeing that no one answered him, "Swann ! Who on earth is Swann?" he shouted, in a frenzy of anxiety which subsided as soon as Mme. Verdurin had explained, "Why, Odette's friend, whom she told us about."

"Ah, good, good; that's all right, then," answered the Doctor, at once mollified. As for the painter, he was overjoyed at the prospect of Swann's appearing at the Verdurins', because he supposed him to be in love with Odette, and was always ready to assist at lovers' meetings. "Nothing amuses me more than match-making," he confided to Cottard. The painter at once invited Swann to visit his studio with Odette, and Swann found him very pleasant. "Perhaps you will be more highly favoured than I have been," Mme. Verdurin broke in, with mock resentment of the favour, "perhaps you will be allowed to see Cottard's portrait" (for which she had given the painter a commission). "Take care, Master Biche," she reminded the painter, whom it was a time-honoured pleasantry to address as 'Master', "to catch that nice look in his eyes, that witty little twinkle. You know, what I want to have most of all is his smile; that's what I've asked you to paint— the portrait of his smile." And since the phrase struck her as noteworthy, she repeated it very loud, so as to make sure that as many as possible of her guests should hear it, and even made use of some indefinite pretext to draw the circle closer before she uttered it again.

Mme. Verdurin was sitting upon a high Swedish chair of waxed pinewood, which a violinist from that country had given her, and which she kept in her drawing-room, although in appearance it suggested a school 'form', and 'swore', as the saying is, at the really good antique furniture which she had besides; but she made a point of keeping on view the presents which her 'faithful' were in the habit of making her from time to time, so that the donors might have the pleasure of seeing them there when they came to the house. She tried to persuade them to confine their tributes to flowers and sweets, which had at least the merit of mortality; but she was never successful, and the house was gradually filled with a collection of foot-warmers, cushions, clocks, screens, barometers and vases, a constant repetition and a boundless incongruity of useless but indestructible objects.

From this lofty perch she would take her spirited part in the conversation of the 'faithful', and would revel in all their fun; but, since the accident to her jaw, she had abandoned the effort involved in real hilarity, and had substituted a kind of symbolical dumb-show which signified, without endangering or even fatiguing her in any way, that she was 'laughing until she cried'. At the least witticism aimed by any of the circle against a 'bore', or against a former member of the circle who was now relegated to the limbo of ' bores'—and to the utter despair of M. Verdurin, who had always made out that he was just as easily amused as his wife, but who, since his laughter was the 'real thing` was out of breath in a moment, and so was overtaken and vanquished by her device of a feigned but continuous hilarity—she would utter a shrill cry, shut tight her little bird-like eyes, which were beginning to be clouded over by a cataract, and quickly, as though she had only just time to avoid some indecent sight or to parry a mortal blow, burying her face in her hands, which completely engulfed it, and prevented her from seeing anything at all, she would appear to be struggling to suppress, to eradicate a laugh which, were she to give way to it, must inevitably leave her inanimate. So, stupefied with the gaiety of the 'faithful', drunken with comradeship, scandal and asseveration, Mme. Verdurin, perched on her high seat like a cage-bird whose biscuit has been steeped in mulled wine, would sit aloft and sob with fellow-feeling.

Meanwhile M. Verdurin, after first asking Swann's permission to light his pipe (" No ceremony here, you understand ; we're all pals!"), went and begged the young musician to sit down at the piano.

"Leave him alone; don't bother him; he hasn't come here to be tormented," cried Mme. Verdurin. "I won't have him tormented."

"But why on earth should it bother him?" rejoined M. Verdurin. "I'm sure M. Swann has never heard the sonata in F sharp which we discovered; he is going to play us the pianoforte arrangement."

"No, no, no, not my sonata!" she screamed, "I don't want to be made to cry until I get a cold in the head, and neuralgia all down my face, like last time; thanks very much, I don't intend to repeat that performance; you are all very kind and considerate; it is easy to see that none of you will have to stay in bed for a week."

This little scene, which was re-enacted as often as the young pianist sat down to play, never failed to delight the audience, as though each of them were witnessing it for the first time, as a proof of the seductive originality of the 'Mistress' as she was styled, and of the acute sensitiveness of her musical 'ear'. Those nearest to her would attract the attention of the rest, who were smoking or playing, cards at the other end of the room, by their cries of 'Hear, hear!' which, as in Parliamentary debates, showed that something worth listening to was being said. And next day they would commiserate with those who had been prevented from coming that evening, and would assure them that the 'little scene' had never been so amusingly done.

"Well, all right, then," said M. Verdurin, "he can play just the *andante*."

"Just the *andante*! How you do go on," cried his wife. "As if it weren't 'just the *andante*' that breaks every bone in my body. The 'Master' is really too priceless! Just as though he said 'in the Ninth, we need only have the *finale*,' or 'just the overture' of the *Meistersingers*."

The Doctor, however, urged Mme. Verdurin to let the pianist play, not because he supposed her to be malingering when she spoke of the distressing effects that music always had upon her, for he recognised the existence of certain neurasthenic states—but from his habit, common to many doctors, of at once relaxing the strict letter of a prescription as soon as it appeared to jeopardise, what seemed to him far more important, the success of some social gathering at which he was present, and of which the patient whom he had urged for once to forget her dyspepsia or headache formed an essential factor.

"You won't be ill this time, you'll find," he told her, seeking at the same time to subdue her mind by the magnetism of his gaze. "And, if you are ill, we will cure you."

"Will you, really?" Mme. Verdurin spoke as though, with so great a favour in store for her, there was nothing for it but to capitulate. Perhaps, too, by dint of saying that she was going to be ill, she had worked herself into a state in which she forgot, occasionally, that it was all only a 'little scene', and regarded things, quite sincerely, from an invalid's point of view.

Odette had gone to sit on a tapestry-covered sofa near the piano, saying to Mme. Verdurin, "I have my own little corner, haven't I?"

And Mme. Verdurin, seeing Swann by himself upon a chair, made him get up: "You're not at all comfortable there; go along and sit by Odette; you can make room for M. Swann there, can't you, Odette?"

After the pianist had played, Swann felt and showed more interest in him than in any of the other guests, for the following reason. The year before, at an evening party, he had heard a piece of music played on the piano and violin. At first he had appreciated only the material quality of the sounds which those instruments secreted. And it had been a source of keen pleasure when, below the narrow ribbon of the violin-part, delicate, unyielding, substantial and governing the whole, he had suddenly perceived, where it was trying to surge upwards in a flowing tide of sound, the mass of the piano-part, multiform, coherent, level, and breaking everywhere in melody like the deep blue tumult of the sea, silvered and charmed into a minor key by the moonlight. But at a given moment, without being able to distinguish any clear outline, or to give a name to what was pleasing him, suddenly enraptured, he had tried to collect, to treasure in his memory the phrase or harmony—he knew not which—that had just been played, and had opened and expanded his soul, just as the fragrance of certain roses, wafted upon the moist air of evening, has the power of dilating our nostrils. Perhaps it was owing to his own ignorance of music that he had been able to receive so confused an impression, one of those that are, notwithstanding, our only purely musical impressions, limited in their extent, entirely original, and irreducible into any other kind.

And so, hardly had the delicious sensation, which Swann had experienced, died away, before his memory had furnished him with an immediate transcript, summary, it is true, and provisional, but one on which he had kept his eyes fixed while the playing continued, so effectively that, when the same impression suddenly returned, it was no longer uncapturable. He was able to picture to himself its extent, its symmetrical arrangement, its notation, the strength of its expression; he had before him that definite object which was no longer pure music, but rather design, architecture, thought, and which allowed the actual music to be recalled. This time he had distinguished, quite clearly, a phrase which emerged for a few moments from the waves of sound. It had at once held out to him an invitation to partake of intimate pleasures, of whose existence, before hearing it, he had never dreamed, into which he felt that nothing but this phrase could initiate him; and he had been filled with love for it, as with a new and strange desire. With a slow and rhythmical movement it led him here, there, everywhere, towards a state of happiness noble, unintelligible, yet clearly indicated. And then, suddenly, having reached a certain point from which he was prepared to follow it, after pausing for a moment, abruptly it changed its direction, and in a fresh movement, more rapid, multiform, melancholy, incessant, sweet, it bore him off with it towards a vista of joys unknown. Then it vanished. He hoped, with a passionate longing, that he might find it again, a third time. And reappear it did, though without speaking to him more clearly, bringing him, indeed, a pleasure less profound. But when he was once more at home he needed it, he was like a man into whose life a woman, whom he has seen for a moment passing by, has brought a new form of beauty, which strengthens and enlarges his own power of perception, without his knowing even whether he is ever to see her again, whom he loves already, although he knows nothing of her, not even her name.

But to-night, at Mme. Verdurin's, scarcely had the little pianist begun to play when, suddenly, after a high note held on through two whole bars, Swann saw it approaching, stealing forth from underneath that resonance, which was prolonged and stretched out over it, like a curtain of sound, to veil the mystery of its birth—and recognised, secret, whispering, articulate, the airy and fragrant phrase that he had loved. And it was so peculiarly itself, it had so personal a charm, which nothing else could have replaced, that Swann felt as though he had met, in a friend's drawing-room, a woman whom he had seen and admired, once, in the street, and had despaired of ever seeing again. Finally the phrase withdrew and vanished, pointing, directing, diligent among the wandering currents of its fragrance, leaving upon Swann's features a reflection of its smile. But now, at last, he could ask the name of his fair unknown (and was told that it was the *andante* movement of Vinteuil's sonata for the piano and violin), he held it safe, could have it again to himself, at home, as often as he would, could study its language and acquire its secret.

And so, when the pianist had finished, Swann crossed the room and thanked him with a vivacity which delighted Mme. Verdurin.

"Isn't he charming?" she asked Swann, "doesn't he just understand it, his sonata, the little wretch? You never dreamed, did you, that a piano could be made to express all that? Upon my word, there's everything in it except the piano! I'm caught out every time I hear it; I think I'm listening to an orchestra. Though it's better, really, than an orchestra, more complete." The young pianist bent over her as he answered, smiling and underlining each of his words as though he were making an epigram: "You are most generous to me." And while Mme. Verdurin was saying to her husband, "Run and fetch him a glass of orangeade; it's well earned!" Swann began to tell Odette how he had fallen in love with that little phrase. When their hostess, who was a little way off, called out, "Well! It looks to me as though some one was saying nice things to you, Odette!" she replied, "Yes, very nice," and he found her simplicity delightful. Then he asked for some information about this Vinteuil; what else he had done, and at what period in his life he had composed the sonata;—what meaning the little phrase could have had for him, that was what Swann wanted most to know.

Swann discovered no more than that the recent publication of Vinteuil's sonata had caused a great stir among the most advanced school of musicians, but that it was still unknown to the general public. " I know some one, quite well, called Vinteuil," said Swann, thinking of the old music-master at Combray who had taught my grandmother's sisters.

"Perhaps that's the man!" cried Mme. Verdurin.

"Oh, no!" Swann burst out laughing. "If you had ever seen him for a moment you wouldn't put the question."

"Then to put the question is to solve the problem?" the Doctor suggested.

"But it may well be some relative;" Swann went on. "That would be bad enough; but, after all, there is no reason why a genius shouldn't have a cousin who is a silly old fool. And if that should be so, I swear there's no known or unknown form of torture I wouldn't undergo to get the old fool to introduce me to the man who composed the sonata; starting with the torture of the old fool's company, which would be ghastly."

"D'you know; we like your friend so very much," said Mme. Verdurin, later, when Odette was bidding her good night. "He is so unaffected, quite charming. If they're all like that, the friends you want to bring here, by all means bring them,"

M. Verdurin remarked that Swann had failed, all the same, to appreciate the pianist's aunt. I dare say he felt a little strange, poor man," suggested Mme. Verdurin. "You can't expect him to catch the tone of the house the first time he comes; like Cottard, who has been one of our little 'clan' now for years. The first time doesn't count; it's just for looking round and finding out things. Odette, he understands all right, he's to join us tomorrow at the Châtelet. Perhaps you might call for him and bring him."

"No, he doesn't want that."

"Oh, very well; just as you like. Provided he doesn't fail us at the last moment."

Greatly to Mme. Verdurin' s surprise, he never failed them. He would go to meet them, no matter where, at restaurants outside Paris, (not that they went there much at first, for the season had not yet begun) and more frequently at the play, in which Mme. Verdurin delighted. One evening, when they were dining at home, he heard her complain that she had not one of those permits which would save her the trouble of waiting at doors and standing in crowds, and say how useful it would be to them at first-nights, and gala performances at the Opéra, and what a nuisance it had been, not having one, on the day of Gambetta's funeral. Swann never spoke of his distinguished friends, but only of such as might be regarded as detrimental, whom, therefore, he thought it snobbish, and in not very good taste to conceal; while he frequented the Faubourg Saint-Germain he had come to include, in the latter class, all his friends in the official world of the Third Republic, and so broke in, without thinking : " I'll see to that, all right. You shall have it in time for the *Danicheff* revival. I shall be lunching with the Prefect of Police to-morrow, as it happens, at the Elysée."

"What's that? The Elysée?" Dr. Cottard roared in a voice of thunder.

"Yes, at M. Grévy's," replied Swann, feeling a little awkward at the effect which his announcement had produced.

"Are you often taken like that?" the painter asked Cottard, with mock-seriousness. As a rule, once an explanation had been given, Cottard would say: "Ah, good, good; that's all, right, then," after which he would show not the least trace of emotion. But this time Swann's last words, instead of the usual calming effect, had that of heating, instantly, to boiling-point his astonishment at the discovery that a man with whom he himself was actually sitting at table, a man who had no official position, no honours or distinction of any sort, was on visiting terms with the Head of the State.

"What's that you say? M. Grévy? Do you know M. Grévy?" he demanded of Swann, in the stupid and incredulous tone of a constable on duty at the palace, when a stranger has come up and asked to see the President of the Republic; until, guessing from his words and manner what, as the newspapers say, 'sort of man he is dealing with' he assures the poor lunatic that he will be admitted at once, and points the way to the reception ward of the police infirmary. "I know him slightly; we have some friends in common" (Swann dared not add that one of these friends was the Prince of Wales). "Anyhow, he is very free with his invitations, and, I assure you, his luncheon-parties are not the least bit amusing; they're very simple affairs, too, you know; never more than eight at table," he went on, trying desperately to cut out everything that seemed to show off his relations with the President in a light too dazzling for the Doctor's eyes. Whereupon Cottard, at once conforming in his mind to the literal interpretation of what Swann was saying, decided that invitations from M. Grévy were very little sought after, were sent out, in fact, into the highways and hedgerows. And from that moment he never seemed at all surprised to hear that Swann, or anyone else, was 'always at the Elysée'; he even felt a little sorry for a man who had to go to luncheon-parties which, he himself admitted, were a bore.

"Ah, good, good; that's quite all right, then," he said, in the tone of a customs official who has been suspicious up to now, but, after hearing your explanations, stamps your passport and lets you proceed on your journey without troubling to examine your luggage.

"I can well believe you don't find them amusing, those parties; indeed, it's very good of you to go to them!" said Mme. Verdurin, who regarded the President of the Republic only as a 'bore' to be especially dreaded, since he had at his disposal means of seduction, and even of compulsion, which, if employed to captivate her 'faithful,' might easily make them 'fail'. " It seems, he's as deaf as a post; and eats with his fingers."

"Upon my word! Then it can't be much fun for you, going there." A note of pity sounded in the Doctor's voice; and then struck by the number—only eight at table— "Are these luncheons what you would describe as 'intimate'?" he inquired briskly, not so much out of idle curiosity as in his linguistic zeal. But so great and glorious a figure was the President of the French Republic in the eyes of Dr. Cottard that neither the modesty of Swann nor the spite of Mme. Verdurin could ever wholly efface that first impression, and he never sat down to dinner with the Verdurins without asking anxiously, "D'you think we shall see M. Swann here this evening? He is a personal friend of M. Grévy's. I suppose that means he's what you'd call a 'gentleman'?" He even went to the length of offering Swann a card of invitation to the Dental Exhibition.

"This will let you in, and anyone you take with you," he explained, "but dogs are not admitted. I'm just warning you, you understand, because some friends of mine went there once, who hadn't been told, and there was the devil to pay." As for M. Verdurin, he did not fail to observe the distressing effect upon his wife of the discovery that Swann had influential friends of whom he had never spoken.

If no arrangement had been made to 'go anywhere', it was at the Verdurins' that Swann would find the 'little nucleus' assembled, but he never appeared there except in the evenings, and would hardly ever accept their invitations to dinner, in spite of Odette's entreaties.

"I could dine with you alone somewhere, if you'd rather," she suggested.

"But what about Mme. Verdurin?"

"Oh, that's quite simple. I need only say that my dress wasn't ready, or that my cab came late. There is always some excuse."

"How charming of you."

But Swann said to himself that, if he could make Odette feel (by consenting to meet her only after dinner) that there were other pleasures which he preferred to that of her company, then the desire that she felt for his would be all the longer in reaching the point of satiety. Besides, as he infinitely preferred to Odette's style of beauty that of a little working girl, as fresh and plump as a rose, with whom he happened to be simultaneously in love, he preferred to spend the first part of the evening with her, knowing that he was sure to see Odette later on. For the same reason, he would never allow Odette to call for him at his house, to take him on to the Verdurins' The little girl used to wait, not far from his door, at a street corner; Rémi, his coachman, knew where to stop; she would jump in beside him, and hold him in her arms until the carriage drew up at the Verdurins'. He would enter the drawing-room; and there, while Mme. Verdurin, pointing to the roses which he had sent her that morning, said: "I am furious with you!" and sent him to the place kept for him, by the side of Odette; the pianist would play to them—for their two selves, and for no one else—that little phrase by Vinteuil which was, so to speak, the national anthem of their love. He began, always, with a sustained *tremolo* from the violin part, which, for several bars, was unaccompanied, and filled all the foreground; until suddenly it seemed to be drawn aside, and—just as in those interiors by Pieter de Hooch, where the subject is set back a long way through the narrow framework of a half-opened door—infinitely remote, in colour quite different, velvety with the radiance of some intervening light, the little phrase appeared, dancing, pastoral, interpolated, episodic, belonging to another world. It passed, with simple and immortal movements, scattering on every side the bounties of its grace, smiling ineffably still; but Swann thought that he could now discern in it some disenchantment. It seemed to be aware how vain, how hollow was the happiness to which it showed the way. In its airy grace there was, indeed, something definitely achieved, and complete in itself, like the mood of philosophic detachment which follows an outburst of vain regret. But little did that matter to him; he looked upon the sonata less in its own light—as what it might express, had, in fact, expressed to a certain musician, ignorant that any Swann or Odette, anywhere in the world, existed, when he composed it, and would express to all those who should hear it played in centuries to come—than as a pledge, a token of his love,which made even the Verdurins and their little pianist think of Odette and, at the same time, of himself— which bound her to him by a lasting tie; and at that point he had (whimsically entreated by Odette) abandoned the idea of getting some 'professional' to play over to him the whole sonata, of which he still knew no more than this one passage. "Why do you want the rest?" she had asked him, "Our little bit: that's all we need."

  It would happen, as often as not, that he had stayed so long outside, with his little girl, before going to the Verdurins' that, as soon as the little phrase had been rendered by the pianist, Swann would discover that it was almost time for Odette to go home. He used to take her back as far as the door of her little house in the Rue La Pérouse, behind the Arc de Triomphe. And it was perhaps on this account, and so as not to demand the monopoly of her favours, that he sacrificed the pleasure (not so essential to his well-being) of seeing her earlier in the evening, of arriving with her at the Verdurins', to the exercise of this other privilege, for which she was grateful, of their leaving together; a privilege which he valued all the more because, thanks to it, he had the feeling that no one else would see her, no one would thrust himself between them, no one could prevent him from remaining with her in spirit, after he had left her for the night.

  And so, night after night, she would be taken home in Swann`s carriage and one night , after she had got down, and while he stood at the gate and murmured "Till to-morrow, then!" she turned impulsively from him, plucked a last lingering chrysanthemum in the tiny garden which flanked the pathway from the street to her house, and as he went back to his carriage thrust it into his hand. He held it pressed to his lips during the drive home, and when, in due course, the flower withered, locked it away, like something very precious, in a secret drawer of his desk.

He would escort her to her gate, but no farther. Twice only had he gone inside to take part in the ceremony—of such vital importance in her life—of 'afternoon tea'. The loneliness and emptiness of those short streets (consisting, almost entirely, of low-roofed houses, self-contained but not detached, their monotony interrupted here and there by the dark intrusion of some sinister little shop, at once an historical document and a sordid survival from the days when the district was still one of ill repute), the snow which had lain on the garden-beds or clung to the branches of the trees, the careless disarray of the season, the assertion, in this man-made city, of a state of nature, had all combined to add an element of mystery to the warmth, the flowers, the luxury which he had found inside.

Passing by (on his left-hand side, and on what, although raised some way above the street, was the ground floor of the house) Odette's bedroom, which looked out to the back over another little street running parallel with her own; he had climbed a staircase that went straight up between dark painted walls, from which hung Oriental draperies, strings of Turkish beads, and a huge Japanese lantern, suspended by a silken cord from the ceiling (which last, however, so that her visitors should not have to complain of the want of any of the latest comforts of Western civilisation, was lighted by a gas-jet inside), to the two drawing-rooms, large and small. These were entered through a narrow lobby, the wall of which, chequered with the lozenges of a wooden trellis such as you see on garden walls, only gilded, was lined from end to end by a long rectangular box in which bloomed, as though in a hothouse, a row of large chrysanthemums, at that time still uncommon, though by no means so large as the mammoth blossoms which horticulturists have since succeeded in making grow. Swann was irritated, as a rule, by the sight of these flowers, which had then been 'the rage' in Paris for about a year, but it had pleased him, on this occasion, to see the gloom of the little lobby shot with rays of pink and gold and white by the fragrant petals of these ephemeral stars, which kindle their cold fires in the murky atmosphere of winter afternoons. Odette had received him in a tea-gown of pink silk, which left her neck and arms bare. She had made him sit down beside her in one of the many mysterious little retreats which had been contrived in the various recesses of the room, sheltered by enormous palm-trees growing out of pots of Chinese porcelain, or by screens upon which were fastened photographs and fans and bows of ribbon. She had said at once, "You're not comfortable there; wait a minute, I'll arrange things for you;" and with a titter of laughter, the complacency of which implied that some little invention of her own was being brought into play, she had installed behind his head and beneath his feet great cushions of Japanese silk, which she pummelled and buffeted as though determined to lavish on him all her riches, and regardless of their value. But when her footman began to come into the room, bringing, one after another, the innumerable lamps which (contained, mostly, in porcelain vases) burned singly or in pairs upon the different pieces of furniture as upon so many altars, rekindling in the twilight, already almost nocturnal, of this winter afternoon, the glow of a sunset more lasting, more roseate, more human—filling, perhaps, with romantic wonder the thoughts of some solitary lover, wandering in the street below and brought to a standstill before the mystery of the human presence which those lighted windows at once revealed and screened from sight—she had kept an eye sharply fixed on the servant, to see whether he set each of the lamps down in the place appointed it. She felt that, if he were to put even one of them where it ought not to be, the general effect of her drawing-room would be destroyed, and that her portrait, which rested upon a sloping easel draped with plush, would not catch the light. And so, with feverish impatience, she followed the man's clumsy movements, scolding him severely when he passed too close to a pair of jardinieres, which she made a point of always tidying herself, in case the plants should be knocked over—and went across to them now to make sure that he had not broken off any of the flowers. She found something 'quaint' in the shape of each of her Chinese ornaments, and also in her orchids, the cattleyas especially (these being, with chrysanthemums, her favourite flowers), because they had the supreme merit of not looking in the least like other flowers, but of being made, apparently, out of scraps of silk or satin. "It looks just as though it had been cut out of the lining of my cloak," she said to Swann, pointing to an orchid, with a shade of respect in her voice for so smart a flower, for this distinguished unexpected sister whom nature had suddenly bestowed upon her, so far removed from her in the scale of existence, and yet so delicate, so refined, so much more worthy than many real women of admission to her drawing-room. As she drew his attention, now to the fiery-tongued dragons painted upon a bowl or stitched upon a fire-screen, now to a fleshy cluster of orchids, now to a dromedary of inlaid silver-work with ruby eyes, which kept company, upon her mantelpiece, with a toad carved in jade, she would pretend now to be shrinking from the ferocity of the monsters or laughing at their absurdity, now blushing at the indecency of the flowers, now carried away by an irresistible desire to run across and kiss the toad and dromedary, calling them 'darlings'. And these affectations were in sharp contrast to the sincerity of some of her attitudes, notably her devotion to Our Lady of the Laghetto, who had once, when Odette was living at Nice, cured her of a mortal illness, and whose medal, in gold, she always carried on her person, attributing to it unlimited powers. She poured out Swann's tea, inquired "Lemon or cream?" and, on his answering "Cream, please," went on, smiling, "A cloud!" And as he pronounced it excellent, "You see, I know just how you like it." This tea had indeed seemed to Swann, just as it seemed to her, something precious, and love is so far obliged to find some justification for itself, some guarantee of its duration in pleasures which, on the contrary, would have no existence apart from love and must cease with its passing, that when he left her, at seven o'clock, to go and dress for the evening, all the way home, sitting bolt upright in his brougham, unable to repress the happiness with which the afternoon's adventure had-filled him, he kept on repeating to himself: "What fun it would be to have a little woman like that in a place where one could always be certain of finding, what one never can be certain of finding, a really good cup of tea." An hour or so later he received a note from Odette, and at once recognised that florid handwriting in which an affectation of British stiffness imposed an apparent discipline upon its shapeless characters, significant, perhaps, to less intimate eyes than his, of an untidiness of mind, a fragmentary education, a want of sincerity and decision. Swann had left his cigarette-case at her house. "Why," she wrote, "did you not forget your heart also? I should never have let you have that back."

More important, perhaps, was a second visit which he paid her, a little later. On his way to the house, as always when he knew that they were to meet, he formed a picture of her in his mind; and the necessity, if he was to find any beauty in her face, of fixing his eyes on the fresh and rosy protuberance of her cheekbones, and of shutting out all the rest of those cheeks which were so often languorous and sallow, except when they were punctuated with little fiery spots, plunged him in acute depression, as proving that one's ideal is always unattainable, and one's actual happiness, mediocre. He was taking her an engraving which she had asked to see. She was not very well; she received him, wearing a wrapper of mauve *crêpe de Chine,* which draped her bosom, like a mantle, with a richly embroidered web. As she stood there beside him, brushing his cheek with the loosened tresses of her hair, bending one knee in what was almost a dancer's pose, so that she could lean without tiring herself over the picture, at which she was gazing, with bended head, out of those great eyes, which seemed so weary and so sullen when there was nothing to animate her, Swann was struck by her resemblance to the figure of Zipporah, Jethro's Daughter, which is to be seen in one of the Sixtine frescoes.

It was with an unusual intensity of pleasure, a pleasure destined to have a lasting effect upon his character and conduct, that Swann remarked Odette's resemblance to the Zipporah of that Alessandro de Mariano, to whom one shrinks from giving his more popular surname, now that 'Botticelli' suggests not so much the actual work of the Master as that false and banal conception of it which has of late obtained common currency. He no longer based his estimate of the merit of Odette's face on the more or less good quality of her cheeks, and the softness and sweetness—as of carnation-petals—which, he supposed, would greet his lips there, should he ever hazard an embrace, but regarded it rather as a skein of subtle and lovely silken threads, which his gazing eyes collected and wound together, following the curving line from the skein to the ball, where he mingled the cadence of her neck with the spring of her hair and the droop of her eyelids, as though from a portrait of herself, in which her type was made clearly intelligible.

He stood gazing at her; traces of the old fresco were apparent in her face and limbs, and these he tried incessantly, afterwards, to recapture, both when he was with Odette, and when he was only thinking of her in her absence; and, albeit his admiration for the Florentine masterpiece was probably based upon his discovery that it had been reproduced in her, the similarity enhanced her beauty also, and rendered her more precious in his sight. The words 'Florentine painting' were invaluable to Swann. They enabled him (gave him, as it were, a legal title) to introduce the image of Odette into a world of dreams and fancies which, until then, she had been debarred from entering, and where she assumed a new and nobler form. And whereas the mere sight of her in the flesh, by perpetually reviving his misgivings as to the quality of her face, her figure, the whole of her beauty, used to cool the ardour of his love, those misgivings were swept away and that love confirmed now that he could re-erect his estimate of her on the sure foundations of his aesthetic principles; while the kiss, the bodily surrender which would have seemed natural and but moderately attractive, had they been granted him by a creature of somewhat withered flesh and sluggish blood, coming, as now they came, to crown his adoration of a masterpiece in a gallery, must, it seemed, prove as exquisite as they would be supernatural.

And when he was tempted to regret that, for months past, he had done nothing but visit Odette, he would assure himself that he was not unreasonable in giving up much of his time to the study of an inestimably precious work of art, cast for once in a new, a different, an especially charming metal, in an unmatched exemplar which he would —contemplate at one moment with the humble, spiritual, disinterested mind of an artist; at another with the pride, the selfishness, the sensual thrill of a collector.

On his study table, at which he worked, he had placed, as it were a photograph of Odette, a reproduction of Jethro's Daughter. He would gaze in admiration at the large eyes, the delicate features in which the imperfection of her skin might be surmised, the marvellous locks of hair that fell along her tired cheeks; and, adapting what he had already felt to be beautiful, on aesthetic grounds, to the idea of a living woman, he converted it into a series of physical merits which he congratulated himself on finding assembled in the person of one whom he might, ultimately, possess. The vague feeling of sympathy which attracts a spectator to a work of art, now that he knew the type, in warm flesh and blood, of Jethro's Daughter, became a desire which more than compensated, thenceforward, for that with which Odette's physical charms had at first failed to inspire him. When he had sat for a long time gazing at the Botticelli, he would think of his own living Botticelli, who seemed all the lovelier in contrast, and as he drew towards him the photograph of Zipporah he would imagine that he was holding Odette against his heart.

It was not only Odette's indifference, however, that he must take pains to circumvent; it was also, not infrequently, his own. Feeling that, since Odette had had every facility for seeing him, she seemed no longer to have very much to say to him when they did meet, he was afraid lest the manner— at once trivial, monotonous, and seemingly unalterable— which she now adopted when they were together should ultimately destroy in him that romantic hope, that a day might come when she would make avowal of her passion, by which hope alone he had become and would remain her lover. And so to alter, to give a fresh moral aspect to that Odette, of whose unchanging mood he was afraid of growing weary, he wrote, suddenly, a letter full of hinted discoveries and feigned indignation, which he sent off so that it should reach her before dinner-time. He knew that she would be frightened, and that she would reply, and he hoped that, when the fear of losing him clutched at her heart, it would force from her words such as he had never yet heard her utter: and he was right—by repeating this device he had won from her the most affectionate letters that she had, so far, written him, one of them (which she had sent to him at midday by a special messenger from the Maison Dorée—it was the day of the Paris-Murcie Fête given for the victims of the recent floods in Murcia) beginning " My dear, my hand trembles so that I can scarcely write—"; and these letters he had kept in the same drawer as the withered chrysanthemum. Or else, if she had not had time to write, when he arrived at the Verdurins' she would come running up to him with an "I've something to say to you!" and he would gaze curiously at the revelation in her face and speech of what she had hitherto kept concealed from him of her heart.

Even as he drew near to the Verdurins' door, and caught sight of the great lamp-lit spaces of the drawing-room windows, whose shutters were never closed, he would begin to melt at the thought of the charming creature whom he would see, as he entered the room, basking in that golden light. Here and there the figures of the guests stood out, sharp and black, between lamp and window, shutting off the light, like those little pictures which one sees sometimes pasted here and there upon a glass screen, whose other panes are mere transparencies. He would try to make out Odette. And then, when he was once inside, without thinking, his eyes sparkled suddenly with such radiant happiness that M. Verdurin said to the painter: "Hmm. Seems to be getting warm." Indeed, her presence gave the house what none other of the houses that he visited seemed to possess; a sort of tactual sense, a nervous system which ramified into each of its rooms and sent a constant stimulus to his heart.

And so the simple and regular manifestations of a social organism, namely the 'little clan', were transformed for Swann into a series of daily encounters with Odette, and enabled him to feign indifference to the prospect of seeing her, or even a desire not to see her; in doing which he incurred no very great risk since, even although he had written to her during the day, he would of necessity see her in the evening and accompany her home.

But one evening, when, irritated by the thought of that inevitable dark drive together, he had taken his other 'little girl' all the way to the Bois, so as to delay as long as possible the moment of his appearance at the Verdurins', he was so late in reaching them that Odette, supposing that he did not intend to come, had already left.

On the landing Swann had run into the Verdurins' butler, who had been somewhere else a moment earlier, when he arrived, and who had been asked by Odette to tell Swann (but that was at least an hour ago) that she would probably stop to drink a cup of chocolate at Prévost's on her way home. Swann set off at once for Prévost's, but every few yards his carriage was held up by others, or by people crossing the street, loathsome obstacles each of which he would gladly have crushed beneath his wheels, were it not that a policeman fumbling with a notebook would delay him even longer than the actual passage of the pedestrian. He counted the minutes feverishly, adding a few seconds to each so as to be quite certain that he had not given himself short measure, and so, possibly, exaggerated whatever chance there might actually, be of his arriving at Prévost's in time, and of finding her still there. And then, in a moment of illumination, like a man in a fever who awakes from sleep and is conscious of the absurdity of the dream-shapes among which his mind has been wandering without any clear distinction between himself and them, Swann suddenly perceived how foreign to his nature were the thoughts which he had been revolving in his mind ever since he had heard at the Verdurins' that Odette had left, how novel the heartache from which he was suffering, but of which he was only now conscious, as though he had just woken up. What! All this disturbance simply because he would not see Odette, now, till, tomorrow, exactly what he had been hoping, not an hour before, as he drove towards Mme. Verdurin's. He was obliged to admit also that now, as he sat in the same carriage and drove to Prévost's, he was no longer the same man, was no longer alone even—but that a new personality was there beside him, adhering to him, amalgamated with him, a creature from whom he might, perhaps, be unable to liberate himself, towards whom he might have to adopt some such stratagem as one uses to outwit a master or a malady. And yet, during this last moment in which he had felt that another, a fresh personality was thus conjoined with his own, life had seemed, somehow, more interesting. It was in vain that he assured himself that this possible meeting at Prévost's (the tension of waiting for which so ravished, stripped so bare the intervening moments that he could find nothing, not one idea, not one memory in his mind beneath which his troubled spirit might take shelter and repose) would probably, after all, should it take place, be much the same as all their meetings, of no great importance

She was not at Prévost's; he must search for her then, in every restaurant upon the boulevards. To save time, while he went in one direction, he sent in the other his coachman Rémi (Rizzo's Doge Loredan) for whom he presently— after a fruitless search—found himself waiting at the spot where the carriage was to meet him.

The coachman came back with the report that he could not find her anywhere, and added the advice, as an old and privileged servant, "I think, sir, that all we can do now is to go home."

But the air of indifference which Swann could so lightly assume when Rémi uttered his final, unalterable response, fell from him like a cast-off cloak when he saw Rémi attempt to make him abandon hope and retire from the quest.

"Certainly not!" he exclaimed. "We must find the lady. It is most important. She would be extremely put out —it's a business matter— and vexed with me if she didn't see me."

"But I do not see how the lady can be vexed, sir," answered Rémi, "since it was she that went away without waiting for you, sir, and said she was going to Prévost's and then wasn't there."

Meanwhile the restaurants were closing, and their lights began to go out. Under the trees of the boulevards there were still a few people strolling to and fro, barely distinguishable in the gathering darkness. Now and then the ghost of a woman glided up to Swann, murmured a few words in his ear, asked him to take her home, and left him shuddering. Anxiously he explored every one of these vaguely seen shapes, as though among the phantoms of the dead, in the realms of darkness, he had been searching for a lost Eurydice.

Swann made Rémi drive him to such restaurants as were still open; it was the sole hypothesis, now, of that happiness which he had contemplated so calmly; he no longer concealed his agitation, the price he set upon their meeting, and promised, in case of success, to reward his coachman, as though, by inspiring in him a will to triumph which would reinforce his own, he could bring it to pass, by a miracle, that Odette—assuming that she had long since gone home to bed,—might yet be found seated in some restaurant on the boulevards. He pursued the quest as far as the Maison Dorée, burst twice into Tortoni's and, still without catching sight of her, was emerging from the Café Anglais, striding with haggard gaze towards his carriage, which was waiting for him at the corner of the Boulevard des Italiens, when he collided with a person coming in the opposite direction it was Odette; she explained, later, that there had been no room at Prévost's, that she had gone, instead, to sup at the Maison Dorée, and had been sitting there in an alcove where he must have overlooked her, and that she was now looking for her carriage.

He climbed after her into the carriage which she had kept waiting, and ordered his own to follow. She had in her hand a bunch of cattleyas, and Swann could see, beneath the film of lace that covered her head, more of the same flowers fastened to a swansdown plume. She was wearing, under her cloak, a flowing gown of black velvet, caught up on one side so as to reveal a large triangular patch of her white silk skirt, with an 'insertion', also of white silk, in the cleft of her low-necked bodice, in which were fastened a few more cattleyas. She had scarcely recovered from the shock which the sight of Swann had given her, when some obstacle made the horse start to one side. They were thrown forward from their seats; she uttered a cry, and fell back quivering and breathless.

"It's all right," he assured her, "don't be frightened." And he slipped his arm round her shoulder, supporting her body against his own; then went on: "Whatever you do, don't utter a word; just make a sign, yes or no, or you'll be out of breath again. You won't mind if I put the flowers straight on your bodice; the jolt has loosened them. I'm afraid of their dropping out; I'm just going to fasten them a little more securely." She was not used to being treated with so much formality by men, and smiled as she answered: "No, not at all, I don't mind in the least."' But he, chilled a little by her answer, perhaps, also, to bear out the pretence that he had been sincere in adopting the stratagem, or even because he was already beginning to believe that he had been, exclaimed: "No, no; you mustn't speak. You will be out of breath again. You can easily answer in signs I shall understand. Really and truly now, you don't mind my doing this? Look, there is a little—I think it must be pollen, spilt over your dress,—may I brush it off with my hand? That's not too hard; I'm not hurting you, am I? I'm tickling you, perhaps, a little; but I don't want to touch the velvet in case I rub it the wrong way. But, don't you see, I really had to fasten the flowers; they would have fallen out if I hadn't. Like that, now; if I just push them a little farther down.... Seriously, I'm not annoying you, am I? And if I just sniff them to see whether they've totally lost all their scent? I don't believe I ever smelt any before; may I? Tell the truth, now." Still smiling, she shrugged her shoulders ever so slightly, as who should say, "You're quite mad; you know very well that I like it." He slipped his other hand upwards along Odette's cheek; she fixed her eyes on him with that languishing and solemn air which marks the women of the old Florentine's paintings, in whose faces he had found the type of hers; swimming at the brink of her fringed lids, her brilliant eyes, large and finely drawn as theirs, seemed on the verge of breaking from her face and rolling down her cheeks like two great tears. She bent her neck, as all their necks may be seen to bend, in the pagan scenes as well as in the scriptural. And although her attitude was, doubtless, habitual and instinctive, one which she, knew to be appropriate to such moments, and was careful not to forget to assume, she seemed to need all her strength to hold her face back, as though some invisible force were drawing it down towards Swann's. And Swann it was who, before she allowed her face, as though despite her efforts, to fall upon his lips, held it back for a moment longer, at a little distance, between his hands. He had intended to leave time for her mind to overtake her body's movements, to recognise the dream which she had so long cherished and to assist at its realisation, like a mother invited as a spectator when a prize is given to the child whom she has reared and loves. Perhaps, moreover, Swann himself was fixing upon these features of an Odette not yet possessed, not even kissed by him, on whom he was looking now for the last time, that comprehensive gaze with which, on the day of his departure, a traveller strives to bear away with him in memory the view of a country to which he may never return. But he was so shy in approaching her that, after this evening which had begun by his arranging her cattleyas and had, ended in her complete surrender, whether from fear of chilling her, or from reluctance to appear, even retrospectively, to have lied, or perhaps because he lacked the audacity to formulate a more urgent requirement than this (which could always be repeated, since it had not annoyed her on the first occasion) he resorted to the same pretext on the following days. If she had any cattleyas pinned to her bodice, he would say: "It is most unfortunate; the cattleyas don't need tucking in this evening; they've not been disturbed as they were the other night; I think, though, that this one isn't quite straight. May I see if they have more scent than the others?" Or else, if she had none: "Oh ! No cattleyas this evening; then there's nothing for me to arrange." So that for some time there was no change from the procedure which he had followed on that first evening, when he had started by touching her throat, with his fingers first and then with his lips, but their caresses began invariably with this modest exploration. And long afterwards, when the arrangement (or, rather, the ritual pretence of an arrangement) of her cattleyas had quite fallen into desuetude, the metaphor 'Do a cattleya', transmuted into a simple verb which they would employ without a thought of its original meaning when they wished to refer to the act of physical possession (in which, paradoxically, the possessor possesses nothing), survived to commemorate in their vocabulary the long forgotten custom from which it sprang. And yet possibly this particular manner of saying "to make love" had not the precise significance of its synonyms.

The ice once broken, every evening, when he had taken her home, he must follow her into the house; and often she would come out again in her dressing-gown, and escort him to his carriage, and would kiss him before the eyes of his coachman, saying: "What on earth does it matter what people see?" And on evenings when he did not go to the Verdurins' (which happened occasionally, now that he had opportunities of meeting Odette elsewhere), when—more and more rarely—he went into society, she would beg him to come to her on his way home, however late he might be.

No one ever received a letter from him now demanding an introduction to a woman. He had ceased to pay any attention to women, and kept away from the places in which they were ordinarily to be met. In a restaurant, or in the country, his manner was deliberately and directly the opposite of that by which, only a few days earlier, his friends would have recognised him, that manner which had seemed permanently and unalterably his own.

Now, wherever Swann might be spending the evening, he never failed to go on afterwards to Odette. If he arrived after the hour at which she sent her servants to bed, before ringing the bell at the gate of her little garden, he would go round first into the other street, over which, at the ground-level, among the windows (all exactly alike, but darkened) of the adjoining houses, shone the solitary lighted window of her room. He would rap upon the pane, and she would hear the signal, and answer, before running to meet him at the gate. He would find, lying open on the piano, some of her favourite music, the *Valse des Roses*, the *Pauvre Fou* of Tagliafico (which, according to the instructions embodied in her will, was to be played at her funeral), but he would ask her, instead, to give him the little phrase from Vinteuil's sonata. It was true that Odette played vilely, but often the fairest impression that remains in our minds of a favourite air is one which has arisen out of a jumble of wrong notes struck by unskilful fingers upon a tuneless piano. The little phrase was associated still, in Swann's mind, with his love for Odette.

He would make Odette play him the phrase again, ten, twenty times on end, insisting that, while she played, she must never cease to kiss him. Every kiss provokes another. Ah, in those earliest days of love how naturally the kisses spring into life. How closely, in their abundance, are they pressed one against another; until lovers would find it as hard to count the kisses exchanged in an hour, as to count the flowers in a meadow in May. Then she would pretend to stop, saying: "How do you expect me to play when you keep on holding me? I can't do everything at once. Make up your mind what you want; am I to play the phrase or do you want to play with me?" Then he would become annoyed, and she would burst out with a laugh which was transformed as it left her lips, and descended upon him in a shower of kisses. Or else she would look at him sulkily, and he would see once again a face worthy to figure in Botticelli's 'Life of Moses', he would place it there, giving to Odette's neck the necessary inclination; and when he had finished her portrait in distemper, in the fifteenth century, on the wall of the Sixtine, the idea that she was, none the less, in the room with him still, by the piano, at that very moment, ready to be kissed and won, the idea of her material existence, of her being alive, would sweep over him with so violent an intoxication that, with eyes starting from his head and jaws that parted as though to devour her, he would fling himself upon this Botticelli maiden and kiss and bite her cheeks.

He went to her only in the evenings, and knew nothing of how she spent her time during the day, any more than he knew of her past; so little, indeed, that he had not even the tiny initial clue which, by allowing us to imagine what we do not know, stimulates a desire for knowledge. And he never asked himself what she might be doing, or what her life had been. Only he smiled sometimes at the thought of how, some years earlier, when he still did not know her, someone had spoken to him of a woman who, if he remembered rightly, must certainly have been Odette, as of a 'tart', a 'kept' woman, one of those women to whom he still attributed (having lived but little in their company) the entire set of characteristics, fundamentally perverse, with which they had been, for many years, endowed by the imagination of certain novelists. He would say to himself that one has, as often as not, only to take the exact counterpart of the reputation created by the world in order to judge a person fairly, when with such a character he contrasted that of Odette, so good, so simple, so enthusiastic in the pursuit of ideals, so nearly incapable of not telling the truth that, when he had once begged her, so that they might dine together alone, to write to Mme. Verdurin, saying that she was unwell, the next day he had seen her, face to face with Mme. Verdurin, who asked whether she had recovered, blushing, stammering, and, in spite of herself, revealing in every feature how painful, what a torture it was to her to act a lie; and, while in her answer she multiplied the fictitious details of an imaginary illness, seeming to ask pardon, by her suppliant look and her stricken accents, for the obvious falsehood of her words.

On certain days, however, though these came seldom, she would call upon him in the afternoon, to interrupt his musings or the essay on Vermeer to which he had latterly returned. His servant would come in to say that Mme. de Crécy was in the small drawing-room. He would go in search of her, and, when he opened the door, on Odette's blushing countenance, as soon as she caught sight of Swann, would appear— changing the curve of her lips, the look in her eyes, the moulding of her cheeks—an all-absorbing smile. Once he was left alone he would see again that smile, and her smile of the day before, another with which she had greeted him sometime else, the smile which had been her answer, in the carriage that night, when he had asked her whether she objected to his rearranging her cattleyas.

Like everything else that formed part of Odette's environment, and was no more, in a sense, than the means whereby he might see and talk to her more often, he enjoyed the society of the Verdurins. There, since, at the heart of all their entertainments, dinners, musical evenings, games, suppers in fancy dress, excursions to the country, theatre parties, even the infrequent 'big evenings' when they entertained 'bores', there were the presence of Odette, the sight of Odette, conversation with Odette, an inestimable boon which the Verdurins, by inviting him to their house, bestowed on Swann, he was happier in the little 'nucleus' than anywhere else, and tried to find some genuine merit in each of its members, imagining that his tastes would lead him to frequent their society for the rest of his life. Never daring to whisper to himself, lest he should doubt the truth of the suggestion, that he would always be in love with Odette, at least when he tried to suppose that he would always go to the Verdurins' (a proposition which, a *priori*, raised fewer fundamental objections on the part of his intelligence), he saw himself for the future continuing to meet Odette every evening; that did not, perhaps, come quite to the same thing as his being permanently in love with her, but for the moment, while he was in love with her, to feel that he would not, one day, cease to see her was all that he could ask. "What a charming atmosphere!" he said to himself. "How entirely genuine life is to these people! They are far more intelligent, far more artistic, surely, than the people one knows. Mme. Verdurin, in spite of a few trifling exaggerations which are rather absurd, has a sincere love of painting and music! What a passion for works of art, what anxiety to give pleasure to artists! Her ideas about some of the people one knows are not quite right, but then their ideas about artistic circles are altogether wrong! Possibly I make no great intellectual demands upon conversation, but I am perfectly happy talking to Cottard, although he does trot out those idiotic puns. And as for the painter, if he is rather unpleasantly affected when he tries to be paradoxical, still he has one of the finest brains that I have ever come across. Besides, what is most important, one feels quite free there, one does what one likes without constraint or fuss. What a flow of humour there is every day in that drawing-room! Certainly, with a few rare exceptions, I never want to go anywhere else again. It will become more and more of a habit, and I shall spend the rest of my life among them."

And as the qualities which he supposed to be an intrinsic part of the Verdurin character were no more, really, than the superficial reflection of the pleasure which he had enjoyed in their society through his love for Odette, those qualities became more serious, more profound, more vital, as that pleasure increased. Since Mme. Verdurin gave Swann, now and then, what alone could constitute his happiness; since, on an evening when he felt anxious because Odette had talked rather more to one of the party than to another, and, in a spasm of irritation, would not take the initiative by asking her whether she was coming home, Mme. Verdurin brought peace and joy to his troubled spirit by the spontaneous exclamation: "Odette! You'll see M. Swann home, won't you?"; and since, when the summer holidays came, and after he had asked himself uneasily whether Odette might not leave Paris without him, whether he would still be able to see her every day, Mme. Verdurin was going to invite them both to spend the summer with her in the country; Swann, unconsciously allowing gratitude and self-interest to filter into his intelligence and to influence his ideas, went so far as to proclaim that Mme. Verdurin was "a great and noble soul."

And so there was probably not, in the whole of the Verdurin circle, a single one of the 'faithful' who loved them, or believed that he loved them as dearly as did Swann. And yet, when M. Verdurin said that he was not satisfied with Swann, he had not only expressed his own sentiments, he had unwittingly discovered his wife's. Doubtless Swann had too particular an affection for Odette, as to which he had failed to take Mme. Verdurin daily into his confidence; doubtless the very discretion with which he availed himself of the Verdurins' hospitality, refraining, often, from coming to dine with them for a reason which they never suspected, and in place of which they saw only an anxiety on his part not to have to decline an invitation to the house of some 'bore' or other; doubtless, also, and despite all the precautions which he had taken to keep it from them, the gradual discovery which they were making of his brilliant position in society— doubtless all these things contributed to their general annoyance with Swann. But the real, the fundamental reason was quite different. What had happened was that they had at once discovered in him a locked door, a reserved, impenetrable chamber in which he still professed silently to himself that the Princesse de Sagan was not grotesque, and that Cottard's jokes were not amusing; in a word (and for all that he never once abandoned his friendly attitude towards them all, or revolted from their dogmas), they had discovered an impossibility of imposing those dogmas upon him, of entirely converting him to their faith, the like of which they had never come across in anyone before. They would have forgiven his going to the houses of 'bores' (to whom, as it happened, in his heart of hearts he infinitely preferred the Verdurins and all their little 'nucleus.') had he consented to set a good example by openly renouncing those 'bores' in the presence of the 'faithful.' But that was an abjuration which, as they well knew, they were powerless to extort.

What a difference was there in a 'newcomer' whom Odette had asked them to invite, although, she herself had met him only a few times, and on whom they were building great hopes—the Comte de Forcheville! (It turned out that he was nothing more nor less than the brother-in-law of Saniette, a discovery which filled all the 'faithful' with amazement: the manners of the old palaeographer were so humble that they had always supposed him to be of a class inferior, socially, to their own, and had never expected to learn that he came of a rich and relatively aristocratic family.) Of course, Forcheville was enormously the 'swell', which Swann was not or had quite ceased to be; of course he would never dream of placing, as Swann now placed, the Verdurin circle above any other. But he lacked that natural refinement which prevented Swann from associating himself with the criticisms (too obviously false to be worth his notice) that Mme. Verdurin levelled at people whom he knew. As for the vulgar and affected tirades in which the painter sometimes indulged, the bagman's pleasantries which Cottard used to hazard—whereas Swann, who liked both men sincerely, could easily find excuses for these without having either the courage or the hypocrisy to applaud them, Forcheville, on the other hand, was on an intellectual level which permitted him to be stupefied, amazed by the invective (without in the least understanding what it all was about), and to be frankly delighted by the wit. And the very first dinner at the Verdurins' at which Forcheville was present threw a glaring light upon all the differences between them, made his qualities start into prominence and precipitated the disgrace of Swann.

When the guests had gone, Mme. Verdurin said to her husband, "Did you notice the way Swann laughed, such an idiotic laugh, when we spoke about Mme. La Trémoille? The *Duchess*, as Swann calls her," she added ironically, with a smile which proved that she was merely quoting, and would not, herself, accept the least responsibility for a classification so puerile and absurd. "I don't mind saying that I thought him extremely stupid."

M. Verdurin took it up. "He's not sincere. He's a crafty customer, always hovering between one side and the other. He's always trying to run with the hare and hunt with the hounds. What a difference between him and Forcheville. There, at least, you have a man who tells you straight out what he thinks. Either you agree with him or you don't. Not like the other fellow, who`s never definitely fish or fowl. Did you notice, by the way, that Odette seemed all out for Forcheville, and I don't blame her, either. And then, after all, if Swann tries to come the man of fashion over us, the champion of distressed Duchesses, at any rate the other man has got a title; he's always Comte de Forcheville!" he let the words slip delicately from his lips, as though, familiar with every page of the history of that dignity, he were making a scrupulously exact estimate of its value, in relation to others of the sort.

"I don't mind saying," Mme. Verdurin went on, "that he saw fit to utter some most venomous, and quite absurd insinuations against Brichot. Naturally, once he saw that Brichot was popular in this house, it was a way of hitting back at us, of spoiling our party. I know his sort, the dear, good friend of the family, who pulls you all to pieces on the stairs as he's going away."

"Didn't I say so?" retorted her husband. "He's simply a failure; a poor little wretch who goes through life mad with jealousy of anything that's at all big."

Had the truth been known, there was not one of the 'faithful' who was not infinitely more malicious than Swann; but the others would all take the precaution of tempering their malice with obvious pleasantries, with little sparks of emotion and cordiality; while the least indication of reserve on Swann's part, undraped in any such conventional formula as "Of course, I don't want to say anything—" to which he would have scorned to descend, appeared to them a deliberate act of treachery.

Swann was still unconscious of the disgrace that threatened him at the Verdurins', and continued to regard all their absurdities in the most rosy light, through the admiring eyes of love.

As a rule he made no appointments with Odette except for the evenings; he was afraid of her growing tired of him if he visited her during the day as well; at the same time he was reluctant to forfeit, even for an hour, the place that he held in her thoughts, and so was constantly looking out for an opportunity of claiming her attention, in any way that would not be displeasing to her. If, in a florist's or a jeweller's window, a plant or an ornament caught his eye, he would at once think of sending them to Odette, imagining that the pleasure which the casual sight of them had given him would instinctively be felt, also, by her, and would increase her affection for himself; and he would order them to be taken at once to the Rue La Pérouse, so as to accelerate the moment in which, as she received an offering from him, he might feel himself, in a sense, transported into her presence. He was particularly anxious, always, that she should receive these presents before she went out for the evening, so that her sense of gratitude towards him might give additional tenderness to her welcome when he arrived at the Verdurins', might even—for all he knew—if the shopkeeper made haste, bring him a letter from her before dinner, or herself, in person, upon his doorstep, come on a little extraordinary visit of thanks. As in an earlier phase, when he had experimented with the reflex action of anger and contempt upon her character, he sought now by that of gratification to elicit from her fresh particles of her intimate feelings, which she had never yet revealed.

Often she was embarrassed by lack of money, and under pressure from a creditor would come to him for assistance. He enjoyed this, as he enjoyed everything which could impress Odette with his love for herself, or merely with his influence, with the extent of the use that she might make of him. Probably if anyone had said to him, at the beginning, "It's your position that attracts her," or at this stage, "It's your money that she's really in love with," he would not have believed the suggestion, nor would he have been greatly distressed by the thought that people supposed her to be attached to him, that people felt them to be united by any ties so binding as those of snobbishness or wealth. But even if he had accepted the possibility, it might not have caused him any suffering to discover that Odette's love for him was based on a foundation more lasting than mere affection, or any attractive qualities which she might have found in him; on a sound, commercial interest; an interest which would postpone for ever the fatal day on which she might be tempted to bring their relations to an end.

One day, when reflections of this order had brought him once again to the memory of the time when some one had spoken to him of Odette as of a 'kept' woman, and when, once again, he had amused himself with contrasting that strange personification, the 'kept' woman—an iridescent mixture of unknown and demoniacal qualities embroidered, as in some fantasy of Gustave Moreau, with poison-dripping flowers, interwoven with precious jewels—with that Odette upon whose face he had watched the passage of the same expressions of pity for a sufferer, resentment of an act of injustice, gratitude for an act of kindness, which he had seen, in earlier days, on his own mother's face, and on the faces of friends; that Odette, whose conversation had so frequently turned on the things that he himself knew better than anyone, his collections, his room, his old servant, his banker; who kept all his title-deeds and bonds ;—the thought of the banker reminded him that he must call on him shortly, to draw some money. And indeed, if, during the current month, he were to come less liberally to the aid of Odette in her financial difficulties than in the month before, when he had given her five thousand francs, if he refrained from offering her a diamond necklace for which she longed, he would be allowing her admiration for his generosity to decline that gratitude which had made him so happy, and would even be running the risk of her imagining that his love for her (as she saw its visible manifestations grow fewer) had itself diminished. And then, suddenly, he asked himself whether that was not precisely what was implied by 'keeping' a woman (as if, in fact, that idea of 'keeping' could be derived from elements not at all mysterious nor perverse, but belonging to the intimate routine of his daily life, such as that thousand-franc note, a familiar and domestic object, torn in places and mended with gummed paper, which his valet, after paying the household accounts and the rent, had locked up in a drawer in the old writing-desk whence he had extracted it to send it, with four others, to Odette) and whether it was not possible to apply to Odette, since he had known her (for he never imagined for a moment that she could ever have taken a penny from anyone else before), that title, which he had believed so wholly inapplicable to, her, of 'kept' woman.

    He could not explore the idea further, for a sudden access of that mental lethargy which was, with him, congenital, intermittent and providential, happened, at that moment, to extinguish every particle of light in his brain, as instantaneously as, at a later period, when electric lighting had been everywhere installed, it became possible, merely by fingering a switch, to cut off all the supply of light from a house. His mind fumbled, for a moment, in the darkness, he took off his spectacles, wiped the glasses, passed his hands over his eyes, but saw no light until he found himself face to face with a wholly different idea, the realisation that he must endeavour, in the coming month, to send

Odette six or seven thousand-franc notes instead of five, simply as a surprise for her and to give her pleasure.

One evening, when Swann had consented to dine with the Verdurins, and had mentioned during dinner that he had to attend, next day, the annual banquet of an old comrades' association, Odette had at once exclaimed across the table, in front of everyone, in front of Forcheville, who was now one of the 'faithful', in front of the painter, in front of Cottard: "Yes, I know, you have your banquet to-morrow; I shan't see you, then, till I get home; don't be too late."

When he came away from his banquet, the next evening, it was pouring with rain, and he had nothing but his victoria. A friend offered to take him home in a closed carriage, and as Odette, by the fact of her having invited him to come, had given him an assurance that she was expecting no one else, he could, with a quiet mind and an untroubled heart, rather than set off thus, in the rain, have gone home and to bed. But perhaps, if she saw that he seemed not to adhere to his resolution to end every evening, without exception, in her company, she might grow careless, and fail to keep free for him just the one evening on which he particularly desired it.

It was after eleven when he reached her door, and as he made his apology for having been unable to come away earlier, she complained that it was indeed very late; the storm had made her unwell, her head ached, and she warned him that she would not let him stay longer than half an hour, that at midnight she would send him away; a little while later she felt tired and wished to sleep.

No cattleya, then, to-night?" he asked, "and I've been looking forward so to a nice little cattleya." But she was irresponsive; saying nervously: " No, dear, no cattleya to-night. Can't you see, I'm not well?" "It might have done you good, but I won't bother you."

She begged him to put out the light before he went; he drew the curtains close round her bed and left her. But, when he was in his own house again, the idea suddenly struck him that, perhaps, Odette was expecting someone else that evening, that she had merely pretended to be tired, that she had asked him to put the light out only so that he should suppose that she was going to sleep, that the moment he had left the house ,she had lighted it again, and had reopened her door to the stranger who was to be her guest for the night. He looked at his watch. It was about an hour and a half since he had left her; he went out, took a cab, and stopped it close to her house, in a little street running at right angles to that other street, which lay at the back of her house, and along which he used to go sometimes, to tap upon her bedroom window, for her to let him in. He left his cab; the streets were all deserted and dark; he walked a few yards and came out almost opposite her house. Amid the glimmering blackness of all the row of windows, the lights in which had long since been put out, he saw one, and only one, from which overflowed, between the slats of its shutters, closed like a wine-press over its mysterious golden juice, the light that filled the room within, a light which on so many evenings, as soon as he saw it, far off, as he turned into the street, had rejoiced his heart with its message: "She is there—expecting you," and now tortured him with "She is there with the man she was expecting." He must know who; he tiptoed along by the wall until he reached the window, but between the slanting bars of the shutters he could see nothing; he could hear, only, in the silence of the night, the murmur of conversation. What agony he suffered as he watched that light, in whose golden atmosphere were moving, behind the closed sash, the unseen and detested pair, as he listened to that murmur which revealed the presence of the man who had crept in after his own departure, the perfidy of Odette, and the pleasures which she was at that moment tasting with the stranger.

And yet he was not sorry that he had come; the torment which had forced him to leave his own house had lost its sharpness when it lost its uncertainty, now that Odette's other life, of which he had had, at that first moment, a sudden helpless suspicion, was definitely there, almost within his grasp, before his eyes, in the full glare of the lamplight, caught and kept there, an unwitting prisoner, in that room into which, when he would, he might force his way to surprise and seize it; or rather he would tap upon the shutters as he had often done when he had come there very late, and by that signal Odette would at least learn that he knew, that he had seen the light and had heard the voices; while he himself, who a moment, ago had been picturing her as laughing at him, as sharing with that other the knowledge of how effectively he had been tricked, now it was he that saw them, confident and persistent in their error, tricked and trapped by none other than himself, whom they believed to be a mile away, but who was there, in person, therewith a plan, there with the knowledge that he was going, in another minute, to tap upon the shutter.

As his hand stole out towards the shutters he felt a pang of shame at the thought that Odette would now know that he had suspected her, that, he had returned, that he had posted himself outside her window. She had often told him what a horror she had of jealous men, of lovers who spied. What he was going to do would be extremely awkward, and she would detest him for ever after, whereas now, for the moment, for so long as he refrained from knocking, perhaps even in the act of infidelity, she loved him still. How often is not the prospect of future happiness thus sacrificed to one's impatient insistence upon an immediate gratification. But his desire to know the truth was stronger, and seemed to him nobler than his desire for her. He knew that the true story of certain events, which he would have given his life to be able to reconstruct accurately and in full, was to be read within that window, streaked with bars of light, as within the illuminated, golden boards of one of those precious manuscripts, by whose wealth of artistic treasures the scholar who consults them cannot. remain unmoved. He yearned for the satisfaction of knowing the truth which so impassioned him in that brief, fleeting, precious transcript, on that translucent page, so warm, so beautiful. And besides, the advantage which he felt—which he so desperately wanted to feel—that he had over them, lay perhaps not so much in knowing as in being able to show them that he knew. He drew himself up on tiptoe. He knocked. They had not heard; he knocked again; louder; their conversation ceased. A man's voice—he strained his ears to distinguish whose, among such of Odette's friends as he knew, the voice could be—asked: "Who's that" .

He could not be certain of the voice. He knocked once again. The window first, then the shutters were thrown open. It was too late, now, to retire, and since he must know all, so as not to seem too contemptible, too jealous and inquisitive, he called out in a careless, hearty, welcoming tone: "Please don't bother; I just happened to be passing, and saw the light. I wanted to know if you were feeling better."

He looked up. Two old gentlemen stood facing him, in the window, one of them with a lamp in his hand; and beyond them he could see into the room, a room that he had never seen before. Having fallen into the habit, when he came late to Odette, of identifying her window by the fact that it was the only one still lighted in a row of windows otherwise all alike, he had been misled, this time, by the light, and had knocked at the window beyond hers, in the adjoining house. He made what apology he could and hurried home, overjoyed that the satisfaction of his curiosity had preserved their love intact, and that, having feigned for so long, when in Odette's company, a sort of indifference; he had not now, by a demonstration of jealousy, given her that proof of the excess of his own passion which, in a pair of lovers, fully and finally dispenses the recipient from the obligation to love the other enough. He never spoke to her of this misadventure.

One day when Swann had gone out early in the afternoon to pay a call, and had failed to find the person at home whom he wished to see, it occurred to him to go, instead, to Odette, at an hour when, although he never went, to her house then as a rule, he knew that she was always at home, resting or writing letters until tea-time, and would enjoy seeing her for a moment, if it did not disturb her. The porter told him that he believed Odette to be in; Swann rang the bell, thought that he heard a sound, that he heard footsteps, but no one came to the door. Anxious and annoyed, he went round to the other little street, at the back of her house, and stood beneath her bedroom window; the curtains were drawn and he could see nothing; he knocked loudly upon the pane, he shouted; still no one came. He could see that the neighbours were staring at him. He turned away, thinking that, after all, he had perhaps been mistaken in believing that he heard footsteps; but he remained so preoccupied with the suspicion that he could turn his mind to nothing else. After waiting for an hour, he returned. He found her at home; she told him that she had been in the house when he rang, but had been asleep; the bell had awakened her; she had guessed that it must be Swann and had run out to meet him, but he had already gone. She had, of course, heard him knocking at the window. Swann could at once detect in this story one of those fragments of literal truth which liars, when taken by surprise, console themselves by introducing into the composition of the falsehood which they have to invent, thinking that it can be safely incorporated, and will lend the whole story an air of verisimilitude. It was true that, when Odette had just done something which she did not wish to disclose, she would take pains to conceal it in a secret place in her heart. But as soon as she found herself face to face with the man to whom she was obliged to lie, she became uneasy, all her ideas melted like wax before a flame, her inventive and her reasoning faculties were paralysed, she might ransack her brain but would find only a void; still, she must say something, and there lay within her reach precisely the fact which she had wished to conceal, which, being the truth, was the one thing that had remained. She broke off from it a tiny fragment, of no importance in itself, assuring herself that, after all, it was the best thing to do, since it was a detail of the truth, and less dangerous, therefore, than a falsehood. "At any rate, this is true;" she said to herself; "that's always something to the good; he may make inquiries; he will see that this is true; it won't be this, anyhow, that will give me away." But she was wrong; it was what gave her away; she had not taken into account that this fragmentary detail of the truth had sharp edges which could not be made to fit in.

"She admits that she heard me ring, and then knock, that she knew it was myself, that she wanted to see me," Swann thought to himself. "But that doesn't correspond with the fact that she did not let me in." He did not, however, draw her attention to this inconsistency, for he thought that, if left to herself, Odette might perhaps produce some falsehood which would give him a faint indication of the truth. It was true that he had, now and then, a strong suspicion that Odette's daily activities were not in themselves passionately interesting, and that such relations as she might have with other men did not exhale, naturally, in a universal sense, or for every rational being, a spirit of morbid gloom capable of infecting with fever or of inciting to suicide. He realised, at such moments, that that interest, that gloom, existed in him only as a malady might exist, and that, once he was cured of the malady, the actions of Odette, the kisses that she might have bestowed, would become once again as innocuous as those of countless other women.

Swann deemed it wise to make allowance in his life for the suffering which he derived from not knowing what Odette had done, just as he made allowance for the impetus which a damp climate always gave to his eczema; to anticipate in his budget the expenditure of a considerable sum on procuring, with regard to the daily occupations of Odette, information the lack of which would make him unhappy, just as he reserved a margin for the gratification of other tastes from, which he knew that pleasure was to be expected (at least, before he had fallen in love) such as his taste for collecting things, or for good cooking.

When he proposed to take leave of Odette, and to return home, she begged him to stay a little longer, and even, detained him forcibly, seizing him by the arm as he was opening the door to go. He knew very well that she was not sufficiently in love with him to be so keenly distressed merely at having missed his visit, but as she was a good-natured woman, anxious to give him pleasure, and often sorry when she had done anything that annoyed him; he found it quite natural that she should be sorry, on this occasion, that she had deprived him of that pleasure of spending an hour in her company, which was so very great a pleasure, if not to herself, at any rate to him. All the same, it was a matter of so little importance that her air of unrelieved sorrow began at length to bewilder him. She reminded him, even more than was usual, of the faces of some of the women created by the painter of the 'Primavera'. She had, at that moment, their downcast, heartbroken expression, which seems ready to succumb beneath the burden of a grief too heavy to be borne, when they are merely allowing the Infant Jesus to play with a pomegranate, or watching Moses pour water into a trough. He had seen the same sorrow once before on her face, but when, he could no longer say. Then, suddenly, he remembered; it was when Odette had lied, in apologising to Mme. Verdurin on the evening after the dinner from which she had stayed away on a pretext of illness, but really so that she. might be alone with Swann. Surely, even had she been the most scrupulous of women, she could hardly have felt remorse for so innocent a lie. But the lies which Odette ordinarily told were less innocent, and served to prevent discoveries which might have involved her in the most terrible difficulties with one or another of her friends. And so, when she lied, smitten with fear, feeling herself to be but feebly armed for her defence, unconfident of success, she was inclined to weep from sheer exhaustion, as children weep sometimes when they have not slept. She knew also, that her lie, as a rule, was doing a serious injury to the man to whom she was telling it, and that she might find herself at his mercy if she told it badly. Therefore she felt at once humble and culpable in his presence. And when she had to tell an insignificant social lie, its hazardous associations, and the memories which it recalled, would leave her weak with a sense of exhaustion and penitent with a consciousness of wrongdoing.

What depressing lie was she now concocting for Swann's benefit, to give her that pained expression, that plaintive voice, which seemed to falter beneath the effort that she was forcing herself to make, and to plead for pardon? He had an idea that it was not merely the truth about what had occurred that afternoon that she was endeavouring to hide from him, but something more immediate, something, possibly, which had not yet happened, but might happen now at any time, and, when it did, would throw a light upon that earlier event. At that moment, he heard the front-door bell ring. Odette never stopped speaking, but her words dwindled into an inarticulate moan. Her regret at not having seen Swann that afternoon, at not having opened the door to him, had melted into a universal despair.

He could hear the gate being closed, and the sound of a carriage, as though some one were going away—probably the person whom Swann must on no account meet—after being told that Odette was not at home. And then, when he reflected that, merely by coming at an hour when he was not in the habit of coming, he had managed to disturb so many arrangements of which she did not wish him to know, he had a feeling of discouragement that amounted, almost, to distress. The pity with which he might have been inspired for himself he felt, for her only, and murmured: " Poor darling!" When finally he left her, she took up several letters which were lying on the table, and asked him if he would be so good as to post them for her. He walked along to the post office, took the letters from his pocket; and, before dropping each of them into the box, scanned its address. They were all to tradesmen, except the last, which was to Forcheville. He kept it in his hand. If I saw what was in this," he argued, " I should know what she calls him, what she says to him, whether there really is anything between them. Perhaps, if I don't look inside, I shall be lacking in delicacy towards Odette, since in this way alone I can rid myself of a suspicion which is, perhaps, a calumny on her, which must in any case, cause her suffering, and which can never possibly be set at rest, once the letter is posted."

He left the post-office and went home, but he had kept the last letter in his pocket. He lighted a candle, and held up close to its flame the envelope which he had not dared to open. At first he could distinguish nothing, but the envelope was thin, and by pressing it down on to the stiff card which it enclosed he was able, through the transparent paper, to read the concluding words. They were a coldly formal signature. If, instead of its being himself who was looking at a letter addressed to Forcheville, it had been Forcheville who had read a letter addressed to Swann, he might have found words in it of another, a far more tender kind! He took a firm hold of the card, which was sliding to and fro, the envelope being too large for it, and then, by moving it with his finger and thumb, brought one line after another beneath the part of the envelope where the paper was not doubled, through which alone it was possible to read.

In spite of all these manoeuvres he could not make it out clearly. Not that it mattered, for he had seen enough to assure himself that the letter was about some trifling incident of no importance, and had nothing at all to do with love; it was something to do with Odette's uncle. Swann had read quite plainly at the beginning of the line "I was right," but did not understand what Odette had been right in doing, until suddenly a word which he had not been able, at first, to decipher, came to light and made the whole sentence intelligible: "I was right to open the door; it was my uncle." To open the door! Then Forcheville had been there when Swann rang the bell, and she had sent him away, hence the sound that Swann had heard.

After that he read the whole letter; at the end she apologised for having treated Forcheville with so little ceremony, and reminded him that he had left his cigarette-case at her house, precisely what she had written to Swann after one of his first visits. But to Swann. she had added: "Why did you not forget your heart also? I should never have let you have that back." To Forcheville nothing of that sort; no allusion that could suggest any intrigue between them. And, really, he was obliged to admit that in all this business Forcheville had been worse treated than himself, since Odette was writing to him to make him believe that her visitor had been an uncle. From which it followed that he, Swann, was the man to whom she attached importance, and for whose sake she had sent the other away. And yet, if there had been nothing between Odette and Forcheville, why not have opened the door at once, why have said, "I was right to open the door; it was my uncle." Right? if she was doing nothing wrong at that moment how could Forcheville possibly have accounted for her not opening the door? For a time Swann stood still there, heartbroken, bewildered, and yet happy; gazing at this envelope which Odette had handed to him without a scruple, so absolute was her trust in his honour; through its transparent window there had been disclosed to him, with the secret history of an incident which he had despaired of ever being able to learn, a fragment of the life of Odette, seen as through a narrow, luminous incision, cut into its surface without her knowledge. Then his jealousy rejoiced at the discovery, as though that jealousy had had an independent existence, fiercely egotistical, gluttonous of everything that would feed its vitality, even at the expense of Swann himself. Now it had food in store, and Swann could begin to grow uneasy afresh every evening, over the visits that Odette had received about five o'clock, and could seek to discover where Forcheville had been at that hour. For Swann's affection for Odette still preserved the form, which had been imposed on it, from the beginning, by his ignorance of the occupations in which she passed her days, as well as by the mental lethargy which prevented him from supplementing that ignorance by imagination. He was not jealous, at first, of the whole of Odette's life, but of those moments only in which an incident, which he had perhaps misinterpreted, had led him to suppose that Odette might have played him false. His jealousy, like an octopus which throws out a first, then a second, and finally a third tentacle, fastened itself irremovably first to that moment, five o'clock in the afternoon, then to another, then to another again. But Swann was incapable of inventing his sufferings. They were only the memory, the perpetuation of a suffering that had come to him from without.

From without, however, everything brought him fresh suffering. He decided to separate Odette from Forcheville, by taking her away for a few days to the south. But. he imagined that she was coveted by every male, person in the hotel, and that she coveted them in return. And so he, who, in old days, when he travelled, used always to seek out new people and crowded places, might now be seen fleeing savagely from human society as if it had cruelly injured him. And how could he not have turned misanthrope, when in every man he saw a potential lover for Odette? Thus his jealousy did even more than the happy, passionate desire which he had originally felt for Odette had done to alter Swann's character, completely changing, in the eyes of the world, even the outward signs by which that character had been intelligible.

A month after the evening on which he had intercepted and read Odette's letter to Forcheville, Swann went to a dinner which the Verdurins were giving in the Bois. As the party. was breaking up he noticed a series of whispered discussions between Mme. Verdurin and several of her guests, and thought that he heard the pianist being reminded to come next day to a party at Chatou;. now he, Swann, had not been invited to any party.

The Verdurins had spoken only in whispers, and in vague terms, but the painter, perhaps without thinking, shouted out: "There must be no lights of any sort, and he must play the Moonlight Sonata in the dark, for us to see by."

Mme. Verdurin, seeing that Swann was within earshot, assumed that expression in which the two-fold desire to make the speaker be quiet and to preserve, oneself, an appearance of guilelessness in the eyes of the listener, is neutralised in an intense vacuity; in which the unflinching signs of intelligent complicity are overlaid by the smiles of innocence, an expression invariably adopted by anyone who has noticed a blunder, the enormity of which is thereby at once revealed if not to those who have made it, at any rate to him in whose hearing it ought not to have been made. Odette seemed suddenly to be in despair as though she had decided not to struggle any longer against the crushing difficulties of life, and Swann was anxiously counting the minutes that still separated him from the point at which, after leaving the restaurant, while he drove her home, he would be able to ask for an explanation, to make her promise, either that she would not go to Chatou next day, or that she would procure an invitation for him also, and to lull to rest in her arms the anguish that still tormented him. At last the carriages were ordered, Mme. Verdurin said to Swann: "Good-bye, then. We shall see you soon, I hope," trying, by the friendliness of her manner and the constraint of her smile, to prevent him from noticing that she was not saying, as she would always have until then: "To-morrow, then, at Chatou and at my house the day after."

M. and Mme. Verdurin made Forcheville get into their carriage; Swann's was drawn up behind it, and he waited for theirs to start before helping Odette into his own.

"Odette, we'll take you," said Mme. Verdurin, "we've kept a little corner specially for you, beside M. de Forcheville."

"Yes, Mme.Verdurin," said Odette meekly.

"What! I thought, I was to take, you home," cried Swann, flinging discretion to the winds, for the carriage-door hung open, time was precious, and he could not, in his present state, go home without her.

"But Mme. Verdurin has asked me."

"That's all right, you can quite well go home alone; we've left you like this dozens of times," said Mme. Verdurin.

"But I had something important to tell Mme de Crécy."

"Very well, you can write it to her instead."

"Good-bye," said Odette, holding out her hand. He tried hard to smile, but could only succeed in looking utterly dejected.

"What do you think of the airs that Swann is pleased to put on with us?" Mme. Verdurin asked her husband when they had reached home. "I was afraid he was going to eat me, simply because we offered to take Odette back. It really is too bad; that sort of thing. Why doesn't he say, straight out, that we keep a disorderly house?   I can't conceive how Odette can stand such manners. He positively seems to be saying, all the time, "You belong to me." I shall tell Odette exactly what I think about it all, and I hope she will have the sense to understand me."

Dr. Cottard, who, having been summoned to attend a serious case in the country, had not seen the Verdurins for some days, and had been prevented from appearing at Chatou, said, on the evening after this dinner, as he sat down to table at. their house: "Why, aren't we going to see M. Swann this evening? He is quite what you might call a personal friend of . . ..

"I sincerely trust that we shan't'!" cried Mme. Verdurin. "Heaven preserve us from him; he's too deadly for words, a stupid, ill-bred boor."

On hearing these words Cottard exhibited an intense astonishment blended with entire submission, as though in the face of a scientific truth which contradicted everything that he had previously believed, but was supported by an irresistible weight of evidence; with timorous emotion he bowed his head over his plate, and merely replied: "Oh—oh—oh—-oh—-oh!" traversing, in an orderly retirement of his forces, into the depths of his being, along a descending scale, the whole compass of his voice. After which there was no more talk of Swann at the Verdurins'.

And so that drawing-room which had brought Swann. and Odette together became an obstacle in the way of their meeting. She no longer said to him, as she had said in the early days of their love: "We shall meet, anyhow, tomorrow evening; there's a supper-party at the Verdurins," but "We shan't be able to meet to-morrow evening; there's a supper-party at the Verdurins." Or else the Verdurins were taking her to the Opéra-Comique, to see *Une Nuit de Cléopâtre.* and Swann could read in her eyes that terror lest he should ask her not to go, which, but a little time before, he could not have refrained from greeting with a kiss as it flitted across the face of his mistress, but which now exasperated him. "Yet I'm not really angry," he assured himself, "when I see how she longs to run away and scratch for maggots in that dunghill of cacophony. I'm disappointed; not for myself, but for her; disappointed to find that, after living for more than six months in daily contact with myself, she has not been capable of improving her mind even to the point of spontaneously eradicating from it a taste for Victor Massé! More than that, to find that she has not arrived at the stage of understanding that there are evenings on which anyone with the least shade of refinement of feeling should be willing to forego an amusement when she is asked to do so. She ought to have the sense to say : "I shall not go," if it were only from policy, since it is by what she answers now that the quality of her soul will be determined once and for all." And having persuaded himself that it was solely, after all, in order that he might arrive at a favourable estimate of Odette's spiritual worth that he wished her to stay at home with him that evening instead of going to the Opéra-Comique, he adopted the same line of reasoning with her, with the same degree of insincerity as he had used with himself, or even with a degree more, for in her case he was yielding also to the desire to capture her by her own self-esteem.

Meanwhile, Odette had shown signs of increasing emotion and uncertainty. Although the meaning of his tirade was beyond her, she grasped that it was to be included among the scenes of reproach or supplication, scenes which her familiarity with the ways of men enabled her, without paying any heed to the words that were uttered, to conclude that men would not make unless they were in love; that, from the moment when they were in love, it was superfluous to obey them, since they would only be more in love later on. And so, she would have heard Swann out with the utmost tranquillity had she not noticed that it was growing late, and that if he went on speaking for any length of time she would "never" as she told him with a fond smile, obstinate but slightly abashed, "get there in time for the Overture."

On other occasions he had assured himself that the one thing which, more than anything else, would make him cease to love her, would be her refusal to abandon the habit of lying. "Even from the point of view of coquetry, pure and simple," he had told her, "can't you see how much of your attraction you throw away when you stoop to lying? By a frank admission—how many faults you might redeem! Really, you are far less intelligent than I supposed!" In vain, however, did Swann expound to her thus all the reasons that she had for not lying; they might have succeeded in overthrowing any universal system of mendacity, but Odette had no such system; she contented herself, merely, whenever she wished Swann to remain in ignorance of anything that she had done, with not telling him of it. So that a lie was, to her, something to be used only as a special expedient; and the one thing that could make her decide whether she should avail herself of a lie or not was a reason which, too, was of a special and contingent order, namely the risk of Swann's discovering that she had not told him the truth.

Sometimes she would be absent for several days on end, when the Verdurins took her to see the tombs at Dreux, or to Compiègne, on the painter's advice, to watch the sun setting through the forest—after which they went on to the Château of Pierrefonds. But when she had set off for Dreux or Pierrefonds—alas, without allowing him to appear there, as though by accident, at her side, for, as she said, that would "create a dreadful impression,"—he would plunge into the most intoxicating romance in the lover's library, the railway time-table, from which he learned the ways of joining her there in the afternoon, in the evening, even in the morning. The ways? More than that, the authority, the right to join her. For, after all, the time-table, and the trains themselves, were not meant for dogs. If the public were carefully informed, by means of printed advertisements, that at eight o'clock in the morning a train started for Pierrefonds which arrived there at ten, that could only be because going to Pierrefonds was a lawful act, for which permission from Odette would be superfluous; an act, moreover which might be performed from a motive altogether different from the desire to see Odette, since persons who had never even heard of her performed it daily, and in such numbers as justified the labour and expense of stoking the engines.

So it came to this; that she could not prevent him from going to Pierrefonds if he chose to do so. Now that was precisely what he found that he did choose to do, and would at that moment be doing were he, like the travelling public, not acquainted with Odette. But it was better not to risk a quarrel with her, to be patient, to wait for her return. He spent his days in poring over a map of the forest of Compiègne, as though it had been that of the 'Pays du Tendre'; he surrounded himself with photographs of the Château of Pierrefonds. When the day dawned on which it was possible that she might return, he opened the timetable again, calculated what train she must have taken, and, should she have postponed her departure, what trains were still left for her to take. He did not leave the house, for fear of missing a telegram, he did not go to bed, in case, having come by the last train, she decided to surprise him with a midnight visit. Yes! The front-door bell rang. There seemed some delay in opening the door, he wanted to awaken the porter, he leaned out of the window to shout to Odette, if it was Odette, for in spite of the orders which he had gone downstairs a dozen times to deliver in person, they were quite capable of telling her that he was not at home. It was only a servant coming in. He noticed the incessant rumble of passing carriages, to which he had never before paid any attention. He could hear them, one after another, a long way off, coming nearer, passing his door without stopping, and bearing away into the distance a message which was not for him. He waited all night, to no purpose, for the Verdurins had returned unexpectedly, and Odette had been in Paris since midday; it had not occurred to her to tell him; not knowing what to do with herself she had spent the evening alone at a theatre, had long since gone home to bed, and was peacefully asleep.

As a matter of fact, she had never given him a thought. And such moments as these, in which she forgot Swann's very existence, were of more value to Odette, did more to attach him to her, than all her infidelities. For in this way Swann was kept in that state of painful agitation which had once before been effective in making his interest blossom into love, on the night when he had failed to find Odette at the Verdurins' and had hunted for her all evening .

Sometimes, when she had been away on a short visit somewhere, several days would elapse before she thought of letting him know that she had returned to Paris. And then she would say quite simply, without taking (as she would once have taken) the precaution of covering herself, at all costs, with a little fragment borrowed from the truth, that she had just, at that very moment arrived by the morning train. What she said was a falsehood; at least for Odette it was a falsehood, inconsistent, lacking (what it would have had, if true) the support of her memory of her actual arrival at the station; she was even prevented from forming a mental picture of what she was saying, while she said it, by the contradictory picture, in her mind, of whatever quite different thing she had indeed been doing at the moment when she pretended to have been alighting from the train. In Swann's mind, however, these words, meeting no opposition, settled and hardened until they assumed the indestructibility of a truth so indubitable that, if some friend happened to tell, him that he had come by the same train and had not seen Odette, Swann would have been convinced that it was his friend who had made a mistake as to the day or hour, since his version did not agree with the words uttered by Odette.

On one occasion, he had looked in for a moment at a revel in the painter's studio, and was getting ready to go home; leaving behind him Odette, transformed into a brilliant stranger, surrounded by men to whom her glances and her gaiety, which were not for him, seemed to hint at some voluptuous pleasure to be enjoyed there or elsewhere (possibly at the Bal des Incohérents, to which he trembled to think that she might be going on afterwards) which made Swann more jealous than the thought of their actual physical union, since it was more difficult to imagine; he was opening the door to go, when he heard himself called back in these words (which, by cutting off from the party that possible ending which had so appalled him, made the party itself seem innocent in retrospect, made Odette's return home a thing no longer inconceivable and terrible, but tender and familiar, a thing that kept close to his side, like a part of his own daily life, in his carriage; a thing that stripped Odette herself of the excess of brilliance and gaiety in her appearance, showed that it was only a disguise which she had assumed for a moment, for his sake and not in view of any mysterious pleasures, a disguise of which she had already wearied)—in these words, which Odette flung out after him as he was crossing the threshold: "Can't you wait a minute for me? I'm just going; we'll drive back together and you can drop me." It was true that on one occasion Forcheville had asked to be driven home at the same time, but when, on reaching Odette's gate, he had begged to be allowed to come in too, she had replied, with a finger pointed at Swann: "Ah That depends on this gentleman. You must ask him. Very well, you may come in, just for a minute, if you insist, but you mustn't stay long, for, I warn you, he likes to sit and talk quietly with me, and he's not at all pleased if I have visitors when he's here. Oh, if you only knew the creature as I know him; isn't that so, my love, there's no one that really knows you, is there, except me?"

And Swann was, perhaps, even more touched by the spectacle of her addressing him thus, in front of Forcheville, not only in these tender words of predilection, but also with certain criticisms, such as: "I feel sure you haven't written yet to your friends, about dining with them on Sunday. You needn't go if you don't want to, but you might at least be polite," or, "Now, have you left your essay on Vermeer here, so that you can do a little more to it to-morrow. What a lazy-bones! I'm going to make you work, I can tell you," which proved that Odette kept herself in touch with his social engagements and his literary work, that they had indeed a life in common. And as she spoke she bestowed on him a smile which he interpreted as meaning that she was entirely his.

Ah! had fate but allowed him to share a single dwelling with Odette, so that in her house he should be in his own; if, when asking his servant what there would be for luncheon, it had been Odette's bill of fare that he had learned from the reply; if, when Odette wished to go for a walk, in the morning, along the Avenue du Bois-de-Boulogne, his duty as a good husband had obliged him, though he had no desire to go out, to accompany her, carrying her cloak when she was too warm; and in the evening, after dinner, if she wished to stay at home, and not to dress, if he had been forced to stay beside her, to do what she asked; then how completely would all the trivial details of Swann's life, which seemed to him now so gloomy, simply because they would, at the same time, have formed part of the life of Odette, have taken on—like that lamp, that orangeade, that armchair, which had absorbed so much of his dreams, which materialised so much of his longing,—a sort of superabundant sweetness and a mysterious solidity.

And yet he was inclined to suspect that the state for which he so much longed was a calm, a peace, which would not have created an atmosphere favourable to his love. When Odette ceased to be for him a creature always absent, regretted, imagined; when the feeling that he had for her was no longer the same mysterious disturbance that was wrought in him by the phrase from the sonata, but constant affection and gratitude, when those normal relations were established between them which would put an end to his melancholy madness; then, no doubt, the actions of Odette's daily life would appear to him as being of but little intrinsic interest—as he had several times, already, felt that they might be, on the day, for instance, when he had read, through its envelope, her letter to Forcheville. Examining his complaint with as much scientific detachment as if he had inoculated himself with it in order to study its effects, he told himself that, when he was cured of it, what Odette might or might not do would be indifferent to him. But in his morbid state, to tell the truth, he feared death itself no more than such a recovery, which would, in fact, amount to the death of all that he then was.

And so, by the chemical process of his malady, after he had created jealousy out of his love, he began again to generate tenderness, pity for Odette. She had become once more the old Odette, charming and kind. He was full of remorse for having treated her harshly. He wished her to come to him, and, before she came, he wished to have already procured for her some pleasure, so as to watch her gratitude taking shape in her face and moulding her smile.

So too, Odette, certain of seeing him come to her in a few days, as tender and submissive as before, and plead with her for a reconciliation, became inured, was no longer afraid of displeasing him or even of making him angry, and refused him whenever it suited her, the favours by which he set most store.

Odette was now frequently away from Paris, even when she was there he scarcely saw her; that she who, when she was in love with him, used to say, "I am always free" and "What can it matter to me, what other people think?" now, whenever he wanted to see her, appealed to the proprieties or pleaded some engagement. When he spoke of going to a charity entertainment, or a private view, or a first night at which she was to be present, she would expostulate that he wished to advertise their relations in public, that he was treating her like a woman off the streets. Things came to such a pitch that, in an effort to save himself from being altogether forbidden to meet her anywhere, Swann remembering that she knew and was deeply attached to my great-uncle Adolphe, whose friend he himself also had been, went to see him in his little flat in the Rue de Bellechasse, to ask him to use his influence with Odette. As it happened, she invariably adopted, when she spoke to Swann about my uncle, a poetic tone, saying: "Ah, he! He is not in the least like you; it is an exquisite thing, a great beautiful thing, his friendship for me. He is not the sort of man who would have so little consideration for me as to let himself be seen everywhere in public" This was embarrassing for Swann, who did not know quite to what rhetorical pitch he should screw himself up in speaking of Odette to my uncle. He began by alluding to her excellence, a priori, the axiom of her seraphic super-humanity, the revelation of her inexpressible virtues, no conception of which could possibly be formed. " I should like to speak to you about her" he went on, "you, who know what a woman supreme above all women, what an adorable being, what an angel Odette is. But you know, also, what life is in Paris. Everyone doesn't see Odette in the light which you and I have been privileged to see her. So there are people who think I am behaving rather foolishly; she won't even allow me to meet her out of doors, at the theatre. Now you, in whom she has such enormous confidence, couldn't you say a few words for me to her, just to assure her that she exaggerates the harm which my bowing to her in the street would do to her?"

My uncle advised Swann not to see Odette for some days after which she would love him all the more; he advised Odette to let Swann meet her everywhere, and as often as he pleased.

One evening, Swann had gone out to a party at the Marquise de Saint-Euverte's on the last, for that season, of the evenings on which she invited people to listen to the musicians who would serve, later on, for her charity concerts. He had gone forward into the room and had taken up a position in a corner from which, unfortunately, his horizon was bounded by two ladies of 'uncertain' age, seated side by side. He suffered greatly from being shut up among all these people whose stupidity and absurdities wounded him all the more cruelly since, being ignorant of his love, incapable, had they known of it, of taking any interest, or of doing more than smile at it as at some childish joke, or deplore it as an act of insanity.

He suffered overwhelmingly, to the point at which even the sound of the instruments made him want to cry, from having to prolong his exile in this place to which Odette would never come, in which no one, nothing was aware of her existence, from which she was entirely absent. But suddenly it was as though she had entered, and this apparition tore him with such anguish that his hand rose impulsively to his heart. What had happened was that the violin had risen to a series of high notes, on which it rested as though expecting something, an expectancy which it prolonged without ceasing to hold on to the notes, in the exaltation with which it already saw the expected object approaching, and with a desperate effort to continue until its arrival, to welcome it before itself expired, to keep the way open for a moment longer, with all its remaining strength, that the stranger might enter in, as one holds a door open that would otherwise automatically close. And before Swann had had time to understand what was happening, to think: "It is the little phrase from Vinteuil's sonata. I mustn't listen! ", all his memories of the days when Odette had been in love with him, which he had succeeded, up till that evening, in keeping invisible in the depths of his being, deceived by this sudden reflection of a season of love, whose sun, they supposed, had dawned again, had awakened from their slumber, had taken wing and risen to sing maddeningly in his ears, without pity for his present desolation, the forgotten strains of happiness.

In place of the abstract expressions, "the time when I was happy", "the time when I was loved ", which he had often used until then, and without much suffering, for his intelligence had not embodied in them anything of the past save fictitious extracts which preserved none of the reality, he now recovered everything that had fixed unalterably the peculiar, volatile essence of that lost happiness; he could see it all; the snowy, curled petals of the chrysanthemum which she had tossed after him into his carriage, which he had kept pressed to his lips—the address 'Maison Dorée', embossed on the note-paper on which he had read "My hand trembles so as I write to you", the frowning contraction of her eyebrows when she said pleadingly : "You won't let it be very long before you send for me? At that time he had been satisfying a sensual curiosity to know what were the pleasures of those people who lived for love alone. He had supposed that he could stop there, that he would not be obliged to learn their sorrows also; how small a thing the actual charm of Odette was now in comparison with that formidable terror which extended it like a cloudy halo all around her, that enormous anguish of not knowing at every hour of the day and night what she had been doing, of not possessing her wholly, at all times and in all places ! Alas, he recalled the accents in which she had exclaimed: " But I can see you at any time; I am always free! "—she, who was never free now; the interest, the curiosity that she had shewn in his life, her passionate desire that he should do her the favour—of which it was he who, then, had felt suspicious, as of a possibly tedious waste of his time and disturbance of his arrangements—of granting her access to his study; how she had been obliged to beg that he would let her take him to the Verdurins'; and, when he did allow her to come to him once a month, how she had first, before he would let himself be swayed, had to repeat what a joy it would be to her, that custom of their seeing each other daily, for which she had longed at a time when to him it had seemed only a tiresome distraction, for which, since that time, she had conceived a distaste and had definitely broken herself of it, while it had become for him so insatiable, so dolorous a need. Little had he suspected how truly he spoke when, on their third meeting, as she repeated: "But why don't you let me come to you oftener?" he had told her, laughing, and in a vein of gallantry, that it was for fear of forming a hopeless passion.

The little phrase was present, like a protective goddess, a confidant of his love, who, so as to be able to come to him through the crowd, and to draw him aside to speak to him, had disguised herself in this sweeping cloak of sound. And as she passed him, light, soothing, as softly murmured as the perfume of a flower, telling him what she had to say, every word of which he closely scanned, sorry to see them fly away so fast, he made involuntarily with his lips the motion of kissing, as it went by him, the harmonious, fleeting form. He felt that he was no longer in exile and alone since she, who addressed herself to him, spoke to him in a whisper of Odette. For he had no longer, as of old, the impression that Odette and he were not known to the little phrase. Had it not often been the witness of their joys? True that, as often, it had warned him of their frailty. It seemed to say to him, as once it had said of his happiness: "What does all that matter; it is all nothing."

Swann now understood that the feeling which Odette had once had for him would never revive, that his hopes of happiness would not be realized now. And the days on which, by a lucky chance, she had once more shown herself kind and loving to him, or if she had paid him any attention, he recorded those apparent and misleading signs of slight movement on her part towards him with the same tender and sceptical solicitude, the desperate joy that people reveal who, when they are nursing a friend in the last days of an incurable malady, relate, as significant facts of infinite value: "Yesterday he went through his accounts himself and actually corrected a mistake that we had made in adding them up; he ate an egg to-day and seemed quite to enjoy it, if he digests it properly we shall try him with a cutlet to-morrow,"— although they themselves know that these things are meaningless on the eve of an inevitable death. No doubt Swann was assured that if he had now been living at a distance from Odette he would gradually have lost all interest in her, so that he would have been glad to learn that she was leaving Paris for ever; he would have had the courage to remain there; but he had not the courage to go.

One day he received an anonymous letter which told him that Odette had been the mistress of countless men (several of whom it named, among them Forcheville, M. de Bréauté and the painter) and women, and that she frequented houses of ill-fame. He was tormented by the discovery that there was to be numbered among his friends a creature capable of sending him such a letter (for certain details betrayed in the writer a familiarity with his private life). He wondered who it could be. But he had never had any suspicion with regard to the unknown actions of other people, those which had no visible connection with what they said. And when he wanted to know whether it was rather beneath the apparent character of M. de Charlus, or of M. des Laumes, or of M. d'Orsan that he must place the untravelled region in which this ignoble action might have had its birth; as none of these men had ever, in conversation with Swann, suggested that he approved of anonymous letters, and as everything that they had ever said to him implied that they strongly disapproved, he saw no further reason for associating this infamy with the character of any one of them more than with the rest. M. de Charlus was somewhat inclined to eccentricity, but he was fundamentally good and kind; M. des Laumes was a trifle dry, but wholesome and straight. As for M. d'Orsan, Swann had never met anyone who, even in the most depressing circumstances, would come to him with a more heartfelt utterance, would act more properly or with more discretion. But then, after not having been able to suspect anyone, he was forced to suspect everyone that he knew. After all, M. de Charlus might be most fond of him, might be most good-natured; but he was a neuropath; to-morrow, perhaps, he would burst into tears on hearing that Swann was ill; and to-day, from jealousy, or in anger, or carried, away by some sudden idea, he might have wished to do him a deliberate injury. Really, that kind of man was the worst of all.

After all, there was not a single one of the people whom he knew who might not, in certain circumstances, prove capable of a shameful action. Must he then cease to see them all? His mind grew clouded; he passed his hands two or three times across his brow, wiped his glasses with his handkerchief, and remembering that, after all, men who were as good as himself frequented the society of M. de Charlus, the Prince des Laumes and the rest, he persuaded himself that this meant, if not that they were incapable of shameful actions, at least that it was a necessity in human life, to which everyone must submit, to frequent the society of people who were, perhaps, not incapable of such actions. And he continued to shake hands with all the friends whom he had suspected, with the purely formal reservation that each one of them had, possibly, been seeking to drive him to despair. As for the actual contents of the letter, they did not disturb him; for in not one of the charges which it formulated against Odette could he see the least vestige of fact. Like many other men, Swann had a naturally lazy mind, and was slow in invention. He knew quite well as a general truth, that human life is full of contrasts, but in the case of any one human being he imagined all that part of his or her life with which he was not familiar as being identical with the part with which he was. He imagined what was kept secret from him in the light of what was revealed. At such times as he spent with Odette, if their conversation turned upon an indelicate act committed, or an indelicate sentiment expressed by some third person, she would ruthlessly condemn the culprit by virtue of the same moral principles which Swann had always heard expressed by his own parents, and to which he himself had remained loyal; **and** then, she would arrange her flowers, would sip her tea, would show an interest in his work. So Swann extended those habits to fill the rest of her life, he reconstructed those actions when he wished to form a picture of the moments in which he and she were apart. If anyone had portrayed her to him as she was, or rather as she had been for so long with himself, but had substituted some other man, he would have been distressed, for such a portrait would have struck him as lifelike. But to suppose that she went to bad houses, that she abandoned herself to orgies with other women, that she led the crapulous existence of the most abject, the most contemptible of mortals—would be an insane wandering of the mind, for the realisation of which, thank heaven, the chrysanthemums that he could imagine, the daily cups of tea, the virtuous indignation left neither time nor place. Only, now and again, he gave Odette to understand that people maliciously kept him informed of everything that she did and making opportune use of some detail—insignificant but true—which he had accidentally learned, as though it were the sole fragment which he would allow, in spite of himself, to pass his lips, out of the numberless other fragments of that complete reconstruction of her daily life which he carried secretly in his mind, he led her to suppose that he was perfectly informed upon matters, which, in reality, he neither knew nor suspected, for if he often adjured Odette never to swerve from or make alteration of the truth, that was only, whether he realised it or no, in order that Odette should tell him everything that she did. No doubt, as he used to assure Odette, he loved sincerity, but only as he might love a pander who could keep him in touch with the daily life of his mistress. Moreover, his love of sincerity, not being disinterested, had not improved his character. The truth which he cherished was that which Odette would tell him; but he himself, in order to extract that truth from her, was not afraid to have recourse to falsehood, that very falsehood which he never ceased to depict to Odette as leading every human creature down to utter degradation. In a word, he lied as much as did Odette, because, while more unhappy than she, he was no less egotistical. And she, when she heard him repeating thus to her the things that she had done, would stare at him with a look of distrust and, at all hazards, of indignation, so as not to appear to be humiliated, and to be blushing for her actions.

One day he went to see Odette. He sat down, keeping at a distance from her. He did not dare to embrace her, not knowing whether in her, in himself, it would be affection or anger that a kiss would provoke. He sat there silent, watching their love expire. Suddenly he made up his mind. "Odette, my darling," he began, "I know, I am being simply odious, but I must ask you a few questions. You remember what I once thought about you and Mme. Verdurin?' Tell me, was it true? Have you, with her or anyone else, ever?"

She shook her head, pursing her lips together a sign which people commonly employ to signify that they are not going, because it would bore them to go, when some one has asked, "Are you coming to watch the procession go by?" or "Will you be at the review?" But this shake of the head, which is thus commonly used to decline participation in an event that has yet to come, imparts for that reason an element of uncertainty to the denial of participation in an event that is past. Furthermore, it suggests reasons of personal convenience, rather than any definite repudiation, any moral impossibility. When he saw Odette thus make him a sign that the insinuation was false, he realised that it was quite possibly true.

"I have told you, I never did; you know quite well," she added, seeming angry and uncomfortable.

"Yes, I know all that; but are you quite sure? Don't say to me, "You know quite well" say, "I have never done anything of that sort with any woman." She repeated his words like a lesson learned by rote, and as though she hoped, thereby, to be rid of him: "I have never done anything of that sort with any woman."

"'Can you swear it to me on your Laghetto medal ?"
Swann knew that Odette would never perjure herself on that.

"Oh, you. do make me so miserable," she cried, with a jerk of her body as though to shake herself free of the constraint of his question. "Have you nearly done. What is the matter with you to-day? You seem to have made up your mind that I am to be forced to hate you, to curse you! Look, I was anxious to be friends with you again, for us to have a nice time together, like the old days; and this is all the thanks I get!" However, he would not let her go, but sat there like a surgeon who waits for a spasm to subside that has interrupted his operation but need not make him abandon it.

"You are quite wrong in supposing that I bear you the least ill-will in the world, Odette," he began with a persuasive and deceitful gentleness. "I never speak to you except of what I already know, and I always know a great deal more than I say. But you alone can mollify by your confession what makes me hate you so long as it has been reported to me only by other people. My anger with you is never due to your actions; I can and do forgive you everything because I love you; but to your untruthfulness, the ridiculous untruthfulness which makes you persist in denying things which I know to be true. How can you expect that I shall continue to love you, when I see you maintain, when I hear you swear to me a thing which I know to be false? Odette, do not prolong this moment which is torturing us both. If you are willing to end it at once, you shall be free of it for ever. Tell me, upon your medal, yes or no, whether you have ever done those things."

"How on earth can I tell ?" she was furious. " Perhaps I have, ever so long ago, when I didn't know what I was doing, perhaps, two or three times."

Swann had prepared himself for all possibilities. Reality must, therefore, be something which bears no relation to possibilities, any more than the stab of a knife in one's body bears to the gradual movement of the clouds overhead, since those words "two or three times" carved, as it were, a cross upon the living tissues of his heart. A strange thing, indeed, that those words, "two or three times," nothing more than a few words, words uttered in the air, at a distance, could so lacerate a man's heart, as if they had actually pierced it, could sicken a man, like a poison that he had drunk. Like an evil deity, his jealousy was inspiring Swann, was thrusting him on towards destruction. It was not his fault, but Odette's alone, if at first his punishment was not more severe.

"My darling," he began again, "it's all over now; was it with anyone I know?"

"No, I swear it wasn't; besides, I think I exaggerated, I never really went as far as that." He smiled, and resumed with: "Just as you like. It doesn't really matter, but it's unfortunate that you can't give me any name. If I were able to form an idea of the person that would prevent my ever thinking of her again. I say it for your own sake, because then I shouldn't bother you any more about it. It's so soothing to be able to form a clear picture of things in one's mind. What is really terrible is what one cannot imagine. But you've been so sweet to me; I don't want to tire you. I do thank you, with all my heart, for all the good that you have done me. I've quite finished now. Only one word more: how many times?"

"Oh, Charles I can't you see, you're killing me? It's all ever so long ago. I've never given it a thought. Anyone would say that you were positively trying to put those ideas into my head again. And then you'd be a lot better off!" she concluded, with unconscious stupidity but with intentional malice.

"I only wished to know whether it had been since I knew you. It's only natural. Did it happen here, ever? You can't give me any particular evening, so that I can remind myself what I was doing at the time? You understand, surely, that it's not possible that you don't remember with whom, Odette, my love."

"But I don't know; really, I don't. I think it was in the Bois, one evening when you came to meet us on the Island. You had been dining with the Princesse des Laumes," she added, happy to be able to furnish him with an exact detail, which testified to her veracity. "At the next table there was a woman whom I hadn't seen for ever so long. She said to me, 'Come along round behind the rock, there, and look at the moonlight on the water !' At first I just yawned, and said, 'No, I'm too tired, and I'm quite happy where I am, thank you.' She swore there'd never been anything like it in the way of moonlight. 'I've heard that tale before', I said to her; you see, I knew quite well what she was after." Odette narrated this episode almost as if it were a joke, either because it appeared to her to be quite natural, or because she thought that she was thereby minimising its importance, or else so as not to appear ashamed. But, catching sight of Swann's face, she changed her tone, and "You are a fiend!" she flung at him, "you enjoy tormenting me, making me tell you lies, just so that you'll leave me in peace."

This second blow struck at Swann was even more excruciating than the first. Never had he supposed it to have been so recent an affair, hidden from his eyes that had been too innocent to discern it, not in a past which he had never known, but in evenings which he so well remembered, which he had lived through with Odette, of which he had supposed himself to have such an intimate, such an exhaustive knowledge, and which now assumed, retrospectively, an aspect of cunning and deceit and cruelty. In the midst of them parted, suddenly, a gaping chasm, that moment on the Island in the Bois de Boulogne. Without being intelligent, Odette had the charm of being natural. She had recounted, she had acted the little scene with so much simplicity that Swann, as he gasped for breath, could vividly see it: Odette yawning, the "rock, there". He could hear her answer—alas, how lightheartedly—"I've heard that tale before!" He felt that she would tell him nothing more that evening, that no further revelation was to be expected for the present. He was silent for a time, then said to her:

"My poor darling, you must forgive me; I know, I am hurting you dreadfully, but it's all over now; I shall never think of it again."

One day, he was trying—without hurting Odette—to discover from her whether she had ever had any dealings with procuresses. He was, as a matter of fact, convinced that she had not; the anonymous letter had put the idea into his mind, but in a purely mechanical way; it had been received there with no credulity, but it had, for all that, remained there, and Swann, wishing to be rid of the burden— a dead weight, but none the less disturbing—of this suspicion, hoped that Odette would now extirpate it for ever.

"Oh dear, no! Not that they don't simply persecute me to go to them," her smile revealed a gratified vanity which she no longer saw that it was impossible should appear legitimate to Swann. "There was one of them waited more than two hours for me yesterday, said she would give me any money I asked. It seems, there's an Ambassador who said to her, ' I'll kill myself if you don't bring her to me' — meaning me! They told her I'd gone out, but she waited and waited, and in the end I had to go myself and speak to her, before she'd go away. I do wish you could have seen the way I tackled her; my maid was in the next room, listening, and told me I shouted fit to bring the house down:—"But when you hear me say that I don't want to! The idea of such a thing, I don't like it at all! I should hope I'm still free to do as I please and when I please and where I please! If I needed the money, I could understand. The porter has orders not to let her in again; he will tell her that I am out of town. Oh, I do wish I could have had you hidden somewhere in the room while I was talking to her. I know, you'd have been pleased, my dear. There's some good in your little Odette, you see, after all, though people do say such dreadful things about her."

Her very admissions—when she made any—of faults which she supposed him to have discovered, rather served Swann as a startingpoint for fresh doubts than they put an end to the old. For her admissions never exactly coincided with his doubts. In vain might Odette expurgate her confession of all its essential part, there would remain in the accessories something which Swann had never yet imagined, which crushed him anew, and was to enable him to alter the terms, of the problem of his jealousy. And. these admissions he could never forget. His spirit carried them along, cast them aside, then cradled them again in its bosom, like corpses in a river. And they poisoned it.

She spoke to him once of a visit that Forcheville had paid her on the day of the Paris-Murcie Fête. "What! you knew him as long ago as that? Oh, yes, of course you did," he corrected himself, so as not to show that he had been ignorant of the fact. And suddenly he began to tremble at the thought that, on the day of the Paris-Murcie Fête, when he had received that letter which he had so carefully preserved, she had been having luncheon, perhaps, with Forcheville at the Maison d'Or. She swore that she had not. "Still, the Maison d'Or reminds me of something or other which, I knew at the time, wasn't true," he pursued, hoping to frighten her. "Yes, that I hadn't been there at all that evening, when I told you I had just come from there, and you had been looking for me at Prévost's," she replied (judging by his manner that he knew) with a firmness that was based not so much upon cynicism as upon timidity, a fear of crossing Swann, which her own self-respect made her anxious to conceal, and a desire to show him that she could be perfectly frank if she chose. And so she struck him with all the sharpness and force of a headsman wielding his axe, and yet could not be charged with cruelty, since she was quite unconscious of hurting him; she even began to laugh, though this may perhaps, it is true, have been chiefly to keep him from thinking that she was ashamed, at all, or confused. "It's quite true, I hadn't been to the Maison Dorée. I was coming away from Forcheville's. I had, really, been to Prévost's— that wasn't a story—and he met me there and asked me to come in and look at his prints. But some one else came to see him. I told you that I was coming from the Maison d'Or because I was afraid you might be angry with me. It was rather nice of me, really, don't you see? I admit, I did wrong, but at least I'm telling you all about it now, arn't I? What have I to gain by not telling you, straight, that I lunched with him on the day of the Paris-Murcie Fête, if it were true? Especially as at that time we didn't know one another quite so well as we do now, did we, dear?"

He smiled back at her with the sudden, craven weakness of the utterly spiritless creature which these crushing words had made of him. And so, even in the months of which he had never dared to think again, because they had been too happy, in those months when she had loved him, she was already lying to him! Besides that moment (that first evening on which they had 'done a cattleya') when she had told him that she was coming from the Maison Dorée, how many others must there have been, each of them covering a falsehood of which Swann had had no suspicion. He recalled how she had said to him once: " I need only tell Mme. Verdurin that my dress wasn't ready, or that my cab came late. There is always some excuse." From himself too, probably, many times when she had glibly uttered such words as explain a delay or justify an alteration of the hour fixed for a meeting, those moments must have hidden, without his having the least inkling of it at the time, an engagement that she had had with some other man, some man to whom she had said " I need only tell Swann that my dress wasn't ready, or that my cab came late. There is always some excuse."

The painter having been ill, Dr. Cottard recommended a sea-voyage; several of the 'faithful' spoke of accompanying him; the Verdurins could not face the prospect of being left alone in Paris, so first of all hired, and finally purchased a yacht; thus Odette was constantly going on a cruise. Whenever she had been away for any length of time, Swann would feel that he was beginning to detach himself from her, but, as though this moral distance were proportionate to the physical distance between them, whenever he heard that Odette had returned to Paris, he could not rest without seeing her. Once, when they had gone away, as everyone thought, for a month only either they succumbed to a series of temptations, or else M. Verdurin had cunningly arranged everything beforehand, to please his wife, and disclosed his plans to the 'faithful' only as time went on; anyhow, from Algiers they flitted to Tunis; then to Italy, Greece, Constantinople, Asia Minor. They had been absent for nearly a year, and Swann felt perfectly at ease and, almost happy. Albeit M. Verdurin had endeavoured to persuade the pianist and Dr. Cottard that their respective aunt and patients had no need of them, and that, in any event, it was most rash, to allow Mme. Cottard to return to Paris, where, Mme. Verdurin assured him, a revolution had just broken out, he was obliged to grant them their liberty at Constantinople. And the painter came home with them. One day, shortly after the return of these four travellers, Swann, seeing an omnibus approach him, labelled 'Luxembourg', and having some business there, had jumped on to it and had found himself sitting opposite Mme. Cottard, who was paying a round of visits to people whose 'day' it was, in full review order, with a plume in her hat, a silk dress, a muff, an umbrella (which would do for a parasol if the rain kept off), a card-case, and a pair of white gloves fresh from the cleaners. Wearing these badges of rank, she would, in fine weather, go on foot from one house to another in the same neighbourhood, but when she had to proceed to another district, would make use of a transfer-ticket on the omnibus. For the first minute or two, until the natural courtesy of the woman broke through the starched surface of the doctor's wife, not being certain, either, whether she ought to mention the Verdurins before Swann, she produced, quite naturally, in her slow and awkward, but not unattractive voice, which, every now and then, was completely drowned by the rattling of, the omnibus, topics selected from those which she had picked up and would repeat in each of the score of houses up the stairs of which she clambered in the course of an afternoon.

Having exhausted these topics to which she had been inspired by the loftiness of her plume, the monogram on her card-case, the little number inked inside each of her gloves by the cleaner, and the difficulty of speaking to Swann about the Verdurins, Mme. Cottard, seeing that they had still a long way to go before they would reach the corner of the Rue Bonaparte, where the conductor was to set her down, listened to the promptings of her heart, which counselled other words than these. "Your ears must have been burning," she ventured, "while we were on the yacht with Mme. Verdurin. We were talking about you all the time."

Swann was genuinely astonished, for he supposed that his name was never uttered in the Verdurins' presence.

"You see," Mme. Cottard went on, "Mme. de Crécy was there; need I say more? When Odette is anywhere it's never long before she begins talking about you. And you know quite well, it isn't nasty things she says. What! You don't believe me!" she went on, noticing that Swann looked sceptical. And, carried away by the sincerity of her conviction, without putting any evil meaning into the word,. which she used purely in the sense in which one employs it to speak of the affection that unites a pair of friends; "Why, she *adores* you ! No, indeed; I'm sure it would never do to say anything against you when she was about; one would soon be taught one's place! Whatever we might be doing, if we were looking at a picture for instance, she would say, "If only we had him here, he's the man who could tell us whether it's genuine or not. There's no one like him for that." And all day long she would be saying, "What can he be doing just now? I do hope, he's doing a little work! It's too dreadful that a fellow with such gifts as he has should be so lazy." (Forgive me, won't you.): "I can see him this very moment; he's thinking of us, he's wondering where we are." Indeed, she used an expression which I thought very pretty at the time. M. Verdurin asked her, "How in the world can you see what he's doing when he's a thousand miles away?" And Odette answered, "Nothing is impossible to the eye of a friend."

"No, I assure you, I'm not saying it just to flatter you; you have a true friend in her, such as one doesn't often find. I can tell you, besides, in case you don't know it, that you're the only one. Mme. Verdurin told me as much herself on our last day with them (one talks more freely, don't you know, before a parting), "I don't say that Odette isn't fond of us, but anything that we may say to her counts for very little beside what Swann might say." Oh, mercy, there's the conductor stopping for me; here have I been chatting away to you, and would have gone right past the Rue Bonaparte, and never noticed. Will you be so very kind as to tell me whether my plume is straight?"

And Mme. Cottard withdrew from her muff, to offer it to Swann, a white-gloved hand from which there floated, with a transfer-ticket, an atmosphere of fashionable life that pervaded the omnibus, blended with the harsher fragrance of newly cleaned kid. And Swann felt himself overflowing with gratitude to her, as well as to Mme. Verdurin (and almost to Odette, for the feeling that he now entertained for her was no longer tinged with pain, was scarcely even to be described, now, as love), while from the platform of the omnibus he followed her with loving eyes, as she gallantly threaded her way along the Rue Bonaparte, her plume erect, her skirt held up in one hand, while in the other she clasped her umbrella and her card-case, so that its monogram could be seen, her muff dancing in the air before her as she went.

To compete with and so to stimulate the moribund feelings that Swann had for Odette, Mme. Cottard, a wiser physician, in this case, than ever her husband would have been, had grafted among them others more normal, feelings of gratitude, of friendship, which in Swann's mind were to make Odette seem again more human (more like other women, since other women could inspire the same feelings in him), were to hasten her final transformation back into that Odette, loved with an undisturbed affection, who had taken him home one evening after a revel at the painter's, to drink orangeade with Forcheville, that Odette with whom Swann had calculated that he might live in happiness.

In former times, having often thought with terror that a day must come when he would cease to be in love with Odette, he had determined to keep a sharp look out, and as soon as he felt that love was beginning to escape him, to cling tightly to it and to hold it back. But now, to the faintness of his love there corresponded a simultaneous faintness in his desire to remain her lover.

When Swann happened to alight upon something which proved that Forcheville had been Odette's lover, he discovered that it caused him no pain, that love was now utterly remote, and he regretted that he had had no warning of the moment in which he had emerged from it for ever.

And with that, old, intermittent fatuity, which reappeared in him now that he was no longer unhappy, and lowered, at the same time, the average level of his morality, he cried out in his heart: "To think that I have wasted years of my life, that I have longed for death, that the greatest love that I have ever known has been for a woman who did not please me, who was not in my style!"

PLACE NAMES: THE NAME

When my father had decided, one year, that we should go for the Easter holidays to Florence and Venice, not finding room to introduce into the name of Florence the elements that ordinarily constitute a town, I was obliged to let a supernatural city emerge from the impregnation by certain vernal scents of what I supposed to be, in its essentials, the genius of Giotto. All the more—and because one cannot make a name extend much further in time than in space—like some of Giotto's paintings themselves which show us at two separate moments the same person engaged in different actions, here lying on his bed, there just about to mount his horse, the name of Florence was divided into two compartments. In one, beneath an architectural dais, I gazed upon a fresco over which was partly drawn a curtain of morning sunlight; dusty, aslant, and gradually spreading; in the other (for, since I thought of names not as an inaccessible ideal but as a real and enveloping substance into which I was about to plunge, the life not yet lived, the life intact and pure which I enclosed in them, gave to the most material pleasures to the simplest scenes, the same attraction that they have in the works of the Primitives), I moved swiftly—so as to arrive, as soon as might be, at the table that was spread for me, with fruit and a flask of Chianti—across a Ponte Vecchio heaped with jonquils, narcissi and anemones. That (for all that I was still in Paris) was what I saw and not what was actually round about me. Even from the simplest, the most realistic point of view, the countries for which we long, occupy, at any given moment, a far larger place in our true life than the country in which we may happen to be. Doubtless, if, at that time, I had paid more attention to what was in my mind when I pronounced the words "going to Florence, to Parma, to Pisa, to Venice," I should have realised that what I saw was in no sense a town; but something as different from anything that I knew, something as delicious as might be for a human race whose whole existence had passed in a series of late winter afternoons, that inconceivable marvel, a morning in spring.

When I repeated to myself, giving thus a special value to what I was going to see, that Venice was the "School of Giorgione, the home of Titian, the most complete museum of the domestic architecture of the Middle Ages," I felt happy indeed. As I was even more when, on one of my walks, as I stepped out briskly on account of the weather, which, after several days of a precocious spring, had relapsed into winter (like the weather that we had invariably found awaiting us at Combray, in Holy Week),—seeing upon the boulevards that the chestnut trees, though plunged in a glacial atmosphere that soaked through them like a stream of water, were none the less beginning, punctual guests, arrayed already for the party, and admitting no discouragement, to shape and chisel and curve in its frozen lumps the irrepressible verdure whose steady growth the abortive power of the cold might hinder but could not succeed in restraining—I reflected that already the Ponte Vecchio was heaped high with an abundance of hyacinths and anemones, and that the spring sunshine was already tingeing the waves of the Grand Canal with so dusky an azure, with emeralds so splendid that when they washed and were broken against the foot of one of Titian's paintings, they could vie with it in the richness of their colouring. I could no longer contain my joy when my father, in the intervals of tapping the barometer and complaining of the cold, began to look out which were the best trains, and when I understood that by making one's way, after luncheon, into the coal-grimed laboratory, the wizard's cell that undertook to contrive a complete transmutation of its surroundings, one could awaken, next morning, in the city of marble and gold, in which 'the building of the wall was of jasper and the foundation of the wall an emerald.' So that it and the City of the Lilies were not just artificial scenes which I could set up at my pleasure in front of my imagination, but did actually exist at a certain distance from Paris which must inevitably be, traversed if I wished to see them, at their appointed place on the earth's surface, and at no other; in a word they were entirely real. They became even more real to me when my father, by saying: "Well, you can stay in Venice from the 20th to the

29th, and reach Florence on Easter morning," made them both emerge, no longer only from the abstraction of Space, but from that imaginary Time in which we place not one, merely, but several of our travels at once, which do not greatly tax us since they are but possibilities,—that Time which reconstructs itself so effectively that one can spend it again in one town after one has already spent it in another— and consecrated to them some of those actual, calendar days which are certificates of the genuineness of what one does on them, for those unique days are consumed by being used, they do not return, one cannot live them again here when one has lived them elsewhere; I felt that it was towards the week that would begin with the Monday on which the laundress was to bring back the white waistcoat that I had stained with ink, that they were hastening to busy themselves with the duty of emerging from that ideal Time in which they did not, as yet, exist, those two Queen Cities of which I was soon to be able, by the most absorbing kind of geometry, to inscribe the domes and towers on a page of my own life. But I was still on the way, only, to the supreme pinnacle of happiness; I reached it finally (for not until then did the revelation burst upon me that on the clattering streets, reddened by the light reflected from Giorgione's frescoes, it was not, as I had, despite so many promptings, continued to imagine, the men "majestic and terrible as the sea, bearing armour that gleamed with bronze beneath the folds of their blood-red cloaks," who would be walking in Venice next week, on the Easter vigil; but that I myself might be the minute personage whom, in an enlarged photograph of St. Mark's that had been lent to me, the operator had portrayed, in a bowler hat, in front of the portico), when I heard my father say: "It must be pretty cold, still, on the Grand Canal; whatever you do, don't forget to pack your winter greatcoat and your thick suit." At these words I was raised to a sort of ecstasy; a thing that I had until then deemed impossible, I felt myself to be penetrating indeed between those "rocks of amethyst, like a reef in the Indian Ocean"; by a supreme muscular effort, a long way in excess of my real strength, stripping myself, as of a shell that served no purpose, of the air in my own room which surrounded me, I replaced it by an equal quantity of Venetian air, that marine atmosphere, indescribable and peculiar as the atmosphere of the dreams which my imagination had secreted in the name of Venice; I could feel at work within me a miraculous disincarnation; it was at once accompanied by that vague desire to vomit which one feels when one has a very sore throat; and they had to put me to bed with a fever so persistent that the Doctor not only assured my parents that a visit, that spring to Florence and Venice was absolutely out of the question, but warned them that, even when I should have completely recovered, I must, for at least a year, give up all idea of travelling, and be kept from anything that was liable to excite me.

And, alas, he forbade also, most categorically, my being allowed to go to the theatre, to hear Berma; the sublime artist, whose genius Bergotte had proclaimed, might, by introducing me to something else that was, perhaps, as important and as beautiful, have consoled me for not having been to Florence and Venice, for not going to Balbec. My parents had to be content with sending me, every day, to the Champs-Elysées, in the custody of a person who would see that I did not tire myself; this person was none other than Françoise, who had entered our service after the death of my aunt Léonie. Going to the Champs-Elysées I found unendurable. If only Bergotte had described the place in one of his books, I should, no doubt, have longed to see and to know it, like so many things else of which a simulacrum had first found its way into my imagination. That kept things warm, made them live, gave them personality, and I sought then to find their counterpart in reality, but in this public garden there was nothing that attached itself to my dreams.

One day, as I was weary of our usual place, beside the wooden horses, Françoise had taken me for an excursion— across the frontier guarded at regular intervals by the little bastions of the barley-sugar women—into those neighbouring but foreign regions, where the faces of the passers-by were strange, where the goat-carriage went past; then she had gone away to lay down her things on a chair that stood with its back to a shrubbery of laurels; while I waited for her I was pacing the broad lawn, of meagre close-cropped grass already faded by the sun, dominated, at its far end, by a statue rising from a fountain, in front of which a little girl with reddish hair was playing with a shuttlecock; when, from the path, another little girl, who was putting on her cloak and covering up her battledore, called out sharply: "Good-bye, Gilberte, I'm going home now; don't forget, we are coming to you this evening, after dinner." The name Gilberte passed close by me, evoking all the more forcibly her whom it labelled in that it did not merely refer to her, as one speaks of a man in his absence, but was directly addressed to her; it passed thus close by me, in action, so to speak, with a force that increased with the curve of its trajectory and as it drew near to its target,—carrying in its wake, I could feel, the knowledge, the impression of her to whom it was addressed that belonged not to me but to the friend who called to her, everything that, while she uttered the words, she more or less vividly reviewed, possessed in her memory, of their daily intimacy, of the visits that they paid to each other, of that unknown existence which was all the more inaccessible, all the more painful to me from being, conversely, so familiar, so tractable to this happy girl who let her message brush past me without my being able to penetrate its surface, who flung it on the air with a light-hearted cry: letting float in the atmosphere, the delicious attar which that message had distilled, by touching them with precision, from certain invisible points in Mlle. Swann's life, from the evening to come, as it would be, after dinner, at her home,—forming, on its celestial passage through the midst of the children and their nursemaids, a little cloud, exquisitely coloured, like the cloud that,. curling over one of Poussin's gardens, reflects minutely, like a cloud in the opera, teeming with chariots and horses, some apparition of the life of the gods; casting, finally, on that ragged grass, at the spot on which she stood (at once a scrap of withered lawn and a moment in the afternoon of the fair player, who continued to beat up and catch her shuttlecock until a governess, with a blue feather in her hat, had called her away) a marvellous little band of light, of the colour of heliotrope, spread over the lawn like a carpet on which I could not tire of treading to and fro with lingering feet, nostalgic and profane, while Françoise shouted: "Come on, button up your coat, look, and let's get away!" and I remarked for the first time how common her speech was, and that she had, alas, no blue feather in her hat. Only, would *she* come again to the Champs-Elysées? Next day she was not there; but I saw her on the following days; I spent all my time revolving round the spot where she was at play with her friends, to such effect that once, when they found they were not enough to make up a prisoner's base, she sent one of them to ask me if I cared to complete their side, and from that day I played with her whenever she came. But this did not happen every day; there were days when she had been prevented from coming by her lessons, by her catechism, by a luncheon-party, by the whole of that life, separated from my own, which twice only, condensed into the name of Gilberte, I had felt pass so painfully close to me, in the hawthorn lane near Combray and on the grass of the Champs-Elysées. On such days she would have told us beforehand that we should not see her; if it were because of her lessons, she would say: "It is too tiresome, I shan't be able to come to-morrow; you will all be enjoying yourselves here without me," with an air of regret which to some extent consoled me; if, on the other hand, she had been invited to a party, and I, not knowing this, asked her whether she was coming to play with us, she would reply: "Indeed I hope not ! Indeed I hope Mamma will let me go to my friend's." But on these days I did at least know that I should not see her, whereas on others, without any warning, her mother would take her for a drive, or some such thing, and next day she would say: "Oh, yes! I went out with Mamma," as though it had been the most natural thing in the world; and not the greatest possible misfortune for someone else. There were also the days of bad weather on which her governess, afraid, on her own account, of the rain, would not bring Gilberte to the Champs-Elysées.

And on those days when all other vegetation had disappeared, when the fine jerkins of green leather which covered the trunks of the old trees were hidden beneath the snow; after the snow had ceased to fall, but when the sky was still too much overcast for me to hope that Gilberte would venture out, then suddenly—inspiring my mother to say: "Look, it's quite fine now; I think you might perhaps try going to the Champs-Elysées after all."—on the mantle of snow that swathed the balcony, the sun had appeared and was stitching seams of gold, with embroidered patches of dark shadow. That day we found no one there, or else a solitary girl, on the point of departure, who assured me that Gilberte was not coming. The chairs, deserted by the imposing but uninspiring company of governesses, stood empty. Only, near the grass, was sitting a lady of uncertain age who came in all weathers, dressed always in an identical style, splendid and sombre, to make whose acquaintance I would have, at that period, sacrificed, had it lain in my power, all the greatest opportunities in my life to come. For Gilberte went up every day to speak to her; she used to ask Gilberte for news of her "dearest mother" and it struck me that, if I had known her, I should have been for Gilberte someone wholly different, someone who knew people in her parents' world. While her grandchildren played together at a little distance, she would sit and read the *Débats,* which she called "My old *Débats!*" as, with an aristocratic familiarity; she would say, speaking of the police-sergeant or the woman who let the chairs, "My old friend the police-sergeant," or "The chairkeeper and I, who are old friends."

Françoise found it too cold to stand about, so we walked to the Pont de La Concorde to see the Seine frozen over, on to which everyone, even children, walked fearlessly, as though upon an enormous whale, stranded, defenceless, and about to be cut up. We returned to the Champs-Elysées; I was growing sick with misery between the motionless wooden horses and, the white lawn, caught in a net of black paths from which the snow had been cleared, while the statue that surmounted it held in its hand a long pendent icicle which seemed to explain its gesture. The old lady herself, having folded up her *Débats*, asked a passing nursemaid the time, thanking her with "How very, good of you!" then begged the road-sweeper to tell her grandchildren to come, as she felt cold, adding "A thousand thanks. I am sorry to give you so much trouble!" Suddenly the sky was rent in two: between the punch-and-judy and the horses, against the opening horizon, I had just seen, like a miraculous sign, Mademoiselle's blue feather. And now Gilberte was running at full speed towards me, sparkling and rosy beneath cap trimmed with fur, enlivened by the cold, by being late, by her anxiety for a game; shortly before she reached me, she slipped on a piece of ice and; either to regain her balance, or because it appeared to her graceful, or else pretending that she was on skates, it was with outstretched arms that she smilingly advanced, as though to embrace me. "Bravo bravo! that's splendid; 'topping', I should say, like you— 'sporting', I suppose I ought to say, only I'm a hundred-and-one, a woman of the old school," exclaimed the lady, uttering, on behalf of the voiceless Champs-Elysées, their thanks to Gilberte for having come, without letting herself be frightened away by the weather. "You are like me, faithful at all costs to our old Champs-Elysées; we are two brave souls! You wouldn't believe me, I dare say, if I told you that I love them; even like this. This snow (I know, you'll laugh at me), it makes me think of ermine!" And the old lady began to laugh herself.

The first of these days—to which the snow, a symbol of the powers that were able to deprive me of the sight of Gilberte, imparted the sadness of a day of separation almost the aspect of a day of departure, because it changed the outward form and almost forbade the use of the customary scene of our only encounters, altered, covered, as it were, in dust-sheets—that day, none the less, marked a stage in the progress of my love, for it was, in a sense, the first sorrow that she was to share with me. There were only our two selves of our little company, and to be thus alone with her was not merely like beginning of intimacy, but also on her part—as though she had come there solely to please me, and in such weather—it seemed to me as touching as if, on one of those days on which she had been invited to a party, she had given it up in order to come to me in the Champs-Elysées. I acquired more confidence in the vitality, in the future of a friendship which could remain so much alive amid the torpor, the solitude, the decay of our surroundings; and while she dropped pellets of snow down my neck, I smiled lovingly at what seemed to me at once a predilection that she showed for me in thus tolerating me as her travelling companion in this new, this wintry land, and a sort of loyalty to me which she preserved through evil times. Presently, one after another, like shyly hopping sparrows, her friends arrived, black against the snow. We got ready to play and, since this day which had begun so sadly was destined to end in joy, as I went up, before the game started, to the friend with the sharp voice whom I had heard, that first day, calling Gilberte by name, she said to me "No, no, I'm sure you'd much rather be in Gilberte's camp; besides, look, she's signalling to you." She was in fact summoning me to cross the snowy lawn to her camp, to take the field, which the sun, by casting over it a rosy gleam, the metallic lustre of old and worn brocades, had turned into a Field of the Cloth of Gold.

This day, which. I had begun with so many misgivings, was, as it happened, one of the few on which I was not unduly wretched. For, although I no longer thought, now, of anything save not to let a single day pass without seeing Gilberte (so much so that once, when my grandmother had not come home by dinner-time, I could not resist the instinctive reflection that, if she had been run over in the street and killed, I should not for some time be allowed to play in the Champs-Elysées, when one is in love one has no love left for anyone) yet those moments which I spent in her company, for which I had waited with so much impatience all night and morning, for which I had quivered with excitement, to which I would have sacrificed everything else in the world, were by no means happy moments; well did I know it, for they were the only moments in my life on which I concentrated a scrupulous, undistracted attention, and yet I could not discover in them one atom of pleasure. All the time that I was away from Gilberte, I wanted to see her, because, having incessantly sought to form a mental picture of her, I was unable, in the end, to do so, and did not know exactly to what my love corresponded. Besides, she had never yet told me that she loved me. Far from it, she had often boasted that she knew other little boys whom she preferred to myself, that I was a good companion, with whom she was always willing to play, although I was too absent-minded, not attentive enough to the game. Moreover, she had often shown signs of apparent coldness towards me, which might have shaken my faith that I was for her a creature different from the rest had that faith been founded upon a love that Gilberte had felt for me, and not, as was the case, upon the love that I felt for her, which strengthened its resistance to the assaults of doubt by making it depend entirely upon the manner in which I was obliged, by an internal compulsion, to think of Gilberte. But my feelings with regard to her I had never yet ventured to express to her in words.

One day, we had gone with Gilberte to the stall of our own special vendor, who was always particularly nice to us, since it was to her that M. Swann used to send for his gingerbread, of which, for reasons of health, (he suffered from a racial eczema and from the constipation of the prophets) he consumed a great quantity,—Gilberte pointed out to me with a laugh two little boys who were like the little artist and the little naturalist in the children's story-books. For one of them would not have a red stick of rock because he preferred the purple, while the other, with tears in his eyes, refused a plum which his nurse was buying for him, because, as he finally explained in passionate tones: "I want the other plum; it's got a worm in it!"

I purchased two ha'penny marbles. With admiring eyes I saw, luminous and imprisoned in a bowl by themselves, the agate marbles which seemed precious to me because they were as fair and smiling as little girls, and because they cost five pence each,Gilberte, who was given a great deal more pocket money than I ever had, asked me which I thought the prettiest. They were as transparent, as liquid-seeming as life itself. I would not have had her sacrifice a single one of them. I should have liked her to be able to buy them, to liberate them all. Still, I pointed out one that had the same colour as her eyes. Gilberte took it, turned it about until it shone with a ray of gold, fondled it, paid its ransom, but at once handed me her captive, saying: "Take it; it is for you, I give it to you, keep it to remind yourself of me."

Another time, being still obsessed by the desire to hear Berma in classic drama, I had asked her whether she had not a copy of a pamphlet in which Bergotte spoke of Racine, and which was now out of print. She had told me to let her know the exact title of it, and that, evening I had sent her a little telegram, writing on its envelope the name, Gilberte Swann, which I had so often traced in my exercise-books. Next day she brought me in a parcel tied with pink bows and sealed with white wax, the pamphlet, a copy of which she had managed to find. "You see, it is what you asked me for," she said, taking from her muff the telegram that I had sent her. But in the address on the pneumatic message—which, only yesterday, was nothing, was merely a 'little blue' that I had written, and, after a messenger had delivered it to Gilberte's porter and a servant had taken it to her in her room, had become a thing without value or distinction, one of the 'little blues' that she had received in the course of the day— I had difficulty in recognising the futile, straggling lines of my own handwriting beneath the circles stamped on it at the post-office, the inscriptions added in pencil by a postman, signs of effectual realisation, seals of the external world, violet bands symbolical of life itself, which for the first time came to espouse, to maintain, to raise, to rejoice my dream.

On one of these sunny days which had not realised my hopes, I had not the courage to conceal my disappointment from Gilberte.

"I had ever so many things to ask you" I said to her; "I thought that to-day was going to mean so much in our friendship. And no sooner have you come than you go away! Try to come early tomorrow, so that I can talk to you."

Her face lighted up and she jumped for joy as she answered: "Tomorrow, you may make up your mind, my dear friend, I shan't come! First of all I've a big luncheon-party; then in the afternoon I am going to a friend's house to see King Theodosius arrive from her windows; won't that be splendid?—and then, next day, I'm going to *Michel Strogoff,* and after that it will soon be Christmas, and the New Year holidays! Perhaps they'll take me south, to the Riviera; won't that be nice? Though I should miss the Christmas-tree here; anyhow, if I do stay in Paris; I shan't be coming here, because 1 shall be out paying calls with Mamma. Good-bye—there's Papa calling me."

I returned home with Françoise through streets that were still gay with sunshine, as on the evening of a holiday when the merriment is over. I could scarcely drag my legs along.

"I'm not surprised;" said Françoise, "it's not the right weather for the time of year; it's much too warm. Oh dear, oh dear, to think of all the poor sick people there must be everywhere; you would think that up there, too, everything's got out of order."

Once my mother, while she was telling us, as she did every evening at dinner, where she had been and what she had done that afternoon, merely by the words: "By the way, guess whom I saw at the Trois Quartiers—at the umbrella counter— Swann!" caused to burst open in the midst of her narrative (an arid desert to me) a mystic blossom. What a melancholy satisfaction to learn that, that very afternoon, threading through the crowd his supernatural form, Swann had gone to buy an umbrella. Among the events of the day, great and small, but all equally unimportant, that one alone aroused in me those peculiar vibrations by which my love for Gilberte was invariably stirred. My father complained that I took no interest in anything, because I did not listen while he was speaking of the political developments that might follow the visit of King Theodosius,—at that moment in France as the nation's, guest and (it was hinted) ally. And yet how intensely interested I was to know whether Swann had been wearing his hooded cape!

"Did you speak to him.?" I asked.

Why, of course I did," answered my mother, who always seemed afraid lest, were she to admit that we were not on the warmest of terms, with Swann, people would seek to reconcile us more than she cared for, in view of the existence of Mme. Swann, whom she did not wish to know. "It was he who came up and spoke to me, I hadn't seen him."

"Then you haven't quarrelled?"

"Quarrelled? What on earth made you think that we had quarrelled?" she briskly parried, as though I had cast doubt on the fiction of her friendly relations with Swann, and was planning an attempt to 'bring them together.'

"He might be cross with you for never asking him here."

"One isn't obliged to ask everyone to one's house, you know; has he ever asked me to his? I don't know his wife."

"But he used often to come, at Combray."

"I should think he did! He used to come at Combray, and now, in Paris, he has something better to do, and so have I. But I can promise you, we didn't look in the least like people who had quarrelled. We were kept waiting there for some time, while they brought him his parcel. He asked after you; he told me you had been playing with his daughter........" my mother went on, amazing me with the portentous revelation of my own existence in Swann's mind; far more than that, of my existence in so complete, so material a form that when I stood before him, trembling with love, in the Champs Elysées, he had known my name, and who my mother was, and had been able to blend with my quality as his daughter's playmate certain facts with regard to my grandparents and their connections, the place in which we lived, certain details of our past life, all of which I myself perhaps did not know.

Most often of all, on days when I was not to see Gilberte, as I had heard that Mme. Swann walked almost every day along the Allée des Acacias, round the big lake, and in the Allée dé la Reine Marguerite, I would guide Françoise in the direction of the Bois de Boulogne. I had been told that I should see in the alley certain women of fashion, who, in spite of their not all having husbands, were constantly mentioned in conjunction with Mme. Swann, but most often by their professional names;—their new names, when they had any, being but a sort of incognito, a veil which those who would speak of them were careful to draw aside, so as to make themselves understood. But it was Mme.

Swann whom I wished to see, and I waited for her to go past, as deeply moved as though she were Gilberte, whose parents, saturated, like everything in her environment, with her own special charm, excited in me as keen a passion as she did herself, indeed a still more painful disturbance, (since their point of contact with her was that intimate, that internal part of her life which was hidden from me), and furthermore, for I very soon learned, as we shall see in due course, that they did not like my playing with her, that feeling of veneration which we always have for those who hold, and exercise without restraint, the power to do us an injury. -

I assigned the first place, in the order of aesthetic merit and of social grandeur, to simplicity, when I saw Mme. Swann on foot, in a 'polonaise' of plain cloth, a little toque on her head trimmed with a pheasant's wing, a bunch of violets in her bosom, hastening along the Allée des Acacias as if it had been merely the shortest way back to her own house, and acknowledging with a rapid glance the courtesy of the gentlemen in carriages, who, recognising her figure at a distance, were raising their hats to her and saying to one another that there was never anyone so well turned out as she. But instead of simplicity it was to ostentation that I must assign the first place if, after I had compelled Françoise, who could hold out no longer, and complained that her legs were 'giving' beneath her, to stroll up and down with me for another hour, I saw at length, emerging from the Porte Dauphine, figuring for me a royal dignity, the passage of a sovereign, an impression such as no real Queen has ever since been able to give me, because my notion of their power has been less vague, and more founded upon experience—borne along by the flight of a pair of fiery horses, slender and shapely as one sees them in the drawings of Constantin Guys, carrying on its box an enormous coachman, furred like a cossack, and, by his side a diminutive groom, like Toby, "the late Beaudenord's tiger," I saw—or rather I felt its outlines engraved upon my heart by a clean and killing stab—a matchless victoria, built rather high, and hinting, through the extreme modernity of its appointments, at the forms of an earlier day, deep down in which lay negligently back Mme. Swann, her hair, now quite pale with one grey lock, girt with a narrow band of flowers, usually violets, from which floated down long veils, a lilac parasol in her hand, on her lips an ambiguous smile in which I read only the benign condescension of Majesty, though it was pre-eminently the enticing smile of the courtesan, which she graciously bestowed upon the men who bowed to her. That smile was, in reality, saying to one: "Oh yes, I do remember, quite well; it was wonderful!" to another:

"How I should have loved to! We were unfortunate! to a third: "Yes, if you like! I must just keep in the line for a minute, then as soon as I can I will break away." When strangers passed she still allowed to linger about her lips a lazy smile, as though she expected or remembered some friend, which made them say: "What a lovely woman!" And for certain men only she had a sour, strained, shy, cold smile which meant; "Yes, you old goat, I know that you've got a tongue like a viper, that you can't keep quiet for a moment. But do you suppose that I care what you say?" Coquelin passed, talking, in a group of listening friends, and with a sweeping wave of his hand bade a theatrical good day to the people in the carriages. But I thought only of Mme. Swann, and pretended to have not yet seen her, for I knew that, when she reached the pigeon-shooting ground, she would tell her coachman to 'break away' and to stop the carriage, so that she might come back on foot. And on days when I felt that I had the courage to pass close by her I would drag Françoise off in that direction; until the moment came when I saw Mme. Swann, letting trail behind her the long train of her lilac skirt, dressed, as the populace imagine queens to be dressed, in rich attire such as no other woman might wear, lowering her eyes now and then to study the handle of her parasol, paying scant attention to the passers-by, as though the important thing for her, her one object in being there was to take exercise, without thinking that she was seen, and that every head was turned towards her. Sometimes, however, when she had looked back to call her dog to her, she would cast, almost imperceptibly, a sweeping, glance round about.

Those even who did not know her were warned by something exceptional, something beyond the normal in her—or perhaps by a telepathic suggestion such as would move an ignorant audience to a frenzy of applause when Berma was 'sublime'—that she must be some one well-known. They would ask one another, "Who is she?" or sometimes would interrogate a passing stranger, or, would make a mental note of how she was dressed so as to fix her identity, later, in the mind of a friend better informed than themselves, who would at once enlighten them. Another pair, half-stopping in their walk, would exchange: "You know who that is? Mme. Swann! That conveys nothing to you? Odette de Crécy, then?"

"Odette de Crécy! Why, I thought as much. Those great, sad eyes..... But I say, you know, she can't be as young as she was once, eh? I remember, I had her on the day that MacMahon went."

"I shouldn't remind her of it, if I were you. She is now Mme. Swann, the wife of a gentleman in the Jockey Club, a friend of the Prince of

Wales. Apart from that, though, she is wonderful still."

"Oh, but you ought to have known her then; Gad, she was lovely! She lived in a very odd little house with a lot of Chinese stuff. I remember, we were bothered all the time by the newsboys, shouting outside; in the end she made me get up and go."

Without listening to these memories, I could feel all about her the indistinct murmur of fame. My heart leaped with impatience when I thought that a few seconds must still elapse before all these people, among whom I was dismayed not to find a certain mulatto banker who (or so I felt) had a contempt for me, were to see the unknown youth, to whom they had not, so far, been paying the slightest attention, salute (without knowing her, it was true, but I thought that I had sufficient authority since my parents knew her husband and I was her daughter's playmate) this woman whose reputation for beauty, for misconduct, and for elegance was universal. But I was now close to Mme. Swann; I pulled off my hat with so lavish, so prolonged a gesture that she could not repress a smile. People laughed. As for her, she had never seen me with Gilberte, she did not know my name, but I was for her—like one of the keepers in the Bois, like the boatman, or the ducks on the lake, to which she threw scraps of bread—one of the minor personages, familiar, nameless, as devoid of individual character as a stage-hand in a theatre, of her daily walks abroad.

WITHIN A BUDDING GROVE

MADAME SWANN AT HOME

My mother, when it was a question of our having M. de Norpois to dinner for the first time, having expressed her regret that Professor Cottard was away from home, and that she herself had quite ceased to see anything of Swann, since either of these might have helped to entertain the old Ambassador, my father replied that so eminent a guest, so distinguished a man of science as Cottard could never be out of place at a dinner-table, but that Swann, with his ostentation, his habit of crying aloud from the house-tops the name of everyone that he knew, however slightly, was an impossible vulgarian whom the Marquis de Norpois would be sure to dismiss as—to use his own epithet—a 'pestilent' fellow. Now, this attitude on my father's part may be felt to require a few words of explanation, inasmuch as some of us, no doubt, remember a Cottard of distinct mediocrity and a Swann by whom modesty and discretion, in all his social relations, were carried to the utmost refinement of delicacy. But in his case, what had happened was that, to the original 'young Swann' and also to the Swann of the Jockey Club, our old friend had added a fresh personality (which was not to be his last) that of Odette's husband. Adapting to the humble ambitions of that lady the instinct, the desire, the industry which he had always had, he had laboriously constructed for himself, a long way beneath the old, a new position more appropriate to the companion who was to share it with him. In this he showed himself another man. Since (while he continued to go, by himself, to the houses of his own friends, on whom he did not care to inflict Odette unless they had expressly asked that she should be introduced to them) it was a new life that he had begun to lead, in common with his wife, among a new set of people, it was quite intelligible that, in order to estimate the importance of these new friends and thereby the pleasure, the self-esteem that were to be derived from entertaining them, he should have made use, as a standard of comparison, not of the brilliant society in which he himself had moved before his marriage but of the earlier environment of Odette. And yet, even when one knew that it was with unfashionable officials and their faded wives, the wallflowers of ministerial ball-rooms, that he was now anxious to associate, it was still astonishing to hear him, who in the old days, and even still, would so gracefully refrain from mentioning an invitation to Twickenham or to

Marlborough House, proclaim with quite unnecessary emphasis that the wife of some Assistant Under-Secretary for Something had returned Mme. Swann's call. It will perhaps be objected here that what this really implied was that the simplicity of the fashionable Swann had been nothing more than a supreme refinement of vanity, and that, like certain other Israelites, my parents' old friend had contrived to illustrate in turn all the stages through which his race had passed, from the crudest and coarsest form of snobbishness up to the highest pitch of good manners.

    With Cottard, on the contrary the epoch in which we have seen him assisting at the first introduction of Swann to the Verdurins was now buried in the past; whereas honours, offices and titles come with the passage of years; moreover, a man may be illiterate, and make stupid puns, and yet have a special gift, which no amount of general culture can replace— such as the gift of a great strategist or physician. And so it was not merely as an obscure practitioner, who had attained in course of time to European celebrity, that the rest of his profession regarded Cottard. The most intelligent of the younger doctors used to assert—for a year or two, that is to say, for fashions, being themselves begotten of the desire for change, are quick to change also—that if they themselves ever fell ill Cottard was the only one of the leading men to whom they would entrust their lives. No doubt they preferred, socially, to meet certain others who were better read, more artistic, with whom they could discuss Nietzsche and Wagner. When there was a musical party at Mme. Cottard's, on the evenings when she entertained—in the hope that it might one day make him Dean of the Faculty—the colleagues and pupils of her husband, he, instead of listening, preferred to play cards in another room. Yet everybody praised the quickness, the penetration, the unerring confidence with which, at a glance, he could diagnose disease. Thirdly, in considering the general impression which Professor Cottard must have made on a man like my father, we must bear in mind that the character which a man exhibits in the latter half of his life is not always, even if it is often his original character developed or withered, attenuated or enlarged; it is sometimes the exact opposite, like a garment that has been turned. Except from the Verdurins, who were infatuated with him, Cottard's hesitating manner, his excessive timidity and affability had, in his young days, called down upon him endless taunts and sneers. What charitable friend counselled that glacial air? The importance of his professional standing made it all the more easy to adopt. Wherever he went, save at the Verdurins', where he instinctively became himself again, he would assume a repellent coldness, remain silent as long as possible, be peremptory when he was obliged to speak, and not forget to say the most cutting things. He had every opportunity of rehearsing this new attitude before his patients, who, seeing him for the first time, were not in a position to make comparisons, and would have been greatly surprised to learn that he was not at all a rude man by nature. Complete impassivity was what he strove to attain, and even while visiting his hospital wards, when he allowed himself to utter one of those puns which left everyone, from the house physician to the junior student, helpless with laughter, he would always make it without moving a muscle of his face, while even that was no longer recognisable now that he had shaved off his beard and moustache.

But who, the reader has been asking, was the Marquis de Norpois. Well, he had been Minister Plenipotentiary before the War, and was actually an Ambassador on the Sixteenth of May; in spite of which, and to the general astonishment, he had since been several times chosen to represent France on Extraordinary Missions,—even as Controller of the Public Debt in Egypt, where, thanks to his great capability as a financier, he had rendered important services—by Radical Cabinets under which a reactionary of the middle classes would have declined to serve, and in whose eyes M. de Norpois, in view of his past, his connections and his opinions, ought presumably to have been suspect. But these advanced Ministers seemed to consider that, in making such an appointment, they were showing how broad their own minds were, when the supreme interests of France were at stake, were raising themselves above the general run of politicians, were meriting, from the *Journal des Débats* itself, the title of 'Statesmen', and were reaping direct advantage from the weight that attaches to an aristocratic name and the dramatic interest always aroused by an unexpected appointment.

But in the character of M. de Norpois there was this predominant feature, that, in the course of a long career of diplomacy, he had become imbued with that negative, methodical, conservative spirit, called 'governmental', which is common to all Governments and, under every Government, particularly inspires its Foreign Office.

M. de Norpois was considered very stiff, at the Commission, where he sat next to my father, whom everyone else congratulated on the astonishing way in which the old Ambassador unbent to him. My father was himself more astonished than anyone. For not being, as a rule, very affable, his company was little sought outside his own intimate circle, a limitation which he used modestly and frankly to avow. "De Norpois has asked me to dinner again; it's quite extraordinary; everyone on the Commission is amazed, as he never has any personal relations with any of us. I am sure he's going to tell me something thrilling, again, about the 'Seventy war'. My father knew that M. de Norpois had warned, had perhaps been alone in warning the Emperor of the growing strength and bellicose designs of Prussia, and that Bismarck rated his intelligence most highly. Only the other day, at the Opéra, during the gala performance given for King Theodosius, the newspapers had all drawn attention to the long conversation which that Monarch had held with M. de Norpois. "I must ask him whether the King's visit had any real significance," my father went on, for he was keenly interested in foreign politics. "I know old Norpois keeps very close as a rule, but when he's with me he opens out quite charmingly."

The evening on which M. de Norpois first appeared at our table, in a year when I still went to play in the Champs-Elysées, has remained fixed in my memory because the afternoon of the same day was that upon which I at last went to hear Berma, at a *matinée*, in *Phèdre*, and also because in talking to M. de Norpois I realised suddenly, and in a new and different way, how completely the feelings aroused in me by all that concerned Gilberte Swann and her parents differed from any that the same family could inspire in anyone else.

It was no doubt the sight of the depression in which I was plunged by the approach of the New Year holidays, in which, as she herself had informed me, I was to see nothing of Gilberte, that prompted my mother one day, in the hope of distracting my mind, to suggest, "If you are still so anxious to hear Berma, I think that your father would allow you perhaps to go; your grandmother can take you."

But it was because M. de Norpois had told him that he ought to let me hear Berma, that it was an experience for a young man to remember in later life, that my father, who had hitherto been so resolutely opposed to my going and wasting my time, with the added risk of my falling ill again, on what he used to shock my grandmother by calling 'futilities', was now not far from regarding this manner of spending an afternoon as included, in some vague way, in the list of precious formulae for success in a brilliant career. My grandmother, who, in renouncing on my behalf the profit which, according to her, I should have derived from hearing Berma, had made a considerable sacrifice in the interests of my health, was surprised to find that this last had become of no account at a mere word from M. de Norpois. Reposing the unconquerable hopes of her rationalist spirit in the strict course of fresh air and early hours which had been prescribed for me, she now deplored, as something disastrous, this infringement that I was to make of my rules, and in a tone of despair protested, "How easily led you are!" to my father, who replied angrily "What ! So it's you that are for not letting him go, now. That is really too much, after your telling us all day and every day that it would be so good for him."

M. de Norpois had also brought about a change in my father's plans in a matter of far greater importance to myself. My father had always meant me to become a diplomat, and I could not endure the thought that, even if I did have to stay for some years, first, at the Ministry, I should run the risk of being sent, later on, as Ambassador, to capitals in which no Gilberte dwelt. I should have preferred to return to the literary career that I had planned for myself, and had then abandoned, years before, in my wanderings along the Guermantes way. But my father had steadily opposed my devoting myself to literature, which he regarded as vastly inferior to diplomacy, refusing even to dignify it with the title of career, until the day when M. de Norpois, who had little love for the more recent generations of diplomatic agents, assured him that it was quite possible, by writing, to attract as much attention, to receive as much consideration, to exercise as much influence, and at the same time to preserve more independence than in the Embassies.

"Well, well, I should never have believed it. Old Norpois doesn't at all disapprove of your idea of taking up writing," my father had reported. And as he had a certain amount of influence himself; he imagined that there was nothing that could not be 'arranged', no problem for which a happy solution might not be found in the conversation of people who 'counted'. "I shall bring him back to dinner, one of these days, from the Commission. You must talk to him a little, and let him see what he thinks of you. Write something good that you can show him; he is an intimate friend of the editor of the *Deux Monde*; he will get you in there; he will arrange it all, the cunning old fox; and, upon my soul, he seems to think that diplomacy, nowadays—!"

My happiness in the prospect of not being separated from Gilberte made me desirous, but not capable, of writing something good which could be shown to M. de Norpois. After a few laboured pages, weariness made the pen drop from my fingers; I cried with anger at the thought that I should never have any talent, that I was not 'gifted', that I could not even take advantage of the chance that M. de Norpois's coming visit was to offer me of spending the rest of my life in Paris. The recollection that I was to be taken to hear Berma alone distracted me from my grief. But just as I did not wish to see any storms except on those coasts where they raged with most violence, so I should not have cared to hear the great actress except in one of those classic parts in which Swann had told me that she touched the sublime.

The doctor who was attending me—the same who had forbidden me to travel—advised my parents not to let me go to the theatre; I should only be ill again afterwards, perhaps for weeks, and should in the long run derive more pain than pleasure from the experience.

I implored my parents, who, after the doctor's visit, were no longer inclined to let me go to *Phèdre*. I repeated, all day long, to myself, the speech beginning,

"*On dit qu'un prompt depart vous éloigne de nous,—*"

seeking out every intonation that could be put into it, so as to be able better to measure my surprise at the way which Berma would have found of uttering the lines.

And with my eyes fixed upon that inconceivable image, I strove from morning to night to overcome the barriers which my family were putting in my way. But when those had at last fallen; when my mother—albeit this *matinée* was actually to coincide with the meeting of the Commission from which my father had promised to bring M. de Norpois home to dinner—had said to me, "Very well, we don't wish you to be unhappy;—if you think that you will enjoy it so very much, you must go; that's all;" when this day of theatre-going, hitherto forbidden and unattainable, depended now only upon myself, then for the first time, being no longer troubled by the wish that it might cease to be impossible, I asked myself if it were desirable, if there were not other reasons than my parents' prohibition which should make me abandon my design. "I would rather not go, if it hurts you," I told my mother, who, on the contrary, strove hard to expel from my mind any lurking fear that she might regret my going, since that, she said, would spoil the pleasure that I should otherwise derive from *Phèdre*, and it was the thought of my pleasure that had induced my father and her to reverse their earlier decision. But then this sort of obligation to find a pleasure in the performance seemed to me very burdensome. Besides, if I returned home ill, should I be well again in time to be able to go to the Champs-Elysées as soon as the holidays were over and Gilberte returned?

Alas! that first *matinée* was to prove a bitter disappointment. My father offered to drop my grandmother and me at the theatre, on his way to the Commission. Before leaving the house he said to my mother: "See that you have a good dinner for us to-night; you remember, I'm bringing de Norpois back with me." My mother had not forgotten. And all that day, and overnight, Françoise, rejoicing in the opportunity to devote herself to that art of the kitchen,—of which she was indeed a past-master, stimulated, moreover, by the prospect of having a new guest to feed, the consciousness that she would have to compose, by methods known to her alone, a dish of beef in jelly, had been living in the effervescence of creation; since she attached the utmost importance to the intrinsic quality of the materials which were to enter into the fabric of her work, she had gone herself to the Halles to procure the best cuts of rump-steak, shin of beef, calves'-feet, as Michelangelo passed eight months in the mountains of Carrara choosing the most perfect blocks of marble for the monument of Julius 11.—Françoise expended on these comings and goings so much ardour that Mamma, at the sight of her flaming cheeks, was alarmed lest our old servant should make herself ill with overwork, like the sculptor of the Tombs of the Medici in the quarries of Pietrasanta. And overnight Françoise had sent to be cooked in the baker's oven, shielded with breadcrumbs, like a block of pink marble packed in sawdust, what she called a 'Nev' York ham. Believing the language to be less rich than it actually was in words, and her own ears less trustworthy, the first time that she heard anyone mention York ham she had thought, no doubt,—feeling it to be hardly conceivable that the dictionary could be so prodigal as to include at once a 'York' and a 'New York'—that she had misheard what was said, and that the ham was really called by the name already familiar to her. And so, ever since, the word York was preceded in her ears, or before her eyes when she read it in an advertisement, by the affix 'New' which she pronounced 'Nev'. And it was with the most perfect faith that she would say to her kitchen-maid "Go and fetch me a ham from Olida's. Madame told me especially to get a 'Nev' York."

On that particular day, if Françoise was consumed by the burning certainty of creative genius, my lot was the cruel anxiety of the seeker after truth. No doubt, so long as I had not yet heard Berma speak, I still felt some pleasure. I felt it in the little square that lay in front of the theatre, in which, in two hours' time, the bare boughs of the chestnut trees would gleam with a metallic lustre as the lighted gas-lamps shewed up every detail of their structure; before the attendants in the box-office, the selection of whom, their promotion, all their destiny depended upon the great artist—for she alone held power in the theatre, where ephemeral managers followed one after the other in an obscure succession—who took our tickets without even glancing at us, so preoccupied were they with their anxiety lest any of Mme. Berma's instructions had not been duly transmitted to the new members of the staff, lest it was not clearly, everywhere, understood that the hired applause must never sound for her, that the windows must all be kept open so long as she was not on the stage, and every door closed tight the moment that she appeared; that a bowl of hot water must be concealed somewhere close to her, to make the dust settle: and, for that matter, at any moment now her carriage, drawn by a pair of horses with flowing manes, would be stopping outside the theatre, she would alight from it muffled in furs, and, crossly acknowledging everyone's salute, would send one of her attendants to find out whether a stage box had been kept for her friends, what the temperature was 'in front', who were in the other boxes, if the programme sellers were looking smart; theatre and public being to her no more than a second, an outermost cloak which she would put on, and the medium, the more or less 'good' conductor through which her talent would have to pass. I was happy, too, in the theatre itself; since I had made the discovery that—in contradiction of the picture so long entertained by my childish imagination— there was but one stage for everybody, I had supposed that I should be prevented from seeing it properly by the presence of the other spectators, as one is when in the thick of a crowd; now I registered the fact that, on the contrary, thanks to an arrangement which is, so to speak, symbolical of all spectatorship, everyone feels himself to be the centre of the theatre; which explained to me why, when Françoise had been sent once to see some melodrama from the top gallery, she had assured us on her return that her seat had been the best in the house, and that instead of finding herself too far from the stage she had been positively frightened by the mysterious and living proximity of the curtain. My pleasure increased further when I began to distinguish behind the said lowered curtain such confused rappings as one hears through the shell of an egg before the chicken emerges, sounds which speedily grew louder and suddenly, from that world which, impenetrable by our eyes, yet scrutinised us with its own, addressed themselves, and to us indubitably, in the imperious form of three consecutive hammer-blows as moving as any signals from the planet Mars. And— once this curtain had risen,—when on the stage a writing-table and a fireplace, in no way out of the ordinary, had indicated that the persons who were about to enter would be, not actors come to recite, as I had seen them once and heard them at an evening party, but real people, just living their lives at home, on whom I was thus able to spy without their seeing me—my pleasure still endured; it was broken by a momentary uneasiness; just as I was straining my ears in readiness before the piece began, two men entered the theatre from the side of the stage, who must have been very angry with each other, for they were talking so loud that in the auditorium, where there were at least a thousand people, we could hear every word, whereas in quite a small *café* one is obliged to call the waiter and ask what it is that two men, who appear to be quarrelling, are saying; but at that moment, while I sat astonished to find that the audience was listening to them without protest, drowned as it was in a universal silence upon which broke, presently, a laugh here and there, I understood that these insolent fellows were the actors, and that the short piece known as the 'curtain-raiser' had now begun. It was followed by an interval so long that the audience, who had returned to their places, grew impatient and began to stamp their feet. I was terrified at this; for just as in the report of a criminal trial, when I read that some noble-minded person was coming, against his own interests, to testify on behalf of an innocent prisoner, I was always afraid that they would not be nice enough to him, would not show enough gratitude, would not recompense him lavishly, and that he, in disgust, would then range himself on the side of injustice so now attributing to genius, in this respect, the same qualities as to virtue, I was afraid lest Berma, annoyed by the bad behaviour of so ill-bred an audience—in which, on the other hand, I should have liked her to recognise, with satisfaction, a few celebrities to whose judgment she would be bound to attach importance—should express her discontent and disdain by acting badly. And I gazed appealingly round me at these stamping brutes who were about to shatter, in their insensate rage, the rare and fragile impression which I had come to seek. The last moments of my pleasure were during the opening scenes of *Phèdre*. The heroine herself does not appear in these first scenes of the second act; and yet, as soon as the curtain rose, and another curtain, of red velvet this time, was parted in the middle (a curtain which was used to halve the depth of the stage in all the plays in which the 'star' appeared), an actress entered from the back who had the face and voice which, I had been told, were those of Berma. The cast must therefore have been changed; all the trouble that I had taken in studying the part of the wife of Theseus was wasted. But a second actress now responded to the first. I must, then, have been mistaken in supposing that the first was Berma, for the second even more closely resembled her, and, more than the other, had her diction. Both of them, moreover, enriched their parts with noble gestures—which I could vividly distinguish, and could appreciate in their relation to the text, while they raised and let fall the lovely folds of their tunics—and also with skilful changes of tone, now passionate, now ironical, which made me realise the significance of lines that I had read to myself at home without paying sufficient attention to what they really meant. But all of a sudden, in the cleft of the red curtain that veiled her sanctuary, as in a frame, appeared a woman, and simultaneously with the fear that seized me, far more vexing than Berma's fear could be, lest someone should upset her by opening a window, or drown one of her lines by rustling a programme, or annoy her by applauding the others and by not applauding her enough ;—in my own fashion, still more absolute than Berma's, of considering from that moment theatre, audience, play and my own body only as an acoustic medium of no importance, save in the degree to which it was favourable to the inflexions of that voice,—I realised that the two actresses whom I had been for some minutes admiring bore not the least resemblance to her whom I had come to hear. But at the same time all my pleasure had ceased; in vain might I strain towards Berma eyes, ears, mind, so as not to let one morsel escape me of the reasons which she would furnish for my admiring her, I did not succeed in gathering a single one. I could not even, as I could with her companions, distinguish in her diction and in her playing intelligent intonations, beautiful gestures. I listened to her as though I were reading *Phèdre*, or as though Phaedra herself had at that moment uttered the words that I was hearing, without its appearing that Berma's talent had added anything at all to them. I could have wished, so as to be able to explore them fully, so as to attempt to discover what it was in them that was beautiful, to arrest, to immobilise for a time before my senses, every intonation of the artist`s voice, every expression of her features; at least I did attempt, by dint of my mental agility in having, before a line came, my attention ready and tuned to catch it, not to waste upon preparations any morsel of the precious time that each word, each gesture occupied, and, thanks to the intensity of my observation, to manage to penetrate as far into them as if I had had whole hours to spend upon them, by myself. But how short their duration was! Scarcely had a sound been received by my ear than it was displaced there by another. In one scene, where Berma stands motionless for a moment, her arm raised to the level of a face bathed, by some piece of stagecraft, in a greenish light, before a back-cloth painted to represent the sea, the whole house broke out in applause; but already the actress had moved, and the picture that I should have liked to study existed no longer. I told my grandmother that I could not see very well; she handed me her glasses. Only, when one believes in the reality of a thing, making it visible by artificial means is not quite the same as feeling that it is close at hand. I thought now that it was no longer Berma at whom I was looking, but her image in a magnifying glass. I put the glasses down, but then possibly the image that my eye received of her, diminished by distance, was no more exact; which of the two Bermas was the real? As for her speech to Hippolyte, I had counted enormously upon that, since, to judge by the ingenious significance which her companions were disclosing to me at every moment in less beautiful parts, she would certainly render it with intonations more surprising than any which, when reading the play at home, I had contrived to imagine; but she did not attain to the heights which Oenone or Aricie would naturally have reached, she planed down into a uniform flow of melody the whole of a passage in which there were mingled together contradictions so striking that the least intelligent of tragic actresses, even the pupils of an academy could not have missed their effect; besides which, she ran through the speech so rapidly that it was only when she had come to the last line that my mind became aware of the deliberate monotony which she had imposed on it throughout.

Then, at last, a sense of admiration did possess me, provoked by the frenzied applause of the audience. I mingled my own with theirs, endeavouring to prolong the general sound so that Berma, in her gratitude, should surpass herself, and I be certain of having heard her on one of her great days. A curious thing, by the way, was that the moment when this storm of public enthusiasm broke loose was, as I afterwards learned, that in which Berma reveals one of her richest treasures. It would appear that certain transcendent realities emit all around them a radiance to which the crowd is sensitive. So it is that when any great event occurs, when on a distant frontier an army is in jeopardy, or defeated, or victorious, the vague and conflicting reports which we receive, from which an educated man can derive little enlightenment, stimulate in the crowd an emotion by which that man is surprised, and in which, once expert criticism has informed him of the actual military situation, he recognises the popular perception of that 'aura' which surrounds momentous happenings, and which may be visible hundreds of miles away. One learns of a victory either after the war is over, or at once, from the hilarious joy of one's hall porter. One discovers the touch of genius in Berma's acting a week after one has heard her, in the criticism of some review, or else on the spot, from the thundering acclamation of the stalls. But this immediate recognition by the crowd was mingled with a hundred others, all quite erroneous; the applause came, most often at wrong moments, apart from the fact that it was mechanically produced by the effect of the applause that had gone before, just as in a storm, once the sea is sufficiently disturbed, it will continue to swell, even after the wind has begun to subside. No matter; the more I applauded, the better, it seemed to me, did Berma act. "I say," came from a woman sitting near me, of no great social pretensions, "she fairly gives it you, she does, you'd think she'd do herself an injury, the way she runs about. I call that acting, don't you?" And happy to find these reasons for Berma's superiority, though not without a suspicion that they no more accounted for it than would for that of the Gioconda or of Benvenuto's Perseus a peasant's gaping "That's a good bit of work. It's all gold, look! Fine, ain't it ?" I greedily imbibed the strong wine of this popular enthusiasm. I felt, all the same, when the curtain had fallen for the last time, disappointed that the pleasure for which I had so longed had been no greater, but at the same time I felt the need to prolong it, not to depart for ever, when I left the theatre, from this strange life of the stage which had, for a few hours, been my own, from which I should be tearing myself away, as though I were going into exile, when I returned to my own home, had I not hoped there to learn a great deal more about Berma from her admirer, to whom I was indebted already for the permission to go to *Phèdre,* M. de Norpois. I was introduced to him before dinner by my father, who summoned me into his study for the purpose. As I entered, the Ambassador rose, held out his hand, bowed his tall figure and fixed his blue eyes attentively on my face. As the foreign visitors who used to be presented to him, in the days when he still represented France abroad, were all more or less (even the famous singers) persons of note, with regard to whom he could tell, when he met them, that he would be able to say, later on, when he heard their names mentioned in Paris or in Petersburg, that he remembered perfectly the evening he had spent with them at Munich or Sofia, he had formed the habit of impressing upon them, by his affability, the pleasure with which he was making their acquaintance; but in addition to this, being convinced that in the life of European capitals, in contact at once with all the interesting personalities that passed through them and with the manners and customs of the native populations, one acquired a deeper insight than could be gained from books into the intellectual movement throughout Europe, he would exercise upon each newcomer his keen power of observation, so as to decide at once with what manner of man he had to deal. The Government had not for some time now entrusted to him a post abroad, but still, as soon as anyone was introduced to him, his eyes, as though they had not yet been informed of their master's retirement, began their fruitful observation, while by his whole attitude he endeavoured to convey that the stranger's name was not unknown to him. And so, all the time, while he spoke to me kindly and with the air of importance of a man who is conscious of the vastness of his own experience, he never ceased to examine me with a sagacious curiosity, and to his own profit, as though I had been some exotic custom, some historic and instructive building or some 'star' upon his course. And in this way he gave proof at once, in his attitude towards me, of the majestic benevolence of the sage Mentor and of the zealous curiosity of the young Anacharsis.

He offered me absolutely no opening to the *Revue des Deux-Mondes;* but put a number of questions to me on what I had been doing and reading; asked what were my own inclinations, which I heard thus spoken of for the first time as though it might be a quite reasonable thing to obey their promptings, whereas hitherto I had always supposed it to be my duty to suppress them. Since they attracted me towards Literature, he did not dissuade me from that course; on the contrary, he spoke of it with deference, as of some venerable personage whose select circle, in Rome or at Dresden, one remembers with pleasure, and regrets only that one's multifarious duties in life enable one to revisit it so seldom. He appeared to be envying me, with an almost jovial smile, the delightful hours which, more fortunate than himself and more free, I should be able to spend with such a Mistress. But the very terms that he employed showed me Literature as something entirely different from the image that I had formed of it at Combray, and I realised that I had been doubly right in abandoning my intention. Until now, I had reckoned only that I had not the 'gift' for writing; now M. de Norpois took from me the ambition also. I wanted to express to him what had been my dreams; trembling with emotion, I was painfully apprehensive that all the words which I could utter would not be the sincerest possible equivalent of what I had felt, what I had never yet attempted to formulate; that is to say that my words had no clear significance. Perhaps by a professional habit, perhaps by virtue of the calm that is acquired by every important personage whose advice is commonly sought, and who, knowing that he will keep the control of the conversation in his own hands, allows the other party to fret, to struggle, to take his time; perhaps also to emphasise the dignity of his head (Greek, according to himself, despite his sweeping whiskers), M. de Norpois, while anything was being explained to him, would preserve a facial immobility as absolute as if you had been addressing some ancient and unhearing bust in a museum. Until suddenly, falling upon you like an auctioneer's hammer, or a Delphic oracle, the Ambassador's voice, as he replied to you, would be all the more impressive, in that nothing in his face had allowed you to guess what sort of impression you had made on him, or what opinion he was about to express.

"Precisely;" he suddenly began, as though the case were now heard and judged, and after allowing me to writhe in increasing helplessness beneath those motionless eyes which never for an instant left my face. "There is the case of the son of one of my friends, which, *mutatis mutandis*, is very much like yours." He adopted in speaking of our common tendency the same reassuring tone as if it had been a tendency not to literature but to rheumatics, and he had wished to assure me that it would not necessarily prove fatal. "He too has chosen to leave the Quai d'Orsay, although the way had been paved for him there by his father, and without caring what people might say, he has settled down to write. And certainly, he's had no reason to regret it. He published two years ago— of course, he's much older than you, you understand— a book dealing with the Sense of the Infinite on the Western Shore of Victoria Nyanza, and this year he has brought out a little thing, not so important as the other, but very brightly, in places perhaps almost too pointedly written, on the Repeating Rifle in the Bulgarian Army; and these have put him quite in a class by himself. He's gone pretty far already, and he's not the sort of man to stop half way; I happen to know that (without any suggestion, of course, of his standing for election) his name has been mentioned several times, in conversation, and not at all unfavourably, at the Academy of Moral Sciences. And so, one can't say yet, of course, that he has reached the pinnacle of fame, still he has made his way, by sheer industry, to a very fine position indeed, and success—which doesn't always come only to agitators and mischief-makers and men who make trouble which is usually more than they are prepared to take—success has crowned his efforts."

My father, seeing me already, in a few years' time, an Academician, was tasting a contentment which M. de Norpois raised to the supreme pitch when, after a momentary hesitation in which he appeared to be calculating the possible consequences of so rash an act, he handed me his card and said: "Why not go and see him yourself? Tell him, I sent you. He may be able to give you some good advice," plunging me by his words into as painful a state of anxiety as if he had told me that, next morning, I was to embark as cabin-boy on board a sailing ship, and to go round the world.

My Aunt Léonie had bequeathed to me, together with all sorts of other things and much of her furniture, with which it was difficult to know what to do, almost all her unsettled estate—revealing thus after her death an affection for me which I had hardly suspected in her lifetime. My father, who was trustee of this estate until I came of age, now consulted M. de Norpois with regard to several of the investments. He recommended certain stocks bearing a low rate of interest, which he considered particularly sound, notably English consols and Russian four per cents. "With absolutely first class securities such as those," said M. de Norpois, "even if your income from them is nothing very great, you may be certain of never losing any of your capital." My father then told him, roughly, what else he had bought. M. de Norpois gave a just perceptible smile of congratulation; like all capitalists, he regarded wealth as an enviable thing, but thought it more delicate to compliment people upon their possessions only by a half-indicated sign of intelligent sympathy; on the other hand, as he was himself immensely rich, he felt that he showed his good taste by seeming to regard as considerable the meagre revenues of his friends, with a happy and comforting resilience to the superiority of his own.

The contempt which my father had for my kind of intelligence was so far tempered by his natural affection for me that, in practice, his attitude towards anything that I might do was one of blind indulgence. And so he had no qualm about telling me to fetch a little 'prose poem' which I had made up, years before, at Combray, while coming home from a walk. I had written it down in a state of exaltation which must, I felt certain, infect everyone who read it. But it was not destined to captivate M. de Norpois, for he handed it back to me without a word.

"Well, did you enjoy your *matinée?*" asked my father, as we moved to the dining-room; meaning me to 'show off' and with the idea that my enthusiasm would give M. de Norpois a good opinion of me. "He has just been to hear Berma. You remember, we were talking about it the other day," he went on, turning towards the diplomat, in the same tone of retrospective, technical, mysterious allusiveness as if he had been referring to a meeting of the Commission.

"You must have been enchanted, especially if you had never heard her before. Your father was alarmed at the effect that the little jaunt might have upon your health, which is none too good, I am told, none too robust. But I soon set his mind at rest. Theatres today are not what they were even twenty years ago. You have more, or less comfortable seats now, and a certain amount of ventilation, although we have, still a long way to go before we come up to Germany or England, which in that respect as in many others are immeasurably ahead of us. I have never seen Mme. Berma in *Phèdre,* but I have always heard that she is excellent in the part. You were charmed with her, of course."

M. de Norpois, a man a thousand times more intelligent than myself, must know that hidden truth which I had failed to extract from Berma's playing; he knew, and would reveal it to me; in answering his question I would implore him to let me know in what that truth consisted; and he would tell me, and so justify me in the longing that I had felt to see and hear the actress. I had only a moment, I must make what use I could of it and bring my cross-examination to bear upon the essential points. But what were they? Fastening my whole attention upon my own so confused impressions, with no thought of making M. de Norpois admire me, but only that of learning from him the truth that I had still to discover, I made no attempt to substitute ready-made phrases for the words that failed me—I stood there stammering, until finally, in the hope of provoking him into declaring what there was in Berma that was admirable, I confessed that I had been disappointed.

"What's that?" cried my father, annoyed at the bad impression which this admission of my failure to appreciate the performance must make on M. de Norpois, "What on earth do you mean; you didn't enjoy it? Why, your grandmother has been telling us that you sat there hanging on every word that Berma uttered, with your eyes starting out of your head; that everyone else in the theatre seemed quite bored, beside you."

"Oh, yes, I was listening as hard as I could, trying to find out what it was that was supposed to be so wonderful about her. Of course, she's frightfully good, and all that. "If she is 'frightfully good', what more do you want?"

"One of the things that have undoubtedly contributed to the success of Mme. Berma," resumed M. de Norpois, turning with elaborate courtesy towards mother, so as not to let her be left out of the conversation, and in conscientious fulfilment of his duty of politeness to the lady of the house, "is the perfect taste that she shows in selecting her parts; thus she can always be assured of success, and success of the right sort. She hardly ever appears in anything trivial. Look how she has thrown herself into the part of Phèdre. And then, she brings the same good taste to the choice of her costumes, and to her acting. In spite of her frequent and lucrative tours in England and America, the vulgarity—I will not say of John Bull; that would be unjust, at any rate to the England of the Victorian era—but of Uncle Sam has not infected her. No loud colours, no rant. And then that admirable voice, which has been of such service to her, with which she plays so delightfully—I should almost be tempted to describe it as a musical instrument"

"He is right!" I told myself. "What a charming voice, what an absence of shrillness, what simple costumes, what intelligence to have chosen *Phèdre*. No; I have not been disappointed!"

The cold beef, spiced with carrots, made its appearance, couched by the Michelangelo of our kitchen upon enormous crystals of jelly, like transparent blocks of quartz.

"You have a chef of the first order, Madame," said M. de Norpois, "and that is no small matter. I myself, who have had, when abroad, to maintain a certain style in housekeeping, I know how difficult it often is to find a perfect master-cook. But this is a positive banquet that you have set before us!"

And indeed Françoise, in the excitement of her ambition to make a success, for so distinguished a guest, of a dinner the preparation of which had been obstructed by difficulties worthy of her powers, had given herself such trouble as she no longer took when we were alone, and had recaptured her incomparable Combray manner.

"That is a thing you can't get in a chophouse,—in the best of them, I mean; a spiced beef in which the jelly does not taste of glue and the beef has caught the flavour of the carrots; it is admirable. Allow me to come again," he went on, making a sign to show that he wanted more of the jelly. " I should be interested to see how your Vatel managed a dish of quite a different kind I should like, for instance, to see him tackle a *boeuf Stroganoff*,"

"My husband tells me, sir, that you are perhaps going to take him to Spain one summer; that will be nice for him; I am so glad."

"Why, yes; it is an idea that greatly attracts me; I amuse myself, planning a tour. I should like to go there with you, my dear fellow. But what about you, Madame; have you decided yet how you are going to spend your holidays?"

"I shall perhaps go with my son to Balbec, but I am not certain."

"Oh, but Balbec is quite charming, I was down that way a few years ago. They are beginning to build some very pretty little villas there; I think you'll like the place. But may I ask what has made you choose Balbec?"

"My son is very anxious to visit some of the churches in that neighbourhood, and Balbec church in particular. I was a little afraid that the tiring journey there, and the discomfort of staying in the place might be too much for him. But I hear that they have just opened an excellent hotel, in which he will be able to get all the comfort that he requires."

"Indeed I must make a note of that, for a certain person who will not turn up her nose at a comfortable hotel."

"The church at Balbec is very beautiful, sir, is it not?" I inquired, repressing my sorrow at learning that one of the attractions of Balbec consisted in its pretty little villas.

"No, it is not bad; but it cannot be compared for a moment with such positive jewels in stone as the Cathedrals of Rheims and Chartres, or with what is to my mind the pearl among them all, the Sainte-Chapelle here in Paris."

"But, surely, Balbec church is partly romanesque, is it not?"

"Why, yes, it is in the romanesque style, which is to say very cold and lifeless, with no hint in it anywhere of the grace, the fantasy of the later gothic builders, who worked their stone as if it had been so much lace. Balbec church is well worth a visit, if you are in those parts it is decidedly quaint; on a wet day, when you have nothing better to do, you might look inside; you will see the tomb of Tourville."

"Tell me, were you at the Foreign Ministry dinner last night?" asked my father. "I couldn't go."

"No," M. de Norpois smiled, "I must confess that I renounced it for a party of a very different sort. I was dining with a lady whose name you may possibly have heard, the beautiful Mme. Swann." My mother checked an impulsive movement, for, being more rapid in perception than my father, she used to alarm herself on his account over things which only began to upset him a moment later. Anything unpleasant that might occur to him was discovered first by her, just as bad news from France is always known abroad sooner than among ourselves. But she was curious to know what sort of people the Swanns managed to entertain, and so inquired of M. de Norpois as to whom he had met there.

"Why, my dear lady, it is a house which (or so it struck me) is especially attractive to gentlemen. There were several married men there last night, but their wives were all, as it happened, unwell, and so had not come with them," replied the Ambassador with a mordancy sheathed in good humour, casting on each of us a glance the gentleness and discretion of which appeared to be tempering while in reality they deftly intensified its malice.

"In all fairness," he went on, "I must add that women do go to the house, but women who belong rather—what shall I say—to the Republican world than to Swann's" (he pronounced it 'Svann's') "circle. Still, you can never tell. Perhaps it will turn into a political or a literary salon some day. Anyhow, they appear to be quite happy as they are. It is true that for some years before the marriage she was always trying to blackmail him in a rather disgraceful way; she would take the child away whenever Swann refused her anything. Poor Swann, who is, unsophisticated as he is, for all that, sharp, believed every time, that the child's disappearance was a coincidence, and declined to face the facts. Apart from that, she made such continual scenes that everyone expected that, from the day she attained her object and was safely married, nothing could possibly restrain her and that their life would be a hell on earth. Instead of which, just the opposite has happened. People are inclined to laugh at the way in which Swann speaks of his wife; it's become a standing joke. Of course, one could hardly expect that, conscious, more or less of being a ….. (you remember Molière's word) he would go and proclaim it *urbi et orbi;* still that does not prevent one from finding a tendency in him to exaggerate when he declares that she makes an excellent wife. And yet that is not so far from the truth as people imagine. In her own way— which is not, perhaps, what all husbands would prefer, but then, between you and me, I find it difficult to believe that Swann, who has known her for ever so long and is far from being an utter fool, did not know what to expect— there can be no denying that she does seem to have a certain regard for him. I do not say that she is not flighty, and Swann himself has no fault to find with her for that, if one is to believe the charitable tongues which, as you may suppose, continue to wag. But she is distinctly grateful to him for what he has done for her, and, despite the fears that were everywhere expressed of the contrary, her temper seems to have become angelic."

This alteration was perhaps not so extraordinary as M. de Norpois professed to find it. Odette had not believed that Swann would ever consent to marry her; each time that she made the suggestive announcement that some man about town had just married his mistress she had seen him stiffen into a glacial silence, or at the most, if she were directly to challenge him, asking "Don't you think it very nice, a very fine thing that he has done, for a woman who sacrificed all her youth to him?" had heard him answer dryly "But I don't say that there's anything wrong in it. Everyone does what he himself thinks right." She came very near, indeed, to believing that (as he used to threaten in moments of anger) he was going to leave her altogether, for she had heard it said, not long since, by a woman sculptor, that "You cannot be surprised at anything men do, they're such brutes," and impressed by the profundity of this maxim of pessimism she had appropriated it for herself, and repeated it on every possible occasion with an air of disappointment which seemed to imply "After all, it's not impossible in any way; it would be just my luck." Meanwhile all the virtue had gone from the optimistic maxim which had hitherto guided Odette through life "You can do anything with men when they're in love with you, they're such idiots!" a doctrine which was expressed on her face by the same tremor of an eyelid that might have accompanied such words as "Don't be frightened; he won't break anything." While she waited, Odette was tormented by the thought of what one of her friends, who had been married by a man who had not lived with her for nearly so long as Odette herself had lived with Swann, and had had no child by him, and who was now in a definitely respectable position, invited to the balls at the Elysée and so forth, must think of Swann's behaviour. A consultant more discerning than M. de Norpois would doubtless have been able to diagnose that it was this feeling of shame and humiliation that had embittered Odette, that the devilish characteristics which she displayed were no essential part of her, no irremediable evil, and so would easily have foretold what had indeed come to pass; namely that a new rule of life, the matrimonial, would put an end, with almost magic swiftness, to these painful incidents, of daily occurrence but in no sense organic. Practically everyone was surprised at the marriage, and this, in itself, is surprising.

There was not on Swann's part, when he married Odette, any renunciation of his social ambitions, for from these ambitions Odette had long ago, in the spiritual sense of the word, detached him. There had been but one person in all the world whose opinion he took into consideration whenever he thought of his possible marriage with Odette; that was, and from no snobbish motive, the Duchesse de Guermantes. With whom Odette, on the contrary, was but little concerned, thinking only of those people whose position was immediately above her own rather than in so vague an empyrean. But when Swann in his daydreams saw Odette as already his wife he invariably formed a picture of the moment in which he would take her—her, and above all her daughter—to call upon the Princesse des Laumes, (who was shortly, on the death of her father-in-law, to become Duchesse de Guermantes). He had no desire to introduce them anywhere else, but his heart would soften as he invented—uttering their actual words to himself—all the things that the Duchess would say of him to Odette, and Odette to the Duchess, the affection that she would show for Gilberte, spoiling her, making him proud of his child. He enacted to himself the scene of this introduction with the same precision in each of its imaginary details that people show when they consider how they would spend, supposing they were to win it, a lottery prize the amount of which they have arbitrarily determined. In so far as a mental picture which accompanies one of our resolutions may be said to be its motive, so it might be said that if Swann married Odette it was in order to present her and Gilberte, without anyone's else being present, without, if need be, anyone's else ever coming to know of it, to the Duchesse de Guermantes. We shall see how this sole social ambition that he had entertained for his wife and daughter was precisely that one the realisation of which proved to be forbidden him by a veto so absolute that Swann died in the belief that the Duchess would never possibly come to know them. We shall see also that, on the contrary the Duchesse de Guermantes did associate with Odette and Gilberte after the death of Swann. And doubtless he would have been wiser—seeing that he could attach so much importance to so small a matter—not to have formed too dark a picture of the future, in this connection, but to have consoled himself with the hope that the meeting of the ladies might indeed take place when he was no longer there to enjoy it.

"Was there a writer of the name of Bergotte at this dinner, sir?" I asked timidly, still trying to keep the conversation to the subject of the Swanns.

"Yes, Bergotte was there," replied M. de Norpois, inclining his head courteously towards me, as though in his desire to be pleasant to my father he attached to everything connected with him a real importance, even to the questions of a boy of my age who was not accustomed to see such politeness shown to him by persons of his. "Do you know him?" he went on, fastening on me that clear gaze, the penetration of which had won the praise of Bismarck.

"My son does not know him, but he admires his work immensely," my mother explained.

"Good heavens!" exclaimed M. de Norpois, inspiring me with doubts of my own intelligence far more serious than those that ordinarily distracted me, when I saw that what I valued a thousand thousand times more than myself, what I regarded as the most exalted thing in the world, was for him at the very foot of the scale of admiration. "I do not share your son's point of view. I can now understand more easily, when I bear in mind your altogether excessive regard for Bergotte, the few lines that you showed me just now, which it would have been unfair to you not to overlook, since you yourself told me in all simplicity, that they were merely a childish scribbling." (I had, indeed, said so, but I did not think anything of the sort.) "For every sin there is forgiveness, and especially for the sins of youth. After all, others as well as yourself have such sins upon their conscience, and you are not the only one who has believed himself to be a poet in his day. But one can see in what you have shown me the evil influence of Bergotte. You will not, of course, be surprised when I say that there was in it none of his good qualities, since he is a past-master in the art— incidentally quite superficial—of handling a certain style of which, at your age, you cannot have acquired even the rudiments. But already there is the same fault, that paradox of stringing together fine-sounding words and only afterwards troubling about what they mean."

Paralysed by what M. de Norpois had just said to me with regard to the fragment which I had submitted to him, and remembering at the same time the difficulties that I experienced when I attempted to write an essay or merely to devote myself to serious thought, I felt conscious once again of my intellectual nullity and that I was not born for a literary life.

At length Gilberte returned to play in the Champs-Elysées almost every day, setting before me fresh pleasures to desire, to demand of her for the morrow, indeed making my love for her every day, in this sense, a new love. But an incident was to change once again, and abruptly, the manner in which, at about two o'clock every afternoon, the problem of my love confronted me. Had M. Swann intercepted the letter that I had written to his daughter, or was Gilberte merely confessing to me long after the event, and so that I should be more prudent in future, a state of things already long established? As I was telling her how greatly I admired her father and mother, she assumed that vague air, full of reticence and kept secrets, which she invariably wore when anyone spoke to her of what she was going to do, her walks, drives, visits— then suddenly expressed it with: "You know, they can't abide you!" and, slipping from me; like the Undine that she was, burst out laughing. Often her laughter, out of harmony with her words, seemed, as music seems, to be tracing an invisible surface on another plane. M. and Mme. Swann did not require Gilberte to give up playing with me, but they would have been just as well pleased, she thought, if we had never begun. They did not look upon our relations with a kindly eye; they believed me to be a young person of low moral standard and imagined that my influence over their daughter must be evil. This type of unscrupulous young man whom the Swanns thought that I resembled, I pictured him to myself as detesting the parents of the girl he loved, flattering them to their faces but, when he was alone with her, making fun of them, urging her on to disobey them and, when once he had completed his conquest, not allowing them even to set eyes on her again. With these characteristics (though they are never those under which the basest of scoundrels recognises himself) how vehemently did my heart contrast the sentiments that did indeed animate it with regard to Swann, so passionate, on the contrary, that I never doubted that, were he to have the least suspicion of them, he must repent of his condemnation of me as of a judicial error. All, that I felt about him I made bold to express to him in a long letter which I entrusted to Gilberte, with the request that she would deliver it. She consented. Alas! So he saw in me an even greater impostor than I had feared; those sentiments which I had supposed myself to be portraying, in sixteen pages, with such amplitude of truth, so he had suspected them; in short, the letter that I had written him, as ardent and as sincere as the words that I had uttered to M. de Norpois, met with no more success. Gilberte told me next day, after taking me aside behind a clump of laurels, along a little path by which we sat down on a couple of chairs, that as he read my letter, which she had now brought back to me, her father had shrugged his shoulders, with: "All this means nothing; it only goes to prove how right I was." I asked her if there was not some way for me to have it out with her father, face to face. Gilberte said that she had suggested that to him, but that he had not thought it of any use. "Look," she went on, "don't go away without your letter; I must run along to the others, as they haven't caught me."

Had Swann appeared on the scene then before I had recovered it, this letter, by the sincerity of which I felt that he had been so unreasonable in not letting himself be convinced, perhaps he would have seen that it was he who had been in the right. For as I approached Gilberte, who, leaning back in her chair, told me to take the letter but did not hold it out to me, I felt myself so irresistibly attracted by her body that I said to her "Look ! You try to stop me from getting it; we'll see which is the stronger." She thrust it behind her back; I put my arms round her neck, raising the plaits of hair which she wore over her shoulders, either because she was still of an age for that or because her mother chose to make her look a child for a little longer so that she herself might still seem young; and we wrestled, locked together. I tried to pull her towards me, she resisted; her cheeks, inflamed by the effort, were as red and round as two cherries; she laughed as though I were tickling her; I held her gripped between my legs like a young tree which I was trying to climb; and, in the middle of my gymnastics, when I was already out of breath with the muscular exercise and the heat of the game, I felt, as it were a few drops of sweat wrung from me by the effort, my pleasure express itself in a form which I could not even pause for a moment to analyse; immediately I snatched the letter from her. Whereupon Gilberte said, good-naturedly:

"You know, if you like, we might go on wrestling for a little."

Perhaps she was dimly conscious that my game had had another object than that which I had avowed, but too dimly to have been able to see that I had attained it. And I, who was afraid that she had seen (and a slight recoil, as though of offended modesty which she made and checked a moment later made me think that my fear had not been unfounded), agreed to go on wrestling, lest she should suppose that I had indeed no other object than that, after which I wished only to sit quietly by her side.

For some time now I had been liable to choking fits, and our doctor, braving the disapproval of my grandmother, who could see me already dying a drunkard's death, had, recommended me to take, as well as the caffeine which had been prescribed to help me to breathe, beer, champagne or brandy when I felt an attack coming. These attacks would subside, he told me, in the 'euphoria' brought about by the alcohol. I was often obliged, so that my grandmother should allow them to give it to me instead of dissembling, almost to make a display of my state of suffocation.

As my chokings had persisted long after any congestion remained that could account for them, my parents asked for a consultation with Professor Cottard. It is not enough that a physician who is called in to treat cases of this sort should be learned. Brought face to face with symptoms which may or may not be those of three or four different complaints, it is in the long run his instinct, his eye that must decide with which, despite the more or less similar appearance of them all, he has to deal. This mysterious gift does not imply any superiority in the other departments of the intellect, and a creature of the utmost vulgarity, who admires the worst pictures, the worst music, in whose mind there is nothing out of the common, may perfectly well possess it. In my case, what was physically evident might equally well have been due to nervous spasms, to the first stages of tuberculosis, asthma, to a toxi-alimentary dyspnoea with renal insufficiency, to chronic bronchitis, or to a complex state into which more than one of these factors entered. Now, nervous spasms required to be treated firmly, and discouraged, tuberculosis with infinite care and with a 'feeding up' process which would have been bad for an arthriticcondition such as asthma, and might indeed have been dangerous in a case of toxi-alimentary dyspnoea, this last calling for a strict diet which, in return, would be fatal to a tuberculous patient. But Cottard's hesitations were brief and his prescriptions imperious. "Purges; violent and drastic purges; milk for some days, nothing but milk. No meat. No alcohol." My mother murmured that I needed, all the same, to be 'built up', that my nerves were already weak, that drenching me like a horse and restricting my diet would make me worse. I could see in Cottard's eyes, as uneasy as though he were afraid of missing a train, that he was asking himself whether he had not allowed his natural good-humour to appear. He was trying to think whether he had remembered to put on his mask of coldness, as one looks for a mirror to see whether one has not forgotten to tie one's tie. In his uncertainty, and, so as, whatever he had done, to put things right, he replied brutally: "I am not in the habit of repeating my instructions. Give me a pen. Now remember, milk! Later on, when we have got the crises and the agrypnia by the throat, I should like you to take a little clear soup, and then a little broth, but always with milk; au *lait* ! You'll enjoy that, since Spain is all the rage just now; *ollé, ollé!*" His pupils knew this joke well, for he made it at the hospital whenever he had to put a heart or liver case on a milk diet. "After that, you will gradually return to your normal life. But whenever there is any coughing or choking—purges, injections, bed, milk!" He listened with icy calm, and without uttering a word, to my mother's final objections, and as he left us without having condescended to explain the reasons for this course of treatment, my parents concluded that it had no bearing on my case, and would weaken me to no purpose, and so they did not make me try it. Naturally they sought to conceal their disobedience from the Professor, and to succeed in this avoided all the houses in which he was likely to be found. Then, as my health became worse, they decided to make me follow out Cottard's prescriptions to the letter; in three days my 'rattle' and cough had ceased, I could breathe freely. Whereupon we realised that Cottard, while finding, as he told us later on, that I was distinctly asthmatic, and still more inclined to imagine things, had seen that what was really the matter with me at the moment was intoxication, and that by loosening my liver and washing out my kidneys he would get rid of the congestion of my bronchial tubes and thus give me back my breath, my sleep and my strength. And we realised that this imbecile was a clinical genius. At last I was able to get up. But they spoke of not letting me go any more to the Champs-Elysées. They said that it was because the air there was bad; but I felt sure that this was only a pretext so that I should not see Mlle. Swann, and I forced myself to repeat the name of Gilberte all the time, like the native tongue which peoples in captivity endeavour to preserve among themselves so as not to forget the land that they will never see again.

One day, after the postman had called, my mother laid a letter upon my bed. I opened it carelessly, since it could not bear the one signature that would have made me happy, the name of Gilberte, with whom I had no relations outside the Champs-Elysées. And lo, at the foot of the page, embossed with a silver seal representing a man's head in a helmet, and under him a scroll with the device *Per viam rectam,* beneath a letter written in a large and flowing hand, in which almost every word appeared to be underlined, simply because the crosses of the 't' s ran not across but over them, and so drew a line beneath the corresponding letters of the word above, it was indeed Gilberte's signature and nothing else that I saw. "My dear Friend," said the letter, "I hear that you have been very ill and have given up going to the Champs-Elysées. I hardly ever go there either because there has been such an enormous lot of illness. But I'm having my friends to tea here every Monday and Friday. Mamma asks me to tell you that it will be a great pleasure to us all if you will come too, as soon as you are well again, and we can have some more nice talks here, just like the Champs-Elysées. Good-bye, dear friend; I hope that your parents will allow you to come to tea very often. With all my kindest regards. GILBERTE."

While I was reading these words, my nervous system was receiving, with admirable promptitude, the news that a piece of great good fortune had befallen me. But my mind, that is to say myself, and in fact the party principally concerned, was still in ignorance. Such good fortune, coming from Gilberte, was a thing of which I had never ceased to dream; a thing wholly in my mind, it was, as Leonardo says of painting, *cosa mentale.* Now, a sheet of paper covered with writing is not a thing that the mind assimilates at once. But as soon as I had finished reading the letter, I thought of it, it became an object of my dreams, became, it also, *cosa mentale,* and I loved it so much already that every few minutes I must read it, kiss it again. Then at last I was conscious of my happiness.

So far as concerns this letter, at the foot of which Françoise declined to recognise Gilberte's name, because the elaborate capital 'G' leaning against the undotted 'i`' looked more like an 'A', while the final syllable was indefinitely prolonged by a waving flourish, if we persist in looking for a rational explanation of the sudden reversal of her attitude towards me which it indicated, and which made me so radiantly happy, we may perhaps find that I was to some extent indebted for it to an incident which I should have supposed, on the contrary, to be calculated to ruin me for ever in the sight of the Swann family. A short while back, Bloch had come to see me at a time when Professor Cottard, whom, now that I was following his instructions, we were again calling in, happened to be in my room. As his examination of me was over, and he was sitting with me simply as a visitor because my parents had invited him to stay to dinner, Bloch was allowed to come in. While we were all talking, Bloch having mentioned that he had heard it said that Mlle. Swann was very fond of me, by a lady with whom he had been dining the day before, who was herself very intimate with Mme. Swann, I should have liked to reply that he was most certainly mistaken, and to establish the fact (from the same scruple of conscience that had made me proclaim it to M. de Norpois, and for fear of Mme. Swann's taking me for a liar) that I did not know her and had never spoken to her. But I had not the courage to correct Bloch's mistake, because I could see quite well that it was deliberate, and that, if he invented something that Mme. Swann could not possibly have said, it was simply to let us know (what he considered flattering to himself, and was not true either) that he had been dining with one of that lady's friends. And so it fell out that, whereas M. de Norpois, on learning that I did not know but would very much like to know Mme. Swann, had taken great care to avoid speaking to her about me, Cottard, who was her doctor also, having gathered from what he had heard Bloch say that she knew me quite well and thought highly of me, concluded that to remark, when next he saw her, that I was a charming young fellow and a great friend of his could not be of the smallest use to me and would be of advantage to himself, two reasons which made him decide to speak of me to Odette whenever an opportunity arose.

Thus at length I found my way into that abode from which was wafted even on to the staircase the scent that Mme. Swann used, though it was embalmed far more sweetly still by the peculiar, disturbing charm that emanated from the life of Gilberte. The implacable porter, transformed into a benevolent Eumenid, adopted the custom, when I asked him if I might go upstairs, of indicating to me, by raising his cap with a propitious hand, that he gave ear to my prayer. Those windows which, seen from outside, used to interpose between me and the treasures within, which were not intended for me, a polished, distant and superficial stare, which seemed to me the very stare of the Swanns themselves, it fell to my lot, when in the warm weather I had spent a whole afternoon with Gilberte in her room, to open them myself, so as to let in a little air, and even to lean over the sill of one of them by her side, if it was her mother's at home day, to watch the visitors arrive who would often, raising their heads as they stepped out of their carriages, greet me with a wave of the hand, taking me for some nephew of their hostess. At such moments Gilberte's plaits used to brush my cheek. They seemed to me, in the fineness of their grain, at once natural and supernatural, and in the strength of their constructed tracery, a matchless work of art, in the composition of which had been used the very grass of Paradise. To a section of them, even infinitely minute, what celestial herbary would I not have given as a reliquary. But since I never hoped to obtain an actual fragment of those plaits, if at least I had been able to have their photograph, how far more precious than one of a sheet of flowers traced by Vinci's pencil! To acquire one of these, I stooped—with friends of the Swanns, and even with photographers to servilities which did not procure for me what I wanted, but tied me for life to a number of extremely tiresome people.

Gilberte's parents, who for so long had prevented me from seeing her, now would come and shake hands with a smile, and say "How d'e do?" (They both pronounced it in the same clipped way, which, you may well imagine, once I was back at home, I made an incessant and delightful practice of copying.) "Does Gilberte know you're here? She does ? Then I'll leave you to her."

Better still, the tea-parties themselves to which Gilberte invited her friends, parties which for so long had seemed to me the most insurmountable of the barriers heaped up between her and myself, became now an opportunity for uniting us of which she would inform me in a few lines, written (because I was still a comparative stranger) upon sheets that were always different. One was adorned with a poodle embossed in blue, above a fantastic inscription in English with an exclamation mark after it; another was stamped with an anchor, or with the monogram G. S. preposterously elongated in a rectangle which ran from top to bottom of the page, or else with the name Gilberte, now traced across one corner in letters of gold which imitated my friend's signature and ended in a flourish, beneath an open umbrella printed in black, now enclosed in a monogram in the shape of a Chinaman's hat, which contained all the letters of the word in capitals without its being possible to make out a single one of them. At last, as the series of different writing-papers which Gilberte possessed, numerous as it might be, was not unlimited, after a certain number of weeks I saw reappear the sheet that bore (like the first letter she had written me) the motto *Per viam rectam*, and over it the man's head in a helmet, set in a medallion of tarnished silver. And each of them was chosen, on one day rather than another, by virtue of a certain ritual, as I then supposed, but more probably, as I now think, because she tried to remember which of them she had already used, so as never to send the same one twice to any of her correspondents, of those at least whom she took special pains to please, save at the longest possible intervals.

Meanwhile on those tea-party days, pulling myself up the staircase step by step, reason and memory already cast off like outer garments, and myself no more now than the sport of the basest reflexes, I would arrive in the zone in which the scent of Mme. Swann greeted my nostrils. I felt that I could already behold the majesty of the chocolate cake, encircled by plates heaped with little cakes, and by tiny napkins of grey damask with figures on them, as required by convention but peculiar to the Swanns. But this unalterable and governed whole seemed, like Kant's necessary universe, to depend on a supreme act of free will. For when we were all together in Gilberte's little sitting-room, suddenly she would look at the clock and exclaim:

"I say! It's getting a long time since luncheon, and we aren't having dinner till eight. I feel as if I could eat something. What do you say?"

And she would make us go into the dining-room, as sombre as the interior of an Asiatic Temple painted by Rembrandt, in which an architectural cake, as gracious and sociable as it was imposing, seemed to be enthroned there in any event, in case the fancy seized Gilberte to discrown it of its chocolate battlements and to hew down the steep brown slopes of its ramparts, baked in the oven like the bastions of the palace of Darius. Better still, in proceeding to the demolition of that Babylonitish pastry, Gilberte did not consider only her own hunger; she inquired also after mine, while she extracted for me from the crumbling monument a whole glazed slab jewelled with scarlet fruits, in the oriental style. She asked me even at what o'clock my parents were dining, as if I still knew, as if the disturbance that governed me had allowed to persist the sensation of satiety or of hunger, the notion of dinner or the picture of my family in my empty memory and paralysed stomach. Alas, its paralysis was but momentary. The cakes that I took without noticing them, a time would come when I should have to digest them. But that time was still remote. Meanwhile Gilberte was making 'my' tea. I went on drinking it indefinitely, whereas a single cup would keep me awake for twenty-four hours. Which explains why my mother used always to say: "What a nuisance it is; he can never go to the Swanns' without coming home ill." But was I aware even, when I was at the Swanns', that it was tea that I was drinking? Had I known, I should have taken it just the same, for even supposing that I had recovered for a moment the sense of the present, that would not have restored to me the memory of the past or the apprehension of the future. My imagination was incapable of reaching to the distant time in which I might have the idea of going to bed, and the need to sleep.

Gilberte's girl friends were not all plunged in that state of intoxication in which it is impossible to make up one's mind. Some of them refused tea! Then Gilberte would say, using a phrase highly fashionable that year: "I can see I'm not having much of a success with my tea!" And to destroy more completely any idea of ceremony, she would disarrange the chairs that were drawn up round the table, with: "We look just like a wedding breakfast. Good lord, what fools servants are!"

She nibbled her cake, perched sideways upon a cross-legged seat placed at an angle to the table. And then, just as though she could have had all those cakes at her disposal without having first asked leave of her mother, when Mme. Swann, whose 'day' coincided as a rule with Gilberte's tea-parties, had shown one of her visitors to the door, and came sweeping in, a moment later, dressed sometimes in blue velvet, more often in a black satin gown draped with white lace, she would say with an air of astonishment: "I say, that looks good, what you've got there. It makes me quite hungry to see you all eating cake."

"But, Mamma, do! We invite you !" Gilberte would answer.

"Thank you, no, my precious ; what would my visitors say ? I've still got Mme. Trombert and Mme. Cottard and Mme. Bontemps; you know dear Mme. Bontemps never pays very short visits, and she has only just come. What would all those good people say if I never went back to them ? If no one else calls, I'll come in again and have a chat with you (which will be far more amusing) after they've all gone. I really think I've earned a little rest I have had forty-five different people today, and forty-two of them told me about Gérôme's picture! But you must come along one of these days," she turned to me, "and take 'your' tea with Gilberte. She will make it for you just as you like it, as you have it in your own little 'studio', she went on, flying off to her visitors, as if it had been something as familiar to me as my own habits (such as the habit that I should have had of taking tea, had I ever taken it; as for my 'studio', I was uncertain whether I had one or not) that I had come to seek in this mysterious world. "When can you come? Tomorrow ? We will make you 'toast' every bit as good as you get at Colombin's. No? You are horrid," for, since she also had begun to form a salon, she had borrowed Mme. Verdurin's mannerisms, and notably her tone of petulant autocracy. 'Toast' being as incomprehensible to me as

'Colombin's' could not add to my temptation. It will appear stranger still, now that everyone uses such expressions—and perhaps even at Combray they are creeping in—that I had not at first understood of whom Mme. Swann was speaking when I heard her sing the praises of our old 'nurse' I did not know any English; I gathered, however, as she went on that the word was intended to denote Françoise. I who, in the Champs-Elysées, had been so terrified of the bad impression that she must make, I now learned from Mme. Swann that it was all the things that Gilberte had told them about my 'nurse' that had attracted her husband and her to me. "One feels that she is so devoted to you; she must be nice!" (At once my opinion of Françoise was diametrically changed. By the same token, to have a governess equipped with a waterproof and a feather in her hat no longer appeared quite so essential.) Finally I learned from some words which Mme. Swann let fall with regard to Mme. Blatin (whose good nature she recognised but dreaded her visits) that personal relation with that lady would have been of less value to me than I had supposed, and would not in any way have improved my standing with the Swanns.

It was not only in those tea-parties, on account of which I had formerly had the sorrow of seeing Gilberte leave me and go home earlier than usual, that I was henceforth to take part, but the engagements that she had with her mother, to go for a walk or to some afternoon party, which by preventing her from coming to the Champs-Elysées had deprived me of her, on those days when I loitered alone upon the lawn or stood before the wooden horses,— to these outings M. and Mme. Swann henceforth admitted me, I had a seat in their landau, and indeed it was me that they asked if I would rather go to the theatre, to a dancing lesson at the house of one of Gilberte's friends, to some social gathering given by friends of her parents (what Odette called "a little meeting") or to visit the tombs at Saint-Denis.

As a rule, however, we did not stay indoors, we went out. Sometimes, before going to dress, Mme. Swann would sit down at the piano. Her lovely hands, escaping from the pink, or white, or, often, vividly coloured sleeves of her *crêpe-de-Chine* wrapper, drooped over the keys with that same melancholy which was in her eyes but was not in her heart. It was on one of those days that she happened to play me the part of Vinteuil's sonata that contained the little phrase of which Swann had been so fond. But often one listens and hears nothing, if it is a piece of music at all complicated to which one is listening for the first time. Since I was able only in successive moments to enjoy all the pleasures that this sonata gave me, I never possessed it in its entirety: it was like life itself. But, less disappointing than life is, great works of art do not begin by giving us all their best. In Vinteuil's sonata the beauties that one discovers at once are those also of which one most soon grows tired, and for the same reason, no doubt, namely that they are less different from what one already knows. But when those first apparitions have withdrawn, there is left for our enjoyment some passage which its composition, too new and strange to offer anything but confusion to our mind, had made indistinguishable and so preserved intact; and this, which we have been meeting every day and have not guessed it, which has thus been held in reserve for us, which by the sheer force of its beauty has become invisible and has remained unknown, this comes to us last of all. But this also must be the last that we shall relinquish. And we shall love it longer than the rest because we have taken longer to get to love it. The time, moreover, that a person requires—as I required in the matter of this sonata—to penetrate a work of any depth is merely an epitome, a symbol, one might say, of the years, the centuries even that must elapse before the public can begin to cherish a masterpiece that is really new. So that the man of genius, to shelter himself from the ignorant contempt of the world, may say to himself that, since one's contemporaries are incapable of the necessary detachment, works written for posterity should be read by posterity alone, like certain pictures which one cannot appreciate when one stands too close to them. But, as it happens, any such cowardly precaution to avoid false judgments is doomed to failure; they are inevitable. The reason for which a work of genius is not easily admired from the first is that the man who has created it is extraordinary, that few other men resemble him. It was Beethoven's Quartets themselves (the Twelfth, Thirteenth, Fourteenth and Fifteenth) that devoted half a century to forming, fashioning and enlarging a public for Beethoven's Quartets, marking in this way, like every great work of art, an advance if not in artistic merit at least in intellectual society, largely composed to-day of what was not to be found when the work first appeared, that is to say of persons capable of enjoying it.

"It is rather charming, don't you think," Swann remarked "that sound can give a reflection, like water, or glass. It is curious, too, that Vinteuil's phrase now shows me only the things to which I paid no attention then. Of my troubles, my loves of those days it recalls nothing, it has altered all my values." "Charles, I don't think that's very polite to me, what you're saying." "Not polite? Really, you women are superb! I was simply trying to explain to this young man that what the music shows—to me, at least—is not for a moment 'Free-will' or 'In Tune with the Infinite', but shall we say old Verdurin in his frock coat in the palm-house at the Jardin d'Acclimatatjon. Hundreds of times, without my leaving this room, the little phrase has carried me off to dine with it at Armenonville. "Since what I'm playing reminds you of the Jardin d'Acclimatation," his wife went on, with a playful semblance of being offended, "we might take him there some day in the carriage, if it would amuse him. It's lovely there just now, and you can recapture your fond impressions !"

In the Jardin d'Acclimatation, how proud I was when we had left the carriage to be walking by the side of Mme. Swann! While she strolled carelessly on, letting her cloak stream on the air behind her, I kept eyeing her with an admiring gaze to which she coquettishly responded in a lingering smile. And now, were we to meet one or other of Gilberte's friends, boy or girl, who saluted us from afar, I would in my turn be looked upon by them as one of those happy creatures whose lot I had envied, one of those friends of Gilberte who knew her family and had a share in that other part of her life, the part which was not spent in the Champs-Elvsées.

Often upon the paths of the Bois or the Jardin we passed, we were greeted by some great lady who was Swann's friend, whom he perchance did not see, so that his wife must rally him with a "Charles Don't you see Mme. de Montmorency?" And Swann, with that amicable smile, bred of a long and intimate friendship, bared his head, but with a slow sweeping gesture, with a grace peculiarly his own. Sometimes the lady would stop, glad of an opportunity to show Mme. Swann a courtesy which would involve no tiresome consequences, by which they all knew that she would never seek to profit, so thoroughly had Swann trained her in reserve. She had none the less acquired all the manners of polite society, and however smart, however stately the lady might be, Mme. Swann was invariably a match for her; halting for a moment before the friend whom her husband had recognised and was addressing, she would introduce us, Gilberte and myself, with so much ease of manner, would remain so free, so tranquil in her exercise of courtesy, that it would have been hard to say, looking at them both, which of the two was the aristocrat.

A favour still more precious than their taking me with them to the Jardin d'Acclimatation, the Swanns did not exclude me even from their friendship with Bergotte, which had been at the root of the attraction that I had found in them when, before I had even seen Gilberte, I reflected that her intimacy with that godlike elder would have made her, for me, the most passionately enthralling of friends, had not the disdain that I was bound to inspire in her forbidden me to hope that she would ever take me, in his company, to visit the towns that he loved. And lo, one day, came an invitation from Mme. Swann to a big luncheon-party. I did not know who else were to be the guests. There were, however, sixteen of us, among whom I never suspected for a moment that I was to find Bergotte. Mme. Swann, who had already 'named' me, as she called it, to several of her guests, suddenly, after my name, in the same tone that she had used in uttering it (in fact, as though we were merely two of the guests at her party, who ought each to feel equally flattered on meeting the other), pronounced that of the sweet Singer with the snowy locks. The name Bergotte made me jump like the sound of a revolver fired at me point blank, but instinctively, for appearance's sake, I bowed; there, straight in front of me, as by one of those conjurers whom we see standing whole and unharmed, in their frock coats, in the smoke of a pistol shot out of which a pigeon has just fluttered, my salute was returned by a young common little thickset peering person, with a red nose curled like a snail-shell and a black tuft on his chin. I was cruelly disappointed, for what had just vanished in the dust of the explosion was not only the feeble old man, of whom no vestige now remained; there was also the beauty of an immense work which I had contrived to enshrine in the frail and hallowed organism that I had constructed, like a temple, expressly for itself, but for which no room was to be found in the squat figure, packed tight with blood-vessels, bones, muscles, sinews, of the little man with the snub nose and black beard who stood before me.

It seemed quite clear, however, that it really was he who had written the books that I had so greatly enjoyed, for Mme. Swann having thought it incumbent upon her to tell him of my admiration for one of these, he showed no surprise that she should have mentioned this to him rather than to any other of the party, nor did he seem to regard her action as due to a misapprehension, but, swelling out the frock coat which he had put on in honour of all these distinguished guests with a body distended in anticipation of the coming meal, while his mind was completely occupied by other, more real and more important considerations, it was only as at some finished episode in his early life, as though one had made an allusion to a costume of the Duc de Guise which he had worn, one season, at a fancy dress ball, that he smiled as he bore his mind back to the idea of his books; which at once began to fall in my estimation (dragging down with them the whole value of Beauty, of the world, of life itself), until they seemed to have been merely the casual amusement of a man with a little beard.

It was about this period that Bloch overthrew my conception of the world and opened for me fresh possibilities of happiness (which, for that matter, were to change later on into possibilities of suffering), by assuring me that, in contradiction of all that I had believed at the time of my walks along the 'Méséglise' way, women never asked for anything better than to make love. He added to this service a second, the value of which I was not to appreciate until much later; it was he who took me for the first time into a disorderly house. But the house to which Bloch led me, (and which he himself, for that matter, had long ceased to visit) was of too humble a grade, its denizens were too inconspicuous and too little varied to be able to satisfy my old or to stimulate new curiosities. The mistress of this house knew none of the women with whom one asked her to negotiate, and was always suggesting others whom one did not want. She boasted to me of one in particular, one of whom, with a smile full of promise (as though this had been a great rarity and a special treat) she would whisper "She is a Jewess ! Doesn't that make you want to?" (That, by the way, was probably why the girl's name was Rachel.) And with a silly and affected excitement which, she hoped, would prove contagious, and which ended in a hoarse gurgle, almost of sensual satisfaction "Think of that, my boy, a Jewess! Wouldn't that be lovely? Rrrr!" This Rachel, of whom I caught a glimpse without her seeing me, was dark and not good looking, but had an air of intelligence, and would pass the tip of her tongue over her lips as she smiled, with a look of boundless impertinence at the 'boys' who were introduced to her and whom I could hear making conversation. Her small and narrow face was framed in short curls of black hair, irregular as though they were outlined in pen-strokes upon a wash-drawing in Indian ink. Every evening I promised the old woman who offered her to me with a special insistence, boasting of her superior intelligence and her education, that I would not fail to come some day on purpose to make the acquaintance of Rachel, whom I had nicknamed 'Rachel when from the Lord'. But the first evening I had heard her, as she was leaving the house, say to the mistress "That's settled then; I shall be free to-morrow, if you have anyone you won't forget to send for me." And these words had prevented me from recognising her as a person because they had made me classify her at once in a general category of women whose habit, common to all of them, was to come there in the evening to see whether there might not be a louis or two to be earned. She would simply vary her formula, saying indifferently: "If you want me" or "If you want anybody".

The mistress, who was not familiar with Halévy's opera, did not know why I always called the girl 'Rachel when from the Lord'. But failure to understand a joke has never yet made anyone find it less amusing, and it was always with a whole-hearted laugh that she would say to me "Then there's nothing doing to-night? When am I going to fix you up with 'Rachel when from the Lord'? Why do you always say that, 'Rachel when from the Lord'? Oh, that's very smart, that is. I'm going to make a match of you two. You won't be sorry for it, you'll see."

Once I was just making up my mind, but she was 'in the press', another time in the hands of the hairdresser, an elderly gentleman who never did anything for the women except pour oil on their loosened hair and then comb it. And I grew tired of waiting, even though several of the humbler frequenters of the place (working girls, they called themselves, but they always seemed to be out of work), had come to mix drinks for me and to hold long conversations to which, despite the gravity of the subjects discussed, the partial or total nudity of the speakers gave an attractive simplicity. I ceased moreover to go to this house because, anxious to present a token of my good-will to the woman who kept it and was in need of furniture, I had given her several pieces, notably a big sofa, which I had inherited from my aunt Léonie. I used never to see them, for want of space had prevented my parents from taking them in at home, and they were stored in a warehouse. But as soon as I discovered them again in the house where these women were putting them to their own uses, all the virtues that one had imbibed in the air of my aunt's room at Combray became apparent to me, tortured by the cruel contact to which I had abandoned them in their helplessness. Had I outraged the dead, I should not have suffered such remorse. I returned no more to visit their new mistress, for they seemed to me to be alive, and to be appealing to me, like those objects, apparently inanimate, in a Persian fairy-tale, in which are embodied human souls that are undergoing martyrdom and plead for deliverance. Besides, as our memory presents things to us, as a rule, not in their chronological sequence but as it were by a reflection in which the order of the parts is reversed, I remembered only long afterwards that it was upon that same sofa that, many years before, I had tasted for the first time the sweets of love with one of my girl cousins, with whom I had not known where to go until she somewhat rashly suggested our taking advantage of a moment in which aunt Léonie had left her room.

My parents meanwhile would have liked to see the intelligence that Bergotte had discerned in me made manifest in some remarkable achievement. When I still did not know the Swanns I thought that I was prevented from working by the state of agitation into which I was thrown by the impossibility of seeing Gilberte when I chose. But, now that their door stood open to me, scarcely had I sat down at my desk than I would rise and run to them.

Had I been less firmly resolved upon setting myself definitely to work, I should perhaps have made an effort to begin at once. But since my resolution was explicit, since within twenty-four hours, in the empty frame of that long morrow in which everything was so well arranged because I myself had not yet entered it, my good intentions would be realised without difficulty, it was better not to select an evening on which I was ill-disposed for a beginning for which the following days were not, alas, to show themselves any more propitious. But I was reasonable. It would have been puerile, on the part of one who had waited now for years, not to put up with a postponement of two or three days. Confident that by the day after next I should have written several pages, I said not a word more to my parents of my decision; I preferred to remain patient for a few hours and then to bring to a convinced and comforted grandmother a sample of work that was already under way. Unfortunately the morrow was not that vast, external day to which I in my fever had looked forward. When it drew to a close, my laziness and my painful struggle to overcome certain internal obstacles had simply lasted twenty-four hours longer. And at the end of several days, my plans not having matured, I had no longer the same hope that they would be realised at once, no longer the courage, therefore, to subordinate everything else to their realisation. I began again to keep late hours, having no longer, to oblige me to go to bed early on any evening, the certain hope of seeing my work begun next morning. I needed, before I could recover my creative energy, several days of relaxation, and the only time that my grandmother ventured, in a gentle and disillusioned tone, to frame the reproach: "Well, and that work of yours; aren't we even to speak of it now?" I resented her intrusion, convinced that in her inability to see that my mind was irrevocably made up, she had further and perhaps for a long time postponed the execution of my task, by the shock which her denial of justice to me had given my nerves, since until I had recovered from that shock I should not feel inclined to begin my work. She felt that her scepticism had charged blindly into my intention. She, apologised, kissing me: "I am sorry; I shall not say anything again," and, so that I should not be discouraged, assured me that, from the day on which I should be quite well again, the work would come of its own accord from my superfluity of strength.

On several occasions I felt that Gilberte was anxious to put off my visits. It is true that when I was at all anxious to see her I had only to get myself invited by her parents who were increasingly persuaded of my excellent influence over her. "Thanks to them," I used to think, "my love is running no risk; the moment I have them on my side, I can set my mind at rest; they have full authority over Gilberte." Until, alas, I detected certain signs of impatience which she allowed to escape her when her father made me come to the house, almost against her will, and asked myself whether what I had regarded as a protection for my happiness was not in fact the secret reason why that happiness could not endure.

The last time that I called to see Gilberte, it was raining; she had been asked to a dancing lesson in the house of some people whom she knew too slightly to be able to take me there with her. In view of the dampness of the air I had taken rather more caffeine than usual. Perhaps on account of the weather, or because she had some objection to the house in which this party was being given, Mme. Swann, as her daughter was leaving the room, called her back in the sharpest of tones: "Gilberte", and pointed to me, to indicate that I had come there to see her and that she ought to stay with me, This "Gilberte!" had been uttered, or shouted rather, with the best of intentions towards myself, but from the way in which Gilberte shrugged her shoulders as she took off her outdoor clothes I divined that her mother had unwittingly hastened the gradual evolution, which until then it had perhaps been possible to arrest, which was gradually drawing away from me my friend. She confined herself to exchanging with me, now and again, on the weather, the increasing violence of the rain, the fastness of the clock, a conversation punctuated with silences and monosyllables, in which I lashed myself on, with a sort of desperate rage, to the destruction of those moments which we might have devoted to friendship and happiness. In vain was my polite: "I thought, the other day, that the clock was slow, if anything;" she evidently understood me to mean: "How tiresome you are being!" I knew that my coldness was not so unalterably fixed as I pretended, and that Gilberte must be fully aware that if, after already saying it to her three times, I had hazarded a fourth repetition of the statement that the evenings were drawing in, I should have had difficulty in restraining myself from bursting into tears. When she was like that, when no smile filled her eyes or unveiled her face, I cannot describe the devastating monotony that stamped her melancholy eyes and sullen features. At length, as I saw no sign in

Gilberte of the happy change for which I had been waiting now for some hours, I told her that she was not being nice. "It is you that are not being nice," was her answer. "Oh, but surely—" I asked myself what I could have done, and, finding no answer, put the question to her. "Naturally, you think yourself nice!" she said to me with a laugh, and went on laughing. "But how am I not being nice," I asked her, "tell me; I will do anything you want." "No; that wouldn't be any good. I can't explain." For a moment I was afraid that she thought that I did not love her, and this was for me a fresh agony, no less keen, but one that required treatment by a different conversational method. "If you knew how much you were hurting me you would tell me." But this pain which, had she doubted my love for her, must have rejoiced her, seemed instead to make her more angry. Then, realising my mistake, making up my mind to pay no more attention to what she said, letting her (without bothering to believe her) assure me: "I do love you, indeed I do; you will see one day," I had the courage to make a sudden resolution not to see her again, and without telling her of it yet since she would not have believed me. I must cease for the present to attempt to see Gilberte. She would be certain to write to me, to apologise. In spite of which, I should not return at once to see her, so as to prove to her that I was capable of living without her. Besides, once I had received her letter, Gilberte's society was a thing with which I should be more easily able to dispense for a time, since I should be certain of finding her ready to receive me whenever I chose.

Not having had any letter from Gilberte that evening, I had attributed this to her carelessness, to her other occupations, I did not doubt that I should find something from her in the morning's post. This I awaited, every day, with a beating heart which subsided, leaving me utterly prostrate, when I had found in it only letters from people who were not Gilberte, or else nothing at all, which was no worse, the proofs of another's friendship making all the more cruel those of her indifference. I transferred my hopes to the afternoon post. Even between the times at which letters were delivered I dared not leave the house, for she might be sending hers by a messenger. Then, the time coming at last when neither the postman nor a footman from the Swanns' could possibly appear that night, I must procrastinate my hope of being set at rest, and thus, because I believed that my sufferings were not destined to last, I was obliged, so to speak, incessantly to renew them.

So my punishment was infinitely more cruel than in those New Year holidays long ago, because this time there was in me, instead of the acceptance, pure and simple, of that punishment, the hope, at every moment, of seeing it come to an end. And yet at this state of acceptance I ultimately arrived; then I understood that it must be final, and I renounced Gilberte for ever, in the interests of my love itself and because I hoped above all that she would not retain any contemptuous memory of me. Indeed, from that moment, so that she should not be led to suppose any sort of lover's spite on my part, when she made appointments for me to see her I used often to accept them and then, at the last moment, write to her that I was prevented from coming, but with the same protestations of my disappointment that I should have made to anyone whom I had not wished to see. These expressions of regret, which we keep as a rule for people who do not matter, would do more, I imagined, to persuade Gilberte of my indifference than would the tone of indifference which we affect only to those whom we love. When, better than by mere words, by a course of action indefinitely repeated, I should have proved to her that I had no appetite for seeing her, perhaps she would discover once again an appetite for seeing me.

In the meantime, what made it easier for me to sentence myself to this separation was the fact that (in order to make it quite clear to her that despite my protestations to the contrary it was my own free will and not any conflicting engagement, not the state of my health that prevented me from seeing her), whenever I knew beforehand that Gilberte would not be in the house, was going out somewhere with a friend and would not be home for dinner, I went to see Mme. Swann who had once more become to me what she had been at the time when I had such difficulty in seeing her daughter and (on days when the latter was not coming to the Champs-Elysées) used to repair to the Allée des Acacias. In this way I should be hearing about Gilberte, and could be certain that she would in due course hear about me, and in terms which would show her that I was not interested in her. And I found, as all those who suffer find, that my melancholy condition might have been worse. For being free at any time to enter the habitation in which Gilberte dwelt, I constantly reminded myself, for all that I was firmly resolved to make no use of that privilege, that if ever my pain grew too sharp there was a way of making it cease. I was not unhappy, save only from day to day. And even that is an exaggeration. How many times in an hour (but now without that anxious expectancy which had strained every nerve of me in the first weeks after our quarrel, before I had gone again to the Swanns') did I not repeat to myself the words of the letter which, one day soon, Gilberte would surely send, would perhaps even bring to me herself. The perpetual vision of that imagined happiness helped me to endure the desolation of my real happiness.

Ever so long ago, before I had even thought of breaking with her daughter, Mme. Swann had said to me: "It is all very well your coming to see Gilberte; I should like you to come sometimes for my sake, not to my 'kettle-drums', which would bore you because there is such a crowd, but on the other days, when you will always find me at home if you come fairly late." So I might be thought, when I came to see her, to be yielding only after a long resistance to a desire which she had expressed in the past. And very late in the afternoon, when it was quite dark, almost at the hour at which my parents would be sitting down to dinner, I would set out to pay Mme. Swann a visit, in the course of which I knew that I should not see Gilberte, and yet should be thinking only of her. And when it was time to return home Mme. Swann allowed the servants to carry away the tea-things, as who should say "Time, please, gentlemen!" And at last she did say to me: "Really, must you go? Very well good-bye!"

At least, the object of my visit had been attained; Gilberte would know that I had come to see her parents when she was not at home, and that I had spoken of her as was fitting, with affection, but that I had not that incapacity for living without our seeing one another which I believed to be at the root of the boredom that she had shown at our last meetings. I had told Mme. Swann that I should not be able to see Gilberte again. I had said this as though I had finally decided not to see her any more. And the letter which I was going to send Gilberte would be framed on those lines. Only to myself, to fortify my courage, I proposed no more than a supreme and concentrated effort, lasting a few days only. I said to myself: "This is the last time that I shall refuse to meet her; I shall accept the next invitation." To make our separation less difficult to realise, I did not picture it to myself as final. But I knew very well that it would be.

So, one day, when Mme. Swann was repeating her familiar statement of what a pleasure it would be to Gilberte to see me, thus putting the happiness of which I had now for so long been depriving myself, as it were within arm's length, I was stupefied by the realisation that it was still possible for me to enjoy that pleasure, and I could hardly wait until next day; when I had made up my mind to take Gilberte by surprise, in the evening, before dinner.

What helped me to remain patient throughout the long day that followed was another plan that I had made. From the moment in which everything was forgotten, in which I was reconciled to Gilberte, I no longer wished to visit her save as a lover. Every day she should receive from me, the finest flowers that grew. And if Mme. Swann, albeit she had no right to be too severe a mother, should forbid my making a daily offering of flowers, I should find other gifts, more precious and less frequent. My parents did not give me enough money for me to be able to buy expensive things. I thought of a big bowl of old Chinese porcelain which had been left to me by aunt Léonie, and of which Mamma prophesied daily that Françoise would come running to her with an "Oh, it's all come to pieces!" and that that would be the end of it. Would it not be wiser, in that case, to part with it, to sell it so as to be able to give Gilberte all the pleasure I could. I felt sure that I could easily get a thousand francs for it. I had it tied up in paper, I had grown so used to it that I had ceased altogether to notice it; parting with it had at least the advantage of making me realise what it was like. I took it with me as I started for the Swanns', and, giving the driver their address, told him to go by the Champs-Elysées, at one end of which was the shop of a big dealer in oriental things, who knew my father. Greatly to my surprise he offered me there and then not one thousand but ten thousand francs for the bowl. I took the notes with rapture. Every day, for a whole year, I could smother Gilberte in roses and lilac. When I left the shop and got into my cab again the driver (naturally enough, since the Swanns lived out by the Bois) instead of taking the ordinary way began to drive me along the Avenue des Champs-Elysées. He had just passed the end of the Rue de Bern when, in the failing light, I thought I saw, close to the Swanns' house but going in the other direction, going away from it, Gilberte, who was walking slowly, though with a firm step, by the side of a young man with whom she was conversing, but whose face I could not distinguish. I stood up in the cab, meaning to tell the driver to stop then hesitated. The strolling couple were already some way away, and the parallel lines which their leisurely progress was quietly drawing were on the verge of disappearing in the Elysian gloom. A moment later, I had reached Gilberte's door. I was received by Mme. Swann. "Oh ! she will be sorry!" was my greeting, "I can't think why she isn't in. She came home just now from a lesson, complaining of the heat, and said she was going out for a little fresh air with another girl." "I fancy I passed her in the Avenue des Champs-Elysées." "Oh, I don't think it can have been. Anyhow, don't mention it to her father; he doesn't approve of her going out at this time of night. Must you go? Good bye." I left her, told my driver to go home the same way, but found no trace of the two walking figures. Where had they been? What were they saying to one another in the darkness so confidentially ?

I returned home, desperately clutching my windfall of ten thousand francs, which would have enabled, me to arrange so many pleasant surprises for that Gilberte whom now I had made up my mind never to see again. No doubt my call at the dealer's had brought me happiness by allowing me to expect that in future, whenever I saw my friend, she would be pleased with me and grateful. But if I had not called there, if my cabman had not taken the Avenue des Champs-Elysées, I should not have seen Gilberte with that young man. Thus a single action may have two contradictory effects, and the misfortune that it engenders cancel the good fortune that it has already brought one.

I put my ten thousand francs in a drawer. But they were no longer of any use to me. I ran through them, as it happened, even sooner than if I had sent flowers every day to Gilberte, for when evening came I was always too wretched to stay in the house and used to go and pour out my sorrows upon the bosoms of women whom I did not love. As for seeking to give any sort of pleasure to Gilberte, I no longer thought of that; to visit her house again now could only have added to my sufferings. Even the sight of Gilberte, which would have been so exquisite a pleasure only yesterday, would no longer have sufficed me. For I should have been miserable all the time that I was not actually with her,

I was irritated by the desire that many people showed about this time to ask me to their houses, and refused all their invitations. There was a scene at home because I did not accompany my father to an official dinner at which the Bontemps were to be present with their niece Albertine, a young girl still hardly more than a child. So it is that the different periods of our life overlap one another. We scornfully decline, because of one whom we love and who will some day be of so little account, to see another who is of no account to-day, with whom we shall be in love tomorrow, with whom we might, perhaps, had we consented to see her now, have fallen in love a little earlier and who would thus have put a term to our present sufferings, bringing others, it is true, in their place. Mine were steadily growing less. I had the surprise of discovering in my own heart one sentiment one day, another the next, generally inspired by some hope or some fear relative to Gilberte. To the Gilberte whom I kept within me. I ought to have reminded myself that the other, the real Gilberte was perhaps entirely different from mine, knew nothing of the regrets that I ascribed to her, was thinking probably less about me, not merely than I was thinking about her but than I made her be thinking about me when I was closeted alone with my fictitious Gilberte, wondering what really were her feelings with regard to me and so imagining her attention as constantly directed towards myself.

But, as time went on, every refusal to see her disturbed me less. And as she became less dear to me, my painful memories were no longer strong enough to destroy by their incessant return the growing pleasure which I found in thinking of Florence, or of Venice. I regretted, at such moments, that I had abandoned the idea of diplomacy and had condemned myself to a sedentary existence, in order not to be separated from a girl whom I should not see again and had already almost forgotten. We construct our house of life to suit another person, and when at length it is ready to receive her that person does not come; presently she is dead to us, and we live on, a prisoner within the walls which were intended only for her. If Venice seemed to my parents to be a long way off, and its climate treacherous, it was at least quite easy for me to go, without tiring myself, and settle down at Balbec. But to do that I should have had to leave Paris, to forego those visits thanks to which, infrequent as they were, I might sometimes hear Mme. Swann telling me about her daughter. Besides, I was beginning to find in tbem various pleasures in which Gilberte had no part.

But it was still more than I could endure that these memories should be recalled to me. There was a risk of their reviving what little remained of my love for Gilberte. Besides, albeit I no longer felt the least distress during these visits to Mme. Swann, I extended the intervals between them and endeavoured to see as little of her as possible. At most, since I continued not to go out of Paris, I allowed myself an occasional walk with her. Fine weather had come at last, and the sun was hot. As I knew that before luncheon Mme. Swann used to go out every day for an hour, and would stroll for a little in the Avenue du Bois, near the Etoile—a spot which, at that time, because of the people who, used to collect there to gaze at the 'swells' whom they knew only by name, was known as the 'Shabby-Genteel Club'—I persuaded my parents, on Sundays, (for on weekdays I was busy all morning), to let me postpone my luncheon until long after theirs, until a quarter past one, and go for a walk before it. During May, that year, I never missed a Sunday, for Gilberte had gone to stay with friends in the country: I used to reach the Arc-de-Triomphe about noon. I kept watch at the entrance to the Avenue, never taking my eyes off the corner of the side-street along which Mme. Swann, who had only a few yards to walk, would come from her house. As by this time many of the people who had been strolling there were going home to luncheon, those who remained were few in number and, for the most part, fashionably dressed. Suddenly, on the gravelled path, unhurrying, cool, luxuriant, Mme. Swann appeared displaying around her a toilet which was never twice the same, but which I remember as being typically mauve; then she hoisted and unfurled at the end of its long stalk, just at the moment when her radiance was most complete, the silken banner of a wide parasol of a shade that matched the showering petals of her gown..

On her arrival I would greet Mme. Swann, she would stop me and say (in English) "Good morning," and smile. We would walk a little way together.

Various young men as they passed looked at her anxiously, not knowing whether their vague acquaintance with her (especially since, having been introduced only once, at the most, to Swann, they were afraid that he might not remember them) was sufficient excuse for their venturing to take off their hats. And they trembled to think of the consequences as they made up their minds, asking themselves whether the gesture, so bold, so sacrilegious a tempting of providence, would not let loose the catastrophic forces of nature or bring down upon them the vengeance of a jealous god. It provoked only, like the winding of a piece of clockwork, a series of gesticulations from little, responsive bowing figures, who were none other than Odette's escort, beginning with Swann himself, who raised his tall hat lined in green leather with an exquisite courtesy, which he had acquired in the Faubourg Saint-Germain, but to which was no longer wedded the indifference that he would at one time have shown. Its place was now taken (as though he had been to some extent permeated by Odette's prejudices) at once by irritation at having to acknowledge the salute of a person who was none too well dressed and by satisfaction at his wife's knowing so many people, a mixed sensation to which he gave expression by saying to the smart friends who walked by his side: "What another! Upon my word, I can't imagine where my wife picks all these fellows up!" Meanwhile, having greeted with a slight movement of her head the terrified youth, who had already passed out of sight though his heart was still beating furiously, Mme. Swann turned to me: "Then it's all over?" she put it to me, "You aren't ever coming to see Gilberte again? I'm glad you make an exception of me, and are not going to 'drop' me straight away. I like seeing you, but I used to like also the influence you had over my daughter. I'm sure she's very sorry about it, too. However,

I mustn't bully you, or you'll make up your mind at once that you never want to set eyes on me again." "Odette, Sagan's trying to speak to you!" Swann called his wife's attention. And there, indeed, was the Prince, as in some transformation scene at the close of a play, or in a circus, or an old painting, wheeling his horse round so as to face her, in a magnificent heroic pose, and doffing his hat with a sweeping theatrical and, so to speak, allegorical flourish in which he displayed all the chivalrous courtesy of a great noble bowing in token of his respect for Woman, were she incarnate in a woman whom it was impossible for his mother or his sister to know. And at every moment, recognised in the depths of the liquid transparency and of the luminous glaze of the shadow which her parasol cast over her, Mme. Swann was receiving the salutations of the last belated horsemen, who passed as though in a cinematograph taken as they galloped in the blinding glare of the Avenue, men from the clubs, the names of whom, which meant only celebrities to the public—Antoine de Castellane, Adalbert de Montmorency and the rest—were for Mme. Swann the familiar names of friends. And as the average span of life, the relative longevity of our memories of poetical sensations is much greater than that of our memories of what the heart has suffered, long after the sorrows that I once felt on Gilberte's account have faded and vanished, there has survived them the pleasure, that I still derive—whenever I close my eyes and read, as it were upon the face of a sundial, the minutes that are recorded between a quarter past twelve and one o'clock in the month of May—from seeing myself once again strolling and talking thus with Mme. Swann beneath her parasol, as though in the coloured shade of a wisteria bower.

PLACE NAMES: THE PLACE

I had arrived at a state almost of complete indifference to Gilberte when, two years later, I went with my grandmother to Balbec.

My grandmother, had planned, so that she might be offering me, of this journey, a "print" that was, at least, in parts "old", that we should repeat, partly by rail and partly by road, the itinerary that Mme. de Sévigné followed when she went from Paris to 'L'Orient' by way of Chaulnes and 'the Pont-Audemer'. But my grandmother had been obliged to abandon this project, at the instance of my father who knew, whenever she organised any expedition with a view to extracting from it the utmost intellectual benefit that it was capable of yielding, what a tale there would be to tell of missed trains, lost luggage, sore throats and broken rules. She was free at least to rejoice in the thought that never, when the time came for us to sally forth to the beach, should we be exposed to the risk of being kept indoors by the sudden appearance of what her beloved Sévigné calls a 'beast of a coachload', since we should know not a soul at Balbec, Legrandin having refrained from offering us a letter of introduction to his sister.

And so we were simply to leave Paris by that one twenty-two train which I had too often beguiled myself by looking out in the railway time-table, where its itinerary never failed to give me the emotion, almost the illusion of starting by it, not to feel that I already knew it.

As my grandmother could not bring herself to do anything so 'stupid' as to go straight to Balbec, she was to break the journey half-way, staying the night with one of her friends, from whose house I was to proceed the same evening, so as not to be in the way there and also in order that I might arrive by daylight and see Balbec church , which we had learned, was at some distance from Balbec-Plage, as I might not have a chance to visit it later on, when I had begun my course of baths.

To prevent the choking fits which the journey might otherwise give me the doctor had advised me to take, as we started, a good stiff dose of beer or brandy, so as to begin the journey in a state of what he called 'euphoria', in which the nervous system is for a time less vulnerable. I had not yet made up my mind whether I should do this, but I wished at least that my grandmother should admit that, if I did so decide, I should have wisdom and authority on my side. I spoke therefore as if my hesitation were concerned only with where I should go for my drink, to the bar on the platform or to the restaurant-car on the train. But immediately, at the air of reproach which my grandmother's face assumed, an air of not wishing even to entertain such an idea for a moment, "What!" I said to myself, suddenly determining upon this action of going out to drink, the performance of which became necessary as a proof of my independence since the verbal announcement of it had not succeeded in passing unchallenged, "What ! You know how ill I am, you know what the doctor ordered, and you treat me like this"

When I had explained to my grandmother how unwell I felt, her distress, her kindness were so apparent as she replied, "Run along then, quickly; get yourself some beer or a liqueur if it will do you any good," that I flung myself upon her, almost smothering her in kisses. And if after that I went and drank a great deal too much in the restaurant car of the train, that was because I felt that otherwise I should have a more violent attack than usual, which was just what would vex her most. When at the first stop I clambered back into our compartment I told my grandmother how pleased I was to be going to Balbec, that I felt that everything would go off splendidly, that after all I should soon grow used to being without Mamma, that the train was most comfortable, the steward and attendants in the bar so friendly that I should like to make the journey often so as to have opportunities of seeing them again. My grandmother, however, did not appear to feel the same joy as myself at all these good tidings. She answered, without looking me in the face "Why don't you try to get a little sleep ?" and turned her gaze to the window, the blind of which, though we had drawn it, did not completely cover the glass, so that the sun could and did slip in over the polished oak of the door and the cloth of the seat (like an advertisement of a life shared with nature far more persuasive than those posted higher upon the walls of the compartment, by the railway company, representing places in the country the names of which I could not make out from where I sat) the same warm and slumberous light which lies along a forest glade.

But when my grandmother thought that my eyes were shut I could see her, now and again, from among the large black spots on her veil, steal a glance at me, then withdraw it, and steal back again, like a person trying to make himself, so as to get into the habit, perform some exercise that hurts him. Thereupon I spoke to her, but that seemed not to please her either. And yet to myself the sound of my own voice was pleasant, as were the most imperceptible, the most internal movements of my body. And so I endeavoured to prolong it. I allowed each of my inflexions to hang lazily upon its word, I felt each glance from my eyes arrive just at the spot to which it was directed and stay there beyond the normal period. "Now, now, sit still and rest," said my grandmother. "If you can't manage to sleep, read something." And she handed me a volume of Madame de Sévigné which I opened, while she buried herself in the *Mémoires de Madame de Beausergent*. She never travelled anywhere without a volume of each. They were her two favourite authors. With no conscious movement of my head, feeling a keen pleasure in maintaining a posture after I had adopted it, I lay back holding in my hands the volume of Madame de Sévigné which I had allowed to close, without lowering my eyes to it, or indeed letting them see anything but the blue windowblind.

When, that evening, after having accompanied my grandmother to her destination and spent some hours in her friend's house, I had returned by myself to the train, at any rate I found nothing to distress me in the night which followed; this was because I had not to spend it in a room the somnolence of which would have kept me awake; I was surrounded by the soothing activity of all those movements of the train which kept me company, offered to stay and converse with me if I could not sleep, lulled me with their sounds which I wedded—as I had often wedded the chime of the Combray bells—now to one rhythm now to another hearing as the whim took me first four level and equivalent semi-quavers, then one semi-quaver furiously dashing against a crotchet.

Certain names of towns, Vezelay or Chartres, Bourges or Beauvais, serve to indicate, by abbreviation, the principal church in those towns. This partial acceptation, in which we are so accustomed to take the word, comes at length—if the names in question are those of places that we do not yet know—to fashion for us a mould of the name as a solid whole, which from that time onwards, whenever we wish it to convey the idea of the town—of that town which we have never seen—will impose on it, as on a cast, the same carved outlines, in the same style of art, will make of the town a sort of vast cathedral. It was, nevertheless, in a railway-station, above the door of a refreshment-room, that I read the name—almost Persian in style—of Balbec. I strode buoyantly through the station and across the avenue that led past it, I asked my way to the beach so as to see nothing in the place but its church and the sea; people seemed not to understand what I meant. Old Balbec, Balbec-en-Terre, at which I had arrived, had neither beach nor harbour. It was, most certainly, in the sea that the fishermen had found, according to the legend, the miraculous Christ, of which a window in the church that stood a few yards from where I now was recorded the discovery; it was indeed from cliffs battered by the waves that had been quarried the stone of its nave and towers. But this sea, which for those reasons I had imagined as flowing up to die at the foot of the window, was twelve miles away and more, at Balbec-Plage, and, rising beside its cupola, that steeple, which, because I had read that it was itself a rugged Norman cliff on which seeds were blown and sprouted, round which the sea-birds wheeled, I had always pictured to myself as receiving at its base the last drying foam of the uplifted waves, stood on a Square from which two lines of tramway diverged, opposite a Café which bore, written in letters of gold, the word "Billiards"; it stood out against a background of houses with the roofs of which no upstanding mast was blended. And the church—entering my mind with the Café, with the passing stranger of whom I had had to ask my way, with the station to which presently I should have to return—made part of the general whole, seemed an accident, a by-product of this summer afternoon, in which its mellow and distended dome against the sky was like a fruit of which the same light that bathed the chimneys of the houses was ripening the skin, pink, glowing, melting-soft. But I wished only to consider the eternal significance of the carvings when I recognised the Apostles, which I had seen in casts in the Trocadéro museum, and which on either side of the Virgin, before the deep bay of the porch, were awaiting me as though to do me reverence. With their benign, blunt, mild faces and bowed shoulders they seemed to be advancing upon me with an air of welcome, singing the Alleluia of a fine day. But it was evident that their expression was unchanging as that on a dead man's face, and could be modified only by my turning about to look at them in different aspects. I said to myself "Here I am, this is the Church of Balbec. This square, which looks as though it were conscious of its glory, is the only place in the world that possesses Balbec Church. All that I have seen so far have been photographs of this Church—and of these famous Apostles, this Virgin of the Porch, mere casts only. Now it is the Church itself, the statue itself; these are they; they, the unique things—this is something far greater."

It was something less, perhaps, also. As a young man on the day of an examination or of a duel feels the question that he has been asked, the shot that he has fired, to be a very little thing when he thinks of the reserves of knowledge and of valour that he possesses and would like to have displayed, so my mind, which had exalted the Virgin of the Porch far above the reproductions that I had had before my eyes, inaccessible by the vicissitudes which had power to threaten them, intact although they were destroyed, ideal, endowed with universal value, was astonished to see the statue which it had carved a thousand times, reduced now to its own apparent form in stone, occupying, on the radius of my outstretched arm, a place in which it had for rivals an election placard and the point of my stick, fettered to the Square, inseparable from the head of the main street, powerless to hide from the gaze of the Café and of the omnibus office, receiving on its face half of that ray of the setting sun (half, presently, in a few hours time, of the light of the street lamp) of which the Bank building received the other half, tainted simultaneously with that branch office of a money-lending establishment, by the smells from the pastry-cook's oven, subjected to the tyranny of the Individual to such a point that, if I had chosen to scribble my name upon that stone, it was she, the illustrious Virgin whom until then I had endowed with a general existence and an intangible beauty, the Virgin of Balbec, the unique (which meant, alas, the only one) who, on her body coated with the same soot as defiled the neighbouring houses, would have displayed—powerless to rid herself of them—to all the admiring strangers come there to gaze upon her, the marks of my piece of chalk and the letters of my name; it was she, indeed, the immortal work of art, so long desired, whom I found, transformed, as was the church itself, into a little old woman in stone whose height I could measure and count her wrinkles. But time was passing; I must return to the station, where I was to wait for my grandmother and Françoise, so that we should all arrive at Balbec-Plage together.

In the little train of the local railway company which was to take us to Balbec-Plage I found my grandmother, but found her alone—for, imagining that she was sending Françoise on ahead of her, so as to have everything ready before we arrived, but having mixed up her instructions, she had succeeded only in packing off Françoise in the wrong direction, who at that moment was being carried down all unsuspectingly, at full speed, to Nantes, and would probably wake up next morning at Bordeaux. No sooner had I taken my seat in the carriage, filled with the fleeting light of sunset and with the lingering heat of the afternoon (the former enabling me, alas, to see written clearly upon my grandmother's face how much the latter had tired her), than she began "Well, and Balbec ?" with a smile so brightly illuminated by her expectation of the great pleasure which she supposed me to have been enjoying that I dared not at once confess to her my disappointment. Besides, the impression which my mind had been seeking occupied it steadily less as the place drew nearer to which my body would have to become accustomed. At the end—still more than an hour away of this journey I was trying to form a picture of the manager of the hotel at Balbec, to whom I, at that moment, did not exist, and I should have liked to be going to present myself to him in more impressive company than that of my grandmother, who would be certain to ask for a reduction of his terms. The only thing positive about him was his haughty condescension; his lineaments were still vague.

Every few minutes the little train brought us to a standstill in one of the stations which came before Balbec-Plage, stations the mere names of which, (Incarville, Marcouville, Doville, Pont-à-Couleuvre, Arambouville, Saint-Mars-le-Vieux, Hermonville, Maineville) seemed to me outlandish, whereas if I had come upon them in a book I should at once have been struck by their affinity to the names of certain places in the neighbourhood of Combray.

How much were my sufferings increased when we had finally landed in the hall of the Grand Hotel at Balbec, and I stood there in front of the monumental staircase that looked like marble, while my grandmother, regardless of the growing hostility of the strangers among whom we should have to live, discussed 'terms' with the manager, a sort of nodding mandarin whose face and voice were alike covered with scars (left by the excision of countless pustules from one and from the other, of the divers accents acquired from an alien ancestry and in a cosmopolitan upbringing) who stood there in a smart dinner-jacket, with the air of an expert psychologist, classifying, whenever the 'omnibus' discharged a fresh load, the 'nobility and gentry as 'geesers' and the 'hotel crooks' as nobility and gentry. Forgetting, probably, that he himself was not drawing five hundred francs a month, he had a profound contempt for people to whom five hundred francs—or, as he preferred to put it, "twenty-five louis" was "a lot of money", and regarded them as belonging to a race of pariahs for whom the Grand Hotel was certainly not intended. It is true that even within its walls there were people who did not pay very much and yet had not forfeited the manager's esteem, provided that he was assured that they were watching their expenditure not from poverty so much as from avarice. For this could in no way lower their standing since it is a vice and may consequently be found at every grade of social position. Social position was the one thing by which the manager was impressed, social position, or rather the signs which seemed to him to imply that it was exalted, such as not taking one's hat off when one came into the hail, wearing knickerbockers, or an overcoat with a waist, and taking a cigar with a band of purple and gold out of a crushed morocco case— to none of which advantages could I, alas, lay claim. He would also adorn his business conversation with choice expressions, to which, as a rule, he gave a wrong meaning.   My sense of loneliness was further increased a moment later: when I had confessed to my grandmother that I did not feel well, that I thought that we should be obliged to return to Paris, she had offered no protest, saying merely that she was going out to buy a few things which would be equally useful whether we left or stayed (and which, I afterwards learned, were all for my benefit, François having gone off with certain articles which I might need.

The need that I now had of my grandmother was enhanced by my fear that I had shattered another of her illusions. She must be feeling discouraged, feeling that if I could not stand the fatigue of this journey there was no hope that any change of air could ever do me good. I decided to return to the hotel and to wait for her there. The manager himself came forward and pressed a button; and a person whose acquaintance I had not yet made, labelled 'LIFT' (who at that highest point in the building, which corresponded to the lantern in a Norman church, was installed like a photographer in his darkroom or an organist in his loft) came rushing down towards me with the agility of a squirrel, tamed, active, caged. Then, sliding upwards again along a steel pil1ar, he bore me aloft in his train towards the dome of this temple of Mammon. On each floor, on either side of a narrow communicating stair; opened out fanwise a range of shadowy galleries, along one of which, carrying a bolster, a chambermaid came past. I lent to her face, which the gathering dusk made featureless, the mask of my most impassioned dreams of beauty, but read in her eyes as they turned towards me the horror of my own nonentity. Meanwhile, to dissipate, in the course of this interminable assent, the mortal anguish which I felt in penetrating thus in silence the mystery of this chiaroscuro so devoid of poetry, lighted by a single vertical line of little windows which were those of the solitary water-closet on each landing, I addressed a few words to the young organist, artificer of my journey and my partner in captivity, who continued to manipulate the registers of his instrument and to finger the stops. I apologised for taking up so much room, for giving him so much trouble, and asked whether I was not obstructing him in the practice of an art to which, so as to flatter the performer, I did more than display curiosity, I confessed my strong attachment. But he vouchsafed no answer, whether from astonishment at my words, preoccupation with what he was doing, regard for convention, hardness of hearing, respect for holy ground, fear of danger, slowness of understanding, or by the manager's orders.

I was half dead with exhaustion, I was burning with fever; I would gladly have gone to bed, but I had no night things. I should have liked at least to lie down for a little while on the bed, but what good would that have done me, seeing that I should not have been able to find any rest there for that mass of sensations which is for each of us his sentient if not his material body, and that the unfamiliar objects which encircled that body, forcing it to set its perceptions on the permanent footing of a vigilant and defensive guard, would have kept my sight, my hearing, all my senses in a position as cramped and comfortless (even if I had stretched out my legs) as that of Cardinal La Balue in the cage in which he could neither stand nor sit. It is our noticing them that puts things in a room, our growing used to them that takes them away again and clears a space for us. Space there was none for me in my bedroom (mine in name only) at Balbec; it was full of things which did not know me, which flung back at me the distrustful look that I had cast at them, and, without taking any heed of my existence, showed that I was interrupting the course of theirs. The clock—whereas at home I heard my clock tick only a few seconds in a week, when I was coming out of some profound meditation—continued without a moment's interruption to utter, in an unknown tongue, a series of observations which must have been most uncomplimentary to myself, for the violet curtains listened to them without replying, but in an attitude such as people adopt who shrug their shoulders to indicate that the sight of a third person irritates them. They gave to this room with its lofty ceiling a semi-historical character which might have made it a suitable place for the assassination of the Duc de Guise, and afterwards for parties of tourists personally conducted by one of Messrs. Thomas Cook and Son's guides, but for me to sleep in—no. I was tormented by the presence of some little bookcases with glass fronts which ran along the walls, but especially by a large mirror with feet which stood across one corner, for I felt that until it had left the room there would be no possibility of rest for me there. I kept raising my eyes—which the things in my room in Paris disturbed no more than did my eyelids themselves, for they were merely extensions of my organs, an enlargement of myself—towards the fantastically high ceiling of this belvedere planted upon the summit of the hotel which my grandmother had chosen for me; and in that region more intimate than those in which we see and hear, that region in which we test the quality of odours, almost in the very heart of my inmost self, the smell of flowering grasses next launched its offensive against my last feeble line of trenches, where I stood up to it, not without tiring myself still further, with the futile incessant defence of an anxious sniffing. Having no world, no room, no body now that was not menaced by the enemies thronging round me, invaded to the very bones by fever, I was utterly alone; I longed to die. Then my grandmother came in, and to the expansion of my ebbing heart there opened at once an infinity of space.

    I threw myself into the arms of my grandmother and clung with my lips to her face as though I had access thus to that immense heart which she opened to me. And when I felt my mouth glued to her cheeks, to her brow, I drew from them something so beneficial, so nourishing that I lay in her arms as motionless, as solemn, as calmly gluttonous as a babe at the breast.

    At last I let go, and lay and gazed, and could not tire of gazing at her large face, as clear in its outline as a fine cloud, glowing and serene, behind which I could discern the radiance of her tender love. And everything that received, in however slight a degree, any share of her sensations, everything that could be said to belong in any way to her was at once so spiritualised, so sanctified that with outstretched hands I smoothed her dear hair, still hardly grey, with as much respect, precaution, comfort as if I had actually been touching her goodness. She found a similar pleasure in taking any trouble that saved me one, and in a moment of immobility and rest for my weary limbs something so delicious that when, having seen that she wished to help me with my undressing and to take my boots off, I made as though to stop her and began to undress myself, with an imploring gaze she arrested my hands as they fumbled with the top buttons of my coat and boots.

"Oh, do let me !" she begged. "It is such a joy for your Granny. And be sure you knock on the wall if you want anything in the night. My bed is just on the other side, and the partition is quite thin. Just give a knock now, as soon as you are ready so that we shall know where we are."

And, sure enough, that evening I gave three knocks— a signal which, the week after, when I was ill, I repeated every morning for several days, because my grandmother wanted me to have some milk early. Then, when I thought that I could hear her stirring, so that she should not be kept waiting but might, the moment she had brought me the milk, go to sleep again, I ventured on three little taps, timidly, faintly, but for all that distinctly, for if I was afraid of disturbing her, supposing that I had been mistaken and that she was still asleep, I should not have wished her either to lie awake listening for a summons which she had not at once caught and which I should not have the courage to repeat. And scarcely had I given my taps than I heard three others, in a different intonation from mine, stamped with a calm authority, repeated twice over so that there should be no mistake, and saying to me plainly "Don't get excited; I heard you; I shall be with you in a minute!" and shortly afterwards my grandmother appeared. I explained to her that I had been afraid that she would not hear me, or might think that it was some one in the room beyond who was tapping; at which she smiled "Mistake my poor chick's knocking for anyone else! Why, Granny could tell it among a thousand! Do you suppose there's anyone else in the world who's such a silly-billy, with such feverish little knuckles, so afraid of waking me up and of not making me understand? Even if he just gave the least scratch, Granny could tell her mouse's sound at once, especially such a poor miserable little mouse as mine is. I could hear it just now, trying to make up its mind, and rustling the bedclothes, and going through all its tricks."

She pushed open the shutters; where a wing of the hotel jutted out at right angles to my window, the sun was already installed upon the roof, like a slater who is up betimes, and starts early and works quietly so as not to rouse the sleeping town, whose stillness seems to enhance his activity. She told me what o'clock, what sort of day it was; that it was not worth while my getting up and coming to the window, that there was a mist over the sea; if the baker's shop had opened yet; what the vehicle was that I could hear passing. All that brief, trivial curtain-raiser, that negligible *introit* of a new day, performed without any spectator, a little scrap of life which was only for our two selves, which I should have no hesitation in repeating, later on, to Françoise or even to strangers, speaking of the fog "which you could have cut with a knife" at six o'clock that morning, with the ostentation of one who was boasting not of a piece of knowledge that he had acquired but of a mark of affection shown to himself alone; dear morning moment, opened like a symphony by the rhythmical dialogue of my three taps, to which the thin wall of my bedroom, steeped in love and joy, grown melodious, immaterial, singing like the angelic choir, responded with three other taps, eagerly awaited, repeated once and again, in which it contrived to waft to me the soul of my grandmother, whole and perfect, and the promise of her coming, with a swiftness of annunciation and melodic accuracy. But on this first night after our arrival, when my grandmother had left me, I began again to feel as I had felt, the day before, in Paris, at the moment of leaving home.

But next morning!—after a servant had come to call me, and had brought me hot water, and while I was washing and dressing myself and trying in vain to find the things that I wanted in my trunk, from which I extracted, pell-mell, only a lot of things that were of no use whatever, what a joy it was to me, thinking already of the delights of luncheon and of a walk along the shore, to see in the window, and in all the glass fronts of the bookcases as in the portholes of a ship's cabin, the open sea, naked, unshadowed, and yet with half of its expanse in shadow, bounded by a thin and fluctuant line, and to follow with my eyes the waves that came leaping towards me, one behind another, like divers along a springboard. Every other moment, holding in one hand the starched, unyielding towel, with the name of the hotel printed upon it, with which I was making futile efforts to dry myself, I returned to the window to gaze once more upon that vast amphitheatre, dazzling, mountainous, and upon the snowy crests of its emerald waves, here and there polished and translucent, which with a placid violence, a leonine bending of the brows, let their steep fronts, to which the sun now added a smile without face or features, run forward to their goal, totter and melt and be no more. The window in which I was, henceforward, to plant myself every morning, as at the pane of a mail coach in which one has slept, to see whether, in the night, a long sought mountain-chain has come nearer or withdrawn—only here it was those hills of the sea which, before they come dancing back towards us, are apt to retire so far that often it was only at the end of a long and sandy plain that I would distinguish, miles it seemed away, their first undulations upon a background transparent, vaporous, bluish, like the glaciers that one sees in the backgrounds of the Tuscan Primitives.

On this first morning the sun pointed out to me far off with a jovial finger those blue peaks of the sea, which bear no name upon any geographer's chart, until, dizzy with its sublime excursion over the thundering and chaotic surface of their crests and avalanches, it came back to take shelter from the wind in my bedroom, swaggering across the unmade bed and scattering its riches over the splashed surface of the basin-stand, and into my open trunk, where by its very splendour and ill-matched luxury it added still further to the general effect of disorder. Alas, that wind from the sea; an hour later, in the great dining-room— while we were having our luncheon, and from the leathern gourd of a lemon were sprinkling a few golden drops on to a pair of soles which presently left on our plates the plumes of their picked skeletons, curled like stiff feathers and resonant as citherns,—it seemed to my grandmother a cruel deprivation not to be able to feel its life-giving breath on her cheek, on account of the window, transparent but closed, which like the front of a glass-case in a museum divided us from the beach while allowing us to look out upon its whole extent, and into which the sky entered so completely that its azure had the effect of being the colour of the windows and its white clouds only so many flaws in the glass. Unfortunately, it was not only in its outlook that it differed from our room at Combray, giving upon the houses over the way, this dining-room at Balbec, bare-walled, filled with a sunlight green as the water in a marble font, while a few feet away the full tide and broad daylight erected as though before the gates of the heavenly city an indestructible and moving rampart of emerald and gold. At Combray, since we were known to everyone, I took heed of no one. In life at the seaside one knows only one's own party. I was not yet old enough, I was still too sensitive to have outgrown the desire to find favour in the sight of other people and to possess their hearts. Nor had I acquired the more noble indifference which a man of the world would have felt, with regard to the people who were eating their luncheon in the room, nor to the boys and girls who strolled past the window, with whom I was pained by the thought that I should never be allowed to go on expeditions, though not so much pained as if my grandmother, contemptuous of social formalities and concerned about nothing but my health, had gone to them with the request, humiliating for me to overhear, that they would consent to let me accompany them. Whether they were returning to some villa beyond my ken, or had emerged from it, racquet in hand, on their way to some lawn-tennis court, or were mounted on horses whose hooves trampled and tore my heart, I gazed at them with a passionate curiosity, in that blinding light of the beach by which social distinctions are altered, I followed all their movements through the transparency of that great bay of glass which allowed so much light to flood the room. But it intercepted the wind, and this seemed wrong to my grandmother, who, unable to endure the thought that I was losing the benefit of an hour in the open air, surreptitiously unlatched a pane and at once set flying, with the bills of fare, the newspapers, veils and hats of all the people at the other tables; she herself, fortified by the breath of heaven, remained calm and smiling like Saint Blandina, amid the torrent of invective which, increasing my sense of isolation and misery, those scornful, dishevelled, furious visitors combined to pour on us. To a certain extent—and this, at Balbec, gave to the population, as a rule monotonously rich and cosmopolitan, of that sort of smart and 'exclusive' hotel, a quite distinctive local character—they were composed of eminent persons from the departmental capitals of that region of France, a chief magistrate from Caen, a leader of the Cherbourg bar, a big solicitor from Le Mans, who annually, when the holidays came round, starting from the various points over which, throughout the working year, they were scattered like snipers in a battle, or draughtsmen upon a board, concentrated their forces upon this hotel. They always reserved the same rooms, and with their wives, who had pretensions to aristocracy, formed a little group, which was joined by a leading barrister and a leading doctor from Paris, who on the day of their departure would say to the others "Oh, yes, of course; you don't go by our train. You are fortunate, you will be home in time for luncheon." "Fortunate, do you say? You, who live in the Capital, in 'Paris, the great town`, while I have to live in a wretched county town of a hundred thousand souls (it is true, we managed to muster a hundred and two thousand at the last census, but what is that compared to your two and a half millions ?)

going back, too, to asphalt streets and all the bustle and gaiety of Paris life."

The barrister and his friends could not exhaust their flow of sarcasm on the subject of a wealthy old lady of title, because she never moved anywhere without taking her whole household with her.

This old lady sent down in advance a servant, who would inform the hotel of the personality and habits of his mistress, and, cutting short the manager's greetings, made, with an abruptness in which there was more timidity than pride, for her room, where her own curtains, substituted for those that draped the hotel windows, her own screens and photographs set up so effectively between her and the outside world, to which otherwise she would have had to adapt herself, the barrier of her private life that it was her home (in which she had comfortably stayed) that travelled rather than herself.

Thenceforward, having placed between herself, on the one hand, and the staff of the hotel and its decorators on the other, the servants who bore instead of her the shock of contact with all this strange humanity, and kept up around their mistress her familiar atmosphere, having set her prejudices between herself and the other visitors, indifferent whether or not she gave offence to people whom her friends would not have had in their houses, it was in her own world that she continued to live, by correspondence with her friends, by memories, by her intimate sense of and confidence in her own position, the quality of her manners, the competence of her politeness. And everyday, when she came downstairs to go for a drive in her own carriage, the lady's-maid who came after her carrying her wraps, the footman who preceded her seemed like sentries who, at the gate of an embassy, flying the flag of the country to which she belonged, assured to her upon foreign soil the privilege of extra-territoriality. She did not leave her room until late in the afternoon on the day following our arrival, so that we did not see her in the dining-room, into which the manager, since we were strangers there, conducted us, taking us under his wing, as a corporal takes a squad of recruits to the master-tailor, to have them fitted; we did see however, a moment later, a country gentleman and his daughter, of an obscure but very ancient Breton family, M. and Mlle. de Stermaria, whose table had been allotted to us, in the belief that they had gone out and would not be back until the evening. Having come to Balbec only to see various country magnates whom they knew in that neighbourhood, they spent in the hotel dining-room, what with the invitations they accepted and the visits they paid, only such time as was strictly unavoidable. It was their stiffness that preserved them intact from all human sympathy, from interesting at all the strangers seated round about them, among whom M. de Stermaria kept up the glacial, preoccupied, distant, rude, punctilious and distrustful air that we assume in a railway refreshment-room, among fellow-passengers whom we have never seen before and will never see again, and with whom we can conceive of no other relations than to defend from their onslaught our 'portion' of cold chicken and our corner seat in the train. No sooner had we begun our luncheon than we were asked to leave the table, on the instructions of M. de Stermaria who had just arrived and, without the faintest attempt at an apology to us, requested the headwaiter, in our hearing to "see that such a mistake did not occur again," for it was repugnant to him that "people whom he did not know" should have taken his table.

At night, hidden springs of electricity flooded the great dining-room with light and it became as it were an immense and wonderful aquarium against whose wall of glass the working population of Balbec, the fishermen and also the tradesmen's families, clustering invisibly in the outer darkness, pressed their faces to watch, gently floating upon the golden eddies within, the luxurious life of its occupants, a thing as extraordinary to the poor as the life of strange fishes or molluscs (an important social question, this; whether the wall of glass will always protect the wonderful creatures at their feasting, whether the obscure folk who watch them hungrily out of the night will not break in some day to gather them from their aquarium and devour them.) Meanwhile there may have been, perhaps, among the gazing crowd, a motionless, formless mass there in the dark, some writer, some student of human ichthyology who, as he watched the jaws of old feminine monstrosities close over a mouthful of food which they proceeded then to absorb, was amusing himself by classifying them according to their race, by their innate characteristics as well as by those acquired characteristics which bring it about that an old Serbian lady whose buccal protuberance is that of a great sea-fish, because from her earliest years she has moved in the fresh waters of the Faubourg Saint-Germain, eats her salad for all the world like a La Rochefoucauld.

Alas for my peace of mind, I had none of the detachment that all these people showed. To many of them I gave constant thought; I should have liked not to pass unobserved by a man with a receding brow and eyes that dodged between the blinkers of his prejudices and his education, the great nobleman of the district, who was none other than the brother-in-law of Legrandin, and came every now and then to see somebody at Balbec and on Sundays, by reason of the weekly garden party that his wife and he gave, robbed the hotel of a large number of its occupants, because one or two of them were invited to these entertainments and the others, so as not to appear to have been not invited, chose that day for an expedition to some distant spot. He had had, as it happened, an exceedingly bad reception at the hotel on the first day of the season, when the staff, freshly imported from the Riviera, did not yet know who or what he was. Not only was he not wearing white flannels, but, with old-fashioned French courtesy and in his ignorance of the ways of smart hotels, on coming into the hall in which there were ladies sitting, he had taken off his hat at the door, the effect of which had been that the manager did not so much as raise a finger to his own in acknowledgment, concluding that this must be some one of the most humble extraction, what he called "sprung from the ordinary." The solicitor's wife, alone, had felt herself attracted by the stranger, who exhaled all the starched vulgarity of the really respectable, and had declared, with the unerring discernment and the indisputable authority of a person from whom the highest society of Le Mans held no secrets, that one could see at a glance that one was in the presence of a gentleman of great distinction, of perfect breeding, a striking contrast to the sort of people one usually saw at Balbec, whom she condemned as impossible to know so long as she did not know them. This favourable judgment which she had pronounced on Legrandin's brother-in-law was based perhaps on the spiritless appearance of a man about whom there was nothing to intimidate anyone; perhaps also she had recognised in this gentleman farmer with the gait of a sacristan, the Masonic signs of her own inveterate clericalisrn.

Alas, none of these people's contempt for me was so unbearable as that of M. de Stermaria. For I had noticed his daughter, the moment she came into the room, her pretty features, her pallid, almost blue complexion, what there was peculiar in the carriage of her tall figure, in her gait, which suggested to me—and rightly—her long descent, her aristocratic upbringing, all the more vividly because I knew her name, like those expressive themes composed by musicians of genius which paint in splendid colours the glow of fire, the rush of water, the peace of fields and woods, to audiences who, having first let their eyes run over the programme, have their imaginations trained in the right direction. The label 'Centuries of Breeding', by adding to Mlle. de Stermaria's charms the idea of their origin, made them more desirable also, advertising their rarity as a high price enhances the value of a thing that has already taken our fancy. And its stock of heredity gave to her complexion, in which so many selected juices had been blended, the savour of an exotic fruit or of a famous vintage.

And then mere chance put into our hands my grandmother's and mine, the means of giving ourselves an immediate distinction in the eyes of all the other occupants of the hotel. On that first afternoon, at the moment when the old lady came downstairs from her room, producing, thanks to the footman who preceded her, the maid who came running after her with a book and a rug that had been left behind, a marked effect upon all who beheld her and arousing in each of them a curiosity from which it was evident that none was so little immune as M. de Stermaria, the manager leaned across to my grandmother and, from pure kindness of heart (as one might point out the Shah, or Queen Ranavalo to an obscure onlooker who could obviously have no sort of connexion with so mighty a potentate, but might be interested, all the same, to know that he had been standing within a few feet of one) whispered in her ear, "The Marquise de Villeparisis!", while at the same moment the old lady, catching sight of my grandmother, could not repress a start of pleased surprise. It may be imagined that the sudden appearance, in the guise of a little old woman, of the most powerful of fairies would not have given me so much pleasure, destitute as I was of any means of access to Mlle. de Stermaria, in a strange place where I knew no one: no one, that is to say, for any practical purpose. Mme. de Villeparisis was capable, of putting at the service of my power an enchantment which would multiply it an hundred fold, and thanks to which, as though I had been swept through the air on the wings of a fabulous bird, I was to cross in a few moments the infinitely wide (at least, at Balbec) social gulf which separated me from Mlle. de Stermaria.

Unfortunately, if there was one person in the world who, more than anyone else, lived shut up in a little world of her own, it was my grandmother. She would not, indeed, have despised me, she would simply not have understood what I meant had she been told that I attached importance to the opinions, that I felt an interest in the persons of people the very existence of whom she had never noticed and would, when the time came to leave Balbec, retain no impression of their names. I dared not confess to her that if these same people had seen her talking to Mme. de Villeparisis, I should have been immensely gratified, because I felt that the Marquise counted for much in the hotel and that her friendship would have given us a position in the eyes of Mlle. de Stermaria. Not that my grandmother's friend represented to me, in any sense of the word, a member of the aristocracy; I was too well used to her name, which had been familiar to my ears before my mind had begun to consider it, when as a child I had heard it occur in conversation at home while her title added to it only a touch of quaintness—as some uncommon Christian name would have done, or as in the names of streets, among which we can see nothing more noble in the Rue Lord Byron, in the plebeian and even squalid Rue Rochechouart, or in the Rue Grammont than in the Rue Léonce Reynaud or the Rue Hippolyte Lebas. Mme. de Villeparisis no more made me think of a person who belonged to a special world than did her cousin MacMahon, whom I did not clearly distinguish from M. Carnot, likewise President of the Republic, or from Raspail, whose photograph Françoise had bought with that of Pius IX. It was one of my grandmother's principles that, when away from home, one should cease to have any social intercourse, that one did not go to the seaside to meet people, having plenty of time for that sort of thing in Paris, that they would make one waste on being merely polite, in pointless conversation, the precious time which ought all to be spent in the open air, beside the waves and finding it convenient to assume that this view was shared by everyone else, and that it authorised, between old friends whom chance brought face to face in the same hotel, the fiction of a mutual *incognito*, on hearing her friend's name from the manager she merely looked the other way, and pretended not to see Mme. de Villeparisis, who, realising that my grandmother did not want to be recognised, looked also into the void. She went past, and I was left in my isolation like a shipwrecked mariner who has seen a vessel apparently coming towards him which has then, without lowering a boat, vanished under the horizon.

She, too, had her meals in the dining-room, but at the other end of it. She knew none of the people who were staying in the hotel, or who came there to call, not even M. de Cambremer; in fact, I noticed that he gave her no greeting, one day when, with his wife, he had accepted an invitation to take luncheon with the barrister, who drunken with the honour of having the nobleman at his table avoided his friends of every day, and confined himself to a distant twitch of the eyelid, so as to draw their attention to this historic event but so discreetly that his signal could not be interpreted by them as an invitation to join the party.

"Well, I hope you've got on your best clothes; I hope you feel smart enough," was the magistrate's wife's greeting to him that evening. "Smart? Why should I?" asked the barrister, concealing his rapture in an exaggerated astonishment. "Because of my guests, do you mean?"

he went on, feeling that it was impossible to keep up the farce any longer. "But what is there smart about having a few friends in to luncheon ? After all, they must feed somewhere!" "But it is smart ! They are the *de* Cambremers, aren't they ? I recognised them at once. She is a Marquise. And quite genuine, too. Not through the females." "Oh, she's a very simple soul, she is charming, no stand-offishness about her. I thought you were coming to join us. I was making signals to you . I would have introduced you!" he asserted, tempering with a hint of irony the vast generosity of the offer, like Ahasuerus when he says to Esther

'Of all my Kingdom must I give you half!'

"No, no, no, no! We lie hidden, like the modest violet." "But you were quite wrong, I assure you," replied the barrister, growing bolder now that the danger point was passed. "They weren't going to eat you. I say, aren't we going to have our little game of bezique?" "Why, of course ! We were afraid to suggest it, now that you go about entertaining Marquises." "Oh, get along with you; there's nothing so very wonderful about them. Why, I'm dining there tomorrow. Would you care to go instead of me? I mean it. Honestly, I'd just as soon stay here." "No, no! I should be removed from the bench as a Reactionary," cried the chief magistrate, laughing till the tears stood in his eyes at his own joke. "But you go to Féterne too, don't you?" he went on, turning to the solicitor. "Oh, I go there on Sundays—in at one door and out at the other. But I don't have them here to luncheon, like the Leader."

M. de Stermaria was not at Balbec that day, to the barrister's great regret. But he managed to say a word in season to the head waiter "Aimé, you can tell M. de Stermaria that he's not the only nobleman you've had in here. You saw the gentleman who was with me to-day at luncheon? Eh? A small moustache, looked like a military man. Well, that was the Marquis de Cambremer!" "Was it indeed? I'm not surprised to hear it." "That will show him that he's not the only man who's got a title. That will teach him! It's not a bad thing to take 'em down a peg or two, those noblemen. I say, Aimé, don't say anything to him unless you like: I mean to say, it's no business of mine; besides, they know each other already."

And next day M. de Stermaria, who remembered that the barrister had once held a brief for one of his friends, came up and introduced himself. "Our friends in common, the de Cambremers, were anxious that we should meet; the days didn't fit; I don't know quite what went wrong—" stammered the barrister, who, like most liars, imagined that other people do not take the trouble to investigate an unimportant detail which, for all that, may be sufficient (if chance puts you in possession of the humble facts of the case, and they contradict it) to show the liar in his true colours and to inspire a lasting mistrust.

My life in the hotel was rendered not only dull because I had no friends there but uncomfortable because Françoise had made so many. It might be thought that they would have made things easier for us in various respects. Quite the contrary. The proletariat, if they succeeded only with great difficulty in being treated as people she knew by Françoise, and could not succeed at all unless they fulfilled the condition of showing the utmost politeness to her, were, on the other hand, once they had reached the position, the only people who "counted". Her time-honoured code taught her that she was in no way bound to the friends of her employers, that she might, if she was busy, shut the door without ceremony in the face of a lady who had come to call on my grandmother. But towards her own acquaintance, that is to say, the select handful of the lower orders whom she admitted to an unconquerable intimacy, her actions were regulated by the most subtle and most stringent of protocols. Thus Françoise having made the acquaintance of the man in the coffee-shop and of a little maid who did dressmaking for a Belgian lady, no longer came upstairs immediately after luncheon to get my grandmother's things ready, but came an hour later, because the coffee man had wanted to make her a cup of coffee or a *tisane* in his shop, or the maid had invited her to go and watch her sew, and to refuse either of them would have been impossible, and one of the things that were not done. Moreover, particular attention was due to the little sewing-maid, who was an orphan and had been brought up by strangers to whom she still went occasionally for a few days holiday. Her unusual situation aroused Françoise's pity, and also a benevolent contempt. She, who had a family, a little house that had come to her from her parents, with a field in which her brother kept his cows, how could she regard so uprooted a creature as her equal? And since this girl hoped, on Assumption Day, to be allowed to pay her benefactors a visit, Françoise kept on repeating: "She does make me laugh! She says, "I hope to be going home for the Assumption." "Home!" says she! It isn't just that it's not her own place, they're people who took her in from nowhere, and the creature says 'home' just as if it really was her home. Poor girl! What a wretched state she must be in, not to know what it is to have a home." Still, if Françoise had associated only with the ladies'-maids brought to the hotel by other visitors, who fed with her in the 'service' quarters and, seeing her grand lace cap and her handsome profile, took her perhaps for some lady of noble birth, whom 'reduced circumstances', or a personal attachment had driven to serve as companion to my grandmother, if in a word Françoise had known only people who did not belong to the hotel, no great harm would have been done, since she could not have prevented them from doing us any service, for the simple reason that in no circumstances, even without her knowledge, would it have been possible for them to serve us at all. But she had formed connections also with one of the wine waiters, with a man in the kitchen, and with the head chambermaid of our landing. And the result of this in our every day life was that Françoise, who on the day of her arrival, when she still did not know anyone, would set all the bells jangling for the slightest thing, at an hour when my grandmother and I would never have dared to ring, and if we offered some gentle admonition answered: "Well, we're paying enough for it, aren't we?" as though it were she herself that would have to pay; nowadays, since she had made friends with a personage in the kitchen, which had appeared to us to augur well for our future comfort, were my grandmother or I to complain of cold feet, Françoise, even at an hour that was quite normal, dared not ring; she assured us that it would give offence because they would have to light the furnace again, or because it would interrupt the servants' dinner and they would be annoyed. And she ended with a formula that, in spite of the ambiguous way in which she uttered it, was none the less clear, and put us plainly in the wrong : "The fact is....." We did not insist, for fear of bringing upon ourselves another, far more serious "It's a matter ......! So that it amounted to this, that we could no longer have any hot water because Françoise had become a friend of the man who would have to heat it.

In the end we too formed a connection, in spite of but through my grandmother, for she and Mme. de Villeparisis came in collision one morning in a doorway and were obliged to accost each other, not without having first exchanged gestures of surprise and hesitation, performed movements of recoil and uncertainty, and finally uttered protestations of joy and greeting, as in some of Molière's plays, where two actors who have been delivering long soliloquies from opposite sides of the stage, a few feet apart, are supposed not to have seen each other yet, and then suddenly catch sight of each other, cannot believe their eyes, break off what they are saying and finally address each other (the chorus having meanwhile kept the dialogue going) and fall into each other's arms. Mme. de Villeparisis was tactful, and made as if to leave my grandmother to herself after the first greetings, but my grandmother insisted on her staying to talk to her until luncheon, being anxious to discover how her friend managed to get her letters sent up to her earlier than we got ours, and to get such nice grilled things (for Mme. de Villeparisis, a great epicure, had the poorest opinion of the hotel kitchen which served us with meals that my grandmother, still quoting Mme. de Sévigné, described as "of a magnificence to make you die of hunger.") And the Marquise formed the habit of coming every day, until her own meal was ready, to sit down for a moment at our table in the dining-room, insisting that we should not rise from our chairs or in any way put ourselves out. At the most we would linger, as often as not, in the room after finishing our luncheon, to talk to her, at that sordid moment when the knives are left littering the tablecloth among crumpled napkins.

As a barber, seeing an officer whom he is accustomed to shave with special deference and care recognise a customer who has just entered the shop and stop for a moment to talk to him, rejoices in the thought that these are two men of the same social order, and cannot help smiling as he goes to fetch the bowl of soap, for he knows that in his establishment, to the vulgar routine of a mere barber's shop, are being added social, not to say aristocratic pleasures, so Aimé, seeing that Mme. de Villeparisis had found in us old friends, went to fetch our finger-bowls with precisely the smile, proudly modest and knowingly discreet, of a hostess who knows when to leave her guests to themselves. He suggested also a pleased and loving father who looks on, without interfering, at the happy pair who have plighted their troth at his hospitable board. Besides, it was enough merely to utter the name of a person of title for Aimé to appear pleased.

"I must remember, some time, to ask Mme. de Villeparisis whether I'm not right, after all, in thinking that there is some connection with the Guermantes," said my grandmother to my great indignation. How could I be expected to believe in a common origin uniting two names which had entered my consciousness, one through the low and shameful gate of experience, the other by the golden gate of imagination?

We had several times, in the last few days seen driving past us in a stately equipage, tall, auburn, handsome, with a rather prominent nose, the Princesse de Luxembourg, who was staying in the neighbourhood for a few weeks. Her carriage had stopped outside the hotel, a footman had come in and spoken to the manager, had gone back to the carriage and had reappeared with the most amazing armful of fruit (which combined in a single basket, like the bay itself, different seasons) with a card "La Princesse de Luxembourg", on which were scrawled a few words in pencil. For what princely traveller sojourning here *incognito*, could they be intended, those glaucous plums, luminous and spherical as was at that moment the circumfluent sea, transparent grapes clustering on a shrivelled stick, like a fine day in autumn, pears of a heavenly ultramarine? For it could not be on my grandmother's friend that the Princess had meant to pay a call. And yet on the following evening Mme. de Villeparisis sent us the bunch of grapes, cool, liquid, golden; plums too and pears which we remembered, though the plums had changed, like the sea at our dinner-hour, to a dull purple, and on the ultramarine surface of the pears there floated the forms of a few rosy clouds. A few days later we met Mme. de Villeparisis as we came away from the symphony concert that was given every morning on the beach. Convinced that the music to which I had been listening (the Prelude to *Lohengrin* , the Overture to *Tannhäuser* and suchlike) expressed the loftiest of truths, I was trying to elevate myself, as far as I could, so as to attain to a comprehension of them, I was extracting from myself so as to understand them, and was attributing to them, all that was best and most profound in my own nature at that time.

Well, as we came out of the concert, and, on our way back to the hotel, had stopped for a moment on the front, my grandmother and I, for a few words with Mme. de Villeparisis who told us that she had ordered some *croquemonsieurs* and a dish of creamed eggs for us at the hotel, I saw, a long way away, coming in our direction, the Princesse de Luxembourg, half leaning upon a parasol in such a way as to impart to her tall and wonderful form that slight inclination, to make it trace that arabesque dear to the women who had been beautiful under the Empire, and knew how, with drooping shoulders, arched backs, concave hips and bent limbs, to make their bodies float as gently as a silken scarf about the rigidity of the invisible stem which might be supposed to have been passed diagonally through them. She went out every morning for a turn on the beach almost at the time when everyone else, after bathing, was climbing home to luncheon, and as hers was not until half past one she did not return to her villa until long after the hungry bathers had left the scorching 'front' a desert. Mme. de Villeparisis presented my grandmother and would, have presented me, but had first to ask me my name, which she could not remember. She had, perhaps, never known it, or if she had must have forgotten years ago to whom my grandmother had married her daughter. My name, when she did hear it, appeared to impress Mme. de Villeparisis considerably. Meanwhile the Princesse de Luxembourg had given us her hand and, now and again, while she conversed with the Marquise, turned to bestow a kindly glance on my grandmother and myself, with that embryonic kiss which we put into our smiles when they are addressed to a baby out with its 'Nana'. Indeed, in her anxiety not to appear to be a denizen of a higher sphere than ours, she had probably miscalculated the distance there was indeed between us, for by an error in adjustment she made her eyes beam with such benevolence that I could see the moment approaching when she would put out her hand and stroke us, as if we were two nice beasts and had poked our heads out at her through the bars of our cage in the Gardens. And, immediately, as it happened, this idea of caged animals and the Bois de Boulogne received striking conflrmation. It was the time of day at which the beach is crowded by itinerant and clamorous vendors, hawking cakes and sweets and biscuits. Not knowing quite what to do to show her affection for us, the Princess hailed the next that came by; he had nothing left but one rye-cake, of the kind one throws to the ducks. The Princess took it and said to me: "For your grandmother." And yet it was to me that she held it out, saying with a friendly smile, "You shall give it to her yourself!" thinking that my pleasure would thus be more complete if there were no intermediary between myself and the animals. Other vendors came up; she stuffed my pockets with everything that they had, tied up in packets, comfits, sponge-cakes, sugar-sticks. "You will eat some yourself," she told me, "and give some to your grandmother," and she had the vendors paid by the little negro page, dressed in red satin, who followed her everywhere and was a nine days' wonder upon the beach. Then she said good-bye to Mme. de Villeparisis and held out her hand to us with the intention of treating us in the same way as she treated her friend, as people whom she knew, and of bringing herself within our reach. But this time she must have reckoned our level as not quite so low in the scale of creation, for her and our equality was indicated by the Princess to my grandmother by that tender and maternal smile which a woman gives a little boy when she says good-bye to him as though to a grown-up person. By a miraculous stride in evolution, my grandmother was no longer a duck or an antelope, but had already become what the anglophile Mme. Swann would have called a 'baby'. Finally, having taken leave of us all, the Princess resumed her stroll along the basking 'front', curving her splendid shape which, like a serpent coiled about a wand, was interlaced with the white parasol patterned in blue which Mme. de Luxembourg held, unopened, in her hand. She was my first Royalty. The second, as we shall see in due course, was to astonish me no less by her indulgence. One of the ways in which our great nobles, kindly intermediaries between commoners and kings, can befriend us was revealed to me next day when Mme. de Villeparisis reported: "She thought you quite charming. She is a woman of the soundest judgment, the warmest heart. Not like so many Queens and people! She has real merit." And Mme. de Villeparisis went on in a tone of conviction, and quite thrilled to be able to say it to us: "I am sure she would be delighted to see you again."

But on that previous morning, after we had parted from the Princesse de Luxembourg, Mme. de Villeparisis said a thing which impressed me far more and was not prompted merely by friendly feeling. "Are you," she had asked me, "the son of the Permanent Secretary at the Ministry? Indeed! I am told your father is a most charming man. He is having a splendid holiday just now."

A few days earlier we had heard, in a letter from Mamma, that my father and his friend M. de Norpois had lost their luggage.

"It has been found; as a matter of fact, it was never really lost, I can tell you what happened," explained Mme. de Villeparisis, who, without our knowing how, seemed to be far better informed than ourselves of the course of my father's travels. "I think your father is now planning to come home earlier, next week, in fact, as he will probably give up the idea of going to Algeciras. But he is anxious to devote a day longer to Toledo; it seems, he is an admirer of a pupil of Titian,—I forget the name—whose work can only be seen properly there."

I asked myself by what strange accident, in the impartial glass through which Mme. de Villeparisis considered, from a safe distance, the bristling, tiny, purposeless agitation of the crowd of people, whom she knew, there had come to be inserted at the spot through which she observed my father, a fragment of prodigious magnifying power which made her see in such high relief and in the fullest detail everything that there was attractive about him, the contingencies that were obliging him to return home, his difficulties with the customs, his admiration for El Greco, and, altering the scale of her vision, showed her this one man so large among all the rest quite small, like that Jupiter to whom Gustave Moreau gave, when he portrayed him by the side of a weak mortal, a superhuman stature.

As to the coming of the Princesse de Luxembourg, whose carriage, on the day on which she left the fruit, had drawn up outside the hotel, it had not passed unobserved by the little group of wives, the solicitor's, the barrister's and the magistrate's, who had for some time past been most concerned to know whether she was a genuine Marquise and not an adventuress, that Mme. de Villeparisis whom everyone treated with so much respect, which all these ladies were burning to hear that she did not deserve. Whenever Mme. de Villeparisis passed through the hall the chief magistrate's wife, who scented irregularities everywhere, would raise her eyes from her 'work' and stare at the intruder in a way that made her friends die with laughter.—"Oh, well, you know," she explained with lofty condescension, I always begin by believing the worst. I will never admit that a woman is properly married until she has shown me her birth certificate and her marriage lines. But there's no need to alarm yourselves; just wait till I've finished my little investigation." And so, day after day the ladies would come together, and, laughingly, ask one another: "Any news?"

But on the evening after the Princesse de Luxembourg's call the magistrate's wife laid a finger on her lips. "I've discovered something." "Oh, isn't Mme. Poncin simply wonderful? I never saw anyone. . . . But do tell us, what has happened?" "Just listen to this. A woman with yellow hair and six inches of paint on her face and a carriage like a—you could *smell* it a mile off; which only a creature like that would dare to have—came here to-day to call on the Marquise, by way of!"

"Oh-yow-yow! Tut-tut-tut-tut. Did you ever! Why, it must be that woman we saw—you remember, Leader,—we said at the time we didn't at all like the look of her, but we didn't know that it was the 'Marquise' she'd come to see. A woman with a nigger-boy, you mean?" "That's the one." "D'you mean to say so? You don't happen to know her name?" "Yes, I made a mistake on purpose; I picked up her card; she *trades* under the name of the 'Princesse de Luxembourg'! Wasn't I right to have my doubts about her?"

It must not, however, be supposed that this misunderstanding was merely temporary, like those that occur in the second act of a farce to be cleared up before the final curtain. Mme. de Luxembourg, a niece of the King of England and of the Emperor of Austria, and Mme. de Villeparisis, when one called to take the other for a drive, did look like nothing but two 'old trots' of the kind one has always such difficulty in avoiding at a watering place.

Mme. de Villeparisis gave us warning that presently she would not be able to see so much of us. A young nephew who was preparing for Saumur, and was meanwhile stationed in the neighbourhood, at Doncières, was coming to spend a few weeks furlough with her, and she would be devoting most of her time to him. In the course of our drives together she had boasted to us of his extreme cleverness, and above all of his goodness of heart; already I was imagining that he would have an instinctive feeling for me, that I was to be his best friend; and when, before his arrival, his aunt gave my grandmother to understand that he had unfortunately fallen into the clutches of an appalling woman with whom he was quite infatuated and who would never let him go, since I believed that that sort of love was doomed to end in mental aberration, crime and suicide, thinking how short the time was that was set apart for our friendship, already so great in my heart, although I had not yet set eyes on him, I wept for that friendship and for the misfortunes that were in store for it, as we weep for a person whom we love when some one has just told us that he is seriously ill and that his days are numbered.

One afternoon of scorching heat I was in the dining-room of the hotel, which they had plunged in semi-darkness, to shield it from the glare, by drawing the curtains which the sun gilded, while through the gaps between them I caught flashing blue glimpses of the sea, when along the central gangway leading inland from the beach to the high road I saw, tall, slender, his head held proudly erect upon a springing neck, a young man go past with searching eyes, whose skin was as fair and his hair as golden as if they had absorbed all the rays of the sun. Dressed in a clinging, almost white material such as I could never have believed that any man would have the audacity to wear, the thinness of which suggested no less vividly than the coolness of the dining-room the heat and brightness of the glorious day outside, he was walking fast. His eyes, from one of which a monocle kept dropping, were of the colour of the sea. Everyone looked at him with interest as he passed, knowing that this young Marquis de Saint-Loup-en-Bray was famed for the smartness of his clothes. All the newspapers had described the suit in which he had recently acted as second to the young Duc d'Uzès in a duel. One felt that this so special quality of his hair, his eyes, his skin, his figure, which would have marked him out in a crowd like a precious vein of opal, azure-shot and luminous, embedded in a mass of coarser substance, must correspond to a life different from that led by other men. So that when, before the attachment which Mme. de Villeparisis had been deploring, the prettiest women in society had disputed the possession of him, his presence, at a watering-place for instance, in the company of the beauty of the season to whom he was paying court, not only made her conspicuous, but attracted every eye fully as much to himself. Because of his 'tone', of his impertinence befitting a young 'lion' , and especially of his astonishing good looks, some people even thought him effeminate, though without attaching any stigma, for everyone knew how manly he was and that he was a passionate 'womaniser'. This was Mme. de Villeparisis's nephew of whom she had spoken to us. I was overcome with joy at the thought that I was going to know him and to see him for several weeks on end, and confident that he would bestow on me all his affection.

What a disappointment was mine on the days that followed, when, each time that I met him outside or in the hotel—his head erect, perpetually balancing the movements of his limbs round the fugitive and dangling monocle which seemed to be their centre of gravity—I was forced to admit that he had evidently no desire to make our acquaintance, and saw that he did not bow to us although he must have known that we were friends of his aunt

When Mme. de Villeparisis, doubtless in an attempt to counteract the bad impression that had been made on us by an exterior indicative of an arrogant and evil nature, spoke to us again of the inexhaustible goodness of her great-nephew (he was the son of one of her nieces, and a little older than myself), I marvelled how the world, with an utter disregard of truth, ascribes tenderness of heart to people whose hearts are in reality so hard and dry, provided only that they behave with common courtesy to the brilliant members of their own sets. Mme. de Villeparisis herself confirmed, though indirectly, my diagnosis, which was already a conviction, of the essential points of her nephew's character one day when I met them both coming along a path so narrow that there was nothing for it but to introduce me to him. He seemed not to hear that a person's name was being repeated to him, not a muscle of his face moved; his eyes, in which there shone not the faintest gleam of human sympathy, showed merely in the insensibility, in the inanity of their gaze an exaggeration failing which there would have been nothing to distinguish them from lifeless mirrors. Then fastening on me those hard eyes, as though he wished to make sure of me before returning my salute, by an abrupt release which seemed to be due rather to a reflex action of his muscles than to an exercise of will, keeping between himself and me the greatest possible interval, he stretched his arm out to its full extension and, at the end of it, offered me his hand. I supposed that it must mean, at the very least, a duel when, next day, he sent me his card. But he spoke to me only of literature, declared after a long talk that he would like immensely to spend several hours with me every day. He had not only, in this encounter, given proof of an ardent zest for the things of the spirit, he had shown a regard for myself which was little in keeping with his greeting of me the day before. After I had seen him repeat the same process whenever anyone was introduced to him, I realised that it was simply a social usage peculiar to his branch of the family, to which his mother, who had seen to it that he should be perfectly brought up, had moulded his limbs; he went through those motions without thinking, any more than he thought about his beautiful clothes or hair; they were a thing devoid of the moral significance which I had at first ascribed to them, a thing purely acquired like that other habit that he had of at once demanding an introduction to the family of anyone whom he knew which had become so instinctive in him that, seeing me again the day after our talk, he fell upon me and without asking how I did, begged me to make him known to my grandmother, who was with me, with the same feverish haste as if the request had been due to some instinct of self-preservation, like the act of warding off a blow, or of shutting one's eyes to avoid a stream of boiling water, without which precautions it would have been dangerous to stay where one was a moment longer.

The first rites of exorcism once performed, as a wicked fairy discards her outer form and endues all the most enchanting graces, I saw this disdainful creature become the most friendly, the most considerate young man that I had ever met. "Good," I said to myself, "I've been mistaken about him once already; I was taken in by a mirage; but I have corrected the first only to fall into a second; for he must be a great gentleman who has, grown sick of his nobility and is trying to hide it." As a matter of fact it was not long before all the exquisite breeding, all the friendliness of Saint-Loup were indeed to let me see another creature but one very different from what I had suspected.

This young man who had the air of a scornful, sporting aristocrat had in fact no respect, no interest save for and in the things of the spirit, and especially those modern manifestations of literature and art which seemed so ridiculous to his aunt; he was imbued, moreover, with what she called "Socialistic spoutings," was filled with the most profound contempt for his caste and spent long hours in the study of Nietzsche and Proudhon.

It was promptly settled between us that he and I were to be great friends for ever, and he would say "our friendship" as though he were speaking of some important and delightful thing which had an existence independent of ourselves, and which he soon called—not counting his love for his mistress—the great joy of his life.

One day when we were sitting on the sands, Saint-Loup and I, we heard issuing from a canvas tent against which we were leaning a torrent of imprecation against the swarm of Israelites that infested Balbec. "You can't go a yard without meeting them," said the voice "I am not in principle irremediably hostile to the Jewish nation, but here there is a plethora of them. You hear nothing but, I thay, Apraham, I've chust theen Chacop. You would think you were in the Rue d'Aboukir." The man who thus inveighed against Israel emerged at last from the tent; we raised our eyes to behold this antisemite. It was my old friend Bloch. Saint-Loup at once begged me to remind him that they had met before the Board of Examiners, when Bloch had carried off the prize of honour, and since then at a popular university course.

Personally, I was not particularly anxious that Bloch should come to the hotel. He was at Balbec not by himself, unfortunately, but with his sisters, and they in turn had innumerable relatives and friends staying there. Now this Jewish colony was more picturesque than pleasant. Balbec was in this respect like such countries as Russia or Rumania, where the geography books teach us that the Israelite population does not enjoy anything approaching the same esteem and has not reached the same stage of assimilation as, for instance, in Paris. Always together, with no blend of any other element, when the cousins and uncles of Bloch or their coreligionists male or female repaired to the Casino, the ladies to dance, the gentlemen branching off towards the baccarat-tables, they formed a solid troop, homogeneous within itself, and utterly dissimilar to the people who watched them go past and found them there again every year without ever exchanging a word or a sign with them, whether these were on the Cambremers' list, or the presiding magistrate's little group, professional or 'business' people, or even simple corn-chandlers from Paris, whose daughters, handsome, proud, derisive and French as the statues at Rheims, would not care to mix with that horde of ill-bred tomboys, who carried their zeal for 'seaside fashions' so far as to be always apparently on their way home from shrimping or out to dance the tango. As for the men, despite the brilliance of their dinner-jackets and patent-leather shoes; the exaggeration of their type made one think of what people call the "intelligent research" of painters who, having to illustrate the Gospels or the Arabian Nights, consider the country in which the scenes are laid, and give to Saint Peter or to Ali-Baba the identical features of the heaviest "punter" at the Balbec tables. Bloch introduced his sisters, who, though he silenced their chatter with the utmost rudeness, screamed with laughter at the mildest sallies of this brother, their blindly worshipped idol. So that it is probable that this set of people contained, like every other, perhaps more than any other, plenty of attractions, merits and virtues. But in order to experience these; one had first to penetrate its enclosure. Now it was not popular; it could feel this; it saw in its unpopularity the mark of an antisemitism to which it presented a bold front in a compact and closed phalanx into which, as it happened, no one ever dreamed of trying to make his way.

Bloch made me the prettiest speeches. He was certainly anxious to be on the best of terms with me. And yet he asked me: "Is it because you've taken a fancy to raise yourself to the peerage that you run after de Saint-Loup-en-Bray? You must be going through a fine crisis of snobbery. Tell me, are you a snob? I think so, what?" Not that his desire to be friendly had suddenly changed. But what is called, in not too correct language, "ill breeding" was his defect, and therefore the defect which he was bound to overlook, all the more the defect by which he did not believe that other people could be shocked.

Bloch was ill-bred, neurotic, a snob, and, since he belonged to a family of little repute, had to support, as on the floor of ocean, the incalculable pressure that was imposed on him not only by the Christians upon the surface but by all the intervening layers of Jewish castes superior to his own, each of them crushing with its contempt the one that was immediately beneath it. To carve his way through to the open air by raising himself from Jewish family to Jewish family would have taken Bloch many thousands of years. It was better worth his while to seek an outlet in another direction. When Bloch spoke to me of the crisis of snobbery through which I must be passing, and bade me confess that I was a snob, I might well have replied: "If I were, I should not be going about with you." I said merely that he was not being very polite. Then he tried to apologise, but in the way that is typical of the ill-bred man who is only too glad to hark back to whatever it was if he can find an opportunity to aggravate his offence. "Forgive me," he used now to plead, whenever we met, "I have vexed you, tormented you; I have been wantonly mischievous.. And yet—man in general and your friend in particular is so singular an animal—you cannot imagine the affection that I, I who tease you so cruelly, have for you. It carries me often, when I think of you, to tears." And he gave an audible sob.

Saint-Loup could not leave the hotel, where he was waiting for an uncle who was coming to spend a few days with Mme. de Villeparisis. Since—for he was greatly addicted to physical culture, and especially to long walks—it was largely on foot, spending the night in wayside farms, that this uncle was to make the journey from the country house in which he was staying, the precise date of his arrival at Balbec was by no means certain. And Saint-Loup, afraid to stir out of doors, even entrusted me with the duty of taking to Incauville, where the nearest telegraph-office was, the messages that he sent every day to his mistress. The uncle for whom we were waiting was called Palamède, a name that had come down to him from his ancestors the Princes of Sicily. Saint-Loup told me that even in the most exclusive aristocratic society, his uncle Palamède had the further distinction of being particularly difficult to approach, contemptuous, double-dyed in his nobility, forming with his brother's wife and a few other chosen spirits what was known as the Phoenix Club. There even his insolence was so much dreaded that it had happened more than once that people of good position who had been anxious to meet him and had applied to his own brother for an introduction had met with a refusal "Really, you mustn't ask me to introduce you to my brother Palamède. My wife and I, we would all of us do our best for you, but it would be no good. Besides, there's always the danger of his being rude to you, and I shouldn't like that."

The morning after Robert had told me about his uncle, while he waited for him (and waited, as it happened, in vain), as I was coming by myself past the Casino on my way back to the hotel, I had the sensation of being watched by somebody who was not far off. I turned my head and saw a man of about forty, very tall and rather stout, with a very dark moustache, who, nervously slapping the leg of his trousers with a switch, kept fastened upon me a pair of eyes dilated with observation. Every now and then those eyes were shot through by a look of intense activity such as the sight of a person whom they do not know excites only in men to whom, for whatever reason, it suggests thoughts that would not occur to anyone else—madmen, for instance, or spies. He trained upon me a supreme stare at once bold, prudent, rapid and profound, like a last shot which one fires at an enemy at the moment when one turns to flee, and, after first looking all round him, suddenly adopting an absent and lofty air, by an abrupt revolution of his whole body turned to examine a playbill on the wall in the reading of which he became absorbed, while he hummed a tune and fingered the moss-rose in his buttonhole. He drew from his pocket a note-book in which he appeared to be taking down the title of the performance that was announced, looked two or three times at his watch, pulled down over his eyes a black straw hat the brim of which he extended with his hand held out over it like a visor, as though to see whether someone were at last coming, made the perfunctory gesture of annoyance by which people mean to show that they have waited long enough, although they never make it when they are really waiting, then pushing back his hat and exposing a scalp cropped close except at the sides where he allowed a pair of waved "pigeon's-wings." to grow quite long, he emitted the loud panting breath that people give who are not feeling too hot but would like it to be thought that they were. He gave me the impression of a 'hotel crook' who had been watching my grandmother and myself for some days, and while he was planning to rob us had just discovered that I had surprised him in the act of spying; to put me off the scent, perhaps he was seeking only, by his new attitude, to express boredom and detachment; but it was with an exaggeration so aggressive that his object appeared to be—at least as much as the dissipating of the suspicion that I must have had of him— to avenge a humiliation which quite unconsciously I must have inflicted on him; to give me the idea not so much that he had not seen me as that I was an object of too little importance to attract his attention. He threw back his shoulders with an air of bravado, bit his lips, pushed up his moustache, and in the lens of his eyes made an adjustment of something that was indifferent, harsh, almost insulting. So effectively that the singularity of his expression made me take him at one moment for a thief and at another for a lunatic. And yet his scrupulously ordered attire was far more sober and far more simple than that of any of the summer visitors I saw at Balbec, and gave a reassurance to my own suit, so often humiliated by the dazzling and commonplace whiteness of their holiday garb. But my grandmother was coming towards me, we took a turn together, and I was waiting for her, an hour later, outside the hotel into which she had gone for a moment, when I saw emerge from it Mme. de Villeparisis with Robert de Saint-Loup and the stranger who had stared at me so intently outside the Casino. Swift as a lightning-flash his look shot through me, just as at the moment when I first noticed him, and returned, as though he had not seen me, to hover, slightly lowered, before his eyes, dulled, like the neutral look which feigns to see nothing without and is incapable of reporting anything to the mind within: the look which expresses merely the satisfaction of feeling round it the eyelids which it cleaves apart with its sanctimonious roundness, the devout, the steeped look that we see on the faces of certain hypocrites, the smug look on those of certain fools. I saw that he had changed his clothes. The suit he was wearing was darker even than the other; and no doubt this was because the true distinction in dress lies nearer to simplicity than the false but there was something more; when one came near him one felt that if colour was almost entirely absent from these garments it was not because he who had banished it from them was indifferent to it but rather because for some reason he forbade himself the enjoyment of it. And the sobriety which they displayed seemed to be of the kind that comes from obedience to a rule of diet rather than from want of appetite. A dark green thread harmonised, in the stuff of his trousers, with the stripe on his socks, with a refinement which betrayed the vivacity of a taste that was everywhere else conquered, to which this single concession had been made out of tolerance for such a weakness, while a spot of red on his necktie was imperceptible, like a liberty which one dares not take.

"How are you? Let me introduce my nephew, the Baron de Guermantes," Mme. de Villeparisis greeted me, while the stranger without looking at me, muttering a vague "Charmed!" which he followed with a "H'm, h'm, h'm" to give his affability an air of having been forced, and doubling back his little finger, forefinger and thumb, held out to me his middle and ring fingers, the latter bare of any ring, which I clasped through his suede glove; then, without lifting his eyes to my face, he turned towards Mme. de Villeparisis.

"Good gracious; I shall be forgetting my own name next!" she exclaimed. "Here am I calling you Baron de Guermantes. Let me introduce the Baron de Charlus. After all, it's not a very serious mistake,"she went on, "for you're a thorough Guermantes whatever else you are."

By this time my grandmother had reappeared, and we all set out together. Saint-Loup's uncle declined to honour me not only with a word, with so much as a look, even, in my direction. If he stared strangers out of countenance (and during this short excursion he two or three times hurled his terrible and searching scrutiny like a sounding lead at insignificant people of obviously humble extraction who happened to pass), to make up for that he never for a moment, if I was to judge by myself, looked at the people whom he did know, just as a detective on special duty might except his personal friends from his professional vigilance. Leaving them, my grandmother, Mme. de Villeparisis and him to talk to one another, I fell behind with Saint-Loup.

"Tell me, am I right in thinking I heard Mme.de Villeparisis say just now to your uncle that he was a Guermantes?" "Of course he is; Palamède de Guermantes." "Not the same Guermantes who have a place near Combray, and claim descent from Geneviève de Brabant.?" "Most certainly, my uncle, who is the very last word in heraldry and all that sort of thing, would tell you that our 'cry', our war-cry, that is to say, which was changed afterwards to 'Passavant' was originally 'Combraysis' ", he said, smiling so as not to appear to be priding himself on this prerogative of a "cry", which only the semi-royal houses, the great chiefs of feudal bands enjoyed. "It's his brother who has the place now."

And so she was indeed related, and quite closely, to the Guermantes, this Mme. de Villeparisis who had so long been for me the lady who had given me a duck filled with chocolates, when I was little, more remote then from the Guermantes way than if she had been shut up somewhere on the Méséglise, less brilliant, less highly placed by me than was the Combray optician, and who now suddenly went through one of those fantastic rises in value, parallel to the depreciations, no less unforeseen, of other objects in our possession, which—rise and fall alike—introduce in our youth and in those periods of our life in which a trace of youth persists, changes as numerous as the Metamorphoses of Ovid.

"Haven't they got, down there, the busts of all the old lords of Guermantes?"

"Yes; and a lovely sight they are!" Saint-Loup was ironical, "Between you and me, I look on all that sort of thing as rather a joke. But they have got at Guermantes, what is a little more interesting, and that is quite a touching portrait of my aunt by Carrière. It's as fine as Whistler or Velasquez;" went on Saint-Loup, who in his neophyte zeal was not always very exact about degrees of greatness. "There are also some moving pictures by Gustave Moreau. My aunt is the niece of your friend Mme. de Villeparisis; she was brought up by her, and married her cousin, who was a nephew, too, of my aunt Villeparisis, the present Duc de Guermantes."

"Then who is this uncle?"

"He bears the title of Baron de Charlus. Properly speaking, when my great-uncle died, my uncle Palamède ought to have taken the title of Prince des Laumes, which his brother used before he became Duc de Guermantes, for in that family they change their names as you'd change your shirt. But my uncle has peculiar ideas about all that sort of thing. And as he feels that people are rather apt to overdo the Italian Prince and Grandee of Spain business nowadays, though he had half-a-dozen titles of 'Prince' to choose from, he has remained Baron de Charlus, as a protest, and with an apparent simplicity which really covers a good deal of pride. "In these days", he says, "everybody is Prince something-or-other; one really must have a title that will distinguish one, I shall call myself Prince when I wish to travel incognito." According to him there is no older title than the Charlus barony; to prove to you that it is earlier than the Montmorency title, though they used to claim, quite wrongly, to be the premier barons of

France when they were only premier in the Ile-de-France, where their fief was, my uncle will explain to you for hours on end and enjoy doing it, because, although he's a most intelligent man, really gifted, he regards that sort of thing as quite a live topic of conversation," Saint-Loup smiled again. "But as I am not like him, you mustn't ask me to talk pedigrees; I know nothing more deadly, more perishing; really, life is not long enough."

I now recognised in the hard look which had made me turn round that morning outside the Casino the same that I had seen fixed on me at Tansonville, at the moment when Mme. Swann called Gilberte away.

"But, I say, all those mistresses that, you told me, your uncle M. de Charlus had had, wasn't Mme. Swann one of them?" "Good lord, no!" That is to say, my uncle's a great friend of Swann, and has always stood up for him. But no one has ever suggested that he was his wife's lover. You would make a great sensation in Paris society if people thought you believed that."

I dared not reply that it would have caused an even greater sensation in Combray society if people had thought that I did not believe it.

Outside the Grand Hotel the three Guermantes left us; they were going to luncheon with the Princesse de Luxembourg. While my grandmother was saying good-bye to Mme. de Villeparisis and Saint-Loup to my grandmother, M. de Charlus who, so far, had not uttered a word to me, drew back a little way from the group and, when he reached my side, said "I shall be taking tea this evening after dinner in my aunt Villeparisis's room; I hope that you will give me the pleasure of seeing you there, and your grandmother." With which he rejoined the Marquise.

I had supposed that in thus inviting us to take tea with his aunt, whom I never doubted that he would have warned that we were coming, M. de Charlus wished to make amends for the impoliteness which he had shown me during our walk that morning. But when, on our entering Mme. de Villeparisis's room, I attempted to greet her nephew, even although I walked right round him, while in shrill accents he was telling a somewhat spiteful story about one of his relatives, I did not succeed in catching his eye; I decided to say "Good evening" to him, and fairly loud, to warn him of my presence; but I realised that he had observed it, for before ever a word had passed my lips, just as I began to bow to him, I saw his two fingers stretched out for me to shake without his having turned to look at me or paused in his story. He had evidently seen me, without letting it appear that he had, and I noticed then that his eyes, which were never fixed on the person to whom he was speaking, strayed perpetually in all directions, like those of certain animals when they are frightened, or those of street hawkers who, while they are bawling their patter and displaying their illicit merchandise, keep a sharp look-out, though without turning their heads, on the different points of the horizon, from any of which may appear, suddenly, the police. At the same time I was a little surprised to find that Mme. de Villeparisis, while glad to see us, did not seem to have been expecting us, and I was still more surprised to hear M. de Charlus say to my grandmother: "Ah ! that was a capital idea of yours to come and pay us a visit; charming of them, is it not, my dear aunt?" No doubt he had noticed his aunt's surprise at our entry and thought, as a man accustomed to set the tone, to strike the right note, that it would be enough to transform that surprise into joy were he to show that he himself felt it, that it was indeed the feeling which our arrival there ought to have prompted. In which he calculated wisely; for Mme. de Villeparisis, who had a high opinion of her nephew and knew how difficult it was to please him, appeared suddenly to have found new attractions in my grandmother and continued to make much of her. But I failed to understand how M. de Charlus could, in the space of a few hours, have forgotten the invitation—so curt but apparently so intentional, so premeditated—which he had addressed to me that same morning, or why he called a "capital idea" on my grandmother's part an idea that had been entirely his own. With a scruple of accuracy which I retained until I had reached the age at which I realised that it is not by asking him questions that one learns the truth of what another man has had in his mind, and that the risk of a misunderstanding which will probably pass unobserved is less than that which may come from a purblind insistence: "But, sir," I reminded him, "you remember, surely, that it was you who asked me if we would come in this evening?" Not a sound, not a movement betrayed that M. de Charlus had so much as heard my question. Seeing which I repeated it, like a diplomat, or like young men after a misunderstanding who endeavour, with untiring and unrewarded zeal, to obtain an explanation which their adversary is determined not to give them. Still M. de Charlus answered me not a word. I seemed to see hovering upon his lips the smile of those who from a great height pass judgment on the characters and breeding of their inferiors.

Meanwhile my grandmother had been making signs to me to go up to bed, in spite of the urgent appeals of Saint-Loup who, to my utter confusion, had alluded in front of M. de Charlus to the depression that used often to come upon me at night before I went to sleep, which his uncle must regard as betokening a sad want of virility. I lingered a few moments still; then went upstairs, and was greatly surprised when, a little later, having heard a knock at my bedroom door and asked who was there, I heard the voice of M. de Charlus saying dryly: "It is Charlus. May I come in, sir ? Sir," he began again in the same tone as soon as he had shut the door, "my nephew was saying just now that you were apt to be worried at night before going to sleep, and also that you were an admirer of Bergotte's books. As I had one here in my luggage which you probably do not know, I have brought it to help you to while away these moments in which you are not comfortable."

I thanked M. de Charlus with some warmth and told him that, on the contrary, I had been afraid that what Saint-Loup had said to him about my discomfort when night came would have made me appear in his eyes more stupid even than I was.

"No; why?" he answered, in a gentler voice. "You have not, perhaps, any personal merit; so few of us have! But for a time at least you have youth, and that is always a charm. Besides, sir, the greatest folly of all is to laugh at or to condemn in others what one does not happen oneself to feel. I love the night, and you tell me that you are afraid of it. I love the scent of roses, and I have a friend whom it throws into a fever. Do you suppose that I think, for that reason, that he is inferior to me? I try to understand everything and I take care to condemn nothing. After all, you must not be too sorry for yourself; I do not say that these moods of depression are not painful, I know that one can be made to suffer by things which the world would not understand. But at least you have placed your affection wisely, in your grandmother. You see a great deal of her. And besides, that is a legitimate affection, I mean one that is repaid. There are so many of which one cannot say that."

He began walking up and down the room, looking at one thing, taking up another. I had the impression that he had something to tell me, and could not find the right words to express it. "I have another volume of Bergotte here; I will fetch it for you," he went on, and rang the bell. Presently a page came. "Go and find me your head waiter. He is the only person here who is capable of obeying an order intelligently," said M. de Charlus stiffly. "Monsieur Aimé, sir?" asked the page. "I cannot tell you his name; yes, I remember now, I did hear him called Aimé. Run along, I am in a hurry." "He won't be a minute, sir, I saw him downstairs just now," said the page, anxious to appear efficient. There was an interval of silence. The page returned. "Sir, M. Aimé has gone to bed. But I can take your message." "No, you have only to get him out of bed." "But I can't do that, sir;' he doesn't sleep here." "Then you can leave us alone." "But, sir," I said when the page had gone, "you are too kind; one volume of Bergotte will be quite enough." "That is just what I was thinking." M. de Charlus walked up and down the room. Several minutes passed in this way, then after a prolonged hesitation, and several false starts, he swung sharply round and, his voice once more stinging, flung at me : "Good night, sir!" and left the room. After all the lofty sentiments which I had heard him express that evening, next day, which was the day of his departure, on the beach, before noon, when I was on my way down to bathe, and M. de Charlus had come across to tell me that my grandmother was waiting for me to join her as soon as I left the water, I was greatly surprised to hear him say, pinching my neck as he spoke, with a familiarity and a laugh that were frankly vulgar "But he doesn't give a damn for his old grandmother, does he, eh ? Little rascal!"

"What, sir I adore her!"

"Sir," he said, stepping back a pace, and with a glacial air, "you are still young; you should profit by your youth to learn two things; first, to refrain from expressing sentiments that are too natural not to be taken for granted; and secondly not to dash into speech to reply to things that are said to you before you have penetrated their meaning. If you had taken this precaution a moment ago you would have saved yourself the appearance of speaking at cross-purposes like a deaf man, thereby adding a second absurdity to that of having anchors embroidered on your bathing-dress. I have lent you a book by Bergotte which I require. See that it is brought to me within the next hour by that head waiter with the silly and inappropriate name, who, I suppose, is not in bed at this time of day. You make me see that I was premature in speaking to you last night of the charms of youth; I should have done you a better service had I pointed out to you its thoughtlessness, its inconsequence, and its want of comprehension. I hope, sir, that this little douche will be no less salutary to you than your bathe. But don't let me keep you standing: you may catch cold. Good day, sir."

No doubt he was sorry afterwards for this speech, for some time later I received—in a morocco binding on the front of which was inlaid a panel of tooled leather representing in demi-relief a spray of forget-me-not —the book which he had lent me, and I had sent back to him, not by Aimé who was apparently "off duty" , but by the lift-boy.

Having a strong prejudice against the people who frequented it, Saint-Loup went rarely into 'Society' and the contemptuous or hostile attitude which he adopted towards it served to increase, among all his near relatives, the painful impression made by his intimacy with a woman on the stage, a connection which, they declared, would be his ruin, blaming it specially for having bred in him that spirit of denigration, that bad spirit, and for having led him astray, after which it was only a matter of time before he would have dropped out altogether. And so, many easy-going men of the Faubourg Saint-Germain were without compunction when they spoke of Robert's mistress. "Those girls do their job," they would say, they are as good as anybody else. But that one; no thank you ! We cannot forgive her. She has done too much harm to a fellow we were fond of."

Saint-Loup's mistress—as the first monks of the middle ages taught Christendom—had taught him to be kind to animals, for which she had a passion, never moving without her dog, her canaries, her love-birds; Saint-Loup looked after them with motherly devotion and treated as brutes the people who were not good to dumb creatures. On the other hand, an actress, or so-called actress, like this one who was living with him,—whether she were intelligent or not, and as to that I had no knowledge—by making him find the society of fashionable women boring, and look upon having to go out to a party as a painful duty, had saved him from snobbishness and cured him of frivolity. If, thanks to her, his social engagements filled a smaller place in the life of her young lover, at the same time, whereas if he had been simply a drawing-room man, vanity or self-interest would have dictated his choice of friends as rudeness would have characterised his treatment of them, his mistress had taught him to bring nobility and refinement into his friendship. With her feminine instinct, with a keener appreciation in men of certain qualities of sensibility which her lover might perhaps, without her guidance, have misunderstood and laughed at them, she had always been swift to distinguish from among the rest of Saint-Loup's friends the one who had a real affection for him, and to make that one her favourite. She knew how to make him feel grateful to such a friend, show his gratitude, notice what things gave his friend pleasure and what pain.

His mistress had opened his mind to the invisible, had brought a serious element into his life, delicacy into his heart, but all this escaped his sorrowing family who repeated "That creature will be the death of him; meanwhile she's doing what she can to disgrace him." It is true that he had succeeded in getting out of her all the good that she was capable of doing him; and that she now caused him only incessant suffering, for she had taken an intense dislike to him and tormented him in every possible way. She had begun, one fine day, to look upon him as stupid and absurd because the friends that she had among the younger writers and actors had assured her that he was, and she duly repeated what they had said with that passion, that want of reserve which we show whenever we receive from without and adopt as our own opinions or customs of which we previously knew nothing. She readily professed, like her actor friends, that between Saint-Loup and herself there was a great gulf fixed, and not to be crossed, because they were of different races, because she was an intellectual and he, whatever he might pretend, the born enemy of the intellect. This view of him seemed to her profound, and she sought confirmation of it in the most insignificant words, the most trivial actions of her lover. But when the same friends had further convinced her that she was destroying, in company so ill-suited to her, the great hopes which she had, they said, aroused in them, that her lover would leave a mark on her, that by living with him she was spoiling her future as an artist; to her contempt for Saint-Loup was added the same hatred that she would have felt for him if he had insisted upon inoculating her with a deadly germ. She saw him as seldom as possible, at the same time postponing the hour of a definite rupture, which seemed to me a highly improbable event. Saint-Loup made such sacrifices for her that unless she was ravishingly beautiful (but he had always refused to show me her photograph, saying: "For one thing, she's not a beauty, and besides she always takes badly. These are only some snapshots that I took myself with my kodak; they would give you a wrong idea of her.") it would surely be difficult for her to find another man who would consent to anything of the sort.

This dramatic period of their connection, which had now reached its most acute stage, the most cruel for Saint-Loup, for she had forbidden him to remain in Paris, where his presence exasperated her, and had forced him to spend his leave at Balbec, within easy reach of his regiment— had begun one evening at the house of one of Saint-Loup's aunts, on whom he had prevailed to allow his friend to come there, before a large party, to recite some of the speeches from a symbolical play in which she had once appeared in an "advanced" theatre, and for which she had made him share the admiration that she herself professed.

But when she appeared in the room, with a large lily in her hand, and wearing a costume copied from the *Ancilia Domini,* which she had persuaded Saint-Loup was an absolute 'vision of beauty' , her entrance had been greeted, in that assemblage of club men and duchesses, with smiles which the monotonous tone of her chantings, the oddity of certain words and their frequent recurrence had changed into fits of laughter, stifled at first but presently so uncontrollable that the wretched reciter had been unable to go on. Next day Saint-Loup's aunt had been universally censured for having allowed so grotesque an actress to appear in her drawingroom. A well-known duke made no bones about telling her that she had only herself to blame if she found herself criticised. "Damn it all, people really don't come to see 'turns` like that! If the woman had talent even; but she has none and never will have any. 'Pon my soul, Paris is not such a fool as people make out. Society does not consist exclusively of imbeciles. This little lady evidently believed that she was going to take Paris by surprise. But Paris is not so easily surprised as all that, and there are still some things that they can't make us swallow."

As for the actress, she left the house with Saint-Loup, exclaiming "What do you mean by letting me in for those geese, those uneducated bitches, those dirty corner-boys? I don't mind telling, you, there wasn't a man in the room who didn't make eyes at me or squeeze my foot, and it was because I wouldn't look at them that they were out for revenge."

Words which had changed Robert's antipathy for people in society into a horror that was at once deep and distressing, and was provoked in him most of all by those who least deserved it, devoted kinsmen who, on behalf of the family, had sought to persuade Saint-Loup's lady to break with him, a move which she represented to him as inspired by their passion for her. Robert, although he had at once ceased to see them, used to imagine when he was parted from his mistress as he was now, that they or others like them were profiting by his absence to return to the charge and had possibly prevailed over her. And when he spoke of the sensualists who were disloyal to their friends, who sought to seduce their friends' wives, tried to make them come to houses of assignation, his whole face would glow with suffering and hatred.

"I would kill them with less compunction than I would kill a dog, which is at least a well-behaved beast, and loyal and faithful. There are men who deserve the guillotine if you like, far more than poor wretches who have been led into crime by poverty and by the cruelty of the rich."

When, some days later, my grandmother told me with a joyful air that Saint-Loup had just been asking her whether, before he left Balbec, she would not like him to take a photograph of her, and when I saw that she had put on her nicest dress on purpose, and was hesitating between several of her best hats, I felt a little annoyed by this childishness, which surprised me coming from her. I even went the length of asking myself whether I had not been mistaken in my grandmother, whether I did not esteem her too highly, whether she was as unconcerned as I had always supposed in the adornment of her person, whether she had not indeed the very weakness that I believed most alien to her temperament, namely coquetry.

Unfortunately, this displeasure that I derived from the prospect of a photographic 'sitting', and more particularly from the satisfaction with which my grandmother appeared to be looking forward to it, I made so apparent that Françoise remarked it and did her best, unintentionally, to increase it by making me a sentimental, gushing speech, by which I refused to appear moved.

"Oh, Master; my poor Madame will be so pleased at having her likeness taken, she is going to wear the hat that her old Françoise has trimmed for her, you must allow her, Master."

I acquired the conviction that I was not cruel in laughing at Françoise's sensibility, by reminding myself that my mother and grandmother, my models in all things, often did the same. But my grandmother, noticing that I seemed cross, said that if this plan of her sitting for her photograph offended me in any way she would give it up. I would not let her; I assured her that I saw no harm in it, and left her to adorn herself, but, thinking that I showed my penetration and strength of mind, I added a few stinging words of sarcasm, intended to neutralise the pleasure which she seemed to find in being photographed, so that if I was obliged to see my grandmother's magnificent hat, I succeeded at least in driving from her face that joyful expression which ought to have made me glad.

SEASCAPE, WITH FRIEZE OF GIRLS

That day, as for some days past, Saint-Loup had been obliged to go to Doncières, where, until his leave finally expired, he would be on duty now until late every afternoon. I was sorry that he was not at Balbec. I had seen alight from carriages and pass, some into the ball-room of the Casino, others into the ice-cream shop, young women who at a distance had seemed to me lovely.

Charming women I seemed to see all round me, because I was too tired, if it was on the beach, too shy if it was in the Casino or at a pastry-cook's, to go anywhere near them. And yet if I was soon to die I should have liked first to know the appearance at close quarters, in reality of the prettiest girls that life had to offer, even although it should be another than myself or no one at all who was to take advantage of the offer. (I did not, in fact, appreciate the desire for possession that underlay my curiosity.) I should have had the courage to enter the ballroom if Saint-Loup had been with me. Left by myself, I was simply hanging about in front of the Grand Hotel until it was time for me to join my grandmother, when, still almost at the far end of the paved 'front' along which they projected in a discordant spot of colour, I saw coming towards me five or six young girls, as different in appearance and manner from all the people whom one was accustomed to see at Balbec as could have been, landed there none knew whence, a flight of gulls which performed with measured steps upon the sands— the dawdlers using their wings to overtake the rest—a movement the purpose of which seems as obscure to the human bathers, whom they do not appear to see, as it is clearly determined in their own birdish minds.

One of these strangers was pushing as she came, with one hand, her bicycle; two others carried golf-clubs ; and their attire generally was in contrast to that of the other girls at Balbec, some of whom, it was true, went in for games; but without adopting any special outfit.

It was the hour at which ladies and gentlemen came out every day for a turn on the 'front', exposed to the merciless fire of the long glasses fastened upon them, as if they had each borne some disfigurement which she felt it her duty to inspect in its minutest details, by the chief magistrate's wife, proudly seated there with her back to the band-stand, in the middle of that dread line of chairs on which presently they too, actors turned critics, would come and establish themselves, to scrutinise in their turn those others who would then be filing past them.

Among all these people, the girls whom I had noticed, with that mastery over their limbs which comes from perfect bodily condition and a sincere contempt for the rest of humanity, were advancing straight ahead, without hesitation or stiffness, performing exactly the movements that they wished to perform, each of their members in full independence of all the rest, the greater part of their bodies preserving that immobility which is so noticeable in a good waltzer. They were now quite near me. Although each was a type absolutely different from the others, they all had beauty; but to tell the truth I had seen them for so short a time, and without venturing to look them straight in the face, that I had not yet individualised any of them. Save one, whom her straight nose, her dark complexion set her out from the rest, like (in a renaissance picture of the Epiphany) a king of Arab cast; the rest were known to me, one by a pair of eyes hard, set and mocking; another by cheeks in which the pink had that coppery tint which makes one think of geraniums; and even of these points I had not yet indissolubly attached any one to one of these girls rather than to another; and when I saw emerge a pallid oval, black eyes, green eyes, I knew not if these were the same that had already charmed me a moment ago, I could not bring them home to any one girl whom I might thereby have set apart from the rest and so identified. And this want, in my vision, of the demarcations which I should presently establish between them sent flooding over the group a wave of harmony, the continuous transfusion of a beauty fluid, collective and mobile.

Just as if, in the heart of their band, which progressed along the 'front' like a luminous comet, they had decided that the surrounding crowd was composed of creatures of another race whose sufferings even could not awaken in them any sense of fellowship, they appeared not to see them, forced those who had stopped to talk to step aside, as though from the path of a machine that had been set going by itself, so that it was no good waiting for it to get out of their way, their utmost sign of consciousness being when, if some old gentleman of whom they did not admit the existence and thrust from them the contact, had fled with a frightened or furious, but a headlong or ludicrous motion, they looked at one another and smiled. They had, for whatever did not form part of their group, no affectation of contempt; their genuine contempt was sufficient. But they could not set eyes on an obstacle without amusing themselves by crossing it, either in a running jump or with both feet together, because they were all filled to the brim, exuberant with that youth which we need so urgently to spend that even when we are unhappy or unwell, obedient rather to the necessities of our age than to the mood of the day, we can never pass anything that can be jumped over or slid down without indulging ourselves conscientiously, interrupting, interspersing our slow progress—as Chopin his most melancholy phrase—with graceful deviations in which caprice is blended with virtuosity.

The wife of an elderly banker, after hesitating between various possible exposures for her husband, had settled him on a folding chair, facing the 'front', sheltered from wind and sun by the bandstand. Having seen him comfortably installed there, she had gone to buy a newspaper which she would read aloud to him, to distract him, one of her little absences which she never prolonged for more than five minutes, which seemed long enough to him but which she repeated at frequent intervals so that this old husband on whom she lavished an attention that she took care to conceal, should have the impression that he was still quite alive and like other people and was in no need of protection. The platform of the band-stand provided, above his head, a natural and tempting springboard, across which, without a moment's hesitation, the eldest of the little band began to run; she jumped over the terrified old man; whose yachting cap was brushed by the nimble feet, to the great delight of the other girls, especially of a pair of green eyes in a 'dashing' face, which expressed, for that bold act, an admiration and a merriment in which I seemed to discern a trace of timidity, a shamefaced and blustering timidity which did not exist in the others. "Oh, the poor old man; he makes me sick; he looks half dead;" said a girl with a croaking voice, but with more sarcasm than sympathy. They walked on a little way, then stopped for a moment in the middle of the road, with no thought whether they were impeding the passage of other people, and held a council, a solid body of irregular shape, compact, unusual and shrill, like birds that gather on the ground at the moment of flight; then they resumed their leisurely stroll along the 'front', against a background of sea.

By this time their charming features had ceased to be indistinct and impersonal. I had dealt them like cards into so many heaps to compose (failing their names, of which I was still ignorant) the big one who had jumped over the old banker; the little one who stood out against the horizon of sea with her plump and rosy cheeks, her green eyes; the one with the straight nose and dark complexion, in such contrast to all the rest, another, with a white face like an egg on which a tiny nose described an arc of a circle like a chicken's beak yet another, wearing a hooded cape (which gave her so poverty-stricken an appearance, and so contradicted the smartness of the figure beneath, that the explanation which suggested itself was that this girl must have parents of high position who valued their self-esteem so far above the visitors to Balbec and the sartorial elegance of their own children that it was a matter of the utmost indifference to them that their daughter should stroll on the 'front' dressed in a way which humbler people would have considered too modest); a girl with brilliant, laughing eyes and plump, colourless cheeks, a black polo-cap pulled down over her face, who was pushing a bicycle with so exaggerated a movement of her hips, with an air borne out by her language, which was so typically of the gutter and was being shouted so loud, when I passed her (although among her expressions I caught that irritating "live my own life") that, abandoning the hypothesis which her friend's hooded cape had made me construct, I concluded instead that all these girls belonged to the population which frequents the racing-tracks, and must be the very juvenile mistresses of professional bicyclists. In any event, in none of my suppositions was there any possibility of their being virtuous. At first sight—in the way in which they looked at one another and smiled, in the insistent stare of the one with the dull cheeks—I had grasped that they were not. Besides, my grandmother had always watched over me with a delicacy too timorous for me not to believe that the sum total of the things one ought not to do was indivisible or that girls who were lacking in respect for their elders would suddenly be stopped short by scruples when there were pleasures at stake more tempting than that of jumping over an octogenarian.

I asked myself whether the girls I had just seen lived at Balbec, and who they could be. When our desire is thus concentrated upon a little tribe of humanity which it singles out from the rest, everything that can be associated with that tribe becomes a spring of emotion and then of reflection. I had heard a lady say on the 'front' "She is a friend of the little Simonet girl" with that self-important air of inside knowledge, as who should say: "He is the inseparable companion of young La Rochefoucauld." And immediately she had detected on the face of the person to whom she gave this information a curiosity to see more of the favoured person who was "a friend of the little Simonet"

I do not know why I said to myself from the first that the name Simonet must be that of one of the band of girls; from that moment I never ceased to ask myself how I could get to know the Simonet family, get to know them, moreover, through people whom they considered superior to themselves (which ought not to be difficult if the girls were only common little 'bounders') so that they might not form a disdainful idea of me. The little Simonet must be the prettiest of them all—she who, I felt moreover, might yet become my mistress, for she was the only one who, two or three times half-turning her head, had appeared to take cognisance of my fixed stare. I asked the lift-boy whether he knew of any people at Balbec called Simonet. Not liking to admit that there was anything which he did not know, he replied that he seemed to have heard the name somewhere. As we reached the highest landing I told him to have the latest lists of visitors sent up to me.

There was a knock at my door; it was Aimé who had come upstairs in person with the latest lists of visitors. It was not without a slight throb of the heart that on the first page of the list I caught sight of the words "Simonet and family." I had in me a store of old dream-memories which dated from my childhood, and in which all the tenderness (tenderness that existed in my heart, but, when my heart felt it, was not distinguishable from anything else) was wafted to me by a person as different as possible from myself. This person, once again I fashioned her, utilising for the purpose the name Simonet and the memory of the harmony that had reigned between the young bodies which I had seen displaying themselves on the beach, in a sportive procession worthy of Greek art or of Giotto. I knew not which of these girls was Mlle. Simonet, if indeed any of them were so named, but I did know that I was loved by Mlle. Simonet and that I was going, with Saint-Loup's help, to attempt to know her. Unfortunately, having, on that condition only, obtained an extension of his leave, he was obliged to report for duty every day at Doncières but to make him forsake his military duty I had felt that I might count, more even than on his friendship for myself, on that same curiosity, as a human naturalist, which I myself had so often felt—even without having seen the person mentioned, and simply on hearing someone say that there was a pretty cashier at a fruiterer's—to acquaint myself with a new variety of feminine beauty. But that curiosity I had been wrong in hoping to excite in Saint-Loup by speaking to him of my band of girls. For it had been and would long remain paralysed in him by his love for that actress whose lover he was. And even if he had felt it lightly stirring him he would have repressed it, from an almost superstitious belief that on his own fidelity might depend that of his mistress. And so it was without any promise from him that he would take an active interest in my girls that we started out to dine at Rivebelle.

Saint-Loup and I entered the dining-room to the sound of some warlike march played by the gypsies, we advanced between two rows of tables laid for dinner as along an easy path of glory, and, feeling a happy glow imparted to our bodies by the rhythms of the orchestra which rendered us its military honours, gave us this unmerited triumph, we concealed it beneath a grave and frozen mien, beneath a languid, casual gait, so as not to be like those music-hall 'mashers' who, having wedded a ribald verse to a patriotic air, come running on to the stage with the martial countenance of a victorious general.

From that moment I was a new man, who was no longer my grandmother's grandson and would remember her only when it was time to get up and go, but the brother, for the time being, of the waiters who were going to bring us our dinner.

The dose of beer—all the more, that of champagne— which at Balbec I should not have ventured to take in a week, albeit to my calm and lucid consciousness the flavour of those beverages represented a pleasure clearly appreciable, since it was also one that could easily be sacrificed, I now imbibed at a sitting, adding to it a few drops of port wine, too much distracted to be able to taste it, and I gave the violinist who had just been playing the two louis which I had been saving up for the last month with a view to buying something, I could not remember what. Several of the waiters, set going among the tables, were flying along at full speed, each carrying on his outstretched palms a dish which it seemed to be the object of this kind of race not to let fall. And in fact the chocolate *soufflés* arrived at their destination unspilled, the potatoes *à l'anglaise,* in spite of the pace which ought to have sent them flying, came arranged as at the start round the Pauilhac lamb. I noticed one of these servants, very tall, plumed with superb black locks, his face dyed in a tint that suggested rather certain species of rare birds than a human being, who, running without pause (and, one would have said, without purpose) from one end of the room to the other, made me think of one of those macaws which fill the big aviaries in zoological gardens with their gorgeous colouring and incomprehensible agitation.

I had already drunk a good deal of port wine, and if I now asked for more, it was not so much with a view to the comfort which the additional glasses would bring me as an effect of the comfort produced by the glasses that had gone before.

I knew none of the women who were at Rivebelle and, because they formed a part of my intoxication just as its reflections form part of a mirror, appeared to me now a thousand times more to be desired than the less and less existent Mlle. Simonet. One of them, young, fair, by herself, with a sad expression on a face framed, in a straw hat trimmed with field-flowers, gazed at me for a moment with a dreamy air and struck me as being attractive. Then it was the turn of another, and of a third; finally of a dark one with glowing cheeks. Almost all of them were known, if not to myself, to Saint-Loup.

He had, in fact, before he made the acquaintance of his present mistress, lived so much in the restricted world of amorous adventure that all the women who would be dining on these evenings at Rivebelle, where many of them had appeared quite by chance, having come to the coast some to join their lovers, others in the hope of finding fresh lovers there, there was scarcely one that he did not know from, having spent—or if not he, one or other of his friends—at least one night in their company. He did not bow to them if they were with men, and they, albeit they looked more at him than at anyone else, for the indifference which he was known to feel towards every woman who was not his actress gave him in their eyes an exceptional interest, appeared not to know him. But you could hear them whispering: "That's young Saint-Loup. It seems he's still quite gone on that girl of his. Got it bad, he has. What a dear boy ! I think he's just wonderful; and what style. Some girls do have all the luck, don't they? And he's so nice in every way. I saw a lot of him when I was with d'Orléans. They were quite inseparable, those two. He was going the pace, that time. But he's given it all up now, she can't complain. She's had a good run of luck, that she can say. And I ask you, what in the world can he see in her? He must be a bit of a chump, when all's said and done. She's got feet like boats, whiskers like an American, and her undies are filthy. I can tell you, a little shop girl would be ashamed to be seen in her knickers. Do just look at his eyes a moment; you would jump into the fire for a man like that. Hush, don't say a word; he's seen me, look, he's smiling. Oh, he remembers me all right. Just you mention my name to him, and see what he says!" Between these girls and him I surprised a glance of mutual understanding. On our way back to Balbec, of those of the fair strangers to whom he had introduced me I would repeat to myself without a moment's interruption, and yet almost unconsciously: "What a delightful woman!" as one chimes in with the refrain of a song. I admit that these words were prompted rather by the state of my nerves than by any lasting judgment. It was nevertheless true that if I had had a thousand francs on me and if there had still been a jeweller's shop open at that hour, I should have bought the lady a ring.

Presently Saint- Loup's visit drew to an end. I had not seen that party of girls again on the beach. He was too little at Balbec in the afternoons to have time to bother about them, or to attempt, in my interest, to make their acquaintance. In the evenings he was more free, and continued to take me constantly to Rivebelle. There are, in those restaurants, as there are in public gardens and railway trains, people embodied in a quite ordinary appearance, whose name astonishes us when, having happened to ask it, we discover that this is not the mere inoffensive stranger whom we supposed, but nothing less than the Minister or Duke of whom we have so often heard. Two or three times already, in the Rivebelle restaurant, we had—Saint-Loup and I—seen come in and sit down at a table when everyone else was getting ready to go, a man of large stature, very muscular, with regular features and a grizzled beard, gazing, with concentrated attention, into the empty air. One evening, on our asking the landlord who was this obscure, solitary and belated diner, "What!" he exclaimed, "do you mean to say you don't know the famous painter Elstir?" Swann had once mentioned his name to me, I had entirely forgotten in what connection; but the omission of a particular memory, like that of part of a sentence when we are reading, leads sometimes not to uncertainty but to a birth of certainty that is premature. "He is a friend of Swann, a very well known artist, extremely good," I told Saint-Loup. Whereupon there passed over us both, like a wave of emotion, the thought that Elstir was a great artist, a celebrated man, and that, confounding us with the rest of the diners, he had no suspicion of the ecstasy into which we were thrown by the idea of his talent. Doubtless, his unconsciousness of our admiration and of our acquaintance with Swann would not have troubled us had we not been at the seaside. But since we were still at an age when enthusiasm cannot keep silence, and had been transported into a life in which not to be known is unendurable, we wrote a letter, signed with both our names, in which we revealed to Elstir in the two diners seated within a few feet of him, two passionate admirers of his talent, two friends of his great friend Swann, and asked to be allowed to pay our homage to him in person. A waiter undertook to convey this missive to the celebrity.

A celebrity Elstir was, perhaps, not yet at this period quite to the extent claimed by the landlord, though he was to reach the height of his fame within a very few years. But he had been one of the first to frequent this restaurant when it was still only a sort of farmhouse, and had brought to it a whole colony of artists (who had all, as it happened, migrated elsewhere as soon as the farm-yard in which they used to feed in the open air, under a lean-to roof, had become a fashionable centre); Elstir himself had returned to Rivebelle this evening only on account of a temporary absence of his wife, from the house which he had taken in the neighbourhood. But great talent, even when its existence is not yet recognised, will inevitably provoke certain phenomena of admiration, such as the landlord had managed to detect in the questions asked by more than one English lady visitor, athirst for information as to the life led by Elstir, or in the number of letters that he received from abroad. Then the landlord had further remarked that Elstir did not like to be disturbed when he was working, that he would rise in the middle of the night and take a little model down to the water's edge to pose for him, nude, if the moon was shining; and had told himself that so much labour was not in vain, nor the admiration of the tourists unjustified when he had, in one of Elstir's pictures, recognised a wooden cross which stood by the roadside as you came into Rivebelle.

"It's all right!" he would repeat with stupefaction, "there are all the four beams!" Oh, he does take a lot of trouble.

And he did not know whether a little *Sunrise over the Sea* which Elstir had given him might not be worth a fortune.

We watched Elstir read our letter, put it in his pocket, finish his dinner, begin to ask for his things, get up to go; and we were so convinced that we had shocked him by our overture that we would now have hoped, (as keenly as at first we had dreaded) to make our escape without his noticing us. We did not bear in mind for a single instant a consideration which should, nevertheless, have seemed to us most important, namely that our enthusiasm for Elstir, on the sincerity of which we should not have allowed the least doubt to be cast, which we could indeed have supported with the evidence of our breathing arrested by expectancy, our desire to do no matter what that was difficult or heroic for the great man, was not, as we imagined it to be, admiration, since neither of us had ever seen anything that he had painted; our feeling might have as its object the hollow idea of a 'great artist', but not a body of work which was unknown to us. It was, at the most, admiration in the abstract, the nervous envelope, the sentimental structure, of an admiration, without content, that is to say a thing as indissolubly attached to boyhood as are certain organs which have ceased to exist in the adult man; we were still boys. Elstir meanwhile was reaching the door when suddenly he turned and came towards us. I was transported by a delicious thrill of terror such as I could not have felt a few years later, because, while age diminishes our capacity, familiarity with the world has meanwhile destroyed in us any inclination to provoke such strange encounters, to feel that kind of emotion.

In the course of the few words that Elstir had come back to say to us, sitting down at our table, he never gave any answer on the several occasions on which I spoke to him of Swann. I began to think that he did not know him. He asked me, nevertheless, to come and see him at his Balbec studio, an invitation which he did not extend to Saint-Loup, and which I had earned (as I might not, perhaps, from Swann's recommendation, had Elstir been intimate with him, for the part played by disinterested motives is greater than we are inclined to think in people's lives) by a few words which made him think that I was devoted to the arts. He lavished on me a friendliness which was as far above that of Saint-Loup as that was above the affability of a mere tradesman. Compared with that of a great artist, the friendliness of a great gentleman, charming as it may be, has the effect of an actor's playing a part, of being feigned. Saint-Loup sought to please; Elstir loved to give, to give himself. Everything that he possessed, ideas, work, and the rest which he counted for far less, he would have given gladly to anyone who could understand him. But, failing society that was endurable, he lived in an isolation, with a savagery which fashionable people called pose and ill-breeding, public authorities a recalcitrant spirit, his neighbours madness, his family selfishness and pride. Elstir did not stay long talking to us. I made up my mind that I would go to his studio during the next few days, but on the following afternoon, when I had accompanied my grandmother right to the point at which the 'front' ended, near the cliffs of Canapville, on our way back, at the foot of one of the little streets which ran down at right angles to the beach, we came upon a girl who, with lowered head like an animal that is being driven reluctant to its stall, and carrying golf-clubs, was walking in front of a person in authority, in all probability her or her friends 'Miss', who suggested a portrait of Jeffreys by Hogarth, with a face as red as if her favourite beverage were gin rather than tea, on which a dried smear of tobacco at the corner of her mouth prolonged the curve of a moustache that was grizzled but abundant. The girl who preceded her was like that one of the little band who, beneath a black polo-cap, had shown in an inexpressive chubby face, a pair of laughing eyes. Now, the girl who was now passing me had also a black polo-cap, but she struck me as being even prettier than the other, the line of her nose was straighter, the curve of nostril at its base fuller and more fleshy. Besides, the other had seemed a proud, pale girl, this one a child well-disciplined and of rosy complexion. And yet, as she was pushing a bicycle just like the other's, and was wearing the same reindeer gloves, I concluded that the differences arose perhaps from the angle and circumstances in which I now saw her, for it was hardly likely that there could be at Balbec a second girl, with a face that, when all was said, was so similar and with the same details in her accoutrements. She cast a rapid glance in my direction; for the next few days, when I saw the little band again on the beach, and indeed long afterwards when I knew all the girls who composed it, I could never be absolutely certain that any of them—even she who among them all was most like her, the girl with the bicycle—was indeed the one that I had seen that evening at the end of the 'front', where a street ran down to the beach, a girl who differed hardly at all, but was still just perceptibly different from her whom I had noticed in the procession..

My grandmother, who had been told of my meeting with Elstir, and rejoiced at the thought of all the intellectual profit that I might derive from his friendship, considered it absurd and none too polite of me not to have gone yet to pay him a visit. But I could think only of the little band, and being uncertain of the hour at which the girls would be passing along the front, I dared not absent myself. My grandmother was astonished, too, at the smartness of my attire, for I had suddenly remembered suits which had been lying all this time at the bottom of my trunk. I put on a different one every day, and had even written to Paris ordering new hats and neckties.

I seized every pretext for going down to the beach at the hours when I hoped to succeed in finding them there. Having caught sight of them once while we were at luncheon, I now invariably came in late for it, waiting interminably upon the 'front' for them to pass; devoting all the short time that I did spend in the dining-room to interrogating with my eyes its azure wall of glass; rising long before the dessert, so as not to miss them should they have gone out at a different hour, and chafing with irritation at my grandmother, when, with unwitting malevolence, she made me stay with her past the hour that seemed to me propitious.

I was in love with none of them, loving them all, and yet the possibility of meeting them was in my daily life the sole element of delight, alone made to burgeon in me those high hopes by which every obstacle is surmounted, hopes ending often in fury if I had not seen them. For the moment, these girls eclipsed my grandmother in my affection; the longest journey would at once have seemed attractive to me had it been to a place in which they might be found. It was to them that my thoughts comfortably clung when I supposed myself to be thinking of something else or of nothing. But when, even without knowing it, I thought of them, they, more unconsciously still, were for me the mountainous blue undulations of the sea, a troop seen passing in outline against the waves. Our most intensive love for a person is always the love, really, of something else as well.

Meanwhile my grandmother was showing, because now I was keenly interested in golf and lawn-tennis and was letting slip an opportunity of seeing at work and hearing talk an artist whom she knew to be one of the greatest of his time, a disapproval which seemed to me to be based on somewhat narrow views. I had guessed long ago in the Champs-Elysées, and had since established to my own satisfaction, that when we are in love with a woman we simply project into her a state of our own soul, that the important thing is, therefore, not the worth of the woman but the depth of the state; and that the emotions which a young girl of no kind of distinction arouses in us can enable us to bring to the surface of our consciousness some of the most intimate parts of our being, more personal, more remote, more essential than would be reached by the pleasure that we derive from the conversation of a great man or even from the admiring contemplation of his work.

I was to end by complying with my grandmother's wishes, all the more reluctantly in that Elstir lived at some distance from the 'front' in one of the newest of Balbec's avenues; The heat of the day obliged me to take the tramway which passed along the Rue de la Plage, and I made an effort (so as still to believe that I was in the ancient realm of the Cimmerians, in the country it might be, of King Mark, or upon the site of the Forest of Broceliande) not to see the gimcrack splendour of the buildings that extended on either hand, among which Elstir's villa was perhaps the most sumptuously hideous, in spite of which he had taken it, because, of all that there were to be had at Balbec, it was the only one that provided him with a really big studio.

It was also with averted eyes that I crossed the garden, which had a lawn—in miniature, like any little suburban villa round Paris—a statuette of an amorous gardener; glass balls in which one saw one's distorted reflexion, beds of begonias and a little arbour, beneath which rocking chairs were drawn up round an iron table. But after all these preliminaries hall-marked with philistine ugliness, I took no notice of the chocolate mouldings on the plinths once I was in the studio; I felt perfectly happy, for, with the help of all the sketches and studies that surrounded me, I foresaw the possibility of raising myself to a poetical understanding, rich in delights, of many forms which I had not, hitherto, isolated from the general spectacle of reality. And Elstir's studio appeared to me as the laboratory of a sort of new creation of the world in which, from the chaos that is all the things we see, he had extracted, by painting them on various rectangles of canvas that were hung everywhere about the room, here a wave of the sea crushing angrily, on the sand its lilac foam, there a young man in a suit of white linen, leaning upon the rail of a vessel. His jacket and the spattering wave had acquired fresh dignity from the fact that they continued to exist, even although they were deprived of those qualities in which they might be supposed to consist, the wave being no longer able to splash nor the jacket to clothe anyone.

At the moment at which I entered, the creator was just finishing, with the brush which he had in his hand, the form of the sun at its setting. The shutters were closed almost everywhere round the studio, which was fairly cool and, except in one place where daylight laid against the wall its brilliant but fleeting decoration, dark; there was open only one little rectangular window embowered in honeysuckle, which, over a strip of garden, gave on an avenue; so that the atmosphere of the greater part of the studio was dusky, transparent and compact in the mass, but liquid and sparkling at the rifts where the golden clasp of sunlight banded it, like a lump of rock crystal of which one surface, already cut and polished, here and there, gleams like a mirror with iridescent rays. While Elstir, at my request, went on painting, I wandered about in the half-light, stopping to examine first one picture, then another.

Most of those that covered the walls were not what I should chiefly have liked to see of his work, paintings in what an English art journal, which lay about on the reading-room table in the Grand Hotel, called his first and second manners, the mythological manner and the manner in which he showed signs of Japanese influence, both admirably exemplified, the article said, in the collection of Mme. de Guermantes. Naturally enough, what he had in his studio were almost all seascapes done here, at Balbec.

The effort made by Elstir to strip himself, when face to face with reality, of every intellectual concept, was all the more admirable in that this man who, before sitting down to paint, made himself deliberately ignorant, forgot, in his honesty of purpose, everything that he knew, since what one knows ceases to exist by itself, had in reality an exceptionally cultivated mind. When I confessed to him the disappointment that I had felt upon seeing the porch at Balbec "What!" he had exclaimed, "you were disappointed by the porch! Why, it's the finest illustrated Bible that the people have ever had. That Virgin, and all the bas-reliefs telling the story of her life, they are the most loving, the most inspired expression of that endless poem of adoration and praise in which the middle ages extolled the glory of the Madonna. If you only knew, side by side with the most scrupulous accuracy in rendering the sacred text, what exquisite ideas the old carver had, what profound thoughts, what delicious poetry! A wonderful idea, that great sheet in which the angels are carrying the body of the Virgin, too sacred for them to venture to touch it with their hands; the angel who is carrying the Virgin's soul, to reunite it with her body; in the meeting of the Virgin with Elizabeth, Elizabeth's gesture when she touches the Virgin's Womb and marvels to feel that it is great with child; and the bandaged arm of the midwife who had refused, unless she touched, to believe the Immaculate Conception; and the linen cloth thrown by the Virgin to Saint Thomas to give him a proof of the Resurrection; that veil, too, which the Virgin tears from her own bosom to cover the nakedness of her Son, from Whose Side the Church receives in a chalice the Wine of the Sacrament, while, on His other side the Synagogue, whose kingdom is at an end, has its eyes bandaged, holds a half-broken sceptre and lets fall, with the crown that is slipping from its head, the tables of the old law; and the husband who, on the Day of Judgment, as he helps his young wife to rise from her grave, lays her hand against his own heart to reassure her, to prove to her that it is indeed beating, is that such a trumpery idea, do you think, so stale and commonplace? And the angel who is taking away the sun and the moon, henceforth useless, since it is written that the Light of the Cross shall be seven times brighter than the light of the firmament; and the one who is dipping his hand in the water of the Child's bath, to see whether it is warm enough; and the one emerging from the clouds to place the crown upon the Virgin's brow, and all the angels who are leaning from the vault of heaven, between the balusters of the New Jerusalem, and throwing up their arms with terror or joy at the sight of the torments of the wicked or the bliss of the elect.or it is all the circles of heaven, a whole gigantic poem full of theology and symbolism that you have before you there. It is fantastic, mad, divine, a thousand times better than anything you will see in Italy, where for that matter this very tympanum has been carefully copied by sculptors with far less genius. There never was a time when genius was universal; that is all nonsense; it would be going beyond the age of gold. The fellow who carved that front, you may make up your mind that he was every bit as great, that he had just as profound ideas as the men you admire most at the present day. I could show you what I mean if we went there together. There are certain passages from the Office of the Assumption which have been rendered with a subtlety of expression that Redon himself has never equalled."

This vast celestial vision of which he spoke to me, this gigantic theological poem which, I understood, had been inscribed there in stone, yet when my eyes, big with desire, had opened to gaze upon the front of Balbec church, it was not these things that I had seen. I spoke to him of those great statues of saints, which, mounted on scaffolds, formed a sort of avenue on either side.

"It starts from the mists of antiquity to end in Jesus Christ," he explained. "You see on one side His ancestors after the spirit, on the other the Kings of Judah, His ancestors after the flesh. All the ages are there. And if you had looked more closely at what you took for scaffolds you would have been able to give names to the figures standing on them. At the feet of Moses you would have recognised the calf of gold, at Abraham's the ram and at Joseph's the demon counselling Potiphar's wife."

I told him also that I had gone there expecting to find an almost

Persian building, and that this had doubtless been one of the chief factors in my disappointment. "Indeed, no," he assured me, "it is perfectly true. Some parts of it are quite oriental; one of the capitals reproduces so exactly a Persian subject that you cannot account for it by the persistence of Oriental traditions. The carver must have copied some casket brought from the East by explorers." And he did indeed show me, later on, the photograph of a capital on which I saw dragons that were almost Chinese devouring one another, but at Balbec this little piece of carving had passed unnoticed by me in the general effect of the building which did not conform to the pattern traced in my mind by the words, "an almost Persian church".

Elstir and I had meanwhile been walking about the studio, and had reached the window that looked across the garden on to a narrow avenue, a side-street that was almost a country lane. We had gone there to breathe the cooler air of the late afternoon. I supposed myself to be nowhere near the girls of the little band, and it was only by sacrificing for once the hope of seeing them that I had yielded to my grandmother's prayers and had gone to see Elstir. For where the thing is to be found that we are seeking, we never know, and often we steadily, for a long time, avoid the place to which, for quite different reasons, everyone has been asking us to go. But we never suspect that we shall there see the very person of whom we are thinking. I looked out vaguely over the country road which, outside the studio, passed quite close to it but did not belong to Elstir. Suddenly there appeared on it, coming along it at a rapid pace, the young bicyclist of the little band, with, over her dark hair, her polo-cap pulled down towards her plump cheeks, her eyes merry and almost importunate; and on that auspicious path, miraculously filled with promise of delights, I saw her beneath the trees throw to Elstir the smiling greeting of a friend, a rainbow that bridged the gulf for me between our terraqueous world and regions which I had hitherto regarded as inaccessible. She even came up to give her hand to the painter, though without stopping, and I could see that she had a tiny beauty spot on her chin. "Do you know that girl, sir?" I asked Elstir, realising that he could if he chose make me known to her, could invite us both to the house. And this peaceful studio with its rural horizon was at once filled with a surfeit of delight such as a child might feel in a house where he was already happily playing when he learned that, in addition, out of that bounteousness which enables lovely things and noble hosts to increase their gifts beyond all measure, there was being prepared for him a sumptuous repast. Elstir told me that she was called Albertine Simonet, and gave me the names also of her friends, whom I described to him with sufficient accuracy for him to identify them almost without hesitation. I had, with regard to their social position, made a mistake, but not the mistake that I usually made at Balbec. I was always ready to take for princes the sons of shopkeepers when they appeared on horseback. This time I had placed in an interloping class the daughters of a set of respectable people, extremely rich, belonging to the world of industry and business. Before I had time to register the social metamorphosis of these girls—so are these discoveries of a mistake, these modifications of the notion one has of a person instantaneous as a chemical combination.....there was already installed behind their faces, so street arab in type that I had taken them for the mistresses of racing bicyclists, of boxing champions, the idea that they might easily be connected with the family of some lawyer or other whom we knew. I was barely conscious of what was meant by Albertine Simonet; she had certainly no conception of what she was one day to mean to me. Even the name, Simonet, which I had already heard spoken on the beach, if I had been asked to write it down I should have spelt with a double 'n', never dreaming of the importance which this family attached to there being but one in their name.

In proportion as we descend the social scale our snobbishness fastens on to mere nothings which are perhaps no more null than the distinctions observed by the aristocracy, but, being more obscure, more peculiar to the individual, take us more by surprise. Possibly there had been Simonnets who had done badly in business, or something worse still even. The fact remains that the Simonets never failed, it appeared, to be annoyed if anyone doubted their 'n'. They wore the air of being the only Simonets in the world with one 'n' instead of two, and were as proud of it, perhaps, as the Montmorency family were of being the premier barons of France. I asked Elstir whether these girls lived at Balbec; yes, he told me, some of them at any rate. The villa in which one of them lived was at that very spot, right at the end of the beach, where the cliffs of Canapville began. As this girl was a great friend of Albertine Simonet, this was another reason for me to believe that it was indeed the latter whom I had met that day when I was with my grandmother.

"Not a day passes but one or the other of them comes by here, and looks in for a minute or two," Elstir told me, plunging me in despair when I thought that if I had gone to see him at once, when my grandmother had begged me to do so, I should, in all probability, long since have made Albertine's acquaintance.

She had passed on; from the studio she was no longer in sight. I supposed that she had gone to join her friends on the 'front'. Could I have appeared there suddenly with Elstir, I should have got to know them all. I thought of endless pretexts for inducing him to take a turn with me on the beach. I had no longer the same peace of mind as before the apparition of the girl in the frame of the little window; so charming until then in its fringe of honeysuckle, and now so drearily empty. Elstir caused me a joy that was tormenting also when he said that he would go a little way with me, but that he must first finish the piece of work on which he was engaged. It was a flower study but not one of any of the flowers, portraits of which I would rather have commissioned him to paint than the portrait of a person, so that I might learn from the revelation of his genius what I had so often sought in vain from the flowers themselves—hawthorn white and pink, cornflowers, appleblossom. Elstir as he worked talked botany to me, but I scarcely listened; he was no longer sufficient in himself, he was now only the necessary intermediary between these girls and me; the distinction which, only a few moments ago, his talent had still given him in my eyes was now worthless save in so far as it might confer a little on me also in the eyes of the little band to whom I should be presented by him.

I paced up and down the room, impatient for him to finish what he was doing; I picked up and examined various sketches, any number of which were stacked against the walls. In this way I happened to bring to light a water-colour which evidently belonged to a much earlier period in Elstir's life, and gave me that particular kind of enchantment which is diffused by works of art not only deliciously executed but representing a subject so singular and so seductive that it is to it that we attribute a great deal of their charm, as if the charm were something that the painter had merely to uncover, to observe, realised already in a material form by nature, and to reproduce in art. It was—this water-colour— the portrait of a young woman, by no means beautiful but of a curious type, in a close-fitting mob-cap not unlike a 'billy-cock' hat, trimmed with a ribbon of cherry coloured silk; in one of her mittened hands was a lighted cigarette, while the other held, level with her knee, a sort of broad-brimmed garden hat, nothing more than a firescreen of plaited straw to keep off the sun. On a table by her side, a tall vase filled with pink carnations. At the foot of the picture was inscribed *"Miss Sacripant* October, 1872." I could not contain my admiration. "Oh, it's nothing, only a rough sketch I did when I was young; it was a costume for a variety show. It's all ages ago now." "And what has become of the model?" A bewilderment provoked by my words preceded on Elstir's face the indifferent, absent-minded air which, a moment later, he displayed there. "Quick, give it to me!" he cried, "I hear Madame Elstir coming, and, though, I assure you, the young person in the billy-cock hat never played any part in my life, still there's no point in my wife's coming in and finding it staring her in the face. I have kept it only as an amusing sidelight on the theatre of those days."

"I should very much like, if you have such a thing, a photograph of the little picture of Miss Sacripant. 'Sacripant'—that's not a real name, surely?" "It is the name of a character the sitter played in a stupid little musical comedy." "But, I assure you, sir, I have never set eyes on her; you look as though you thought that I knew her." Elstir was silent. "It isn't Mme. Swann, before she was married?" I hazarded, in one of those sudden fortuitous stumblings upon the truth, which are rare enough in all conscience, and yet give, in the long run, a certain cumulative support to the theory of presentiments, provided that one takes care to forget all the wrong guesses that would invalidate it. Elstir did not reply. The portrait was indeed that of Odette de Crécy. She had preferred not to keep it for many reasons, some of them obvious. But there were others less apparent. The portrait dated from before the point at which Odette, disciplining her features, had made of her face and figure that creation the broad outlines of which her hairdressers, her dressmakers, she herself—in her way of standing, of speaking, of smiling, of moving her hands, her eyes, of thinking—were to respect throughout the years to come.

It was along this train of thought, meditated in silence by the side of Elstir as I accompanied him to his door, that I was being led by the discovery that I had just made of the identity of his model, when this original discovery caused me to make a second, more disturbing still, involving the identity of the artist. He had painted the portrait of Odette de Crécy. Could it possibly be that this man of genius, this sage, this eremite, this philosopher with his marvellous flow of conversation, who towered over everyone and everything, was the foolish, corrupt little painter who had at one time been 'taken up' by the Verdurins? I asked him if he had known them, whether by any chance it was he that they used to call M. Biche. He answered me in the affirmative, with no trace of embarrassment, as if my question referred to a period in his life that was ended and already somewhat remote, with no suspicion of what a cherished illusion his words were shattering in me, until looking up he read my disappointment upon my face.

Meanwhile we had reached his door. I was disappointed at not having met the girls. But after all there was now the possibility of meeting them again later on; they had ceased to do no more than pass beyond a horizon on which I had been ready to suppose that I should never see them reappear. Around them no longer swirled that sort of great eddy which had separated me from them, which had been merely the expression of the perpetually active desire, mobile, compelling, fed ever on fresh anxieties, which was aroused in me by their inaccessibility, their flight from me, possibly for ever. My desire for them, I could now set it at rest, hold it in reserve, among all those other desires the realisation of which, as soon as I knew it to be possible, I would cheerfully postpone. I took leave of Elstir; I was alone once again.

The sense of comfort that I drew from the probability of my now being able to meet the little band whenever I chose was all the more precious to me because I should not have been able to keep watch for them during the next few days, which would be taken up with preparations for Saint-Loup's departure. My grandmother was anxious to offer my friend some proof of her gratitude for all the kindnesses that he had shown to her and myself. I told her that he was a great admirer of Proudhon, and this put it into her head to send for a collection of autograph letters by that philosopher which she had once bought; Saint-Loup came to her room to look at them on the day of their arrival, which was also his last day at Balbec. He read them eagerly, fingering each page with reverence, trying to get the sentences by heart; and then, rising from the table, was beginning to apologise to my grandmother for having stayed so long, when he heard her say "No, no; take them with you; they are for you to keep; that was why I sent for them, to give them to you."

He was overpowered by a joy which he could no more control than we can a physical condition that arises without the intervention of our will. He blushed scarlet as a child who has just been whipped, and my grandmother was a great deal more touched to see all the efforts that he was making (without success) to control the joy that convulsed him than she would have been to hear any words of thanks that he could have uttered. But he, fearing that he had failed to show his gratitude properly, begged me to make his excuses to her again, next day, leaning from the window of the little train of the local railway company which was to take him back to his regiment.

When, some days after Saint-Loup's departure, I had succeeded in persuading Elstir to give a small tea-party, at which I was to meet Albertine, that freshness of appearance, that smartness of attire, both (alas) fleeting, which were to be observed in me at the moment of my starting out from the Grand Hotel, and were due respectively to a longer rest than usual and to special pains over my toilet, I regretted my inability to reserve them (and also the credit accruing from Elstir's friendship) for the captivation of some other, more interesting person; I regretted having to use them all up on the simple pleasure of making Albertine's acquaintance. My brain assessed this pleasure at a very low value now that it was assured me.

When I arrived at Elstir's, a few minutes later, my first impression was that Mlle. Simonet was not in the studio. There was certainly a girl sitting there in a silk frock, bareheaded, but one whose marvellous hair, her nose, meant nothing to me, in whom I did not recognise the human entity that I had formed out of a young cyclist strolling past, in a polo-cap, between myself and the sea. It was Albertine, nevertheless.

When Elstir asked me to come with him so that he might introduce me to Albertine, who was sitting a little farther down the room, I first of all finished eating a coffee *éclair* and, with a show of keen interest, asked an old gentleman whose acquaintance I had just made (and thought that I might, perhaps, offer him the rose in my buttonhole which he had admired) to tell me more about the old Norman fairs. This is not to say that the introduction which followed did not give me any pleasure, nor assume a definite importance in my eyes. But so far as the pleasure was concerned, I was not conscious of it, naturally, until some time later, when, once more in the hotel, and in my room alone, I had become myself again.

Whatever my disappointment in finding in Mlle. Simonet a girl so little different from those that I knew already, just as my rude awakening when I saw Balbec church did not prevent me from wishing still to go to Quimperlé, Pont-Aven and Venice, I comforted myself with the thought that through Albertine at any rate, even if she herself was not all that I had hoped, I might make the acquaintance of her comrades of the little band.

I thought at first that I should fail. As she was to be staying (and I too) for a long time still at Balbec, I had decided that the best thing was not to make my efforts to meet her too apparent, but to wait for an accidental encounter. But should this occur every day, even, it was greatly to be feared that she would confine herself to acknowledging my bow from a distance, and such meetings, repeated day after day throughout the whole season, would benefit me not at all.

Shortly after this, one morning when it had been raining and was almost cold, I was accosted on the 'front' by a girl wearing a close fitting toque and carrying a muff, so different from the girl whom I had met at Elstir's party that to recognise in her the same person seemed an operation beyond the power of the human mind; mine was, nevertheless, successful in performing it, but after a momentary surprise which did not, I think, escape Albertine's notice. On the other hand, when I instinctively recalled the good breeding which had so impressed me before, she filled me with a converse astonishment by her rude tone and manners typical of the 'little band'. Apart from these, her temple had ceased to be the optical centre, on which the eye might comfortably rest, of her face, either because I was now on her other side, or because her toque hid it, or else possibly because its inflammation was not a constant thing. "What weather!" she began. "Really the perpetual summer of Balbec is all stuff and nonsense. You don't go in for anything special here, do you? We don't ever see you playing golf, or dancing at the Casino. You don't ride, either. You must be bored stiff. You don't find it too deadly, staying about on the beach all day. I see, you just bask in the sun like a lizard; you enjoy that. You must have plenty of time on your hands. I can see you're not like me; I simply adore all sports. You weren't at the Sogne races! We went in the ' tram', and I can quite believe you don't see the fun of going in an old 'tin-pot' like that. It took us two whole hours! I could have gone there and back three times on my bike." I, who had been lost in admiration of Saint-Loup when he, in the most natural manner in the world, called the little local train the 'crawler', because of the ceaseless windings of its line, was positively alarmed by the glibness with which Albertine spoke of the 'tram', and called it a 'tin-pot'. I could feel her mastery of a form of speech in which I was afraid of her detecting and scorning my inferiority. And yet the full wealth of the synonyms that the little band possessed to denote this railway had not yet been revealed to me. In speaking, Albertine kept her head motionless, her nostrils closed, allowing only the corners of her lips to move. The result of this was a drawling, nasal sound, into the composition of which there entered perhaps a provincial descent, a juvenile affectation of British phlegm, the teaching of a foreign governess and a congestive hypertrophy of the mucus of the nose. This enunciation which, as it happened, soon disappeared when she knew people better, giving place to a natural girlish tone, might have been thought unpleasant. But it was peculiar to herself, and delighted me. Whenever I had gone for several days without seeing her, I would refresh my spirit by repeating to myself "We don't ever see you playing golf," with the nasal intonation in which she had uttered the words, point blank, without moving a muscle of her face. And I thought then that there could be no one in the world so desirable.

We parted, Albertine and I, after promising to take a walk together later. I had talked to her without being any more conscious of where my words were falling, of what became of them, than if I were dropping pebbles into a bottomless pit. That our words are, as a general rule, filled, by the person to whom we address them, with a meaning which that person derives from her own substance, a meaning widely different from that which we had put into the same words when we uttered them, is a fact which the daily round of life is perpetually demonstrating. But if we find ourself as well in the company of a person whose education is inconceivable (as Albertine's was to me), her tastes, her reading, her principles unknown, we cannot tell whether our words have aroused in her anything that resembles their meaning, any more than in an animal, although there are things that even an animal may be made to understand. So that to attempt any closer friendship with Albertine seemed to me like placing myself in contact with the unknown, if not the impossible, an occupation as arduous as breaking a horse, as reposeful as keeping bees or growing roses.

I had thought, a few hours before, that Albertine would acknowledge my bow but would not speak to me. We had now parted, after planning to make some excursion soon together. I vowed that when I next met Albertine I would treat her with greater boldness, and I had sketched out in advance a draft of all that I would say to her, and even (being now quite convinced that she was not strait-laced) of all the favours that I would demand of her. But the mind is subject to external influences, as plants are, and cells and chemical elements, and the medium in which its immersion alters it is a change of circumstances, or new surroundings. Grown different by the mere fact of her presence, when I found myself once again in Albertine's company, what I said to her was not at all what I had meant to say. Remembering her flushed temple, I asked myself whether she might not appreciate more keenly a polite attention which she knew to be disinterested. Besides, I was embarrassed by certain things in her look, in her smile. They might equally well signify a laxity of morals or the rather silly merriment of a girl who though full of spirits was at heart thoroughly respectable. A single expression, on a face as in speech, is susceptible of divers interpretations, and I stood hesitating like a schoolboy faced by the difficulties of a piece of Greek prose.

On this occasion we met almost immediately the tall one, Andrée, the one who had jumped over the old banker, and Albertine was obliged to introduce me. Her friend had a pair of eyes of extraordinary brightness, like, in a dark house, a glimpse through an open door of a room into which the sun is shining with a greenish reflection from the glittering sea.

    A party of five were passing, men whom I had come to know very well by sight during my stay at Balbec. I had often wondered who they could be. "They're nothing very wonderful," said Albertine with a sneering laugh. "The little old one with dyed hair and yellow gloves has a fine touch; he knows how to draw all right, he's the Balbec dentist; he's a good sort. The fat one is the Mayor, not the tiny little fat one, you must have seen him before, he's the dancing master; he's rather a beast, you know; he can't stand us, because we make such a row at the Casino; we smash his chairs, and want to have the carpet up when we dance; that's why he never gives us prizes, though we're the only girls there who can dance a bit. The dentist is a dear, I would have said how d'ye do to him, just to make the dancing master swear, but I couldn't because they've got M. de Sainte-Croix with them; he's on the General Council he comes of a very good family, but he's joined the Republicans, to make more money. No nice people ever speak to him now. He knows my uncle, because they're both in the Government, but the rest of my family always cut him. The thin one in the waterproof is the bandmaster. You know him, of course. You don't? Oh, he plays divinely. You haven't been to *Cavalleria Rusticana?* I thought it too lovely! He's giving a concert this evening, but we can't go because it's to be in the town hall. In the Casino it wouldn't matter, but in the town hall, where they've taken down the crucifix, Andrée's mother would have a fit if we went there. You're going to say that my aunt's husband is in the Government. But what difference does that make? My aunt is my aunt. That's not why I'm fond of her. The only thing she has ever wanted has been to get rid of me. No, the person who has really been a mother to me, and all the more credit to her because she's no relation at all, is a friend of mine whom I love just as much as if she was my mother. I will let you see her 'photo'." We were joined for a moment by the golf champion and baccarat plunger, Octave. I thought that I had discovered a bond between us, for I learned in the course of conversation that he was some sort of relative, and even more, a friend of the Verdurins. But he spoke contemptuously of the famous Wednesdays, adding that M. Verdurin had never even heard of a dinner-jacket, which made it a horrid bore when one ran into him in a music hall, where one would very much rather not be greeted with "Well, you young rascal," by an old fellow in a frock coat and black tie, for all the world like a village lawyer. Octave left us, and soon it was Andrée's turn, when we came to her villa, into which she vanished without having uttered a single word to me during the whole of our walk. I regretted her departure, all the more in that, while I was complaining to Albertine how chilling her friend had been with me, two girls came by to whom I lifted my hat, the young Ambresacs, whom Albertine greeted also. I felt that, in Albertine's eyes, my position would be improved by this meeting. They were the daughters of a kinswoman of Mme. de Villeparisis, who was also a friend of Mme. de Luxembourg. M. and Mme. d'Ambresac, who had a small villa at Balbec and were immensely rich, led the simplest of lives there, and always went about dressed, he in an unvarying frock coat, she in a dark gown. Both of them used to make sweeping bows to my grandmother, which never led to anything further. The daughters, who were very pretty, were dressed more fashionably, but in a fashion suited rather to Paris than to the seaside. With their long skirts and large hats, they had the look of belonging to a different race from Albertine. She, I discovered, knew all about them.

"Oh, so you know the little d'Ambresacs, do you? Dear me, you have some swagger friends. After all, they're very simple souls," she went on as though this might account for it. They're very nice, but so well brought up that they aren't allowed near the Casino, for fear of us—we've such a bad tone. They attract you, do they? Well, it all depends on what you like. They're just little white rabbits, really. There may be something in that, of course. If little white rabbits are what appeals to you, they may supply a long-felt want. It seems, there must be some attraction, because one of them has got engaged already to the Marquis de Saint-Loup. Which is a cruel blow to the younger one, who is madly in love with that young man. I'm sure, the way they speak to you with their lips shut is quite enough for me. And then they dress in the most absurd way. Fancy going to play golf in silk frocks at their age, they dress more showily than grown-up women who really know about clothes. Look at Mme. Elstir; there's a well dressed woman if you like," I answered that she had struck me as being dressed with the utmost simplicity. Albertine laughed. "She does put on the simplest things, I admit, but she dresses wonderfully, and to get what you call simplicity costs her a fortune." Mme. Elstir's gowns passed unnoticed by any one who had not a sober and unerring taste in matters of attire. This was lacking in me. Elstir possessed it in a supreme degree, or so Albertine told me. I had not suspected this, nor that the beautiful but quite simple objects which littered his studio were treasures long desired by him which he had followed from sale room to sale room, knowing all their history, until he had made enough money to be able to acquire them. But as to this Albertine, being as ignorant as myself, could not enlighten me. Whereas when it came to clothes, prompted by a coquettish instinct, and perhaps by the regretful longing of a penniless girl who is able to appreciate with greater disinterestedness, more delicacy of feeling, in other, richer people the things that she will never be able to afford for herself, she expressed herself admirably on the refinement of Elstir's taste, so hard to satisfy that all women appeared to him badly dressed, while, attaching infinite importance to right proportions and shades of colour, he would order to be made for his wife, at fabulous prices, the sunshades, hats and cloaks which he had learned from Albertine to regard as charming, and which a person wanting in taste would no more have noticed than myself. Apart from this, Albertine, who had done a little painting, though without, she confessed, having any 'gift' for it, felt a boundless admiration for Elstir, and, thanks to his precept and example, showed a judgment of pictures which was in marked contrast to her enthusiasm for *Cavalleria Rusticana*. The truth was, though as yet it was hardly apparent, that she was highly intelligent, and that in the things that she said the stupidity was not her own but that of her environment and age. Elstir's had been a good but only a partial influence. All the branches of her intelligence had not reached the same stage of development. The taste for pictures had almost caught up the taste for clothes and all forms of smartness, but had not been followed by the taste for music, which was still a long way behind.

Albertine might know all about the Ambresacs; but as he who can achieve great things is not necessarily capable of small, I did not find her, after I had bowed to those young ladies, any better disposed to make me known to her friends. "It's too good of you to attach any importance to them. You shouldn't take any notice of them; they don't count. What on earth can a lot of kids like them mean to a man like you? Now Andrée, I must say, is remarkably clever. She is a good girl, that, though she is perfectly fantastic at times, but the others are really dreadfully stupid." When I had left Albertine, I felt suddenly a keen regret that Saint-Loup should have concealed his engagement from me and that he should be doing anything so improper as to choose a wife before breaking with his mistress. And then, shortly afterwards, I met Andrée, and as she went on talking to me for some time I seized the opportunity to tell her that I would very much like to see her again next day, but she replied that this was impossible, because her mother was not at all well, and she would have to stay beside her. The next day but one, when I was at Elstir's, he told me how greatly Andrée had been attracted by me; on my protesting: "But it was I who was attracted by her from the start I asked her to meet me again yesterday, but she could not." "Yes, I know she told me all about that," was his reply, "she was very sorry, but she had promised to go to a picnic, somewhere miles from here. They were to drive over in a break, and it was too late for her to get out of it." Albeit this falsehood (Andrée knowing me so slightly) was of no real importance, I ought not to have continued to seek the company of a person who was capable of uttering it for what people have once done they will do again indefinitely.

Within the next few days, in spite of the reluctance that Albertine had shown to introduce me to them, I knew all the little band of that first afternoon and two or three other girls as well to whom at my request they introduced me. And thus, my expectation of the pleasure which I should find in a new girl springing from another girl through whom I had come to know her, the latest was like one of those new varieties of rose which gardeners get by using first a rose of another kind. And as I passed from blossom to blossom along this flowery chain, the pleasure of knowing one that was different would send me back to her to whom I was indebted for it, with a gratitude in which desire was mingled fully as much as in my new expectation. Presently I was spending all my time among these girls.

It was not merely a social engagement, a drive with Mme. de Villeparisis, that I would have sacrificed to the 'Ferret' or 'Guessing Games' of my friends. More than once, Robert de Saint-Loup had sent word that, since I was not coming to see him at Doncières, he had applied for twenty-four hours' leave, which he would spend at Balbec. Each time I wrote back that he was on no account to come, offering the excuse that I should be obliged to be away myself that very day, when I had some duty call to pay with my grandmother on family friends in the neighbourhood. No doubt I fell in his estimation when he learned from his aunt in what the "duty call" consisted, and who the persons were who combined to play the part of my grandmother.

Now and then a pretty attention from one or another of them would stir in me vibrations which dissipated for a time my desire for the rest. Thus one day Albertine had suddenly asked: "Who has a pencil?" Andrée had provided one, Rosemonde the paper; Albertine had warned them: "Now, young ladies, you are not to look at what I write." After carefully tracing each letter, supporting the paper on her knee, she had passed it to me with: "Take care no one sees." Whereupon I had unfolded it and read her message, which was: "I love you."

"But we mustn't sit here scribbling nonsense," she cried, turning impetuously, with a sudden gravity of demeanour, to Andrée and Rosemonde, "I ought to show you the letter I got from Gisèle this morning.

An hour later, as I scrambled down the paths which led back, a little too vertically for my liking, to Balbec, I said to myself that it was with her that I would have my romance.

As for the harmonious cohesion in which had been neutralised for some time, by the resistance that each brought to bear against the expansion of the others, the several waves of sentiment set in motion in me by these girls, it was broken in Albertine's favour one afternoon when we were playing the game of 'ferret'. It was in a little wood on the cliff. Stationed between two girls, strangers to the little band, whom the band had brought in its train because we wanted that day to have a bigger party than usual, I gazed enviously at Albertine's neighbour, a young man, saying to myself that if I had been in his place I could have been touching my friend's hands all those miraculous moments which might perhaps never recur, and that this would have been but the first stage in a great advance. I let myself deliberately be caught with the ring, and, having gone into the middle, when the ring passed I pretended not to see it but followed its course with my eyes, waiting for the moment when it should come into the hands of the young man next to Albertine, who herself, pealing with helpless laughter, and in the excitement and pleasure of the game, was blushing like a rose. The players began to show surprise at my stupidity in never getting the ring. I was looking at Albertine, so pretty, so indifferent, so gay, who, though she little knew it, was to be my neighbour when at last I should catch the ring in the right hands, thanks to a stratagem which she did not suspect, and would certainly have resented if she had. Suddenly the ring passed to her neighbour. I sprang upon him at once, forced open his hands and seized it; he was obliged now to take my place inside the circle, while I took his beside Albertine. A few minutes earlier I had been envying this young man, when I saw that his hands as they slipped over the cord were constantly brushing against hers. Now that my turn was come, too shy to seek, too much moved to enjoy this contact, I no longer felt anything save the rapid and painful beating of my heart. At one moment Albertine leaned towards me, with an air of connivance, her round and rosy face, making a show of having the ring, so as to deceive the ferret, and keep him from looking in the direction in which she was just going to pass it. I realised at once that this was the sole object of Albertine's mysterious, confidential gaze, but I was a little shocked to see thus kindle in her eyes the image—purely fictitious, invented to serve the needs of the game—of a secret, an understanding between her and myself which did not exist, but which from that moment seemed to me to be possible and would have been divinely sweet. While I was still being swept aloft by this thought, I felt a slight pressure of Albertine's hand against mine, and her caressing finger slip under my finger along the cord, and I saw her, at the same moment, give me a wink which she tried to make pass unperceived by the others. At once, a mass of hopes, invisible hitherto by myself, crystallised within me. "She is taking advantage of the game to let me feel that she really does love me," I thought to myself, in an acme of joy, from which no sooner had I reached it than I fell, on hearing Albertine mutter furiously: "Why can't you take it? I've been shoving it at you for the last hour." Stunned with grief, I let go the cord, the ferret saw the ring and swooped down on it, and I had to go back into the middle, where I stood helpless, in despair, looking at the unbridled rout which continued to circle round me, stung by the jeering shouts of all the players, obliged, in reply, to laugh when I had so little mind for laughter, while Albertine kept on repeating: "People can't play if they don't pay attention, and spoil the game for the others. He shan't be asked again when we're going to play, Andrée; if he is, I don't come." Andrée, with a mind above the game, sought to make a diversion from Albertine's reproaches by saying to me: "We're quite close to those old Creuniers you wanted so much to see. Look, I'll take you there by a dear little path, and we'll leave these silly idiots to go on playing like babies in the nursery." As Andrée was extremely nice to me, as we went along I said to her everything about Albertine that seemed calculated to make me attractive to the latter. Andrée replied that she too was very fond of Albertine, thought her charming; in spite of which the compliments that I was paying to her friend did not seem altogether to please her. It was inconceivable to me that she would not repeat what I said to her friend, seeing the emphasis that I put into it. And yet I never heard that Albertine had been told.

When I listened to all the charming things Andrée was saying to me about a possible affection between Albertine and myself it seemed as though she were bound to do everything in her power to bring it to pass. Whereas, by mere chance perhaps, not even of the least of the various minor opportunities which were at her disposal and might have proved effective in uniting me to Albertine did she ever make any use, and I would not swear that my effort to make myself loved by

Albertine did not—if not provoke in her friend secret stratagems destined to bring it to nought—at any rate arouse in her an anger which however she took good care to hide and against which even, in her delicacy of feeling, she may herself have fought.

We had left the little wood and had followed a network of overgrown paths through which Andrée managed to find her way with great skill. Suddenly, "Look now," she said to me, "there are your famous Creuniers, and, I say, you are in luck, it's just the time of day, and the light is the same as when Elstir painted them." But I was still too wretched at having fallen, during the game of 'ferret', from such a pinnacle of hopes. And so it was not with the pleasure which otherwise I should doubtless have felt that I caught sight, almost below my feet, crouching among the rocks, where they had gone for protection from the heat, of marine goddesses for whom Elstir had lain in wait and surprised them there, beneath a dark glaze as lovely as Leonardo would have painted, the marvellous Shadows, sheltered and furtive, nimble and voiceless, ready at the first glimmer of light to slip behind the stone, to hide in a cranny, and prompt, once the menacing ray had passed, to return to rock or seaweed beneath the sun that crumbled the cliffs and the colourless ocean, over whose slumbers they seemed to be watching, motionless lightfoot guardians letting appear on the water's surface their viscous bodies and the attentive gaze of their deep blue eyes.

We went back to the wood to pick up the other girls and go home together. I knew now that I was in love with Albertine; but, alas, I had no thought of letting her know it. This was because, since the days of our games in the Champs-Elysées, my conception of love had become different, even if the persons to whom my love was successively assigned remained practically the same. For one thing, the avowal, the declaration of my passion to her whom I loved no longer seemed to me one of the vital and necessary incidents of love, nor love itself an external reality, but simply a subjective pleasure. And as for this pleasure, I felt that Albertine would do everything necessary to furnish it, all the more since she would not know that I was enjoying it.

About a month after the day on which we had played 'ferret' together, I learned that Albertine was going away next morning to spend a couple of days with Mme. Bontemps, and, since she would have to start early, was coming to sleep that night at the Grand Hotel, from which, by taking the omnibus, she would be able, without disturbing the friends with whom she was staying, to catch the first train in the morning. I mentioned this to Andrée. "I don't believe a word of it," she replied, with a look of annoyance. Anyhow it won't help you at all, for I'm quite sure Albertine won't want to see you if she goes to the hotel by herself. It wouldn't be 'regulation' she added, employing an epithet which had recently come into favour with her, in the sense of 'what is done'. "I tell you this because I understand Albertine. What difference do you suppose it makes to me whether you see her or not? Not the slightest, I can assure you!"

We were joined by Octave who had no hesitation in telling Andrée the number of strokes he had gone round in, the day before, at golf, then by Albertine, counting her diabolo as she walked along, like a nun telling her beads. Thanks to this pastime she could be left alone for hours on end without growing bored. As soon as she joined us I became conscious of the obstinate tip of her nose, which I had omitted from my mental pictures of her during the last few days; beneath her dark hair the vertical front of her brow controverted—and not for the first time—the indefinite image that I had preserved of her, while its whiteness made a vivid splash in my field of vision; emerging from the dust of memory, Albertine was built up afresh before my eyes. Golf gives one a taste for solitary pleasures. The pleasure to be derived from diabolo is undoubtedly one of these. And yet, after she had joined us, Albertine continued to toss up and catch her missile, just as a lady on whom friends have come to call does not on their account stop working at her crochet. "I hear that Mme. de Villeparisis," she remarked to Octave, "has been complaining to your father. She's not written only to your father, either, she wrote to the Mayor of Balbec at the same time, to say that we must stop playing diabolo on the 'front' as somebody hit her in the face with one." "Yes, I was hearing about that. It's too silly. There's little enough to do here as it is." Andrée did not join in the conversation; she was not acquainted, any more than was Albertine or Octave, with Mme. de Villeparisis. She did, however, remark "I can't think why this lady should make such a song about it. Old Mme. de Cambremer got hit in the face, and she never complained." "I will explain the difference," replied Octave gravely, striking a match as he spoke. "It's my belief that Mme. de Cambremer is a woman of the world, and Mme. de Villeparisis is just an upstart. Are you playing golf this afternoon?" and he left us, followed by Andrée. I was alone now with Albertine. "Do you see," she began, "I'm wearing my hair now the way you like—look at my ringlet. They all laugh at me and nobody knows who I'm doing it for. My aunt will laugh at me too. But I shan't tell her why, either." I had a sidelong view of Albertine's cheeks, which often appeared pale, but, seen thus, were flushed with a coursing stream of blood which lighted them up, gave them that dazzling clearness which certain winter mornings have when the stones sparkling in the sun seem blocks of pink granite and radiate joy. The joy that I was drawing at this moment from the sight of Albertine's cheeks was equally keen, but led to another desire on my part, which was not to walk with her but to take her in my arms. I asked her if the report of her plans which I had heard were correct. "Yes," she told me, "I shall be sleeping at your hotel tonight, and in fact as I've got rather a chill, I shall be going to bed before dinner. You can come and sit by my bed and watch me eat, if you like, and afterwards we'll play at anything you choose. I should have liked you to come to the station to-morrow morning, but I'm afraid it might look rather odd, I don't say to Andrée, who is a sensible person, but to the others who will be there; if my aunt got to know, I should never hear the last of it. But we can spend the evening together, at any rate. My aunt will know nothing about that. I must go and say good-bye to Andrée. So long, then. Come early, so that we can have a nice long time together," she added, smiling.

I went in to dinner with my grandmother. I felt within me a secret which she could never guess. Similarly with Albertine; to-morrow her friends would be with her, not knowing what novel experience she and I had in common; and when she kissed her niece on the brow Mme. Bontemps would never imagine that I stood between them, in that arrangement of Albertine's hair which had for its object, concealed from all the world, to give me pleasure, me who had until then so greatly envied Mme. Bontemps because, being related to the same people as her niece, she had the same occasions to don mourning, the same family visits to pay; and now I found myself meaning more to Albertine than did the aunt herself. When she was with her aunt, it was of me that she would be thinking. What was going to happen that evening, I scarcely knew. In any event, the Grand Hotel, the evening would no longer seem empty to me; they contained my happiness. I rang for the liftboy to take me up to the room which Albertine had engaged, a room that looked over the valley. The slightest movements, such as that of sitting down on the bench in the lift, were satisfying, because they were in direct relation to my heart; I saw in the ropes that drew the cage upwards, in the few steps that I had still to climb, only a materialisation of the machinery, the stages of my joy. I had only two or three steps to take now along the corridor before coming to that room in which was enshrined the precious substance of that rosy form—that room which, even if there were to be done in it delicious things, would keep that air of permanence, of being, to a chance visitor who knew nothing of its history, just like any other room, which makes of inanimate things the obstinately mute witnesses, the scrupulous confidants, the inviolable depositaries of our pleasure. Those few steps from the landing to Albertine's door, those few steps which no one now could prevent my taking, I took with delight, with prudence, as though plunged into a new and strange element, as if in going forward I had been gently displacing the liquid stream of happiness, and at the same time with a strange feeling of absolute power, and of entering at length into an inheritance which had belonged to me from all time. Then suddenly I reflected that it was wrong to be in any doubt; she had told me to come when she was in bed. It was as clear as daylight; I pranced for joy, I nearly knocked over Françoise who was standing in my way, I ran, with glowing eyes, towards my friend's room. I found Albertine in bed. Leaving her throat bare, her white nightgown altered the proportions of her face, which, flushed by being in bed or by her cold or by dinner, seemed pinker than before; I thought of the colours which I had had a few hours earlier, displayed beside me, on the 'front', the savour of which I was now at last to taste; her cheek was crossed obliquely by one of those long, dark, curling tresses, which, to please me, she had undone altogether. She looked at me and smiled. Beyond her, through the window, the valley lay bright beneath the moon. The sight of Albertine's bare throat, of those strangely vivid cheeks, had so intoxicated me (that is to say had placed the reality of the world for me no longer in nature, but in the torrent of my sensations. which it was all I could do to keep within bounds), as to have destroyed the balance between the life, immense and indestructible, which circulated in my being, and the life of the universe, so puny in comparison. The sea, which was visible through the window as well as the valley, the swelling breasts of the first of the Maineville cliffs, the sky in which the moon had not yet climbed to the zenith, all of these seemed less than a featherweight on my eyeballs, which between their lids I could feel dilated, resisting, ready to bear very different burdens, all the mountains of the world upon their fragile surface. Their orbit no longer found even the sphere of the horizon adequate to fill it. And everything that nature could have brought me of life would have seemed wretchedly meagre, the sigh of the waves far too short a sound to express the enormous aspiration that was surging in my breast. I bent over Albertine to kiss her. Death might have struck me down in that moment; it would have seemed to me a trivial, or rather an impossible thing, for life was not outside, it was in me; I should have smiled pityingly had a philosopher then expressed the idea that some day, even some distant day, I should have to die, that the external forces of nature would survive me, the forces of that nature beneath whose godlike feet I was no more than a grain of dust; that, after me, there would still remain those rounded, swelling cliffs, that sea, that moonlight and that sky! How was that possible; how could the world last longer than myself, since it was it that was enclosed in me, in me whom it went a long way short of filling, in me, where, feeling that there was room to store so many other treasures, I flung contemptuously into a corner, sky, sea and cliffs.

"Stop that, or I'll ring the bell!" cried Albertine, seeing that I was flinging myself upon her to kiss her. But I reminded myself that it was not for no purpose that a girl made a young man come to her room in secret, arranging that her aunt should not know—that boldness, moreover, rewards those who know how to seize their opportunities; in the state of exaltation in which I was, the round face of Albertine, lighted by an inner flame, like the glass bowl of a lamp, started into such prominence that, copying the rotation of a burning sphere, it seemed to me to be turning, like those faces of Michael Angelo which are being swept past in the arrested headlong flight of a whirlwind. I was going to learn the fragrance, the flavour which this strange pink fruit concealed. I heard a sound, precipitous, prolonged, shrill. Albertine had pulled the bell with all her might.

I had supposed that the love which I felt for Albertine was not based on the hope of carnal possession. And yet, when the lesson to be drawn from my experience that evening was, apparently, that such possession was impossible; when, after having had not the least doubt, that first day, on the beach, of Albertine's being unchaste, and having then passed through various intermediate assumptions, I seemed to have quite definitely reached the conclusion that she was absolutely virtuous when, on her return from her aunt's, a week later, she greeted me coldly with "I forgive you; in fact I'm sorry to have upset you, but you must never do it again,"—then, in contrast to what I had felt on learning from Bloch that one could always have all the women one liked, and as if, in place of a real girl, I had known a wax doll, it came to pass, that gradually there detached itself from her my desire to penetrate into her life, to follow her through the places in which she had spent her childhood, to be initiated by her into the athletic life; my intellectual curiosity to know what were her thoughts on this subject or that did not survive my belief that I might take her in my arms if I chose. My dreams abandoned her, once they had ceased to be nourished by the hope of a possession of which I had supposed them to be independent.

Attracting people more easily than she wished, and having no need to proclaim her conquests abroad, Albertine kept silence with regard to the scene with myself by her bedside, which a plain girl would have wished the whole world to know. And yet of her attitude during that scene I could not arrive at any satisfactory explanation. Taking first of all the supposition that she was absolutely chaste (a supposition with which I had originally accounted for the violence with which Albertine had refused to let herself be taken in my arms and kissed, though it was by no means essential to my conception of the goodness, the fundamentally honourable character of my friend), I could not accept it without a copious revision of its terms. It ran so entirely counter to the hypothesis which I had constructed that day when I saw Albertine for the first time. Then ever so many different acts, all acts of kindness towards myself (a kindness that was caressing, at times uneasy, alarmed, jealous of my predilection for Andrée) came up on all sides to challenge the brutal gesture with which, to escape from me, she had pulled the bell. Why then had she invited me to come and spend the evening by her bedside? Why had she spoken all the time in the language of affection? What object is there in your desire to see a friend, in your fear that he is fonder of another of your friends than of you; why seek to give him pleasure, why tell him, so romantically, that the others will never know that he has spent the evening in your room, if you refuse him so simple a pleasure and if to you it is no pleasure at all? I could not believe, all the same, that Albertine's chastity was carried to such a pitch as that, and I had begun to ask myself whether her violence might not have been due to some reason of coquetry, a disagreeable odour, for instance, which she suspected of lingering about her person, and by which she was afraid that I might be disgusted, or else of cowardice, if for instance she imagined, in her ignorance of the facts of love, that my state of nervous exhaustion was due to something contagious, communicable to her in a kiss.

She was genuinely distressed by her failure to afford me pleasure, and gave me a little gold pencil-case, with that virtuous perversity which people show who, moved by your supplications and yet not consenting to grant you what those supplications demand, are anxious all the same to bestow on you some mark of their affection; the critic, an article from whose pen would so gratify the novelist, asks him, instead to dinner; the duchess does not take the snob with her to the theatre but lends him her box on an evening when she will not be using it herself. So far are those who do least for us, and might easily do nothing, driven by conscience to do something. I told Albertine that in giving me this pencil-case she was affording me great pleasure, and yet not so great as I should have felt if, on the night she had spent at the hotel, she had permitted me to embrace her. "It would have made me so happy; what possible harm could it have done you? I was simply astounded at your refusing to let me do it." "What astounds me," she retorted, "is that you should have thought it astounding. Funny sort of girls you must know if my behaviour surprises you." "I am extremely sorry if I annoyed you, but even now I cannot say that I think I was in the wrong. What I feel is that all that sort of thing is of no importance, really, and I can't understand a girl who could so easily give pleasure not consenting to do so. Let us be quite clear about it," I went on, throwing a sop of sorts to her moral scruples, as I recalled how she and her friends had scarified the girl who went about with the actress Léa, "I don't mean to say for a moment that a girl can behave exactly as she likes, or that there's no such thing as immorality. Take, let me see now, yes, what you were saying the other day about a girl who is staying at Balbec and her relations with an actress; I call that degrading, so degrading that I feel sure it must all have been made up by the girl's enemies, and that there can't be any truth in the story. It strikes me as improbable, impossible. But to let a friend kiss you, and go farther than that even—since you say that I am your friend . "So you are, but I have had friends before now, I have known lots of young men who were every bit as friendly, I can assure you. There wasn't one of them would ever have dared to do a thing like that. They knew they'd get their ears boxed if they tried it on. Besides, they never dreamed of trying, we would shake hands in an open, friendly sort of way, like good pals, but there was never a word said about kissing, and yet we weren't any the less friends for that. Why, if it's my friendship you are after, you've nothing to complain of; I must be jolly fond of you to forgive you. But I'm sure you don't care two straws about me, really. Own up now, it's Andrée you're in love with. After all, you're quite right; she is ever so much prettier than I am, and perfectly charming! Oh! You men!" Despite my recent disappointment, these words so frankly uttered, by giving me a great respect for Albertine, made a very pleasant impression on me. And perhaps this impression was to have serious and vexatious consequences for me later on, for it was round it that there began to form that feeling almost of brotherly intimacy, that moral core which was always to remain at the heart of my love for Albertine. A feeling of this sort may be the cause of the keenest pain. For in order really to suffer at the hands of a woman one must have believed in her completely.

My dreams were now once more at liberty to concentrate on one or another of Albertine's friends, and returned first of all to Andrée, whose kindnesses might perhaps have appealed to me less strongly had I not been certain that they would come to Albertine's ears. Undoubtedly the preference that I had long been pretending to feel for Andrée had furnished me in the habit of conversation with her, of declaring my affection—with, so to speak, the material, prepared and ready, for a love of her which had hitherto lacked only the complement of a genuine sentiment, and this my heart being once more free was now in a position to supply. But for me really to love Andrée, she was too intellectual, too neurotic, too sickly, too much like myself. If Albertine now seemed to me to be void of substance, Andrée was filled with something which I knew only too well. I had thought, that first day, that what I saw on the beach there was the mistress of some racing cyclist, passionately athletic; and now Andrée told me that if she had taken up athletic pastimes, it was under orders from her doctor, to cure her neurasthenia, her digestive troubles, but that her happiest hours were those which she spent in translating one of George Eliot's novels. The misunderstanding, due to an initial mistake as to what Andrée was, had not as a matter of fact, the slightest importance. I had thought to find in Andrée a healthy, primitive creature, whereas she was merely a person in search of health, as were doubtless many of those in whom she herself had thought to find it, and who were in reality no more healthy than a burly arthritic with a red face and in white flannels is necessarily a Hercules.

Then the concerts ended, the bad weather began, my friends left Balbec; not all at once, like the swallows, but all in the same week. Albertine was the first to go, abruptly, without any of her friends understanding, then or afterwards, why she had returned suddenly to Paris whither neither her work nor any amusement summoned her. "She said neither why nor wherefore, and with that she left!" muttered Françoise, who, for that matter, would have liked us to leave as well. We were, she thought, inconsiderate towards the staff, now greatly reduced in number, but retained on account of the few visitors who were still staying on, and towards the manager who was "just eating up money." It was true that the hotel, which would very soon be closed for the winter, had long since seen most of its patrons depart, but never had it been so attractive. This view was not shared by the manager; from end to end of the rooms in which we sat shivering, and at the doors of which no page now stood on guard, he paced the corridors, wearing a new frock coat, so well tended by the hairdresser that his insipid face appeared to be made of some composition in which, for one part of flesh, there were three of cosmetics, incessantly changing his neckties. (These refinements cost less than having the place heated and keeping on the staff, just as a man who is no longer able to subscribe ten thousand francs to a charity can still parade his generosity without inconvenience to himself by tipping the boy who brings him a telegram with five.) He appeared to be inspecting the empty air, to be seeking to give, by the smartness of his personal appearance, a provisional splendour to the desolation that could now be felt in this hotel where the season had not been good, and walked like the ghost of a monarch who returns to haunt the ruins of what was once his palace. He was particularly annoyed when the little local railway company, finding the supply of passengers inadequate, discontinued its trains until the following spring. "What is lacking here," said the manager, "is the means of commotion." In spite of the deficit which his books showed, he was making plans for the future on a lavish scale. And as he was, after all, capable of retaining an exact memory of fine language when it was directly applicable to the hotel-keeping industry and had the effect of enhancing its importance "I was not adequately supported, although in the dining room I had an efficient squad," he explained; "but the pages left something to be desired. You will see, next year, what, a phalanx I shall collect." In the meantime the suspension of the services of the B. C. B. obliged him to send for letters and occasionally to dispatch visitors in a light cart. I would often ask leave to sit by the driver, and in this way I managed to be out in all weathers, as in the winter that I had spent at Combray. Sometimes, however, the driving rain kept my grandmother and me, the Casino being closed, in rooms almost completely deserted, as in the lowest hold of a ship when a storm is raging; and there, day by day, as in the course of a sea-voyage, a new person from among those in whose company we had spent three months without getting to know them, the chief magistrate from Caen, the leader of the Cherbourg bar, an American lady and her daughters, came up to us, started conversation, discovered some way of making the time pass less slowly, revealed some social accomplishment, taught us a new game, invited us to drink tea or to listen to music, to meet them at a certain hour, to plan together some of those diversions which contain the true secret of pleasure-giving, which is to aim not at giving pleasure but simply at helping us to pass the time of our boredom, in a word, formed with us, at the end of our stay at Balbec, ties of friendship which, in a day or two, their successive departures from the place would sever. I even made the acquaintance of the rich young man, of one of his pair of aristocratic friends and of the actress, who had reappeared for a few days; but their little society was composed now of three persons only, the other friend having returned to Paris. They asked me to come out to dinner with them at their restaurant. I think they were just as well pleased that I did not accept. But they had given the invitation in the most friendly way imaginable, and albeit it came actually from the rich young man, since the others were only his guests, as the friend who was staying with him, the Marquis Maurice de Vaudémont, came of a very good family indeed, instinctively the actress, in asking me whether I would come, said, to flatter my vanity "Maurice will be so pleased."

And when in the hall of the hotel I met them all three together, it was M. de Vaudémont (the rich young man effacing himself) who said to me "Won't you give us the pleasure of dining with us."

On the whole I had derived very little benefit from Balbec, but this only strengthened my desire to return there. It seemed to me that I had not stayed there long enough. This was not what my friends at home were thinking, who wrote to ask whether I meant to stay there for the rest of my life. And when I saw that it was the name 'Balbec' which they were obliged to put on the envelope—just as my window looked out not over a landscape or a street but on to the plains of the sea, as I heard through the night its murmur to which I had before going to sleep entrusted my ship of dreams, I had the illusion that this life of promiscuity with the waves must effectively, without my knowledge, pervade me with the notion of their charm, like those lessons which one learns by heart while one is asleep.

The manager offered to reserve better rooms for me next year, but I had now become attached to mine, into which I went without ever noticing the scent of flowering grasses, while my mind, which had once found such difficulty in rising to fill its space had come now to take its measurements so exactly that I was obliged to submit it to a reverse process when I had to sleep in Paris, in my own room, the ceiling of which was low.

It was high time, indeed, to leave Balbec, for the cold and damp had become too penetrating for us to stay any longer in a hotel which had neither fireplaces in the rooms nor a central furnace.

THE GUERMANTES WAY

CHAPTER ONE

The twittering of the birds at daybreak sounded insipid to Françoise. Every word uttered by the maids upstairs made her jump; disturbed by all their running about, she kept asking herself what they could be doing. In other words, we had moved. Certainly the servants had made no less noise in the attics of our old home; but she knew them, she had made of their comings and goings familiar events. Now she faced even silence with a strained attention. And as our new neighbourhood appeared to be as quiet, as the boulevard on to which we had hitherto looked had been noisy, the song of a passer-by (distinct at a distance, when it was still quite faint, like an orchestral *motif*), brought tears to the eyes of a Françoise in exile. And so if I had been tempted to laugh at her in her misery at having to leave a house in which she was "so well respected on all sides" and had packed her trunks with tears, according to the Use of Combray, declaring superior to all possible houses that which had been ours, on the other hand I, who found it as hard to assimilate new as I found it easy to abandon old conditions, I felt myself drawn towards our old servant when I saw that this installation of herself in a building where she had not received from the hall-porter, who did not yet know us, the marks of respect necessary to her moral well being, had brought her positively to the verge of dissolution. She alone could understand what I was feeling; certainly, her young footman was not the person to do so; for him, who was as unlike the Combray type as it was possible to conceive, packing up, moving, living in another district, were all like taking a holiday in which the novelty of one's surroundings gave one the same sense of refreshment as if one had actually travelled; he thought he was in the country; and a cold in the head afforded him, as though he had been sitting in a draughty railway carriage, the delicious sensation of having seen the world; at each fresh sneeze he rejoiced that he had found so smart a place, having always longed to be with people who travelled a lot. And so, without giving him a thought, I went straight to Françoise, who, in return for my having laughed at her tears over a removal which had left me cold, now showed an icy indifference to my sorrow because she shared it. The 'sensibility' claimed by neurotic people is matched by their egotism; they cannot abide the flaunting by others of the sufferings to which they pay an ever increasing attention in themselves. Françoise, who would not allow the least of her own ailments to pass unnoticed, if I were in pain would turn her head from me so that I should not have the satisfaction of seeing my sufferings pitied, or so much as observed. It was the same as soon as I tried to speak to her about our new house. Moreover, having been obliged, a day or two later, to return to the house we had just left, to retrieve some clothes which had been overlooked in our removal, while I, as a result of it, had still a 'temperature', and like a boa constrictor that has just swallowed an ox, felt myself painfully distended by the sight of a long trunk which my eyes had still to digest, Françoise, with true feminine inconstancy, came back saying that she had really thought she would stifle on our old boulevard, it was so stuffy, that she had found it quite a day's journey to get there, that never had she seen such stairs, that she would not go back to live there for a king's ransom, not if you were to offer her millions—a pure hypothesis— and that everything (everything, that is to say, to do with the kitchen and 'usual offices') was much better fitted up in the new house. Which, it is high time now that the reader should be told—and told also that we had moved into it because my grandmother, not having been at all well (though we took care to keep this reason from her), was in need of better air—was a flat forming part of the Hotel de Guermantes.

We had come to live beside Mme. de Villeparisis in one of the flats adjoining that occupied by Mme. de Guermantes in a wing of the Hotel. It was one of those old town houses, a few of which are perhaps still to be found; in which the court of honour—whether they were alluvial deposits washed there by the rising tide of democracy, or a legacy from a more primitive time when the different trades were clustered round the overlord—is flanked by little shops and workrooms, a shoemaker's, for instance, or a tailor's, such as we see nestling between the buttresses of those cathedrals which the aesthetic zeal of the restorer has not swept clear of such accretions; a porter who also does cobbling, keeps hens, grows flowers, and, at the far end, in the main building, a 'Comtesse' who, when she drives out in her old carriage and pair, flaunting on her hat a few nasturtiums which seem to have escaped from the plot by the porter's lodge (with, by the coachman's side on the box, a footman who gets down to leave cards at every aristocratic mansion in the neighbourhood), scatters vague little smiles and waves her hand in greeting to the porter's children and to such of her respectable fellow-tenants as may happen to be passing, who, to her contemptuous affability and levelling pride, seem all the same.

In the house in which we had now come to live, the great lady at the end of the courtyard was a Duchess, smart and still quite young. She was, in fact, Mme. de Guermantes and, thanks to Françoise, I soon came to know all about her household. For the Guermantes (to whom Françoise regularly alluded as the people 'below', or 'downstairs') were her constant preoccupation from the first thing in the morning when, as she did Mamma's hair, casting a forbidden, irresistible, furtive glance down into the courtyard, she would say: "Look at that, now; a pair of holy Sisters; that'll be for downstairs, surely;" or, "Oh! just look at the fine pheasants in the kitchen window; no need to ask where they came from, the Duke will have been out with his gun!"—until the last thing at night when, if her ear, while she was putting out my night-things, caught a few notes of a song, she would conclude: "They're having company down below; gay doings, I'll be bound;" whereupon, in her symmetrical face, beneath the arch of her now snow-white hair, a smile from her young days, sprightly but proper, would for a moment set each of her features in its place, arranging them in an intricate and special order, as though for a country-dance.

But the moment in the life of the Guermantes which excited the keenest interest in Françoise, gave her the most complete satisfaction and at the same time the sharpest annoyance was that at which, the two halves of the great gate having been thrust apart, the Duchess stepped into her carriage. It was generally a little while after our servants had finished the celebration of that sort of solemn passover which none might disturb, called their midday dinner, during which they were so far taboo that my father himself was not allowed to ring for them, knowing moreover that none of them would have paid any more attention to the fifth peal than to the first, and that the discourtesy would therefore, have been a pure waste of time and trouble, though not without trouble in store for himself. For Françoise (who, in her old age, lost no opportunity of standing upon her dignity, would without fail have presented him, for the rest of the day, with a face covered with the tiny red cuneiform hieroglyphs by which she made visible—though by no means legible—to the outer world the long tale of her griefs and the profound reasons for her dissatisfactions. She would enlarge upon them too, in a running 'aside', but not so that we could catch her words. She called this practice—which, she imagined, must be infuriating, 'mortifying' as she herself put it 'vexing' to us— "saying low masses all the blessed day."

The last rites accomplished, Françoise, who was at one and the same time, as in the primitive church, the celebrant and one of the faithful, helped herself to a final glass, undid the napkin from her throat, folded it after wiping from her lips a stain of watered wine and coffee, slipped it into its ring, turned a doleful eye to thank 'her' young footman who, to show his zeal in her service was saying: "Come, ma'am, a drop more of the grape; it's d'licious to-day," and went straight across to the window, which she flung open, protesting that it was too hot to breathe in "this wretched kitchen". Dexterously casting, as she turned the latch and let in the fresh air, a glance of studied indifference into the courtyard below, she furtively elicited the conclusion that the Duchess was not ready yet to start, brooded for a moment with contemptuous, impassioned eyes over the waiting carriage, and, this meed of attention once paid to the things of the earth, raised them towards the heavens, whose purity she had already divined from the Sweetness of the air and the Warmth of the sun; and let them rest on a corner of the roof, at the place where, every spring, there came and built, immediately over the chimney of my bedroom, a pair of pigeons like those she used to hear cooing from her kitchen at Combray.

She was interrupted by the voice of the waistcoat-maker downstairs, who occupied an exalted a place in Françoise's affections. Having raised his head when he heard our window open, he had already been trying for some time to attract his neighbour's attention, in order to bid her good day. The coquetry of the young girl that Françoise had once been, softened and refined for M. Jupien the querulous face of our old cook, dulled by age, ill-temper and the heat of the kitchen fire, and it was with a charming blend of reserve, familiarity and modesty that she bestowed a gracious salutation on the waistcoat-maker, but without making any audible response, for if she did infringe Mamma's orders by looking into the courtyard, she would never have dared to go the length of talking from the window, which would have been quite enough (according to her) to bring down on her "a whole chapter" from the Mistress. She pointed to the waiting carriage, as who should say: "A fine pair, eh!" though what she actually muttered was: "What an old rattle-trap!" but principally because she knew that he would be bound to answer, putting his hand to his lips so as to be audible without having to shout:*"You* could have one too if you liked, as good as they have and better, I dare say, only you don't care for that sort of thing."

This new friend of Françoise was very little at home, having obtained a post in one of the Government offices. A waistcoat-maker first of all, with the 'chit of a girl' whom my grandmother had taken for his daughter, he had lost all interest in the exercise of that calling after his assistant had turned to ladies' fashions and become a seamstress. A prentice hand to begin with, in a dressmaker's workroom, set to stitch a seam, to fasten a flounce, to sew on a button or to press a crease, to fix a waistband with hooks and eyes, she had quickly risen to be second and then chief assistant, and having formed a connection of her own among ladies of fashion, now worked at home, that is to say in our courtyard, generally with one or two of her young friends from the workroom, whom she had taken on as apprentices. After this, Jupien's presence in the place had ceased to matter. No doubt the little girl (a big girl by this time) had often to cut out waistcoats still. But with her friends to assist her she needed no one besides. And so Jupien, her uncle, had sought employment outside. He was free at first to return home at midday, then, when, he had definitely succeeded the man whose substitute only, he had begun by being, not before dinner-time. His appointment to the 'regular establishment' was, fortunately, not announced until some weeks after our arrival, so that his courtesy could be brought to bear on her long enough to help Françoise to pass through the first, most difficult phase without undue suffering. At the same time, and without underrating his value to Françoise as, so to speak, a sedative during the period of transition, I am bound to say that my first impression of Jupien had been far from favourable. At a little distance, entirely ruining the effect that his plump cheeks and vivid colouring would otherwise have produced, his eyes, brimming with a compassionate, mournful, dreamy gaze, led one to suppose that he was seriously ill or had just suffered a great bereavement. Not only was he nothing of the sort, but as soon as he opened his mouth (and his speech, by the way, was perfect) he was quite markedly cynical and cold. There resulted from this discord between eyes and lips a certain falsity which was not attractive, and by which he had himself the air of being made as uncomfortable as a guest who arrives in morning dress at a party where everyone else is in evening dress, or as a commoner who having to speak to a Royal Personage does not know exactly how he ought to address him, and gets round the difficulty by cutting down his remarks to almost nothing. Jupien's (there the comparison ends) were, on the contrary, charming. Indeed, corresponding possibly to this overflowing of his face by his eyes, (which one ceased to notice when one came to know him), I soon discerned in him a rare intellect, and one of the most spontaneously literary that it has been my privilege to come across, in the sense that, probably without education, he possessed or had assimilated, with the help only of a few books skimmed in early life, the most ingenious turns of speech. The most gifted people that I had known had died young. And so I was convinced that Jupien's life would soon be cut short. Kindness was among his qualities, and pity, the most delicate and the most generous feelings for others.

One day an old friend of my father said to us, speaking of the Duchess: "She is the first lady in the Faubourg Saint-Germain; hers is the leading house in the Faubourg Saint-Germain." No doubt the most exclusive drawing-room, the leading house in the Faubourg Saint-Germain was little or nothing after all those other mansions of which in turn I had dreamed. And yet in this one too, (and it was to be the last of the series) there was something, however humble, quite apart from its material components, a secret differentiation.

And it became all the more essential that I should be able to explore in the drawing-room of Mme. de Guermantes, among her friends, the mystery of her name, since I did not find it in her person when I saw her leave the house in the morning on foot, or in the afternoon in her carriage. Once before, indeed, in the church at Combray, she had appeared to me in the blinding flash of a transfiguration, with cheeks irreducible to, impenetrable by the colour of the name Guermantes and of afternoons on the banks of the Vivonne, taking the place of my shattered dream like a swan or willow into which has been changed a god or nymph, and which henceforward, subjected to natural laws, will glide over the water or be shaken by the wind. And yet, when that radiance had vanished, hardly had I lost sight of it before it formed itself again, like the green and rosy afterglow of sunset after the sweep of the oar that has broken it, and in the solitude of my thoughts the name had quickly appropriated to itself my impression of the face. But now, frequently, I saw her at her window, in the courtyard, in the street, and for myself at least if I did not succeed in integrating in her the name Guermantes, I cast the blame on the impotence of my mind to accomplish the whole act that I demanded of it; but she, our neighbour, she seemed to make the same error, nay more, to make it without discomfiture, without any of my scruples, without even suspecting that it was an error. Thus Mme. de

Guermantes showed in her dresses the same anxiety to follow the fashions as if, believing herself to have become simply a woman like all the rest, she had aspired to that elegance in her attire in which other ordinary women might equal and perhaps surpass her; I had seen her in the street gaze admiringly at a well-dressed actress; and in the morning, before she sallied forth on foot, as if the opinion of the passers-by, whose vulgarity she accentuated by parading familiarly through their midst her inaccessible life, could be a tribunal competent to judge her, I would see her before the glass playing, with a conviction free from all pretence or irony, with passion, with ill-humour, with conceit, like a queen who has consented to appear as a servant-girl in theatricals at court, this part, so unworthy of her, of a fashionable woman; and in this mythological oblivion of her natural grandeur, she looked to see whether her veil was hanging properly, smoothed her cuffs, straightened her cloak, as the celestial swan performs all the movements natural to his animal species, keeps his eyes painted on either side of his beak without putting into them any glint of life, and darts suddenly after a bud or an umbrella, as a swan would, without remembering that he is a god. But as the traveller, disappointed by the first appearance of a strange town, reminds himself that he will doubtless succeed in penetrating its charm if he visits its museums and galleries, so I assured myself that, had I been given the right of entry into Mme. de Guermantes's house, were I one of her friends, were I to penetrate into her life, I should then know what, within its glowing orange-tawny envelope, her name did really, objectively enclose for other people, since, after all, my father's friend had said that the Guermantes set was something quite by itself in the Faubourg Saint-Germain.

The life which I supposed them to lead there flowed from a source so different from anything in my experience, and must, I felt, be so indissolubly associated with that particular house that I could not have imagined the presence, at the Duchess's parties, of people in whose company I myself had already been, of people who really existed. For not being able suddenly to change their nature, they would have carried on conversations there of the sort that I knew; their partners would perhaps have stooped to reply to them in the same human speech, and, in the course of an evening spent in the leading house in the Faubourg Saint-Germain, there would have been moments identical with moments that I had already lived. Which was impossible. It was thus that my mind was embarrassed by certain difficulties, and the Presence of Our Lord's Body in the Host seemed to me no more obscure a mystery than this leading house in the Faubourg, situated here, on the right bank of the river, and so near that from my bed, in the morning, I could hear its carpets being beaten. But the line of demarcation that separated me from the Faubourg Saint-Germain seemed to me all the more real because it was purely ideal. I felt clearly that it was already part of the Faubourg, when I saw the Guermantes doormat, spread out beyond that intangible Equator, of which my mother had made bold to say, having like myself caught a glimpse of it one day when their door stood open, that it was in a shocking state. For the rest, how could their dining-room, their dim gallery upholstered in red plush, into which I could see sometimes from our kitchen window, have failed to possess in my eyes the mysterious charm of the Faubourg Saint-Germain, to form part of it in an essential fashion, to be geographically situated within it, since to have been entertained to dinner in that room was to have gone into the Faubourg Saint-Germain, to have breathed its atmosphere, since the people who, before going to table, sat down by the side of Mme. de Guermantes on the leather covered sofa in that gallery were all of the Faubourg Saint-Germain.

But if the Hotel de Guermantes began for me at its hall-door, its 'dependencies' must he regarded as extending a long way farther, according to the Duke, who, looking on all the other tenants as farmers, peasants, purchasers of forfeited estates, whose opinion was of no account, shaved himself every morning in his nightshirt at the window, came down into the courtyard, according to the warmth or coldness of the day, in his shirt-sleeves, in pyjamas, in a plaid coat of startling colours, with a shaggy nap, in little light-coloured covert coats shorter than the jackets beneath, and made one of his grooms lead past him at a trot some horse that he had just been buying. More than once, indeed, the horse broke the window of Jupien's shop, whereupon Jupien, to the Duke's indignation, demanded compensation. " If it were only in consideration of all the good that Madame la Duchesse does in the house, here, and in the parish," said M. de Guermantes, "it is an outrage on this fellow's part to claim a penny from us." But Jupien had stuck to his point, apparently not having the faintest idea what 'good' the Duchess had ever done. And yet she did do good, but— since one cannot do good to everybody at once—the memory of the benefits that we have heaped on one person is a valid reason for our abstaining from helping another, whose discontent we thereby make all the stronger. From other points of view than that of charity the quarter appeared to the Duke—and this over a considerable area— to be only an extension of his courtyard, a longer track for his horses. After seeing how a new acquisition trotted by itself he would have it harnessed and taken through all the neighbouring streets, the groom running beside the carriage holding the reins, making it pass to and fro before the Duke who stood on the pavement, erect, gigantic, enormous in his vivid clothes, a cigar, between his teeth, his head in the air, his eyeglass scrutinous, until the moment when he sprang on to the box, drove the horse up and down for a little to try it, then set off with his new turn out to pick up his mistress in the Champs-Elysées. M. de Guermantes bade good day, before leaving the courtyard, to two couples who belonged more or less to his world; the first, some cousins of his who, like working-class parents, were never at home to look after their children, since every morning, the wife went off to the Schola to study counterpoint and fugue, and the husband to his studio to carve wood and beat leather; and after them the Baron and Baronne de Norpois, always dressed in black, she like a pew-opener and he like a mute at a funeral, who emerged several times daily on their way to church. They were the nephew and niece of the old Ambassador who was our friend, and whom my father had, in fact, met at the foot of the staircase without realising from where he came; for my father supposed that so important a personage, one who had come, in contact with the most eminent men in Europe and was probably quite indifferent to the empty distinctions of rank, was hardly likely to frequent the society of these obscure, clerical and narrow-minded nobles. They had not been long in the place; Jupien, who had come out into the courtyard to say a word to the husband just as he was greeting M. de Guermantes, called him "M. Norpois," not being certain of his name.

"Monsieur Norpois, indeed! Oh, that really is good! Just wait a little! This individual will be calling you Comrade Norpois next!" exclaimed M. de Guermantes, turning to the Baron. He was at last able to vent his spleen against Jupien who addressed him as "Monsieur," instead of "Monsieur le Duc."

One day when M. de Guermantes required some information upon a matter of which my father had professional knowledge, he had introduced himself to him with great courtesy. After that, he had often some neighbourly service to ask of my father and, as soon as he saw him begin to come downstairs, his mind occupied with his work and anxious to avoid any interruption, the Duke, leaving his stable-boys, would come up to him in the courtyard, straighten the collar of his great-coat, with the serviceable deftness inherited from a line of royal body-servants in days gone by, take him by the hand, and, holding it in his own, patting it even to prove to my father, with a courtesan's or courtier's shamelessness, that he, the Duc de Guermantes, made no bargain about my father's right to the privilege of contact with the ducal flesh, lead him, so to speak, on leash, extremely annoyed and thinking only how he might escape, through the carriage entrance out into the street. He had given us a sweeping bow one day when we had come in just as he was going out in the carriage with his wife; he was bound to have told her my name, but what likelihood was there of her remembering it, or my face either? And besides, what a feeble recommendation to be pointed out simply as being one of her tenants! Another, more valuable, would have been my meeting the Duchess in the drawing-room of Mme. de Villeparisis, who, as it happened, had just sent word by my grandmother that I was to go and see her, and, remembering that I had been intending to go in for literature, had added that I should meet several authors there. But my father felt that I was still a little young to go into society, and as the state of my health continued to give him uneasiness he did not see the use of establishing precedents that would do me no good As one of Mme. de Guermantes's footmen was in the habit of talking to Françoise, I picked up the names of several of the houses which she frequented, but formed no impression of any of them; from the moment in which they were a part of her life, of that life which I saw only through the veil of her name, were they not inconceivable?

"To-night there's a big party with a Chinese shadow show at the Princesse de Parme's," said the footman, "but we shan't be going, because at five o'clock Madame is taking the train to Chantilly, to spend a few days with the Duc d'Aumale, but it'll be the lady's maid and valet that are going with her. I'm to stay here. She won't be at all pleased, the Princesse de Parme won't, that's four times already she's written to Madame la Duchesse."

"Then you won't be going down to Guermantes Castle this year?"

"It's the first time we shan't be going there: it's because of the Duke's rheumatics, the doctor says he's not to go there till the hot pipes are in, but we've been there every year till now, right on to January. If the hot pipes aren't ready, perhaps Madame will go for a few days to Cannes, to the Duchesse de Guise, but nothing's settled yet."

"And do you go to the theatre sometimes?"

" We go now and then to the Opéra, usually on the evenings when the Princesse de Parme has her box, that's once a week; it seems it's a fine show they give there, plays, operas, everything. Madame refused to subscribe to it herself, but we go all the same to the boxes Madame's friends take, on one night, another, often with the Princesse de Guermantes, the Duke's cousin's lady. She's sister to the Duke of Bavaria. And so you've got to rush upstairs again now, have you?" went on the footman, who, albeit identified with the Guermantes, looked upon masters in general as a political estate, a view which allowed him to treat Françoise with as much respect as if she too were in service with a duchess. "You enjoy good health, ma'am?"

"Oh, if it wasn't for these cursed legs of mine! On the plain I can still get along" ('on the plain' meant in the courtyard or in the streets, where Françoise had no objection to walking, in other words 'on a plane surface') "but it's these stairs that do me in, devil take them. Good day to you sir, see you again, perhaps this evening."

She was all the more anxious to continue her conversations with the footman after he mentioned to her that the sons of dukes often bore a princely title which they retained until their fathers were dead. Evidently the cult of the nobility, blended with and accommodating itself to a certain spirit of revolt against it, must, springing hereditarily from the soil of France, be very strongly implanted still in her people. For Françoise, to whom, you might speak of the genius of Napoleon or of wireless telegraphy without succeeding in attracting her attention, and without her slackening for an instant the movements with which she was scraping the ashes from the grate or laying the table, if she were simply to be told these idiosyncrasies of nomenclature, and that the younger son of the Duc de Guermantes was generally called Prince d'Oléron, would at once exclaim: "That's fine, that is!" and stand there dazed, as though in contemplation of a stained window in church.

Françoise learned also from the Prince d'Agrigente's valet, who had become friends with her by coming often to the house with notes for the Duchess, that he had been hearing a great deal of talk in society about the marriage of the Marquis de Saint-Loup to Mlle. d'Ambresac, and that it was practically settled.

My father had a friend at the Ministry, one A.J.Moreau, who, to distinguish him from the other Moreaus, took care always to prefix both initials to his name, with the result that people called him, for short, "A. J.". Well, somehow or other, this A. J. found himself entitled to a stall at the Opéra-Comique on a gala night; he sent the ticket to my father, and as Berma, whom I had not been again to see since my first disappointment, was to give an act of *Phèdre*, my grandmother persuaded my father to pass it on to me.

To tell the truth, I attached no importance to this possibility of hearing Berma which, a few years earlier, had plunged me in such a state of agitation. And it was not without a sense of melancholy that I realised the fact of my indifference to what at one time I had put before health, comfort, everything. It was not that there had been any slackening of my desire, for an opportunity to contemplate close at hand, the precious particles of reality of which my imagination caught a broken glimpse. But my imagination no longer placed these in the diction of a great actress; since my visits to Elstir, it was on certain tapestries, certain modern paintings that I had brought to bear the inner faith I had once had in this acting, in this tragic art of Berma; my faith, my desire, no longer coming forward to pay incessant worship to the diction, the attitudes of Berma; the counterpart that I possessed of them in my heart had gradually perished, like those other counterparts of the dead in ancient Egypt which had to be fed continually in order to maintain their originals in eternal life. This art had become a feeble, tawdry thing. No deep-lying soul inhabited it any more.

That evening, armed with the ticket my father had received from his friend, I climbed the grand staircase of the Opéra; I took my seat and at length the curtain went up and Berma came on to the stage. And then—oh, the miracle— like those lessons which we laboured in vain to learn overnight, and find intact, got by heart, on waking up next morning; like, too, those faces of dead friends which the impassioned efforts of our memory pursue without recapturing them, and which, when we are no longer thinking of them, are there before our eyes just as they were in life—the talent of Berma, which had evaded me when I sought so greedily to seize its essential quality, now, after these years of oblivion, in this hour of indifference, imposed itself, with all the force of a thing directly seen, on my admiration. Berma's interpretation was, around Racine's work, a second work, quickened also by the breath of genius.

My own impression, to tell the truth, though more pleasant than on the earlier occasion, was not really different. Only, I no longer put it to the test of a pre-existent, abstract and false idea of dramatic genius, and I understood now that dramatic genius was precisely this. It had just occurred to me that if I had not derived any pleasure from my first hearing of Berma, it was because, as earlier still when I used to meet Gilberte in the Champs-Elysées, I had come to her with too strong a desire. Between my two disappointments there was perhaps not only this resemblance, but another more profound. The impression given us by a person or a work (or a rendering, for that matter) of marked individuality is peculiar to that person or work. We have brought to it the ideas of 'beauty', 'breadth of style', 'pathos' and so forth which we might, failing anything better, have had the illusion of discovering in the commonplace show of a 'correct' face or talent, but our critical spirit has before it the insistent challenge of a form of which it possesses no intellectual equivalent, in which it must detect and isolate the unknown element. It hears a shrill sound, an oddly interrogative intonation. It asks itself: "Is that good? Is what I am feeling just now admiration? Is that richness of colouring, nobility, strength?" And what answers it again is a shrill voice, a curiously questioning tone, the despotic impression caused by a person whom one does not know, wholly material, in which there is no room left for 'breadth of interpretation'. And for this reason it is the really beautiful works that, if we listen to them with sincerity, must disappoint us most keenly, because in the storehouse of our ideas there is none that corresponds to an individual impression.

This was precisely what Berma's acting showed me. This was what was meant by nobility, by intelligence of diction. Now I could appreciate the worth of a broad, poetical, powerful interpretation, or rather it was to this that those epithets were conventionally applied, but only as we give the names of Mars, Venus, Saturn to planets which have no place in classical mythology. We feel in one world, we think, we give names to things in another; between the two we can establish a certain correspondence, but not bridge the interval. It was quite narrow, this interval, this fault that I had had to cross when, that afternoon on which I went first to hear Berma, having strained my ears to catch every word, I had found some difficulty in correlating my ideas of 'nobility of interpretation', of 'originality', and had broken out in applause only after a moment of unconsciousness and as if my applause sprang not from my actual impression but was connected in some way with my preconceived ideas, with the pleasure that I found in saying to myself: "At last I am listening to Berma." And the difference that there is between a person, or a work of art which is markedly individual, and the idea of beauty, exists just as much between what they make us feel and the idea of love, or of admiration. Wherefore we fail to recognise them. I had found no pleasure in listening to Berma (any more than, earlier still, in, seeing Gilberte). I had said to myself: "Well, I do not admire this." But then I was thinking only of mastering the secret of Berma's acting, I was preoccupied with that alone, I was trying to open my mind as wide as possible to receive all that her acting contained. I understood now that all this amounted to nothing more nor less than admiration.

This genius of which Berma's rendering of the part was only the revelation, was it indeed the genius of Racine and nothing more?

The piece that followed was one of those novelties which at one time I had expected, since they were not famous, to be inevitably trivial and of no general application, devoid as they were of any existence outside the performance that was being given of them at the moment. But this part would be set one day in the list of her finest impersonations, next to that of Phèdre. Not that in itself it was not destitute of all literary merit. But Berma was as sublime in one as in the other. I realised then that the work of the playwright was for the actress no more than the material, the nature of which was comparatively unimportant, for the creation of her masterpiece of interpretation, just as the great painter whom I had met at Balbec, Elstir, had found the inspiration for two pictures of equal merit in a school building without any character and a cathedral which was in itself a work of art. And as the painter dissolves houses, carts, people, in some broad effect of light which makes them all, so Berma spread out great sheets of terror or tenderness over words that were all melted together in a common mould, lowered or raised to one level, which a lesser artist would have carefully detached from one another. No doubt each of them had an inflection of its own and Berma's diction did not prevent one from catching the rhythm of the verse. Is it not already a first element of ordered complexity, of beauty, when, on hearing a rhyme, that is to say something which is at once similar to and different from the preceding rhyme, which was prompted by it, but introduces the variety of a new idea, one is conscious of two systems overlapping each other, one intellectual, the other prosodic? But Berma at the same time made her words, her lines, her whole speeches even, flow into lakes of sound vaster than themselves, at the margins of which it was a joy to see them obliged to stop, to break off; thus it is that a poet takes pleasure in making hesitate for a moment at the rhyming point the word which is about to spring forth, and a composer in merging the various words of his libretto in a single rhythm which contradicts, captures and controls them. Thus into the prose sentences of the modern playwright as into the poetry of Racine, Berma managed to introduce those vast images of grief, nobility, passion, which were the masterpieces of her own personal art, and in which she could be recognised as, in the portraits which he has made of different sitters, we recognise a painter.

Just as the curtain was rising on this second play I looked up at Mme. de Guermantes's box. The Princess was in the act—by a movement that called into being an exquisite line which my mind pursued into the void—of turning her head towards the back of the box; her party were all standing, and also turning, towards the back; between the double hedge which they thus formed, with all the assurance, the grandeur of the goddess that she was, but with a strange meekness which so late an arrival, making every one else get up in the middle of the performance, blended with the white muslin in which she was attired, just as an adroitly compounded air of simplicity, shyness and confusion tempered her triumphant smile, the Duchesse de Guermantes, who had at that moment entered the box, came towards her cousin, made a profound obeisance to a young man with fair hair who was seated in the front row, and turning again towards the amphibian monsters who were floating in the recesses of the cavern, gave to these demi-gods of the Jockey Club—who at that moment, and among them all M. de Palancy in particular, were the men who I should most have liked to be—the familiar "good evening" of an old and intimate friend, an allusion to the daily sequence of her relations with them during the last fifteen years. I felt the mystery, but could not solve the riddle of that smiling gaze which she addressed to her friends, in the azure brilliance with which it glowed while she surrendered her hand to one and then to another, a gaze which could I have broken up its prism, analysed its crystallisation might perhaps have revealed to me the essential quality of the unknown form of life which became apparent in it at that moment. The Duc de Guermantes followed his wife, the flash of his monocle, the gleam of his teeth, the whiteness of his carnation or of his pleated shirtfront scattering, to make room for their light, the darkness of his eyebrows, lips and coat; with a wave of his outstretched hand which he let drop on to their shoulders, vertically, without moving his head, he commanded the inferior monsters, who were making way for him, to resume their seats, and made a profound bow to the fair young man. One would have said that the Duchess had guessed that her cousin, of whom, it was rumoured, she was inclined to make fun for what she called her 'exaggerations' (a name which, from her own point of view, so typically French and restrained, would naturally be applied to the poetry and enthusiasm of the Teuton), would be wearing this evening one of those costumes in which the Duchess thought of her as 'dressed up', and that she had decided to give her a lesson in good taste. Instead of the wonderful downy plumage which, from the crown of the Princess's head, fell and swept her throat, instead of her net of shells and pearls, the Duchess wore in her hair, only a simple aigrette, which, rising above her arched nose and level eyes, reminded one of the crest on the head of a bud. Her neck and shoulders emerged from a drift of snow-white muslin, against which fluttered a swansdown fan, but below this her gown, the bodice of which had for its sole ornament innumerable spangles (either little sticks and beads of metal, or possibly brilliants), moulded her figure with a precision that was positively British. But different as their two costumes were, after the Princess had given her cousin the chair in which she herself had previously been sitting, they could be seen turning to gaze at one another in mutual appreciation.

Possibly a smile would curve the lips of Mme. de Guermantes when next day she referred to the headdress, a little too complicated, which the Princess had worn, but certainly she would declare that it had been, all the same, quite lovely and marvellously arranged; and the Princess, whose own tastes found something a little cold, a little austere, a little 'tailor-made' in her cousin's way of dressing; would discover in this rigid sobriety an exquisite refinement. Moreover the harmony that existed in the toilet of these two ladies seemed to me like a materialisation, snow-white or patterned with colour, of their internal activity, and, like the gestures which I had seen the Princesse de Guermantes make, with no doubt in my own mind that they corresponded to some idea latent in hers, the plumes which swept downward from her brow, and her cousin's glittering spangled bodice seemed each to have a special meaning, to be to one or the other lady an attribute which was hers and hers alone, the significance of which I would eagerly have learned; the bird of paradise seemed inseparable from its wearer as her peacock is from Juno, and I did not believe that any other woman could usurp that spangled bodice, any more than the fringed and flashing aegis of Minerva. And when I turned my eyes to their box, far more than on the ceiling of the theatre, painted with cold and lifeless allegories, it was as though I had seen thanks to a miraculous rending of the clouds that ordinarily veiled it, the Assembly of the Gods in the act of contemplating the spectacle of mankind, beneath a crimson canopy, in a clear lighted space, between two pillars of Heaven. I gazed on this brief transfiguration with a disturbance which was partly soothed by the feeling that I myself was unknown to these Immortals; the Duchess had indeed seen me once with her husband, but could surely have kept no memory of that, and it gave me no pain that she found herself, owing to the place that she occupied in the box, in a position to gaze down upon the nameless, collective madrepores of the public in the stalls, for I had the happy sense that my own personality had been dissolved in theirs, when, at the moment in which, by the force of certain optical laws, there must, I suppose, have come to paint itself on the impassive current of those blue eyes the blurred outline of the protozoon, devoid of any individual existence, which was myself, I saw a ray illumine them; the Duchess, goddess turned woman, and appearing in that moment a thousand times more lovely, raised, pointed in my direction the white-gloved hand which had been resting on the balustrade of the box, waved it at me in token of friendship; my gaze felt itself trapped in the spontaneous incandescence of the flashing eyes of the Princess, who had unconsciously set them ablaze merely by turning her head to see who it might be that her cousin was thus greeting, while the Duchess, who had remembered me, showered upon me the sparkling and celestial torrent of her smile.

And now every morning, long before the hour at which she would appear, I went by a devious course to post myself at the corner of the street along which she generally came, and, when the moment of her arrival seemed imminent, strolled homewards with an air of being absorbed in something else, looking the other way and raising my eyes to her face as I drew level with her, but as though I had not in the least expected to see her. Indeed, for the first few mornings, so as to be sure of not missing her, I waited opposite the house. And every time that the carriage gate opened (letting out one after another so many people who were none of them she for whom I was waiting) its grinding rattle continued in my heart in a series of oscillations which it took me a long time to subdue. For never was devotee of a famous actress whom he did not know, posting himself and patrolling the pavement outside the stage door, never was angry or idolatrous crowd, gathered to insult or to carry in triumph through the streets the condemned assassin or the national hero whom it believes to be on the point of coming whenever a sound is heard from the inside of the prison or the palace, never were these so stirred by their emotion as I was, awaiting the emergence of this great lady who in her simple attire was able, by the grace of her movements (quite different from the gait she affected on entering a drawing-room or a box), to make of her morning walk—and for me there was no one in the world but herself out walking—a whole poem of elegant refinement and the finest ornament, the most curious flower of the season. But after the third day, so that the porter should not discover my stratagem, I betook myself much farther afield, to some point upon the Duchess's usual route.

Every morning, certainly at the moment when Mme. de Guermantes emerged from her gateway at the top of the street, I saw again her tall figure, her face with its bright eyes and crown of silken hair—all the things for which I was there waiting; but, on the other hand, a minute or two later, when, having first turned my eyes away so as to appear not to be waiting for this encounter which I had come out to seek, I raised them to look at the Duchess at the moment in which we converged, what I saw then were red patches (as to which I knew not whether they were due to the fresh air or to a faulty complexion) on a sullen face which with the curtest of nods, a long way removed from the affability of the *Phèdre* evening, acknowledged my salute, which I addressed to her daily with an air of surprise, and which did not seem to please her. I had ceased to dream of the little girls coming from their catechism, or of a certain dairy-maid; and yet I had also lost all hope of encountering in the street what I had come out to seek, either the affection promised to me, at the theatre, in a smile, or the profile, the bright face beneath its pile of golden hair which were so only when seen from afar. Now I should not even have been able to say what Mme. de Guermantes was like, by what I recognised her for every day, in the picture which she presented as a whole, the face was different, as were the dress and the hat.

I felt that I was annoying her by crossing her path in this way every morning but even if I had had the courage to refrain, for two or three days consecutively, from doing so, perhaps that inattention, which would have represented so great a sacrifice on my part, Mme. de Guermantes would not have noticed, or would have set it down to some obstacle beyond my control. And indeed I could not have succeeded in making myself cease to track her down except by arranging that it should be impossible for me to do so, for the need incessantly reviving in me to meet her, to be for a moment the object of her attention, the person to whom her bow was addressed, was stronger than my fear of arousing her displeasure. I should have had to go away for some time; and for that I had not the heart. I did think of it more than once. I would then tell Françoise to pack my boxes, and immmediately afterwards to unpack them. And as the spirit of imitation, the desire not to appear behind the times, alters the most natural and most positive form of oneself, Françoise borrowing the expression from her daughter's vocabulary, used to remark that I was 'dippy'. She did not approve of this; she said that I was always 'balancing', for she made use, when she was not aspiring to rival the moderns, of the language of Saint-Simon. It is true that she liked it still less when I spoke to her as master to servant. She knew that this was not natural to me, and did not suit me, a condition which she rendered in words as "where there isn't a will". I should never have had the heart to leave Paris except in a direction that would bring me closer to Mme. de Guermantes.

The friendship, the admiration that Saint-Loup felt for me seemed to me undeserved and had hitherto left me unmoved. All at once I attached a value to them, I would have liked him to disclose them to Mme. de Guermantes, I was quite prepared even to ask him to do so. For when we are in love, all the trifling little privileges that we enjoy, we would like to be able to divulge to the woman we love, as people who have been disinherited and bores of other kinds do to us in everyday life. We are distressed by her ignorance of them; we seek consolation in the thought that just because they are never visible she has perhaps added to the opinion which she already had of us this possibility of further advantages that must remain unknown.

Saint-Loup had not for a long time been able to come to Paris, whether, as he himself explained, on account of his military duties, or, as was more likely, on account of the trouble that he was having with his mistress, with whom he had twice now been on the point of breaking off relations He had often told me what a pleasure it would be to him if I came to visit him at that garrison town, the name of which, a couple of days after his leaving Balbec, had caused me so much joy when I had read it on the envelope of the first letter I received from my friend.

It was not too far away from Paris for me to be able, if I took the express, to return, join my mother and grandmother and sleep in my own bed. As soon as I realised this, troubled by a painful longing, I had too little will power to decide not to return to Paris but rather to stay in this town; but also too little to prevent a porter from carrying my luggage to a cab and not to adopt, as I walked behind him, the unburdened mind of a traveller who is looking after his luggage and for whom no grandmother is waiting anywhere at home, to get into the carriage with the complete detachment of a person who, having ceased to think of what it is that he wants, has the air of knowing what he wants, and to give the driver the address of the cavalry barracks. I thought that Saint-Loup might come to sleep that night at the hotel at which I should be staying, so as to make less painful for me the first shock of contact with this strange town. One of the guard went to find him, and I waited at the barrack gate, before that huge ship of stone, booming with the November wind, out of which, every moment, for it was now six o'clock, men were emerging in pairs into the street, staggering as if they were coming ashore in some foreign port in which they found themselves temporarily anchored.

Saint-Loup appeared, moving like a whirlwind, his eyeglass spinning in the air before him; I had not given my name, I was eager to enjoy his surprise and delight. "Oh! What a bore!" he exclaimed, suddenly catching sight of me and blushing to the tips of his ears. "I have just had a week's leave, and I shan't be off duty again for another week ."

And, preoccupied by the thought of my having to spend this first night alone, for he knew better than anyone my bed-time agonies, which he had often remarked and soothed at Balbec, he broke off his lamentation to turn and look at me, coax me with little smiles, with tender though unsymmetrical glances, half of them coming directly from his eye, the other half through his eyeglass, but both sorts alike an allusion to the emotion that he felt on seeing me again, an allusion also to that important matter which 1 did not always understand but which concerned me now vitally, our friendship.

"I say! Where are you going to sleep? Really, I can't recommend the hotel where we mess; it is next to the Exhibition ground, where there's a show just starting; you'll find it beastly crowded.

And he knitted his brows partly with vexation and also in the effort to decide, like a doctor, what remedy he might best apply to my disease.

"Run along and light the fire in my quarters," he called to a trooper who passed us. "Hurry up; get a move on!"

After which he turned once more to me, and his eyeglass and his peering, myopic gaze hinted an allusion to our great friendship.

"No! To see you here, in these barracks where I have spent so much time thinking about you, I can scarcely believe my eyes. I must be dreaming. And how are you? Better, I hope. You must tell me all about yourself presently. We'll go up to my room; we mustn't hang about too long on the square, there's the devil of a draught; I don't feel it now myself, but you aren't accustomed to it, I'm afraid of your catching cold. And what about your work; have you started yet? No? You are a quaint fellow! If I had your talent I'm sure I should be writing morning, noon and night. It amuses you more to do nothing? What a pity it is that it's the useless fellows like me who are always ready to work, and the ones who could if they wanted to, won't. There, and I've clean forgotten to ask you how your grandmother is. Her Proudhons are in safe keeping. I never part from them."

An officer, tall, handsome, majestic, emerged with slow and solemn gait from the foot of a staircase. Saint-Loup saluted him and arrested the perpetual instability of his body for the moment occupied in holding his hand against the peak of his cap. But he had flung himself into the action with so much force, straightening himself with so sharp a movement, and, the salute ended, let his hand fall with so abrupt a relaxation, altering all the positions of shoulder, leg, and eyeglass, that this moment was one not so much of immobility as if a throbbing tension in which were neutralised the excessive movements which he had just made and those on which he was about to embark. Meanwhile the officer, without coming any nearer us, calm, benevolent, dignified, imperial, representing, in short, the direct opposite of Saint-Loup, himself also, but without haste, raised his hand to the peak of his cap.

"I must just say a word to the Captain," whispered Saint-Loup. "Be a good fellow, and go and wait for me in my room. It's the second on the right, on the third floor; I'll be with you in a minute."

And setting off at the double, preceded by his eyeglass which fluttered in every direction, he made straight for the slow and stately Captain whose horse had just been brought round and who, before preparing to mount, was giving orders with a studied nobility of gesture as in some historical painting, and as though he were setting forth to take part in some battle of the First Empire, whereas he was simply going to ride home, to the house which he had taken for the period of his service at Doncières, and which stood in a Square that was named, as though in an ironical anticipation of the arrival of this Napoleonid, Place de la République. I started to climb the staircase, nearly slipping on each of its nail-studded steps, catching glimpses of barrack-rooms, their bare walls edged with a double line of beds and kits. I was shown Saint-Loup's room. I stood for a moment outside its closed door, for I could hear some one stirring; he moved something, let fall something else; I felt that the room was not empty, that there must be somebody there. But it was only the freshly lighted fire beginning to burn. It could not keep quiet, it kept shifting its faggots about, and very clumsily. I entered the room; it let one roll into the fender and set another smoking. And even when it was not moving, like an ill-bred person it made noises all the time, which, from the moment I saw the flames rising, revealed themselves to me as noises made by a fire, although if I had been on the other side of a wall I should have thought that they came from someone who was blowing his nose and walking about. I sat down in the room and waited. Liberty hangings and old German stuffs of the eighteenth century managed to rid it of the smell that was exhaled by the rest of the building, a coarse, insipid, mouldy smell like that of stale toast. It was here, in this charming room, that I could have dined and slept with a calm and happy mind. Saint-Loup seemed almost to be present by reason of the textbooks which littered his table, between his photographs, among which I could make out my own and that of the Duchesse de Guermantes, by the light of the fire which had at length grown accustomed to the grate, and, like an animal crouching in an ardent, noiseless, faithful watchfulness, let fall only now and then a smouldering log which crumbled into sparks; or licked with a tongue of flame the sides of the chimney.

The silence, though only relative, which reigned in the little barrack-room where I sat waiting was now broken. The door opened and Saint-Loup, dropping his eyeglass, dashed in.

"Ah, my dear Robert, you make yourself very comfortable here" I said to him; "how jolly it would be if one were allowed to dine and sleep here."

So you'd rather stay with me and sleep here, would you, than go to the hotel by yourself?" Saint-Loup asked me, smiling.

"Oh, Robert, it is cruel of you to be sarcastic about it," I pleaded; "you know it's not possible, and you know how wretched I shall be over there."

"Good! You flatter me!" he replied. "It occurred to me just now that you would rather stay here tonight. And that is precisely what I stopped to ask the Captain."

"And he has given you leave?" I cried. "He hadn't the slightest objection." "Oh! I adore him!" "No; that would be going too far. But now, let me just get hold of my batman and tell him to see about our dinner," he went on, while I turned away so as to hide my tears.

We were several times interrupted by one or other of Saint-Loup's friends coming in. He drove them all out again. "Get out of here. Buzz off!" I begged him to let them stay. "No, really; they would bore you stiff; they are absolutely uncultured; all they can talk about is racing, or stable shop. Besides, I don't want them here either; they would spoil these precious moments I've been looking forward to. But you mustn't think, when I tell you that these fellows are brainless, that everything military is devoid of intellectuality. Far from it. We have a major here who is a splendid chap. He's given us a course in which military history is treated like a demonstration, like a problem in algebra. Even from the aesthetic point of view there is a curious beauty, alternately inductive and deductive, about it which you couldn't fail to appreciate." "That's not the officer who's given me leave to stay here tonight?" "No; thank God! The man you adore for so very trifling a service is the biggest fool that ever walked the face of the earth. He is perfect at looking after messing, and at kit inspections; he spends hours with the serjeant major and the master tailor. There you have his mentality. Apart from that, he has a vast contempt, like everyone here, for the excellent major I was telling you about. No one will speak to him because he's a freemason and doesn't go to confession. The Prince de Borodina would never have an outsider like that in his house. Which is pretty fair cheek, when all's said and done, from a man whose great-grandfather was a small farmer, and who would probably be a small farmer himself if it hadn't been for the Napoleonic wars. Not that he hasn't a lurking sense of his own rather ambiguous position in society, where he's neither flesh nor fowl. He hardly ever shows his face at the jockey, it makes him feel so deuced awkward, this so-called Prince," added Robert, who, having been led by the same spirit of imitation to adopt the social theories of his teachers and the worldly prejudices of his relatives, had unconsciously wedded the democratic love of humanity to a contempt for the nobility of the Empire.

After that first night I had to sleep at the hotel. And I knew beforehand that I was doomed to find there nothing but sorrow. As it happened, I was mistaken. I had no time to be sad, for I was not left alone for an instant.

On certain days, I was agitated by the desire to see my grandmother again, or by the fear that she might be ill, or else it was the memory of some undertaking which I had left half-finished in Paris, and which seemed to have made no progress; sometimes again it was some difficulty in which, even here, I had managed to become involved. One or other of these anxieties had kept me from sleeping, and I was without strength to face my sorrow which in a moment grew to fill the whole of my existence. Then from the hotel I sent a messenger to the barracks, with a line to Saint-Loup: I told him that, should it be materially possible—I knew that it was extremely difficult for him—I should be most grateful if he would look in for a minute.

An hour later he arrived; and on hearing his ring at the door I felt myself liberated from my obsessions. I knew that, if they were stronger than I, he was stronger than they, and my attention was diverted from them and concentrated on him, who would have to settle them. He had come into the room and already he had enveloped me in the gust of fresh air in which from before dawn he had been displaying so much activity, a vital atmosphere very different from that of my room, to which I at once adapted myself by appropriate reactions.

"I hope you weren't angry with me for bothering you; there is something that is worrying me, as you probably guessed." "Not at all, I just supposed you wanted to see me; and I thought it very nice of you. I was delighted that you should have sent for me. But what is the trouble? Things not going well? What can I do to help?" He listened to my explanations, and gave careful answers; but before he had uttered a word, he had transformed me to his own likeness; compared with the important occupations which kept him so busy, so alert, so happy, the worries which, a moment ago, I had been unable to endure for another instant seemed to me, as to him, negligible; I was like a man who, not having been able to open his eyes for some days, sends for a doctor, who neatly and gently raises his eyelid, removes from beneath it and shows, him a grain of sand; the sufferer is healed and comforted. All my cares resolved themselves into a telegram which Saint-Loup undertook to dispatch. Life seemed to me so different so delightful; I was flooded with such a surfeit of strength that I longed for action. "What are you doing now?" I asked him. "I must leave you, I'm afraid; we're going on a route march in three quarters of an hour, and I have to be on parade." "Then it's been a great bother to you, coming here?" "No, no bother at all, the Captain was very good about it; he told me that if it was for you I must go at once; but you understand, I don't like to seem to be abusing the privilege." "But if I got up and dressed quickly and went by myself to the place where you'll be training, it would interest me immensely, and I could perhaps talk to you during the breaks." "I shouldn't advise you to do that; you have been lying awake racking your brains over a thing which, I assure you, is not of the slightest importance, but now that it has ceased to worry you, lay your head down on the pillow and go to sleep, which you will find an excellent antidote to the demineralisation of your nerve-cells; only you mustn't go to sleep too soon, because our band-boys will be coming along under your windows; but as soon as they've passed I think you'll be left in peace, and, we shall meet again this evening, at dinner."

At the hotel where I was to meet Saint-Loup and his friends, I went to the smaller room in which Saint-Loup's table was laid. I found there several of his friends who dined with him regularly, nobles except for one or two commoners in whom the young nobles had, in their schooldays, detected likely friends, and with whom they readily associated, proving thereby that they were not on principle hostile to the middle class, even though it were Republican, provided it had clean hands, and went to mass. On the first of these evenings, before we sat down to dinner, I drew Saint-Loup into a corner and in front of all the rest but so that they should not hear me, said to him: "Robert, this is hardly the time or the place for what I am going to say, but I shan't be a second. I keep on forgetting to ask you when I'm in the barracks; isn't that Mme. de Guermantes's photograph that you have on your table? I can't tell you how funny it is that it should be her photograph, because we're living in her house now, in Paris, and I've been hearing the most astounding things" (I should have been hard put to it to say what) "about her which have made me immensely interested in her, only from a literary point of view, don't you know, from a—how shall I put it—from a Balzacian point of view; but you're so clever you can see what I mean; I don't need to explain things to you; but we must hurry up; what on earth will your friends think of my manners?"

"They will think absolutely nothing; I have told them that you are sublime, and they are a great deal more alarmed than you are."

"You are too kind. But listen, what I want to say is this: I suppose Mme. de Guermantes hasn't any idea that I know you, has she?" "I can't say; I haven't seen her since the summer, because I haven't had any leave since she's been in town." "What I was going to say is this: I've been told that she looks on me as an absolute idiot." "That I do not believe; Oriane is not exactly an eagle, but all the same she's by no means stupid." "You know that, as a rule, I don't approve of your advertising the good opinion you're kind enough to hold of me; I'm not conceited. That's why I'm sorry you should have said flattering things about me to your friends here (we will go back to them in two seconds). But Mme. de Guermantes is different; if you could let her know—if you would even exaggerate a trifle—what you think of me, you would give me great pleasure."

"Why, of course I will, if that's all you want me to do; it's not very difficult; but what difference can it possibly make to you what she thinks of you? I suppose you think her no end of a joke, really."

"I've mentioned only one of the two things I wanted to ask you, the less important; the other is more important to me, but I'm afraid you will never consent. Would it bore you if we were to call each other *tu*?" "Bore me? My dear fellow! Joy! Tears of joy! Undreamed of happiness!" "Thank you—tu I mean; you begin first—ever so much. It is such a pleasure to me that you needn't do anything about Mme. de Guermantes if you'd rather not, this is quite enough for me." "I can do both." "You wouldn't care to give me her photograph, I suppose?"

I had meant to ask him only for the loan of it. But when the time came to speak I felt shy, I decided that the request was indiscreet, and in order to, hide my confusion I put the question more bluntly, and increased my demand, as if it had been quite natural. "No; I should have to ask her permission first," was his answer. He blushed as he spoke. I could see that he had a reservation in his mind, that he credited me also with one, that he would give only a partial service to my love, under the restraint of certain moral principles, and for this I hated him.

I could not help asking Robert, whether it were really settled that he was to marry Mlle. d'Ambresac He assured me that not only was it not settled, but there had never been any thought of such a match, he had never seen her, he did not know who she was. If at that moment I had happened to see any of the social gossipers who had told me of this coming event, they would promptly have announced the betrothal of Mlle. d'Ambresac to some one who was not Saint-Loup and that of Saint-Loup to some one who was not Mlle. d'Ambresac. I should have surprised them greatly had I reminded them of their incompatible and still so recent predictions. In order that this little game may continue, and multiply false reports by attaching the greatest possible number to every name in turn, nature has furnished those who play it with a memory as short as their credulity is long.

One evening when, I passed through the town on my way to the restaurant I said to myself: "Perhaps there will be a letter tonight;" and on entering the dining-room I found courage to ask Saint-Loup: "You don't happen to have had any news from Paris?"

"Yes," he replied gloomily; " bad news."

I breathed a sigh of relief when I realised that it was only he who was unhappy, and that the news came from his mistress. But I soon saw that one of its consequences would be to prevent Robert, for ever so long, from taking me to see his aunt.

I learned that a quarrel had broken out between him and his mistress, through the post presumably, unless she had come down to pay him a flying visit between trains. And the quarrels, even when relatively slight, which they had previously had, had always seemed as though they must prove insoluble. For she was a girl of violent temper, who would stamp her foot and burst into tears for reasons as incomprehensible as those that make children shut themselves into dark cupboards, not come out for dinner, refuse to give any explanation, and only redouble their sobs when, our patience exhausted, we visit them with a whipping.

At length she wrote to ask whether he would consent to forgive her. As soon as he realised that a definite rupture had been avoided, he saw all the disadvantages of a reconciliation. Besides, he had already begun to suffer less acutely, and had almost accepted a grief the sharp tooth of which he would have, in a few months perhaps, to feel again if their intimacy were to be resumed. He did not hesitate for long. And perhaps he hesitated only because he was now certain of being able to recapture his mistress, of being able to do it and therefore of doing it. Only she asked him, so that she might have time to recover her equanimity, not to come to Paris at the New Year. Now he had not the heart to go to Paris without seeing her. On the other hand, she had declared her willingness to go abroad with him, but for that he would need to make a formal application for leave, which Captain de Borodino was unwilling to grant.

"I'm sorry about it, because of your meeting with my aunt, which will have to be put off. I dare say I shall be in Paris at Easter."

"We shan't be able to call on Mme. de Guermantes then, because I shall have gone to Balbec. But, really, it doesn't matter in the least, I assure you."

"To Balbec? But you didn't go there till August."

"I know; but next year they're making me go there earlier, for my health."

All that he feared was that I might form a bad impression of his mistress, after what he had told me "She is violent simply because she is too frank, too thorough in her feelings. But she is a sublime creature. You can't imagine what exquisite poetry there is in her. She goes every year to spend All Souls Day at Bruges. Nice of her, don't you think? If you ever do meet her you'll see what I mean; she has a greatness........" And, as he was infected with certain of the mannerisms used in the literary circles in which the lady moved: "There is something sidereal about her, in fact something bardic; you know what I mean, the poet merging into the priest." I was searching all through dinner for a pretext which would enable Saint-Loup to ask his aunt to see me without my having to wait until he came to Paris. Now such a pretext was furnished by the desire that I had to see some more pictures by Elstir, the famous painter whom Saint-Loup and I had met at Balbec. Three important works by my favourite painter were described as belonging to Mme. de Guermantes. So that it was, after all, quite sincerely that, on the evening on which Saint-Loup told me of his lady's projected visit to Bruges, I was able, during dinner, in front of his friends, to let fall, as though on the spur of the moment:

"Listen, if you don't mind. Just one last word, on the subject of the lady we were speaking about. You remember Elstir, the painter I met at Balbec?" "Why, of course I do." "You remember how much I admired his work?" "I do, quite well; and the letter we sent him." "Very well, one of the reasons—not one of the chief reasons, a subordinate reason—why I should like to meet the said lady—you do know who I mean, don't you?" "Of course I do. How involved you're getting." "Is that she has in her house one very fine picture, at least, by Elstir." "' I say, I never knew that." "Elstir will probably be at Balbec at Easter; you know he stays down there now all the year round, practically. I should very much like to have seen this picture before I leave Paris. I don't know whether you're on sufficiently intimate terms with your aunt: but couldn't you manage, somehow, to give her so good an impression of me that she won't refuse, and then ask her if she'll let me come and see the picture without you, since you won't be there?"

"That's all right. I'll answer for her; I'll make a special point of it." "Oh, Robert, you are an angel; I do love you." "It's very nice of you to love me, but it would be equally nice if you were to call me *tu,* as you promised, and as you began to do."

One morning, Saint-Loup confessed to me that he had written to my grandmother to give her news of me, with the suggestion that, since there was telephonic connexion between Paris and Doncières, she might make use of it to speak to me. In short, that very day she was to give me a call, and he advised me to be at the post office at about a quarter to four. The telephone was not yet at that date as commonly in use as it is today. When I reached the post office, my grandmother's call had already been received; I stepped into the box;

the line was engaged; some one was talking who probably did not realise that there was nobody to answer him, for when I raised the receiver to my ear, the lifeless block began squeaking like Punchinello; I silenced it, as one silences a puppet, by putting it back on its hook, but, like Punchinello, as soon as I took it again in my hand, it resumed its gabbling. At length, giving it up as hopeless, by hanging up the receiver once and for all, I stifled the convulsions of this vociferous stump which kept up its chatter until the last moment, and went in search of the operator, who told me to wait a little; then I spoke, and, after a few seconds of silence, suddenly I heard that voice which I supposed myself, mistakenly, to know so well; for, always until then, every time that my grandmother had talked to me, I had been accustomed to follow what she was saying on the open score of her face, in which the eyes figured so largely; but her voice itself I was hearing this afternoon for the first time. And because that voice appeared to me to have altered in its proportions from the moment that it was a whole, and reached me in this way alone and without the accompaniment of her face and features, I discovered for the first time how sweet that voice was; perhaps, too, I noticed for the first time the sorrows that had scarred it in the course of a lifetime.

My grandmother, by telling me to stay, filled me with an anxious, an insensate longing to return. This freedom of action which for the future she allowed me and to which I had never dreamed that she would consent, appeared to me suddenly as sad as might be my freedom of action after her death (when I should still love her and she would for ever have abandoned me) "Granny!" I cried to her; "Granny!" and would fain have kissed her, but I had beside me only that voice, a phantom, as impalpable as that which would come perhaps to revisit me when my grandmother was dead. "Speak to me!" but then it happened that, left more solitary still, I ceased to catch the sound of her voice. My grandmother could no longer hear me; she was no longer in communication with me; we had ceased to stand face to face, to be audible to one another.

When I came among Robert and his friends, I withheld the confession that my heart was no longer with them, that my departure was now irrevocably fixed. Saint-Loup appeared to believe me, but I learned afterwards that he had from the first moment realised that my uncertainty was feigned and that he would not see me again next day.

"I don't doubt the truth of what you're saying, Or that you aren't thinking of leaving us just yet," said Saint-Loup, smiling; "but pretend you are going, and come and say good-bye to me tomorrow morning early, otherwise there's a risk of my not seeing you; I'm going out to luncheon, I've got leave from the Captain; I shall have to be back in barracks by two, as we are to be on the march all afternoon I suppose the man to whose house I'm going, a couple of miles out, will manage to get me back in time.

The following morning I rose late and failed to catch Saint-Loup, who had already started for the country house where he was invited to luncheon. About half past one, I had decided to go in any case to the barracks, so as to be there before he arrived, when, as I was crossing one of the avenues on the way there, I noticed, coming behind me in the same direction as myself, a tilbury which, as it overtook me, obliged me to jump out of its way, an N.C.O. was driving it, wearing an eyeglass; it was Saint-Loup. By his side was the friend whose guest he had been at luncheon, and whom I had met once before at the hotel where we dined. I did not dare shout to Robert since he was not alone, but, in the hope that he would stop and pick me up, I attracted his attention by a sweeping wave of my hat, which might be regarded as due to the presence of a stranger. I knew that Robert was short-sighted; still, I should have supposed that, provided he saw me at all, he could not fail to recognise me; he did indeed see my salute, and returned it, but without stopping; driving on at full speed, without a smile, without moving a muscle of his face, he confined himself to keeping his hand raised for a minute to the peak of his cap as though he were acknowledging the salute of a trooper whom he did not know personally. I ran to the barracks, but it was a long way; when I arrived, the regiment was parading on the square, on which I was not allowed to stand, and I was heart-broken at not having been able to say good-bye to Saint-Loup.

I was wretched at not having said good-bye to Saint-Loup, but I went nevertheless, for my one anxiety was to return to my grandmother; always until then, in this little country town, when I thought of what my grandmother must be doing by herself, I had pictured her as she was when with me, suppressing my own personality but without taking into account the effects of such a suppression; now I had to free myself, at the first possible moment, in her arms, from the phantom, hitherto unsuspected and suddenly called into being by her voice, of a grandmother really separated from me, resigned, having, what I had never yet thought of her as having, a definite age, who had just received a letter from me in an empty house, as I had once before imagined Mamma in a house by herself, when I had left her to go to Balbec.

Alas, this phantom was just what I did see when, entering the drawing-room before my grandmother had been told of my return, I found her there, reading. For the first time and for a moment only, since she vanished at once, I saw, sitting on the sofa, beneath the lamp, red-faced, heavy and common, sick, lost in thought, following the lines of a book with eyes that seemed hardly sane, a dejected old woman whom I did not know.

My request to be allowed to inspect the Elstirs in Mme.de Guermantes's collection had been met by Saint-Loup with: "I will answer for her." During the long weeks in which Saint-Loup still did not come to Paris, his aunt, to whom I had no doubt of his having written begging her to do so, never once asked me to call at her house to see the Elstirs.

When Saint-Loup did come to Paris, it was for a few hours only. He came with assurances that he had had no opportunity of mentioning me to his cousin. "She's not being at all nice just now, Oriane isn't," he explained, with innocent self-betrayal. "She's not my old Oriane any longer, they've gone and changed her. I assure you, it's not worth while bothering your head about her. You pay her far too great a compliment. You wouldn't care to meet my cousin Poictiers?" he went on, without stopping to reflect that this could not possibly give me any pleasure. "Quite an intelligent young woman, she is; you'd like her. She's married to my cousin, the Duc de Poictiers, who is a good fellow, but a bit slow for her. I've told her about you. She said I was to bring you to see her. She's much better looking than Oriane, and younger too. Really a nice person, don't you know, really a good sort."

My father had informed us that he now knew, from his friend A. J., where M. de Norpois was going when he met him about the place. "It's to see Mme. de Villeparisis, they are great friends; I never knew anything about it. It seems she's a delightful person, a most superior woman: you ought to go and call on her," he told me. "Another thing that surprised me very much. He spoke to me of M. de Guermantes as quite a distinguished man; I had always taken him for a boor. It seems he knows an enormous amount, and has perfect taste, only he's very proud of his name and his connections. But for that matter, according to Norpois, he has a tremendous position, not only here but all over Europe. It appears, the Austrian Emperor and the Tsar treat him just like one of themselves. Old Norpois told me that Mme. de Villeparisis had taken quite a fancy to you and that you would meet all sorts of interesting people in her house. He paid a great tribute to you; you will see him if you go there, and he may have some good advice for you if you are going to be a writer. For you're not likely to do anything else; I can see that. It might turn out quite a good career; it's not what I should have chosen for you myself; but you'll be a man in no time now, we shan't always be here to look after you, and we mustn't prevent you from following your vocation.

If only I had been able to start writing. But whatever the conditions in which I approached the task (as, too, alas, the undertakings not to touch alcohol, to go to bed early, to sleep, to keep fit), whether it were with enthusiasm, with method, with pleasure, in depriving myself of a walk, or postponing my walk and keeping it in reserve as a reward of industry, taking advantage of an hour of good health, utilising the inactivity forced on me by a day of illness, what always emerged in the end from all my effort was a virgin page, undefiled by any writing, ineluctable as that forced card which in certain tricks one invariably is made to draw, however carefully one may first have shuffled the pack. I was merely the instruments of habits of not working, of not going to bed, of not sleeping, which must find expression somehow, cost what it might; if I offered them no resistance, they acted as they chose from the first opportunity that the day afforded and I escaped without serious injury! I slept for a few hours after all, towards morning, I read a little, I did not over exert myself; but if I attempted to thwart them, if I pretended to go to bed early, to drink only water, to work, they grew restive, they adopted strong measures, they made me really ill, I was obliged to double my dose of alcohol, did not lie down in bed for two days and nights on end, could not even read, and I vowed that another time I would be more reasonable, that is to say less wise, like the victim of an assault who allows himself to be robbed for fear, should he offer resistance, of being murdered.

Saint-Loup, who was coming anyhow to Paris, had promised to take me to Mme. de Villeparisis's, where I hoped, though I had not said so to him, that we might meet Mme. de Guermantes. He invited me to luncheon in a restaurant with his mistress, whom we were afterwards to accompany to a rehearsal. We were to go out in the morning and call for her at her home on the outskirts of Paris.

"If she is nice to me today;" he confided to me, "I am going to give her something that she'll like. It's a necklace she saw at Boucheron's. It's rather too much for me just at present—thirty thousand francs. But, poor puss, she gets so little pleasure out of life. She will be jolly pleased with it, I know. She mentioned it to me and told me she knew somebody who would perhaps give it to her. I don't believe that is true, really, but I wasn't taking any risks, so I've arranged with Boucheron, who is our family jeweller, to keep it for me. I am glad to think that you're going to meet her; she's nothing so very wonderful to look at, you know," (I could see that he thought just the opposite and had said this only so as to make me, when I did see her, admire her all the more) "what she has got is a marvellous judgment; she'll perhaps be afraid to talk much before you, but, by Jove! the things she'll say to me about you afterwards, you know she says things one can go on thinking about for hours; there's really something about her that's quite Pythian."

On our way to her house we passed by a row of little gardens, and I was obliged to stop, for they were all aflower with pear and cherry blossom; as empty, no doubt, and lifeless only yesterday as a house that no tenant has taken, they were suddenly peopled and adorned by these newcomers, arrived during the night, whose lovely white garments we could see through the railings along the garden paths.

"Listen; I can see you'd rather stop and look at that stuff, and grow poetical about it," said Robert, "so just wait for me here, will you; my friend's house is quite close, I will go and fetch her."

Suddenly Saint-Loup appeared, accompanied by his mistress, and then, in this woman who was for him all the love, every possible delight in life, whose personality, mysteriously enshrined in a body as in a Tabernacle, was the object that still occupied incessantly the toiling imagination of my friend, whom he felt that he would never really know, as to whom he was perpetually asking himself what could be her secret self, behind the veil of eyes and flesh, in this woman I recognised at once 'Rachel when from the Lord', her who, but a few years since—women change their position so rapidly in that world, when they do change—used to say to the procuress: "To-morrow evening, then, if you want me for anyone, you will send round, won't you?"

And when they had 'come round' for her, and she found herself alone in the room with the 'anyone', she had known so well what was required of her that, after locking the door as a prudent woman's precaution or a ritual gesture, she would begin to take off all her things, as one does before the doctor who is going to sound one's chest, never stopping in the process unless the 'someone' not caring for nudity, told her that she might keep on her shift, as specialists do sometimes who, having an extremely fine ear and being afraid of their patient's catching a chill, are satisfied with listening to his breathing and the beating of his heart through his shirts. On this woman, whose whole life, all her thoughts, all her past, all the men who at one time or another had had her were to me so utterly unimportant that if she had begun to tell me about them I should have listened to her only out of politeness, and should barely have heard what she said, I felt that the anxiety, the torment, the love of Saint-Loup had been concentrated in such a way as to make—out of what was for me a mechanical toy, nothing more—the cause of endless suffering, the very object and reward of existence. Seeing these two elements separately (because I had known 'Rachel when from the Lord' in a house of ill fame), I realised that many women for the sake of whom men live, suffer, take their lives, may be in themselves or for other people, what Rachel was for me. The idea that anyone could be tormented by curiosity with regard to her life stupefied me. I could have told Robert of any number of her unchastities, which seemed to me the most uninteresting things in the world. And how they would have pained him! And what had he not given to learn them, without avail!

I realised also then all that the human imagination can put behind a little scrap of face, such as this girl's face was, if it is the imagination that was the first to know it; and conversely into what wretched elements, crudely material and utterly without value, might be decomposed what had been the inspiration of countless dreams if, on the contrary, it should be so to speak controverted by the slightest actual acquaintance. I saw that what had appeared to me to be not worth twenty francs when it had been offered to me for twenty francs in the house of ill fame, where it was then for me simply a woman desirous of earning twenty francs, might be worth more than a million, more than one's family, more than all the most coveted positions in life if one had begun by imagining her to embody a strange creature; interesting to know, difficult to seize and to hold. No doubt it was the same thin and narrow face that we saw, Robert and I. But we had arrived at it by two opposite ways, between which there was no communication, and we should never both see it from the same side. That face, with its stares, its smiles, the movements of its lips, I had known from outside as being simply that of a woman of the street who for twenty francs would do anything that I asked. And so her stares, her smiles, the movements of her lips had seemed to me significant merely of the general actions of a class without any distinctive quality. And beneath them I should not have had the curiosity to look for a person. But what to me had in a sense been offered at the start, that consenting face, had been for Robert an ultimate goal towards which he had made his way through endless hopes and doubts, suspicions, dreams. He gave more than a million francs in order to have for himself, in order that there might not be offered to others what had been offered to me, as to all and sundry, for twenty.

As soon as Saint-Loup found himself in a public place with his mistress, he would imagine that she was looking at every other man in the room, and his brow would darken; she would remark his ill-humour, which she may have thought it amusing to encourage, or, as was more probable, by a foolish piece of conceit preferred, feeling wounded by his tone, not to appear to be seeking to disarm; and would make a show of being unable to take her eyes off some man or other, not that this was always a mere pretence. In fact, the gentleman who, in theatre or café, happened to sit next to them, or, to go no farther, the driver of the cab they had engaged need only have something attractive about him, no matter what, and Robert, his perception quickened by jealousy, would have noticed it before his mistress; he would see in him immediately one of those foul creatures whom he had denounced to me at Balbec, who corrupted and dishonoured women for their own amusement, would beg his mistress to take her eyes off the man, thereby drawing her attention to him. And sometimes she found that Robert had shown such good judgment in his suspicion that after a little, she even left off teasing him in order that he might calm down and consent to go off by himself on some errand which would give her time to begin conversation with the stranger, often to make an assignation, sometimes even to bring matters quickly to a head.

But the opening scene of this afternoon's performance interested me in quite another way. It made me realise in part the nature of the illusion of which Saint-Loup was a victim with regard to Rachel, and which had set a gulf between the images that he and I respectively had in mind of his mistress, when we beheld her that morning among the blossoming pear trees; Rachel was playing a part which involved barely more than her walking on in the little play. But seen thus, she was another woman. She had one of those faces to which distance and not necessarily that between stalls and stage, the world being in this respect only a larger theatre—gives, form and outline and which, seen close at hand, dissolve back into dust. Standing beside her one saw only a nebula, a milky way, of freckles, of tiny spots, nothing more. At a proper distance all this ceased to be visible and from cheeks that withdrew, were reabsorbed into her face, rose like a crescent moon, a nose so fine, so pure that one would have liked to be the object of Rachel's attention, to see her again as often as one chose, to keep her close to one, provided that one had not already seen her differently and at close range.

When, the curtain having fallen, we moved on to the stage, the stage scenery, still in its place, seen, thus at close range and without the advantage of any of those effects of lighting and distance on which the eminent artist whose brush had painted it had calculated, was a depressing sight and Rachel, when I came near her, was subjected to a no less destructive force. The curves of her charming nose had stood out in perspective between stalls and stage, like the relief of the scenery. It was no longer herself; I recognised her only thanks to her eyes, in which her identity had taken refuge. The form, the radiance of this young star, so brilliant a moment, ago, had vanished. On the other hand---as though we came close to the moon and it ceased to present the appearance of a disk of rosy gold---on this face, so smooth a surface until now, I could distinguish only protuberances, discolourations and cavities.

I had realised that morning beneath the pear blossom, how illusory were the grounds upon which Robert's love for 'Rachel when from the Lord' was based; I was bound now to admit how very real were the sufferings to which that love gave rise which seemed to have prompted in Robert a desire to be left alone for a while and he asked me to leave him, and to go by myself to call on Mme. de Villeparisis. He would join me there, but preferred that we should not enter the room together, so that he might appear to have only just arrived in Paris, instead of having spent half the day already with me.

As I had supposed before making the acquaintance of Mme. de Villeparisis at Balbec, there was a vast difference between the world in which she lived and that of Mme. de Guermantes. Mme. de Villeparisis was one of those women who, born of a famous house, entering by marriage into another no less famous, do not for all that enjoy any great position in the social world, and, apart from a few duchesses who are their nieces or sisters-in-law, perhaps even a crowned head or two, old family friends, see their drawing-rooms filled only by the third rate, either provincial or tainted in some way, whose presence there has long since driven, away all such: smart and snobbish folk as are not obliged to come to the house by ties of blood or the claims of a friendship too old to be ignored. Certainly I had no difficulty after the first few minutes in understanding how Mme. de

Villeparisis, at Balbec, had come to be so well informed, better than ourselves even, as to the smallest details of the tour through Spain which my father was then making with M. de Norpois. Even this, however, did not make it possible to rest content with the theory that the intimacy—of more than twenty years standing—between Mme. de Villeparisis and the Ambassador could have been responsible for the lady's loss of caste in a world where the smartest women boasted the attachment of lovers far less respectable than him, not to mention that it was probably years since he had been anything more to the Marquise than just an old friend. Had Mme. de Villeparisis then had other adventures in days gone by?

Whether or not there had been in the life of Mme. de Villeparisis any of those scandals, which (if there had) the lustre of her name would have blotted out, it was this intellect, resembling rather that of a writer of the second order than that of a woman of position, that was undoubtedly the cause of her social degradation. A bluestocking Mme. de Villeparisis had perhaps been in her earliest youth, and, intoxicated with the ferment of her own knowledge, had perhaps failed to realise the importance of not applying to people in society, less intelligent and less educated than herself, those cutting strokes which the injured party never forgets.

Certainly, if at a given moment in her youth Mme. de Villeparisis, surfeited with the satisfaction of belonging to the fine flower of the aristocracy, had found a sort of amusement in scandalising the people among whom she lived, and in deliberately impairing her own position in society, she had begun to attach its full importance to that position once it was definitely lost. She had wished to show the Duchesses that she was better than they, by saying and doing all the things that they dared not say or do. But now that they all, save such as were closely related to her, had ceased to call, she felt herself diminished, and sought once more to reign, but with another sceptre than that of wit. She would have liked to attract to her house all those women whom she had taken such pains to drive away.

On the occasion of this first call which, after leaving Saint-Loup, I went to pay on Mme. de Villeparisis, following the advice given by M. de Norpois to my father, I found her in her drawing-room hung with yellow silk, against which the sofas and the admirable armchairs upholstered in Beauvais tapestry stood out with the almost purple redness of ripe raspberries. Side by side with the Guermantes and Villeparisis portraits one saw those—gifts from the sitters themselves—of Queen Marie-Amélie, the Queen of the Belgians, the

Prince de Joinville and the Empress of Austria. Mme. de Vileparisis herself, capped with an old-fashioned bonnet of black lace (which she preserved with the same instinctive sense of local or historical colour as a Breton innkeeper who, however Parisian his customers may have become, feels it more in keeping to make his maids dress in coifs and wide sleeves), was seated at a little desk on which in front of her, as well as her brushes, her palette and an unfinished flower-piece in water-colours, were arranged in glasses, in saucers, in cups, moss-roses, zinnias, maidenhair ferns, which on account of the sudden influx of callers she had just left off painting, and which had the effect of being piled on a florist's counter in some eighteenth-century mezzotint. In this drawing-room, which had been slightly heated on purpose because the Marquise had caught cold on the journey from her house in the country, there were already when I arrived a librarian with whom Mme. de Villeparisis had spent the morning in selecting the autograph letters to herself from various historical personages which were to figure in facsimile as documentary evidence in the *Memoirs* which she was preparing for the press, and a historian, solemn and tongue-tied, who hearing that she had inherited and still possessed a portrait of the Duchesse de Montmorency had come to ask her permission to reproduce it as a plate in his work on the Fronde; a party strengthened presently by the addition of my old friend Bloch, now a rising dramatist, upon whom she counted to secure the gratuitous services of actors and actresses at her next series of afternoon parties. It was true that the social kaleidoscope was in the act of turning and that the Dreyfus case was shortly to hurl the Jews down to the lowest rung of the social ladder. But, for one thing, the anti-Dreyfus cyclone might rage as it would, it is not in the first hour of a storm that the waves are highest. In the second place, Mme. de Villeparisis, leaving a whole section of her family to fulminate against the Jews, had hitherto kept herself entirely aloof from the Case and never gave it a thought. Lastly, a young man like Bloch, whom no one knew, might pass unperceived, whereas leading Jews, representatives of their party, were already threatened. He had his chin pointed now by a goat-beard, wore double glasses and a long frock coat, and carried a glove like a roll of papyrus in his hand. The Rumanians, the Egyptians, the Turks may hate the Jews. But in a French drawing-room the differences between those peoples are not so apparent, and an Israelite making his entry as though he were emerging from the heart of the desert, his body crouching like a hyena's, his neck thrust obliquely forward, spreading himself in profound 'salaams', completely satisfies a certain taste for the oriental. Only it is essential that the Jew should not be actually 'in' society, otherwise he will readily assume the aspect of a lord and his manners become so Gallicised that on his face a rebellious nose, growing like a nasturtium in any but the right direction, will make one think rather of Mascarille's nose than of Solomon's. But Bloch, not having been rendered supple by the gymnastics of the Faubourg, nor ennobled by a crossing with England or Spain, remained for a lover of the exotic as strange and savoury a spectacle, in spite of his European costume, as one of Decamps's Jews. (Later in the afternoon Bloch might have imagined that it was out of anti-semitic malice that M. de Charlus inquired whether his first name was Jewish, whereas it was simply from aesthetic interest and love of local colour.)

"I understand, sir, that you are thinkin' of writin' somethin' about Mme. la Duchesse de Montmorency," said Mme. de Villeparisis to the historian of the Fronde in that grudging tone which she allowed, quite unconsciously, to spoil the effect of her great and genuine kindness, a tone due to the shrivelling crossness, the sense of grievance that is a physiological accompaniment of age, as well as to the affectation of imitating the almost rustic speech of the old nobility: "I'm goin' to let you see her portrait, the original of the copy they have in the Louvre."

She rose, laying down her brushes beside the flowers, and the little apron which then came into sight at her waist, and which she wore so as not to stain her dress with paints, added still further to the impression of an old peasant given by her bonnet and her big spectacles, and offered a sharp contrast to the luxury of her appointments, the butler who had brought in the tea and cakes, the liveried footman for whom she now rang to light up the portrait of the Duchesse de Montmorency, Abbess of one of the most famous Chapters in the East of France. Everyone had risen. "What is rather amusin'," said our hostess, "is that in these Chapters where our great-aunts were so often made Abbesses, the daughters of the King of France would not have been admitted. They were very close corporations." "Not admit the King's daughters," cried Bloch in amazement, "why ever not?" "Why, because the House of France had not enough quarterings after that low marriage." Bloch's bewilderment increased. "A low marriage? The House of France? When was that?" "Why, when they married into the Medicis," replied Mme. de Villeparisis in the most natural manner. "It's a fine picture, ain't it, and in a perfect state of preservation," she added.

The door opened and the Duchesse de Guermantes entered the

room. "Well, how are you?" Mme. de Villeparisis greeted her without moving her head, taking from her apron-pocket a hand which she held out to the newcomer; and then ceasing at once to take any notice of her niece, in order to return to the historian: "That is the portrait of the Duchesse de La Rochefoucauld........."

A young servant with a bold manner and a charming face (but so finely chiselled, to ensure its perfection, that the nose was a little red and the rest of the skin slightly flushed as though they were still smarting from the recent and sculptural incision) came in bearing a card on a salver.

"It is that gentleman who has been several times to see Mme. la Marquise."

"Did you tell him I was at home?" "He heard the voices." "Oh, very well then, show him in. It's a man who was introduced to me," she explained. "He told me he was very anxious to come to the house. I certainly never said he might. But here he's taken the trouble to call five times now; it doesn't do to hurt people's feelings. Sir," she went on to me, "and you, Sir," to the historian of the Fronde, "let me introduce my niece, the Duchesse de Guermantes."

The historian made a low bow, as I did also, and since he seemed to suppose that some friendly remark ought to follow this salute, his eyes brightened and he was preparing to open his mouth when he was once more frozen by the sight of Mme. de Guermantes who had taken advantage of the independence of her torso to throw it forward with an exaggerated politeness and bring it neatly back to a position of rest without letting face or eyes appear to have noticed that anyone was standing before them; after breathing a gentle sigh she contented herself with manifesting the nullity of the impression that had been made on her by the sight of the historian and myself by performing certain movements of her nostrils, with a precision that testified to the absolute inertia of her unoccupied attention.

The importunate visitor entered the room, making straight for Mme de Villeparisis with an ingenuous, fervent air: it was Legrandin.

"Thank you so very much for letting me come and see you," he began, laying stress on the word 'very' "it is a pleasure of a quality altogether rare and subtle that you confer on an old solitary; I assure you that its repercussion ......" He stopped short on catching sight of me. "I was just showing this gentleman a fine portrait of the Duchesse de La Rochefoucauld, the wife of the author of the *Maxims*; it's a family picture."

Mme. de Guermantes had sat down. Her name, accompanied as it was by her title, added to her corporeal dimensions the duchy which projected itself round about her and brought the shadowy, sun-splashed coolness of the woods of Guermantes into this drawing-room, to surround the tuffet on which she was sitting.

Mme de Villeparisis rang the bell and, when the servant had appeared, as she made no secret, and indeed, liked to advertise the fact that her old friend spent the greater part of his time in her house: "Go and tell M. de Norpois to come in," she ordered him, "he is sorting some papers in my library; he said he would be twenty minutes, and I've been waiting now for an hour and three-quarters. He will tell you about the Dreyfus case, anything you want to know," she said gruffly to Bloch. "He doesn't approve much of the way things are going."

The butler could not have delivered his mistress's message properly, for M. de Norpois, to make believe that he had just come in from the street, and had not yet seen his hostess, had picked up the first hat that he had found in the hall, and came forward to kiss Mme. de Villeparisis's hand with great ceremony, asking after her health with all the interest that people show after a long separation. He was not aware that the Marquise had already destroyed any semblance of reality in this charade, which she cut short by taking M. de Norpois and Bloch into an adjoining room. Bloch, who had observed all the courtesy that was being shown to a person whom he had not yet discovered to be M. de Norpois, had said to me, trying to seem at his ease: "Who is that old idiot?" Perhaps, too, all this bowing and scraping by M. de Norpois had really shocked the better element in Bloch's nature, the freer and more straightforward manners of a younger generation, and he was partly sincere in condemning it as absurd. However that might be, it ceased to appear absurd, and indeed delighted him the moment it was himself, Bloch, to whom the salutations were addressed.

"Monsieur l'Ambassadeur," said Mme. de Villeparisis, "I should like you to know this gentleman. Monsieur Bloch, Monsieur le Marquis de Norpois. Just ask him anything you want to know; he will be delighted to talk to you. I think you wished to speak to him about the Dreyfus case," she went on, no more considering whether this would suit M. de Norpois than she would have thought of asking leave of the Duchesse de Montmorency's portrait before having it lighted up for the historian, or of the tea before pouring it into a cup. "

I heard you refusing to let Robert bring his woman." said Mme. de Guermantes to her aunt, after Bloch had taken the Ambassador aside. " I don't think you'll miss much, she's a perfect horror, as you know, without a vestige of talent, and besides she's grotesquely ugly."

"Do you mean to say, you know her, Duchess? "asked M. d'Argencourt.

"Yes, didn't you know that she performed in my house before the whole of Paris, not that that's anything for me to be proud of," explained Mme. de Guermantes with a laugh, glad nevertheless, since the actress was under discussion, to let it be known that she herself had had the first fruits of her foolishness. " Hallo, I suppose I ought to be going now" she added, without moving. She had just seen her husband enter the room and these words were an allusion to the absurdity of their appearing to be paying a call together, like a newly married couple, rather than to the often strained relations that existed between her and the enormous fellow she had married, who, despite his increasing years, still led the life of a gay bachelor. Ranging over the considerable party that was gathered round the tea-table the genial, cynical gaze—dazzled a little by the brightness of the setting sun—of the little round pupils lodged in the exact centre of his eyes, like the " bulls " which the excellent marksman that he was could always hit with such perfect aim and precision, the Duke came forward with a bewildered cautious slowness as though, alarmed by so brilliant a gathering, he was afraid of treading on ladies' skirts and interrupting conversations. A permanent smile—suggesting a "Good King of Yvetot"—slightly pompous, a half-open hand floating like a shark's fin by his side, which he allowed to be vaguely clasped by his old friends and by the strangers who were introduced to him, enabled him, without his having to make a single movement, or to interrupt his genial, lazy, royal progress, to reward the assiduity of them all by simply murmuring: " How do, my boy; how do, my dear friend; charmed, Monsieur Bloch; how do, Argencourt; " and, on coming to myself, who was the most highly favoured, when he had been told my name: " How do, my young neighbour, how's your father? What a splendid fellow he is! ". He made no great demonstration except to Mme. de Villeparisis, who gave him good-day with a nod of her head, drawing one hand from a pocket of her little apron.

Being formidably rich in a world where everyone was steadily growing poorer, and having secured the permanent attachment to his person of the idea of this enormous fortune, he displayed all the vanity of the great nobleman reinforced by that of the man of means, the refinement and breeding of the former just managing to control the latter's self-sufficiency. One could understand, moreover, that his success with women, which made his wife so unhappy, was not due merely to his name and fortune, for he was still extremely good looking, and his profile retained the purity, the firmness of outline of a Greek god's.

Before M. de Norpois, under constraint from his hostess, had taken Bloch into the little recess where they could talk more freely, I went up to the old diplomat for a moment and put in a word about my father's Academic chair. He tried first of all to postpone the conversation to another day. I pointed out that I was going to Balbec. "What? Going again to Balbec? Why, you're a regular globe-trotter." He listened to what I had to say. All at once he seemed animated by a positive affection for my father. And after one of those opening hesitations out of which suddenly a word explodes as though in spite of the speaker, whose irresistible conviction prevails over his half-hearted efforts at silence: "No, no," he said to me with emotion, "your father *must not* stand. In his own interest he must not; it is not fair to himself; he owes a certain respect to his own really great merits, which would be compromised by such an adventure. He is too big a man for that. If he should be elected, he will have everything to lose and nothing to gain. He is not an orator, thank heaven. And that is the one thing that counts with my dear colleagues, even if you only talk platitudes. Your father has an important goal in life; he should march straight ahead towards it, and not allow himself to turn aside to beat bushes, even the bushes (more thorny for that matter than flowery) of the grove of Academe. Besides, he would not get many votes. The Academy likes to keep a postulant waiting for some time before taking him to its bosom. For the present, there is nothing to be done. Later on, I don't say. But he must wait until the Society itself comes in quest of him. It makes a practice, not a very fortunate practice, a fetish rather, of the *farà da sè* of our friends across the Alps. But, whatever happens, your father must on no account put himself forward as a candidate. *Principis obsta.* His friends would find themselves placed in a delicate position if he suddenly called upon them for their votes. Indeed," he broke forth, with an air of candour, fixing his blue eyes on my face, "I am going to say a thing that you will be surprised to hear coming from me, who am so fond of your father. Well, simply because I am fond of him (we are known as the inseparables—*Arcades ambo*), simply because I know the immense service that he can still render to his country, the reefs, from which he can steer her if he remains at the helm; out of affection, out of high regard for him, out of patriotism, I should not vote for him. I fancy, moreover, that I have given him to understand that I should not." " So that to give him my vote now would be a sort of recantation on my part." M. de Norpois repeatedly dismissed his brother Academicians as old fossils. Other reasons apart, every member of a club or academy likes to ascribe to his fellow members the type of character that is the direct converse of his own, less for the advantage of being able to say: "Ah! If It only rested with me!" than for the satisfaction of making the election which he himself has managed to secure seem more difficult, a greater distinction. "I may tell you," he concluded, "that in the best interests of you all, I should prefer to see your father triumphantly elected in ten or fifteen years time." Words which I assumed to have been dictated if not by jealousy, at any rate by an utter lack of any willingness to oblige.

After a while Bloch and M. de Norpois returned from the other room and came towards us. "Well, sir," asked Mme. de Villeparisis, "have you been talking to him about the Dreyfus case?"

M. de Norpois raised his eyes to the ceiling, but with a smile, as though calling on heaven, to witness the monstrosity of the caprices to which his Dulcinea compelled him to submit. Nevertheless he spoke to Bloch with great affability of the terrible, perhaps fatal period through which France was passing. As this presumably meant that M. de Norpois (to whom Bloch had confessed his belief in the innocence of Dreyfus) was an ardent anti-Dreyfusard, the Ambassador's geniality, his air of tacit admission that his listener was in the right, of never doubting that they were both of the same opinion, of being prepared to join forces with him to overthrow the Government, flattered Bloch's vanity and aroused his curiosity. What were the important points which M. de Norpois never specified but on which he seemed implicitly to affirm that he was in agreement with Bloch; what opinion, then, did he hold of the case, that could bring them together? Bloch was all the more astonished at the mysterious unanimity which seemed to exist between him and M. de Norpois, in that it was not confined to politics, Mme. de Villeparisis having spoken at some length to M. de Norpois of Bloch's literary work.

"You are not of your age," the former Ambassador told him, "and I congratulate you upon that. You are not of this age in which disinterested work no longer exists, in which writers offer the public nothing but obscenities or ineptitudes. Efforts such as yours ought to be encouraged, and would be, if we had a Government."

Bloch was flattered by this picture of himself swimming alone amid a universal shipwreck. But here again he would have been glad of details, would have liked to know what were the ineptitudes to which M. de Norpois referred. Bloch had the feeling that he was working along the same lines as plenty of others; he had never supposed himself to be so exceptional. He returned to the Dreyfus case, but did not succeed in elucidating M. de Norpois's own views.

"What are those two palavering about over there?" M. de Guermantes asked Mme. de Villeparisis, indicating M. de Norpois and Bloch. "The Dreyfus case." "The devil they are. By the way, do you know who is a red-hot supporter of Dreyfus? I give you a thousand guesses. My nephew Robert! I can tell you that, at the Jockey, when they heard of his goings on, there was a fine gathering of the clans, a regular hue and cry. And as he's coming up for election next week..........

"Of course," broke in the Duchess, "if they're all like Gilbert, who keeps on saying that all the Jews ought to be sent back to Jerusalem.".

The Duke made a show of his wife, but did not love her. Extremely self-centred, he hated to be interrupted, besides he was in the habit, at home, of treating her brutally. Convulsed with the twofold rage of a bad husband when his wife speaks to him, and a good talker when he is not listened to, he stopped short and transfixed the Duchess with a glare which made everyone feel uncomfortable.

"What makes you think we want to hear about Gilbert and Jerusalem? It's nothing to do with that. But," he went on in a gentler tone, "you will agree that if one of our family were to be pilled at the Jockey, especially Robert, whose father was chairman for ten years, it would be a pretty serious matter. What can you expect my dear, it's got em on the raw, those fellows; they're all over it. I don't blame them either; personally you know that I have no racial prejudice, all that sort of thing seems to me out of date, and I do claim to move with the times; but damn it all, when one goes by the name of 'Marquis de Saint-Loup,' one isn't a Dreyfusard; what more can I say?"

M.de Guermantes uttered the words: "When one goes by the name of Marquis de Saint-Loup," with some emphasis. He knew very well that it was a far greater thing to go by that of Duc de Guermantes.

A lady came in who was the Comtesse de Marsantes, Robert's mother. Mme. de Marsantes was regarded in the Faubourg Saint--

Germain as a superior being, of a goodness, a resignation that were positively angelic. So I had been told, and had had no particular reason to feel surprised, not knowing at the same time that she was the sister of the Duc de Guermantes. Later, I have always been taken aback, whenever I have learned that such women, melancholy, pure, victimised, venerated like the ideal forms of saints in church windows, had flowered from the same genealogical stem as brothers brutal debauched and vile. Brothers and sisters, when they are closely alike in features as were the Duc de Guermantes and Mme. de Marsantes, ought (I felt) to have a single intellect in common, the same heart, as a person would have who might vary between good and evil moods but in whom one could not, for all that, expect to find a vast breadth of outlook if he had a narrow mind, or a sublime abnegation if his heart was hard.

Mme. de Marsantes was wearing a gown of white surah embroidered with large palms, on which stood out flowers of a different material, these being black. This was because, three weeks earlier, she had lost her cousin, M. de Montmorency, a bereavement which did not prevent her from paying calls or even from going to small dinners, but always in mourning. She was a great lady. Atavism had filled her with the frivolity of generations of life at court, with all the superficial, rigorous duties that that implies. Mme. de Marsantes had not had the strength of character to regret for any length of time the death of her father and mother, but she would not for anything in the world have appeared in colours in the month following that of a cousin. She was more than pleasant to me, both because I was Robert's friend and because I did not move in the same world as he. This pleasantness was accompanied by a pretence of shyness, by that sort of intermittent withdrawal of the voice, the eyes, the mind, which a woman draws back to her like a skirt that has indiscreetly spread, so as not to take up too much room, to remain stiff and erect even in her suppleness, as a good upbringing teaches. A good upbringing which must not, however, be taken too literally, many of these ladies passing very swiftly into a complete dissolution of morals without ever losing the almost childlike correctness of their manners.

At this point the door opened again and Robert himself entered the room.

"Well, talk of the Saint!" said Mme. de Guermantes.

Mme. de Marsantes, who had her back to the door, had not seen her son come in. When she did catch sight of him, her motherly bosom was convulsed with joy, as by the beating of a wing, her body half rose from her seat, her face quivered and she fastened on Robert eyes big with astonishment: "What! You've come! How delightful! What a surprise!"

"Ah! *Talk of the Saint!*—I see," cried the Belgian diplomat, with a shout of laughter.

"Delicious, ain't it?" came tartly from the Duchess, who hated puns, and had ventured on this one only with a pretence of making fun of herself.

"Good afternoon, Robert," she said, "I believe he's forgotten his aunt."

They talked for a moment, probably about myself for as Saint-Loup was leaving her to join his mother Mme. de Guermantes turned to me: "Good afternoon; how are you?" was her greeting. She allowed to rain on me the light of her azure gaze, hesitated for a moment, unfolded and stretched towards me the stem of her arm, leaned forward her body which sprang rapidly backwards like a bush that has been pulled down to the ground and, on being released, returns to its natural position. Thus she acted under the fire of Saint-Loup's eyes, which kept her under observation and were making frantic efforts to obtain some further concession still from his aunt. Fearing that our conversation might fail altogether, he joined in, to stimulate it and answered for me: "He's not very well just now, he gets rather tired; I think he would be a great deal better, by the way, if he saw you more often, for I can't help telling you that he admires you immensely."

"Oh, but that's very nice of him," said Mme. de Guermantes in a deliberately casual tone, as if I had brought her her cloak. "I am most flattered."

"Look, I must go and talk to my mother for a minute; take my chair," said Saint-Loup, thus forcing me to sit down next to his aunt. We were both silent.

"I see you sometimes in the morning," she said, as though she were telling me something that I did not know, and I for my part had never seen her. "It's so good for one, a walk."

Mme. de Guermantes lowered her eyes and gave a semicircular turn to her wrist to look at the time. "Gracious! I must fly at once if I'm to get to Mme. de Saint-Ferréol's, and I'm dining with Mme. Leroi." And she rose without bidding me goodbye. She had just caught sight of Mme. Swann, who appeared considerably embarrassed at finding me in the room. She remembered, doubtless, that she had been the first to assure me that she was convinced of

Dreyfus's innocence.

" I don't want my mother to introduce me to Mme. Swann,," Saint-Loup said to me. "She's an ex-whore. Her husband's a Jew, and she comes here to pose as a Nationalist. Hallo, here's uncle Palamède."

The arrival of Mme Swann had a special interest for me, due to an incident which had occurred a few days earlier and which I am obliged to record on account of the consequences which it was to have at a much later date, as the reader will learn in due course. Well, a few days before this visit to Mme. de Villeparisis, I had myself received a visitor whom I little expected, namely Charles Morel, the son (though I had never heard of his existence) of my great-uncle's old servant. This great-uncle (he in whose house I had met the lady in pink) had died the year before. His servant had more than once expressed his intention of coming to see me; I had no idea of the object of his visit, but should have been glad to see him for I had learned from Françoise that he had a genuine veneration for my uncle's memory and made a pilgrimage regularly to the cemetery in which he was buried. But, being obliged for reasons of health, to retire to his home in the country, where he expected to remain for some time, he delegated the duty to his son. I was surprised to see come into my room a handsome young fellow of eighteen, dressed with expensive rather than good taste, but looking, all the same, like anything in the world except the son of a gentleman's servant. He made a point moreover, at the start of our conversation, of severing all connection with the domestic class from which he sprang, by informing me, with a smile of satisfaction, that he had won the first prize at the Conservatoire. The object of his visit to me was as follows: his father, when going through the effects of my uncle Adolphe, had set aside some, which he felt could not very well be sent to my parents but were at the same time of a nature likely to interest a young man of my age. These were the photographs of the 'famous' actresses, the notorious courtesans whom my uncle had known, the last fading pictures of that gay life of a man about town which he divided by a watertight compartment from his family life. While young Morel was showing them to me, I noticed that he addressed me as though he were speaking to an equal. He derived from saying 'you' to me as often, and 'sir' as seldom as possible, the pleasure natural in one whose father had never ventured, when addressing my parents, upon anything but the third person. Almost all these photographs bore an inscription such as: 'To my best friend.' One actress, less grateful and more circumspect than the rest, had written: 'To the best of friends,' which enabled her (so I was assured) to say afterwards that my uncle was in no sense and had never been her best friend but was merely the friend who had done the most little services for her, the friend she made use of, a good, kind man, in other words an old fool. In vain might young Morel seek to divest himself of his lowly origin, one felt that the shade of my uncle Adolphe, venerable and gigantic in the eyes of the old servant, had never ceased to hover, almost a holy vision, over the childhood and boyhood of the son. While I was turning over the photographs Charles Morel examined my room. And as I was looking for some place in which I might keep them, "How is it," he asked me (in a tone in which the reproach had no need to find expression, so implicit was it in the words themselves), "that I don't see a single photograph of your uncle in your room?" I felt the blood rise to my cheeks and stammered: "Why, I don't believe I have such a thing." "What, you haven't one photograph of your uncle Adolphe, who was so devoted to you! I will send you one of my governor's—he has quantities of them— and I hope you will set it up in the place of honour above that chest of drawers, which came to you from your uncle." It is true that, as I had not even a photograph of my father or mother in my room, there was nothing so very shocking in there not being one of my uncle Adolphe. But it was easy enough to see that for old Morel, who had trained his son in the same way of thinking, my uncle was the important person in the family, my parents only reflecting a diminished light from his. I was in higher favour, because my uncle used constantly to say that I was going to turn out a sort of Racine, or Vaulabelle, and Morel regarded me almost as an adopted son, as a child by election of my uncle. I soon discovered that this young man was extremely 'pushing'. Thus at this first meeting he asked me, being something of a composer as well and capable of setting short poems to music, whether I knew any poet who had a good position in society. I mentioned one. He did not know the work of this poet and had never heard his name, of which he made a note. Well, I found out that shortly afterwards he wrote to the poet telling him that, a fanatical admirer of his work, he, Morel, had composed a musical setting for one of his sonnets and would be grateful if the author would arrange for its performance at the Comtesse so-and-so's. This was going a little too fast, and exposing his hand. The poet, taking offence, made no reply.

For the rest, Charles Morel seemed to have, besides his ambition, a strong leaning towards more concrete realities. He had noticed, as he came through the courtyard, Jupien's niece at work upon a waistcoat, and although he explained to me only that he happened to want a fancy waistcoat at that very moment, I felt that the girl had made a vivid impression on him. He had no hesitation about asking me to come downstairs and introduce him to her, "but not as a connection of your family, you follow me, I rely on your discretion not to drag in my father, say just a distinguished artist of your acquaintance, you know how important it is to make a good impression on tradespeople." Albeit he had suggested to me that, not knowing him well enough to call him, he quite realised, "dear friend," I might address him, before the girl, in some such terms as "not dear master, of course, . . although. . . well, if you like, dear distinguished artist." Once in the shop, I avoided 'qualifying' him as Saint-Simon would have expressed it, and contented myself with reiterating his "you". He picked out from several patterns of velvet one of the brightest red imaginable and so loud that, for all his bad taste, he was never able to wear the waistcoat when it was made. The girl settled down to work again with her two apprentices, but it struck me that the impression had been mutual, and that Charles Morel, whom she regarded as of her own 'station' (only smarter and richer), had proved singularly attractive to her. As I had been greatly surprised to find among the photographs which his father had sent me one of the portrait of Miss Sacripant (otherwise Odette) by Elstir, I said to Charles Morel as I went with him to the outer gate: "I don't suppose you can tell me, but did my uncle know this lady well? I don't see at what stage in his life I can fit her in exactly; and it interests me, because of M. Swann ..." "Why, if I wasn't forgetting to tell you that my father asked me specially to draw your attention to that lady's picture. As a matter of fact, she was, 'lunching' with your uncle the last time you ever saw him. My father was in two minds whether to let you in. It seems you made a great impression on the wench and she hoped to see more of you. But just at that time there was some trouble in the family, by what my father tells me and you never set eyes on your uncle again." He broke off with a smile of farewell across the courtyard at Jupien's niece. She was watching him and admiring, no doubt, his thin face and regular features, his fair hair and sparkling eyes. I, as I gave him my hand, was thinking of Mme. Swann and saying to myself with amazement, so far apart, so different were they in my memory, that I should have henceforth to identify her with the 'Lady in pink.'

M. de Charlus was not long in taking his place by the side of Mme.

Swann, At every social gathering at which he appeared and, contemptuous towards the men, courted by the women, he promptly attached himself to the smartest of the latter, whose garments he seemed almost to put on as an ornament to his own; the Baron's frock coat or swallowtails made one think of a portrait by some great painter of a man dressed in black but having by his side, thrown over a chair, the brilliantly coloured cloak which he is about to wear at some costume ball. This partnership, generally with some royal lady, secured for M. de Charlus various privileges which he liked to enjoy. For instance, one result of it was that his hostesses, at theatricals or concerts, allowed the Baron alone to have a front seat, in a row of ladies, while the rest of the men were crowded together at the back of the room. And then besides, completely absorbed it seemed, in repeating, at the top of his voice, amusing stories to the enraptured lady, M. de Charlus was dispensed from the necessity of going to shake hands with any of the others, was set free, in other words, from all social duties. Behind the scented barrier in which the beauty of his choice enclosed him, he was isolated amid a crowded drawing-room, as in a crowded theatre or concert-hall, behind the rampart of a box; and when anyone came up to greet him, through, so to speak, the beauty of his companion, it was permissible for him to reply quite curtly and without interrupting his business of conversation with a lady. Certainly Mme. Swann was scarcely of the rank of the people with whom he liked thus to flaunt himself. But he professed admiration for her and friendship for Swann, he knew that she would be flattered by his attentions and was himself flattered at being compromised by the prettiest woman in the room.

Mme. Swann, finding herself alone and having realised that I was a friend of Saint-Loup, beckoned to me to come and sit beside her. Not having seen her for so long I did not know what to talk to her about: I was keeping an eye on my hat, among the crowd of hats that littered the carpet, and I asked myself with a vague curiosity to whom one of them could belong which was not that of the Duc de Guermantes and yet in the lining of which a capital 'G' was surmounted by a ducal coronet. I knew who everyone in the room was, and could not think of anyone whose hat this could possibly be.

" What a pleasant man M. de Norpois is," I said to Mme. Swann, looking at the Ambassador. "It is true Robert de Saint-Loup says he's a pest, but ......"

"He is quite right," she replied. Seeing from her face that she was thinking of something which she was keeping from me, I plied her with questions. For the satisfaction of appearing to be greatly taken up by some one in this room where she knew hardly anyone, she took me into a corner.

"I am sure this is what M. de Saint-Loup meant," she began, "but you must never tell him I said so, for he would think me indiscreet, and I value his esteem very highly; I am an 'honest Injun', don't you know. The other day, Charlus was dining at the Princesse de Guermantes's; I don't know how it was, but your name was mentioned. M. de Norpois seems to have told them— it's all too silly for words, don't go and worry yourself to death over it, nobody paid any attention, they all knew only too well the mischievous tongue that said it—that you were a hypocritical little flatterer."

I have recorded a long way back my stupefaction at the discovery that a friend of my father, such as M. de Norpois was, could have expressed himself, thus in speaking of me.

A few years earlier I should have been only too glad to tell Mme. Swann in what connection I had fawned upon M. de Norpois, since the connection had been my desire to know her. But I no longer felt this desire, I was no longer in love with Gilberte. On the other hand I had not succeeded in identifying Mme. Swann with the lady in pink of my childhood. Accordingly I spoke of the woman who was on my mind at the moment.

"Did you see the Duchesse de Guermantes just now?" I asked Mme. Swann.

But since the Duchess did not bow to Mme. Swann when they met, the latter chose to appear to regard her as a person of no importance whose presence in a room one did not even remark.   "I don't know; I didn't *realise* she was here," she replied sourly, using an expression borrowed from England.

Robert called me away to the far end of the room where he and his mother were. "You have been good to me," I said, "how can I thank you? Can we dine together to-morrow?" "Tomorrow? Yes, if you like, but it will have to be with Bloch. I met him just now on the doorstep. As for being good," went on Saint-Loup, "you say I have been to you, but I haven't been good at all, my aunt tells me that it's you who avoid her, that you never utter a word to her. She wonders whether you have anything against her."

Fortunately for myself, if I had been taken in by this speech, our departure for Balbec, which I believed to be imminent, would have prevented my making any attempt to see Mme. de Guermantes again, to assure her that I had nothing against her, and so to put her under the necessity of proving that it was she who had something against me. But I had only to remind myself that she had not even offered to let me see her Elstirs. Besides, this was not a disappointment; I had never expected her to begin talking to me about them; I knew that I did not appeal to her, that I need have no hope of ever making her like me; the most that I had been able to look forward to was that, thanks to her kindness, I might there and then receive, since I should not be seeing her again before I left Paris, an entirely pleasing impression, which I could take with me to Balbec indefinitely prolonged, intact, instead of a memory broken by anxiety and sorrow.

Now that Mme. de Guermantes had left the room, I had more leisure to observe Robert, and I noticed then for the first time that, once again, a sort of flood of anger seemed to be coursing through him rising to the surface of his stern and sombre features. I was afraid lest, he might be feeling humiliated in my presence at having allowed himself to be treated so harshly by his mistress without making any rejoinder.

Suddenly he broke away from his mother, who had put her arm round his neck, and, coming towards me, led me behind the little flower-strewn counter at which Mme. de Villeparisis had resumed her seat, making a sign to me to follow him, into the smaller room. I was hurrying after him when. M. de Charlus, who must have supposed that I was leaving the house turned abruptly from Prince von Faffenheim, to whom he had been talking, and made a rapid circuit which brought him face to face with me. I saw with alarm that he had taken the hat in the lining of which were a capital 'G' and a ducal coronet. In the doorway into the little room he said, without looking at me: "As I see that you have taken to going into society, you must do me the pleasure of coming to see me. But its a little complicated," he went on with a distracted, calculating air, as if the pleasure had been one that he was afraid of not securing again once he had let slip the opportunity of arranging with me the means by which it might be realised. "I am very seldom at home; you will have to write to me. But I should prefer to explain things to you more quietly. I am just going. Will you walk a short way with me? I shall only keep you a moment."

"You'd better take care sir," I warned him; "you have picked up the wrong hat by mistake."

"Do you want to stop me taking my own hat?"

I assumed, a similar mishap having recently occurred to myself, that someone else having taken his hat he had seized upon one at random, so as not to go home bare-headed, and that I had placed him in a difficulty by exposing his strategem. I told him that I must say a few words to Saint-Loup. "He is still talking to that idiot the Duc de Guermantes," I added. "That really is charming; I shall tell my brother." "Oh! you think that would interest M. de Charlus?" (I imagined that, if he had a brother, that brother must be called Charlus also. Saint-Loup had indeed explained his family tree to me at Balbec, but I had forgotten the details) "Who is talking about M.de Charlus?" replied the Baron in an arrogant tone. "Go to Robert. I hear," he went on, "that you took part this morning in one of those orgies that he has with a woman who is disgracing him. You would do well to use your influence with him to make him realise the pain he is causing his poor mother, and all of us, by dragging our name in the dirt."

I should have liked to reply that at this degrading luncheon the conversation had been entirely about Emerson, Ibsen and Tolstoy, and that the young woman had lectured Robert to make him drink nothing but water. In the hope of bringing some balm to Robert, whose pride had, I felt, been wounded, I sought to find an excuse for his mistress. I did not know that at that moment in spite of his anger with her, it was on himself that he was heaping reproaches.

"I've come to the conclusion I was wrong about that matter of the necklace," Robert said to me. "Of course, I never meant for a moment to do anything wrong, but, I know very well, other people don't look at things in the same way as oneself. She had a very hard time when she was young. In her eyes, I was bound to appear just the rich man who thinks he can get anything he wants with his money, and with whom a poor person cannot compete, whether in trying to influence Boucheron or in a lawsuit. Of course she has been horribly cruel to me, when I have never thought of anything but her good. But I do see clearly, she believes that I wanted to make her feel that one could keep a hold on her with money, and that's not true. And she's so fond of me; what must she be thinking of me? Poor darling, if you only knew, she has such charming ways, I simply can't tell you, she has often done the most adorable things for me. How wretched she must be feeling now! In any case, whatever happens in the long run, I don't want to let her think me a cad; I shall dash off to Boucheron's and get the necklace. You never know; very likely when she sees me with it, she will admit that she's been in the wrong. Don't you see, it's the idea that she is suffering at this moment that I can't bear. What one suffers oneself one knows; that's nothing. But with her—to say to oneself that she's suffering and not to be able to form any idea of what she feels—I think I shall go mad in a minute—I'd much rather never see her again than let her suffer. "!

Robert swept me back to his mother. "Good-bye," he said to her. " I've got to go now. I don't know when I shall get leave again. Probably not for a month. I shall write as soon as I know myself."

Robert went to his mistress, taking with him the splendid ornament which, after what had been said on both sides, he ought not to have given her. But it came to the same thing, for she would not look at it, and even after their reconciliation he could never persuade her to accept it. Certain of Robert's friends thought that these proofs of disinterestedness which she furnished were deliberately planned to draw him closer to her. And yet she was not greedy about money, except perhaps to be able to spend it without thought. I have seen her bestow recklessly on people whom she believed to be in need, the most insensate charity.

"I blame myself for one thing only," Mme. de Marsantes murmured in my ear, "and that was my telling him that he wasn't nice to me: He, such an adorable, unique son, there's no one else like him in the world, the only time I see him, to have told him he wasn't nice to me, I would far rather he'd beaten me, because I am sure that whatever pleasure he may be having this evening, and he hasn't many, will be spoiled for him by that unfair word. But, Sir, I mustn't keep you, since you're in a hurry."

"But I am in no hurry," I replied; "besides, I must wait for M. de Charlus; I am going with him."

"You're going from here with my nephew Palamède?" she asked me.

Thinking that it might produce a highly favourable impression on Mme. de Villeparisis if she learned that I was on intimate terms with a nephew whom she esteemed so greatly, "He has asked me to go home with him," I answered blithely. "I am so glad. Besides we are greater friends than you think and I've quite made up my mind that we're going to be better friends still."

From being vexed, Mme. de Villeparisis seemed to have grown anxious. "Don't wait for him," she said to me, with a preoccupied air. "He is talking to M. de Faffenheim. He's certain to have forgotten what he said to you. You'd much better go, now, quickly, while his back is turned."

The first emotion shown by Mme. de Villeparisis would have suggested, but for the circumstances, offended modesty. Her insistence, her opposition might well, if one had studied her face alone, have appeared to be dictated by virtue. I was not, myself, in any hurry to join Robert and his mistress. But Mme. de Villeparisis seemed to make such a point of my going that, thinking perhaps that she had some important business to discuss with her nephew, I bade her good-bye. Next to her M. de Guermantes, superb and Olympian, was ponderously seated. One would have said that the notion, omnipresent in all his members, of his vast riches gave him a particular high density, as though they had been melted in a crucible into a single human ingot to form this man whose value was so immense. At the moment of my saying good-bye to him he rose politely from his seat, and I could feel, the dead weight of thirty mlllions which his old-fashioned French breeding set in motion, raised until it stood before me.

As I went downstairs I heard behind me a voice calling out to me: "So this is how you wait for me, is it?" It was M. de Charlus.

"You don't mind if we go a little, way on foot?" he asked dryly, when we were in the courtyard. "We can walk until I find a cab that suits me." "You wished to speak to me about something, Sir?" "Oh yes, as a matter of fact there were some things I wished to say to you, but I am not so sure now whether I shall. As far as you are concerned, I am sure that they might be the starting-point which would lead you to inestimable benefits. But I see also that they would bring into my existence, at an age when one begins to value tranquillity, a great loss of time, great inconvenience. I ask myself whether you are worth all the pains that I should have to take with you, and I have not the pleasure of knowing you well enough to be able to say. Perhaps also to you yourself what I could do for you does not appear sufficiently attractive for me to give myself so much trouble, for I repeat quite frankly that for me it can only be trouble." I protested that, in that case, he must not dream of it. This summary end to the discussion did not seem to be to his liking.

"That sort of politeness means nothing," he rebuked me coldly. "There is nothing so pleasant as to give oneself trouble for a person who is worth one's while. For the best of us, the study of the arts, a taste for old things, collections, gardens are all mere ersatz, substitutes, alibis. In the heart of our tub, like Diogenes, we cry out for a man. We cultivate begonias, we trim yews, as a last resort, because yews and begonias submit to treatment. But we should like to give our time to a plant of human growth, if we were sure that he was worth the trouble. That is the whole question: you must know something about yourself. Are you worth my trouble or not?"

"I would not for anything in the world, Sir; be a cause of anxiety to you," I said to him, "but so far as I am concerned you may be sure that everything which comes to me from you will be a very great pleasure to me. I am deeply touched that you should be so kind as to take notice of me in this way and try to help me."

Greatly to my surprise, it was almost with effusion that he thanked me for this speech, slipping his arm through mine with that intermittent familiarity which had already struck me at Balbec, and was in such contrast to the coldness of his tone.

"With the want of consideration common at your age," he told me, "you are liable to say things at times which would open an unbridgeable gulf between us. What you have said just now, on the other hand, is exactly the sort of thing that touches me, and makes me want to do a great deal for you."

As he walked arm in arm with me and uttered these words, which, albeit tinged with contempt, were so affectionate, M. de Charlus now fastened his gaze on me with that intense fixity which had struck me the first morning, when I saw him outside the casino at Balbec, and indeed many years before that, through the pink hawthorns, standing beside Mme. Swann, whom I supposed then to be his mistress, in the park at Tansonville; now let it stray around him and examine the cabs which at this time of the day were passing in considerable numbers on the way to their stables, looking so determinedly at them that several stopped, the drivers supposing that he wished to engage them. But M. de Charlus immediately dismissed them. "They're not what I want," he explained to me, "all a question of the colour of their lamps, and the direction they're going in. I hope, Sir," he went on, "that you will not in any way misinterpret the purely disinterested and charitable nature of the proposal which I am going to make to you." I was struck by the similarity of his diction to Swann's, closer now than at Balbec. "You have enough intelligence, I suppose, not to imagine that it is from want of society, from any fear of solitude and boredom that I have recourse to you. I do not, as a rule, care to talk about myself, but you may possibly have heard—it was alluded to in a leading article in *The Times*, which made a considerable impression— that the Emperor of Austria, who has always honoured me, with his friendship, and is good enough to insist on keeping up terms of cousinship with me, declared the other day in an interview which was made public that if the Comte de Chambord had had by his side a man as thoroughly conversant with the undercurrents of European politics as myself, he would be King of France to-day. I have often thought, sir, that there was in me, thanks not to my own humble talents but to circumstances which you may one day have occasion to learn, a sort of secret record of incalculable value, of which I have not felt myself at liberty to make use personally but which would be a priceless acquisition to a young man to whom I would hand over in a few months what it has taken me more than thirty years to collect, what I am perhaps alone in possessing. I do not speak of the intellectual enjoyment which you would find in learning certain secrets which, a Michelet of our day would give years of his life to know, and in the light of which certain events would assume for him an entirely different aspect. And I do not speak only of events that have already occurred, but of the chain of circumstances." (This was a favourite expression with M. de Charlus, and often, when he used it, he joined his hands as if in prayer, but with his fingers stiffened, as though to illustrate by their complexity the said circumstances, which he did not specify, and the chain that linked them.) "I could give you an explanation that no one has dreamed of, not only of the past but of the future. Let us return to yourself," he said, "and my plans for you. There exists among certain men, sir, a free-masonry of which I cannot now say more than that it numbers in its ranks four of the reigning sovereigns of Europe. Now, the courtiers of one of these are trying to cure him of his fancy. That is a very serious matter, and may bring us to war. Yes sir, that is a fact.   Given a very considerable advantage over people of your age, for all one knows, you will perhaps become what some eminent man of the past might have been if a good angel had revealed to him, in the midst of a humanity that knew nothing of them, the secrets of steam and electricity. Do not be foolish, do not refuse from discretion. Understand that, if I do you a great service, I expect my reward from you to be no less great. It is many years now since people in society ceased to interest me. I have but one passion left, to seek to redeem the mistakes of my life by conferring the benefit of my knowledge on a soul that is still virgin and capable of being inflamed by virtue. I have had great sorrows, sir, of which I may tell you perhaps some day; I have lost my wife, who was the loveliest; the noblest, the most perfect creature that one could dream of seeing. I have young relatives who are not—I do not say worthy, but who are not capable of accepting the moral heritage of which I have been speaking. For all I know, you may be he into whose hands it is to pass, he whose life I shall be able to direct and to raise to so lofty a plane. My own would gain in return. Perhaps in teaching you the great secrets of diplomacy I might recover a taste for them myself, and begin at last to do things of real interest in which. you would have an equal share. But before I can tell I must see you often, very often, every day."

"The Duchesse de Guermantes seems to be very clever. We were talking this afternoon about the possibility of war. It appears that she is specially well informed on that subject."

"She is nothing of the sort," replied M. de Charlus tartly. "Women, and most men for that matter, understand nothing of what I was going to tell you. My sister-in-law, is a charming woman who imagines that we are still living in the days of Balzac's novels, when women had an influence on politics. Going to her house could at present have only a bad effect on you, as for that matter going anywhere. The first sacrifice that you must make for me—I shall claim them from you in proportion to the gifts I bestow on you—is to give up going into society. It distressed me this afternoon to see you at that idiotic tea-party. You may remind me that I was there myself, but for me it was not a social gathering, it was simply a family visit. Later on, when you have established your position, if it amuses you to step down for a little into that sort of thing, it may, perhaps, do no harm. And then, I need not point out how invaluable I can be to you. The 'Open Sesame' to the Guermantes house and any others that it is worth while throwing open the doors of to you, rests with me. I shall be the judge, and intend to remain master of the situation."

I thought I would take advantage of what M. de Charlus had said about my call on Mme. de Villeparisis to try to find out what position exactly she occupied in society, but the question took another form on my lips than I had intended, and I asked him instead what the Villeparisis family was.

"That is absolutely as though you had asked me what the Nobody family was," replied M. de Charlus. "My aunt married for love, a M.Thirion, who was extremely rich for that matter, and whose sisters had married surprisingly well; and from that day onwards he called himself Marquis de Villeparisis. It did no harm to anyone, at the most a little to himself, and very little! What his reason was I cannot tell; I suppose he was actually a 'Monsieur de Villeparisis', a gentleman born at Villeparisis, which as you know is the name of a little place outside Paris. My aunt tried to make out that there was such a Marquisate in the family; she wanted to put things on a proper footing; I can't tell you why. When one takes a name to which one has no right it is better not to copy the regular forms."

Mme.de Villeparisis being merely Mme.Thirion completed the fall which had begun in my estimation of her when I had seen the composite nature of her party. I felt it to be unfair that a woman whose title and name were of quite recent origin should be able thus to impose upon her contemporaries, with the prospect of similarly imposing upon posterity, by virtue of her friendships with royal personages. Now that she had become once again what I had supposed her to be in my childhood, a person who had nothing aristocratic about her, these distinguished kinsfolk who gathered round her seemed to remain alien to her. She did not cease to be charming to us all. I went occasionally to see her and she sent me little presents from time to time. But I had never any impression that she. belonged to the Faubourg Saint-Germain, and if I had wanted any information about it she would have been one of the last people to whom I should have applied.

"At present," went on M. de Charlus, "by going into society, you will only damage your position, warp your intellect and character. Also, you must be particularly careful in choosing your friends. Keep mistresses, if your family have no objection, that doesn't concern me, indeed I can only advise it, you young rascal, young rascal who will soon have to start shaving," he rallied me; passing his fingers over my chin. "But the choice of your men friends is more important. Eight out of ten young men are little scoundrels, little wretches capable of doing you an injury which you will never be able to repair. Wait now, my nephew Saint-Loup is quite a suitable companion for you, at a pinch. As far as your future is concerned, he can be of no possible use to you; but for that I am sufficient. And really, when all's said and done, as a person to go about with, at times when you have had enough of me, he does not seem to present any serious drawback that I know of. At any rate he is a man, not one of those effeminate creatures one sees so many of nowadays, who look like little renters, and at any moment may bring their innocent victims to the gallows." I did not know the meaning of this slang word 'renter', anyone who had known it, would have been as greatly surprised by his use of it as myself. People in society always like talking slang, and people against whom certain, things may be hinted, like to show that they are not afraid to mention them. A proof of innocence in their eyes. But they have lost their sense of proportion, they are no longer capable of realising the point at which a certain pleasantry will become too technical, too shocking, will be a proof rather of corruption than of simplicity. "He is not like the rest of them; he has nice manners; he is really serious."

I could not help smiling, at this epithet 'serious', to which the intonation that M. de Charlus gave to it seemed to impart the sense of 'virtuous', of 'steady', as one says of a little shopgirl that she is 'serious'. At this moment a cab passed, zigzagging along the street; a young cabman, who had deserted his box, was driving it from inside, where he lay sprawling upon the cushions, apparently half drunk. M. de Charlus instantly stopped him. The driver began to argue: "Which way are you going?" "Yours," This surprised me, for M. de Charlus had already refused several cabs with similarly coloured lamps.

"Well, I don't want to get up on the box. D'you mind if I stay down here?"

"No; but you must put down the hood. Well, think over my proposal," said M. de Charlus, preparing to leave me, "I give you a few days to consider my offer; write to me. I repeat, I shall need to see you every day, and to receive from you guarantees of loyalty, of discretion which for that matter, you do appear, I must say, to furnish. But in the course of my life I have been so often taken in by appearances that I never wish to trust them again. Damn it, it's the least you can expect that before giving up a treasure, I should know into what hands it is going to pass. Very well, bear in mind what I'm offering you; you are like Hercules (though, unfortunately for yourself, you do not appear to me to have quite his muscular development) at the parting of the ways. Try not to have to regret all your life not having chosen the way that leads to virtue. Hallo!" he turned to the cabman, "haven't you put the hood down? I'll do it myself. I think too, I'd better drive, seeing the state you appear to be in." He jumped in beside the cabman, took the reins, and the horse trotted off.

For some time past, without knowing exactly what was wrong, my grandmother had been complaining of her health. As I knew that du Boulbon was a great physician, a superior man, of a profound and inventive intellect, I begged my mother to send for him, and the hope that, by a clear perception of the malady, he might perhaps cure it, carried the day finally over the fear that we had of (if we called in a specialist) alarming my grandmother. What decided my mother was the fact that, encouraged unconsciously by Cottard, my grandmother no longer went out of doors, and scarcely rose from her bed. In vain might she answer us in the words of Mme. de Sévigné's letter on Mme. de la Fayette: "Everyone said she was mad not to wish to go out. I said to these persons, so headstrong in their judgment: Mme. de

La Fayette is not mad! and I stuck to that. It has taken her death to prove that she was quite right not to go out."

Du Boulbon, when he came, decided against—if not Mme. de Sévigné, whom we did not quote to him—my grandmother, at any rate. Instead of sounding her chest, fixing on her steadily his wonderful eyes, in which there was perhaps the illusion that he was making a profound scrutiny of his patient, or the desire to give her that illusion, which seemed spontaneous but must be mechanically produced, or else not to let her see that he was thinking of something quite different, or simply to obtain the mastery over her, he began talking about Bergotte.

"I should think so, indeed, he's magnificent, you are quite right to admire him. But which of his books do you prefer? Indeed! Well, perhaps that is the best after all. In any case it is the best composed of his novels. Claire is quite charming in it; of his male characters which appeals to you most?"

I supposed at first that he was making her talk like this about literature because he himself found medicine boring, perhaps also to display his breadth of mind and even, with a more therapeutic aim, to restore confidence to his patient, to show her that he was not alarmed, to take her mind from the, state of her health. But afterwards I realised that, being distinguished particularly as an alienist and by his work on the brain, he had been seeking to ascertain by these questions whether my grandmother's memory was in good order. As though reluctantly, he began to enquire about her past life, fixing a stern and sombre eye on her. Then suddenly, as though catching sight of the truth and determined to reach it at all costs, with a preliminary rubbing of his hands, which he seemed to have some difficulty in wiping dry of the final hesitations which he himself might feel and of all the objections which we might have raised, looking down at my grand-mother with a lucid eye, boldly and as though he were at last upon solid ground, punctuating his words in a quiet, impressive tone, every inflection of which bore the mark of intellect, he began. (His voice, for that matter, throughout this visit remained what it naturally was, caressing. And under his bushy brows his ironical eyes were full of kindness.)

"You will be quite well, Madame, on the day—when it comes, and it rests entirely with you whether, it comes to-day—on which you realise that there is nothing wrong with you, and resume your ordinary life. You tell me that you have not been taking your food, not going out?"

"But, sir, I have a temperature." He laid a finger on her wrist. "Not just now, at any rate. Besides, what an excuse! Don't you know that we keep out in the open air and overfeed tuberculous patients with temperatures of 102?"

"But I have a little albumen as well."

"You ought not to know anything about that. You have what I have had occasion to call 'mental albumen'. We have all of us had, when we have not been very well, little albuminous phases which our doctor has done his best to make permanent by calling our attention to them. For one disorder that doctors cure with drugs (as I am told that they do occasionally succeed in doing) they produce a dozen others in healthy subjects by inoculating them with that pathogenic agent a thousand times more virulent than all the microbes in the world, the idea that one is ill.

"Your grandmother might perhaps go and sit, if the Doctor allows it, in some quiet path in the Champs-Elysées, near that laurel shrubbery where you used to play when you were little," said my mother to me, thus indirectly consulting Dr. du Boulbon, her voice for that reason assuming a tone of timid deference which it would not have had if she had been addressing me alone. The Doctor turned to my grandmother and, being apparently as well-read in literature as in science, adjured her as follows: "Go to the Champs-Elysées, Madame, to the laurel shrubbery which your grandson loves. The laurel you will find healthgiving. It purifies. After he had exterminated the serpent Python, it was with a bough of laurel in his hand that Apollo made his entry into Delphi. He sought thus to guard himself from the deadly germs of, the venomous monster. So you see that the Laurel is the most ancient, the most venerable and, I will add— what is of therapeutic as well as of prophylactic value—the most beautiful of antiseptics. The symptoms which you describe will vanish at my bidding. Besides, you have with you a very efficient person whom I appoint as your doctor from now onwards. That is your trouble itself the super-activity of your nerves. Even if I knew how to cure you of that, I should take good care not to. All I need do is to control it. I see on your table there one of Bergotte's books. Cured of your neurosis you would no longer care for it. Well, I might feel it my duty to substitute for the joys that it procures for you, a nervous stability which would be quite incapable of giving you those joys. But those joy's themselves are a strong remedy, the strongest of all perhaps. No; I have nothing to say against your nervous energy. All I ask is that it should listen to me; I leave you in its charge. It must reverse its engines. The force which it is now using to prevent you from getting up, from taking sufficient food, let it employ in making you eat, in making you read, in making you go out, and in distracting you in every possible way. You needn't tell me that you are fatigued. Fatigue is the organic realisation of a preconceived idea. Begin by not thinking it. And if ever you have a slight indisposition, which is a thing that may happen to anyone, it will be just as if you hadn't it, for your nervous energy will have endowed you with what M. de Talleyrand, in an expression full of meaning, called 'imaginary health'. See, it has begun to cure you already, you have been sitting up in bed listening to me without once leaning back on your pillows; your eye is bright, your complexion is good, I have been talking to you for half an hour by the clock and you have never noticed the time. Well, Madame, I shall now bid you good-day."

During the last few days people had begun to hear of my grandmother's illness and to inquire for news of her. Saint-Loup had written to me: "I do not wish to take advantage of a time when your dear grandmother is unwell to convey to you what is far more than mere reproaches, on a matter with which she has no concern. But I should not be speaking the truth were I to say to you, even out of politeness, that I shall ever forget the perfidy of your conduct, or that there can ever be any forgiveness for so scoundrelly a betrayal."

But some other friends, supposing that my grandmother was not seriously ill, (they may not even have known that she was ill at all), had asked me to meet them next day in the Champs-Elysées, to go with them from there to pay a call together, ending up with a dinner in the country, the thought of which appealed to me. I had no longer any reason to forego these two pleasures. When my grandmother had been told that it was now imperative, if she was to obey Dr. du Boulbon's orders, that .she should go out as much as possible, she had herself at once suggested the Champs-Elysées. It would be easy for me to escort her there; and, while she sat reading, to arrange with my friends where I should meet them later; and I should still be in time, if I made haste, to take the train with them to Ville d'Avray. When the time came, my grandmother did not want to go out; she felt tired. But my mother, acting on du Boulbon's instructions, had the strength of mind to be firm and to insist on obedience. She was almost in tears at the thought that my grandmother was going to relapse again into her nervous weakness, which she might never be able to shake off. It was time for my grandmother to get ready. Having obstinately refused to let Mamma stay in the room with her, she took, left to herself, an endless time over her dressing, and now that I knew her to be quite well, with that strange indifference which we feel towards our relatives so long as they are alive, which makes us put everyone else before them, I felt it to be very selfish of her to take so long, to risk making me late when she knew that I had an appointment with my friends and was dining at Ville d'Avray. In my impatience I finally went downstairs without waiting for her, after I had twice been told that she was just ready. At last she joined me, without apologising to me, as she generally did, for having kept me waiting, flushed and bothered like a person who has come to a place in a hurry and has forgotten half her belongings, just as I was reaching the half-opened glass door which, without warming them with it in the least, let in the liquid, throbbing, tepid air from the street (as though the sluices of a reservoir had been opened) between the frigid walls of the passage.

"Oh, dear, if you're going to meet your friends I ought to have put on another cloak. I look rather poverty stricken in this one."

I was startled to see her so flushed and supposed that having begun by making herself late she had had to hurry over her dressing. When we left the cab at the end of the Avenue Gabriel, in the Champs-Elysées, I saw my grandmother, without a word to me, turn aside and make her way to the little old pavilion with its green trellis, at the door of which I had once waited for Françoise. The same park-keeper who had been standing there then was still talking to Françoise's 'Marquise' when, following my grandmother who, doubtless because she was feeling sick, had her hand in front of her mouth, I climbed the steps of that little rustic theatre, erected there among the gardens. At the entrance, as in those circus booths where the clown, dressed for the ring and smothered in flour, stands at the door and takes the money himself for the seats, the 'Marquise', at the receipt of custom, was still there in her place with her huge, uneven face smeared with a coarse plaster and her little bonnet of red flowers and black lace surmounting her auburn wig. But I do not suppose that she recognised me.

Finally my grandmother emerged, and feeling that she probably would not seek to atone by a lavish gratuity for the indiscretion that she had shown by remaining so long inside, I beat a retreat, so as not to have to share in the scorn which the 'Marquise' would no doubt heap on her, and began strolling along a path, but slowly, so that my grandmother should not have to hurry to overtake me; as presently she did. I expected her to begin:"I am afraid I've kept you waiting; I hope you'll still be in time for your friends," but she did not utter a single word, so much so that, feeling a little hurt, I was disinclined to speak first; until looking up at her I noticed that as she walked beside me she kept her face turned the other way. I was afraid that her heart might be troubling her again. I studied her more carefully and was struck by the disjointedness of her gait. Her hat was crooked, her cloak stained; she had the confused and worried look, the flushed, slightly dazed face of a person who has just been knocked down by a carriage or pulled out of a ditch.

"I was afraid you were feeling sick, Grandmamma; are you feeling better now?" I asked her. Probably she thought that it would be impossible for her, without alarming me, not to make some answer.

"I heard the whole of her conversation with the keeper," she told me. "Could anything have been more typical of the Guermantes, or the Verdurins and their little circle? Heavens, what fine language. she put it all in!" And she quoted, with deliberate application, this sentence from her own special Marquise, Mme. de Sévigné: "As I listened to them I thought that they were preparing for me the pleasures of a farewell."

Such was the speech that she made me, a speech into which she had put all her critical delicacy, her love of quotations, her memory of the classics, more thoroughly even than she would naturally have done, and as though to prove that she retained possession of all these faculties. But I guessed rather than heard what she said, so inaudible was the voice in which she muttered her sentences, clenching her teeth more than could be accounted for by the fear of being sick again.

"Come!" I said lightly, so as not to seem to be taking her illness too seriously, "since your heart is bothering you, shall we go home now? I don't want to trundle a grandmother with indigestion about the Champs-Elysées."

"I didn't like to suggest it, because of your friends," she replied. "Poor boy! But if you don't mind, I think it would be wiser."

I was afraid of her noticing the strange way in which she uttered these words. "Come!" I said to her sharply, "you mustn't tire yourself talking; if your heart is bad, it's silly; wait till we get home."

She smiled at me sorrowfully and gripped my band. She had realised that there was no need to hide from me what I had at once guessed, she had had a slight stroke.

We made our way back along the Avenue Gabriel, through the strolling crowd. I left my grandmother to rest on a seat and went in search of a cab.

"Well, sir, I don't like to say no, but you have not made an appointment, you have no time fixed. Besides, this is not my day for seeing patients. You surely have a doctor of your own. I cannot interfere with his practice, unless he were to call me in for a consultation. It's a question of professional etiquette."

Just as I was signalling to a cabman, I had caught sight of the famous Professor E—, almost a friend of my father and grandfather, acquainted at any rate with them both, who lived in the Avenue Gabriel, and, with a sudden inspiration, had stopped him just as he was entering his house, thinking that he would perhaps be the very person to advise my grandmother. But he was evidently in a hurry and, after calling for his letters, seemed anxious to get rid of me, so that my only chance of speaking to him lay in going up with him in the lift, of which he begged me to allow him to work the switches himself, this being a mania with him.

"But, sir, I am not asking you to see my grandmother here; you will realise from what I am trying to tell you that she is not in a fit state to come; what I am asking is that you should call at our house in half an hour's time, when I have taken her home."

"Call at your house! Really, sir, you must not expect me to do that. I am dining with the Minister of Commerce. I have a call to pay first. I must change at once and to make matters worse I have torn my coat and my other one has no buttonholes for my decorations. I beg you, please, to oblige me by not touching the switches. You don't know how the lift works; one can't be too careful. Getting that buttonhole made means more delay. Well, as I am a friend of your people, if your grandmother comes here at once I will see her. But I warn you that I shall be able to give her exactly a quarter of an hour, not a moment more."

I had started off at once, without even getting out of the lift which Professor E had himself set in motion to take me down again, casting a suspicious glance at me as he did so.

I helped my grandmother into Professor E---'s lift and a moment later he came to us and took us into his consulting room. But there, busy as he was, his bombastic manner changed, such is the force of habit; for his habit was to be friendly, that is to say lively with his patients. Since he knew that my grandmother was a great reader, and was himself one also, he devoted the first few minutes to quoting various favourite passages of poetry appropriate to the glorious summer weather. He had placed her in an armchair and himself with his back to the light so as to have a good view of her. His examination was minute and thorough, even obliging me at one moment to leave the room. He continued it after my return, then, having finished, went on, although the quarter of an hour was almost at an end, repeating various quotations to my grandmother. He even made a few jokes, which were witty enough, though I should have preferred to hear them on some other occasion, but which completely reassured me by the tone of amusement in which he uttered them. I then remembered that M. Fallières, the President of the Senate, had, many years earlier, had a false seizure, and that to the consternation of his political rivals he had returned a few days later to his duties and had begun, it was said, his preparations for a more or less remote succession to the Presidency of the Republic. My confidence in my grandmother's prompt recovery was all the more complete in that, just as I was recalling the example of M. Fallières, I was distracted from following up the similarity by a shout of laughter, which served as conclusion to one of the Professor's jokes. After which he took out his watch, wrinkled his brows petulantly on seeing that he was five minutes late, and while he bade us good-bye rang for his other coat to be brought to him at once. I waited until my grandmother had left the room, closed the door and asked him to tell me the truth.

"There is not the slightest hope," he informed me. "It is a stroke brought on by uraemia. In itself, uraemia is not necessarily fatal, but this case seems to me desperate. I need not tell you that I hope I am mistaken. Anyhow, you have Cottard, you're in excellent hands. Excuse me"; he broke off as a maid came into the room with his coat over her arm. "I told you, I'm dining with the Minister of Commerce, and I have a call to pay first. Ah! Life is not all a bed of roses, as one is apt to think at your age."

And he graciously offered me his hand. I had shut the door behind me, and a footman was showing us into the hall when we heard a loud shout of rage. The maid had forgotten to cut and hem the buttonhole for the decorations. This would take another ten minutes. The Professor continued to storm while I stood on the landing gazing at a grandmother for whom there was not the slightest hope. Each of us is indeed alone. We started for home.

My mother and I (whose falsehood was exposed before we spoke by the obnoxious perspicacity of Françoise) would not even admit that my grandmother was seriously ill, as though such an admission might give pleasure to her enemies (not that she had any) and it was more loving to feel that she was not so bad as all that. The same individual phenomena are reproduced in the mass, in great crises. In a war, the man who does not love his country says nothing against it, but regards it as lost, commiserates it, sees everything in the darkest colours.

Françoise was of infinite value to us owing to her faculty of doing without sleep, of performing the most arduous tasks. And if, when she had gone to bed after several nights spent in the sickroom, we were obliged to call her a quarter of an hour after she had fallen asleep, she was so happy to be able to do the most tiring duties as if they had been the simplest things in the world that, so far from looking cross, her face would light up with a satisfaction tinged with modesty. Only when the time came for mass, or for breakfast, then, had my grand-mother been in her death agony, still Françoise would have quietly slipped away so as not to make herself late. She neither could nor would let her place be taken by her young footman.

There came a time when her uraemic trouble affected my grandmother's eyes. For some days she could not see at all. Her eyes were not at all like those of a blind person, but remained just the same as before. And I gathered that she could see nothing only from the strangeness of a certain smile of welcome which she assumed the moment one opened the door, until one had come up to her and taken her hand, a smile which began too soon and remained stereotyped on her lips, fixed, but always full-faced, and endeavouring to be visible from all points, because she could no longer rely upon her sight to regulate it, to indicate the right moment, the proper direction, to bring it to the point, to make it vary according to the change of position or of facial expression of the person who had come in; because it was left isolated, without the accompanying smile in her eyes which would have distracted a little from it the attention of the visitor, it assumed in its awkwardness an undue importance, giving one the impression of an exaggerated friendliness. Then her sight was completely restored; from her eyes the wandering affliction passed to her ears. For several days my grandmother was deaf. And as she was afraid of being taken by surprise by the sudden entry of some one whom she would not have heard come in, all day long, albeit she was lying with her face to the wall, she kept turning her head sharply towards the door. But the movement of her neck was clumsy, for one cannot adapt oneself in a few days to this transposition of faculties, so as, if not actually to see sounds, to listen with one's eyes. Finally her pain grew less, but the impediment of her speech increased. We were obliged to ask her to repeat almost everything that she said.

And now my grandmother, realising that we could no longer understand her, gave up altogether the attempt to speak and lay perfectly still. When she caught sight of me she gave a sort of convulsive start like a person who suddenly finds himself unable to breathe, but could make no intelligible sound. Then, overcome by her sheer powerlessness, she let her head drop on to the pillows, stretched herself out flat in her bed, her face grave, like a face of marble, her hands motionless on the sheet or occupied in some purely physical action such as that of wiping her fingers with her handkerchief. She made no effort to think. Then came a state of perpetual agitation. She was incessantly trying to get up. But we restrained her so far as we could from doing so, for fear of her discovering how paralysed she was. One day when she had been left alone for a moment I found her standing on the floor in her nightgown trying to open the window.

We were just in time to catch my grandmother, she put up an almost violent resistance to my mother, then, overpowered, seated forcibly in an armchair, she ceased to wish for death, to regret being alive, her face resumed its impassivity and she began laboriously to pick off the hairs that had been left on her nightgown by a fur cloak which somebody had thrown over her shoulders.

The look in her eyes changed completely; often uneasy, plaintive, haggard, it was no longer the look we knew, it was the sullen expression of a doddering old woman.

By dint of repeatedly asking her whether she would not like her hair done, Françoise managed to persuade herself that the request had come from my grandmother. She armed herself with brushes, combs, eau de Cologne, a wrapper. "It can't hurt Madame Amédée," she said to herself, "if I just comb her; nobody's ever too ill for a good combing." In other words, one was never too weak for another person to be able, for her own satisfaction, to comb one. But when I came into the room I saw between the cruel hands of Françoise, as blissfully happy as though she were in the act of restoring my grandmother to health, beneath a thin rain of aged tresses which had not the strength to resist the action of the comb, a head which, incapable of maintaining the position into which it had been forced, was rolling to and fro with a ceaseless swirling motion in which sheer debility alternated with spasms of pain. I felt that the moment at which Françoise would have finished her task was approaching, and I dared not hasten it by suggesting to her: "That is enough," for fear of her disobeying me. But I did forcibly intervene when, in order that my grandmother might see whether her hair had been done to her liking, Françoise, with innocent savagery, brought her a glass. I was glad for the moment that I had managed to snatch it from her in time, before my grandmother, whom we had carefully kept without a mirror, could catch even a stray glimpse of a face unlike anything she could have imagined. But, alas, when, a moment later, I leaned over her to kiss that dear forehead which had been so harshly treated, she looked up at me with a puzzled, distrustful, shocked expression: she did not know me.

According to our doctor, this was a symptom that the congestion of her brain was increasing. It must be relieved in some way. Cottard was in two minds. Françoise hoped at first that they were going to apply 'clarified cups'. She looked for the effects of this treatment in my dictionary, but could find no reference to it. Even if she had said 'scarified' instead of 'clarified' she still would not have found any reference to this adjective, since she did not look any more for it under 'S' than under 'C', she did indeed say 'clarified' but she wrote (and consequently assumed that the printed word was) 'esclarified'. Cottard, to her disappointment, gave the preference, though without much hope, to leeches. When, a few hours later, I went into my grandmother's room, fastened to her neck, her temples, her ears, the tiny black serpents were writhing among her bloodstained locks, as on the head of Medusa. But in her pale and peaceful, entirely motionless face I saw wide open, luminous and calm, her own beautiful eyes, as in days gone by (perhaps even more charged with the light of intelligence than they had been before her illness, since, as she could not speak and must not move, it was to her eyes alone that she entrusted her thought, that thought which at one time occupies an immense place in us, offering us undreamed-of treasures, at another time seems reduced to nothing, then may be reborn, as though by spontaneous generation, by the withdrawal of a few drops of blood), her eyes, soft and liquid like two pools of oil in which the rekindled fire that was now burning, lighted before the face of the invalid a reconquered universe. Her calm was no longer the wisdom of despair, but that of hope. She realised that she was better, wished to be careful, not to move, and made me the present only of a charming smile so that I should know that she was feeling better, as she gently pressed my hand.

I knew the disgust that my grandmother felt at the sight of certain animals, let alone being touched by them. I knew that it was in consideration of a higher utility that she was enduring the leeches. And so it infuriated me to hear Françoise repeating to her with that laugh which people use to a baby, to make it crow: "Oh, look at the little beasties running about on Madame." This was, moreover, treating our patient with a want of respect, as though she were in her second childhood. But my grandmother, whose face had assumed the calm fortitude of a stoic, did not seem even to hear her.

Alas! No sooner had the leeches been taken off than the congestion returned and grew steadily worse. I was surprised to find that at this stage, when my grandmother was so ill, Françoise was constantly disappearing. The fact was that she had ordered herself a mourning dress, and did not wish to keep her dressmaker waiting. In the lives of most women everything, even the greatest sorrow, resolves itself into a question of 'trying-on'.

A few days later, when I was in bed and sleeping, my mother came to call me in the early hours of the morning. With that tender consideration which, in great crises, people who are crushed by grief shew even for the slightest discomfort of others: "Forgive me for disturbing your sleep," she said to me. "I was not asleep," I answered as I awoke.

In a voice so gentle that she seemed to be afraid of hurting me, my mother asked whether it would tire me too much to get out of bed, and, stroking my hands, went on: "My poor boy, you have only your Papa and Mamma to help you now."

We went into the sickroom. Bent in a semi-circle on the bed a creature other than my grandmother, a sort of wild beast which was coated with her hair and couched amid her bedclothes lay panting, groaning, making the blankets heave with its convulsions. The eyelids were closed, and it was because the one nearer me did not shut properly, rather than because it opened at all that it left visible a chink of eye, misty, filmed, reflecting the dimness both of an organic sense of vision and of a hidden, internal pain. All this agitation was not addressed to us, whom she neither saw nor knew. But if this was only a beast that was stirring there, where could my grandmother be? Yes, I could recognise the shape of her nose, which bore no relation now to the rest of her face, but to the corner of which a beauty spot still adhered, and the hand that kept thrusting the blankets aside with a gesture which formerly would have meant that those blankets were pressing upon her, but now meant nothing.

Mamma asked me to go for a little vinegar and water with which to sponge my grandmother's forehead. It was the only thing that refreshed her, thought Mamma, who saw that she was trying to push back her hair. But now one of the servants was signalling to me from the doorway. The news that my grandmother was in the last throes had spread like wildfire through the house. One of those 'extra helps' whom people engage at exceptional times to relieve the strain on their servants (a practice which gives deathbeds an air of being social functions) had just opened the front door to the Duc de Guermantes, who was now waiting in the hail and had asked for me: I could not escape him.

"I have just, my dear Sir, heard your tragic news. I should like, as a mark of sympathy, to shake hands with your father." I made the excuse that I could not very well disturb him at the moment. M. de Guermantes was like a caller who turns up just as one is about to start on a journey. But he felt so intensely the importance of the courtesy he was showing us that it blinded him to all else, and he insisted upon being taken into the drawing-room. As a general rule, he made a point of going resolutely through the formalities with which he had decided to honour anyone, and took little heed that the trunks were packed or the coffin ready.

"Have you sent for Dieulafoy? No? That was a great mistake. And if you had only asked me, I would have got him to come, he never refuses me anything, although he has refused the Duchesse de Chartres before now. You see, I set myself above a Princess of the Blood. However, in the presence of death we are all equal," he added, not that he meant to suggest that my grandmother was becoming his equal, but probably because he felt that a prolonged discussion of his power over Dieulafoy and his pre-eminence over the Duchesse de Chartres would not be in very good taste.

This advice did not in the least surprise me. I knew that, in the Guermantes set, the name of Dieulafoy was regularly quoted (only with slightly more respect) among those of other tradesmen who were 'quite the best' in their respective lines. And the old Duchesse de Mortemart *née* Guermantes (I never could understand, by the way, why, the moment one speaks of a Duchess, one almost invariably says: "The old Duchess of So-and-so," or, alternatively, in a delicate Watteau tone, if she is still young: "The little Duchess of So-and-so,") would prescribe almost automatically, with a droop of the eyelid, in serious cases: "Dieulafoy, Dieulafoy!" as, if one wanted a place for ices, she would advise: 'Poiré Blanche'" or for small pastry 'Rebattet, Rebattet'. But I was not aware that my father had, as a matter of fact, just sent for Dieulafoy.

At this point my mother, who was waiting impatiently for some cylinders of oxygen which would help my grandmother to breathe more easily, came out herself to the hall where she little expected to find M. de Guermantes. I should have liked to conceal him, had that been possible. But convinced in his own mind that nothing was more essential, could be more gratifying to her or more indispensable to the maintenance of his reputation as a perfect gentleman, he seized me violently by the arm and, although I defended myself as against an assault with repeated protestations of "Sir, Sir, Sir," dragged me across to Mamma, saying: "Will you do me the great honour of presenting me to your mother?" letting go a little as he came to the last word. And it was so plain to him that the honour was hers that he could not help smiling at her even while he was composing a grave face. There was nothing for it but to mention his name, the sound of which at once started him bowing and scraping, and he was just going to begin the complete ritual of salutation. He apparently proposed to enter into conversation, but my mother, overwhelmed by her grief, told me to come at once and did not reply to the speeches of M. de Guermantes who, expecting to be received as a visitor and finding himself instead left alone in the hall, would have been obliged to retire had he not at that moment caught sight of Saint-Loup who had arrived in Paris that morning and had come to us in haste to inquire for news. "I say, this is a piece of luck!" cried the Duke joyfully, catching his nephew by the sleeve, which he nearly tore off, regardless of the presence of my mother who was again crossing the hall. Saint-Loup was not sorry, I fancy, despite his genuine sympathy, at having missed seeing me, considering his attitude towards myself. He left the house, carried off by his uncle who, having had something very important to say to him and having very nearly gone down to Doncières on purpose to say it, was beside himself with joy at being able to save himself so much exertion. "Upon my soul, if anybody had told me I had only to cross the courtyard and I should find you here, I should have thought it a huge joke; as your friend M. Bloch would say, it's a regular farce." And as he disappeared down the stairs with Robert whom he held by the shoulder: "All the same," he went on, "it's quite clear I must have touched the hangman's rope or something; I do have the most astounding luck." Not that the Duc de Guermantes was ill-bred; far from it. But he was one of those men who are incapable of putting themselves in the place of other people, who resemble in that respect undertakers and the majority of doctors, and who, after composing their faces and saying: "This is a very painful occasion," after, if need be, embracing you and advising you to rest, cease to regard a deathbed or a funeral as anything but a social gathering of a more or less restricted kind at which, with a joviality that has been checked for a moment only, they scan the room in search of the person whom they can tell about their own little affairs, or ask to introduce them to some one else, or offer a lift in their carriage when it is time to go home. The Duc de Guermantes, while congratulating himself on the 'good wind' that had blown him into the arms of his nephew, was still so surprised at the reception—natural as it was—that had been given him by my mother, that he declared later on that she was as disagreeable as my father was civil, that she had 'absent fits' during which she seemed literally not to hear a word you said to her, and that in his opinion she had no self-possession and perhaps even was not quite 'all there'. At the same time he had been quite prepared (according to what I was told) to put this state of mind down, in part at any rate, to the circumstances, and declared that my mother had seemed to him greatly 'affected' by the sad event. But he had still stored up in his limbs all the residue of bows and reverences which he had been prevented from using up, and had so little idea of the real nature of Mamma's sorrow that he asked me, the day before the funeral, if I was not doing anything to distract her.

A half-brother of my grandmother, who was a monk, and whom I had never seen, had telegraphed to Austria, where the head of his Order was, and having as a special privilege obtained leave, arrived that day. Bowed down with grief, he sat by the bedside reading prayers and meditations from a book, without, however, taking his gimlet eyes from the invalid's face. At one point, when my grandmother was unconscious, the sight of this cleric's grief began to upset me, and I looked at him tenderly. He appeared surprised by my pity, and then an odd thing happened, he joined his hands in front of his face, like a man absorbed in painful meditation, but, on the assumption that I would then cease to watch him, left, as I observed, a tiny chink between his fingers. And at the moment when my gaze left his face, I saw his sharp eye, which had been making use of its vantage-point behind his hands to observe whether my sympathy were sincere. He was hidden there as in the darkness of a confessional. He saw that I was still looking and at once shut tight the lattice which he had had left ajar. I have met him again since then, but never has any reference been made by either of us to that minute. It was tacitly agreed that I had not noticed that he was spying on me. In the priest as in the alienist, there is always an element of the examining magistrate. Besides, what friend is there, however cherished, in whose and our common past there has not been some such episode which we find it convenient to believe that he must have forgotten?

The doctor gave my grandmother an injection of morphine, and to make her breathing less troublesome ordered cylinders of oxygen. My mother, the doctor, the nursing sister held these in their hands; as soon as one was exhausted another was put in its place. I had left the room for a few minutes. When I returned I found myself face to face with a miracle. Accompanied on a muted instrument by an incessant murmur, my grandmother seemed to be greeting us with a long and blissful chant, which filled the room, rapid and musical. I soon realized that this was scarcely less unconscious, that it was as purely mechanical as the hoarse rattle that I had heard before leaving the room. Perhaps to a slight extent it reflected some improvement brought about by the morphine. Principally it was the result (the air not passing quite in the same way through the bronchial tubes) of a change in the register of her breathing. Released by the twofold action of the oxygen and the morphine, my grandmother's breath no longer laboured, panted, groaned, but, swift and light, shot like a skater along the delicious stream. The hiss of the oxygen ceased for a few moments. But the happy plaint of her breathing poured out steadily, light, troubled, unfinished, without end, beginning afresh. Now and then it seemed that all was over, her breath stopped, whether owing to one of those transpositions to another octave that occur in the breathing of a sleeper, or else from a natural interruption, an effect of unconsciousness, the progress of asphyxia, some failure of the heart. The doctor stooped to feel my grandmother's pulse, but already, as if a tributary were pouring its current into the dried river-bed, a fresh chant broke out from the interrupted measure. And the first was resumed in another pitch with the same inexhaustible force. Who knows whether, without indeed my grandmother's being conscious of them, a countless throng of happy and tender memories compressed by suffering were not escaping from her now, like those lighter gases which had long been compressed in the cylinders? One would have said that everything that she had to tell us was pouring out, that it was to us that she was addressing herself with this prolixity, this earnestness, this effusion. At the foot of the bed, convulsed by every gasp of this agony, not weeping but now and then drenched with tears, my mother presented the unreasoning desolation of a leaf which the rain lashes and the wind twirls on its stem. They made me dry my eyes before I went up to kiss my grandmother.

"But I thought she couldn't see anything now?" said my father. "One can never be sure," replied the doctor.

When my lips touched her face, my grandmother's hands quivered, a long shudder ran through her whole body, reflex perhaps, perhaps because certain affections have their hyperaesthesia which recognises through the veil of unconsciousness what they barely need senses to enable them to love. Suddenly my grandmother half rose, made a violent effort, as though struggling to resist an attempt on her life. Françoise could not endure this sight and burst out sobbing. Remembering what the doctor had just said I tried to make her leave the room. At that moment my grandmother opened her eyes. I thrust myself hurriedly in front of Françoise to hide her tears, while my parents were speaking to the sufferer. The sound of the oxygen had ceased; the doctor moved away from the bedside. My grandmother was dead.

An hour or two later Françoise was able for the last time, and without causing them any pain, to comb those beautiful tresses which had only begun to turn grey and hitherto had seemed not so old as my grandmother herself. But now on the contrary it was they alone that set the crown of age on a face grown young again, from which had vanished the wrinkles, the contractions, the swellings, the strains, the hollows which in the long course of years had been carved on it by suffering. As at the far-off time when her parents had chosen for her a bridegroom, she had the features delicately traced by purity and submission, the cheeks glowing with a chaste expectation, with a vision of happiness, with an innocent gaiety even, which the years had gradually destroyed. Life in withdrawing from her had taken with it the disillusionments of life. A smile seemed to be hovering on my grandmother's lips. On that funeral couch, death, like a sculptor of the middle ages, had laid her in the form of a young maiden.

CHAPTER TWO

Albeit it was simply a Sunday in autumn, I had been born again, life lay intact before me, for that morning, after a succession of mild days, there had been a cold mist which had not cleared until nearly midday. A change in the weather is sufficient to create the world and oneself anew

I had gone back to bed to wait until the hour came at which, taking advantage of the absence of my parents, who had gone for a few days to Combray, I proposed to get up and go to a little play which was being given that evening in Mme. de Villeparisis's drawing-room. Had they been at home I should perhaps not have ventured to go out; my mother, in the delicacy of her respect for my grandmother's memory, wished the tokens of regret that were paid to it to be freely and sincerely given; she would not have forbidden me this outing, she would have disapproved of it. There was no one else in the house but Françoise. The grey light, falling like a fine rain on the earth, wove without ceasing a transparent web through which the Sunday holidaymakers appeared in a silvery sheen. I had flung to the foot of my bed the *Figaro,* for which I had been sending out religiously every morning, ever since I had sent in an article which it had not yet printed; despite the absence of the sun, the intensity of the daylight was an indication that we were still only half-way through the afternoon. The tulle window-curtains, vaporous and friable as they would not have been on a fine day, had that same blend of beauty and fragility that dragon-flies wings have, and Venetian glass. Robert de Saint-Loup, whom his mother had at length succeeded in parting—after painful and abortive attempts—from his mistress, and who immediately afterwards had been sent to Morocco in the hope of his there forgetting one whom he had already for some little time ceased to love, had sent me a line, which had reached me the day before, announcing his arrival, presently, in France for a short spell of leave. I had had no news of him since, at the time of my grandmother's last illness, he had accused me of perfidy and treachery. It had then been quite easy to see what must have happened. Rachel, who liked to provoke his jealousy—she had other reasons also for wishing me harm—had persuaded her lover that I had made a dastardly attempt to have relations with her in his absence. It is probable that he continued to believe in the truth of this allegation, but he had ceased to be in love with her, which meant that its truth or falsehood had become a matter of complete indifference to him, and our friendship alone re mained. When, on meeting him again, I attempted to speak to him about his attack on me his sole answer was a cordial and friendly smile, which gave him the air of begging my pardon; then he turned the conversation to something else.

This afternoon, which I should have to spend by myself, seemed to me very empty and very melancholy. Every now and then, I heard the sound of the lift coming up, but it was followed by a second sound, not that for which I was hoping, namely the sound of it coming to a halt at our landing, but a very different sound which the lift made in continuing its progress to the floors above and which, because it so often meant the desertion of my floor when I was expecting a visitor, remained for me at other times, even when I had no wish to see anyone, a sound lugubrious in itself, in which there echoed, as it were, a sentence of solitary confinement.

Suddenly, although I had heard no bell, Françoise opened the door to let in Albertine, who came forward smiling, silent, plump, containing in the fullness of her body, made ready so that I might continue living them, come in search of me, the days we had spent together at that Balbec to which I had never since returned. On each of Albertine's smiling, questioning, blushing features I could read the questions: "And Madame de Villeparisis? And the dancing-master? And the pastry-cook?" When she sat down her back seemed to be saying: "Gracious! There's no cliff here; you don't mind if I sit down beside you, all the same, as I used to do at Balbec?" She was like an enchantress handing me a mirror that reflected time. In this she was like all the people whom we seldom see now but with whom at one time we lived on more intimate terms. With Albertine, however, there was something more than this.   Certainly, even at Balbec, in our daily encounters, I had always been surprised when she came in sight, so variable was her appearance from day to day. But now it was difficult to recognise her. Cleared of the pink vapour that used to bathe them, her features had emerged like those of a statue. She had another face, or rather she had a face at last; her body too had grown. There remained scarcely anything now of the shell in which she had been enclosed and on the surface of which, at Balbec, her future outline had been barely visible.

Departing from the customary order of her holiday movements, this year she had come straight from Balbec, where furthermore she had not stayed nearly so late as usual. It was a long time since I had seen her, and as I did not know even by name the people with whom she was in the habit of mixing in Paris, I could form no impression of her during the periods in which she abstained from coming to see me. These lasted often for quite a time. Then, one fine day, in would burst Albertine whose rosy apparitions and silent visits left me little if any better informed as to what she might have been doing in an interval which remained plunged in that darkness of her hidden life which my eyes felt little anxiety to pierce. This time, however, certain signs seemed to indicate that some new experience must have entered into that life.

I felt, in this same pretty girl who had just sat down by my bed, something that was different: and in those lines which, in one's eyes and other features, express one's general attitude towards life, a change of front, a partial conversion as though there had now been shattered those resistances against which I had hurled my strength in vain at Balbec, one evening, now remote in time, on which we formed a couple symmetrical with but the converse of our present arrangement, since then it had been she who was lying down and I who sat by her bedside. Wishing and not venturing to make certain whether now she would let herself be kissed, every time that she rose to go I asked her to stay beside me a little longer. This was a concession not very easy to obtain, for albeit she had nothing to do (otherwise she would have rushed from the house) she was a person methodical in her habits and moreover not very gracious towards me, seeming scarcely to be at ease in my company, and yet each time, after looking at her watch, she sat down again at my request until finally she had spent several hours with me without my having asked her for anything; the things I was saying to her followed logically those that I had said during the hours before, and bore no relation to what I was thinking about, what I desired from her, remained indefinitely parallel. There is nothing like desire for preventing the thing one says from bearing any resemblance to what one has in one's mind.

Certainly I was not in the least in love with Albertine; child of the mists outside, she could merely content the imaginative desire which the change of weather had awakened in me and which was midway between the desires that are satisfied by the arts of the kitchen and of monumental sculpture respectively, for it made me dream simultaneously of mingling with my flesh a substance different and warm, and of attaching at some point to my outstretched body a body divergent, as the body of Eve barely holds by the feet to the side of Adam, to whose body hers is almost perpendicular, in those romanesque bas-reliefs on the church at Balbec which represent in so noble and so reposeful a fashion, still almost like a classical frieze, the Creation of Woman; God in them is everywhere followed, as by two ministers, by two little angels in whom the visitor recognises—like winged, swarming summer creatures which winter has surprised and spared—cupids from Herculaneum, still surviving well into the thirteenth century, and winging their last slow flight, weary but never failing in the grace, that might be expected of them, over the whole front of the porch.

Not only did I no longer feel any love for her, but I had no longer to consider, as I should have had at Balbec, the risk of shattering in her an affection for myself, which no longer existed. There could be no doubt that she had long since become quite indifferent to me. I was well aware that to her I was in no sense a member now of the 'little band' into which I had at one time so anxiously sought and had then been so happy to have secured admission. Besides, as she had no longer even, as in Balbec days, an air of frank good nature, I felt no serious scruples: still I believe that what made me finally decide was another philological discovery. As, continuing to add fresh links to the external chain of talk behind which I hid my intimate desire, I spoke, having Albertine secure now on the corner of my bed, of one of the girls of the little band, one smaller than the rest, whom, nevertheless, I had thought quite pretty, "Yes," answered Albertine, "she reminds me of a little *mousmé*.." There had been nothing in the world to show, when I first knew Albertine, that she had ever heard the word *mousmé*. It was probable that, had things followed their normal course, she would never have learned it, and for my part I should have seen no cause for regret in that, for there is no more horrible word in the language. The mere sound of it makes one's teeth ache as they do when one has put too large a spoonful of ice in one's mouth. But coming from Albertine, as she sat there looking so pretty, not even *"mousmé"* could strike me as unpleasant. On the contrary, I felt it to be a revelation, if not of an outward initiation, at any rate of an inward evolution. Unfortunately it was now time for me to bid her good-bye if I wished her to reach home in time for her dinner, and myself to be out of bed and dressed in time for my own. It was Françoise who was getting it ready; she did not like having to keep it back, and must already have found it an infringement of one of the articles of her code that Albertine, in the absence of my parents, should be paying me so prolonged a visit, and one which was going to make everything late. But before. *"mousmé"* all these arguments fell to the ground and I hastened to say:

"Just fancy; I'm not in the least ticklish; you can go on tickling me for an hour on end and I won't even feel it." "Really?" "I assure you."

She understood, doubtless, that this was the awkward expression of a desire on my part, for, like a person who offers to give you an introduction for which you have not ventured to ask him, though what you have said has shown him that it would be of great service to you, she inquired, with womanly meekness: "Would you like me to try?"

"Just as you like, but you would be more comfortable if you lay down properly on the bed." "Like that?" "No; get right on top." "You're sure I'm not too heavy?"

As she uttered these words the door opened and Françoise, carrying a lamp, came in. Albertine had just time to fling herself back upon her chair. Perhaps Françoise had chosen this moment to confound us, having been listening at the door or even peeping through the keyhole. Holding over Albertine and myself the lighted lamp whose searching beams missed none of the still visible depressions which the girl's body had hollowed in the counterpane, Françoise made one think of a picture of "Justice throwing light upon Crime." Albertine's face did not suffer by this illumination. It revealed on her cheeks the same sunny burnish that had charmed me at Balbec. This face of Albertine, the general effect of which sometimes was, out of doors, a sort of milky pallor, now showed, according as the lamp shone on them, surfaces so dazzlingly, so uniformly coloured, so firm, so glowing that one might have compared them to the sustained flesh tints of certain flowers. Taken aback meanwhile by the unexpected entry of Françoise, I exclaimed:

"What? The lamp already? I say, the light is strong!" My object, as may be imagined, was by the second of these ejaculations to account for my confusion, by the first to excuse my lateness in rising. Françoise replied with a cruel ambiguity: "Do you want me to extinglish it?"

—guish! "Albertine slipped into my ear, leaving me charmed by the familiar vivacity with which, taking me at once for teacher and for accomplice, she insinuated this psychological affirmation as though asking a grammatical question.

When Françoise had left the room and Albertine was seated once again on my bed: "Do you know what I'm afraid of?" I asked her. "It is that if we go on like this I may not be able to resist the temptation to kiss you." "That would be a fine pity."

I did not respond at once to this invitation, which another man might even have found superfluous, for Albertine's way of pronouncing her words was so carnal, so seductive that merely in speaking to you she seemed to be caressing you. A word from her was a favour, and her conversation covered you with kisses. And yet it was highly attractive to me, this invitation. It would have been so, indeed, coming from any pretty girl of Albertine's age; but that Albertine should be now so accessible to me gave me more than pleasure, brought before my eyes a series of images that bore the stamp of beauty. I recalled the original

Albertine standing between me and the beach, almost painted upon a background of sea, having for me no more real existence than those figures seen on the stage, when one knows not whether one is looking at the actress herself who is supposed to appear, at an understudy who for the moment is taking her principal's part, or at a mere projection from a lantern. Then the real woman had detached herself from the luminous mass, had come towards me, with the sole result that I had been able to see that she had nothing in real life of that amorous facility which one supposed to be stamped upon her in the magic pictures. I had learned that it was not possible to touch her, to embrace her, that one might only talk to her, that for me she was no more a woman than the jade grapes, an inedible decoration at one time in fashion on dinner tables, were really fruit. And now she was appearing to me in a third plane, real as in the second experience that I had had of her but facile as in the first, facile, and all the more deliciously so in that I had so long imagined that she was not. My surplus knowledge of life (of a life less uniform, less simple than I had at first supposed it to be) inclined me provisionally towards agnosticism. What can one positively affirm, when the thing that one thought probable at first has then shown itself to be false and in the third instance turns out true? And alas, I was not yet at the end of my discoveries with regard to Albertine. In any case, "If you really don't mind my kissing you, I would rather put it off for a little and choose a good moment. Only you mustn't forget that you've said I may. I shall want a voucher: Valid for one kiss."

"Shall I have to sign it?" "But if I took it now, should I be entitled to another later on?"

"You do make me laugh with your vouchers; I shall issue a new one now and then."

"Tell me just one thing more. You know, at Balbec, before I had been introduced to you, you used often to have a hard, calculating look; you can't tell me what you were thinking about when you looked like that?" "No; I don't remember at all."

"Wait; this may remind you: one day your friend Gisèle put her feet together and jumped over the chair an old gentleman was sitting in. Try to remember what was in your mind at that moment.

"Gisèle was the one we saw least of; she did belong to the band, I suppose, but not properly. I expect I thought that she was very illbred and common." "Oh, is that all?"

I should certainly have liked, before kissing her, to be able to fill her afresh with the mystery which she had had for me on the beach before I knew her, to find latent in her the place in which she had lived earlier still; for that, at any rate, if I knew nothing of it, I could substitute all my memories of our life at Balbec, the sound of the waves rolling up and breaking beneath my window, the shouts of the children. But when I let my eyes glide over the charming pink globe of her cheeks, the gently curving surfaces of which ran up to expire beneath the first foothills of her piled black tresses which ran in undulating mountain chains, thrust out escarped ramparts and moulded the hollows of deep valleys, I could not help saying to myself: "Now at last, after failing at Balbec, I am going to learn the fragrance of the secret rose that blooms in Albertine's cheeks.

To begin with, as my mouth began gradually to approach the cheeks which my eyes had suggested to it that it should kiss, my eyes, changing their position, saw a different pair of cheeks; the throat, studied at closer range and as though through a magnifying glass shewed in its coarse grain a robustness which modified the character of the face. In this brief passage of my lips towards her cheek it was ten Albertines that I saw; this single girl being like a goddess with several heads, that which I had last seen, if I tried to approach it, gave place to another. At least so long as I had not touched it, that head, I could still see it, a faint perfume reached me from it. But alas---for in this matter of kissing, our nostrils and eyes are as ill placed as our lips are shaped— suddenly my eyes ceased to see; next, my nose, crushed by the collision, no longer perceived any fragrance, and, without thereby gaining any clearer idea of the taste of the rose of my desire, I learned, from these unpleasant signs, that at last I was in the act of kissing Albertine's cheek.

Was it because we were enacting—as may be illustrated by the rotation of a solid body—the converse of our scene together at Balbec, because it was I, now, who was lying in bed and she who sat beside me, capable of evading any brutal attack and of dictating her pleasure to me, that she allowed me to take so easily now what she had refused me on the former occasion with so forbidding a frown? It was quite another explanation, however, that Albertine offered me; this, in short: "Oh, well, you see, that time at Balbec I didn't know you properly. For all I knew, you might have meant mischief." This argument left me in perplexity. Albertine was no doubt sincere in advancing it. So difficult is it for a woman to recognise in the movements of her limbs, in the sensations felt by her body in the course of an intimate conversation with a friend, the unknown sin into which she would tremble to think that a stranger was planning her fall.

In any case, whatever the modifications that had occurred at some recent time in her life, which might perhaps have explained why it was that she now readily accorded to my momentary and purely physical desire, what at Balbec she had with horror refused to allow to my love, another far more surprising manifested itself in Albertine that same evening as soon as her caresses had procured in me the satisfaction which she could not have failed to notice, which, indeed, I had been afraid might provoke in her the instinctive movement of revulsion and offended modesty which Gilberte had given at a corresponding moment behind the laurel shrubbery in the Champs-Elysées.

The exact opposite happened. Already, when I had first made her lie on my bed and had begun to fondle her, Albertine had assumed an air which I did not remember in her, of docile good will, of an almost childish simplicity. Obliterating every trace of her customary anxieties and interests, the moment preceding pleasure, similar in this respect to the moment after death, had restored to her rejuvenated features what seemed like the innocence of earliest childhood. And no doubt everyone whose special talent is suddenly brought into play becomes modest, devoted, charming; especially if by this talent he knows that he is giving us a great pleasure, he is himself happy in the display of it, anxious to present it to us in as complete a form as possible. But in this new expression on Albertine's face there was more than a mere profession of disinterestedness, conscience, generosity, a sort of conventional and unexpected devotion; and it was farther than to her own childhood, it was to the infancy of the race that she had reverted, Very different from myself who had looked for nothing more than a physical alleviation, which I had finally secured, Albertine seemed to feel that it would indicate a certain coarseness on her part were she to seem to believe that this material pleasure could be unaccompanied by a moral sentiment or was to be regarded as terminating anything. She, who had been in so great a hurry a moment ago, now, presumably because she felt that kisses implied love and that love took precedence of all other duties, said when I reminded her of her dinner: "Oh, but that doesn't matter in the least; I have plenty of time."

She seemed embarrassed by the idea of getting up and going immediately after what had happened, embarrassed by good manners, just as Françoise when, without feeling thirsty, she had felt herself bound to accept with a seemly gaiety the glass of wine which Jupien offered her, would never have dared to leave him as soon as the last drops were drained, however urgent the call of duty. Albertine—and this was perhaps, with another which the reader will learn in due course, one of the reasons which had made me unconsciously desire her—was one of the incarnations of the little French peasant whose type may be seen in stone at Saint-André-des-Champs. As in Françoise, who presently nevertheless was to become her deadly enemy, I recognised in her a courtesy towards friend and stranger, a sense of decency, of respect for the bedside.

Françoise who, after the death of my aunt, felt obliged to speak only in a plaintive tone, would, in the months that preceded her daughter's marriage, have been quite shocked if, when the young couple walked out together, the girl had not taken her lover's arm. Albertine lying motionless beside me said: "What nice hair you have; what nice eyes; you are a dear boy."

When, after pointing out to her that it was getting late, I added: "You don't believe me?" she replied, what was perhaps true but could be so only since the minute before and for the next few hours: "I always believe you."

I insisted upon her going home, and finally she did go, but so ashamed on my account at my discourtesy that she laughed almost as though to apologise for me, as a hostess to whose party you have gone without dressing, makes the best of you but is offended nevertheless. "Are you laughing at me?" I inquired. "I am not laughing, I am smiling at you," she replied lovingly. "When am I going to see you again?" she went on, as though declining to admit that what had just happened between us, since it is generally the crowning consummation, might not be at least the prelude to a great friendship, a friendship already existing which we should have to discover, to confess, and which alone could account for the surrender we had made of ourselves.

"Since you give me leave, I shall send for you when I can." "It will have to be at short notice, unfortunately," I went on, "I never know beforehand. Would it be possible for me to send round for you in the evenings, when I am free?" "It will be quite possible in a little while, I am going to have a latch-key of my own. But just at present. it can't be done. Anyhow I shall come round to-morrow or next day in the afternoon. You needn't see me if you're busy."

On reaching the door, surprised that I had not anticipated her, she offered me her cheek, feeling that there was no need now for any coarse physical desire to prompt us to kiss one another. The brief relations in which we had just indulged being of the sort to which an absolute intimacy and a heartfelt choice often tend, Albertine had felt it incumbent upon her to improvise and add provisionally to the kisses which we had exchanged on my bed the sentiment of which those kisses would have been the symbol for a knight and his lady such as they might have been conceived in the mind of a gothic minstrel.

Albertine had made me so late that the play had just finished when I entered Mme. de Villeparisis's drawing-room; and having little desire to be caught in the stream of guests who were pouring out, discussing the great piece of news, the separation, said to be already effected, of the Duc de Guermantes from his wife, I had, until I should have an opportunity of shaking hands with my hostess, taken my seat on an empty sofa in the outer room, when from the other, in which she had no doubt had her chair in the very front row of all, I saw emerging, majestic, ample and tall in a flowing gown of yellow satin upon which stood out in relief huge black poppies, the Duchess herself. The sight of her no longer disturbed me in the least. There had been a day when my mother, laying her hands on my forehead (as was her habit when she was afraid of hurting my feelings) said: "You really must stop hanging about trying to meet Mme. de Guermantes. All the neighbours are talking about you. Besides, look how ill your grandmother is, you really have something more serious to think about than waylaying a woman who only laughs at you," in a moment, like a hypnotist who brings one back from the distant country in which one imagined oneself to be, and opens one's eyes for one, or like the doctor who, by recalling one to a sense of duty and reality, cures one of an imaginary disease in which one has been indulging one's fancy, my mother had awakened me from an unduly protracted dream.

As the Duchess swept through the room in which I was sitting, her mind filled with thoughts of friends whom I did not know and whom she would perhaps be meeting presently at some other party, Mme. de Guermantes caught sight of me on my sofa, genuinely indifferent and seeking only to be polite whereas while I was in love I had tried so desperately, without ever succeeding, to assume an air of indifference; she swerved aside, came towards me and, reproducing the smile she had worn that evening at the Opéra-Comique, which the unpleasant feeling of being cared for by some one for whom she did not care was no longer there to obliterate: "No, don't move; you don't mind if I sit down beside you for a moment?" she asked, gracefully gathering in her immense skirt which otherwise would have covered the entire sofa.

Of less stature than she, who was further expanded by the volume of her gown, I was almost brushed by her exquisite bare arm round which a faint, luminous down rose in perpetual smoke like a golden mist, and by the fringe of her fair tresses which wafted their fragrance over me. Having barely room to sit down, she could not turn easily to face me, and so, obliged to look straight before her rather than in my direction, assumed the sort of dreamy, sweet expression one sees in a portrait.

"Have you any news of Robert?" she inquired.

At that moment Mme. de Villeparisis entered the room. "Well, sir, you arrive at a fine time, when we do see you here for once in a way!" And noticing that I was talking to her niece, concluding, perhaps, that we were more intimate than she had supposed: "But don't let me interrupt your conversation with Oriane," she went on, and (for these good offices as pander are part of the duties of the perfect hostess): "You wouldn't care to dine with her here on Thursday?"

It was a day on which I was already committed, so I declined. "Saturday, then?" As my mother was returning on Saturday or Sunday, it would never do for me not to stay at home every evening to dine with her; I therefore declined this invitation also.

"Ah, you're not an easy person to get hold of!"

"Why do you never come to see me?" inquired Mme. de Guermantes when Mme. de Villeparisis had left us to go and congratulate the performers and present the leading lady with a bunch of roses upon which the hand that offered it conferred all its value, for it had cost no more than twenty francs. (This, incidentally, was as high as she ever went when an artist had performed only once. Those who gave their services at all her afternoons and evenings throughout the season received roses painted by the Marquise.)

"It's such a bore that we never see each other except in other people's houses. Since you won't meet me at dinner at my aunt's, why not come and dine with me?" Various people who had stayed to the last possible moment, upon one pretext or another, but were at length preparing to leave, seeing that the Duchess had sat down to talk to a young man on a seat so narrow as just to contain them both, thought that they must have been misinformed, that it was the Duchess, and not the Duke, who was seeking a separation, and on my account. Whereupon they hastened to spread abroad this intelligence. I had better grounds than anyone to be aware of its falsehood. But I was myself surprised that at one of those difficult periods in which a separation that is not yet completed is beginning to take effect, the Duchess, instead of withdrawing from society, should go out of her way to invite a person whom she knew so slightly. The suspicion crossed my mind that it had been the Duke alone who had been opposed to her having me in the house, and that now that he was leaving her she saw no further obstacle to her surrounding herself with the people that she liked.

A minute earlier I should have been stupefied had anyone told me that Mme. de Guermantes was going to ask me to call on her, let alone to dine with her To dine with the Guermantes was like travelling to a place I had long wished to see, making a desire emerge from my brain and take shape before my eyes, forming acquaintance with a dream. At the most, I might have supposed that it would be one of those dinners to which one's hosts invite one with: "Do come; there'll, be *absolutely* nobody but ourselves," pretending to attribute to the pariah the alarm which they themselves feel at the thought of his mixing with their other friends, seeking indeed to convert into an enviable privilege, reserved for their intimates alone, the quarantine of the outsider, hopelessly uncouth, whom they are befriending. I felt on the contrary that Mme. de Guermantes was anxious for me to enjoy the most delightful society that she had to offer me when she went on:

"On Friday, now, couldn't you? There are just a few people coming; the Princesse de Parme, who is charming, not that I'd ask you to meet anyone who wasn't nice."

Discarded in the intermediate social grades which are engaged in a perpetual upward movement, the family still plays an important part in certain stationary grades, such as the lower middle class and the semi-royal aristocracy, which latter cannot seek to raise itself since above it, from its own special point of view, there exists nothing higher. The friendship shown me by her 'aunt Villeparisis' and Robert had perhaps made me, for Mme. de Guermantes and her friends, living always upon themselves and in the same little circle, the object of a curious interest of which I had no suspicion.

She had of those two relatives a familiar, everyday, homely knowledge, of a sort, utterly different from what we imagine, in which if we happen to be comprised in it, so far from our actions being at once ejected, like the grain of dust from the eye or the drop of water from the windpipe, they are capable of remaining engraved, and will still be related and discussed years after we ourselves have forgotten them, in the palace in which we are astonished to find them preserved, like a letter in our own handwriting among a priceless collection of autographs.

People who are merely fashionable may set a guard upon doors which are too freely invaded. But the Guermantes door was not that. Hardly ever did a stranger have occasion to pass by it. If, for once in a way, the Duchess had one pointed out to her, she never dreamed of troubling herself about the social increment that he would bring, since this was a thing that she conferred and could not receive. She thought only of his real merits. Both Mme. de Villeparisis and Saint-Loup had testified to mine. Doubtless she might not have believed them if she had not at the same time observed that they could never manage to secure me when they wanted me, and therefore that I attached no importance to worldly things, which seemed to the Duchess a sign that the stranger was to be numbered among what she called 'nice people'.

Was the true motive in the mind of Mme. de Guermantes for thus inviting me (now that I was no longer in love with her) that I did not run after her relatives, although apparently run after myself by them? I cannot say. In any case, having made up her mind to invite me, she was anxious to do me the honours of the best company at her disposal and to keep away those of her friends whose presence might have dissuaded me from coming again, those whom she knew to be boring. I had not known to what to attribute her change of direction, when I had seen her deviate from her stellar path, come to sit down beside me and had heard her invite me to dinner, the effect of causes unknown for want of a special sense to enlighten us in this respect. We picture to ourselves the people who know us but slightly—such as, in my case, the Duchesse de Guermantes—as thinking of us only at the rare moments at which they set eyes on us.

I must at the same time add that a surprise of a totally different sort was to follow that which I had felt on hearing Mme. de Guermantes ask me to dine with her. Since I had decided that it would show greater modesty, on my part, and gratitude also not to conceal this initial surprise, but rather to exaggerate my expression of the delight that it gave me, Mme. de Guermantes, who was getting ready to go on to another final party, had said to me, almost as a justification and for fear of my not being quite certain who she was, since I appeared so astonished at being invited to dine with her: "You know I'm the aunt of Robert de Saint-Loup, who is such a friend of yours; besides we have met before." In replying that I was aware of this, I added that I knew also M. de Charlus, "who had been very good to me at Balbec and in Paris." Mme. de Guermantes appeared dumbfounded, and her eyes seemed to turn, as though for a verification of this statement, to some page, already filled and turned, of her internal register of events. "What, so you know Palamède, do you? What a humbug Mémé is!" she exclaimed. "We talked to him about you for hours; he told us that he would be delighted to make your acquaintance, just as if he had never set eyes on you. You must admit he's odd, and — though it's not very nice of me to say such a thing about a brother-in-law I'm devoted to, and really do admire immensely — a trifle mad at times."

The next day was cold and fine; winter was in the air—indeed the season was so far advanced that it had seemed miraculous that we should find in the already pillaged Bois a few domes of gilded green. When I awoke I saw, as from the window of the barracks at Doncières, a uniform, dead white mist which hung gaily in the sunlight, consistent and sweet as a web of spun sugar. Then the sun withdrew, and the mist thickened still further in the afternoon.

As I passed through the dining-room, where suddenly my feet ceased to sound on the bare boards as they had been doing and were hushed to a silence which, even before I had realised the explanation of it, gave me a feeling of suffocation and confinement. It was the carpets which, in view of my parents' return, the servants had begun to put down again, those carpets which look so well on bright mornings when amid their disorder the sun stays and waits for you like a friend come to take you out to luncheon in the country, and casts over them the dappled light and shade of the forest, but which now on the contrary were the first installation of the wintry prison from which, obliged as I should be to live, to take my meals at home, I should no longer be free now to escape when I chose.

"Take care you don't slip, Sir; they're not tacked yet," Françoise called to me. "I ought to have lighted up. Oh, dear, it's the end of September already, the fine days are over." She left me by myself in the dining room with the remark that it was foolish of me to stay there before she had lighted the fire. She went to get me some dinner, for even before the return of my parents, from this very evening my seclusion was to begin

Suddenly I heard a voice: "May I come in? Françoise told me you would be in here. I looked in to see whether you would care to come out and dine somewhere, if it isn't bad for your throat—there's a fog outside you could cut with a knife."

It was—arrived in Paris that morning, when I imagined him to be still in Morocco or on the sea—Robert de Saint-Loup.

When he first appeared Robert warned me that there was a good deal of fog outside, but while we were indoors, talking, it had grown steadily thicker. It was no longer merely the light mist which I had seen earlier. A few feet away from us the street lamps were blotted out and then it was night, as dark as in the open fields, in a forest, or rather on a mild Breton island whither I would fain have gone; I lost myself, as on the stark coast of some Northern sea where one risks one's life twenty times over before coming to the solitary inn; ceasing to be a mirage for which one seeks, the fog became one of those dangers against which one has to fight, so that we had, in finding our way and reaching a safe haven, the difficulties, the anxiety and finally the joy which safety, so little perceived by him who is not threatened with the loss of it, gives to the perplexed and benighted traveller. One thing only came near to destroying my pleasure during our adventurous ride, owing to the angry astonishment into which it flung me for a moment. "You know, I told Bloch," Saint-Loup suddenly informed me, "that you didn't really think all that of him, that you found him rather vulgar at times. I'm like that, you see, I want people to know where they stand," he wound up with a satisfied air and in a tone which brooked no reply. I was astounded. Not only had I the most absolute confidence in Saint-Loup, in the loyalty of his friendship, and he had betrayed it by what he had said to Bloch, but it seemed to me that he of all men ought to have been restrained from doing so, by his defects as well as by his good qualities, by that astonishing veneer of breeding which was capable of carrying politeness to what was positively a want of frankness. His triumphant air, was it what we assume to cloak a certain embarrassment in admitting a thing which we know that we ought not to have done, or did it mean complete unconsciousness; stupidity making a virtue out of a defect which I had not associated with him; a passing fit of ill humour towards me, prompting him to make an end of our friendship, or the notation in words of a passing fit of ill humour in the company of Bloch to whom he had felt that he must say something disagreeable, even although I should be compromised by it? However that might be, his face was seared, while he uttered this vulgar speech, by a frightful sinuosity which I saw on it once or twice only in all the time I knew him, and which, beginning by running more or less down the middle of his face, when it came to his lips twisted them, gave them a hideous expression of baseness, almost of bestiality, quite transitory and no doubt inherited. There must have been at such moments, which recurred probably not more than once every other year, a partial eclipse of his true self by the passage across it of the personality of some ancestor whose shadow fell on him. Fully as much as his satisfied air, the words: "I want people to know where they stand," encouraged the same doubt and should have incurred a similar condemnation. I felt inclined to say to him that if one wants people to know where they stand, one ought to confine these outbursts of frankness to one's own affairs and not to acquire a too easy merit at the expense of others. But by this time the carriage had stopped outside the restaurant, the huge front of which, glazed and streaming with light, alone succeeded in piercing the darkness. The fog itself, beside the comfortable brightness of the lighted interior, seemed to be waiting outside on the pavement to show one the way in with the joy of servants whose faces reflect the hospitable instincts of their master; shot with the most delicate shades of light, it pointed the way like the pillar of fire which guided the Children of Israel. Many of whom, as it happened, were to be found inside. For this was the place to which Bloch and his friends had long been in the habit, maddened by a hunger as famishing as the Ritual Fast, which at least occurs only once a year, for coffee and the satisfaction of political curiosity, of repairing in the evenings. But they were not viewed with favour by the young nobles who composed the rest of its patrons and had taken possession of a second room, separated from the other only by a flimsy parapet topped with a row of plants.

As ill luck would have it, Saint-Loup remaining outside for a minute to explain to the driver that he was to call for us again after dinner, I had to make my way in by myself. In the first place, once I had involved myself in the spinning door, to which I was not accustomed, I began to fear that I should never succeed in escaping from it. This evening the proprietor, not venturing either to brave the elements outside or to desert his customers, remained standing near the entrance so as to have the pleasure of listening to the joyful complaints of the new arrivals, all aglow with the satisfaction of people who have had difficulty in reaching a place and have been afraid of losing their way. The smiling cordiality of his welcome was, however, dissipated by the sight of a stranger incapable of disengaging himself from the rotating sheets of glass. This flagrant sign of social ignorance made him knit his brows like an examiner who has a good mind not to utter the formula: *Dignus est intrare.* As a crowning error I went to look for a seat in the room set apart for the nobility, from which he at once expelled me, indicating to me, with a rudeness to which all the waiters at once conformed, a place in the other room. This was all the less to my liking because the seat was in the middle of a crowded row and I had opposite me the door reserved for the Hebrews which, as it did not revolve, opening and shutting at every moment kept me in a horrible draught. But the proprietor declined to move me, saying: "No, sir, I cannot have the whole place upset for you." Presently, however, he forgot this belated and troublesome guest, captivated as he was by the arrival of each newcomer who, before calling for his beer, his wing of cold chicken or his hot grog (it was by now long past dinner-time), must first, as in the old romances, pay his scot by relating his adventure at the moment of his entry into this asylum of warmth and security where the contrast with the perils just escaped made that gaiety and sense of comradeship prevail which create a cheerful harmony round the camp fire.

One reported that his carriage, thinking it had got to the Pont de la Concorde had circled three times round the Invalides, another that his, in trying to make its way down the Avenue des Champs-Elysées, had driven into a clump of trees at the Rond Point, from which it had taken him three quarters of an hour to get clear. Then followed lamentations upon the fog, the cold, the deathly stillness of the streets, uttered and received with the same exceptionally jovial air, which was accounted for by the pleasant atmosphere of the room which, except where I sat, was warm, the dazzling light which set blinking eyes already accustomed to not seeing, and the buzz of talk which restored their activity to deafened ears.

It was all the newcomers could do to keep silence. The singularity of the mishaps which each of them thought unique burned their tongues, and their eyes roved in search of some one to engage in conversation. The proprietor himself lost all sense of social distinction. "M. le Prince de Foix lost his way three times coming from the Porte Saint-Martin," he was not afraid to say with a laugh, actually pointing out, as though introducing one to the other, the illustrious nobleman to an Israelite barrister, who, on any evening but this, would have been divided from him by a barrier far harder to surmount than the ledge of greenery. "Three times—fancy that!" said the barrister, touching his hat. This note of personal interest was not at all to the Prince's liking. He formed one of an aristocratic group for whom the practice of impertinence, even at the expense of their fellow-nobles when these were not of the very highest rank, seemed the sole possible occupation. Not to acknowledge a bow, and, if the polite stranger repeated the offence, to titter with sneering contempt or fling back one's head with a look of fury, to pretend not to know some elderly man who might have done them a service, to reserve their handclasp for dukes and the really intimate friends of dukes whom the latter introduced to them, such was the attitude of these young men, and especially of the Prince de Foix.

Suddenly I saw the landlord's body whipped into a series of bows, the head waiters hurrying to support him in a full muster which drew every eye towards the door. "Quick, send Cyprien here, lay a table for M. le Marquis de Saint-Loup," cried the proprietor, for whom Robert was not merely a great nobleman possessing a real importance even in the eyes of the Prince de Foix, but a client who drove through life four-in-hand, so to speak, and spent a great deal of money in this restaurant.

The customers in the big room looked on with interest, those in the small room shouted simultaneous greetings to their friend as he finished wiping his shoes. But just as he was about to make his way into the small room he caught sight of me in the big one. "Good God," he exclaimed, "what on earth are you doing there? And with the door wide open too?" he went on, with an angry glance at the proprietor, who ran to shut it, throwing the blame on his staff: "I'm always telling them to keep it shut."

I had been obliged to shift my own table and to disturb others which stood in the way in order to reach him. " Why did you move? Would you sooner dine here than in the little room? Why, my poor fellow, you're freezing. You will oblige me by keeping that door locked;" he turned to the proprietor. "This very instant, M. le Marquis; the gentlemen will have to go out of this room through the other, that is all." And the better to show his zeal he detailed for this operation a head waiter and several satellites, vociferating the most terrible threats of punishment were it not properly carried out. He began to show me exaggerated marks of respect, so as to make me forget that these had begun not upon my arrival but only after that of Saint-Loup, while, lest I should think them to have been prompted by the friendliness shown me by his rich and noble client, he gave me now and again a surreptitious little smile which seemed to indicate a regard that was wholly personal.

After leaving us for a moment in order to supervise personally the barring of the door and the ordering of our dinner (he laid great stress on our choosing 'butcher's meat', the fowls being presumably nothing to boast of) the proprietor came back to inform us that M. le Prince de Foix would esteem it a favour if M. le Marquis would allow him to dine at a table next to ours. "But they are all taken," objected Robert, casting an eye over the tables which blocked the way to mine. "That doesn't matter in the least, if M. le Marquis would like it, I can easily ask these people to move to another table. It is always a pleasure to do anything for M. le Marquis!" "But you must decide," said Saint-Loup to me. "Foix is a good fellow, he may bore you or he may not; anyhow he's not such a fool as most of them." I told Robert that of course I should like to meet his friend but that now that I was for once in a way dining with him and was so entirely happy, I should be just as well pleased to have him all to myself. "He's got a very fine cloak, the Prince has," the proprietor broke in upon our deliberation. "Yes, I know," said Saint-Loup. I wanted to tell Robert that M. de Charlus had disclaimed all knowledge of me to his sister-in-law, and to ask him what could be the reason of this, but was prevented by the arrival of M. de Foix, come to see whether his request had been favourably received, we caught sight of him standing beside our table. Robert introduced us, but did not hide from his friend that as we had things to talk about he would prefer not to be disturbed. The Prince withdrew, adding to the farewell bow which he made me, a smile which, pointed at Saint-Loup, seemed to transfer to him the responsibility for the shortness of a meeting which the Prince himself would have liked to see prolonged. As he turned to go, Robert, struck, it appeared, by a sudden idea, dashed off after his friend, with a "Stay where you are, and get on with your dinner, I shall be back in a moment," to me; and vanished into the smaller room.

While waiting for Saint-Loup to return I asked the proprietor to get me some bread. "Certainly, Monsieur le Baron!" "I am not a Baron," I told him. "Oh, beg pardon, Monsieur le Comte!" I had no time to lodge a second protest which would certainly have promoted me to the rank of marquis; when faithful to his promise of an immediate return, Saint-Loup reappeared in the doorway carrying over his arm the thick vicuna cloak of the Prince de Foix, from whom I guessed that he had borrowed it in order to keep me warm. He signed to me not to get up, and came towards me, but either my table would have to be moved again or I must change my seat if he was to get to his. Entering the big room he sprang lightly on to one of the red plush benches which ran round its walls and on which, apart from myself, there were sitting only three or four of the young men from the Jockey Club, friends of his own, who had not managed to find places in the other room. Between the tables and the wall electric wire's were stretched at a certain height; without the least hesitation Saint-Loup jumped nimbly over them like a horse in a steeplechase; embarrassed that it should be done wholly for my benefit and to save me the trouble of a slight movement, I was at the same time amazed at the precision with which my friend performed this exercise in levitation; and in this I was not alone; for, albeit they would probably have had but little admiration for a similar display on the part of a more humbly born and less generous client, the proprietor and his staff stood fascinated, like race-goers in the enclosure; one underling, apparently rooted to the ground, stood there gaping with a dish in his hand for which a party close beside him were waiting; and when Saint-Loup, having to get past his friends, climbed on the narrow ledge behind them and ran along it, balancing himself with his arms, discreet applause broke from the body of the room. On coming to where I was sitting he stopped short in his advance with the precision of a tributary chieftain before the throne of a sovereign, and, stooping down, handed to me with an air of courtesy and submission the vicuna cloak which, a moment later, having taken his place beside me, without my having to make a single movement he arranged as a light but warm shawl about my shoulders.

"By the way, while I think of it, my uncle Charlus has something to say to you. I promised I'd send you round to him to-morrow evening."

"I was just going to speak to you, about him. But to-morrow evening I am dining with your aunt Guermantes."

"Yes there's a regular beanfeast to-morrow at Oriane's. I'm not asked. But my uncle Palamède don't want you to go there. You can't get out of it, I suppose? Well, anyhow, go on to my uncle's afterwards. I'm sure he really does want to see you. Look here, you can easily manage to get there by eleven. Eleven o'clock; don't forget; I'll let him know. He's very touchy. If you don't turn up he'll never forgive you. And Oriane's parties are always over quite early. If you are only going to dine there you can quite easily be at my uncle's by eleven. I ought really to go and see Oriane, about getting shifted from Morocco; I want an exchange. She is so nice about all that sort of thing, and she can get anything she likes out of General de Saint-Joseph, who runs that branch. But don't say anything about it to her. I've mentioned it to the Princesse de Parme, everything will be all right. Interesting place, Morocco. I could tell you all sorts of things. Very fine lot of men out there. One feels they're on one's own level, mentally."

"You don't think the Germans are going to go to war about it?"

"No; they're annoyed with us, as after all they have every right to be. But the Emperor is out for peace. They are always making us think they want war, to force us to give in. Pure bluff, you know, like poker. The Prince of Monaco, one of Wilhelm's agents, comes and tells us in confidence that Germany will attack us. Then we give way. But if we didn't give way, there wouldn't be war in any shape or form. You have only to think what a comic spectacle a war would be in these days. It'd be a bigger catastrophe than the Flood and the *Götterdämmerung* rolled in one. Only it wouldn't last so long."

He spoke to me of friendship, affection, regret, albeit like all visitors of his sort he was going off the next morning for some months, which he was to spend in the country, and would only be staying a couple of nights in Paris on his way back to Morocco (or elsewhere); but the words which he thus let fall into the heated furnace which my heart was this evening, kindled a pleasant glow there. Our infrequent meetings, this one in particular, have since formed a distinct episode in my memories. For him, as for me, this was the evening of friendship.

And yet the friendship that I felt for him at this moment was scarcely, I feared (and felt therefore some remorse at the thought), what he would have liked to inspire. Filled still with the pleasure that I had had in seeing him come bounding towards me and gracefully pause on arriving at his goal, I felt that this pleasure lay in my recognising that each of the series of movements which he had developed against the wall, along the bench, had its meaning, its cause in Saint-Loup's own personal nature possibly, but even more in that which by birth and upbringing he had inherited from his race.

How much familiar intercourse with a Guermantes could disclose of vulgar arrogance I had had an opportunity of seeing, not in M. de Charlus, in whom certain characteristic faults, for which I had been unable, so far, to account, were overlaid upon his aristocratic habits, but in the Duc de Guermantes. And yet he too, in the general impression of commonness which had so strongly repelled my grandmother when she had met him once, years earlier, at Mme. de Villeparisis's, included glimpses of historic grandeur of which I became conscious when I went to dine in his house, on the evening following that which I had spent with Saint-Loup.

They had not been apparent to me either in himself or in the Duchess when I had met them first in their aunt s drawing-room, any more than I had discerned, on first seeing her, the differences that set Berma apart from her fellow-players, all the more that in her the individuality was infinitely more striking than in any social celebrity, such distinctions becoming more marked in proportion as the objects are more real, more conceivable by the intellect. And yet, however slight the shades of social distinction may be (and so slight are they that when an accurate portrayer like Sainte-Beuve tries to indicate the shades of difference between the salons of Mme. Geoffrin, Mme. Récamier and Mme. de Boigne, they appear so much alike that the cardinal truth which, unknown to the author, emerges from his investigations, is the vacuity of that form of life), nevertheless, and for the same reason as with Berma, when the Guermantes had ceased to impress me and the tiny drop of their originality was no longer vaporised by my imagination, I was able to distil and analyse it, imponderable as it was.

The Duchess having made no reference to her husband when she talked to me at her aunt's party, I wondered whether, in view of the rumours of a divorce that were current, he would be present at the dinner. But my doubts were speedily set at rest, for through the crowd of footmen who stood about in the hall and who (since they must until then have regarded me much as they regarded the children of the evicted cabinet-maker, that is to say with more fellow-feeling perhaps than their master but as a person incapable of being admitted to his house) must have been asking themselves to what this social revolution could be due, I saw slip towards me M. de Guermantes himself, who had been watching for my arrival so as to receive me upon his threshold and take off my greatcoat with his own hands.

"Mme. de Guermantes will be as pleased as punch," he greeted me in a glibly persuasive tone. "Let me help you off with your duds." (He felt it to be at once companionable and comic to employ the speech of the people.) "My wife was just the least bit afraid you might fail us, although you had fixed a date. We've been saying to each other all day long: Depend upon it, he'll never turn up. I am bound to say, Mme. de Guërmantes was a better prophet than I was. You are not an easy man to get hold of, and I was quite sure you were going to play us false." And the Duke was so bad a husband, so brutal even (people said), that one felt grateful to him, as one feels grateful to wicked people for their occasional kindness of heart, for those words "Mme. de Guermantes" with which he appeared to be spreading out over the Duchess a protecting wing, that she might be but one flesh with him. Meanwhile, taking me familiarly by the hand, he began to lead the way, to introduce me into his household. As we left the outer hall, I had mentioned to M. de Guermantes that I was extremely anxious to see his Elstirs. "I am at your service. Is M. Elstir a friend of yours, then? If so, it is most vexing, for I know him slightly; he is a pleasant fellow, what our fathers used to call an ' honest fellow', I might have asked him to honour us with his company, and to dine tonight. I am sure he would have been highly flattered at being invited to spend the evening in your society." Very little suggestive of the old order when he tried thus to assume its manner, the Duke relapsed unconsciously into it. After inquiring whether I wished him to show me the pictures, he conducted me to them, gracefully standing aside for me at each door, apologising when, to show me the way, he was obliged to precede me, a little scene which (since the days when Saint-Simon relates that an ancestor of the Guermantes did him the honours of his town house with the same punctilious exactitude in the performance of the frivolous duties of a gentleman) must, before coming gradually down to us, have been enacted by many other Guermantes for numberless other visitors. And as I had said to the Duke that I would like very much to be left alone for a few minutes with the pictures, he discreetly withdrew; telling me that I should find him in the drawing-room when I was ready.

Only, once I was face to face with the Elstirs, I completely forgot about dinner and the time; here again as at Balbec I had before me fragments of that strangely coloured world which was no more than the projection, the way of seeing things peculiar to that great painter, which his speech in no way expressed. The parts of the walls that were covered by paintings from his brush, all homogeneous with one another, were like the luminous images of a magic lantern, which would have been in this instance the brain of the artist, and the strangeness of which one could never have suspected so long as one had known only the man, which was like seeing the iron lantern boxing its lamp before any coloured slide had been slid into its groove. Among these pictures several of the kind that seemed most absurd to ordinary people, interested me more than the rest because they recreated those optical illusions which prove to us that we should never succeed in identifying objects if we did not make some process of reasoning intervene. How often, when driving in the dark, do we not come upon a long, lighted street which begins a few feet away from us, when what we have actually before our eyes is nothing but a rectangular patch of wall with a bright light falling on it, which has given us the mirage of depth. In view of which is it not logical, not by any artifice of symbolism but by a sincere return to the very root of the impression, to represent one thing by that other for which, in the flash of a first illusion, we mistook it? Surfaces and volumes are in reality independent of the names of objects which our memory imposes on them after we have recognised them. Elstir attempted to wrest from what he had just felt what he already knew, his effort had often been to break up that aggregate of impressions which we call vision.

The people who detested these 'horrors' were astonished to find that Elstir admired Chardin, Perroneau, any number of painters whom they, the ordinary men and women of society, liked. They did not take into account that Elstir had had to make, for his own part, in striving to reproduce reality (with the particular index of his taste for certain lines of approach), the same effort as a Chardin or a Perroneau and that he admired in them attempts of the same order, fragments anticipatory so to speak of works of his own. Nor did these society people include in their conception of Elstir's work that temporal perspective which enabled them to like, or at least to look without discomfort at Chardin's painting. And yet the older among them might have reminded themselves that in the course of their lives they had seen gradually, as the years bore them away from it, the unbridgeable gulf between what they considered a masterpiece by Ingres and what, they had supposed, must remain for ever a 'horror' (Manet's *Olympia,* for example) shrink until the two canvases seemed like twins. But we learn nothing from any lesson because we have not the wisdom to work backwards from the particular to the general, and imagine ourselves always to be going through an experience which is without precedents in the past.

I was moved by the discovery in two of the pictures (more realistic, these, and in an earlier manner) of the same person, in one in evening dress in his own drawing-room, in the other wearing a frock coat and tall hat at some popular regatta where he had evidently no business to be, which proved that for Elstir he was not only a regular sitter but a friend, perhaps a patron whom it pleased him to introduce into his pictures, (just as Carpaccio used to introduce prominent figures, and in speaking likenesses, from contemporary life in Venice) just as Beethoven, too, found pleasure in inscribing at the top of a favourite work the beloved name of the Archduke Rudolph. There was something enchanting about this waterside carnival. The river, the women's dresses, the sails of the boats, the innumerable reflections of one thing and another came crowding into this little square panel of beauty which Elstir had cut out of a marvellous afternoon. What delighted one in the dress of a woman who had stopped for a moment in the dance because it was hot and she was out of breath, was irresistible also in the same way in the canvas of a motionless sail, in the water of the little harbour, in the wooden bridge, in the leaves of the trees and in the sky. As in one of the pictures that I had seen at Balbec, the hospital, as beautiful beneath its sky of lapis lazuli as the cathedral itself, seemed (more bold than Elstir the theorician, than Elstir the man of taste, the lover of things mediaeval) to be intoning: "There is no such thing as gothic, there is no such thing as a masterpiece; this tasteless hospital is just as good as the glorious porch," so I now heard: "The slightly vulgar lady at whom a man of discernment would refrain from glancing as he passed her by, whom he would exclude from the poetical composition which nature has set before him—she is beautiful too; her dress is receiving the same light as the sail of that boat, and there are no degrees of value and beauty; the commonplace dress and the sail, beautiful in itself, are two mirrors reflecting the same gleam; the value is all in the painter's eye." This eye had had the skill to arrest for all time the motion of the hours at this luminous instant, when the lady had felt hot and had stopped dancing, when the tree was fringed with a belt of shadow, when the sails seemed to be slipping over a golden glaze. But just because the depicted moment pressed on one with so much force, this so permanent canvas gave one the most fleeting impression, one felt that the lady would presently move out of it, the boats drift away, the night draw on, that pleasure comes to an end, that life passes and that the moments illuminated by the convergence, at once, of so many lights do not recur. I recognised yet another aspect, quite different it is true, of what the moment means in a series of water-colours of mythological subjects, dating from Elstir's first period, which also adorned this room. Society people who held 'advanced' views on art went 'as far as' this earliest manner, but no farther.

While I was examining Elstir's paintings the bell, rung by arriving guests, had been pealing uninterruptedly, and had lulled me into a pleasing unconsciousness. But the silence which followed its clangour and had already lasted for some time succeeded — less rapidly, it is true — in awakening me from my dream, as the silence that follows Lindor's music arouses Bartolo from his sleep. I was afraid that I had been forgotten, that they had sat down to dinner, and hurried to the drawing-room. At the door of the Elstir gallery I found a servant waiting for me, white-haired, though whether with age or powder I cannot say, with the air of a Spanish Minister, but treating me with the same respect that he would have shown to a King. I felt from his manner that he must have been waiting for at least an hour, and I thought with alarm of the delay I had caused in the service of dinner, especially as I had promised to be at M. de Charlus's by eleven.

It was the Spanish Minister (though I also met on the way the footman persecuted by the porter, who, radiant with delight when I inquired after his girl, told me that the very next day they were both to be off duty, so that he would be able to spend the whole day with her, and extolled the generosity of Madame la Duchesse) who conducted me to the drawing-room, where I was afraid of finding M. de Guermantes in an ill humour. He welcomed me, on the contrary, with a joy that was evidently to a certain extent artificial and dictated by politeness, but was also sincere, prompted both by his stomach, which so long a delay had begun to famish, and his consciousness of a similar impatience in all his other guests, who completely filled the room. Indeed I heard afterwards that I had kept them waiting for nearly three-quarters of an hour. The Duc de Guermantes probably thought that to prolong the general torment for two minute's more would not intensify it and that, politeness having driven him to postpone for so long the moment of moving into the dining-room, this politeness would be more complete if, by not having dinner announced immediately, he could succeed in persuading me that I was not late, and that they had not been waiting for me. And so he asked me, as if we had still an hour before dinner and some of the party had not yet arrived, what I thought of his Elstirs. But at the same time, and without letting the cravings of his stomach become apparent, so as not to lose another moment, without even allowing me time to shake hands with the Duchess, led me, as though I were a delightful surprise to the person in question to whom he seemed to be saying: "Here's your friend! You see, I'm bringing him to you by the scruff of his neck," towards a lady of smallish stature. Whereupon, long before, thrust forward by the Duke, I had reached her chair, the lady had begun to flash at me continuously from her large, soft, dark eyes the thousand smiles of understanding which we address to an old friend who perhaps has not recognised us. As this was precisely my case and I could not succeed in calling to mind who she was, I averted my eyes from her as I approached so as not to have to respond until our introduction should have released me from my predicament. Meanwhile the lady continued to maintain in unstable equilibrium the smile intended for myself. She looked as though she were anxious to be relieved of it and to hear me say: "Oh, but this is a pleasure! Mamma will be pleased when I tell her I've met you! " I was as impatient to learn her name as she was to see that I did finally greet her, fully aware of what I was doing, so that the smile which she was holding on indefinitely, like the note of a tuning-fork, might at length be let go. But M. de Guermantes managed things so badly (to my mind, at least) that I seemed to have heard only my own name uttered and was given no clue to the identity of my unknown friend, to whom it never occurred to tell me herself what her name was, so obvious did the grounds of our intimacy, which baffled me completely, seem to her. Indeed, as soon as I had come within reach, she did not offer me her hand, but took mine in a familiar clasp, and spoke to me exactly as though I had been equally conscious with herself of the pleasant memories to which her mind reverted. She told me how sorry Albert (who, I gathered, was her son) would be to have missed seeing me. I tried to remember who, among the people I had known as boys, was called Albert, and could think only of Bloch, but this could not be Bloch's mother that I saw before me since she had been dead for some time. In vain I struggled to identify the past experience common to herself and me to which her thoughts had been carried back. But I could no more distinguish it through the translucent jet of her large, soft pupils which allowed only her smile to pierce their surface than one can distinguish a landscape that lies on the other side of a smoked glass, even when the sun is blazing on it. She asked me whether my father was not working too hard, if I would not come to the theatre some evening with Albert, if I was stronger now, and as my replies, stumbling through the mental darkness in which I was plunged, became distinct only to explain that I was not feeling well that evening, she pushed forward a chair for me herself, going to all sorts of trouble which I was not accustomed to see taken by my parents' friends. At length the clue to the riddle was furnished me by the Duke: "She thinks you're charming," he murmured in my ear, which felt somehow that it had heard these words before. They were what Mme. de Villeparisis had said to my grandmother and myself after we had made the acquaintance of the Princesse de Luxembourg. Everything became clear; the lady I now saw had nothing in common with Mme. de Luxembourg, but from the language of him who thus served me with her I could discern the nature of the animal. It was a Royalty. She had never before heard of either my family or myself, but, a scion of the noblest race and endowed with the greatest fortune in the world (for, a daughter of the Prince de Parme, she had married a cousin of equal princelihood), she sought always, in gratitude to her Creator, to testify to her neighbour, however poor or lowly he might be, that she did not look down upon him. Really, I might have guessed this from her smile. I had seen the Princesse de Luxembourg buy little rye-cakes on the beach at Balbec to give to my grandmother, as though to a caged deer in the zoological gardens. But this was only the second Princess of the Blood Royal to whom I had been presented, and I might be excused my failure to discern in her the common factors of the friendliness of the great. Besides, had not they themselves gone out of their way to warn me not to count too much on this friendliness, since the Duchesse de Guermantes, who had waved me so effusive a greeting with her gloved hand at the Opéra-Comique, had appeared furious when I bowed to her in the street, like people who, having once given somebody a sovereign, feel that this has set them free from any further obligation towards him. As for M. de Charlus, his ups and downs were even more sharply contrasted. While in the sequel I have known, as the reader will learn, Highnesses and Majesties of another sort altogether, Queens who play the Queen and speak not after the conventions of their kind but like the Queens in Sardou's plays.

    If M. de Guermantes had been in such haste to present me, it was because the presence at a party of anyone not personally known to a Royal Personage is an intolerable state of things which must not be prolonged for a single instant. It was similar to the haste which Saint-Loup had shown in making me introduce him to my grandmother. By the same token, by a fragmentary survival of the old life of the court which is called social courtesy and is not superficial, in which, rather, by a centripetal reversion, it is the surface that becomes essential and profound, the Duc and Duchesse de Guermantes regarded as a duty more essential than those (which one at least of the pair neglected often enough) of charity, chastity, pity and justice, that of never addressing the Princesse de Parme save in the third person.

I then asked the Duke to present me to the Prince d'Agrigente. "What! Do you mean to say you don't know our excellent Gri-gri!" cried M. de Guermantes, and gave M. d'Agrigente my name. His own, so often quoted by Françoise, had always appeared to me like a transparent sheet of coloured glass through which I beheld, struck, on the shore of the violet sea, by the slanting rays of a golden sun, the rosy marble cubes of an ancient city of which I had not the least doubt that the Prince—happening for a miraculous moment to be passing through Paris—was himself, as luminously Sicilian and gloriously mellowed, the absolute sovereign. Alas, the vulgar drone to whom I was introduced, and who wheeled round to bid me good evening with a ponderous ease which he considered elegant, was as independent of his name as of any work of art that he might have owned without bearing upon his person any trace of its beauty, without, perhaps, ever having stopped to examine it. The Prince d'Agrigente was so entirely devoid of anything princely, anything that might make one think of Agrigento, that one was led to suppose that his name, entirely distinct from himself, bound by no ties to his person, had had the power of attracting to itself the whole of whatever vague poetical element there might have been in this man as in any other, and isolating it, after the operation, in the enchanted syllables. If any such operation had been performed, it had certainly been done most efficiently, for there remained not an atom of charm to be drawn from this kinsman of the Guermantes. With the result that he found himself at one and the same time, the only man in the world who was Prince d'Agrigente and the man who, of all the men in the world was, perhaps, least so. He was, for all that, very glad to be what he was, but as a banker is glad to hold a number of shares in a mine without caring whether the said mine answers to the charming name of Ivanhoe or Primrose, or is called merely the Premier. Meanwhile, as these introductions, which it has taken me so long to recount but which, beginning as I entered the room, had lasted only a few seconds, were coming to an end, and Mme. de Guermantes, in an almost suppliant tone, was saying to me: "I am sure Basin is tiring you, dragging you round like that; we are anxious for you to know our friends, but we are a great deal more anxious not to tire you, so that you may come again often," the Duke, with a somewhat awkward and timid wave of the hand, gave (as he would gladly have given it at any time during the last hour, filled for me by the contemplation of his Elstirs) the signal that dinner might now be served.

No sooner was the order to serve dinner given than with a vast gyratory whirr, multiple and simultaneous, the double doors of the dining-room swung apart; a chamberlain with the air of a Lord Chamberlain bowed before the Princesse de Parme and announced the tidings "Madame is served," in a tone such as he would have employed to say "Madame is dead," which, however, cast no gloom over the assembly for it was with an air of unrestrained gaiety and as, in summer, at 'Robinson' that the couples moved forward one behind another to the dining-room, separating when they had reached their places where footmen thrust their chairs in behind them; last of all, Mme. de Guermantes advanced upon me, that I might lead her to the table, and without my feeling the least shadow of the, timidity that I might have feared, for, like a huntress to whom her great muscular prowess has made graceful motion an easy thing, observing no doubt that I had placed myself on the wrong side of her, she pivoted with such accuracy round me that I found her arm resting on mine and attuned in the most natural way to a ryhthm of precise and noble movements. I yielded to these with all the more readiness in that the Guermantes attached no more importance to them than does to learning a truly learned man in whose company one is less alarmed than in that of a dunce; other doors opened through which there entered the steaming soup, as though the dinner were being held in a puppet theatre of skilful mechanism where the belated arrival of the young guest set, on a signal from the puppet-master, all the machinery in motion.

I asked myself where in her mansion could be hiding the familiar spirit whose duty it was to ensure the maintenance of the aristocratic standard of living, and which, always invisible but evidently crouching at one moment in the entrance hall, at another in the drawing-room, at a third in her dressing-room, reminded the servants of this woman who did not believe in titles to address her as Mme. la Duchesse, reminding also herself who cared only for reading and had no respect for persons to go out to dinner with her sister-in-law when eight o'clock struck, and to put on a low gown. The same familiar spirit represented to Mme. de Guermantes the social duties of duchesses, of the foremost among them, that was, who like herself were multi-millionaires, the sacrifice to boring tea, dinner and evening parties of hours in which she might have read interesting books, as unpleasant necessities like rain, which Mme. de Guermantes accepted, letting play on them her biting humour, but without seeking in any way to justify her acceptance of them. The curious accident by which the butler of Mme. de Guermantes invariably said "Madame la Duchesse" to this woman who believed only in the intellect, did not however appear to shock her. Never had it entered her head to request him to address her simply as "Madame". Giving her the utmost benefit of the doubt one might have supposed that, thinking of something else at the time, she had heard only the word "Madame" and that the suffix appended to it had not caught her attention. Only, though she might feign deafness, she was not dumb. In fact, whenever she had a message to give to her husband she would say to the butler: "Remind Monsieur le Duc—"

All the Guermantes, when you were introduced to them proceeded to perform a sort of ceremony almost as though the fact that they held out their hand to you had been as important as the conferring of an order of knighthood. At the moment when a Guermantes, were he no more than twenty, but treading already in the footsteps of his ancestors, heard your name uttered by the person who introduced you, he let fall on you as though he had by no means made up his mind to say "How d'ye do?" a gaze generally blue, always of the coldness of a steel blade which he seemed ready to plunge into the deepest recesses of your heart. Which was as a matter of fact what the Guermantes imagined themselves to be doing, each of them regarding himself as a psychologist of the highest order. They thought moreover that they increased by this inspection the affability of the salute which was to follow it, and would not be rendered you without full knowledge of your deserts. All this occurred at a distance from yourself which, little enough had it been a question of a passage of arms, seemed immense for a handclasp, and had as chilling an effect in this connection as in the other, so that when the Guermantes, after a rapid twisting thrust that explored the most intimate secrets of your soul and laid bare your title to honour, had deemed you worthy to associate with him thereafter, his hand, directed towards you at the end of an arm stretched out to its fullest extent, appeared to be presenting a rapier at you for a single combat, and that hand was in fact placed so far in advance of the Guermantes himself at that moment that when he afterwards bowed his head it was difficult to distinguish whether it was yourself or his own hand that he was saluting.

Guermantes of the gentler sex had a feminine form of greeting. At the moment when you were presented to one of these, she made you a sweeping bow in which she carried towards you, almost to an angle of forty-five degrees, her head and bust, the rest of her body (which came very high, up to the belt which formed a pivot) remaining stationary. But no sooner had she projected thus towards you the upper part of her person than she flung it backwards beyond the vertical line by a sudden retirement through almost the same angle. This subsequent withdrawal neutralised what appeared to have been conceded to you; the ground which you believed yourself to have gained did not even remain a conquest as in a duel; the original positions were retained.

Among the elements which, absent from the three or four other more or less equivalent drawing-rooms that set the fashion for the Faubourg Saint-Germain, differentiated from them that of the Duchesse de Guermantes, one of the least attractive was regularly furnished by one or two extremely good-looking women who had no title to be there apart from their beauty and the use that M. de Guermantes had made of them, and whose presence revealed at once, as does in other drawing-rooms that of certain otherwise unaccountable pictures, that in this household the husband was an ardent appreciator of feminine graces. They were all more or less alike, for the Duke had a taste for large women, at once statuesque and loose-limbed, of a type half-way between the Venus of Milo and the Samothracian Victory; often fair, rarely dark, sometimes auburn, like the most recent, who was at this dinner, that Vicomtesse d'Arpajon whom he had loved so well that for a long time he had obliged her to send him as many as ten telegrams daily (which slightly annoyed the Duchess), corresponded with her by carrier pigeon when he was at Guermantes, and from whom moreover he had long been so incapable of tearing himself away that, one winter which he had had to spend at Parma, he travelled back regularly every week to Paris, spending two days in the train, in order to see her.

As a rule these handsome 'supers' had been his mistresses but were no longer (as was Mme. d'Arpajon's case) or were on the point of ceasing to be so. It may well have been that the importance which the Duchess enjoyed in their sight and the hope of being invited to her house, though they themselves came of thoroughly aristocratic, but still not quite first-class stock, had prompted them, even more than the good looks and generosity of the Duke, to yield to his desires. Not that the Duchess would have placed any insuperable obstacle in the way of their crossing her threshold: she was aware that in more than one of them she had found an ally, thanks to whom she had obtained a thousand things which she wanted but which M. de Guermantes pitilessly denied his wife so long as he was not in love with some one else. And so the reason why they were not invited by the Duchess until their intimacy with the Duke was already far advanced lay principally in the fact that he, every time that he had embarked on the deep waters of love, had imagined nothing more than a brief flirtation, as a reward for which he considered an invitation from his wife to be more than adequate. And yet he found himself offering this as the price of far less, for a first kiss in fact, because a resistance upon which he had never reckoned had been brought into play or because there had been no resistance. In love it often happens that gratitude, the desire to give pleasure, makes us generous beyond the limits of what the other person's expectation and self-interest could have anticipated. But then the realisation of this offer was hindered by conflicting circumstances. In the first place, all the women who had responded to M. de Guerrnantes's love, and sometimes even when they had not yet surrendered themselves to him, he had, one after another, segregated from the world. He no longer allowed them to see anyone, spent almost all his time in their company, looked after the education of their children to whom now and again, if one was to judge by certain, speaking likenesses later on, he had occasion to present a little brother or sister. And so if, at the start of the connection, the prospect of an introduction to Mme. de Guermantes, which had never crossed the mind of the Duke, had entered considerably into the thoughts of his mistress, their connection had by itself altered the whole of the lady's point of view; the Duke was no longer for her merely the husband of the smartest woman in Paris, but a man with whom his new mistress was in love, a man moreover who had given her the means and the inclination for a more luxurious style of living and had transposed the relative importance in her mind of questions of social and of material advantage; while now and then a composite jealousy, into which all these factors entered, of Mme. de Guermantes, animated the Duke's mistresses. But this case was the rarest of all; besides, when the day appointed for the introduction at length arrived (at a point when as a rule the Duke had lost practically all interest in the matter, his actions, like everyone's else, being generally dictated by previous actions, the prime motive of which had already ceased to exist), it frequently happened that it was Mme. de Guermantes who had sought the acquaintance of the mistress in whom she hoped, and so greatly needed, to discover, against her dread husband, a valuable ally. This is not to say that, save at rare moments, in their own house, where, when the Duchess talked too much, he let fall a few words or, more dreadful still, preserved a silence which rendered her speechless, M. de Guermantes failed in his outward relations with his wife to observe what are called the forms. People who did not know them might easily misunderstand. Sometimes between the racing at Deauville, the course of waters and the return to Guermantes for the shooting, in the few weeks which people spend in Paris, since the Duchess had a liking for café-concerts, the Duke would go with her to spend the evening at one of these. The audience remarked at once, in one of those little open boxes in which there is just room for two, this Hercules in his 'smoking' (for in France we give to everything that is more or less British the one name that it happens not to bear in England), his monocle screwed in his eye, in his plump but finely shaped hand, on the ring-finger of which there glowed a sapphire, a plump cigar from which now and then he drew a puff of smoke, keeping his eyes for the most part on the stage but, when he did let them fall upon the audience in which there was absolutely no one whom he knew, softening them with an air of gentleness, reserve, courtesy and consideration. When a verse struck him as amusing and not too indecent, the Duke would turn round with a smile to his wife, letting her share, by a twinkle of good-natured understanding, the innocent merriment which the new song had aroused in himself. And the spectators might believe that there was no better husband in the world than this, nor anyone more enviable than the Duchess—that woman outside whom every interest in the Duke's life lay, that woman with whom he was not in love, to whom he had been consistently unfaithful; when the Duchess felt tired, they saw M. de Guermantes rise, put on her cloak with his own hands, arranging her necklaces so that they did not catch in the lining, and clear a path for her to the street with an assiduous and respectful attention which she received with the coldness of the woman of the world who sees in such behaviour simply conventional politeness, at times even with the slightly ironical bitterness of the disabused spouse who has no illusion left to shatter. But despite these externals (another element of that politeness which has made duty evolve from the depths of our being to the surface, at a period already remote but still continuing for its survivors) the life of the Duchess was by no means easy. M. de Guermantes never became generous or human save for a new mistress who would take, as it generally happened, the Duchess's part; the latter saw becoming possible for her once again generosities towards inferiors, charities to the poor, even for herself, later on, a new and sumptuous motor-car. But from the irritation which developed as a rule pretty rapidly in Mme. de Guermantes at people whom she found too submissive, the Duke's mistresses were not exempt. Presently the Duchess grew tired of them. Simultaneously, at this moment, the Duke's intimacy with Mme. d'Arpajon was drawing to an end. Another mistress dawned on the horizon.

"Wait a minute, now," Mme. de Guermantes turned to me, fixing on me a tender, smiling gaze, because, as an accomplished hostess, she was anxious to display her own knowledge of the artist who interested me specially, to give me, if I required it an opportunity for exhibiting mine. "Wait," she urged me, gently waving her feather fan, so conscious was she at this moment that she was performing in full the duties of hospitality, and, that she might be found wanting in none of them, making a sign also to the servants to help me to more of the asparagus and *mousseline* sauce: "wait, now, I do believe that Zola has actually written an essay on Elstir, the painter whose things you were looking at just now—the only ones of his, really, that I care for," she concluded. As a matter of fact she hated Elstir's work, but found a unique quality in anything that was in her own house. I asked M. de Guermantes if he knew the name of the gentleman in the tall hat who figured in the picture of the crowd and whom I recognised as the same person whose portrait the Guermantes also had and had hung, beside the other, both dating more or less from the same early period in which Elstir's personality was not yet completely established and he derived a certain inspiration from Manet. "Good Lord, yes," he replied, " I know it's a fellow who is quite well-known and no fool either, in his own line, but I have no head for names. I have it on the tip of my tongue, Monsieur . . . Monsieur . . . . oh, well, it doesn't matter, I can't remember it. Swann would be able to tell you, it was he who made Mme. de Guermantes buy all that stuff; she is always too good-natured, afraid of hurting people's feelings if she refuses to do things; between ourselves, I believe he's landed us with a lot of rubbish. What I can tell you is that the gentleman you mean has been a sort of Maecenas to M. Elstir, he started him and has often helped him out of tight places by ordering pictures from him. As a compliment to this man—if you can call that sort of thing a compliment—he has painted him standing about among that crowd, where with his Sunday-go-to-meeting look he creates a distinctly odd effect. He may be a big gun in his own way but he is evidently not aware of the proper time and place for a top hat. With that thing on his head, among all those bare-headed girls, he looks like a little country lawyer on the razzle-dazzle. But tell me, you seem quite gone on his pictures. If I had only known, I should have got up the subject properly. Not that there's any need to rack one's brains over the meaning of M. Elstir's work, as one would for Ingres's *Source* or the *Princes in the Tower* by Paul Delaroche. What one appreciates in his work is that it's shrewdly observed, amusing, Parisian, and then one passes on to the next thing. One doesn't need to be an expert to look at that sort of thing. I know of course that they're merely sketches, still, I don't feel myself that he puts enough work into them. Swann was determined that we should buy a *Bundle of Asparagus*. In fact it was in the house for several days. There was nothing else in the picture, a bundle of asparagus exactly like what you're eating now. But I must say I declined to swallow M. Elstir's asparagus. He asked three hundred francs for them. Three hundred francs for a bundle of asparagus. A louis, that's as much as they're worth, even if they are out of season. I thought it a bit stiff. When he puts real people into his pictures as well, there's something rather caddish, something detrimental about him which does not appeal to me. I am surprised to see a delicate mind, a superior brain like yours admire that sort of thing." "I don't know why you should say that, Basin," interrupted the Duchess, who did not like to hear people run down anything that her rooms contained. "I am by no means prepared to admit that there's nothing distinguished in Elstir's pictures. You have to take it or leave it. But it's not always lacking in talent. And you must admit that the ones I bought are singularly beautiful." "Well, Oriane, in that style of thing I'd a thousand times rather have the little study by M. Vibért we saw at the water-colour exhibition. There's nothing much in it, if you like, you could take it in the palm of your hand, but you can see the man's clever through and through: that unwashed scarecrow of a missionary standing before the sleek prelate who is making his little dog do tricks, it's a perfect little poem of subtlety, and in fact goes really deep." "I believe you know M. Elstir," the Duchess went on to me,"' as a man, he's quite pleasant." "He is intelligent," said the Duke; "one is surprised, when one talks to him, that his painting should be so vulgar." "He is more than intelligent, he is really quite clever," said the Duchess in the confidently critical tone of a person who knew what she was talking about. "Didn't he once start a portrait of you, Oriane?" asked the Princesse de Parme. "Yes, in shrimp pink," replied Mme. de Guermantes, "but that's not going to hand his name down to posterity. It's a ghastly thing; Basin wanted to have it destroyed." This last statement was one which Mme. de Guermantes often made. But at other times her appreciation of the picture was different: "I do not care for his painting, but he did once do a good portrait of me." The former of these judgments was addressed as a rule to people who spoke to the

Duchess of her portrait, the other to those who did not refer to it and whom therefore she was anxious to inform of its existence. The former was inspired in her by coquetry, the latter by vanity.

"I fancy Mme de Villeparisis is not absolutely . . . moral," said the Princesse de Parme, who knew that the best people did not visit the Duchess's aunt, and from what the Duchess herself had just been saying that one might speak freely about her. But, Mme. de Guermantes not seeming to approve of this criticism, she hastened to add: "Though, of course, intellect carried to that degree excuses everything." "But you take the same view of my aunt that everyone else does," replied the Duchess, "which is really quite mistaken. It's just what Mémé was saying to me only yesterday." She blushed; a reminiscence unknown to me filmed her eyes. I formed the supposition that M. de Charlus had asked her to cancel my invitation, as he had sent Robert to ask me not to go to her house. I had the impression that the blush—equally incomprehensible to me—which had tinged the Duke's cheek when he made some reference to his brother could not be attributed to the same cause. "My poor aunt—she will always have the reputation of being a lady of the old school, of sparkling wit and uncontrolled passions. And really there's no more middle-class, serious, commonplace mind in Paris. She will go down as a patron of the arts, which means to say that she was once the mistress of a great painter, though he was never able to make her understand what a picture was; and as for her private life, so far from being a depraved woman, she was so much made for marriage, conjugal from her cradle that, not having succeeded in keeping a husband, who incidentally was a cad, she has never had a love affair which she hasn't taken just as seriously as if it were holy matrimony, with the same susceptibilities, the same quarrels, the same fidelity. By which token, those relations are often the most sincere; you'll find, in fact, more inconsolable lovers than husbands." "Yet, Oriane, if you take the case of your brother-in-law Palamède you were speaking about just now; no mistress in the world could ever dream of being mourned as that poor Mme. de Charlus has been." "Ah!" replied the Duchess, "Your Highness must permit me to be not altogether of her opinion. People don't all like to be mourned in the same way, each of us has his preferences." "Still, he did make a regular cult of her after her death. It is true that people sometimes do for the dead what they would not have done for the living." "For one thing," retorted Mme. de Guermantes in a dreamy tone which belied her teasing purpose, "we go to their funerals, which we never do for the living!" M. de Guermantes gave a sly glance at M. de Bréauté as though to provoke him into laughter at the Duchess's wit. "At the same time I frankly admit," went on Mme. de Guermantes, "that the manner in which I should like to be mourned by a man I loved would not be that adopted by my brother-in-law." The Duke's face darkened. He did not like to hear his wife utter rash judgments, especially about M. de Charlus. "You are very particular. His grief set an example to everyone," he reproved her stiffly. But the Duchess had in dealing with her husband that sort of boldness which animal tamers show, or people who live with a madman and are not afraid of making him angry: "Oh, very well, just as you like—he does set an example, I never said he didn't, he goes every day to the cemetery to tell her how many people he has had to luncheon, he misses her enormously, but— as he'd mourn for a cousin, a grandmother, a sister. It is not the grief of a husband. It is true that they were a pair of saints, which makes it all rather exceptional." M. de Guermantes, infuriated by his wife's chatter, fixed on her with a terrible immobility a pair of eyes already loaded. "I don't wish to say anything against poor Mémé, who, by the way, could not come this evening," went on the Duchess, "I quite admit there's no one like him, he's delightful; he has a delicacy, a warmth of heart that you don't as a rule find in men. He has a woman's heart, Mémé has!" "What you say is absurd," M. de Guermantes broke in sharply "There's nothing effeminate about Mémé, I know nobody so manly as he is." "But I am not suggesting that he's the least bit in the world effeminate. Do at least take the trouble to understand what I say," retorted the Duchess. "He's always like that the moment anyone mentions his brother," she added, turning to the Princesse de Parme. "It's very charming, it's a pleasure to hear him. There's nothing so nice as two brothers who are fond of each other," replied the Princess, as many a humbler person might have replied, for it is possible to belong to a princely race by birth and at the same time to be mentally affiliated to a race that is thoroughly plebeian.

"As we're discussing your family, Oriane," said the Princess, "I saw your nephew Saint-Loup yesterday; I believe he wants to ask you to do something for him." The Duc de Guermantes bent his Olympian brow. When he did not himself care to do a service, he preferred his wife not to assume the responsibility for it, knowing that it would come to the same thing in the end and that the people to whom the Duchess would be obliged to apply would put this concession down to the common account of the household, just as much as if it had been asked of them by the husband alone. "Why didn't he tell me about it himself?" said the Duchess, "he was here yesterday and stayed a couple of hours, and heaven only knows what a bore he managed to make himself. He would be no stupider than anyone else if he had only the sense, like many people we know, to be content with being a fool. It's his veneer of knowledge that's so terrible. He wants to preserve an open mind—open to all the things he doesn't understand. He talks to you about Morocco. It's appalling."

"He can't go back there, because of Rachel," said the Prince de Foix. "Surely, now that they've broken it off," interrupted M. de Bréauté. "So far from breaking it off, I found her a couple of days ago in Robert's rooms, they didn't look at all like people who'd quarrelled, I can assure you," replied the Prince de Foix, who loved to spread abroad every rumour that could damage Robert's chances of marrying, and might for that matter have been misled by one of the intermittent resumptions of a connection that was practically at an end.

"Why, that's just what it was—Morocco!" exclaimed the Princess, flinging herself into this opening. "What on earth can he want in Morocco?" asked M. de Guermantes sternly; "Oriane can do absolutely nothing for him there, as he knows perfectly well."

He would like not to go back to Morocco," said the Princesse de Parme, alighting hurriedly again upon the perch of Robert's name which had been held out to her, quite unintentionally, by Mme. de Guermantes. "I believe you know General de Monserfeuil." "Very slightly," replied the Duchess, who was an intimate friend of the officer in question. The Princess explained what it was that Saint-Loup wanted. "Good gracious, yes, if I see him—it is possible that I may meet him," the Duchess replied, so as not to appear to be refusing, the occasions of her meeting General de Monserfeuil seeming to extend rapidly farther apart as soon as it became a question of her asking him for anything. This uncertainty did not, however, satisfy the Duke, who interrupted his wife: "You know perfectly well you won't be seeing him, Oriane, and besides you have already asked him for two things which he hasn't done. My wife has a passion for doing good turns to people," he went on, growing more and more furious, in order to force the Princess to withdraw her request, without there being any question made of his wife's good nature and so that Mme. de Parme should throw the blame back upon his own character, which was essentially obstructive. "Robert could get anything he wanted out of Monserfeuil. Only, as he happens not to know himself what he wants, he gets us to ask for it because he knows there's no better way of making the whole thing fall through. Oriane has asked too many favours of Monserfeuil. A request from her now would be a reason for him to refuse." "Oh, in that case, it would be better if the Duchess did nothing," said Mme. de Parme.

But it was by the genuine malice of Mme. de Guermantes that I was revolted when, the Princesse de Parme having timidly suggested that she might say something herself and on her own responsibility to the General, the Duchess did everything in her power to dissuade her. "But Ma'am," she cried, "Monserfeuil has no sort of standing or influence whatever with the new Government. You would be wasting your breath." "I think he can hear us," murmured the Princess, as a hint to the Duchess not to speak so loud. Without lowering her voice: "Your Highness need not be afraid, he's as deaf as a post," said the Duchess, every word reaching the General distinctly. "The thing is, I believe M. de Saint-Loup is in a place that is not very safe," said the Princess. "What is one to do?" replied the Duchess. "He's in the same boat as everybody else, the only difference being that it was he who originally asked to be sent there. Besides, no, it's not really dangerous; if it was, you can imagine how anxious I should be to help. I should have spoken to Saint-Joseph about it during dinner. He has far more influence, and he's a real worker. But, as you see, he's gone now. Still, asking him would be less awkward than going to this one, who has three of his sons in Morocco just now and has refused to apply for them to be exchanged; he might raise that as an objection. Since your Highness insists on it, I shall speak to Saint-Joseph—if I see him again, or to Beautreillis. But if I don't see either of them, you mustn't waste your pity on Robert. It was explained to us the other day exactly where he is. I'm sure he couldn't wish for a better place."

Already I had made several attempts to slip away, but the presence of the Princesse de Parme —one must never depart before Royalty— was one of the two reasons, neither of which I had guessed, for which the Duchess had insisted so strongly on my remaining. As soon as Mme. de Parme had risen, it was like a deliverance. Each of the ladies having made a genuflection before the Princess, who raised her up from the ground, they received from her, in a kiss, and like a benediction which they had craved kneeling, the permission to ask for their cloaks and carriages. With the result that there followed, at the front door, a sort of stentorian recital of great names from the History of France. The Princesse de Parme had forbidden Mme. de Guermantes to accompany her downstairs to the hall for fear of her catching cold, and the Duke had added: "There, Oriane, since Ma'am gives you leave, remember what the doctor told you."

"I am sure the Princesse de Parme was *most pleased* to take dinner with you." I knew the formula. The Duke had come the whole way across the drawing-room in order to utter it before me with an obliging, concerned air, as though he were handing me a diploma or offering me a plateful of biscuits. And I guessed from the pleasure which he appeared to be feeling as he spoke, and which brought so sweet an expression momentarily into his face that the effort which this represented for him was of the kind which he would continue to make to the very end of his life, like one of those honorific and easy posts which, even when paralytic, one is still allowed to retain.

Just as I was about to leave, the lady in waiting reappeared in the drawing-room, having forgotten to take away some wonderful carnations, sent up from Guermantes, which the Duchess had presented to Mme. de Parme. The lady in waiting was somewhat flushed, one felt that she had just been receiving a scolding, for the Princess, so kind to everyone else, could not contain her impatience at the stupidity of her attendant. And so the latter picked up the flowers and ran quickly, but to preserve her air of ease and independence flung at me as she passed: "The Princess says I'm keeping her waiting; she wants to be gone, and to have the carnations as well. Good lord! I'm not a little bird, I can't be in two places at once."

In the hall where I asked a footman for my snowboots which I had brought as a precaution against the snow, several flakes of which had already fallen, to be converted rapidly into slush, not having realised that they were hardly fashionable, I felt, at the contemptuous smile on all sides, a shame which rose to its highest pitch when I saw that Mme. de Parme had not gone and was watching me put on my American 'rubbers'. The Princess came towards me. "Oh! What a good idea," she exclaimed, it's so practical! There's a sensible man for you. Madame, we shall have to get a pair of those," she went on to her lady in waiting, while the mockery of the footmen turned to respect and the other guests crowded round me to inquire where I had managed to find these marvels.

"With those on, you will have nothing to fear even if it starts snowing again and you have a long way to go. You're independent of the weather," said the Princess to me. "Oh! If it comes to that, your Royal Highness can be assured," broke in the lady in waiting with a knowing air, "it will not snow again." "What do you know about it, Madame?" came witheringly from the excellent Princesse de Parme, who alone could succeed in piercing the thick skin of her lady in waiting. " I can assure your Royal Highness, it cannot snow again. It is a physical impossibility." " But why?" "It cannot snow any more, they have taken the necessary steps to prevent it, they have put down salt in the streets."

Then, having escorted the Princesse de Parme to her carriage, M. de Guermantes said to me, taking hold of my greatcoat: "Let me help you into your skin." He had ceased even to smile when he employed this expression, for those that were most vulgar had for that very reason, because of the Guermantes affection of simplicity, become aristocratic.

An exaltation that sank only into melancholy, because it was artificial, was what I also, although quite differently from Mme. de Guermantes, felt once I had finally left her house, in the carriage that was taking me to that of M. de Charlus.   I rang the bell at M. de Charlus's door, and it was in long monologues with myself, in which I rehearsed everything that I was going to tell him and gave scarcely a thought to what he might have to say to me, that I spent the whole of the time during which I was kept waiting in a drawing room into which a footman showed me and where I was incidentally too much excited to look at what it contained. I felt so urgent a need that M. de Charlus should listen to the stories which I was burning to tell him that I was bitterly disappointed to think that the master of the house was perhaps in bed, and that I might have to go home to sleep off by myself my drunkenness of words. I had just noticed, in fact, that I had been twenty-five minutes—that they had perhaps forgotten about me—in this room of which, despite this long wait, I could at the most have said that it was very big; greenish in colour, and contained a large number of portraits. The need to speak prevents one not merely from listening but from seeing things, and in this case the absence of any description of my external surroundings is tantamount to a description of my internal state. I was preparing to leave the room to try to get hold of some one, and if I found no one to make my way back to the hall and have myself let out, when, just as I had risen from my chair and taken a few steps across the mosaic parquet of the floor, a manservant came in, with a troubled expression: "Monsieur le Baron has been engaged all evening, Sir," he told me. "There are still several people waiting to see him. I am doing everything I possibly can to get him to receive you, I have already telephoned up twice to the secretary." "No; please don't bother. I had an appointment with M. le Baron, but it is very late already, and if he is busy this evening I can come back another day." "Oh no, Sir, you must not go away," cried the servant. "M. le Baron might be vexed. I will try again."

I waited ten minutes more, and then, after requesting me not to stay too long as M. le Baron was tired and had had to send away several most important people who had made appointments with him many days before, they admitted me to his presence. This setting with which M. de Charlus surrounded himself seemed to me a great deal less impressive than the simplicity of his brother Guermantes, but already the door stood open, I could see the Baron, in a Chinese dressing-gown, with his throat bare, lying upon a sofa. My eye was caught at the same moment by a tall hat, its nap flashing like a mirror which had been left on a chair with a cape, as though the Baron had but recently come in. The valet withdrew. I supposed that M. de Charlus would rise to greet me. Without moving a muscle he fixed on me a pair of implacable eyes. I went towards him, I said good evening; he did not hold out his hand, made no reply, did not ask me to take a chair. After a moment's silence I asked him, as one would ask an ill-mannered doctor, whether it was necessary for me to remain standing. I said this without any evil intention, but my words seemed only to intensify the cold fury on M. de Charlus's face. I was not aware, as it happened, that at home, in the country, at the Chateau de Charlus, he was in the habit, after dinner (so much did he love to play the king), of sprawling in an armchair in the smoking-room, letting his guests remain standing round him. He would ask for a light from one, offer a cigar to another and then, after a few minutes interval, would say: "But Argencourt, why don't you sit down? Take a chair, my dear fellow," and so forth, having made a point of keeping them standing simply to remind them that it was from himself that permission came to them to be seated. "Put yourself in the Louis XIV seat," he answered me with an imperious air, as though rather to force me to move away farther from himself than to invite me to be seated. I took an armchair which was comparatively near. "Ah! so that is what you call a Louis XIV seat, is it? I can see you have been well educated," he cried in derision. I was so much taken aback that I did not move, either to leave the house, as I ought to have done, or to change my seat, as he wished. Sir," he next said to me, weighing each of his words, to the more impertinent of which he prefixed a double yoke of consonants, "the interview which I have condescended to grant you at the request of a person who desires to be nameless, will mark the final point in our relations. I shall not conceal from you that I had hoped for better things! I should perhaps be forcing the sense of the words a little, which one ought not to do, even with people who are ignorant of their value, simply out of the respect due to oneself, were I to tell you that I had felt a certain *attraction* towards you. I think, however, that *benevolence,* in its most actively protecting sense, would exceed neither what I felt nor what I was proposing to display. I had, immediately on my return to Paris, given you to understand, while you were still at Balbec, that you could count upon me." I who remembered with what a torrent of abuse M. de Charlus had parted from me at Balbec made an instinctive gesture of contradiction. "What!" he cried with fury, and indeed his face, convulsed and white, differed as much from his ordinary face as does the sea when on a morning of storm one finds instead of its customary smiling surface a thousand serpents writhing in spray and foam, "do you mean to pretend that you did not receive my message—almost a declaration—that you were to remember me? What was there in the way of decoration round the cover of the book that I sent you?" "Some very pretty twined garlands with tooled ornaments," I told him. "Ah!" he replied, with an air of scorn, "these young Frenchmen know little of the treasures of our land. What would be said of a young Berliner who had never heard of the *Walküre?* Besides, you must have eyes to see and see not, since you yourself told me that you had stood for two hours in front of that particular treasure. I can see that you know no more about flowers than you do about styles; don't protest that you know about styles," he cried in a shrill scream of rage, "you can't even tell me what you are sitting on. You offer your hindquarters a Directory *chauffeuse* as a Louis XIV *bergère*. One of these days you'll be mistaking Mme. de Villeparisis's knees for the seat of the watercloset, and a fine mess you'll make of things then. It's precisely the same; you didn't even recognise on the binding of Bergotte's book the lintel of myosotis over the door of Balbec church. Could there be any clearer way of saying to you: "Forget me not?"

I looked at M: de Charlus. Undoubtedly his magnificent head, though repellent, yet far surpassed that of any of his relatives; you would have called him an Apollo grown old; but an olive-hued, bilious juice seemed ready to start from the corners of his evil mouth; as for intellect one could not deny that his, over a vast compass, had taken in many things which must always remain unknown to his brother Guermantes. But whatever the fine words with which he coloured all his hatreds, one felt that, even if there was now an offended pride, now a disappointment in love, or a rancour, or sadism, a love of teasing, a fixed obsession, this man was capable of doing murder, and of proving by force of logic that he had been right in doing it and was still superior by a hundred cubits in moral stature to his brother, his sister-in-law, or any of the rest. "Just as, in Velazquez's *Lances* " he went on, "the victor advances towards him who is the humbler in rank, as is the duty of every noble nature, since I was everything and you were nothing, it was I who took the first steps towards you. You have made an idiotic reply to what it is not for me to describe as an act of greatness. But I have not allowed myself to be discouraged. Our religion inculcates patience. The patience I have shown towards you will be counted, I hope, to my credit, and also my having only smiled at what might be denounced as impertinence, were it within your power to offer any impertinence to me who surpass you in stature by so many cubits; but after all Sir, all this is now neither here nor there. I have subjected you to the test which the one eminent man of our world has ingeniously named the test of excessive friendliness, and which he rightly declares to be the most terrible of all, the only one that can separate the good grain from the tares. I could scarcely reproach you for having undergone it without success, for those who emerge from it triumphant are very few. But at least, and this is the conclusion which I am entitled to draw from the last words that we shall exchange on this earth, at least I intend to hear nothing more of your calumnious fabrications." So far, I had never dreamed that M. de Charlus's rage could have been caused by an unflattering remark which had been repeated to him; I searched my memory; I had not spoken about him to anyone. Some evil-doer had invented the whole thing. I protested to M. de Charlus that I had said absolutely nothing about him. "I don't think I can have annoyed you by saying to Mme. de Guermantes that I was a friend of yours." He gave a disdainful smile, made his voice climb to the supreme pitch of its highest register; and there, without strain, attacking the shrillest and most insolent note: "Oh! Sir," he said, returning by the most gradual stages to a natural intonation, and seeming to revel as he went in the oddities of this descending scale "I think that you are doing yourself an injustice when you accuse yourself of having said that we were *friends.* I do not look for any great verbal accuracy in anyone who could readily mistake a piece of Chippendale for a rococo *chaire,* but really I do not believe;" he went on, with vocal caresses that grew more and more winning and brought to hover over his lips what was actually a charming smile, "I do not believe that you can ever have said, or thought, that we were *friends!* As for your having boasted that you had been *presented* to me, had *talked* to me, *knew* me slightly, had obtained, almost without solicitation, the prospect of coming one day under my *protection,* I find it on the contrary very natural and intelligent of you to have done so. The extreme difference in age that there is between us enables me to recognise without absurdity that that *presentation,* those *talks,* that vague prospect of future *relations* were for you, it is not for me to say an honour, but still, when all is said and done, an advantage as to which I consider that your folly lay not in divulging it but in not having had the sense to keep it. I will go so far as to say," he went on, passing abruptly for a moment from his arrogant wrath to a gentleness so tinged with melancholy that I expected him to burst into tears, "that when you left unanswered the proposal I made to you here in Paris it seemed to me so unheard of an act on your part, coming from you who had struck me as well brought up and of a good *bourgeois* family," (on this adjective alone his voice sounded a little whistle of impertinence) "that I was foolish enough to imagine all the excuses that never really happen, letters miscarrying, addresses copied down wrong. I can see that on my part it was great foolishness, but Saint Bonaventure preferred to believe that an ox could fly rather than that his brother was capable of lying. Anyhow, that is all finished now, the idea did not attract you, there is no more to be said. It seems to me only that you might have brought yourself," (and there was a genuine sound of weeping in his voice) "were it only out of consideration for my age, to write to me. I had conceived and planned for you certain infinitely seductive things, which I had taken good care not to tell you. You have preferred to refuse without knowing what they were; that is your affair. But, as I tell you, one can always write. In your place, and indeed in my own, I should have done so. I like my place, for that reason, better than yours—I say 'for that reason' because I believe that we are all equal, and I have more fellow-feeling for an intelligent labourer than for many of our dukes. But I can say that I prefer my place to yours, because what you have done, in the whole course of my life, which is beginning now to be a pretty long one, I am conscious that I have never done." His head was turned away from the light, and I could not see if his eyes were dropping tears as I might have supposed from his voice. " I told you that I had taken a hundred steps towards you; the only effect of that has been to make you retire two hundred from me. Now it is for me to withdraw, and we shall know one another no longer. I shall retain not your name but your story, so that at moments when I might be tempted to believe that men have good hearts, good manners, or simply the intelligence not to allow an unparalleled opportunity to escape them, I may remember that that is ranking them too highly. No, that you should have said that you knew me, when it was true— for, henceforward it ceases to be true—I regard that as only natural, and I take it as an act of homage, that is to say something pleasant. Unfortunately, elsewhere and in other circumstances, you have uttered remarks of a very different nature." " Sir, I swear to you that I have said nothing that could insult you." "And who says that I am insulted?" he cried with fury, flinging himself into an erect posture on the seat on which hitherto he had been reclining motionless, while, as the pale frothing serpents stiffened in his face, his voice became alternately shrill and grave, like the deafening onrush of a storm. (The force with which he habitually spoke, which used to make strangers turn round in the street, was multiplied an hundredfold, as is a musical *forte* if, instead of being played on the piano, it is played by an orchestra, and changed into a *fortissimo* as well.) M. de Charlus roared "Do you suppose that it is within your power to insult me? You evidently are not aware to whom you are speaking? Do you imagine that the envenomed spittle of five hundred little gentlemen of your type, heaped one upon another, would succeed in slobbering so much as the tips of my august toes?" A moment before this my desire to persuade M. de Charlus that I had never said, nor heard anyone else say any evil of him had given place to a mad rage, caused by the words which were dictated to him solely, to my mind, by his colossal pride. Perhaps they were indeed the effect, in part at any rate, of this pride. Almost all the rest sprang from a feeling of which I was then still ignorant, and for which I could not therefore be blamed for not making due allowance. I could at least, failing this unknown element, have mingled with his pride, had I remembered the words of Mme. de Guermantes, a trace of madness. But at that moment the idea of madness never even entered my head. There was in him, according to me, only pride, in me there was only fury. This fury (at the moment when M. de Charlus ceased to shout, in order to refer to his august toes, with a majesty that was accompanied by a grimace, a nausea of disgust at his obscure blasphemers), this fury could contain itself no longer. With an impulsive movement, I wanted to strike something, and, a lingering trace of discernment making me respect the person of a man so much older than myself, and even, in view of their dignity as works of art, the pieces of German porcelain that were grouped around him, I flung myself upon the Baron's new silk hat, dashed it to the ground, trampled upon it, began blindly pulling it to pieces, wrenched off the brim, tore the crown in two, without heeding the vociferations of M. de Charlus, which continued to sound, and, crossing the room to leave it, opened the door. One on either side of it, to my intense stupefaction, stood two footmen, who moved slowly away, so as to appear only to have been casually passing in the course of their duty. (I afterwards learned their names; one was called Burnier, the other Charnel.) I was not taken in for a moment by this explanation which their leisurely gait seemed to offer me. It was highly improbable; three others appeared to me to be less so; one, that the Baron sometimes entertained guests against whom, as he might happen to need assistance (but why?), he deemed it necessary to keep reinforcements posted close at hand. The second was that, drawn by curiosity, they had stopped to listen at the keyhole, not thinking that I should come out so quickly. The third, that, the whole of the scene which M. de Charlus had made with me having been prepared and acted, he had himself told them to listen, from a love of the spectacular combined, perhaps, with a *"nunc erudimini"* from which each would derive a suitable profit.

My anger had not calmed that of M. de Charlus, my departure from the room seemed to cause him acute distress; he called me back, made his servants call me back, and finally, forgetting that a moment earlier, when he spoke of his "august toes ", he had thought to make me a witness of his own deification, came running after me at full speed, overtook me in the hall, and stood barring the door. "There, now," he said, "don't be childish ; come back for a minute; he that loveth well chasteneth well, and if I have chastened you well it is because I love you well." My anger had subsided; I let the word "chasten" pass, and followed the Baron, who, summoning a footman, ordered him without a trace of selfconsciousness to clear away the remains of the shattered hat, which was replaced by another. "If you will tell me, Sir, who it is that has treacherously maligned me," I said to M. de Charlus, "I will stay here to learn his name and to confute the impostor." "Who? Do you not know? Do you retain no memory of the things you say? Do you think that the people who do me the service of informing me of those things do not begin by demanding secrecy? And do you imagine that I am going to betray a person to whom I have given my promise?" "Sir, is it impossible then for you to tell me?" I asked, racking my brains in a final effort to discover (and discovering no one) to whom,I could have spoken about M. de Charlus. "You did not hear me say that I had given a promise of secrecy to my informant?" he said in a snapping voice. "I see that with your fondness for abject utterances you combine one for futile persistence. You ought to have at least the intelligence to profit by a final conversation, and so to speak as to say something that does not mean precisely nothing." "Sir," I replied, moving away from him, "you insult me; I am unarmed, because you are several times my age, we are not equally matched; on the other hand, I cannot convince you; I have already sworn to you that I have said nothing." "I am lying, then, am I?" he cried in a terrifying tone, and with a bound forwards that brought him within a yard of myself. "Someone has misinformed you." Then in a gentle, affectionate, melancholy voice, as in those symphonies which are played without any break between the different movements, in which a graceful *scherzo,* amiable and idyllic, follows the thunder-peals of the opening pages: "It is quite possible," he told me. "Generally speaking, a remark repeated at second hand is rarely true. It is your fault if, not having profited by the opportunities of seeing me which I had held out to you, you have not furnished me, by that open speech of daily intercourse which creates confidence, with the unique and sovereign remedy against a spoken word which made you out a traitor. Either way, true or false, the remark has done its work. I can never again rid myself of the impression it made on me. I cannot even say that he who chasteneth well loveth well, for I have chastened you well enough but I no longer love you." While saying this he had forced me to sit down and had rung the bell. A different footman appeared. "Bring something to drink and order the brougham." I said that I was not thirsty and besides had a carriage waiting. "They have probably paid him and sent him away," he told me, "you needn't worry about that. I am ordering a carriage to take you home. If you're anxious about the time . . . I could have given you a room here. ." I said that my mother would be uneasy. "Ah! Of course, yes. Well, true or false, the remark has done its work. My affection, a trifle premature, had flowered too soon, and, like those apple trees of which you spoke so poetically at Balbec, it has been unable to withstand the first frost." If M. de Charlus's affection for me had not been destroyed, he could hardly have acted differently, since, while assuring me that we were no longer acquainted, he made me sit down, drink, asked me to stay the night, and was going now to send me home. He had indeed an air of dreading the moment at which he must part from me and find himself alone, that sort of slightly anxious fear which his sister-in-law and cousin Guermantes had appeared to me to be feeling when she had tried to force me to stay a little longer, with something of the same momentary fondness for myself, of the same effort to prolong the passing minute. "Unfortunately," he went on, "I have not the power to make blossom again what has once been destroyed. My affection for you is quite dead. Nothing can revive it. I believe that it is not unworthy of me to confess that I regret it. I always feel myself to be a little like Victor Hugo's Boaz: 'I am widowed and alone, and the darkness gathers o'er me.'

I passed again with him through the big green drawing-room. I told him, speaking quite at random, how beautiful I thought it. "Ain't it?" he replied. "It's a good thing to be fond of something. The woodwork is Bagard. What is rather charming, d'you see, is that it was made to match the Beauvais chairs and the consoles. You observe, it repeats the same decorative design. There used to be only two places where you could see this, the Louvre and M. d'Hinnisdal's house. But naturally, as soon as I had decided to come and live in this street, there cropped up an old family house of the Chimays which nobody had ever seen before because it came here expressly for *me*. On the whole, it's good. It might perhaps be better, but after all it's not bad. Some pretty things, ain't there? These are portraits of my uncles, the King of Poland and the King of England, by Mignard. But why am I telling you all this? You must know it as well as I do, you were waiting in this room. No? Ah, then they must have put you in the blue drawing-room," he said with an air that might have been either impertinence, on the score of my want of interest, or personal superiority, in not having taken the trouble to ask where I had been kept waiting. "Look now, in this cabinet I have all the hats worn by Mlle. Elisabeth, by the Princesse de Lamballe, and by the Queen. They don't interest you, one would think you couldn't see. Perhaps you are suffering from an affection of the optic nerve. If you like this kind of beauty better, here is a rainbow by Turner beginning to shine out between these two Rembrandts, as a sign of our reconciliation. You hear; Beethoven has come to join him." And indeed one could hear the first chords of the third part of the Pastoral Symphony, 'Joy after the Storm', performed somewhere not far away, on the first landing no doubt, by a band of musicians. I innocently inquired how they happened to be playing that, and who the musicians were. "Ah, well, one doesn't know. One never does know. They are unseen music. Pretty, ain't it?" he said to me in a slightly impertinent tone, which, nevertheless, suggested somehow the influence and accent of Swann. "But you care about as much for it as a fish does for little apples. You want to go home, regardless of any want of respect for Beethoven or for me. You are uttering your own judgment and condemnation," he added, with an affectionate and mournful air, when the moment had come for me to go. "You will excuse my not accompanying you home, as good manners ordain that I should," he said to me. "Since I have decided not to see you again, spending five minutes more in your company would make very little difference to me. But I am tired, and

I have a great deal to do." And then, seeing that it was a fine night: "Very well, yes, I will come in the carriage, there is a superb moon which I shall go on to admire from the Bois after I have taken you home. What, you don't know how to shave; even on a night when you've been dining out, you have still a few hairs here," he said, taking my chin between, two fingers, so to speak magnetised, which after a moments resistance ran up to my ears, like the fingers of a barber. "Ah! It would be pleasant to look at the 'blue light of the moon' in the Bois with some one like yourself," he said to me with a sudden and almost involuntary gentleness, then, in a sadder tone: "For you are nice, all the same; you could be nicer than anyone," he went on, laying his hand in a fatherly way on my shoulder. "Originally, I must say that I found you quite insignificant." I ought to have reflected that he must find me so still. I had only to recall the rage with which he had spoken to me, barely half-an-hour before. In spite of this I had the impression that he was, for the moment, sincere, that his kindness of heart was prevailing over what I regarded as an almost delirious condition of susceptibility and pride. The carriage was waiting beside us, and still he prolonged the conversation. "Come along," he said abruptly, "jump in, in five minutes we shall be at your door. And I shall bid you a good night which will cut short our relations, and for all time. It is better, since we must part for ever, that we should do so, as in music, on a perfect chord." Despite these solemn affirmations that we should never see one another again, I could have sworn that M. de Charlus, annoyed at having forgotten himself earlier in the evening and afraid of having hurt my feelings, would not have been displeased to see me once again. Nor was I mistaken, for, a moment later: "There now," he said, "if I hadn't forgotten the most important thing of all. In memory of your grandmother, I have had bound for you a curious edition of Mme. de Sévigné. That is what is going to prevent this from being our last meeting. One must console oneself with the reflection that complicated affairs are rarely settled in a day. Just look how long they took over the Congress of Vienna." "But I could call for it without disturbing you," I said obligingly. "Will you hold your tongue, you little fool," he replied with anger, "and not give yourself the grotesque appearance of regarding as a small matter the honour of being probably (I do not say certainly, for it will perhaps be one of my servants who hands you the volumes) received by me." Then, regaining possession of himself: "I do not wish to part from you on these words. No dissonance, before the eternal silence of the dominant." It was for his own nerves that he seemed to dread an immediate return home after harsh words of dissension. "You would not care to come to the Bois?" he addressed me in a tone not so much interrogative as affirmative, and that not, as it seemed to me, because he did not wish to make me the offer but because he was afraid that his self-esteem might meet with a refusal. "Oh, very well," he went on, still postponing our separation, "it is the moment when, as Whistler says, the *bourgeois* go to bed" (perhaps he wished now to capture me by my self-esteem) "and the right time to begin to look at things. But you don't even know who Whistler was!" I changed the conversation and asked about the Princesse de Guermantes, "It is really very lovely, isn't it, Sir, the Princesse de Guermantes's mansion?" "Oh, it's not very lovely. It's the loveliest thing in the world. Next to the Princess herself, of course." "The Princesse de Guermantes is better than the Duchesse de Guermantes?" "Oh! There's no comparison." (It is to be observed that, whenever people in society have the least touch of imagination, they will crown or dethrone, to suit their affections or their quarrels, those whose position appeared most solid and unalterably fixed.)

"The Duchesse de Guermantes" (possibly, in not calling her "Oriane", he wished to set a greater distance between her and myself) "is delightful, far superior to anything you can have guessed. But, after all, she is incommensurable with her cousin. The Princess is exactly what the people in the Markets might imagine Princess Metternich to have been, but old Metternich believed she had started Wagner, because she knew Victor Maurel. The Princesse de Guermantes, or rather her mother, knew the man himself. Which is a distinction, not to mention the incredible beauty of the lady. And the Esther gardens alone!" "One can't see them?" "No, you would have to be invited, but they never invite *anyone* unless I intervene." But at once withdrawing, after casting it at me, the bait of this offer, he held out his hand, for we had reached my door. "My part is played, Sir, I will simply add these few words. Another person will perhaps some day offer you his affection, as I have done. Let the present example serve for your instruction. Do not neglect it. Affection is always precious. What one cannot do by oneself in this life, because there are things which one cannot ask, nor do, nor wish, nor learn by oneself, one can do in company, and without needing to be Thirteen, as in Balzac's story, or Four, as in *The Three Musketeers*. Goodbye."

He must have been feeling tired and have abandoned the idea of going to look at the moonlight, for he asked me to tell his coachman to drive home. At once he made a sharp movement as though he had changed his mind. But I had already given the order, and, so as not to lose any more time, went across now to ring the bell, without its entering my head that I had been meaning to tell M. de Charlus, about the German Emperor and General Botha, stories which had been an hour ago such an obsession but which his unexpected and crushing reception had sent flying far out of my mind.

CITIES OF THE PLAIN

PART 1

About two months after my dinner with the Duchess and while she was at Cannes, I opened an envelope and read the following words engraved on a card:

> *"The Princesse de Guermantes , née Duchesse en Bavière,*
> *At Home, the -----th"*

No doubt to be invited to the Princesse de Guermante's was perhaps not, from a social point of view, any more difficult than to dine with the Duchesse, and my slight knowledge of heraldry had taught me that the title of Prince is not superior to that of Duke. However the mysterious utterances of M. de Charlus had led me to imagine the Princesse de Guermantes as an extraordinary creature into whose presence it was highly improbable I should ever make my way so I trembled as I looked at the card of invitation thinking of the probability of its having been sent me by some practical joker.

On the day on which the party was to be given, the Duke and Duchesse had just returned to Paris and I decided to try to find out from them whether the invitation which I had received was genuine and so I stood on our staircase from where I could see the opening of the carriage gate hoping to catch them as they returned from a morning call.

This vigil led me to a discovery concerning M de Charlus so important that I must give it some prominence and treat it with the fullness it demands.

I could see M. de Charlus, on his way to call upon Mme. de Villeparisis, slowly crossing the courtyard, a pursy figure, aged by the strong light, his hair visibly grey. Nothing short of an indisposition of Mme. de Villeparisis could have made M. de Charlus pay a call, perhaps for the first time in his life, at that hour of the day.

Then I saw him coming away from the Marquise. Perhaps he had learned from his elderly relative herself, or merely from a servant, of the great improvement, or rather her complete recovery from what had been nothing more than a slight indisposition. At this moment, when he did not suspect that anyone was watching him, his eyelids lowered as a screen against the sun, M. de Charlus had relaxed that tension in his face, deadened that artificial vitality, which the animation of his talk and the force of his will kept in evidence there as a rule. I regretted for his sake that he should habitually adulterate with so many acts of violence, offensive oddities, tale-bearings, with such harshness, susceptibility and arrogance, that he should conceal beneath a false brutality the amenity, the kindness which, at the moment of his emerging from Mme de Villeparisis's, I could see displayed so innocently upon his face. Blinking his eyes in the sunlight, he seemed almost to be smiling, I found in his face seen thus in repose and, so to speak, in its natural state, something so affectionate, so disarmed that I could not help thinking how angry M de Charlus would have been could he have known that he was being watched; for what was suggested to me by the sight of this man who was so insistent, who prided himself so upon his virility, to whom all other men seemed odiously effeminate, what he made me suddenly think of, so far had he momentarily assumed her features, expression, smile, was a woman.

I was about to change my position again, so that he should not catch sight of me; I had neither the time nor the need to do so. What did I see? Face to face in that courtyard where certainly they had never met before (M. de Charlus coming to the Hotel de Guermantes only in the afternoon, during the time when Jupien was at his office), the Baron, having suddenly opened wide his half shut eyes, was studying with unusual attention the ex-tailor poised on the threshold of his shop, while the latter, fastened suddenly to the ground before M. de Charlus, taking root in it like a plant, was contemplating with a look of amazement the plump form of the middle aged Baron. But, more astounding still, M. de Charlus's attitude having changed, Jupien's, as though in obedience to the laws of an occult art, at once brought itself into harmony with it. The Baron, who was now seeking to conceal the impression that had been made on him, and yet, in spite of his affectation of indifference, seemed unable to move away without regret, came and went, looked vaguely into the distance in the way which, he felt, most enhanced the beauty of his eyes, assumed a complacent, careless, fatuous air. Meanwhile Jupien, shedding at once the humble, honest expression which I had always associated with him, had—in perfect symmetry with the Baron—thrown up his head, given a becoming tilt to his body, placed his hand with a grotesque impertinence on his hip, stuck out his behind, posed himself with the coquetry that the orchid might have adopted on the providential arrival of the bee. I had not supposed that he could appear so repellent. But I was equally unaware that he was capable of improvising his part in this sort of dumb charade, which (albeit he found himself for the first time in the presence of M. de Charlus) seemed to have been long and carefully rehearsed; one does not arrive spontaneously at that pitch of perfection except when one meets in a foreign country a compatriot with whom an understanding then grows up of itself, both parties speaking the same language, even although they have never seen one another before.

This scene was not, however, positively comic, it was stamped with a strangeness, or if you like a naturalness, the beauty of which steadily increased. M. de Charlus might indeed assume a detached air, indifferently let his eyelids droop; every now and then he raised them, and at such moments turned on Jupien an attentive gaze. But (doubtless because he felt that such a scene could not be prolonged indefinitely in this place, whether for reasons which we shall learn later on, or possibly from that feeling of the brevity of all things which makes us determine that every blow must strike home, and renders so moving the spectacle of every kind of love), each time that M. de Charlus looked at Jupien, he took care that his glance should be accompanied by a spoken word, which made it infinitely unlike the glances we usually direct at a person whom we do or do not know; he stared at Jupien with the peculiar fixity of the person who is about to say to us: "Excuse my taking the liberty but you have a long white thread hanging down your back;" or else: "Surely I can't be mistaken; you come from Zurich too; I'm certain I must have seen you there often in the curiosity shop!" Thus every other minute, the same question seemed to be being intensely put to Jupien in the stare of M. de Charlus, like those questioning phrases of Beethoven indefinitely repeated at regular intervals; and intended—with an exaggerated lavishness of preparation—to introduce a new theme, a change of tone, a 're-entry'. On the other hand, the beauty of the reciprocal glances of M. de Charlus and Jupien arose precisely from the fact that they did not, for the moment at least, seem to be intended to lead to anything further. This beauty, it was the first time that I had seen the Baron and Jupien display it. In the eyes of both of them, it was the sky not of Zurich but of some Oriental city, the name of which I had not yet divined, that I saw reflected. Whatever the point might be that held M. de Charlus and the ex-tailor thus arrested, their pact seemed concluded and these superfluous glances to be but ritual preliminaries, like the parties that people give before a marriage which has been definitely 'arranged'.

Nearer still to nature and the multiplicity of these analogies is itself all the more natural in that the same man, if we examine him for a few minutes, appears in turn as a man, a man-bird or man-insect, and so forth—one would have called them a pair of birds, the male and the female, the male seeking to make advances, the female—Jupien—no longer giving any sign of response to these overtures, but regarding her new friend without surprise, with an inattentive fixity of gaze, which she doubtless felt to be more disturbing and the only effective method, once the male had taken the first steps, and had fallen back upon preening his feathers. At length Jupien's indifference seemed to suffice him no longer; from this certainty of having conquered, to making himself be pursued and desired was but the next stage, and Jupien, deciding to go off to his work; passed through the carriage gate. It was only, however, after turning his head two or three times that he escaped into the street towards which the Baron, trembling lest he should lose the trail (boldly humming a tune, not forgetting to fling a "Good day" to the porter, who, half-tipsy himself and engaged in treating a few friends in his back kitchen, did not even hear him), hurried briskly to overtake him. A few minutes later, engaging my attention afresh, Jupien (perhaps to pick up a parcel which he did take away with him ultimately and so, presumably, in the emotion aroused by the apparition of M. de Charlus, had forgotten, perhaps simply for a more natural reason) returned, followed by the Baron. The latter, deciding to cut short the preliminaries, asked the tailor for a light, but at once observed: "I ask you for a light; but I find that I have left my cigars at home." The laws of hospitality prevailed over those of coquetry. "Come inside, you shall have everything you require," said the tailor, on whose features, disdain now gave place to joy. The door of the shop closed behind them and I could hear no more.

M. de Charlus, by the mere accident of Mme. de Villesparisis's illness had encountered the tailor, and with him the good fortune reserved for men of the type of the Baron by one of those fellow-creatures who may indeed be, as we shall see, infinitely younger than Jupien and better looking, the man predestined to exist in order, that they may have their share of sensual pleasure on this earth; the man who cares only for elderly gentlemen.

All that I have just said, however, I was not to understand until several minutes had elapsed; so much is reality encumbered by those properties of invisibility until a chance occurrence has divested it of them. Anyhow for the moment I was greatly annoyed at not being able to hear any more of the conversation between the ex-tailor and the

Baron. I then bethought myself of the vacant shop, separated from Jupien's only by a partition that was extremely slender. I had, in order to get to it, merely to go up to our flat, pass through the kitchen, go down by the service stair to the cellars, make my way through them across the breadth of the courtyard above, and on coming to the right place underground, where the joiner had, a few months ago; still been storing his timber and where Jupien intended to keep his coal, climb the flight of steps which led to the interior of the shop. Thus the whole of my journey would be made under cover, I should not be seen by anyone. This was the most prudent method. It was not the one that I adopted, but, keeping close to the walls, I made a circuit in the open air of the courtyard, trying not to let myself be seen. If I was not, I owe it more, I am sure, to chance than to my own sagacity. And for the fact that I took so imprudent a course, when the way through the cellar was so safe, I can see three possible reasons, assuming that I had any reason at all. First of all, my impatience. Secondly, perhaps, a dim memory of the scene at Montjouvain, when I stood concealed outside Mlle. Vinteuil's window. Certainly, the affairs of this sort of which I have been a spectator have always been presented in a setting of the most imprudent and least probable character, as if such revelations were to be the reward of an action full of risk, though in part clandestine. Lastly, I hardly dare, so childish does it appear, to confess the third reason, which was I am quite sure, unconsciously decisive. Since, in order to follow—and see controverted—the military principles enunciated by Saint-Loup, I had followed in close detail the course of the Boer war, I had been led on from that to read again old accounts of explorations, narratives of travel. These stories had excited me, and I applied them to the events of my daily life to stimulate my courage. When attacks of illness had compelled me to remain for several days and nights on end not only without sleep but without lying down, without tasting food or drink, at the moment when my pain and exhaustion became so intense that I felt that I should never escape from them, I would think of some traveller cast on the beach, poisoned by noxious herbs, shivering with fever in clothes drenched by the salt water, who nevertheless in a day or two felt stronger, rose and went blindly upon his way, in search of possible inhabitants who might, when he came to them, prove cannibals. His example acted on me as a tonic, restored my hope, and I felt ashamed of my momentary discouragement. Thinking of the Boers who, with British armies facing them, were not afraid to expose themselves at the moment when they had to cross, in order to reach a covered position, a tract of open country: "It would be a fine thing," I thought to myself, "if I were to show less courage when the theatre of operations is simply the human heart, and when the only steel that I, who engaged in more than one duel without fear at the time of the Dreyfus case, have to fear is that of the eyes of the neighbours who have other things to do besides looking into the courtyard." But when I was inside the shop, taking care not to let any plank in the floor make the slightest creak, as I found that the least sound in Jupien's shop could be heard from the other, I thought to myself how rash Jupien and M. de Charlus had been, and how wonderfully fortune had favoured them. I did not dare move. The Guermantes groom, taking advantage no doubt of his master's absence, had, as it happened, transferred to the shop in which I now stood, a ladder which hitherto had been kept in the coach-house, and if I had climbed this I could have opened the ventilator above and heard as well as if I had been in Jupien's shop itself. But I was afraid of making a noise. Besides, it was unnecessary. I had not even cause to regret my not having arrived in the shop until several minutes had elapsed. For from what I heard at first in Jupien's shop, which was only a series of inarticulate sounds, I imagine that few words had been exchanged. It is true that these sounds were so violent that, if one set had not always been taken up an octave higher by a parallel plaint, I might have thought that one person was strangling another within a few feet of me, and that subsequently the murderer and his resuscitated victim were taking a bath to wash away the traces of the crime. I concluded from this later on that there is another thing as vociferous as pain, namely pleasure, especially when there is added to it—failing the fear of an eventual parturition, which could not be present in this case, despite the hardly convincing example in the *Golden Legend*— an immediate afterthought of cleanliness. Finally, after about half an hour (during which time I had climbed on tiptoe up my ladder so as to peep through the ventilator which I did not open), a conversation began. Jupien refused with insistence the money that M. de Charlus was pressing upon him. "Why do you have your chin shaved like that," he inquired of the Baron in a cajoling tone. It's so becoming, a nice beard." "Ugh! It's disgusting," the Baron replied. Meanwhile he still lingered upon the threshold and plied Jupien with question about the neighbourhood. "You don't know anything about the man who sells chestnuts at the corner, not the one on the left, he's a horror, but the other way, a great, dark fellow? And the chemist opposite, he has a charming cyclist who delivers his parcels." These questions must have ruffled Jupien, for, drawing himself up with the scorn of a great courtesan who has been forsaken, he replied: "I can see you are completely heartless." Uttered in a pained, frigid, affected tone, this reproach must have made its sting felt by M. de Charlus, who, to counteract the bad impression made by his curiosity, addressed to Jupien, in too low a tone for me to be able to make out his words, a request the granting of which would doubtless necessitate their prolonging their sojourn in the shop, and which moved the tailor sufficiently to make him forget his annoyance, for he studied the Baron's face, plump and flushed beneath his grey hair, with the supremely blissful air of a person whose self-esteem has just been profoundly flattered, and, deciding to grant M. de Charlus the favour that he had just asked of him, after various remarks lacking in refinement such as "Aren't you naughty!" said to the Baron with a smiling, emotional, superior and grateful air: "All right, you big baby, come along!"

"If I hark back to the question of the tram conductor," M. de Charlus went on imperturbably, "it is because; apart from anything else, he might offer me some entertainment on my homeward journey. For it falls to my lot, now and then, like the, Caliph who used to roam the streets of Bagdad in the guise of a, common merchant, to condescend to follow some curious little person whose profile may have taken my fancy." I made at this point the same observation that I had made on Bergotte. If he should ever have to plead before a bench, he would employ not the sentences calculated to convince his judges, but such Bergottesque sentences as his peculiar literary temperament suggested to him and made him find pleasure in using. Similarly M. de Charlus, in conversing with the tailor, made use of the same language that he would have used to fashionable people of his own set, even exaggerating its eccentricities, whether because the shyness which he was striving to overcome drove him to an excess of pride or, by preventing him from mastering himself (for we are always less at our ease in the company of some one who is not of our station), forced him to unveil, to lay bare his true nature, which was, in fact, arrogant and a trifle mad, as Mme. de Guermantes had remarked. "So as not to lose the trail," he went on, "I spring like a little usher; like a young and good looking doctor, into the same car as the little person herself, of whom we speak in the feminine gender only so as to conform with the rules of grammar (as we say, in speaking of a Prince, "Is His Highness enjoying *her* usual health"). If she changes her car, I take, with possibly the germs of the plague, that incredible thing called a transfer, a number, and one which, albeit it is presented to *me*, is not always number one! I change 'carriages' in this way as many as three or four times, I end up sometimes at eleven o'clock at night at the Orléans station and have to come home. Still, if it were only the Orléans station! Once, I must tell you, not having managed to get into conversation sooner, I went all the way to Orléans itself, in one of those frightful compartments where one has, to rest one's eyes upon, between triangles of what is known as 'string-work', photographs of the principal architectural features of the line. There was only one vacant seat; I had in front of me, as an historic edifice, a 'view' of the Cathedral of Orléans, quite the ugliest, in France, and as tiring a thing to have to stare at in that way against my will as if somebody had forced me to focus its towers in the lens of one of those optical penholders which give one ophthalmia. I got out of the train at Les Aubrais together with my young person, for whom alas his family (when I had imagined him to possess every defect except that of having a family) were waiting on the platform! My sole consolation, as I waited for a train to take me back to Paris, was the house of Diane de Poitiers. She may indeed have charmed one of my royal ancestors, I should have preferred a more living beauty. That is why, as an antidote to the boredom of returning home by myself, I should rather like to make friends with a sleeping-car attendant or the conductor of an omnibus, Now, don't be shocked," the Baron wound up, "it is all a question of class. With what you would call 'young gentlemen,' for instance,' I feel no desire actually to have them, but I am never satisfied until I have touched them, I don't mean physically, but touched a responsive, chord. As soon as, instead of leaving my letters unanswered, a young man starts writing to me incessantly; when he is morally at my disposal, I grow calm again, or at least I should grow calm were I not immediately caught by the attraction of another. Rather curious ain't it?—Speaking of 'young gentlemen', those that come to the house here, do you know any of them?" "No, baby. Oh, yes, I do, a dark one, very tall, with an eyeglass, who keeps smiling and turning round." "I don't know who you mean." Jupien filled in the portrait, but M. de Charlus could not succeed in identifying its subject, not knowing that the ex-tailor was one of those persons, more common than is generally supposed, who never remember the colour of the hair of people they do not know well. But to me, who was aware of this infirmity in Jupien and substituted 'fair' for 'dark', the portrait appeared to be an exact description of the Duc de Châtellerault. "To return to young men not of the lower orders;" the Baron went on, "at the present moment my head has been turned by a strange little fellow, an intelligent little cit who shows with regard to myself a prodigious want of civility. He has absolutely no idea of the prodigious personage that I am, and of the microscopic animalcule that he is in comparison. After all, what does it matter, the little ass may bray his head off before my august bishop's mantle." " Bishop!" cried Jupien, who had understood nothing of M. de Charlus's concluding remarks, but was completely taken aback by the word bishop. "But that sort of thing doesn't go with religion," he said. "I have three Popes in my family," replied M. de Charlus, "and enjoy the right to mantle in gules by virtue of a cardinalate title, the niece of the Cardinal, my great-uncle, having conveyed to my grand-father the title of Duke which was substituted for it. I see, though, that metaphor leaves you deaf and French history cold. Besides," he added, less perhaps by way of conclusion than as a warning, "this attraction that I feel towards the young people who avoid me, from fear of course, for only their natural respect stops their mouth's from crying out to me that they love me, requires in them an outstanding social position. And again, their feint of indifference may produce, in spite of that, the directly opposite effect. Fatuously prolonged, it sickens me., To take an example from a class with which you are more familiar, when they were doing up my Hotel, so as not to create jealousies among all the duchesses who were vying with one another for the honour of being able to say that they had given me a lodging, I went for a few days to an 'hotel,' as they call inns nowadays. One of the bedroom valets I knew, I pointed out to him an interesting little page who used to open and shut the front door, and who remained refractory to my proposals. Finally, losing my temper, in order to prove to him that my intentions were pure, I made him an offer of a ridiculously high sum simply to come upstairs and talk to me for five minutes in my room. I waited for him in vain. I then took such a dislike to him that I used to go out by the service door so as not to see his villainous little mug at the other. I learned afterwards that he had never had any of my notes, which had been intercepted, the first by the bedroom valet, who was jealous, the next by the day porter, who was virtuous, the third by the night porter, who was in love with the little page, and used to couch with him at the hour when Dian rose. But my disgust persisted none the less, and were they to bring me the page, simply like a dish of venison on a silver platter, I should thrust him away with a retching stomach. But there's the unfortunate part of it, we have spoken of serious matters, and now all is over between us, there, can be no more question of what I hoped to secure. But you could render me great-services, act as my agent; why no, the mere thought of such a thing restores my vigour, and I can see that all is by no means over."

From the beginning of this scene a revolution, in my unsealed eyes, had occurred in M. de Charlus, as complete, as immediate as if he had been touched by a magician's wand. Until then, because I had not understood, I had not seen. The vice (we use the word for convenience only), the vice of each of us accompanies him through life after the manner of the familiar genius who was invisible to men so long as they were unaware of his presence. Our goodness, our meanness, our name, our social relations do not disclose themselves to the eye, we carry them hidden within us. Even Ulysses did not at once recognise Athena. But the gods are immediately perceptible to one another, as quickly like to like, and so too had M. de Charlus been to Jupien. Until that moment I had been, in the presence of M. de Charlus, in the position of an unobservant man who, standing before a pregnant woman whose distended outline he has failed to remark, persists, while she smilingly reiterates: "Yes, I am a little tired just now," in asking her indiscreetly: "Why, what is the matter with you?" But let some one say to him: "She is expecting a child," suddenly he catches sight of her abdomen and ceases to see anything else. It is the explanation that opens our eyes; the dispelling of an error gives us an additional sense.

The transformation of M. de Charlus into a new person was so complete that not only the contrasts of his face, of his voice, but, in retrospect, the very ups and downs of his relations with myself, everything that hitherto had seemed to my mind incoherent; became intelligible, brought itself into evidence, just as a sentence which presents no meaning so long as it remains broken up in letters scattered at random upon a table, expresses, if these letters be rearranged in the proper order; a thought which one can never afterwards forget. I now understood, moreover, how, earlier in the day, when I had seen him coming away from Mme. de Vileparisis's, I had managed to arrive at the conclusion that M. de Charlus looked like a woman: he was one! He belonged to that race of beings, less paradoxical than they appear, whose ideal is manly simply because their temperament is feminine and who in their life resemble, in appearance only, the rest of men; there where each of us carries, inscribed in those eyes through which he beholds everything in the universe, a human outline engraved on the surface of the pupil, for them, it is that not of a nymph but of a youth.

From this day onwards M. de Charlus was to alter the time of his visits to Mme. de Villeparisis, not that he could not see Jupien elsewhere and with greater convenience, but because to him just as much as to me the afternoon sunshine and the blossoming plant were, no doubt, linked together in memory. Apart from this, he did not confine himself to recommending the Jupiens to Mme. de Villeparisis, to the Duchesse de Guermantes, to a whole brilliant list of patrons, who were all the more assiduous in their attentions to the young seamstress when they saw that the few ladies who had held out, or had merely delayed their submission, were subjected to the direst reprisals by the Baron, whether in order that they might serve as an example, or because they had aroused his wrath and had stood out against his attempted domination; he made Jupien's position more and more lucrative, until he definitely engaged him as his secretary and established him in the state in which we shall see him later on. "Ah now ! There is a happy man, if you like, that Julien," said Françoise, who had a tendency to minimise or exaggerate people's generosity according as it was bestowed on herself or on others. Not that, in this instance, she had any need to exaggerate, nor for that matter did she feel any jealousy, being genuinely fond of Jupien. "Oh, he's such a good man, the Baron," she went on," such a well-behaved, religious, proper sort of man. If I had a daughter to marry and was one of the rich myself, I would give her to the Baron with my eyes shut." "But; Françoise," my mother observed gently, "she'd be well supplied with husbands, that daughter of yours. Don't forget you've already promised her to Jupien." "Ah! Lordy, now," replied Françoise, "there's another of them that would make a woman happy. It doesn't matter whether you're rich or poor, it makes no difference to your nature. The Baron and Julien, they're just the same sort of person."

This revelation about the character of M de Charlus led me to ponder on the role of Sodomites who are so numerous today in London, Berlin, Rome, Petrograd or Paris.

When I knew that the Guermantes had come home, I visited them and was received by the Duke alone in the library and his face grew dark when I told him I had come to ask his wife to find out whether her cousin really had invited me. The Duke explained to me that it was too late, that if the Princesse had not sent me an invitation it would make him appear to be asking for one and he had no wish to appear either directly or indirectly to be interfering with their visiting list, be "meddling. If you do decide to go to the party I have no need to tell you what a pleasure it will be to spend the evening there with you." But we are dining with Mme de Sainte-Euverte before the party and we are already late. "

The Duke was now joined by his wife ready for the evening, tall and proud in a gown of red satin the skirt of which was bordered with spangles. He exclaimed " Come, Oriane, dont stop here chattering, the horses have been waiting for a good five minutes and you know that we have to sit down to table at eight o'clock sharp."

The Duchesse lifted her red skirt and set foot on the step of the carriage, when seeing this foot exposed, the Duke cried in a terrifying voice: "Oriane, what have you been thinking about you wretch! You've kept on your black shoes! With a red dress! Go upstairs quick and put on red shoes, or rather," he said to the footman, "tell the lady's maid at once to bring down a pair of red shoes. It wont matter if we turn up at half past eight they'll have to wait for us.

Part II

Chapter One

As I was in no haste to arrive at this party at the Guermantes' to which I was not certain that I had been invited, I remained sauntering out of doors in the evening twilight. Outside the mansion of the Princesse de Guermantes, I met the Duc de Châtellerault; I greeted the young Duke and made my way into the house. But here I must first of all record a trifling incident, which will enable us to understand something that was presently to occur.

There was one person who, on that evening as on the previous evenings, had been thinking a great deal about the Duc de Châtellerault, without however suspecting who he was: this was the usher (styled at that time the *aboyeur.*) of Mme. de Guermantes. M. de Châtellerault, so far from being one of the Princesses intimate friends, albeit he was one of her cousins, had been invited to her house for the first time. His parents, who had not been on speaking terms with her for the last ten years, had been reconciled to her within the last fortnight, and, obliged to be out of Paris that evening, had requested their son to fill their place. Now, a few days earlier, the Princess's usher had met in the Champs-Elysées a young man whom he had found charming but whose identity he had been unable to establish. Not that the young man had not shown himself as obliging as he had been generous. All the favours that the usher had supposed that he would have to bestow upon so young a gentleman, he had on the contrary received. But M. de Châtellerault was as reticent as he was rash; he was all the more determined not to disclose his incognito since he did not know with what sort of person he was dealing; his fear would have been far greater, although quite unfounded, if he had known. He had confined himself to posing as an Englishman, and to all the passionate questions with which he was plied by the usher, desirous to meet again a person to whom he was indebted for so much pleasure and so ample a gratuity, the Duke had merely replied, from one end of the Avenue Gabriel to the other: "I do not speak French."

The general estimate of the Princesse de Guermantes-Bavière's initiative, spirit and intellectual superiority was based upon an innovation that was to be found nowhere else in her set. After dinner, however important the party that was to follow, the chairs, at the Princesse de Guermantes's, were arranged in such a way as to form little groups, in which people might have to turn their backs upon one another. The Princess then displayed her social sense by going to sit down, as though by preference, in one of these. Not that she was afraid to pick out and attract to herself a member of another group. If for instance, she had remarked to M. Detaille, who naturally agreed with her, on the beauty of Mme. de Villemur's neck, of which that lady's position in another group made her present a back view, the Princess did not hesitate to raise her voice: "Madame de Villemur; M. Detaille, with his wonderful painter's eye, has just been admiring your neck" Mme de Villemur interpreted this as a direct invitation to join in the conversation; with the agility of a practised horsewoman, she made her chair rotate slowly through three quadrants of a circle, and, without in the least disturbing her neighbours, came to rest almost facing the Princess. " You don't know M. Detaille?" exclaimed their hostess; for whom her guest's nimble and modest tergiversation was not sufficient. "I do not know him, but I 'know' his work," replied Mme. de Villemur, with a respectful engaging air, and a promptitude which many of the onlookers envied her, addressing the while to the celebrated painter whom this invocation had not been sufficient to introduce to her in a formal manner an imperceptible bow. "Come, Monsieur Detaille," said the Princess, "let me introduce you to Mme. de Villemur." That lady there upon showed as great ingenuity in making room for the creator of the *Dream* as she had shown a. moment earlier in wheeling round to face him. And the Princess drew forward a chair for herself; she had indeed invoked Mme. de Villemur only to have an excuse for quitting the first group, in which she had spent the statutory ten minutes, and bestowing a similar allowance of her time upon the second in three quarters of an hour, all the groups had received a visit from her, which seemed to have been determined in each instance by impulse and predilection, but had the paramount object of making it apparent how naturally "a great lady knows how to entertain." But now the guests for the party were beginning to arrive, and the lady of the house was seated not far from the door—erect and proud in her semi-regal majesty, her eyes ablaze with their own incandescence—between two unattractive Royalties and the Spanish Ambassadress.

I stood waiting behind a number of guests who had arrived before me. Facing me was the Princess, whose beauty is probably not the only thing, where there were so many beauties, that reminds me of this party. But the face of my hostess was so perfect; stamped like so beautiful a medal, that it has retained a commemorative force in my mind. The Princess was in the habit of saying to her guests when she met them a day or two before one of her parties, " You will come, won't you?" as though she felt a great desire to talk to them. But as on the contrary she had nothing to talk to them about, when they entered her presence she contented herself, without rising, with breaking off for an instant her vapid conversation, with the two Royalties and the Ambassadress and thanking them with: "How good of you to have come," not that she thought that the guest had shown his goodness by coming, but to enhance her own; then, at once dropping him back into the stream, she would add: "You will find M. de Guermantes by the garden door," so that the guest proceeded on his way and ceased to bother her. To some indeed, she said nothing, contenting herself with showing them her admirable onyx eyes, as though they had come merely to visit an exhibition of precious stones.

The person immediately in front of me was the Duc de Châtellerault. Having to respond to all the smiles, all the greetings waved to him from inside the drawing-room, he had not noticed the usher, But from the first moment the usher had recognised him. The identity of this stranger, which he had so ardently desired to learn, in another minute he would know. When he asked his 'Englishman' of the other evening what name he was to announce, the usher was not merely stirred, he considered that he was being indiscreet, indelicate. He felt that he was about to reveal to the whole world (which would, however, suspect nothing) a secret which it was criminal of him to force like this and to proclaim in public. Upon hearing the guest's reply: "Le duc de Châtellerault," he felt such a burst of pride that he remained for a moment speechless. The Duke looked at him, recognised him, saw himself ruined, while the servant, who had recovered his composure and was sufficiently versed in heraldry to complete for himself an appellation that was too modest, shouted with a professional vehemence softened by an emotional tenderness: "Son Altesse Monseigneur le duc de Châtellerault!" But it was now my turn to be announced. Absorbed in contemplation of my hostess, who had not yet seen me, I had not thought of the function—terrible to me, although not in the same sense as to M. de Châtellerault—of this usher garbed in black like a headsman, surrounded by a group of lackeys in the most cheerful livery, lusty fellows ready to seize hold of an intruder and away and cast him out of doors. The usher asked me my name, I told him it as mechanically as the condemned man allows himself to be strapped to the block. At once he lifted his head majestically and, before I could beg him to announce me in a lowered tone so as to spare my own feelings if I were not invited and those of the Princesse de Guermantes if I were, shouted the disturbing syllables with a force capable of bringing down the roof.

The famous Huxley (whose grandson occupies an unassailable position in the English literary world of today) relates that one of his patients dared not continue to go into society because often, on the actual chair that was pointed out to her with a courteous gesture, she saw an old gentleman already seated. She could be quite certain that either the gesture of invitation or the old gentleman's presence was a hallucination, for her hostess would not have offered her a chair that was already occupied. And when Huxley, to cure her, forced her to reappear in society, she felt a moment of painful hesitation when she asked herself whether the friendly sign that was being made to her was the real thing, or, in obedience to a non-existent vision, she was about to sit down in public upon the knees of a gentleman in flesh and blood. Her brief uncertainty was agonising. Less so perhaps than mine. From the moment at which I had taken in the sound of my name like the rumble that warns us of a possible cataclysm, I was bound, to plead my own good faith in either event, and as though I were not tormented by any doubt, to advance towards the Princess with a resolute air.

She caught sight of me when I was still a few feet away and (to leave me in no doubt that I was the victim of a conspiracy), instead of remaining seated, as she had done for her other guests, rose and came towards me. A moment later, I was able to heave the sigh of relief of Huxley's patient, when, having made up her mind to sit down on the chair, she found it vacant and realised that it was the old gentleman that was a hallucination. The Princess had just held out her hand to me with a smile. She remained standing for some moments with the kind

of charm enshrined in the verse of Malherbe which ends:
"*To do them honour all the angels rise.*"

She apologised because the Duchess had not yet come, as though I must be bored there without her. In order to give me this greeting, she wheeled round me, holding me by the hand, in a graceful revolution by the whirl of which I felt myself carried off my feet. I almost expected that she would next offer me like the leader of a cotillon, an ivory headed cane or a watch-bracelet. She did not, however, give me anything of the sort and as though, instead of dancing the Boston, she had been listening to a sacred quartet by Beethoven the sublime strains of which she was afraid of interrupting, she cut short the conversation there and then, or rather did not begin it, and, still radiant at having seen me come in, merely informed me where the Prince was to be found. I moved away from her and did not venture to approach her again, feeling that she had absolutely nothing to say to me and that, in her vast kindness, this woman marvellously tall and handsome, noble as were so many great ladies who stepped so proudly upon the scaffold, could only, short of offering me a draught of honeydew, repeat what she had already said to me twice: "You will find the Prince in the garden." Now, to go in search of the Prince was to feel my doubts revive in a fresh form; I should have to find somebody to introduce me. One could hear, above all the din of conversation, the interminable chatter of M. de Charlus, talking to H. E. the Duke of Sidonia, whose acquaintance he had just made. Members of the same profession find one another out, and so it is with a common vice. M. de Charlus and M. de Sidonia had each of them immediately detected the other's vice which was in both cases, that of soliloquising in society, to the extent of not being able to stand any interruption. Having decided at once that, in the words of a famous sonnet, there was 'no help', they had made up their minds not to be silent but each to go on talking without any regard to what the other might say. This had resulted in the confused babble produced in Molière's comedies by a number of people saying different things simultaneously. The Baron, with his deafening voice, was moreover certain of keeping the upper hand, of drowning the feeble voice of M. de Sidonia; without however discouraging him for, whenever M. de Charlus paused for a moment to breathe, the interval was filled by the murmurs of the Grandee of Spain who had imperturbably continued his discourse. I could easily have asked M. de Charlus to introduce me to the Prince de Guermantes, but I feared (and with good reason) that he might be cross with me. I had treated him in the most ungrateful fashion by letting his offer pass unheeded, for the second time and by never giving him a sign of my existence since the evening when he had so affectionately escorted me home. And yet I could not plead the excuse of having anticipated the scene which I had just witnessed, that very afternoon, enacted by himself and Jupien. I suspected nothing of the sort. It is true that shortly before this, when my parents reproached me with my laziness and with not having taken the trouble to write a line to M. de Charlus, I had violently reproached them with wishing me to accept a degrading proposal. But anger alone and the desire to hit upon the expression that would be most offensive to them had dictated this mendacious retort. In reality, I had imagined nothing sensual, nothing sentimental even, underlying, the Baron's offers. I had said this to my parents with entire irresponsibility. But sometimes the future is latent in us without our knowledge, and our words which we suppose to be false, forecast an imminent reality.

M. de Charlus would doubtless have forgiven me my want of gratitude. But what made him furious was that my presence this evening at the Princesse de Guermantes's, as for some time past at her cousin's, seemed to be a defiance of his solemn declaration: "There is no admission to those houses save through me." A grave fault, a crime that was perhaps inexpiable, I had not followed the conventional path. M. de Charlus knew well that the thunderbolts, which he hurled at those who did not comply with his orders or to whom he had taken a dislike, were beginning to be regarded by many people, however furiously he might brandish them, as mere pasteboard, and had no longer the force to banish anybody from anywhere. But he believed perhaps that his diminished power, still considerable, remained intact in the eyes of novices like myself. And so I did not consider it well advised to ask a favour of him at a party at which the mere fact of my presence seemed an ironical denial of his pretensions.

I could distinguish beneath the trees various women with whom I was more or less closely acquainted, but they seemed transformed because they were at the Princess's and not at her cousin's, and because I saw them seated not in front of Dresden china plates but beneath the boughs of a chestnut. The refinement of their setting mattered nothing. Had it been infinitely less refined than at Oriane's, I should have felt the same uneasiness. When the electric light in our drawing-room fails, and we are obliged to replace it with oil lamps, everything seems altered. I was recalled from my uncertainty by Mme. de Souvré. "Good evening," she said as she approached me. "Have you seen the Duchesse de Guermantes lately?" She excelled in giving to speeches of this sort an intonation which proved that she was not uttering them from sheer silliness, like people who, not knowing what to talk about, come up to you, a thousand times over to mention some bond of common acquaintance, often extremely slight. She had on the contrary a fine conducting wire in her glance which signified: "Don't suppose for a moment that I haven't recognised you. You are the young man I met at the Duchesse de Guermantes. I remember quite well." Unfortunately, this protection, extended over me by this phrase, stupid in appearance but delicate in intention, was extremely fragile, and vanished as soon as I tried to make use of it. Madame de Souvré had the art, if called upon to convey a request to some influential person, of appearing at the same time, in the petitioner's eyes, to be recommending him, and in those of the influential person not to be recommending the petitioner, so that her ambiguous gesture opened a credit balance of gratitude to her with the latter without placing her in any way in debt to the former. Encouraged by this lady's civilities to ask her to introduce me to M. de Guermantes, I found that she took advantage of a moment when our host was not looking in our direction, laid a motherly hand on my shoulder, and, smiling at the averted face of the Prince who was unable to see her, thrust me towards him with a gesture of feigned protection, but deliberately ineffective, which left me stranded almost at my starting point. Such is the cowardice of people in society.

I had no recourse left save to M. de Charlus, who had withdrawn to a room downstairs which opened on the garden. I had plenty of time (as he was pretending to be absorbed in a fictitious game of whist which enabled him to appear not to notice people) to admire the deliberate, artistic simplicity of his evening coat which, by the merest trifles which only a tailor's eye could have picked out, had the air of a 'Harmony in Black and White' by Whistler; black, white and red, rather, for M. de Charlus was wearing, hanging from a broad ribbon pinned to the lapel of his coat, the Cross, in white, black and red enamel, of a Knight of the religious Order of Malta. I might perhaps—despite his ill-humour towards me—have been successful when I asked him to introduce me to the Prince, had I not been so ill-inspired as to add, from a scruple of conscience, and so that he might not suppose me guilty of the indelicacy of entering the house at a venture, counting upon him to enable me to remain there: "You are aware that I know them quite well, the Princess has been very kind to me." "Very well, if you know them, why do you need me to introduce you?" he replied in a sharp tone, and, turning his back, resumed his make-believe game with the Nuncio, the German Ambassador and another personage whom I did not know by sight.

Then, from the depths of those gardens where in days past the Duc d'Aiguillon used to breed rare animals, there came to my ears, through the great open doors, the sound of a sniffing nose that was savouring all those refinements and determined to miss none of them. The sound approached, I moved at a venture in its direction, with the result that the words *good evening* were murmured in my ear by M. de Bréauté, not like the rusty metallic sound of a knife being sharpened on a grindstone, even less like the cry of the wild boar, devastator of tilled fields, but like the voice of a possible saviour.

Less influential than Mme. de Souvré but less deeply ingrained than she with the incapacity to oblige, far more at his ease with the Prince than was Mme. d'Arpajon entertaining some illusion perhaps as to my position in the Guermantes set, or perhaps knowing more about it than myself, I had nevertheless for the first few moments some difficulty in arresting his attention, for, with fluttering, distended nostrils, he was turning in every direction, inquisitively protruding his monocle, as though he found himself face to face with five hundred matchless works of art. But, having heard my request, he received it with satisfaction, led me towards the Prince and presented me to him with a relishing, ceremonious, vulgar air, as though he had been handing him, with a word of commendation, a plate of cakes. Just as the greeting of the Duc de Guermantes was, when he chose, friendly, instinct with good fellowship, cordial and familiar, so I found that of the Prince stiff, solemn, haughty. He barely smiled at me, addressed me gravely as "Sir." I had often heard the Duke make fun of his cousin's stiffness. But from the first words that he addressed to me, which by their cold and serious tone formed the most entire contrast with the language of Basin, I realised at once that the fundamentally disdainful man was the Duke, who spoke to you at your first meeting with him as 'man to man', and that, of the two cousins, the one who was really simple was the Prince. I found in his reserve a stronger feeling, I do not say of equality, for that would have been inconceivable to him, but at least of the consideration which one may show for an inferior, such as may be found in all strongly hierarchical societies, in the Law Courts, for instance; in a Faculty, where a public prosecutor or dean, conscious of their high charge, conceals perhaps more genuine simplicity, and, when you come to know them better, more kindness, true simplicity, cordiality, beneath their traditional aloofness than the more modern brethren beneath their jocular affectation of comradeship. "Do you intend to follow the career of Monsieur, your father?" he said to me with a distant but interested air. I answered his question briefly, realising that he had asked it only out of politeness, and moved away to allow him to greet the fresh arrivals.

I drifted back into the stream of guests who were entering the house. "Have you seen my delicious cousin Oriane lately?" I was asked by the Princess who had now deserted her post by the door and with whom I was making my way back to the rooms. "She's sure to be here to-night, I saw her this afternoon," my hostess added. "She promised me to come. I believe too, that you will be dining with us both to meet the Queen of Italy, at the Embassy, on Thursday. There are to be all the Royalties imaginable, it will be most alarming." They could not in any way alarm the Princesse de Guermantes, whose rooms swarmed with them, and who would say: "My little Coburgs" as she might have said "my little dogs." And so Mme. de Guermantes said: "It will be most alarming," out of sheer silliness, which, among people in society, overrides even their vanity.

While the Princess was talking to me, it so happened that the Duc and Duchesse de Guermantes made their entrance. But I could not go at once to greet them, for I was waylaid by the Turkish Ambassadress, who, pointing to our hostess whom I had just left, exclaimed as she seized me by the arm: "Ah! What a delicious woman the Princess is! What a superior being! I feel sure that, if I were a man," she went on, with a trace of Oriental servility and sensuality, "I would give my life for that heavenly creature." I replied that I did indeed find her charming, but that I knew her cousin, the Duchess, better. "But there is no comparison," said the Ambassadress. "Oriane is a charming society woman who gets her wit from Mémé and Babal, whereas Marie-Gilbert is *somebody*. This same diplomatic personage had said to me, with a purposeful and serious air, that she found the Princesse de Guermantes frankly antipathetic. I felt that I need not stop to consider this change of front: the invitation to the party this evening had brought it about. The Ambassadress was perfectly sincere when she told me that the Princesse de Guermantes was a sublime creature. She had always thought so. But, having never before been invited to the Princess's house, she had felt herself bound to give this non-invitation the appearance of a deliberate abstention on principle. Now that she had been asked, and would presumably continue to be asked in the future, she could give free expression to her feelings.

In the ordinary course of life, the eyes of the Duchesse de Guermantes were absent and slightly melancholy, she made them sparkle with a flame of wit only when she had to say how d'ye do to a friend; precisely as though the said friend had been some witty remark, some charming touch, some titbit for delicate palates, the savour of which has set on the face of the connoisseur an expression of refined joy. But upon big evenings, as she had too many greetings to bestow, she decided that it would be tiring to have to switch off the light after each. Just as an ardent reader, when he goes to the theatre to see a new piece by one of the masters of the stage, testifies to his certainty that he is not going to spend a dull evening by having, while he hands his hat and coat to the attendant, his lip adjusted in readiness for a sapient smile, his eye kindled for a sardonic approval; similarly it was at the moment of her arrival that the Duchess lighted up for the whole evening. And while she was handing over her evening cloak, of a magnificent Tiepolo red, exposing a huge collar of rubies round her neck, having cast over her gown that final rapid, minute and exhaustive dressmaker's glance which is also that of a woman of the world, Oriane made sure that her eyes, just as much as her other jewels, were sparkling.

I was beginning to learn the exact value of the language spoken or mute, of aristocratic affability, an affability that is happy to shed balm upon the sense of inferiority in those persons towards whom it is directed, though not to the point of dispelling that sense, for in that case it would no longer have any reason to exist. "But you are our equal, if not our superior," the Guermantes seemed in all their actions, to be saying; and they said it in the most courteous fashion imaginable, to be loved, admired, but not to be believed; that one should discern the fictitious character of this affability was what they called being well bred; to suppose it to be genuine, a sign of illbreeding. I was to receive, as it happened, shortly after this, a lesson which gave me a full and perfect understanding of the extent and limitations of certain forms of aristocratic affability. It was at an afternoon party given by the Duchesse de Montmorency to meet the Queen of England; there was a sort of royal procession to the buffet, at the head of which walked Her Majesty on the arm of the Duc de Guermantes. I happened to arrive at that moment. With his disengaged hand the Duke conveyed to me, from a distance of nearly fifty yards, a thousand signs of friendly invitation, which appeared to mean that I need not be afraid to approach, that I should not be devoured alive instead of the sandwiches. But I, who was becoming word-perfect in the language of the court, instead of going even one step nearer, keeping my fifty yards interval, made a deep bow, but without smiling, the sort of bow that I should have made to some one whom I scarcely knew, then proceeded in the opposite direction. Had I written a masterpiece, the Guermantes would have given me less credit for it than I earned by that bow. Not only did it not pass unperceived by the Duke, albeit he had that day to acknowledge the greetings of more than five hundred people, it caught the eye of the Duchess, who, happening to meet my mother, told her of it, and, so far from suggesting that I had done wrong, that I ought to have gone up to him, said that her husband had been lost in admiration of my bow, that it would have been impossible for anyone to put more into it.They never ceased to find in that bow every possible merit, without however mentioning that which had seemed the most priceless of all, to wit that it had been discreet.

As she strolled by my side, the Duchesse de Guermantes allowed the azure light of her eyes to float in front of her, but vaguely, so as to avoid the people with whom she did not wish to enter into relations, whose presence she discerned at times like a menacing reef in the distance. We advanced between a double hedge of guests who, conscious that they would never come to know Oriane, were anxious at least to point her out, as a curiosity, to their wives: "Quick, Ursule, come and look at Madame de Guermantes talking to that young man." And one felt that in another moment they would be clambering upon the chairs for a better view, as at the Military Review on the 14th of July, or the Grand Prix.

"What, you don't know these glories?" said the Duchess, referring to the rooms through which we were moving. But, having given its due meed of praise to her cousin's 'palace', she hastened to add that she a thousand times preferred her own 'humble den'. "This is an admirable house to *visit*. But I should die of misery if I had to stay behind and sleep in rooms that have witnessed so many historic events. It would give me the feeling of having been left after closing-time, forgotten, in the Chateau of Blois, or Fontainebleau, or even the Louvre, with no antidote to my depression except to tell myself that I was in the room in which Monaldeschi was murdered. As a sedative, that is not good enough. Why, here comes Mme. de Saint-Euverte. We've just been dining with her. As she is giving her great annual beanfeast to-morrow, I supposed she would be going straight to bed. But she can never miss a party. If this one had been in the country, she would have jumped on a lorry rather than not go to it.

As a matter of fact, Mme. de Saint-Euverte had come this evening, less for the pleasure of not missing another person's party than in order to ensure the success of her own, recruit the latest additions to her list, and, so to speak, hold an eleventh hour review of the troops who were on the morrow to perform such brilliant evolutions at her garden party.

For, in the long course of years, the guests at the Saint-Euverte parties had almost entirely changed. The female celebrities of the Guermantes world, formerly so sparsely scattered, had— with attentions by their hostess—begun gradually to bring their friends. At the same time, by an enterprise equally progressive, but in the opposite direction, Mme.de Saint-Euverte had, year by year, reduced the number of persons unknown to the world of fashion. You had ceased to see first one of them, then another. For some time the 'batch' system was in operation, which enabled her, thanks to parties over which a veil of silence was drawn, to summon the ineligibles separately to entertain one another, which, dispensed her from having to invite them with the nice people. What cause had they for complaint? Were they not given *(panem et circenses)* light refreshments and a select musical programme.

Mme. de Guermantes felt curious as to the subject of the conversation Swann had had with their host. "Do you know what it was about?" the Duke asked M. de Bréauté and went on "So far as Swann is concerned, I can tell you frankly that his conduct towards ourselves has been beyond words. Introduced into society, in the past, by ourselves, by the Duc de Chartres, they tell me now that he is openly a Dreyfusard. I should never have believed it of him, an epicure, a man of practical judgment, a collector, who goes in for old books, a member of the Jockey, a man who enjoys the respect of all that know him, who knows all the good addresses, and used to send us the best port wine you could wish to drink, a dilettante, the father of a family. Oh! I have been greatly deceived. I do not complain for myself, it is understood that I am only an old fool, whose opinion counts for nothing, mere rag tag and bobtail, but if only for Oriane's sake, he ought to have openly disavowed the Jews and the partisans of the man Dreyfus. "Yes, after the friendship my wife has always shown him," went on the Duke, who evidently considered that to denounce Dreyfus as guilty of high treason, whatever opinion one might hold in one's own conscience as to his guilt, constituted a sort of thank-offering for the manner in which one had been received in the Faubourg Saint-Germain, "he ought to have disassociated himself. For, you can ask Oriane, she had a real friendship for him." The Duchess, thinking that an ingenuous, calm tone would give a more dramatic and sincere value to her words, said in a schoolgirl voice, as though she were simply letting the truth fall from her lips, merely giving a slightly melancholy expression to her eyes: "It is quite true, I have no reason to conceal the fact that I did feel a sincere affection for Charles!" "There, you see, I don't have to make her say it. And after that, he carries his ingratitude to the point of being a Dreyfusard!"

"Talking of Dreyfusards," I said, "it appears, Prince Von is one."
"Ah, I am glad you reminded me of him," exclaimed M. de Guermantes, "I was forgetting that he had asked me to dine with him on Monday. But whether he is a Dreyfusard or not is entirely immaterial, since he is a foreigner. I don't give two straws for his opinion. With a Frenchman, it is another matter. It is true that Swann is a Jew. But, until to-day, I have always been foolish enough to believe that a Jew can be a Frenchman, that is to say, an honourable Jew, a man of the world. Now, Swann was that in every sense of the word. Ah, well! He forces me to admit that I have been mistaken, since he has taken the side of this Dreyfus (who, guilty or not, never moved in his world, he cannot ever have met him) against a society that had adopted him, had treated him as one of ourselves. It goes without saying, we were all of us prepared to vouch for Swann, I would have answered for his patriotism as for my own. Ah! He is rewarding us very badly: I must confess that I should never have expected such a thing from him. I thought better of him. He was a man of intelligence (in his own line, of course). I know that he had already made that insane, disgraceful marriage. By which token, shall I tell you some one who was really hurt by Swann's marriage, my wife. Oriane often has what I might call an affectation of insensibility. But at heart she feels things with extraordinary keenness." Mme. de Guermantes, delighted by this analysis of her character, listened to it with a modest air but did not utter a word; from a scrupulous reluctance to acquiesce in it, but principally from fear of cutting it short. M. de Guermantes might have gone on talking for an hour on this subject, she would have, sat as still, or even stiller than if she had been listening to music. "Very well! I remember, when she heard of Swann's marriage, she felt hurt; she considered that it was wrong in a person to whom we had given so much friendship. She was very fond of Swann; she was deeply grieved. Am I not right, Oriane?" Mme. de Guermantes felt that she ought to reply to so direct a challenge, upon a point of fact, which would allow her, unobtrusively, to confirm the tribute which she felt, had come to an end. In a shy and simple tone, and with an air all the more studied in that it sought to show genuine 'feeling', she said with a meek reserve, "It is true, Basin is quite right." "Still, that was not quite the same. After all, love is love, although, in my opinion, it ought to confine itself within certain limits. I might excuse a young fellow, a mere boy, for letting himself be caught by an infatuation. But Swann, a man of intelligence, of proved refinement, a good judge of pictures, an intimate friend of the Duc de

Chartres, of Gilbert himself!" It is true that M. de Guermantes had not displayed so profound and pained an astonishment when he learned that Saint-Loup was a Dreyfusard. But, for one thing, he regarded his nephew as a young man gone astray, as to whom nothing, until he began to mend his ways, would be surprising, whereas Swann was what M. de Guermantes called "a man of weight, a man occupying a position in the front rank." Moreover and above all, a considerable interval of time had elapsed during which, if, from the historical point of view, events had, to some extent, seemed to justify the Dreyfusard argument, the anti-Drefusian opposition had doub!ed its violence, and, from being purely political, had become social. It was now a question of militarism, of patriotism, and the waves of anger that had been stirred up in society had had time to gather the force which they never have at the beginning of a storm. "Don't you see," M, de Guermantes went on, "even from the point of view of his beloved Jews, since he is absolutely determined to stand by them, Swann has made a blunder of an incalculable magnitude. He has shown that they are to some extent forced to give their support to anyone of their own race even if they do not know him personally. It is a public danger. We have evidently been too easy going, and the mistake Swann is making will create all the more stir since he was respected, not to say received, and was almost the only Jew that anyone knew. People will say: *Ab uno disce omnes.*" (His satisfaction at having hit, at the right moment, in his memory, upon so apt a quotation, alone brightened with a proud smile the melancholy of the great nobleman conscious of betrayal.)

I was longing to know what exactly had happened between the Prince and Swann, and to catch the latter, if he had not already gone home. "I don't mind telling you," the Duchess answered me when I spoke to her of this desire, "that I for my part am not over anxious to see him, because it appears, by what I was told just now at Mme. de Saint-Euverte's, that he would like me before he dies to make the acquaintance of his wife and daughter. Good heavens, it distresses me terribly that he should be ill, but, I must say, I hope it is not so serious as all that. And besides, it is not really a reason at all, because if it were it would be so childishly simple." A writer with no talent would have only to say: 'Vote for me at the Academy because my wife is dying and I wish to give her this last happiness. There would be no more entertaining if one was obliged to make friends with all the dying people. My coachman might come to me with: "My daughter is seriously ill, get me an invitation to the Princesse de Parme's." I adore Charles, and I should hate having to refuse him, and so that is why I prefer to avoid the risk of his asking me. I hope with all my heart that he is not dying, as he says, but really, if it has to happen, it would not be the moment for me to make the acquaintance of those two creatures who have deprived me of the most amusing of my friends for the last fifteen years, with the additional disadvantage that I should not even be able to make use of their society to see him, since he would be dead!"

I had at length the pleasure of seeing Swann come into this room, which was very big, so big that he did not at first catch sight of me. A pleasure mingled with sorrow, with a sorrow which the other guests did not, perhaps, feel, their feeling consisting rather in that sort of fascination which is exercised by the strange and unexpected forms of an approaching death, a death that a man already has, in the popular saying, written on his face. And it was with a stupefaction that was almost offensive, into which entered indiscreet curiosity, cruelty, a scrutiny at once quiet and anxious (a blend of *suave mari magno* and *memento quia pulvis*, Robert would have said), that all eyes were fastened upon that face the cheeks of which had been so eaten away by disease, like a waning moon, that, except at a certain angle, the angle doubtless at which Swann looked at himself, they stopped short like a flimsy piece of scenery to which only an optical illusion can add the appearance of solidity. Whether because of the absence of those cheeks, no longer there to modify it, or because arterio-sclerosis, which also is a form of intoxication, had reddened it, as would drunkenness, or deformed it, as would morphine, Swann's punchinello nose, absorbed for long years in an attractive face, seemed now enormous, tumid, crimson, the nose of an old Hebrew rather than of a dilettante Valois.

I was just crossing the room to speak to Swann when unfortunately a hand fell upon my shoulder:

"Hallo, old boy, I am in Paris for forty-eight hours. I called at your house, they told me you were here, so that it is to you that my aunt is indebted for the honour of my company at her party." It was Saint-Loup. I told him how greatly I admired the house. "Yes, it makes quite a historic edifice. Personally, I think it appalling. We mustn't go near my uncle Palamède, or we shall be caught. Now that Mme. Molé has gone (for it is she that is ruling the roost just now), he is quite at a loose end. It seems it was as good as a play, he never let her out of his sight for a moment, and only left her when he had put her safely into her carriage. I bear my uncle no ill will, only I do think it odd that my family council, which has always been so hard on me, should be composed of the very ones who have led giddy lives themselves, beginning with the giddiest of the lot, my uncle Charlus, who is my official guardian, has had more women than Don Juan, and is still carrying on in spite of his age. There was a talk at one time of having me made a ward of court. I bet, when all those gay old dogs met to consider the question, and had me up to preach to me and tell me that I was breaking my mother's heart, they dared not look one another in the face for fear of laughing. Just think of the fellows who formed the council, you would think they had deliberately chosen the biggest womanisers."

When M. de Charlus made indignant remonstrances to Robert, who moreover was unaware of his uncle's true inclinations at that time, and indeed if it had still been the time when the Baron used to scarify his own inclinations, he might perfectly well have been sincere in considering, from the point of view of a man of the world, that Robert was infinitely more to blame than himself. Had not Robert, at the very moment when his uncle had been deputed to make him listen to reason, come within an inch of getting himself ostracised by society, had he not, very nearly been blackballed at the Jockey, had he not made himself a public laughing stock by the vast sums that he threw away upon a woman of the lowest order, by his friendships with people—authors, actors, Jews—not one of whom moved in society, by his opinions, which were indistinguishable from those held by traitors, by the grief he was causing to all his relatives? In what respect could it be compared, this scandalous existence, with that of M. de Charlus who had managed, so far, not only to retain but to enhance still further his position as a Guermantes, being in society an absolutely privileged person, sought after, adulated in the most exclusive circles, and a man who, married to a Bourbon Princess, a woman of eminence, had been able to ensure her happiness, had shewn a devotion to her memory more fervent, more scrupulous than is customary in society, and had thus been as good a husband as a son!

"But are you sure that M. de Charlus has had all those mistresses?" I asked, not, of course, with any diabolical intent of revealing to Robert the secret that I had surprised, but irritated, nevertheless, at hearing him maintain an erroneous theory with so much certainty and assurance. He merely shrugged his shoulders in response to what he took for ingenuousness on my part. "Not that I blame him in the least, I consider that he is perfectly right." And he began to sketch in outline a theory of conduct that would have horrified him at Balbec (where he was not content with denouncing seducers, death seeming to him then the only punishment adequate to their crime). Then, however, he had still been in love and jealous. He went so far as to sing me the praises of houses of assignation: "They're the only places where you can find a shoe to fit you, sheath your weapon, as we say in the regiment." He no longer felt for places of that sort the disgust that had inflamed him at Balbec when I made an allusion to them, and, hearing what he now said, I told him that Bloch had introduced me to one, but Robert replied that the one which Bloch frequented must be "extremely mixed, the poor man's paradise!—It all depends though, where is it?" I remained vague, for I had just remembered that it was the same house at which one used to have for a louis that Rachel whom Robert had so passionately loved. "Anyhow, I can take you to some far better ones, full of stunning women." Hearing me express the desire that he would take me as soon as possible to the ones he knew, which must indeed be far superior to the house to which Bloch had taken me, he expressed a sincere regret that he could not, on this occasion, as he would have to leave Paris next day. "It will have to be my next leave," he said. "You'll see, there are young girls there, even," he added with an air of mystery. "There is a little Mademoiselle de..... I think it's d'Orgeville,. I can let you have the exact name, who is the daughter of quite tip-top people; her mother was by way of being a La Croix-l'Evêque, and they're a really decent family, in fact they're more or less related, if I'm not mistaken, to my aunt Oriane. Anyhow, you have only to see the child, you can tell at once that she comes of decent people (I could detect, hovering for a moment over Robert's voice; the shadow of the genius of the Guermantes, which passed like a cloud, but at a great height and without stopping). "It seems to me to promise marvellous developments. The parents are always ill and can't look after her. Gad, the child must have some amusement, and I count upon you to provide it!" "Oh! When are you coming back?" "I don't know; if you don't absolutely insist upon Duchesses" (Duchess being in aristocracy the only title that denotes a particularly brilliant rank, as the lower orders talk of 'Princesses'), "in a different class of goods, there is that big, fair girl, Mme. Putbus's maid. "She goes with women too, but I don't suppose you mind that, I can tell you frankly, I have never seen such a gorgeous creature." "I imagine her rather Giorgione?" "Wildly Giorgione! Oh, if I only had a little time in Paris, what wonderful things there are to be done! And then, one goes on to the next. For love is all rot, mind you, I've finished with all that." I soon discovered, to my surprise, that he had equally finished with literature, whereas it was merely with regard to literary men that he had struck me as being disillusioned at our last meeting. ("They're practically all a pack of scoundrels," he had said to me, a saying that might be explained by his justified resentment towards certain of Rachel's friends. They had indeed persuaded her that she would never have any talent if she allowed "Robert, scion of an alien race" to acquire an influence over her, and with her used to make fun of him, to his face, at the dinners to which he entertained them.) But in reality Robert's love of Letters was in no sense profound, did not spring from his true nature, was only a by-product of his love of Rachel, and he had got rid of it, at the same time as of his horror of voluptuaries and his religious respect for the virtue of women.

Swann having caught sight of me came over to Saint-Loup and myself. His Jewish gaiety was less refined than his witticisms as a man of the world. "Good evening," he said to us. "Heavens! All three of us together, people will think it is a meeting of the Syndicate. In another minute they'll be looking for the safe!" He had not observed that M. de Monserfeuil was just behind his back and could hear what he said. The General could not help wincing.

"It appears that Loubet is entirely on our side, I have it from an absolutely trustworthy source," Swann informed Saint-Loup, but this time in a lower tone so as not to be overheard by the General. Swann had begun to find his wife's Republican connections more interesting now that the Dreyfus case had become his chief preoccupation. "I tell you this because I know that your heart is with us."

"Not quite to that extent; you are entirely mistaken," was Robert's answer. "It's a bad business, and I'm sorry I ever had a finger in it. It was no affair of mine. If it were to begin over again, I should keep well clear of it. I am a soldier, and my first duty is to support the Army. If you will stay with M. Swann for a moment, I shall be back presently, I must go and talk to my aunt."

I could not bring myself to leave Swann. He had arrived at that stage of exhaustion in which a sick man's body becomes a mere retort in which we study chemical reactions. His face was mottled with tiny spots of Prussian blue, which seemed not to belong to the world of living things, and emitted the sort of odour which at school, after the 'experiments', makes it so unpleasant to have to remain in a science classroom. I asked him whether he had not had a long conversation with the Prince de Guermantes and whether what he had said to the Prince in their conversation in the garden was really what M. de Bréauté (whom I did not name) had reported to us, about a little play by Bergotte. He burst out laughing: "There is not a word of truth in it, not one, it is entirely made up and would have been an utterly stupid thing to say. Really, it is unheard of, this spontaneous generation of falsehood. I do not ask who it was that told you, but it would be really interesting, in a field as limited as this, to work back from one person to another and find out how the story arose. Anyhow; what concern can it be of other people, what the Prince said to me? People are very inquisitive; I have never been inquisitive, except when I was in love, and when I was jealous. And a lot I ever learned! Are you jealous?" I told Swann that I had never experienced jealousy, that I did not even know what it was. "Indeed! I congratulate you. A little jealousy is not at all a bad thing from two points of view. For one thing, because it enables people who are not inquisitive to take an interest in the lives of others, or of one other at any rate. And besides, it makes one feel the pleasure of possession, of getting into a carriage with a woman, of not allowing her to go about by herself. But that occurs only in the very first stages of the disease, or when the cure is almost complete. In the interval, it is the most agonising torment. But, to come back to my conversation with the Prince I shall repeat it to one person only, and that person is going to be yourself."

"Suppose we took a turn in the garden, Sir," I said to Swann. "No," Swann replied, "I am too tired to walk about, let us sit down somewhere in a corner, I cannot remain on my feet any longer." This was true, and yet the act of beginning to talk had already given him back a certain vivacity. "This is word for word," he said to me when we were seated, "my conversation with the Prince, and if you remember what I said to you just now, you will see why I choose you as my confidant. There is another reason as well, which you shall one day learn.

My dear Swann; the Prince de Guermantes said to me, you must forgive me if I have appeared to be avoiding you for some time past. (I had never even noticed it, having been ill and avoiding society myself.) In the first place, I had heard it said that as I fully expected, in the unhappy affair which is splitting the country in two, your views were diametrically opposed to mine. Now, it would have been extremely painful to me to have to hear you express them. So sensitive were my nerves that when the Princess, two years ago, heard her brother-in-law, the Grand Duke of Hesse say that Dreyfus was innocent, she was not content with promptly denying the assertion but refrained from repeating it to me in order not to upset me. About the same time, the Crown Prince of Sweden came to Paris and, having probably heard some one say that the Empress Eugenie was a Dreyfusist, confused her with the Princess (a strange confusion, you will admit, between a woman of the rank of my wife and a Spaniard, a great deal less well born than people make out, and married to a mere Bonaparte), and said to her: Princess, I am doubly glad to meet you, for I know that you hold the same view as myself of the Dreyfus case, which does not surprise me since Your Highness is Bavarian. Which drew down upon the Crown Prince the answer: Sir, I am nothing now but a French Princess, and I share the views of all my fellow countrymen. Now, my dear Swann, about eighteen months ago a conversation I had with General de Beaucerfeuil made me suspect that not an error, but grave illegalities had been committed in the procedure of the trial. Well," the Prince de Guermantes went on to say: "I don't mind telling you that this idea of a possible illegality in the procedure of the trial was extremely painful to me, because I have always, as you know, worshipped the army; I discussed the matter again with the General, and, alas there could be no two ways of looking at it. I don't mind telling you frankly that, all this time, the idea that an innocent man might be undergoing the most degrading punishment had never even entered my mind. But, starting from this idea of illegality, I began to study what I had always declined to read, and then the possibility not this time of illegal procedure, but of the prisoner's innocence began to haunt me. I did not feel that I could talk about it to the Princess. Heaven knows that she has become just as French as myself. You may say what you like, from the day of our marriage, I took such pride in showing her our country in all its beauty, and what to me is the most splendid thing in it, our Army, that it would have been too painful to me to tell her of my suspicions, which involved, it is true, a few officers only. But I come of a family of soldiers, I did not like to think that officers could be mistaken. I discussed the case again with Beaucerfeuil, he admitted that there had been culpable intrigues, that the *bordereau* was possibly not in Dreyfus's writing, but that an overwhelming proof of his guilt did exist. This was the Henry document. And, a few days later, we learned that it was a forgery. After that, without letting the Princess see me, I began to read the *Siècle* and the *Aurore* every day; soon I had no doubt left, it kept me awake all night. I confided my distress to our friend, the abbé Poiré, who, I was astonished to find, held the same conviction, and I got him to say masses for the intention of Dreyfus, his unfortunate wife and their children. Meanwhile, one morning as I was going to the Princess's room, I saw her maid trying to hide something: from me that she had in her hand. I asked her, chaffingly, what it was, she blushed and refused to tell me. I had the fullest confidence in my wife, but this incident disturbed me considerably (and the Princess too, no doubt, who must have heard of it from her woman), for my dear Marie barely uttered a word to me that day at luncheon. I asked the abbé Poiré whether he could say my mass for Dreyfus on the following morning. And so much for that!" exclaimed Swann, breaking off his narrative. I looked up, and saw the Duc de Guermantes bearing down upon us. "Forgive me for interrupting you boys. My lad;" he went on, addressing myself, "I am instructed to give you a message from Oriane. Marie and Gilbert have asked her to stay and have supper at their table with only five or six other people: the Princess of Hesse, Mme. de Ligné, Mme de Tarente, Mme. de Chevreuse, the Duchesse d'Arènberg. Unfortunateiy, we can't wait, we are going on to a little ball of sorts."

I was listening, but whenever we have something definite to do at a given moment, we depute a certain person who is accustomed to that sort of duty to keep an eye on the clock and warn us in time. This indwelling servant reminded me, as I had asked him to remind me a few hours before, that Albertine, who at the moment was far from my thoughts, was to come and see me immediately after the theatre, so I declined the invitation to supper.

"At last we are alone" said Swann, when the Duke left us; "I quite forget where I was. Oh yes, I had just told you, hadn't I, that the Prince asked the abbé Poiré if he could say his mass next day for Dreyfus. No, the abbé informed me ('I say *me* to you," Swann explained to me, "because it is the Prince who is speaking, you understand?), for I have another mass that I have been asked to say for him to-morrow as well— What, I said to him, is there another Catholic as well as myself who is convinced of his innocence?—It appears so.—But this other supporter's conviction must be of more recent growth than mine.—Maybe, but this other was making me say masses when you still believed Dreyfus guilty.—Ah, I can see that it is not anyone in our world.—On the contrary!—Indeed! There are Dreyfusists among us, are there? You intrigue me; I should like to unbosom myself to this rare bird, if I know him.— You do know him.—His name?—The Princesse de Guermantes. 'While I was afraid of shocking the Nationalist opinions, the French faith of my dear wife, she had been afraid of alarming my religious opinions, my patriotic sentiments.   But privately she had been thinking as I did, though for longer than I had. And what her maid had been hiding as she went into her room, what she went out to buy for her every morning, was the *Aurore*. My dear Swann, from that moment I thought of the pleasure that I should give you when I told you how closely akin my views upon this matter were to yours; forgive me for not having done so sooner. If you bear in mind that I had never said a word to the

Princess, it will not surprise you to be told that thinking the same as yourself must at that time have kept me farther apart from you than thinking differently. For it was an extremely painful topic for me to approach. The more I believe that an error, that crimes even, have been committed; the more my heart bleeds for the Army. It had never occurred to me that opinions like mine could possibly cause you similar pain, until I was told the other day that you were emphatically protesting against the insults to the Army and against the Dreyfusists for consenting to ally themselves with those who insulted it. That settled it, I admit that it has been most painful for me to confess to you what I think of certain officers, few in number fortunately, but it is a relief to me not to have to keep at arms length from you any longer, and especially that you should quite understand that if I was able to entertain other sentiments, it was because I had not a shadow, of doubt as to the soundness of the verdict. As soon as my doubts began, I could wish, for only one thing, that the mistake should be rectified.

I must tell you that this speech of the Prince de Guermantes moved me profoundly. If you knew him as I do, if you could realise the distance he has had to traverse in order to reach his present position, you would admire him as he deserves. Not that his opinion surprises me; his is such a straightforward nature.

Swann now found equally intelligent anybody who was of his opinion, his old friend the Prince de Guermantes and my schoolfellow Bloch, whom previously he had avoided and whom he now invited to luncheon. Swann interested Bloch greatly by telling him that the Prince de Guermantes was a Dreyfusard. "We must ask him to sign our appeal for Picquart; a name like his would have a tremendous effect." But Swann, blending with his ardent conviction as an Israelite the diplomatic moderation of a man of the world, whose habits he had too thoroughly acquired to be able to shed them at this late hour, refused to allow Bloch to send the Prince a circular to sign; even on his own initiative. "He cannot do such a thing, we must not expect the impossible," Swann repeated. "There you have a charming man who has travelled thousands of miles to come over to our side. He can be very useful to us. If he were to sign your list, be would simply be compromising himself with his own people, would be made to suffer on our account, might even repent of his confidences and not confide in us again." Nor was this all, Swann refused his own signature. He felt that his name was too Hebraic not to create a bad effect. Besides, even if he approved of all the attempts to secure a fresh trial, he did not wish to be mixed up in any way in the antimilitarist campaign. He wore, a thing he had never done previously, the decoration he had won as a young militiaman in '70 and added a codicil to his will asking that, contrary to his previous dispositions, he might be buried with the military honours due to his rank as Chevalier of the Legion of Honour. A request which assembled round the church of Combray a whole squadron of those troopers over whose fate Françoise used to weep in days gone by, when she envisaged the prospect of a war. In short, Swann refused to sign Bloch's circular, with the result that, if he passed in the eyes of many people as a fanatical Dreyfusard, my friend found him lukewarm, infected with Nationalism, and a militarist.

Swann left me without shaking hands so as not to be forced into a general leave-taking in this room which swarmed with his friends, but said to me: "You ought to come and see your friend Gilberte. She has really grown up now and altered, you would not know her. She would be so pleased!" I was no longer in love with Gilberte. She was for me like a dead person for whom one has long mourned, then forgetfulness has come, and if she were to be resuscitated, she could no longer find any place in a life which has ceased to be fashioned for her. I had no desire now to see her, not even that desire to show her that I did not wish to see her which, every day, when I was in love with her, I vowed to myself that I would flaunt before her, when I should be in love with her no longer.

And so, seeking now only to give myself, in Gilberte's eyes, the air of having longed with all my heart to meet her again and of having been prevented by circumstances of the kind called 'beyond our control' albeit they only occur, with any certainty at least, when we have done nothing to prevent them; so, far from accepting Swann's invitation with reserve, I would not let him go until he had promised to explain in detail to his daughter the mischances that had prevented and would continue to prevent me from going to see her. "Anyhow, I am going to write to her as soon as I go home," I added. "But be sure you tell her it will be a threatening letter, for in a month or two I shall be quite free, and then let her tremble, for I shall be coming to your house as regularly as in the old days."

Before parting from Swann, I said a word to him about his health. "No, it is not as bad as all that," he told me. "Still, as I was saying, I am quite worn out, and I accept with resignation whatever may be in store for me. Only I must say that it would be most annoying to die before the end of the Dreyfus case. Those scoundrels have more than one card up their sleeves. I have no doubt of their being defeated in the end, but still they are very powerful, they have supporters everywhere. Just as everything is going on splendidly, it all collapses. I should like to live long enough to see Dreyfus rehabilitated and Picquart a colonel."

I went to bid the Princesse de Guermantes good night, for her cousins who had promised to take me home, were in a hurry to be gone. M. de Guermantes wished, however, to say goodbye to his brother. At the moment when we were saying good-bye to the Princess he was attempting, without actually thanking M. de Charlus, to give expression to his fondness for him, whether because he really found a difficulty in controlling it or in order that the Baron might remember that actions of the sort that he had performed this evening did not escape the eyes of a brother, just as, with the object of creating a chain of pleasant associations in the future, we give sugar to a dog that has done its trick. "Well, little brother!" said the Duke, stopping M. de Charlus and taking him lovingly by the arm, "so this is how one walks past one's elders and betters without so much as a word. I never see you now, Mémé, and you can't think how I miss you. I was turning over some old letters just now and came upon some from poor Mamma, which are all so full of love for you." "Thank you, Basin," replied M. de Charlus in a broken voice, for he could never speak without emotion of their mother. "You must make up your mind to let me fix up bachelor quarters for you at Guermantes," the Duke went on. " It is nice to see the two brothers so affectionate towards each other," the Princess said to Oriane. "Yes, indeed! I don't suppose you could find many brothers like that. I shall invite you to meet him," she promised me. "You've not quarrelled with him........?

But what can they be talking about?" she added in an anxious tone, for she could catch only an occasional word of what they were saying. She had always felt a certain jealousy of the pleasure that M. de Guermantes found in talking to his brother of a past from which he was inclined to keep his wife shut out. She felt that, when they were happy at being together like this, and she, unable to restrain her impatient curiosity, came and joined them, her coming did not add to their pleasure. "Come along, Basin; good night, Palamède," said the Duchess, who, devoured by rage and curiosity could endure no more, "if you have made up your minds to spend the night here, we might just as well have stayed to supper. You have been keeping Marie and me standing for the last half-hour." The Duke parted from his brother after a significant pressure of his hand, and the three of us began to descend the immense staircase of the Princess's house.

On our homeward drive, in the confined space of the coupé, the red shoes were of necessity very close to mine, and Mme. de Guermantes, fearing that she might actually have touched me, said to the Duke: "This young man will have to say to me, like the person in the caricature: "Madame, tell me at once that you love me, but don't tread on my feet like that." My thoughts however, were far from Mme. de Guermantes. Ever since Saint-Loup had spoken to me of a young girl of good family who frequented a house of ill-fame, and of the Baroness Putbus's maid, it was in these two persons that were coalesced and embodied the desires inspired in me day by day by countless beauties of two classes, on the one hand the plebeian and magnificent, the majestic lady's maids of great houses, swollen with pride and saying "we" when they spoke of Duchesses, on the other hand those girls of whom it was enough for me sometimes, without even having seen them go past in carriages or on foot, to have read the names in the account of a ball for me to fall in love with them and, having conscientiously searched the year-book for the country houses in which they spent the summer (as often as not letting myself be led astray by a similarity of names), to dream alternately of going to live amid the plains of the West, the sandhills of the North, the pine-forests of the South. In the whole universe I desired only two women, of whose faces I could not, it is true, form any picture, but whose names Saint-Loup had told me and had guaranteed their consent. So that, if he had, by what he had said this evening, set my imagination a heavy task, he had at the same time procured an appreciable relaxation, a prolonged rest for my will.

"Well" said the Duchess to me, "apart from your balls, can't I be of any use to you? Have you found a house where you would like me to introduce you?" I replied that I was afraid the only one that tempted me was hardly fashionable enough for her. "Whose is that?" she asked in a hoarse and menacing voice, scarcely opening her lips." "Baroness Putbus." This time she pretended to be really angry. "No, not that! I believe you're trying to make a fool of me. I don't even know how I come to have heard the creature's name. But she is the dregs of society. It's just as though you were to ask me for an introduction to my milliner. And worse than that, for my milliner is charming. You are a little bit cracked, my poor boy. In any case, I beg that you will be polite to the people to whom I have introduced you, leave cards on them, and go and see them, and not talk to them about Baroness Putbus of whom they have never heard."

"You won't come with us to the ball?" the Duke asked me, "I can lend you a Venetian cloak and I know some one who will be damned glad to see you there—Oriane for one, that I needn't say, but the

Princesse de Parme. She's never tired of singing your praises, and swears by you alone. It's fortunate for you—since she is a trifle mature—that she is the model of virtue. Otherwise she would certainly have chosen you as a sigisbee, as it was called in my young days, a sort of cavaliere servente."

I was interested not in the ball but in my appointment with Albertine. And so I refused. The carriage had stopped, the footman was shouting for the gate to be opened, the horses pawing the ground until it was flung apart and the carriage passed into the courtyard. "Till we meet again," said the Duke. "I have sometimes regretted living so close to Marie," the Duchess said to me, "because I may be very fond of her, but I am not quite so fond of her company." But I have never regretted it so much as to-night, since it has allowed me so little of yours." "Come, Oriane, no speechmaking." The Duchess would have liked me to come inside for a minute. She laughed heartily, as did the Duke, when I said that I could not because I was expecting a girl to call at any moment. "You choose a funny time to receive visitors," she said to me.

"Come along, my child, there is no time to waste," said M. de Guermantes to his wife. "It is a quarter to twelve, and time we were dressed....." He came in collision, outside his front door which they were grimly guarding, with the two ladies of the walking-sticks, who had not been afraid to descend at dead of night from their mountain-top to prevent a scandal. "Basin, we felt we must warn you in case you were seen at that ball: poor Amanien has just passed away, an hour ago." The Duke felt a momentary alarm. He saw the delights of the famous ball snatched from him as soon as these accursed mountaineers had informed him of the death of M. d'Osmond. But he quickly recovered himself and flung at his cousins a retort into which he introduced, with his determination not to forego a pleasure, his incapacity to assimilate exactly the niceties of the French language: "He is dead! No, no, they exaggerate, they exaggerate!" And without, giving a further thought to his two relatives who, armed with their alpenstocks, were preparing to make their nocturnal ascent, he fired off a string of questions at his valet: "Are you sure my helmet has come?" "Yes, Monsieur le Duc." "You're sure there's a hole in it I can breathe through? I don't want, to be suffocated, damn it!" "Yes, Monsieur le Duc." "Oh, thunder of heaven, this is an unlucky evening. Oriane, I forgot to ask Babal whether the shoes with pointed toes were for you!" "But, my dear, the dresser from the Opéra-Comique is here, he will tell us. I don't see how they could go with your spurs." "Let us go and find the dresser," said the Duke. "Good-bye, my boy, I should ask you to come in while we are trying on, it would amuse you. But we should only waste time talking, it is nearly midnight and we must not be late in getting there or we shall spoil the set."

I too was in a hurry to get away from M. and Mme. de Guermantes as quickly as possible. *Phèdre* finished at about half past eleven. Albertine must have arrived by now. I went straight to Françoise: "Is Mlle. Albertine in the house?" "No one has called." Good God, that meant that no one would call! I was in torment, Albertine's visit seeming to me now all the more desirable, the less certain it had become.

Since, whenever the outer gate opened, the doorkeeper pressed an electric button which lighted the stairs, and since all the occupants of the building had already come in, I left the kitchen immediately and went to sit down in the hall, keeping watch, at a point where the curtains did not quite meet over the glass panel of the outer door, leaving visible, a vertica1 strip of semi-darkness, on the stair. If, all of a sudden this strip turned to a golden yellow, that would mean that Albertine had just entered the building and would be with me in a minute; nobody else could be coming at that time of night. And I sat there, unable to take my eyes from the strip which persisted in remaining dark; I bent my whole body forward to make certain of noticing any change; but gaze as I might, the vertical black band, despite my impassioned longing, did not give me the intoxicating delight that I should have felt had I seen it changed by a sudden and, significant magic to a luminous bar of gold. This was a great fuss to make about that Albertine to whom I had not given three minutes thought during the Guermantes party!

To make my room look a little brighter, in case Albertine should still come, and because it was one of the prettiest things that I possessed, I set out, for the first time for years, on the table by my bed, the turquoise-studded cover, which Gilberte had had made for me to hold Bergotte's pamphlet, and which, for so long a time, I had insisted on keeping by me while I slept, with the agate marble. Besides, as much perhaps as Albertine herself who still did not come, her presence at that moment in an 'alibi' which she had evidently found more attractive and of which I knew nothing, gave me a painful feeling which, in spite of what I had said, barely an hour before to Swann, as to my incapacity for being jealous, might, if I had seen my friend at less protracted intervals, have changed into an anxious need to know where, with whom, she was spending her time. I dared not send round to Albertine's house, it was too late, but in the hope that having supper perhaps with some other girls in a café she might take it into her head to telephone to me, I turned the switch and, restoring the connection to my own room, cut it off between the post office and the porter's lodge to which it was generally switched at that hour. A receiver in the little passage on which Françoise's room opened would have been simpler, less inconvenient, but useless. The advance of civilisation enables each of us to display unsuspected merits or fresh defects which make him, dearer or more insupportable to his friends. Thus Dr. Bell's invention had enabled Françoise to acquire an additional defect, which was that of refusing, however important, however urgent the occasion might be, to make use of the telephone. She would manage to disappear whenever anybody was going to teach her how to use it, as people disappear when it is time for them to be vaccinated. And the telephone was installed in my bedroom, and that it might not disturb my parents, a rattle had been substituted for the bell.

I was tortured by the incessant recurrence of my longing, ever more anxious and never to be gratified, for the sound of a call; arrived at the culminating point of a tortuous ascent through the coils of my lonely anguish, from the heart of the populous, nocturnal Paris that had suddenly come close to me, there beside my bookcase, I heard all at once, mechanical and sublime, like, in *Tristan*, the fluttering veil or the shepherd's pipe, the purr of the telephone. I sprang to the instrument, it was Albertine.

"I'm not disturbing you, ringing you up at this hour?" "Not at all" I said, restraining my joy, for her remark about the lateness of the hour was doubtless meant as an apology for coming, in a moment, so late, and did not mean that she was not coming. "Are you coming round?" I asked in a tone of indifference. "Why, no, unless you absolutely must see me." Part of me which the other part sought to join was in Albertine. It was essential that she came, but I did not tell her so at first; now that we were in communication, I said to myself that I could always oblige her at the last moment either to come to me or to let me hasten to her. "Yes, I am near home," she said, "and miles away from you; I hadn't read your note properly. I have just found it again and was afraid you might be waiting up for me." I felt sure that she was lying, and it was now, in my fury, from a desire not so much to see her as to upset her plans that I determined to make her come. But I felt it better to refuse at first what in a few moments I should try to obtain from her. But where was she? With the sound of her voice were blended other sounds: the braying of a bicyclist's horn, a woman's voice singing, a brass band in the distance rang out as distinctly, as the beloved voice, as though to show me that it was indeed Albertine in her actual surroundings who was beside me at that moment, like a clod of earth with which we have carried away all the grass that was growing from it. The same sounds that I heard were striking her ear also, and were distracting her attention: details of truth, extraneous to the subject under discussion, valueless in themselves, all the more necessary to our perception of the miracle for what it was; elements sober and charming, descriptive of some street in Paris, elements heartrending also and cruel of some unknown festivity which, after she came away from *Phèdre,* had prevented Albertine from coming to me. "I must warn you first of all that I don't in the least want you to come, because, at this time of night, it will be a frightful nuisance......." I said to her, "I'm dropping with sleep. Besides, oh, well, There are endless complications. I am bound to say that there was no possibility of your misunderstanding my letter. You answered that it was all right. Very well, if you hadn't understood, what did you mean by that?" "I said it was all right, only I couldn't quite remember what we had arranged. But I see you're cross with me, I'm sorry. I wish now I'd never gone to *Phèdre.* If I'd known there was going to be all this fuss about it......." she went on, as people invariably do when, being in the wrong over one thing, they pretend to suppose that they are being blamed for another. "I am not in the least annoyed about *Phèdre,* seeing it was I that asked you to go to it." "Then you are angry with me; it's a nuisance it's so late now, otherwise I. should have come to you, but I shall call tomorrow or the day after and make it up." " Oh, please; Albertine, I beg of you not to; after making me waste an entire evening, the least you can do is to leave me in peace for the next few days. I shan't be free for a fortnight or three weeks. Listen, if it worries you to think that we seem to be parting in anger and perhaps, you are right after all, then I greatly prefer, all things considered, since I have been waiting for you all this time and you have not gone home yet, that you should come at once. I shall take a cup of coffee to keep myself awake." "Couldn't you possibly put it off till to-morrow?' Because, the trouble is......"

"No;" I replied, "I told you a moment ago that I should not be free for the next three weeks—no more to-morrow than any other day." "Very well, in that case I shall come this very instant...... it's a nuisance, because I am at a friend's house, and she......." I saw that she had not believed that I would accept her offer to come, which therefore was not sincere, and I decided to force her hand. "What do you suppose I care about your friend, either come or don't, it's for you to decide, it wasn't I that asked you to come, it was you who suggested it to me." "Don't be angry with me, I am going to jump into a cab now and shall be with you in ten minutes."

I no longer asked myself what could have made Albertine late, and when Françoise came into my room to inform me: "Mademoiselle Albertine is here," if I answered without even turning my head, it was only to conceal my emotion: "What in the world makes Mademoiselle Albertine come at this time of night!" But then, raising my eyes to look at Françoise, as though curious to hear her answer which must corroborate the apparent sincerity of my question, I perceived, with admiration and wrath, that, capable of rivalling Berma herself in the art of endowing with speech inanimate garments and the lines of her face, Françoise had taught their part to her bodice, her hair—the whitest threads of which had been brought to the surface, were displayed there like a birth-certificate—her neck bowed by weariness and obedience. They commiserated her for having been dragged from her sleep and from her warm bed, in the middle of the night, at her age, obliged to bundle into her clothes in haste, at the risk of catching pneumonia. And so, afraid that I might have seemed to be apologising for Albertine's late arrival: "Anyhow, I'm very glad she has come, it's just what I wanted," and I gave free vent to my profound joy. It did not long remain unclouded, when I had heard Françoise's reply. Without uttering a word of complaint, seeming indeed to be doing her best to stifle an irrepressible cough, and simply folding her shawl over her bosom as though she were feeling cold, she began by telling me everything that she had said to Albertine, whom she had not forgotten to ask after her aunt's health. "I was just saying, Monsieur must have been afraid that Mademoiselle was not coming, because this is no time to pay visits, it's nearly morning. But she must have been in some place where she was enjoying herself, because she never even said as much as that she was sorry she had kept Monsieur waiting, she answered me with a devil may care look, "Better late than never!"

I pretended that I was obliged to write a letter: "To whom were you writing?" Albertine asked me as she entered the room. "To a pretty little friend of mine, Gilberte Swann. Don't you know her?" "No." I decided not to question Albertine as to how she had spent the evening, I felt that I should only find fault with her and that we should not have any time left, seeing how late it was already, to be reconciled sufficiently to pass to kisses and caresses. And so it was with these that I chose to begin from the first moment. Besides, if I was a little calmer, I was not feeling happy. The loss of all orientation, of all sense of direction that we feel when we are kept waiting, still continues, after the coming of the person awaited, and taking the place, inside us, of the calm spirit in which we were picturing her coming as so great a pleasure, prevents us from deriving any from it. Albertine was in the room: my unstrung nerves, continuing to flutter, were still expecting her. "I want a nice kiss, Albertine." "As many as you like," she said to me in her kindest manner. I had never seen her looking so pretty. "Another?" "Why, you know it's a great, great pleasure to me." "And a thousand times greater to me," she replied. "Oh! What a pretty book cover you have there" "Take it, I give it to you as a keepsake." "You are too kind......" People would be cured for ever of romanticism if they could make up their minds, in thinking of the girl they love, to try to be the man they will be when they are no longer in love with her. Gilberte's bookcover, her agate marble, must have derived their importance in the past from some purely inward distinction, since now they were to me a book cover, a marble like any others.

I asked Albertine if she would like something to drink. "I seem to see oranges over there and water," she said. "That will be perfect." I was thus able to taste with her kisses that refreshing coolness which had seemed to me to be better than they, at the Princesse de Guermantes's. And the orange squeezed into the water seemed to yield to me, as I drank, the secret life of its ripening growth, its beneficent action upon certain states of that human body which belongs to so different a kingdom, its powerlessness to make that body live, but on the other hand the process of irrigation by which it was able to benefit it, a hundred mysteries concealed by the fruit from my senses, but not from my intellect.

When Albertine had gone, I remembered that I had promised Swann that I would write to Gilberte, and courtesy I felt, demanded that I should do so at once. It was without emotion and as though drawing a line at the foot of a boring school essay that I traced upon the envelope the name *Gilberte Swann,* with which at one time I used to cover my exercise-books to give myself the illusion that I was corresponding with her. For if, in the past, it had been I who wrote that name, now the task had been deputed by Habit to one of the many secretaries whom she employs. He could write down Gilberte's name with all the more calm, in that, placed with me only recently by Habit, having but recently entered my service, he had never known Gilberte, and knew only, without attaching any reality to the words, because he had heard me speak of her, that she was a girl with whom I had once been in love.

There appeared about this time a phenomenon which deserves mention only because it recurs in every important period of history. At the same moment when I was writing to Gilberte, M. de Guermantes, just home from his ball, still wearing his helmet, was thinking that next day he would be compelled to go into formal mourning and decided to proceed a week earlier to the cure that he had been ordered to take. When he returned from it three weeks later (to anticipate for a moment, since I am still finishing my letter to Gilberte), those friends of the Duke who had seen him, so indifferent at the start, turn into a raving anti-Dreyfusard, were left speechless with amazement when they heard him (as though the action of the cure had not been confined to his bladder), answer: "Oh, well, there'll be a fresh trial and he'll be acquitted; you can't sentence a fellow without any evidence against him. Did you ever see anyone so gaga as Froberville? An officer, leading the French people to the shambles, heading straight for war. Strange times we live in." The fact was that in the interval, the Duke had met, at the spa, three charming ladies (an Italian princess and her two sisters-in-law). After hearing them make a few remarks about the books they were reading, a play that was being given at the Casino, the Duke had at once understood that he was dealing with women of superior intellect, by whom, as he expressed it, he would be knocked out in the first round. He was all the more delighted to be asked to play bridge by the Princess. But, the moment he entered her sitting room, as he began, in the fervour of his double dyed anti-Dreyfusism: "Well, we don't hear very much more of the famous Dreyfus and his appeal," his stupefaction had been great when he heard the Princess and her sisters-in-law say: "It's becoming more certain every day. They can't keep a man in prison who has done nothing." "Eh? Eh?" the Duke had gasped at first, as at the discovery of a fantastic nickname employed in this household to turn to ridicule a person whom he had always regarded as intelligent. But, after a few days, as, from cowardice and the spirit of imitation, we shout "Hallo, Jojotte," without knowing why, at a great artist whom we hear so addressed by the rest of the household, the Duke, still greatly embarrassed by the novelty of this attitude, began nevertheless to say: "After all, if there is no evidence against him." The three charming ladies decided that he was not progressing rapidly enough and began to bully him: "But really, nobody with a grain of intelligence can ever have believed for a moment that there was anything." Whenever any revelation came out that was 'damning' to Dreyfus, and the Duke, supposing that now he was going to convert the three charming ladies, came to inform them of it, they burst out laughing and had no difficulty in proving to him, with great dialectic subtlety, that his argument was worthless and quite absurd. The Duke had returned to Paris a frantic Dreyfusard.

I have no time left now, before my departure for Balbec (where to my sorrow I am going to make a second stay which will also be my last), to start upon a series of pictures of society which will find their place in due course. I need here say only that to this first erroneous reason (my relatively frivolous existence which made people suppose that I was fond of society) for my letter to Gilberte, and for that reconciliation with the Swann family to which it, seemed to point, Odette might very well, and with equal inaccuracy, have added a second.

Mme. Swann's drawing-room was crystallised round a man, a dying man, who had almost in an instant passed, at the moment when his talent was exhausted, from obscurity to a blaze of glory. The passion for Bergotte's works was unbounded. He spent the whole day, on show, at Mme. Swann's, who would whisper to some influential man: "I shall say a word to him, he will write an article for you." He was, for that matter, quite capable of doing so and even of writing a little play for Mme. Swann. A stage nearer to death, he was not quite so feeble as at the time when he used to come and inquire after my grandmother. This was because intense physical suffering had enforced a regime on him. Illness is the doctor to whom we pay most heed: to kindness, to knowledge we make promises only; pain we obey.

Mme d'Epinoy, when busy collecting some subscription for the 'Patrie Française', having been obliged to go and see Odette, as she would have gone to her dressmaker, convinced moreover that she would find only a lot of faces that were not so much impossible as completely unknown, stood rooted to the ground when the door opened not upon the drawing-room she imagined but upon a magic ball in which, as in the transformation scene of a pantomime, she recognised in the dazzling chorus, half reclining upon divans, seated in armchairs, addressing their hostess by her Christian name, the royalties, the duchesses, whom she, the Princesse d'Epinoy, had the greatest difficulty in enticing into her own drawing-room, and to whom at that moment, beneath the benevolent eyes of Odette, the Marquis du Lau, Comte Louis de Turenne, Prince Borghese, the Duc d'Estrées, carrying orangeade and cakes were acting as cupbearers and henchmen! The Princesse d'Epinoy, as she instinctively made people's social value inherent in themselves, was obliged to disincarnate Mme. Swann and reincarnate her in a fashionable woman. Our ignorance of the real existence led by the women who do not advertise it in the newspapers draws thus over certain situations (thereby helping to differentiate one house from another) a veil of mystery. In Odette's case, at the start, a few men of the highest society, anxious to meet Bergotte, had gone to dine, quite quietly, at her house. She had had the, tact, recently acquired, not to advertise their presence, they found when they went there, a memory perhaps of the little nucleus, whose traditions Odette had preserved in spite of the schism, a place laid for them at table, and so forth. Odette took them with Bergotte, whom these excursions incidentally finished off, to interesting first nights. They spoke of her to various women of their own world who were capable of taking an interest in such a novelty. These women were convinced that Odette, an intimate friend of Bergotte, had more or less collaborated in his works, and believed her to be a thousand times more intelligent than the most outstanding women of the Faubourg.

This change in Odette's status was carried out, so far as she was concerned, with a discretion that made it more secure and more rapid but allowed no suspicion to filter through to the public that is prone to refer to the social columns of the *Gaulois* for evidence, as to the advance or decline of a house, with the result that one day, at the dress rehearsal of a play by Bergotte, given in one of the most fashionable theatres in aid of a charity, the really dramatic moment was when people saw enter the box opposite, which was that reserved for the author, and sit down by the side of Mme. Swann, Mme. de Marsantes and her who, by the gradual selfeffacement of the Duchesse de Guermantes (glutted with fame, and retiring to save the trouble of going on), was on the way to becoming the lion, the queen of the age, Comtesse Molé. "We never even supposed that she had begun to climb," people said of Odette as they saw Comtesse Molé enter her box, "and look, she has reached the top of the ladder."

So Mme. Swann might suppose that it was from snobbishness that I was taking up again with her daughter.

Odette, notwithstanding her brilliant escort, listened with close attention to the play, as though she had come there solely to see it performed, just as in the past she used to walk across the Bois for her health, as a form of exercise. Men who in the past had shown less interest in her came to the edge of the box, disturbing the whole audience, to reach up to her hand and so approach the imposing circle that surrounded her. She, with a smile that was still more friendly than ironical, replied patiently to their questions, affecting greater calm than might have been expected, a calm which was perhaps sincere; this exhibition being only the belated revelation of a habitual and discreetly hidden intimacy. Behind these three ladies to whom every eye was drawn was Bergotte flanked by the Prince d'Agrigente, Comte Louis de

Turenne and the Marquis de Bréauté

And it is easy to understand that to men who were received everywhere and could not expect any further advancement save as a reward for original research, this demonstration of their merit which they considered that they were making in letting themselves succumb to a hostess with a reputation for profound intellectuality, in whose house they expected to meet all the dramatists and novelists of the day, was more exciting, more lively than those evenings at the Princesse de Guermantes's, which, without any change of programme or fresh attraction, had been going on year after year, all more or less like the one we have described, in such detail. In that exalted sphere, the sphere of the Guermantes, in which people were beginning to lose interest, the latest intellectual fashions were not incarnate in entertainments fashioned in their image, as in those sketches that Bergotte used to write for Mme. Swann, or those positive committees of public safety (had society been capable of taking an interest in the Dreyfus case) at which, in Mme. Verdurin's drawing-room, used to assemble Picquart,. Clemenceau, Zola, Reinach and Labori.

Gilberte, too helped to strengthen her mother's position, for an uncle of Swann had just left nearly twenty-four million francs to the girl, which meant that the Faubourg Saint-Germain was beginning to take notice of her. The reverse of the medal was that Swann (who..however,was dying) held Dreyfusard opinions; though this as a matter of fact did not 'injure' his wife, but was actually of service to her. It did not injure her because people said: "He is dotty, his mind has quite gone, nobody pays any attention to him, his wife is the only person who counts and she is charming. But even Swann's Dreyfusism was useful to Odette. Left to herself, she would quite possibly have allowed herself to make advances to fashionable women which would have been her undoing. Whereas on the evenings when she dragged her husband out to dine in the Faubourg Saint Germain, Swann, sitting sullenly in his corner, would not hesitate, if he saw Odette seeking an introduction to some Nationalist lady, to exclaim aloud: "Really, Odette, you are mad. Why can't you keep yourself to yourself. It is idiotic of you to get yourself introduced to anti-semites. I forbid you." People in society whom everyone else runs after are not accustomed either to such pride or to such ill—breeding. For the first time they beheld some one who thought himself 'superior' to them. The fame of Swann's mutterings was spread abroad, and cards with turned-down corners rained upon Odette.

The Heart's Intermissions

My second arrival at Balbec was very different from the other. The manager had come in person to meet me at Pont-à-Couleuvre, reiterating how greatly he valued his titled patrons, which made me afraid that he had ennobled me, until I realised that, in the obscurity of his grammatical memory, *titré* meant simply *attitré,* or accredited. In fact, the more new languages he learned the worse he spoke the others. He informed he that he had placed me at the very top of the hotel. "I hope," he said, "that you will not interpolate this as a want of discourtesy, I was sorry to give you a room of which you are unworthy, but I did it in connection with the noise, because in that room you will not have anyone above your head, to disturb your trepanum" (tympanum). "Don't be alarmed, I shall have the windows closed, so that they shan't bang. Upon that point, I am intolerable" (the last word expressing not his own thought, which was that he would always be found inexorable in that respect, but, quite possibly, the thoughts of his underlings). The rooms were, as it proved, those we had had before. They were no humbler, but I had risen in the manager's esteem, I could light a fire if I liked (for, by the doctor's orders, I had left Paris, at Easter), but he was afraid there might be 'fixtures' in the ceiling. "See that you always wait before alighting a fire until the preceding one is extenuated" (extinct). "The important thing is to take care not to avoid setting fire to the chimney, especially as to cheer things up a bit, I have put an old china pottage on the mantelpiece which might become insured."

The desires that had led me forth to Balbec sprang to some extent from my discovery that the Verdurins (whose invitations I had invariably declined; and who would certainly be delighted to see me, if I went to call upon them in the country with apologies for never having been able to call upon them in Paris), knowing that several of the faithful would be spending the holidays upon that part of the coast, and having, for that reason, taken for the whole season one of M. de Cambremer's houses (La Raspelière), had invited Mme. Putbus to stay with them. The evening on which I learned this (in Paris) I lost my head completely and sent our young footman to find out whether the lady would be taking her Abigail to Balbec with her. It was eleven o'clock. Her porter was a long time in opening the front door, and for a wonder, did not send my messenger packing, did not call the police, merely gave him a dressing down, but with it the information that I desired. He said that the head lady's maid would indeed be accompanying her mistress, first of all to the waters in Germany, then to Biarritz, and at the end of the season to Mme. Verdurin's: From that moment my mind had been at rest, and glad to have this iron in the fire. I had been able to dispense with those pursuits in the streets, in which I had not that letter of introduction to the beauties I encountered which I should have to the 'Giorgione' in the fact of my having dined that very evening, at the Verdurins', with her mistress. Besides, she might form a still better opinion of me perhaps when she learned that I knew not merely the middle class tenants of Là Raspelière but its owners, and above all Saint-Loup who, prevented from commending me personally to the maid (who did not know him by name), had written an enthusiastic letter about me to the Cambremers. He believed that, quite apart from any service that they might be able to render me, Mme. de Cambremer, the Legrandin daughter-in-law, would interest me by her conversation. "She is an intelligent woman," he had assured me. "She won't say anything final" (*final* having taken the place of *sublime things* with Robert, who, every five or six years, would modify a few of his favourite expressions, while preserving the more important intact), "but it is an interesting nature, she has a personality, intuition; she has the right word for everything. Every now and then she is maddening, she says stupid things on purpose, to seem smart, which is all the more ridiculous as nobody could be less smart than the Cambremers, she is not always in the picture, but, taking her all round, she is one of the people it is more or less possible to talk to."

No sooner had Robert's letter of introduction reached them than the Cambremers, whether from a snobbishness that made them anxious to oblige Saint-Loup, even indirectly, or from gratitude for what he had done for one of their nephews at Doncières, or (what was most likely) from kindness of heart and traditions of hospitality, had written long letters insisting that I should stay with them, or, if I preferred to be more independent, offering to find me lodgings. When Saint-Loup had pointed out that I should be staying at the Grand Hotel, Balbec, they replied that at least they would expect a call from me as soon as I arrived and if I did not appear, would come without fail to hunt me out and invite me to their garden parties.

It was true that Mme. Putbus was not to be at the Verdurins' so early in the season; but these pleasures which we have chosen beforehand may be remote, if their coming is assured, and if, in the interval of waiting, we can devote ourselves to the pastime of seeking to attract, while powerless to love. Moreover, I was not going to Balbec in the same practical frame of mind as before; there is always less egoism in pure imagination than in recollection; and I knew that I was going to find myself in one of those very places where fair strangers most abound; a beach presents them as numerously as a ballroom, and I looked forward to strolling up and down outside the hotel, on the front, with the same sort of pleasure that Mme. de Guermantes would have procured me if, instead of making other hostesses invite me to brilliant dinner-parties, she had given my name more frequenty for their lists of partners to those of them who gave dances. To make female acquaintances at Balbec would be as easy for me now as it had been difficult before, for I was now as well supplied with friends and resources there as I had been destitute of them on my former visit.

Complete physical collapse. On the first night, as I was suffering from cardiac exhaustion, trying to master my pain, I bent down slowly and cautiously to take off my boots. But no sooner had I touched the topmost button than my bosom swelled, filled with an unknown, a divine presence, I shook with sobs, tears streamed from my eyes. I had just perceived, in my memory, bending over my weariness, the tender, preoccupied, dejected face of my grandmother, as she had been on that first evening of our arrival, the face not of that grandmother whom I was astonished—and reproached myself—to find that I regretted so little and who was no more of her than just her name; but of my own true grandmother, of whom, for the first time since that afternoon in the Champs-Elysées on which she had had her stroke, I now recaptured, by an instinctive and complete act of recollection, the living reality. It was not until this moment, more than a year after her burial, because of that anachronism which so often prevents the calendar of facts from corresponding to that of our feelings, that I became conscious that she was dead. I had often spoken about her in the interval, and thought of her also, but behind my words and thoughts, those of an ungrateful, selfish, cruel youngster, there had never been anything that resembled my grandmother, because, in my frivolity, my love of pleasure, my familiarity with the spectacle of her ill health, I retained only in a potential state the memory of what she had been. But as soon as I had succeeded in falling asleep, at that more truthful hour when my eyes closed to the things of the outer world, the world of sleep (on whose frontier intellect and will, momentarily paralysed, could no longer strive to rescue me from the cruelty of my real impressions) reflected, refracted the agonising synthesis of survival and annihilation, in the mysteriously lightened darkness of my organs. World of sleep in which our inner consciousness, placed in bondage to the disturbances of our organs, quickens the rhythm of heart or breath because a similar dose of terror, sorrow, remorse acts with a strength magnified an hundredfold if it is thus injected into our veins; as soon as, to traverse the arteries of the subterranean city, we have embarked upon the dark current of our own blood as upon an inward Lethe meandering sixfold, huge solemn forms appear to us, approach and glide away, leaving us in tears. I sought in vain for my grandmother's form when I had stepped ashore beneath the sombre portals; I knew, indeed, that she did still exist, but with a diminished vitality, as pale as that of memory; the darkness was increasing, and the wind; my father, who was to take me where she was, did not appear. Suddenly my breath failed me, I felt my heart turn to stone; I had just remembered that for week after week I had forgotten to write to my grandmother. What must she be thinking of me? "Great God!" I said to myself; "how wretched she must be in that little room which they have taken for her, no bigger than what one would take for an old servant, where she is all alone with the nurse they have put there to look after her, from which she cannot stir, for she is still slightly paralysed and has always refused to rise from her bed. She must be thinking that I have forgotten her now that she is dead; how lonely she must be feeling, how deserted! Oh, I must run to see her, I mustn't lose a minute, I mustn't wait for my father to come, even—but where is it, how can I have forgotten the address, will she know me again, I wonder? How can I have forgotten her all these months?" It is so dark, I shall not find her; the wind is keeping me back; but look! There is my father walking ahead of me; I call out to him: "Where is grandmother? Tell me her address. Is she all right? Are you quite sure she has everything she wants?" "Why," says my father, "you need not alarm yourself. Her nurse is well trained. We send her a trifle, from time to time, so that she can get your grandmother anything she may need. She asks, sometimes, how you are getting on. She was told that you were going to write a book. She seemed pleased. She wiped away a. tear." And then I fancied I could remember that a little time after her death, my grandmother had said to me, crying, with a humble expression, like an old servant who has been given notice to leave, like a stranger in fact: "You will let me see something of you occasionally, won't you; don't let too many years go by without visiting me. Remember that you were my grandson, once, and that grandmothers never forget." And seeing again that face, so submissive, so sad, so tender, which was hers; I wanted to run to her at once and say to her, as I ought to have said to her then: "Why, grandmother, you can see me as often as you like, I have only you in the world, I shall never leave you any more." What tears my silence must have made her shed through all those months in which I have never been to the place where she lies, what can she have been saying to herself about me? And it is in a voice choked with tears that I too shout to my father "Quick, quick, her address, take me to her." But he says: "Well . . . I don't know whether you will be able to see her. Besides, you know, she is very frail now, very frail, she is not at all herself, I am afraid you would find it rather painful. And I can't be quite certain of the number of the avenue." "But tell me, you who know, it is not true that the dead have ceased to exist. It can't possibly be true, in spite of what they say, because grandmother does exist still." My father smiled a mournful smile: "Oh, hardly at all, you know, hardly at all. I think that it would be better if you did not go. She has everything that she wants. They come and keep the place tidy for her." "But she is often left alone?" "Yes, but that is better for her. It is better for her not to think, which could only be bad for her. It often hurts her, when she tries to think. Besides, you know, she is quite lifeless now. I shall leave a note of the exact address, so that you can go to her; but I don't see what good you can do there, and I don't suppose the nurse will allow you to see her." "You know quite well I shall always stay beside her, dear, deer deer, Francis Jammes, fork." But already I had retraced the dark meanderings of the stream, had ascended to the surface where the world of living people opens, so that if I still repeated: "Francis Jammes, deer, deer, " the sequence of these words no longer offered me the limpid meaning and logic which they had expressed to me so naturally an instant earlier and which I could not now recall. I could not even understand why the word "Aias" which my father had just said to me, had immediately signified: "Take care you don't catch cold," without any possible doubt. I had forgotten to close the shutters, and so probably the daylight had awakened me. But I could not bear to have before my eyes those waves of the sea which my grandmother could formerly contemplate for hours on end; the fresh image of their heedless beauty was at once supplemented by the thought that she did not see them; I should have liked to stop my ears against their sound, for now the luminous plenitude of the beach carved out an emptiness in my heart; everything seemed to be saying to me, like those paths and lawns of a public garden in which I had once lost her, long ago, when I was still a child "We have not seen her," and beneath the hemisphere of the pale vault of heaven I felt myself crushed as though beneath a huge bell of bluish glass, enclosing an horizon within which my grandmother was not. To escape from the sight of it, I turned to the wall, but alas what was now facing me was that partition which used to serve us as a morning messenger, that partition which, as responsive as a violin in rendering every fine shade of sentiment, reported so exactly to my grandmother my fear at once of waking her and, if she were already awake, of not being heard by her and so of her not coming, then immediately, like a second instrument taking up the melody, informed me that she was coming and bade me be calm. I dared not put out my hand to that wall, any more than to a piano on which my grandmother had played and which still throbbed from her touch. I knew that I might knock now, even louder, that I should hear no response, that my grandmother would never come again. And I asked nothing better of God, if a Paradise exists, than to be able, there, to knock upon that wall the three little raps which my grandmother would know among a thousand, and to which she would reply with those other raps which said: "Don't be alarmed, little mouse, I know you are impatient, but I am just coming," and that He would let me remain with her throughout eternity which would not be too long for us.

The manager came in to ask whether I would not like to come down. He had most carefully supervised my 'placement' in the dining-room. As he had seen no sign of me, he had been afraid that I might have had another of my choking fits. He hoped that it might be only a little 'sore throats' and assured me that he had heard it said that they could be soothed with what he called 'calyptus'.

He brought me a message from Albertine. She was not supposed to be coming to Balbec that year but, having changed her plans, had been for the last three days not in Balbec itself but ten minutes away by the tram at a neighbouring watering-place. Fearing that I might be tired after the journey, she had stayed away the first evening, but sent word now to ask when I could see her. I inquired whether she had called in person, not that I wished to see her, but so that I might arrange not to see her. "Yes," replied the manager. "But she would like it to be as soon as possible, unless you have not some quite necessitous reasons. You see" he concluded, "that everybody here desires you, definitively." But for my part, I wished to see nobody.

Despite the manager's promises, they brought me in a little later the turned down card of the Marquise de Cambremer. Having come over to see me, the old lady had sent to inquire whether I was there and when she heard that I had arrived only the day before, and was unwell, had not insisted, but (not without stopping doubtless at the chemist's or the haberdasher's, while the footman jumped down from the box and went in to pay a bill or to give an order) had driven back to Féterne, in her old barouche upon eight springs, drawn by a pair of horses. Not infrequently did one hear the rumble and admire the pomp of this carriage in the streets of Balbec and of various other little places along the coast, between Balbec and Féterne.

On the card that was brought me, Mme. de Cambremer had scribbled the message that she was giving an after-noon party "the day after tomorrow." To be sure, as recently as the day before yesterday, tired as I was of the social round, it would have been a real pleasure to me to taste it, transplanted amid those gardens in which there grew in the open air, thanks to the exposure of Féterne, fig trees, palms, rose bushes extending down to sea as blue and calm often as the Mediterranean upon which the host's little yacht sped across, before the party began, to fetch from the places on the other side of the bay the most important guests, served, with its awnings spread to shut out the sun, after the party had assembled, as an open air refreshment room, and set sail again in the evening to take back those whom it had brought. A charming luxury, but so costly that it was partly to meet the expenditure that it entailed that Mme. de Cambremer had sought to increase her income in various ways, and notably by letting, for the first time, one of her properties, very different from Féterne: La Raspelière. Yes, two days earlier, how welcome such a party, peopled with minor nobles all unknown to me, would have been to me as a change from the 'high life' of Paris. But now pleasures had no longer any meaning for me. And so I wrote to Mme. de Cambremer to decline, just as an hour ago, I had put off Albertine: grief had destroyed in me the possibility of desire as completely as a high fever takes away one's appetite. . . . My mother was to arrive on the morrow. I felt that I was less unworthy to live in her company, that I should understand her better, now that an alien and degrading existence had wholly given place to the resurging heartrending memories that wreathed and ennobled my soul, like her own, with their crown of thorns. I thought so: in reality there is a world of difference between real griefs, like my mother's, which literally crush out our life for years if not for ever; when we have lost the person we love—and those other griefs, transitory when all is said, as mine was to be, which pass as quickly as they have been slow in coming, which we do not realise until long after the event, because, in order to feel them, we need first to understand them; griefs such as so many people feel, from which the grief that was torturing me at this moment differed only in assuming the form of unconscious memory.

What struck me most of all, when I saw her cloak of crepe, was—what had never occurred to me in Paris—that it was no longer my mother that I saw before me, but my grandmother. As, in royal and princely families, upon the death of the head of the house his son takes his title and, from being Duc d'Orléans, Prince de Tarente or Prince des Laumes, becomes King of France, Duc de la Trémoille, Duc de Guermantes, so by an accession of a different order and more remote origin, the dead man takes possession of the living who becomes his image and successor, carries on his interrupted life.

Not only could my mother not bear to be parted from my grandmother's bag, become more precious than if it had been studded with sapphires and diamonds, from her muff, from all those garments which served to enhance their personal resemblance, but even from the volumes of Mme. de Sévigné which my grandmother took with her everywhere, copies which my mother would not have exchanged for the original manuscript of the letters. She had often teased my grandmother who could never write to her without quoting some phrase of Mme. de Sévigné or Mme. de Beausergent. In each of the three letters that I received from Mamma before her arrival at Balbec, she quoted Mme. de Sévigné to me, as though those three letters had been written not by her to me but by my grandmother and to her. She must at once go out upon the front to see that beach of which my grandmother had spoken to her every day in her letters. Carrying her mother's sunshade, I saw her from my window advance, a sable figure, with timid, pious steps, over the sands that beloved feet had trodden before her, and she looked as though she were going down to find a corpse which the waves would cast up at her feet.

Daily after this my mother went down and sat upon the beach, so as to do exactly what her mother had done, and read her mother's two favourite books, the *Memoirs* of Madame de Beausergent and the *Letters* of Madame de Sévigné. She, like all the rest of us, could not bear to hear the latter lady called the 'spirituelle Marquise' any more than to hear La Fontaine called 'le Bonhomme'. But when, in reading the *Letters*, she came upon the words: "My daughter," she seemed to be listening to her mother's voice.

Mamma, who had met Albertine, insisted upon my seeing her, because of the nice things that she had said about my grandmother and myself. I had accordingly made an appointment with her. I told the manager that she was coming, and asked him to let her wait for me in the drawing-room. He informed me that he had known her for years, her and her friends, long before they had attained "the age of purity" but that he was annoyed with them because of certain things that they had said about the hotel. "They can't be very 'gentlemanly' if they talk like that. Unless people have been slandering them." I had no difficulty in guessing that "purity" here meant "puberty." As I waited until it should be time to go down and meet Albertine, I was keeping my eyes fixed, as upon a picture which one ceases to see by dint of staring at it, upon the photograph that Saint-Loup had taken, when all of a sudden I thought once again: "It's grandmother, I am her grandson" as a man who has lost his memory remembers his name, as a sick man changes his personality. Françoise came in to tell me that Albertine was there, and, catching sight of the photograph: "Poor Madame, it's the very image of her, even the beauty spot on her cheek; that day the Marquis took her picture, she was very poorly, she had been taken bad twice. 'Whatever happens, Françoise,' she said, 'you must never let my grandson know.' And she kept it to herself, she was always bright with other people. When she was by herself, though, I used to find that she seemed to be in rather monotonous spirits now and then. But that soon passed away. And then she said to me, she said: 'If anything were to happen to me he ought to have a picture of me to keep. And I have never had one done in my life.' So then she sent me along with a message to the Marquis, and he was never to let you know that it was she who had asked him, but could he take her photograph. But when I came back and told her that he would, she had changed her mind again, because she was looking so poorly. 'It would be even worse,' she said to me,' than no picture at all.' But she was a clever one, she was, and in the end she got herself up so well in that big shady hat that it didn't show at all when she was out of the sun. She was very glad to have that photograph, because at that time she didn't think she would ever leave Balbec alive. It was no use my saying to her: 'Madame, it's wrong to talk like that, I don't like to hear Madame talk like that,' she had got it into her head. And, lord, there were plenty days when she couldn't eat a thing. That was why she used to make Monsieur go and dine away, out in the country with M. le Marquis. Then, instead of going in to dinner, she would pretend to be reading a book, and as soon as the Marquis's carriage had started, up she would go to bed. Some days she wanted to send word to Madame, to come down and see her in time. And then she was afraid of alarming her, as she had said nothing to her about it. 'It will be better for her to stay with her husband, don't you see, Françoise.' " Looking me in the face, Françoise asked me all of a sudden if I was feeling indisposed. I said that I was not; whereupon she said, " And you make me waste my time talking to you. Your visitor has been here all this time. I must go down and tell her. She is not the sort of person to have here. Why, a fast one like that, she may be gone again by now. She doesn't like to be kept waiting. Oh, nowadays, Mademoiselle Albertine, she's somebody!" "You are quite wrong, she is very respectable person, too respectable for this place. But go and tell her that I shan't be able to see her to-day."

To be sure, I suffered agonies, all that day, as I sat gazing at my grandmother's, photograph. It tortured me. Not so acutely, though, as the visit I received that evening from the manager. After I had spoken to him about my grandmother, and he had reiterated his condolences, I heard him say (for he enjoyed using the words that he pronounced wrongly): "Like the day when Madame your grandmother had that sincup, I wanted to tell you about it, because of the other visitors, don't you know, it might have given the place a bad name. She ought really to have left that evening. But she begged me to say nothing about it and promised me that she wouldn't have another sincup, or the first time she had one, she would go. The floor waiter reported to me that she had had another. But, lord, you were old friends that we try to please, and so long as nobody made any complaint." And so my grandmother had had syncopes which she had never mentioned to me. Perhaps at the very moment when I was being most beastly to her, when she was obliged, amid her pain, to see that she kept her temper, so as not to anger me, and her looks, so as not to be turned out of the hotel. '

A few days later I was able to look with pleasure at the photograph that Saint-Loup had taken of her; it did not revive the memory of what Françoise had told me, because that memory had never left me and I was growing used to it. But with regard to the idea that I had received of the state of her health—so grave, so painful—on that day, the photograph, still profiting by the ruses that my grandmother had adopted, which succeeded in taking me in even after they had been disclosed to me, showed me her so smart, so care free, beneath the hat which partly hid her face, that I saw her looking less unhappy and in better health than I had imagined. And yet, her cheeks having unconsciously assumed an expression of their own, livid, haggard, like the expression of an animal that feels that it has been marked down for slaughter, my grandmother had an air of being under sentence of death, an air involuntarily sombre, unconsciously tragic, which passed unperceived by me but prevented Mamma from ever looking at that photograph, that photograph which seemed to her a photograph not so much of her mother as of her mother's disease, of an insult that the disease was offering to the brutally buffeted face of my grandmother.

Then one day I decided to send word to Albertine that I would see her presently. But on the day on which Albertine came, the weather had turned dull and cold again and moreover I had no opportunity of hearing her laugh; she was in a very bad temper. "Balbec is deadly dull this year," she said to me. "I don't mean to stay any longer than I can help. You know I've been here since Easter, that's more than a month. There's not a soul here. You can imagine what fun it is." Notwithstanding the recent rain and a sky that changed every moment, after escorting Albertine as far as Epreville, for she was, to borrow her expression, "on the run" between that little watering place, where Mme. Bontemps had her villa, and Parville, where she had been taken "en pension" by Rosemonde's family, I went off by myself in the direction of the highroad that Mme. de Villeparisis's carriage had taken when we went for a drive with my grandmother; pools of water which the sun, now bright again, had not dried made a regular quagmire of the ground, and I thought of my grandmother who, in the old days, could not walk a yard without covering herself in mud. But on reaching the road I found a dazzling spectacle. Where I had seen with my grandmother in the month of August only the green leaves and, so to speak, the disposition of the apple-trees, as far as the eye could reach they were in full bloom, marvellous in their splendour, their feet in the mire beneath their ball-dresses, taking no precaution not to spoil the most marvellous pink satin that was ever seen, which glittered in the sunlight; the distant horizon of the sea gave the trees the background of a Japanese print; if I raised my head to gaze at the sky through the blossom, which, made its serene blue appear almost violent, the trees seemed to be drawing apart to reveal the immensity of their paradise. Beneath that azure a faint but cold breeze set the blushing bouquets gently trembling. Blue tits came and perched upon the branches and fluttered among the flowers, indulgent, as though it had been an amateur of exotic art and colours who had artificially created this living beauty. But it moved one to tears because, to whatever lengths the artist went in the refinement of his creation, one felt that it was natural, that these apple-trees were there in the heart of the country, like peasants, upon one of the highroads of France. Then the rays of the sun gave place suddenly to those of the rain; they streaked the whole horizon, caught the line of apple-trees in their grey net. But these continued to hold aloft their beauty, pink and blooming, in the wind that had turned icy beneath the drenching rain: it was a day in spring.

Chapter Two

Incapable as I still was of feeling any fresh physical desire, Albertine was beginning nevertheless to inspire in me a desire for happiness. Certain dreams of shared affection, always floating on the surface of our minds, ally themselves readily by a sort of affinity with the memory (provided that this has already become slightly vague) of a woman with whom we have taken our pleasure. This sentiment recalled to me aspects of Albertine's face, more gentle, less gay, quite different from those that would have been evoked by physical desire; and as it was also less pressing than that desire, I would gladly have postponed its realisation until the following winter, without seeking to see Albertine again at Balbec before her departure. But even in the midst of a grief that is still keen, physical desire will revive. From my bed, where I was made to spend hours every day resting, I longed for Albertine to come and resume our former amusements.

I asked Françoise to go and find Albertine, so that she might spend the rest of the afternoon with me. It would be untrue, I think, to say that there were already symptoms of that painful and perpetual mistrust which Albertine was to inspire in me, not to mention the special character, emphatically Gomorrhan, which that mistrust was to assume. Certainly, even, that afternoon—but this was not the first time—I grew anxious as I was kept waiting. Françoise, once she had started, stayed away so long that I began to despair. I had not lighted the lamp. The daylight had almost gone. The wind was making the flag over the Casino flap. And, fainter still in the silence of the beach over which the tide was rising, and like a voice rendering and enhancing the troubling emptiness of this restless, unnatural hour, a little barrel organ that had stopped outside the hotel was playing Viennese waltzes. At length Françoise arrived, but unaccompanied. "I have been as quick as I could but she wouldn't come because she didn't think she was looking smart enough. If she was five minutes painting herself and powdering herself, she was an hour by the clock. You'll be having a regular scentshop in here. She's coming, she stayed behind to tidy herself at the glass. I thought I should find her here." There was still a long time to wait before Albertine appeared. But the gaiety, the charm that she showed on this occasion dispelled my sorrow. She informed me (in contradiction of what she had said the other day) that she would be staying for the whole season and asked me whether we could not arrange, as in the former year, to meet daily. I told her that at the moment I was too melancholy and that I would rather send for her from time to time at the last moment, as I did in Paris. "If ever you're feeling worried, or feel that you want me, do not hesitate," she told me, "to send for me, I shall come immediately, and if you are not afraid of its creating a scandal in the hotel, I shall stay as long as you like." Françoise, in bringing her to me, had assumed the joyous air she wore whenever she had gone out of her way to please me and had been successful. But Albertine herself contributed nothing to her joy, and the very next day Françoise was to greet me with the profound observation: "Monsieur ought not to see that young lady. I know quite well the sort she is, she'll land you in trouble."

Albertine had made me take a note of the dates on which she would be going away for a few days to visit various girl friends, and had made me write down their addresses as well, in case I should want her on one of those evenings, for none of them lived very far away.

I wrote down the names and addresses of the girls with whom I should find her upon the days when she was not to be at Incarville, but privately decided that I would devote those days rather to calling upon Mme. Verdurin. In any case, our desire for different women varies in intensity. One evening we cannot bear to let one out of our sight who, after that, for the next month or two, will never enter our mind. As for Albertine, I saw her seldom, and only upon the very infrequent evenings when I felt that I could not live without her. If this desire seized me when she was too far from Balbec for Françoise to be able to go and fetch her, I used to send the lift-boy to Epreville, to La Sogne, to Saint-Frichoux, asking him to finish his work a little earlier than usual. He would come into my room, but would leave the door open for, albeit he was conscientious at his 'job' which was pretty hard, consisting in endless cleanings from five o'clock in the morning, he could never bring himself to make the effort to shut a door, and, if one were to remark to him that it was open, would turn back and, summoning up all his strength, give it a gentle push. With the democratic pride that marked him, a pride to which, in more liberal careers, the members of a profession that is at all numerous never attain, barristers, doctors and men of letters speaking simply of a 'brother' barrister, doctor or man of letters, he, employing, and rightly, a term that is confined to close corporations like the Academy, would say to me in speaking of a page who was in charge of the lift upon alternate days: "I shall get my *colleague* to take my place." This pride did not prevent him from accepting, with a view to increasing what he called his 'salary', remuneration for his errands, a fact which had made Françoise take a dislike to him: "Yes, the first time you see him you would give him the sacrament without confession, but there are days when his tongue is as smooth as a prison door. It's your money he's after." This was the category in which she had so often included Eulalie, and in which, alas (when I think of all the trouble that was one day to come of it), she already placed Albertine, because she saw me often asking Mamma, on behalf of my impecunious friend, for trinkets and other little presents, which Françoise held to be inexcusable because Mme. Bontemps had only a general servant.

It was not this evening, however that my cruel mistrust began to take solid form. No, to make no mystery about it, although the incident did not occur until some weeks later it arose out of a remark made by Cottard. Albertine and her friends had insisted that day upon dragging me to the casino at Incarville where, as luck would have it, I should not have joined them (having intended to go and see Mme. Verdurin who had invited me again and again), had I not been held up at Incarville itself by a breakdown of the tram which it would take a considerable time to repair. As I strolled up and down waiting for the men to finish working at it, I found myself all of a sudden face to face with Doctor Cottard, who had come to Incarville to see a patient. I almost hesitated to greet him as he had not answered any of my letters. But friendship does not express itself in the same way in different people. Not having been brought up to observe the same fixed rules of behaviour as well-bred people, Cottard was full of good intentions of which one knew nothing, even denying their existence, until the day when he had an opportunity of displaying them. He apologised, had indeed received my letters, had reported my whereabouts to the Verdurins who were most anxious to see me and whom he urged me to go and see. He even proposed to take me to them there and then, for he was waiting for the little local train to take him back there for dinner. As I hesitated and as he had still some time before his train (for there was bound to be still a considerable delay), I made him come with me to the little casino, one of those that had struck me as being so gloomy on the evening of my first arrival, now filled with the tumult of the girls who, in the absence of male partners, were dancing together. Andrée came sliding along the floor towards me; I was meaning to go off with Cottard in a moment to the Verdurins', when I definitely declined his offer, seized by an irresistable desire to stay with Albertine. The fact was, I had just heard her laugh. And her laugh at once suggested the rosy flesh, the fragrant portals between which it had just made its way, seeming also, as strong, sensual and revealing as the scent of geraniums, to carry with it some microscopic particles of their substance, irritant and secret. One of the girls, a stranger to me, sat down at the piano, and Andrée invited Albertine to waltz with her. Happy in the thought that I was going to remain in this little casino with these girls, I remarked to Cottard how well they danced together. But he, taking the professional point of view of a doctor and with an ill-breeding which overlooked the fact that they were my friends, although he must have seen me shaking hands with them, replied: "Yes, but parents are very rash to allow their daughters to form such habits. I should certainly never let mine come here. Are they nice looking, though? I can't see their faces. There now, look," he went on, pointing to Albertine and Andrée who were waltzing slowly, tightly clasped together, "I have left my glasses behind and I don't see very well, but they are certainly keenly roused. It is not sufficiently known that women derive most excitement from their breasts. And theirs as you see, are completely touching." And indeed the contact had been unbroken between the breasts of Andrée and of Albertine. I do not know whether they heard or guessed Cottard's observation, but they gently broke the contact while continuing to waltz. At that moment Andrée said something to Albertine, who laughed, the same deep and penetrating laugh that I had heard before. But all that it wafted to me this time was a feeling of pain; Albertine appeared to be revealing by it, to be making Andrée share some exquisite, secret thrill. It rang out like the first or the last strains of a ball to which one has not been invited. I left the place with Cottard, distracted by his conversation, thinking only at odd moments of the scene I had just witnessed.

The mischief that his remarks about Albertine and Andrée had done me was extreme, but its worst effects were not immediately felt by me, as happens with those forms of poisoning which begin to act only after a certain time.

Some days later, at Balbec, while we were in the ballroom of the casino, there entered Bloch's sister and cousin, who had both turned out quite pretty, but whom I refrained from greeting on account of my girl friends, because the younger one, the cousin, was notoriously living with the actress; whose acquaintance she had made during my first visits . Andrée, at a murmured allusion to this scandal, said to me: "Oh! About that sort of thing I'm like Albertine; there's nothing we both loathe so much as that sort of thing." As for Albertine, on sitting down to talk to me upon the sofa, she had turned her back on the disreputable pair. I had noticed, however, that before she changed her position at the moment when Mlle. Bloch and her cousin appeared, my friend's eyes had flashed with that sudden, close attention which now and again imparted to the face of this frivolous girl a serious, indeed a grave, air, and left her pensive afterwards. But Albertine had at once turned towards myself a gaze which nevertheless remained singularly fixed and meditative. Mlle. Bloch and her cousin having finally left the room after laughing and shouting in a loud and vulgar manner, I asked Albertine whether the little fair one (the one who was so intimate with the actress) was not the girl who had won the prize the day before in the procession of flowers. "I don't know," said Albertine, "is one of them fair? I must confess they don't interest me particularly, I have never looked at them. Is one of them fair?" she asked her three girl friends with a detached air of inquiry. When applied to people whom Albertine passed every day on the front, this ignorance seemed to me too profound to be genuine. "They didn't appear to be looking at us much either," I said to Albertine, perhaps (on the assumption, which I did not however consciously form, that Albertine loved her own sex), to free her from any regret by pointing out to her that she had not attracted the attention of these girls and that, generally speaking, it is not customary even for the most vicious of women to take an interest in girls whom they do not know. "They weren't looking at us," was Albertine's astonished reply. "Why, they did nothing else the whole time." "But you can't possibly tell," I said to her, "you had your back to them." "Very well, and what about that?" she replied, pointing out to me, set in the wall in front of us, a large mirror which I had not noticed and upon which I now realised that my friend, while talking to me, had never ceased to fix her troubled, preoccupied eyes.

I thought then of all that I had been told about Swann's love for Odette, of the way in which Swann had been tricked all his life. Indeed, when I come to think of it, the hypothesis that made me gradually build up the whole of Albertine's character and give a painful interpretation to every moment of a life that I could not control in its entirety, was the memory, the rooted idea of Mme. Swann's character, as it had been described to me. These accounts helped my imagination, in after years, to take the line of supposing that Albertine might, instead of being a good girl, have had the same immorality, the same faculty of deception as a reformed prostitute, and I thought of all the sufferings that would in that case have been in store for me had I ever really been her lover.

One day, outside the Grand Hotel, where we were gathered on the front, I had just been addressing Albertine in the harshest, most humiliating language, and Rosemonde was saying: "Oh, how you have changed your mind about her; why, she used to be everything, it was she who ruled the roost, and now she isn't even fit to be thrown to the dogs." I was beginning, in order to make my attitude towards Albertine still more marked, to say all the nicest things I could think of to Andrée, who, if she was tainted with the same vice, seemed to me to have more excuse for it since she was sickly and neurasthenic, when we saw emerging at the steady trot of its pair of horses into the street at right angles to the front, at the corner of which we were standing, Mme. de Cambremer's barouche. The chief magistrate who, at that moment, was advancing towards us, sprang back upon recognising the carriage, in order not to be seen in our company; then, when he thought that the Marquise's eye might catch his, bowed to her with an immense sweep of his hat. But the carriage, instead of continuing, as might have been expected, along the Rue de la Mer, disappeared through the gate of the hotel. It was quite ten minutes later when the lift-boy, out of breath, came to announce to me: "It's the Marquise de Camembert, she's come here to see Monsieur. I've been, up to the room, I looked in the reading-room, I couldn't find Monsieur anywhere. Luckily I thought of looking on the beach." He had barely ended this speech when, followed by her daughter-in-law and by an extremely ceremonious gentleman, the Marquise advanced towards me, coming on probably from some afternoon tea-party in the neighbourhood, and bowed down not so much by age as by the mass of costly trinkets with which she felt it more sociable and more befitting her rank to cover herself, in order to appear as 'well dressed' as possible to the people whom she went to visit.

It was in fact that 'landing' of the Cambremers at the hotel which my grandmother had so greatly dreaded long ago when she wanted us not to let Legrandin know that we might perhaps be going to Balbec. Then Mamma used to laugh at these fears inspired by an event which she considered impossible. And here it was actually happening, but by different channels and without Legrandin having had any part in it. Do you mind my staying here, if I shan't be in your way?" asked Albertine (in whose eyes there lingered, brought there by the cruel things I had just been saying to her, a pair of tears which I observed without seeming to see them, but not without rejoicing inwardly at the sight), "there is something I want to say to you." A hat with feathers, itself surmounted by a sapphire pin, was perched haphazard upon Mme. de Cambremer's wig, like a badge, the display of which was necessary, but sufficient, its place immaterial, its elegance conventional and its stability superfluous. Notwithstanding the heat, the good lady had put on a jet cloak, like a dalmatic, over which hung an ermine stole the wearing of which seemed to depend not upon the temperature and season, but upon the nature of the ceremony. And on Mme. de

Cambremer's bosom a baronial torse fastened to a chain, dangled like a pectoral cross.

Madame de Cambremer had taken the opportunity, she told me, of a party which some friends of hers had been giving that afternoon in the Balbec direction to come and call upon me, as she had promised Robert de Saint-Loup "You know he's coming down to these parts quite soon for a few days. His uncle Charlus is staying near here with his sister-in-law, the Duchesse de Luxembourg, and M. de Saint-Loup means to take the opportunity of paying his aunt a visit and going to see his old regiment, where he is very popular, highly respected. We often have visits from officers who are never tired of singing his praises. How nice it would be if you, and he would give us the pleasure of coming together to Féterne." I presented Albertine and her friends. Mme. de Cambremer introduced us all to her daughter-in-law. The latter, so frigid towards the petty nobility with whom her seclusion at Féterne forced her to associate, so reserved, so afraid of compromising herself, held out her hand to me with a radiant smile, safe as she felt herself and delighted at seeing a friend of Robert de Saint-Loup, whom he, possessing a sharper social intuition than he allowed to appear, had mentioned to her as being a great friend of the Guermantes. So, unlike her mother-in-law, Mme. de Cambremer employed two vastly different forms of politeness. It was at the most the former kind, dry, insupportable, that she would have conceded me had I met her through her brother Legrandin. But for a friend of the Guermantes she had not smiles enough. At a signal from her daughter-in-law, Mme. de Cambremer prepared to depart, and said to me: "Since you won t come and stay at Féterne, won't you at least come to luncheon, one day this week, to-morrow for instance?" And in her bounty, to make the invitation irresistible, she added: "You will find the Comte de Crisenoy," whom I had never lost, for the simple reason that I did not know him. She was beginning to dazzle me with yet further temptations, but stopped short. The chief magistrate who, on returning to the hotel, had been told that she was on the premises had crept about searching for her everywhere, then waited his opportunity, and pretending to have caught sight of her by chance, came up now to greet her. I gathered that Mme. de Cambremer did not mean to extend to him the invitation to luncheon that she had just addressed to me. And yet he had known her far longer than I, having for years past been one of the regular guests at the afternoon parties at Féterne whom I used so to envy during my former visit to Balbec. But old acquaintance is not the only thing that counts in society. And hostesses are more inclined to reserve their luncheons for new acquaintances who still whet their curiosity, especially when they arrive preceded by a glowing and irresistible recommendation like Saint-Loup's of me. Mme. de Cambremer decided that the chief magistrate could not have heard what she was saying to me, but, to calm her guilty conscience, began addressing him in the kindest tone.

"She has asked you to luncheon," the chief magistrate said to me sternly when the carriage had passed out of sight and I came indoors with the girls. "We're not on the best of terms just now. She feels that I neglect her. You seem to be in her good books. When you reach my age you will see that society is a very trumpery thing, and you will be sorry you attached so much importance to these trifles. Well, I am going to take a turn before dinner. Good-bye, children," he shouted back at us, as though he were already fifty yards away.

When I had said good-bye to Rosemonde and Gisèle, they saw with astonishment that Albertine was staying behind instead of accompanying them. "Why, Albertine, what are you doing, don't you know what time it is?" "Go home," she replied, in a tone of authority. "I want to talk to him" she added; indicating myself with a submissive air. Rosemonde and Gisèle stared at me, filled with a new and strange respect. I enjoyed the feeling that, for a moment at least, in the eyes even of Rosemonde and Gisèle, I was to Albertine something more important than the time, than her friends, and might indeed share solemn secrets with her into which it was impossible for them to be admitted. "Shan't we see you again this evening?" "I don't know, it will depend on this person. Anyhow, to-morrow." "Let us go up to my room," I said to her, when her friends had gone.

As soon as we were alone and had moved along the corridor, Albertine began: "What is it you have got against me?" Had my harsh treatment of her been painful to myself? Had it been merely an unconscious ruse on my part, with the object of bringing my mistress to that attitude of fear and supplication which would enable me to interrogate her, and perhaps to find out which of the alternative hypotheses that I had long since formed about her was correct? However that may be, when I heard her question, I suddenly felt the joy of one who attains to a long desired goal. Before answering her, I escorted her to the door of my room. Opening it, I scattered the roseate light that was flooding the room and turning the white muslin of the curtains drawn for the night to golden damask. I went across to the window; the gulls had settled again upon the waves; but this time they were pink. I drew Albertine's attention to them. "Don't change the subject," she said, "be frank with me." I lied. I declared to her that she must first listen to a confession, that of my passionate admiration, for some time past, of Andrée, and I made her this confession with a simplicity and frankness worthy of the stage, but seldom employed in real life except for a love which people do not feel. Harking back to the fiction I had employed with Gilberte before my first visit to Balbec, but adapting its terms, I went so far (in order to make her more ready to believe me when I told her now that I was not in love with her) as to let fall the admission that at one time I had been on the point of falling in love with her, but that too long an interval had elapsed, that she could be nothing more to me now than a good friend and comrade, and that even if I wished to feel once again a more ardent sentiment for her it would be quite beyond my power.

She thanked me for my sincerity and added that so far from being puzzled she understood perfectly a state of mind so frequent and so natural.

"But tell me, what on earth have I done?" Albertine asked me. There was a knock at the door; it was the lift-boy; Albertine's aunt, who was passing the hotel in a carriage, had stopped on the chance of finding her there, to take her home. Albertine sent word that she could not come, that they were to begin dinner without her, that she could not say at what time she would return. "But won't your aunt be angry?" "What do you suppose? She will understand all right." And so, at this moment at least, a moment such as might never occur again—a conversation with myself was proved by this incident to be in Albertine's eyes a thing of such self evident importance that it must be given precedence over everything, a thing to which, referring no doubt instinctively to a family code, enumerating certain crises in which, when the career of M. Bontemps was at stake, a journey had been made without a thought, my friend never doubted that her aunt would think it quite natural to see her sacrifice the dinner-hour. That remote hour which she passed without my company, among her own people, Albertine, having brought it to me, bestowed it on me; I might make what use of it I chose. I ended by making bold to tell her what had been reported to me about her way of living, and that notwithstanding the profound disgust that I felt for women tainted with that vice, I had not given it a thought until I had been told the name of her accomplice, and that she could readily understand, loving Andrée as I did, the grief that the news had caused me. It would have been more tactful perhaps to say that I had been given the names of other women as well, in whom I was not interested. But the sudden and terrible revelation, that Cottard had made to me had entered my heart to lacerate,it, complete in itself but without accretions., And just as, before that moment, it would never have occurred to me that Albertine was in love with Andrée, or at any rate could, find pleasure in caressing her, if Cottard had not drawn my attention to their attitude as they waltzed together, so I had been incapable of passing from that idea to the idea, so different for me, that Albertine might have, with other women than Andrée, relations for which affection could not be pleaded in excuse. Albertine, before even swearing to me that it was not true, showed, like everyone upon learning that such things are being said about him; anger, concern, and, with regard to the unknown slanderer, a fierce curiosity to know who he was and a desire to be confronted with him so as to be able to confound him. But she assured me that she bore me, at least, no resentment. If it had been true, I should have told you. But Andrée and I both loathe that sort of thing. We have not lived all these years without seeing women with cropped hair who behave like men and do the things you mean, and nothing revolts us more." Albertine gave me merely her word, a peremptory word unsupported by proof. But this was just what was best calculated to calm me, jealousy belonging to that family of sickly doubts which are better purged by the energy than by the probability of an affirmation. I had before me a new Albertine, of whom I had already, it was true, caught more than one glimpse towards the end of my previous visit to Balbec, frank and honest, an Albertine who had, out of affection for myself, forgiven me my suspicions and tried to dispel them. She made me sit down by her side upon my bed. I thanked her for what she had said to me, assured her that our reconciliation was complete, and that I would never be horrid to her again. I suggested to her that she ought, at the same time, to go home to dinner. She asked me whether I was not glad to have her with me. Drawing my head towards her for a caress which she had never before given me and which I owed perhaps to the healing of our rupture, she passed her tongue lightly over my lips which she attempted to force apart. At first I kept them tight shut. "You are a great bear!" she informed me.

    I ought to have left the place that evening and never set eyes on her again. I ought to have left Balbec, to have shut myself up in solitude, to have remained so in harmony with the last vibrations of the voice which I had contrived to render amorous for an instant, and of which I should have asked nothing more than that it might never address another word to me; for fear lest, by an additional word which now could only be different, it might shatter with a discord the sensitive silence in which, as though by the pressure of a pedal, there might long have survived in me the throbbing chord of happiness.

Soothed by my explanation with Albertine, I began once again to live in closer intimacy with my mother. She loved to talk to me gently about the days in which my grandmother had been younger. Fearing that I might reproach myself with the sorrows with which I had perhaps darkened the close of my grandmother's life, she preferred to turn back to the years when the first signs of my dawning intelligence had given my grandmother a satisfaction which until now had always been kept from me. We talked of the old days at Combray. My mother reminded me that there at least I used to read, and that at Balbec I might well do the same, if I was not going to work. I told her that I would read on the days when I felt too tired to go out.

These days were not very frequent however. We used to go out picnicking as before in a band, Albertine, her friends and myself, on the cliff or to the farm called Marie-Antoinette. But there were times when Albertine bestowed on me this great pleasure. She would say to me: "To-day I want to be alone with you for a little, it will be nicer if we are just by ourselves." Then she would give out that she was busy, not that she need furnish any explanation, and so that the others, if they went all the same, without us, for an excursion and picnic, might not be able to find us, we would steal away like a pair of lovers, all by ourselves to Bagatelle or the Cross of Heulan, while the band, who would never think of looking for us there and never went there, waited indefinitely, in the hope of seeing us appear at Marie-Antoinette.

Presently the season was in full swing; every day there was some fresh arrival, and for the sudden increase in the frequency of my outings, there was a reason devoid of pleasure which poisoned them all. The beach was now peopled with girls, and, since the idea suggested to me by Cottard had not indeed furnished me with fresh suspicions but had rendered me sensitive and weak in that quarter and careful not to let any suspicion take shape in my mind, as soon as a young woman arrived at Balbec, I began to feel ill at ease, I proposed to Albertine the most distant excursions, in order that she might not make the newcomer's acquaintance, and indeed, if possible, might not set eyes on her. I would have liked to be sure that no more women were coming to Balbec; I trembled when I thought that, as it was almost time for Mme. Putbus to arrive at the Verdurins', her maid, whose tastes Saint-Loup had not concealed from me, might take it into her head to come down to the beach, and, if it were a day on which I was not with Albertine, might seek to corrupt her.

As it was chiefly the presence of Andrée that was disturbing me, the soothing effect that Albertine's words had had upon me still to some extent persisted—I knew moreover that presently I should have less, need of it, as Andrée would be leaving the place with Rosemonde and Gisèle just about the time when the crowd began to arrive and would be spending only a few weeks more with Albertine. During these weeks, moreover, Albertine seemed to have planned everything that she did, everything that she said with a view to destroying my suspicions if any remained, or to preventing, their recurrence. She contrived never to be left alone with Andrée, and insisted, when we came back from an excursion, upon my accompanying her to her door, upon my coming to fetch her when we were going anywhere. Andrée meanwhile took just as much trouble on her, side, seemed to avoid meeting Albertine. And this apparent understanding between them was not the only indication that Albertine must have informed her friend of our conversation and have asked her to be so kind as to calm my absurd suspicions.

About this time there occurred at the Grand Hotel a scandal which was not calculated to modify the intensity of my torment. Bloch's cousin had for some time past been indulging, with a retired actress, in secret relations which presently ceased to satisfy them. That they should be seen seemed to them to add perversity to their pleasure, they chose to flaunt their perilous sport before the eyes of all the world. They began with caresses, which might after all be set down to a friendly intimacy, in the card-room, by the baccarat-table. Then they grew more bold. And finally, one evening, on a sofa, in a corner of the big ball-room that was not even dark, they made no more attempt to conceal what they were doing than if they had been in bed. Two officers who happened to be near, with their wives, complained to the manager. It was thought for moment that their protest would be effective. But they had this against them that, having come over for the evening from Netteholme, where they were staying, they could not be of any use to the manager. Whereas, without her knowing it even, and whatever remarks the manager may have made to her, there hovered over Mlle. Bloch the protection of M. Nissim Bernard. I must explain why M. Nissim Bernard carried to their highest pitch the family virtues. Every year he took a magnificent villa at Balbec for his nephew, and no invitation would have dissuaded him from going home to dine at his own table, which was really the others. But he never took his luncheon at home. Every day at noon he was at the Grand Hotel. The fact of the matter was that he was keeping, as other men keep a chorus-girl from the opera, an embryo waiter of much the same type as the pages of whom we have spoken, and who made us think of the young Israelites in Esther and Athalie.

Bloch's family might never have suspected the reason which made their uncle never take his luncheon at home and have accepted it from the first as the mania of an elderly bachelor, due perhaps to the demands of his intimacy with some actress; everything that concerned M. Nissim Bernard was taboo to the manager of the Balbec hotel. And that was why, without even referring to the uncle, he had finally not ventured to find fault with the niece, albeit recommending her to be a little more circumspect. And so the girl and her friend who, for some days, had pictured themselves as excluded from the casino and the Grand Hotel, seeing that everything was settled, were delighted to show those fathers of families who held aloof from them that they might with impunity take the utmost liberties. No doubt they did not go so far as to repeat the public exhibition which had revolted everybody but gradually they returned to their old ways. And one evening as I came out of the casino, which was half in darkness, with Albertine and Bloch whom we had met there, they came towards us linked together, kissing each other incessantly, and as they passed us, crowed and laughed, uttering indecent cries. Bloch lowered his eyes, so as to seem not to have recognized his cousin, and as for myself I was tortured by the thought that this occult, appalling language was addressed perhaps to Albertine. Another incident turned my thoughts even more in the direction of Gomorrah. I had noticed upon the beach a handsome young roman, erect and pale, whose eyes, round their centre, scattered rays so geometrically luminous that one was reminded, on meeting her gaze, of some constellation. I thought how much more beautiful this girl was than Albertine, and that it would be wiser to give up the other. Only the face of this beautiful young woman had been smoothed by the invisible plane of an ufterly low life, of the constant acceptance of vulgar expedients, so much so that her eyes, more noble however, than the rest of her face, could radiate nothing but appetites and desires. Well, on the following day, this young woman being seated a long way away from us in the casino, I saw that she never ceased to fasten upon Albertine the recurrent, circling fires of her gaze. One would have said that she was making signals to her from a lighthouse. I dreaded my friend seeing that she was being so closely observed, I was afraid that these incessantly rekindled glances might have the conventional meaning of an amorous assignation for the morrow. For all I knew, this assignation might not be the first. The young woman with the radiant eyes might have come another year to

Balbec? It was perhaps, because Albertine had already yielded to her desires, or to those of a friend, that this woman allowed herself to address to her those flashing signals. If so, they did more than demand something for the present, they found a justification in pleasant hours in the past. This assignation, in that case, must be not the first, but the sequel to adventures shared in past years. And indeed her glance did not say "Will you?" As soon as the young woman had caught sight of Albertine, she had turned her head and beamed upon her glances charged with recollection, as though she were terribly afraid that my friend might not remember. Albertine, who could see her plainly, remained phlegmatically motionless, with the result that the other, with the same sort of discretion as a man who sees his old mistress with a new lover, ceased to look at her and paid no more attention to her than if she had not existed.

But, a day or two later, I received a proof of this young woman's tendencies, and also of the probability of her having known Albertine in the past. Often, in the hall of the casino, when two girls were smitten with mutual desire, a luminous phenomenon occurred, a sort of phosphorescent train passing from one to the other. Let us note in passing that it is by the aid of such materialisations, even if they be imponderable, by these astral signs that set fire to a whole section of the atmosphere, that the scattered Gomorrah tends, in every town, in every village, to reunite its separated members, to reform the biblical city while everywhere the same efforts are being made, be it in view of but a momentary reconstruction, by the nostalgic, the hypocritical, sometimes by the courageous exiles from Sodom.

Once I saw the stranger whom Albertine had appeared not to recognise, just at the moment when Bloch's cousin was approaching her. The young woman's eyes flashed, but it was quite evident that she did not know the Israelite maiden. She beheld her for the first time, felt a desire, a shadow of doubt, by no means the same certainty as in the case of Albertine, Albertine upon whose comradeship she must so far have reckoned that, in the face of her coldness, she had felt the surprise of a foreigner familiar with Paris but not resident there, who, having returned to spend a few weeks there, on the site of the little theatre where he was in the habit of spending pleasant evenings, sees that they have now built a bank.

Bloch's cousin went and sat down at a table where she turned the pages of a magazine. Presently the young woman came and sat down, with an abstracted air, by her side. But under the table one could presently see their feet wriggling, then their legs and hands, in a confused heap. Words followed, a conversation began, and the young woman's innocent husband, who had been looking everywhere for her, was astonished to find her making plans for that very evening with a girl whom he did not know. His wife introduced Bloch's cousin to him as a friend of her childhood, by an inaudible name, for she had forgotten to ask her what her name was. But the husband's presence made their intimacy advance a stage farther, for they addressed each other as *tu*, having known each other at their convent, an incident at which they laughed heartily later on, as well as at the hoodwinked husband, with a gaiety which afforded them an excuse for more caresses.

However, the jealousy that was caused me by the women whom Albertine perhaps loved was, abruptly to cease. We were waiting, Albertine and I, at the Balbec station of the little local railway. We had driven there in the hotel omnibus, because it was raining. Not far away from us was M. Nissim Bernard, with a black eye. He had recently forsaken the chorister from *Athalie* for the waiter at a much frequented farmhouse in the neighbourhood, known as the 'Cherry Orchard'. This rubicund youth, with his blunt features, appeared for all the world to have a tomato instead of a head. A tomato, exactly similar served as head to his twin brother. To the detached observer there is this attraction about these perfect resemblances between pairs of twins, that nature, becoming for the moment industrialised, seems to be offering a pattern for sale. Unfortunately M. Nissim. Bernard looked at it from another point of view, and this resemblance was only external. Tomato II showed a frenzied zeal in furnishing the pleasures exclusively of ladies, Tomato I did not mind condescending to meet the wishes of certain gentlemen. Now on each occasion when, stirred, as though by a reflex action, by the memory of pleasant hours spent with Tomato I, M. Bernard presented himself at the Cherry Orchard, being shortsighted (not that one need be short-sighted to mistake them), the old Israelite, unconsciously playing Amphitryon, would accost the twin brother with: "Will you meet me somewhere this evening?" He at once received a resounding smack in the face. It might even be repeated in the course of a single meal, when he continued with the second brother the conversation he had begun with the first. In the end this treatment so disgusted him, by association of ideas, with tomatoes, even of the edible variety, that whenever he heard a newcomer order that vegetable at the next table to his own, in the Grand Hotel, he would murmur to him: "You must excuse me Sir, for addressing you, without an introduction but I heard you order tomatoes. They are stale to-day. I tell you in your own interest, for it makes no difference to me, I never touch them myself." The stranger would reply with effusive thanks to this philanthropic and disinterested neighbour, call back the waiter, pretend to have changed his mind: "Not on second thoughts, certainly not, no tomatoes." Aimé, who had seen it all before, would laugh to himself, and think: "He's an old rascal, that Monsieur Bernard, he's gone and made another of them change his order." M. Bernard, as he waited for the already overdue tram, showed no eagerness to speak to Albertine and myself, because of his black eye. We were even less eager to speak to him. It would however have been almost inevitable if, at that moment, a bicycle had not come dashing towards us; the lift-boy sprang from its saddle, breathless. Madame Verdurin had telephoned shortly after we left the hotel, to know whether I would dine with her two days later; we shall see presently why. Then, having given me the message in detail, the lift-boy left us, and, being one of these democratic 'employees' who affect independence with regard to the middle classes, and among themselves restore the principle of authority, explained: "I must be off, because of my chiefs."

Albertine's girl friends had gone, and would be away for some time. I was anxious to provide her with distractions.. And so I had asked her that day to come with me to Doncières, where I was going to meet Saint-Loup. With a similar hope of occupying her mind, I advised her to take up painting, in which she had had lessons in the past. While working she would not ask herself whether she was happy or unhappy. I would gladly have taken her also to dine now and again with the Verdurins and the Cambremers, who certainly would have been delighted to see any friend introduced by myself, but I must first make certain that Mme. Putbus was not yet at La Raspelière. It was only by going there in person that I could make sure of this, and, as I knew beforehand that on the next day but one Albertine would be going on a visit with her aunt, I had seized this opportunity to send Mme. Verdurin a telegram asking whether she would be at home upon Wednesday. If Mme. Putbus was there, I would manage to see her maid, ascertain whether there was any danger of her coming to Balbec, and if so find out when, so as to take Albertine out of reach on the day. The little local railway, making a loop which did not exist at the time when I had taken it with my grandmother, now extended to Doncières-la-Goupil, a big station at which important trains stopped, among them the express by which I had come down to visit Saint-Loup, from Paris, and the corresponding express by which I had returned. And, because of the bad weather; the omnibus from the Grand Hotel took Albertine and myself to the station of the little tram, Balbec-Plage.

The little train had not yet arrived but one could see, lazy and slow, the plume of smoke that it had left in its wake, which, confined now to its own power of locomotion as an almost stationary cloud, was slowly mounting the green slope of the cliff of Criquetot. Finally the little tram, which it had preceded by taking a vertical course, arrived in its turn, at a leisurely crawl. The passengers who were waiting to board it stepped back to make way for it, but without hurrying, knowing that they were dealing with a good-natured, almost human traveller, who, guided like the bicycle of a beginner; by the obliging signals of the station-master, in the strong hands of the engine-driver, was in no danger of running over anybody, and would come to a halt at the proper place.

My telegram explained the Verdurins' telephone message and had been all the more opportune since Wednesday (the day I had fixed happened to be a Wednesday) was the day set apart for dinner-parties by Mme. Verdurin, at La Raspelière, as in Paris., a fact of which I was unaware. Mme. Verdurin could not give 'dinners', but she had 'Wednesdays'. These Wednesdays were works of art. While fully conscious that they had not their match anywhere, Mme. Verdurin introduced shades of distinction between them. "Last Wednesday was not as good as the one before," she would say. "But I believe the next will be one of the best I have ever given." Sometimes she went so far as to admit: "This Wednesday was not worthy of the others. But I have a big surprise for you next week." In the closing weeks of the Paris season, before leaving for the country, the Mistress would announce the end of the Wednesdays. It gave her an opportunity to stimulate the faithful. "There are only three more Wednesdays left, there are only two more," she would say, in the same tone as though the world were coming to an end. "You aren't going to miss next Wednesday, for the finale." But this finale was a sham, for she would announce: "Officially, there will be no more Wednesdays. Today was the last for this year. But I shall be at home all the same on Wednesday. We shall have a little Wednesday to ourselves; I dare say these little private Wednesdays will be the nicest of all." At La Raspelière, the Wednesdays were of necessity restricted, and since, if they had discovered a friend who was passing that way, they would invite him for one or another evening, almost every day of the week became a Wednesday. "I don't remember all the guests, but I know there's Madame la Marquise de Camembert," the lift-boy had told me; his memory of our discussion of the name Cambremer had not succeeded in definitely supplanting that of the old word, whose syllables, familiar and full of meaning, came to the young employee's rescue when he was embarrassed by this difficult name, and were immediately preferred and readopted by him, not by any means from laziness or as an old and ineradicable usage, but because of the need for logic and clarity which they satisfied.

We hastened in search of an empty carriage in which I could hold Albertine in my arms throughout the journey. Having failed to find one, we got into a compartment in which there was already installed a lady with a massive face, old and ugly, with a masculine expression, very much in her Sunday best, who was reading the *Revue des Deux Mondes*. Notwithstanding her commonness, she was eclectic in her tastes, and I found amusement in asking myself to what social category she could belong; I at once concluded that she must be the manager of some large brothel, a procuress on holiday. Her face, her manner, proclaimed the fact aloud. Only, I had never yet supposed that such ladies read the *Revue des Deux Mondes*. Albertine drew my attention to her with a wink and a smile. The lady wore an air of extreme dignity; and as I, for my part, bore within me the consciousness that I was invited, two days later, to the terminal point of the little railway, by the famous Mme. Verdurin, that at an intermediate station I was awaited by Robert de Saint-Loup, and that a little farther on I had it in my power to give great pleasure to Mme. de Cambremer, by going to stay at Féterne, my eyes sparkled with irony as I studied this self important lady who seemed to think that, because of her elaborate attire, the feathers in her hat, her *Revue des Deux Mondes*, she was a more considerable personage than myself. I hoped that the lady would not remain in the train much longer than M. Nissim Bernard, and that she would alight at least at Toutainville, but no. The train stopped at Epreville, she remained seated. Similarly at Montmartin-sur-Mer; at Parville-la-Bingard, at Incarville, so that in despair, when the train had left Saint-Frichoux, which was the last station before Doncières, I began to embrace Albertine without bothering about the lady. At Doncières, Saint-Loup had come to meet me at the station, with the greatest difficulty, he told me, for, as he was staying with his aunt, my telegram had only just reached him and he could not, having been unable to make any arrangements beforehand, spare me more than an hour of his time. This hour seemed to me, alas, far too long, for as soon as we had left the train Albertine devoted her whole attention to Saint-Loup. She never talked to me, barely answered me if I addressed her, repulsed me when I approached her. With Robert, on the other hand, she laughed her provoking laugh, talked to him volubly, played with the dog be had brought with him, and, as she excited the animal, deliberately rubbed against its master. I remembered that on the day when Albertine had allowed me to kiss her for the first time, I had had a smile of gratitude for the unknown seducer who had wrought so profound a change in her and had so far simplified my task. I thought of him now with horror. Robert must have noticed that I was not unconcerned about Albertine, for he offered no response to her provocations, which made her extremely annoyed with myself; then he spoke to me as though I had been alone, which, when she realised it, raised me again in her esteem.

He left us at the station. "But you may have about an hour to wait," he told me. "If you spend it here, you will probably see my uncle Charlus, who is going by the train to Paris, ten minutes before yours. I have said good-bye to him already because I have to go back before his train starts. I didn't tell him about you, because I hadn't got your telegram." To the reproaches which I heaped upon Albertine when Saint-Loup had left us, she replied that she had intended, by her coldness towards me, to destroy any idea that he might have formed if, at the moment when the train stopped, he had seen me leaning against her with my arm round her waist. He had indeed noticed this attitude (I had not caught sight of him, otherwise I should have adopted one that was more correct), and had had time to murmur in my ear: "So that's how it is, one of those priggish little girls you told me about, who wouldn't go near Mlle. de Stermaria because they thought her fast?" I had indeed mentioned to Robert, and in all sincerity, when I went down from Paris to visit him at Doncières, and when we were talking about our time at Balbec, that there was nothing to be had from Albertine, that she was the embodiment of virtue. And now that I had long since discovered for myself that this was false, I was even more anxious that Robert should believe it to be true. It would have been sufficient for me to tell Robert that I was in love with Albertine. He was one of those people who are capable of denying themselves a pleasure to spare their friend sufferings which they would feel even more keenly if they themselves were the victims. "Yes, she is still rather childish. But you don't know anything against her?" I added anxiously. "Nothing, except that I saw you clinging together like a pair of lovers."

"Your attitude destroyed absolutely nothing," I told Albertine when Saint-Loup had left us. "Quite true," she said to me, "it was stupid of me, I hurt your feelings, I'm far more unhappy about it than you are. You'll see, I shall never be like that again; forgive me," she pleaded, holding out her hand with a sorrowful air. At that moment, from the entrance to the waiting-room in which we were sitting, I saw advance slowly, followed at a respectful distance by a porter loaded with his baggage, M. de Charlus.

In Paris, where I encountered him only in evening dress, immobile, straitlaced in a black coat, maintained in a vertical posture by his proud aloofness, his thirst for admiration, the soar of his conversation, I had never realised how far he had aged. Now, in a light travelling suit which made him appear stouter, as he swaggered through the room, balancing a pursy stomach and an almost symbolical behind, the cruel light of day broke up into paint, upon his lips, rice-powder fixed by cold cream, on the tip of his nose, black upon his dyed moustaches whose ebon tint formed a contrast to his grizzled hair, all that by artificial light had seemed the animated colouring of a man who was still young.

While I stood talking to him, though briefly because of his train, I kept my eye on Albertine's carriage to show her that I was coming. When I turned my head towards M. de Charlus, he asked me to be so kind as to summon a soldier, a relative of his, who was standing on the other side of the platform, as though he were waiting to take our train, but in the opposite direction, away from Balbec. "He is in his regimental band," said M. de Charlus ,"As you are so fortunate as to be still young enough, and I unfortunately am old enough for you to save me the trouble of going across to him." I took it upon myself to go across to the soldier he pointed out to me, and saw from the lyres embroidered on his collar that he was a bandsman. But, just as I was preparing to execute my commission, what was my surprise, and I may say, my pleasure, on recognising Morel, the son of my uncle's valet, who recalled to me so many memories. They made me forget to convey M. de Charlus's message. "What, you are at Doncières?" " Yes, and they've put me in the band attached to the batteries." But he made this answer in a dry and haughty tone. He had become an intense 'poseur', and evidently the sight of myself, reminding him of his father's profession, was not pleasing to him. Suddenly I saw M. de Charlus descending upon us. My delay had evidently taxed his patience. "I should like to listen to a little music this evening," he said to Morel without any preliminaries, "I pay five hundred francs for the evening, which may perhaps be of interest to one of your friends, if you have any in the band." Knowing as I did the insolence of M. de Charlus, I was astonished at his not even saying how d'ye do to his young friend. The Baron did not however give me time to think. Holding out his hand in the friendliest manner "Good-bye, my dear fellow," he said, as a hint that I might now leave them. I had, as it happened, left my dear

Albertine too long alone. " D'you know," I said to her as I climbed into the carriage, "Life by the seaside, and travelling make me realise that the theatre of the world is stocked with fewer settings than actors, and with fewer actors than situations." "What makes, you say that?" "Because M. de Charlus asked me just now to fetch one of his friends, whom, this instant, on the platform of this station, I have just discovered to be one of my own." But as I uttered these words, I began. to wonder how the Baron could have bridged the social gulf to which I had not given a thought. It occurred to me first of all that it might be through Jupien, whose niece, as the reader may remember, had seemed to show a preference for the violinist. What did baffle me completely was that, when due to leave for Paris in five minutes, the Baron should have asked for a musical evening... But, visualising Jupien's niece again in my memory, I was beginning to find that 'recognitions' did indeed play an important part in life, when all of a sudden the truth flashed across my mind and I realised that I had been absurdly innocent. M. de Charlus had never in his life set eyes upon Morel, nor Morel upon M. de Charlus, who, dazzled but also terrified by a warrior, albeit he bore no weapon but a lyre, had called upon me in his emotion to bring him the person whom he never suspected that I already knew. In any case, the offer of five hundred francs must have made up to Morel for the absence of any previous relations, for I saw that they continued to talk, without reflecting that they were standing close beside our tram. As I recalled the manner in which M. de Charlus had come up to Morel and myself, I saw at once the resemblance to certain of his relatives, when they picked up a woman in the street. Only the desired object had changed its sex. After a certain age, and even if different evolutions are occurring in us, the more we become ourself, the more our characteristic features are accentuated. For Nature, while harmoniously contributing the design of her tapestry, breaks the monotony of the composition thanks to the variety of the intercepted forms. Besides the arrogance with which M. de Charlus had accosted the violinist is relative, and depends upon the point of view one adopts. It would have been recognised by three out of four of the men in society who nodded their heads to him, not by the prefect of police who, a few years later, was to keep him under observation.

"The Paris train is signalled Sir," said the porter who was carrying his luggage. "But I am not going by the train, put it in the cloakroom, damn you!" said M. de Charlus, as he gave twenty francs to the porter, astonished by the change of plan and charmed by the tip. This generosity at once attracted a flower-seller. "Buy these carnations, look, this lovely rose, kind gentlemen, it will bring you luck." M. de Charlus, out of patience, handed her a couple of, francs, in exchange for which the woman gave him her blessing, and her flowers as well. "Good God, why can't she leave us alone," said M. de Charlus, addressing himself in an ironical and complaining tone, as of a man distraught, to Morel, to whom he found a certain comfort in appealing. "We've quite enough to talk about as it is." Perhaps the porter was not yet out of earshot, perhaps M. de Charlus did not care to have too numerous an audience, perhaps these incidental remarks enabled his lofty timidity not to approach too directly the request for an assignation. The musician, turning with a frank imperative and decided air to the flower-seller, raised a hand which repulsed her and indicated to her that they did not want her flowers and that she was to get out of their way as quickly as possible. M. de Charlus observed, with ecstasy this authoritative, virile gesture, made by the graceful hand for which it ought still to have been too weighty, too massively brutal, with a precocious firmness and suppleness which gave to this still beardless adolescent the air of a young David capable of waging war against Goliath. The Baron's admiration was unconsciously blended with the smile with which we observe in a child an expression of gravity beyond his years. "This is a person whom I should like to accompany me on my travels and help me in my business. How he would simplify my life," M. de Charlus said to himself.

    The train for Paris (which M. de Charlus did not take) started. Then we took our seats in our own train, Albertine and I, without my knowing what had become of M. de Charlus and Morel. "We must never quarrel any more, I beg your pardon again," Albertine repeated, alluding to the Saint-Loup incident. "We must always be nice to each other," she said tenderly. "As for your friend Saint-Loup, if you think that I am the least bit interested in him, you are quite mistaken. All that I like about him is that he seems so very fond of you." "He's a very good fellow," I said, taking care not to supply Robert with those imaginary excellences which I should not have failed to invent, out of friendship for himself, had I been with anybody but Albertine. "He's an excellent creature, frank, devoted, loyal, a person you can rely on to do anything.

    Two days later, on the famous Wednesday, in that same little train, which I had again taken at Balbec to go and dine at La Raspelière, I was taking care not to miss Cottard at Graincourt-Saint-Vast, where a second telephone message from Mme. Verdurin had told me that I should find him. He was to join my train and would tell me where we had to get out to pick up the carriages that would be sent from La Raspelière to the station. And so, as the little train barely stopped for a moment at Graincourt, the first station after Doncières, I was standing in readiness, at the open window, so afraid was I of not seeing Cottard or of his not seeing me. Vain fears. I had not realised to what an extent the little clan had moulded all its regular members after the same type, so that they, being moreover in full evening dress, as they stood waiting upon the platform, let themselves be recognised immediately by a certain air of assurance, fashion and familiarity, by a look in their eyes which seemed to sweep, like an empty space in which there was nothing to arrest their attention, the serried ranks of the common herd, watched for the arrival of some fellow-member who had taken the train at an earlier station, and sparkled in anticipation of the talk that was to come. This sign of election, with which the habit of dining together had marked the members of the little group, was not all that distinguished them; when numerous, in full strength, they were massed together, forming a more brilliant patch in the midst of the troop of passengers—what Brichot called the *pecus*—upon whose dull countenances could be read no conception of what was meant by the name Verdurin, no hope of ever dining at La Raspelière.

For the first few moments after the little group had plunged into the carriage, I could not even speak to Cottard, for he was suffocated, not so much by having run in order not to miss the train as by his astonishment at having caught it so exactly. He felt more than the joy inherent in success, almost the hilarity of an excellent joke. "Ah! That was a good one!" he said when he had recovered himself. "A minute later! Pon my soul, that's what they call arriving in the nick of time!" he added, with a wink intended not so much to inquire whether the expression were apt, for he was now overflowing with assurance, but to express his satisfaction. At length he was able to introduce me to the other members of the little clan.

At Harambouville, as the tram was full, a farmer in a blue blouse who had only a third class ticket got into our compartment. The doctor called a porter, showed his card describing him as medical officer to one of the big railway companies, and obliged the station-master to make the farmer get out. This incident so pained and alarmed Saniette's timid spirit that, as soon as he saw it beginning, fearing already lest, in view of the crowd of peasants on the platform, it should assume the proportions of a rising, he pretended to be suffering from a stomachache, and, so that he might not be accused of any share in the responsibility for the doctor's violence, wandered down the corridor, pretending to be looking for what Cottard called the 'water'. Failing to find one, he stood and gazed at the scenery from the other end of the 'twister'.

"It is a charming house," Cottard told me, "you will find a little of everything, for Mme. Verdurin is not exclusive, great scholars like Brichot, the high nobility, such as the Princess Sherbatoff, a great Russian lady, a friend of the Grand Duchess Eudoxie, who even sees her alone at hours when no one else is admitted." As a matter of fact the Grand Duchess Eudoxie, not wishing Princess Sherbatoff, who for years past had been cut by everyone, to come to her house when there might be other people, allowed her to come only in the early morning, when Her Imperial Highness was not at home to any of those friends for whom it would have been as unpleasant to meet the Princess as it would have been awkward for the Princess to meet them.

"Still, no news, I suppose, of the violinist," said Cottard. The event of the day in the little clan was, in fact, the failure of Mme. Verdurin's. favourite violinist. Employed on military service near Doncières, he came three times a week to dine at La Raspelière, having a midnight pass. But two days ago, for the first time, the faithful had been unable to discover him on the tram. It was supposed that he had missed it. But albeit Mme. Verdurin had sent to meet the next tram, and so on until the last had arrived, the carriage had returned empty. "He's certain to have been shoved into the guard-room, there's no other explanation of his desertion. Gad! In soldiering, you know, with those fellows, it only needs a bad-tempered serjeant." "It will be all the more mortifying for Mme. Verdurin," said Brichot, "if he fails again this evening, because our kind hostess has invited to dinner for the first time the neighbours from whom she has taken La Raspelière, the Marquis and Marquise de Cambremer." "This evening, the Marquis and Marquise de Cambremer!" exclaimed Cottard. "But I knew absolutely nothing about it. Naturally, I knew like everybody else that they would be coming one day, but I had no idea that it was to be so soon. Sapristi! He went on, turning to myself, "what did I tell you? The Princess Sherbatoff, the Marquis and Marquise de Cambremer." And, after repeating these names, lulling himself with their melody: "You see that we move in good company;" he said to me. "However, as it's your first appearance, you'll be one of the crowd. It is going to be an exceptionally brilliant gathering." And, turning to Brichot, he went on: "The Mistress will be furious. It is time we appeared to lend her a hand." Ever since Mme. Verdurin had been at La Raspelière she had pretended for the benefit of the faithful to be at once feeling and regretting the necessity of inviting her landlords for one evening. By so doing she would obtain better terms next year, she explained, and was inviting them for business reasons only. For their part, the Cambremers, living far too remote from the social movement ever to suspect that certain ladies of fashion were speaking with a certain consideration of Mme. Verdurin, imagined that she was a person who could know none but Bohemians, was perhaps not even legally married, and so far as people of birth were concerned would never meet any but themselves. They had resigned themselves to the thought of dining with her only to be on good terms with a tenant who, they hoped, would return again for many seasons, especially after they had, in the previous month, learned that she had recently inherited all those millions. It was in silence and without any vulgar pleasantries that they prepared themselves for the fatal day. The faithful had given up hope of its ever coming, so often had Mme. Verdurin already fixed in their hearing a. date that was invariably postponed. These false decisions were intended not merely to make a display of the boredom that she felt at the thought of this dinner-party, but to keep in suspense those members of the little group who were staying in the neighbourhood and were sometimes inclined to fail. Not that the Mistress guessed that the 'great day' was as delightful a prospect to them as to herself, but in order that, having persuaded them that this dinner-party was to her the most terrible of social duties, she might make an appeal to their devotion. "You are not going to leave me all alone with those Chinese mandarins! We must assemble in full force to support the boredom. Naturally, we shan't be able to talk about any of the things in which we are interested. It will be a Wednesday spoiled, but what is one to do!"

"Indeed," Brichot explained, to me, "I fancy that Mme. Verdurin, who is highly intelligent and takes infinite pains in the elaboration of her Wednesdays, was by no means anxious to see these bumpkins of andent lineage but scanty brains. She could not bring herself to invite the dowager Marquise, but has resigned herself to having the son and daughter-in-law." "Ah! We are to see the Marquise de Cambremer?" said Cottard with a smile into which he saw fit to introduce a leer of sentimentality, albeit he had no idea whether Mme. de Cambremer was good-looking or not. But the title Marquise suggested to him fantastic thoughts of gallantry. "Ah! I know her," said Ski, who had met her once when he was out with Mme. Verdurin. "Not in the biblical sense of the word, I trust," said the doctor, darting a sly glance through his eyeglass; this was one of his favourite pleasantries. "She is intelligent," Ski informed me. "'Naturally," he went on, seeing that I said nothing, and dwelling with a smile upon each word, "she is intelligent and at the same time she is not, she lacks education, she is frivolous, but she has an instinct for beautiful things. She may say nothing, but she will never say anything silly. And besides, her colouring is charming. She would be an amusing person to paint," he added, half shutting his eyes, as though he saw her posing in front of him.

As my opinion of her was quite the opposite of what Ski was expressing with so many fine shades, I observed merely that she was the sister of an extremely distinguished engineer, M. Legrandin. "There, you see, you are going to be introduced to a pretty woman," Brichot said to me, "and one never knows what may come of that. Cleopatra was not even a great lady, she was a little woman, the unconscious, terrible little woman of our Meilhac, and just think of the consequences, not only to that idiot Antony, but to the whole of the ancient world." "I have already been introduced to Mme. de Cambremer," I replied. "Ah! In that case, you will find yourself on familiar ground." "I shall be all the more delighted to meet her," I answered him, "because she has prornised me a book by the former curé of Combray about the place-names of this district, and I shall be able to remind her of her promise. I am interested in that priest, and also in etymologies."

"The Princess must be on the train," said Cottard, " she can't have seen us, and will have got into another compartment. Come along and find her. Let's hope this won't land us in trouble!" And he led us all off in search of Princess Sherbatoff. He found her in the corner of an empty compartment, reading the *Revue des Deux Mondes.* She had long ago, from fear of rebuffs, acquired the habit of keeping in her place, or remaining in her corner, in life as on the train, and of not offering her hand until the other person had greeted her. She went on reading as the faithful trooped into her carriage. I recognised her immediately; this woman who might have forfeited her position but was nevertheless of exalted birth, who in any event was the pearl of a salon such as the Verdurins', was the lady whom, on the same train, I had put down, two days earlier, as possibly the keeper of a brothel. Her social personality, which had been so vague, became clear to me as soon as I learned her name; just as when, after racking our brains over a puzzle, we at length hit upon the word which clears up all the obscurity, and which, in the case of a person, is his name. To discover two days later who the person is, with whom one has travelled in the train is a far more amusing surprise than to read in the next number of a magazine the clue to the problem set in the previous number. Big restaurants, casinos, local trains, are the family portrait galleries of these social enigmas. "Princess, we must have missed you at Maineville May we come and sit in your compartment?" "Why, of course," said the Princess who, upon hearing Cottard address her, but only then, raised from her magazine a pair of eyes which, like the eyes of M. de. Charlus, although gentler, saw perfectly well the people of whose presence she pretended to be unaware. Cottard, coming to the conclusion that the fact of my having been invited to meet the Cambremers was a sufficient recommendation, decided, after a momentary hesitation, to introduce me to the Princess, who bowed with great courtesy but appeared to be hearing my name for the first time. The Princess informed us that the young violinist had been found. He had been confined to bed the evening before by a sick headache, but was coming that evening and bringing with him a friend of his father whom he had met at Doncières. She had learned this from Mme. Verdurin with whom she had taken luncheon that morning, she told us in a rapid voice, rolling her rs, with her Russian accent, softly at the back of her throat, as though they were not rs but *is*. "Ah! You had luncheon with her this morning," Cottard said to the Princess; but turned his eyes to myself, the purport of this remark being to show me on what intimate terms the Princess was with the Mistress. "You are indeed a faithful adherent!" "Yes, I love the little ciricle, so intelligent, so agleeable, neverl spiteful, quite simple, not at all snobbish, and clevel to theirl fingle-tips."

"Nom d'une pipe! I must have lost my ticket, I can't find it anywhere," cried Cottard, with an agitation that was, in the circumstances, quite unjustified. He knew that at Douville, where a couple of landaus would be awaiting us, the collector would let him pass without a ticket, and would only bare his head all the more humbly, so that the salute, might furnish an explanation of his indulgence, to wit that he had of course recognised Cottard as one of the Verdurins' regular guests. "They won't shove me in the lock-up for that," the doctor concluded. "You were saying, Sir," I inquired of Brichot, "that there used to be some famous waters near here; how do we know that?" "The name of the next station is one of a multitude of proofs. It is called Fervaches." "I don't undlestand what he's talking about," mumbled the Princess, as though she were saying to me out of politeness: "He's rather a bore, ain't he?" "Why, Princess, Fervaches means hot springs. *Fervidae aquae*. But to return to the young violinist," Brichot went on, "I was quite forgetting, Cottard, to tell you the great news. Had you heard that our poor friend Dechambre, who used to be Mme. Verdurin's favourite pianist, has just died? It is terribly sad."

"He was quite young," replied Cottard, "but he must have had some trouble with his liver; there must have been something sadly wrong in that quarter, he had been looking very queer indeed for a long time past." "But he was not so young as all that," said Brichot; "in the days when Elstir and Swann used to come to Mme. Verdurin's, Dechambre had already made himself a reputation in Paris, and, what is remarkable, without having first received the baptism of success abroad. Ah! He was no follower of the Gospel according to Saint Barnum, that fellow" "You are mistaken, he could not have been going to Mme. Verdurin's, at that time, he was still in the nursery." "But, unless my old memory plays me false, I was under the impression that Dechambre used to play Vinteuil's sonata for Swann, when that clubman, who had broken with the aristocracy, had still no idea that he was one day to become the embourgeoised Prince Consort of our national Odette." "It is impossible, Vinteuil's sonata was played at Mme. Verdurin's long after Swann ceased to come there," said the doctor, who, like all people who work hard and think that they remember many things which they imagine to be of use to them, forget many others, a condition which enables them to go into ecstasies over the memories of people who have nothing else to do. "You are hopelessly muddled, though your brain is as sound as ever," said the doctor with a smile. Brichot admitted that he was mistaken. The train stopped. We were at la Sogne. The name stirred my curiosity. "How I should like to know what all these names mean," I said to Cottard: "You must ask M. Brichot, he may know, perhaps." "Why, la Sogne is la Cicogne, *Siconia,*" replied Brichot, whom I was burning to interrogate about many other names.

Forgetting her attachment to her 'corner', Mme. Sherbatoff kindly offered to change places with me, so that I might talk more easily with Brichot, whom I wanted to ask about other etymologies that interested me, and assured me that she did not mind in the least whether she travelled with her face or her back to the engine, standing, or seated, or anyhow. She remained on the defensive until she had discovered a newcomer's intentions, but as soon as she had realised that these were friendly, she would do everything in her power to oblige. At length the train stopped at the station of Douville-Féterne, which being more or less equidistant from the villages of Féterne and Douville, bore for this reason their hyphenated name. "Saperlipopette!" exclaimed Doctor Cottard, "when we came to the barrier where the tickets were collected, and, pretending to have only just discovered his loss, "I can't find my ticket, I must have lost it." But the collector, taking off his cap, assured him that it did not matter and smiled respectfully. The Princess (giving instructions to the coachman, as though she were a sort of lady in waiting to Mme. Verdurin, who, because of the Cambremers, had not been able to come to the station, as, for that matter, she rarely did) took me, and also Brichot, with herself in one of the carriages. The doctor, Saniette and Ski got into the other.

The driver, although quite young, was the Verdurins' head coachman, the only one who had any right to the title; he took them, in the daytime, on all their excursions, for he knew all the roads, and in the evening went down to meet the faithful and took them back to the station later on. He was accompanied by extra helpers (whom he selected if necessary). He was an excellent fellow, sober and capable, but with one of those melancholy faces on which a fixed stare indicates that the merest trifle will make the person fly into a passion, not to say nourish dark thoughts. But at the moment he was quite happy, for he had managed to secure a place for his brother, another excellent type of fellow, with the Verdurins. We began by driving through Douville. Grassy knolls ran down from the village to the sea, in wide slopes to which their saturation in moisture and salt gave a richness, a softness, a vivacity of extreme tones. The islands and indentations of Rivebelle, far nearer now than at Balbec, gave this part of the coast the appearance, novel to me, of a relief map. We passed by some little bungalows, almost all of which were let to painters; turned into a track upon which some loose cattle, as frightened as were our horses, barred our way for ten minutes, and emerged upon the cliff road.

From the height we had now reached, the sea suggested no longer, as at Balbec, the undulations of swelling mountains, but on the contrary, the view, beheld from a mountain-top or from a road winding round its flank, of a blue-green glacier or a glittering plain, situated at a lower level. The lines of the currents seemed to be fixed upon its surface, and to have traced there for ever their concentric circles; the enamelled face of the sea which changed imperceptibly in colour, assumed towards the head of the bay, where an estuary opened, the blue whiteness of milk, in which little black boats that did not move seemed entangled like flies. I felt that from nowhere could one discover a vaster prospect. But at each turn in the road a fresh expanse was added to it and when we arrived at the Douville toll-house, the spur of the cliff which until then had concealed from us half the bay, withdrew, and all of a sudden I descried upon my left a gulf as profound as that which I had already had before me, but one that changed the proportions of the other and doubled its beauty. The air at this lofty point acquired a keenness and purity that intoxicated me. I adored the Verdurins; that they should have sent a carriage for us seemed to me a touching act of kindness. I should have liked to kiss the Princess. I told her that I had never seen anything so beautiful. She professed that she too loved this spot more than any other. But I could see that to her, as to the Verdurins, the thing that really mattered was not to gaze at the view like tourists, but to partake of good meals there, to entertain people whom they liked, to write letters, to read books, in short to live in these surroundings, passively allowing the beauty of the scene to soak into them, rather than making, it the object of their attention.

After the toll-house, where the carriage had stopped for a moment at such a height above the sea that, as from a mountain-top, the sight of the blue gulf beneath almost made one dizzy, I opened the window; the sound, distinctly caught, of each wave that broke in turn had something sublime in its softness and precision.. It melted my heart that the Verdurins should have sent to meet us at the station. I said as much to the Princess, who seemed to think that I was greatly exaggerating so simple an act of courtesy. I know that she admitted subsequently to Cottard that she found me very enthusiastic; he replied that I was too emotional, required sedatives and ought to take to knitting. I pointed out to the Princess every tree, every little house smothered in its mantle of roses, I made her admire everything, I would have liked to take her in my arms and press her to my heart. She told me that she could see that I had a gift for painting, that of course I must sketch, that she was surprised that nobody had told her about it. And she confessed that the country was indeed picturesque. We drove through, where it perched upon its height, the little village of Englesqueville *(En gleberti villa,* Brichot informed us). "But are you quite sure that there will be a party this evening, in spite of Dechambre's death, Princess?" he went on, without stopping to think that the presence at the station of the carriage in which we were sitting was in itself an answer to his question. "Yes," said the Princess, "M. Verdurin insisted that it should not be put off, simply to keep his wife from thinking. And besides, after never failing for all these years to entertain on Wednesdays, such a change in her habits would have been bound to upset her. Her nerves are velly bad just now. M. Verdurin was particularly pleased that you were coming to dine this evening, because he knew that it would be a great distraction for Mme. Verdurin," said the Princess, forgetting her pretence of having never heard my name before. "I think that it will be as well not to say *anything* in front of Mme. Verdurin," the Princess added. "Ah! I am glad you warned me," Brichot artlessly replied. "I shall pass on your suggestion to Cottard." The carriage stopped for a moment. It moved on again, but the sound that the wheels had been making in the village street had ceased. We had turned into the main avenue of La Raspelière where M. Verdurin stood waiting for us upon the steps. "I did well to put on a dinner-jacket," he said, observing with pleasure that the faithful had put on theirs "since I have such smart gentlemen in my party." And as I apologised for not having changed: "Why that's quite all right. We're all friends here. I should be delighted to offer you one of my own dinner-jackets, but it wouldn't fit you." The handclasp throbbing with emotion which, as he entered the hall of La Raspelière, and by way of condolence at the death of the pianist, Brichot gave our host, elicited no response from the latter. I told him how greatly I admired the scenery. "Ah! All the better, and you've seen nothing, we must take you round. Why not come and spend a week or two here, the air is excellent." Brichot was afraid that his handclasp had not been understood. "Ah! Poor Dechambre!" he said, but in an undertone, in case Mme. Verdurin was within earshot. "It is terrible," replied M. Verdurin lightly. "So young," Brichot pursued the point. Annoyed at being detained over these futilities, M. Verdurin replied in a hasty tone and with an embittered groan, not of grief but of irritated impatience: "Why yes, of course but what's to be done about it, it's no use crying over spilt milk, talking about him won't bring him back to life, will it?" And his civility returning with his joviality: "Come along, my good Brichot, get your things off quickly. We have a bouillabaisse which mustn't be kept waiting. But, in heaven's name, don't start talking about Dechambre to Madame Verdurin. You know that she always hides her feelings, but she is quite morbidly sensitive. I give you my word; when she heard that Dechambre was dead, she almost cried," said M. Verdurin in a tone of profound irony. One might have concluded, from hearing him speak, that it implied a form of insanity to regret the death of a friend of thirty years' standing, and on the other hand one gathered that the perpetual union of M. Verdurin and his wife did not preclude his constantly criticising her and her frequently irritating him. "If you mention it to her, she will go and make herself ill again. It is deplorable, three weeks after her bronchitis. When that happens, it is I who have to be sicknurse., You can understand that I have had more than enough of it. Grieve for Dechambre's fate in your heart as much, as you like. Think of him, but do not speak about him. I was very fond of Dechambre, but you cannot blame me for being fonder still of my wife. Here's Cottard, now, you can ask him." And indeed he knew that a family doctor can do many little services, such as prescribing that one must not give way to grief.

The docile Cottard had said to the Mistress: "Upset yourself like that, and to-morrow you will give me a temperature of 102," as he might have said to the cook: "Tomorrow you will give me a *riz de veau.*" Medicine, when it fails to cure the sick, busies itself with changing the sense of verbs and pronouns.

Mme. Verdurin and her husband had acquired, in their idleness, cruel instincts for which the great occasions, occurring too rarely, no longer sufficed. They had succeeded in effecting a breach between Odette and Swann, between Brichot and his mistress.. They would try it again with some one else, that was understood. But the opportunity did not present itself every day.

"Whatever you do," Brichot reminded Cottard, who had not heard what M. Verdurin was saying, "mum's the word before Mme. Verdurin. Have no fear, 0 Cottard, you are dealing with a sage, as Theocritus says. Besides, M. Verdurin is right, what is the use of lamentations," he went on, for, being capable of assimilating forms of speech and the ideas which they suggested to him, but having no finer perception, he had admired in M. Verdurin's remarks the most courageous stoicism. "All the same, it is a great talent that has gone from the world." "What, are you still talking about Dechambré," said M. Verdurin, who had gone on ahead of us, and, seeing that we were not following him, had turned back. "Listen," he said to Brichot, "nothing is gained by exaggeration. The fact of his being dead is no excuse for making him out a genius, which he was not. He played well, I admit, and what is more, he was in his proper element here; transplanted, he ceased to exist. My wife, was infatuated with him and made his reputation. You know what she is. I will go farther, in the interest of his own reputation he has died at the right moment, he is done to a turn, as the demoiselles de Caen, grilled according to the incomparable recipe of Pampilles, are going to be, I hope (unless you keep us standing here all night with your jeremiads in this Kasbah exposed to all the winds of heaven). You don't seriously expect us all to die of hunger because Dechambre is dead, when for the last year he was obliged to practise scales before giving a concert; to recover for the moment, and for the moment only, the suppleness of his wrists. Besides, you are going to hear this evening, or at any rate to meet, for the rascal is too fond of deserting his art, after dinner, for the card table, somebody who is a far greater artist than Dechambre, a youngster whom my wife has discovered" (as she, had discovered Dechambre, and Paderewski, and everybody else): Morel. He has not arrived yet, the devil. I shall have to send a carriage down to meet the last train. He is coming with an old friend of his family whom he has picked up, and who bores him to tears, but otherwise, not to get into trouble with his father, he would have been obliged to stay down at Doncières and keep him company: the Baron de Charlus." The faithful entered the drawing-room. M. Verdurin, who had remained behind with me while I took off my things, took my arm by way of a joke, as one's host does at a dinner-party when there is no lady for one to take in. "Did, you have a pleasant journey?" "Yes, M. Brichot told me things which interested me greatly," said I, thinking of the etymologies, and because I had heard that the Verdurins greatly admired Brichot. "I am surprised to hear that he told you anything," said M. Verdurin, "he is such a retiring man, and talks so little about the things he knows." This compliment did not strike me as being very apt. "He seems charming," I remarked. "Exquisite, delicious, not the sort of man you meet every day, such a light, fantastic touch, my wife adores him, and so do I!" replied M. Verdurin in an exaggerated tone, as though repeating a lesson. Only then did I grasp that what he had said to me about Brichot was ironical. And I asked myself whether M. Verdurin, since those far-off days of which I had heard reports, had not shaken off the yoke of his wife's tutelage.

Mme. Verdurin who, to welcome us in her immense drawing-room, in which displays of grasses, poppies, field-flowers, plucked only that morning, alternated with a similar theme painted on the walls, two centuries earlier, by an artist of exquisite taste, had risen for a moment from a game of cards which she was playing with an old friend, begged us to excuse her for just one minute while she finished her game, talking to us the while. What I told her about my impressions did not, however, seem altogether to please her. For one thing I was shocked to observe that she and her husband came indoors every day long before the hour of those sunsets which were considered so fine when seen from that cliff, and finer still from the terrace of La Raspelière, and which I would have travelled miles to see. "Yes, it's incomparable," said Mme. Verdurin carelessly, with a glance at the huge windows which gave the room a wall of glass. "Even though we have it always in front of us, we never grow tired of it," and she turned her attention back to her cards. Now my very enthusiasm made me exacting. I expressed my regret that I could not see from the drawing-room the rocks of Darnetal which, Elstir had told me, were quite lovely at that hour, when they reflected so many colours. "Ah! You can't see them from here, you would have to go to the end of the park to the view of the bay. From the seat there, you can take in the whole panorama. But you can't go there by yourself, you will lose your way. I can take you there, if you like," she added kindly." I did not insist and understood that it was enough for the Verdurins to know that this sunset made its way into their drawing-room or dining-room, like a magnificent painting, like a priceless Japanese enamel; justifying the high rent that they were paying for La Raspelière, with plate and linen, but a thing to which they rarely raised their eyes; the important thing, here, for them was to live comfortably, to take drives, to feed well, to talk, to entertain agreeable friends whom they provided with amusing games of billiards, good meals, merry tea-parties. I noticed, however, later on, how intelligently they had learned to know the district, taking their guests for excursions as 'novel' as the music to which they made them listen. The part which the flowers of La Raspelière, the roads by the sea's edge, the old houses, the undiscovered churches, played in the life of M. Verdurin was so great that those people who saw him only in Paris and who, themselves, substituted for the life by the seaside and in the country the refinements of life in town could barely understand the idea that he himself formed of his own life or the importance that his pleasures gave him in his own eyes. This importance was further enhanced by the fact that the Verdurins were convinced that La Raspelière, which they hoped to purchase, was a property without its match in the world. This superiority which their self-esteem made them attribute to La Raspelière justified in their eyes my enthusiasm which, but for that, would have annoyed them slightly, because of the disappointments which it involved (like my disappointment when long ago I had first listened to Berma) and which I frankly admitted to them.

"I hear the carriage coming back," the Mistress suddenly murmured. Let us state briefly that Mme. Verdurin, quite apart from the inevitable changes due to increasing years, no longer resembled what she had been at the time when Swann and Odette used to listen to the little phrase in her house. Even when she heard it played, she was no longer obliged to assume the air of attenuated admiration which she used to assume then, for that had become her normal expression. Under the influence of the countless neuralgias which the music of Bach, Wagner, Vinteuil, Debussy had given her, Mme.Verdurin's brow had assumed enormous proportions, like limbs that are finally crippled by rheumatism. Her temples, suggestive of a pair of beautiful, painstricken, milk-white spheres, in which Harmony rolled endlessly, flung back upon either side her silvered tresses, and proclaimed, on the Mistress's behalf, without any need for her to say a word: "I know what is in store for me tonight." Her features no longer took the trouble to formulate successively aesthetic impressions of undue violence, for they had themselves become their permanent expression on a countenance ravaged and superb. This attitude of resignation to the ever impending sufferings inflicted by Beauty, and of the courage that was required to make her dress for dinner when she, had barely recovered from the effects of the last sonata, had the result that Mme. Verdurin, even when listening to the most heartrending music, preserved a disdainfully impassive countenance, and actually withdrew into retirement to swallow her two spoonfuls of aspirin. "Why, yes, here they are!" M. Verdurin cried with relief when he saw the door open to admit Morel, followed by M. de Charlus. The latter, to whom dining with the Verdurins meant not so much going into society as going into questionable surroundings, was as frightened as a schoolboy making his way for the first time into a brothel with the utmost deference towards its mistress. Moreover the persistent desire that M. de Charlus felt to appear virile and frigid, was overcome (when he appeared in the open doorway) by those traditional ideas of politeness which are awakened as soon as shyness destroys an artificial attitude and makes an appeal to the resources of the subconscious. When it is a Charlus, whether he be noble or plebeian, that is stirred by such a sentiment of instinctive and atavistic politeness to strangers, it is always the spirit of a relative of the female sex, attendant like a goddess, or incarnate as a double, that undertakes to introduce him into a strange drawing-room and to mould his attitude until he comes face to face with his hostess.

The society in which M. de Charlus had lived furnished him at this critical moment, with different examples, with other patterns of affability, and above all with the maxim that one must, in certain cases, when, dealing with people of humble rank, bring into play and make use of one's rarest graces, which one normally holds in reserve, so it was with a flutter, archly, and with the same sweep with which a skirt would have enlarged and impeded his waddling motion that he advanced upon Mme. Verdurin with so flattered and honoured an air that one would have said that to be taken to her house was for him a supreme favour. His head inclined forwards, his face, upon which satisfaction vied with propriety, was creased with little wrinkles of affability. One would have thought that it was Mme. de Marsantes who was entering the room, so prominent at that moment was the woman whom a mistake on the part of Nature had enshrined in the body of M. de Charlus. It was true that the Baron had made every effort to obliterate this mistake and to assume a masculine appearance. But no sooner had he succeeded than, he having in the meantime kept the same tastes, this habit of looking at things through a woman's eyes gave him a fresh feminine appearance, due this time not to heredity but to his own way of living. And as he had gradually come to regard, even social questions from the feminine point of view, and without noticing it, for it is not only by dint of lying to other people, but also by lying to oneself that one ceases to be aware that one is lying, albeit he had called upon his body to manifest, (at the moment of his entering the Verdurins drawing-room) all the courtesy of a great nobleman, that body which had fully understood what M. de Charlus had ceased to apprehend, displayed, to such an extent that the Baron would have deserved the epithet 'ladylike', all the attractions of a great lady.

Morel, who accompanied him, came to shake hands with me. From that first moment, owing to a twofold change that occurred in him I formed (alas, I was not warned in time to act upon it!) a bad impression of him. I have said that Morel, having risen above his father's menial status, was generally pleased to indulge in a contemptuous familiarity. He had talked to me on the day when he brought me the photographs without once addressing me as Monsieur, treating me as an inferior. What was my surprise at Mme. Verdurin's to see him bow very low before me, and before me alone, and to hear, before he had even uttered a syllable to anyone else, words of respect, most respectful—such words as I thought could not possibly flow from his pen or fall from his lips—addressed to myself. I at once suspected that he had some favour to ask of me. Taking me aside a minute later: "Monsieur would be doing me a very great service," he said to me, going so, far this time as to address me in the third person, "by keeping from Mme. Verdurin and her guests the nature of the profession that my father practised with his uncle. It would be best to say that he was, in your family, the agent for estates so considerable as to put him almost on a level with your parents." Morel's request annoyed me intensely because it obliged me to magnify not his father's position, in which I took not the slightest interest, but the wealth— the apparent wealth of my own, which I felt to be absurd. But he appeared so unhappy, so pressing, that I could not refuse him. "No, before dinner," he said in an imploring tone, "Monsieur can easily find some excuse for taking Mme. Verdurin aside." This was what, in the end, I did, trying to enhance to the best of my ability the distinction of Morel's father, without unduly exaggerating the 'style', the 'worldly goods' of my own family. It went like a letter through the post, notwithstanding the astonishment of Mme.

Verdurin, who had had a nodding acquaintance with my grandfather. And as she had no tact, hated family life (that dissolvent of the little nucleus), after telling me that she remembered, long ago, seeing my greatgrandfather, and after speaking of him as of somebody who was almost an idiot, who would have been incapable of understanding the little group, and who, to use her expression, "was not one of us," she said to me: "Families are such a bore, the only thing is to get right away from them;" and at once proceeded to tell me of a trait in my great-grandfather's character of which I was unaware, although I might have suspected it at home (I had never seen him, but they frequently spoke of him), his remarkable stinginess (in contrast to the somewhat excessive generosity of my great-uncle the friend of the lady in pink and Morel's father's employer):

"Why, of course, if your grandparents had such a grand agent, that only shows that there are all sorts of people in a family. Your grandfather's father was so stingy that, at the end of his life, when he was almost half-witted—between you and me, he was never anything very special, you are worth the whole lot of them—he could not bring himself to pay a penny for his ride on the omnibus. So that they were obliged to have him followed by somebody who paid his fare for him, and to let the old miser think that his friend M. de Persigny, the Cabinet Minister, had given him a permit to travel free on the omnibuses. But I am delighted to hear that *our* Morel's father held such a good position. I was under the impression that he had been a schoolmaster, but that's nothing, I must have misunderstood. In any case, it makes not the slightest difference, for I must tell you that here we appreciate only true worth, the personal contribution, what I call the participation. Provided that a person is artistic, provided in a word that he is one of the brotherhood, nothing else matters." The way in which Morel was one of the brotherhood was—so far as I have been able to discover—that he was sufficiently fond of both women and men to satisfy either sex with the fruits of his experience of the other. But what it is essential to note here is that as soon as I had given him my word that I would speak on his behalf to Mme. Verdurin, as soon, moreover, as I had actually done so, and without any possibility of subsequent retraction, Morel's 'respect' for myself vanished as though by magic, the formal language of respect melted away, and indeed for some time he avoided me, contriving to appear contemptuous of me, so that if Mme. Verdurin wanted me to give him a message, to ask him to play something, he would continue to talk to one of the faithful, then move on to another, changing his seat if I approached him. The others were obliged to tell him three or four times that I had spoken to him, after which he would reply, with an air of constraint, briefly, that is to say unless we were by ourselves. When that happened, he was expansive, friendly, for there was a charming side to him. I concluded all the same from this first evening that his must be a vile nature, that he would not, at a pinch, shrink from any act of meanness, was incapable of gratitude. In which he resembled the majority of mankind. But inasmuch as I had inherited a strain of my grandmother's nature, and enjoyed the diversity of other people without expecting anything of them or resenting anything that they did, I overlooked his baseness, rejoiced in his gaiety when it was in evidence, and indeed in what I believe to have been a genuine affection on his part when, having gone the whole circuit of his false ideas of human nature, he realised (with a jerk, for he showed strange reversions to a blind and primitive savagery) that my kindness to him was disinterested, that my indulgence arose not from a want of perception but from what he called goodness; and more, important still, I was enraptured by his art which indeed was little more than an admirable virtuosity, but which made me (without his being in the intellectual sense of the word a real musician) hear again or for the first time so much good music.

I had just given Mme. Verdurin the message with which Morel had charged me and was talking to M. de Charlus about Saint-Loup, when Cottard burst into the room announcing, as though the house were on fire, that the Cambremers had arrived. Mme. Verdurin, not wishing to appear before strangers such as M. de Charlus (whom Cottard had not seen) and myself, to attach any great importance to the arrival of the Cambremers, did not move, made no response to the announcement of these tidings, and merely said to the doctor, fanning herself gracefully, and adopting the tone of a Marquise in the Théâtre-Français: "The Baron has just been telling us......." This was too much for Cottard! Less abruptly than he would have done in the old days, for learning and high positions had added weight to his utterance, but with the emotion, nevertheless, which he recaptured at the Verdurins, he exclaimed: "A Baron! What Baron? Where's the Baron?" staring round the room with an astonishment that bordered on incredulity. Mme. Verdurin, with the affected indifference of a hostess when a servant has, in front of her guests, broken a valuable glass, and with the artificial, high-falutin tone of a conservatoire prize-winner acting in a play by the younger Dumas, replied, pointing with her fan to Morel's patron: "Why, the Baron de Charlus, to whom let me introduce you, M. le Professeur Cottard." Mme. Verdurin was, for that matter, by no means sorry to have an opportunity of playing the leading lady. M. de Charlus proffered two fingers which the Professor clasped with the kindly smile of a 'Prince of Science'. But he stopped short upon seeing the Cambremers enter the room, while M. de Charlus led me into a corner to tell me something, not without feeling my muscles, which is a German habit. M. de Cambremer bore no resemblance to the old Marquise. To anyone who had only heard of him, or of letters written by him, well and forcibly expressed, his personal appearance was startling. No doubt, one would grow accustomed to it. But his nose had chosen to place itself aslant above his mouth, perhaps the only crooked line, among so many, which one would never have thought of tracing upon his face, and one that indicated a vulgar stupidity, aggravated still further by the proximity of a Norman complexion on cheeks that were like two ripe apples. Mme de Cambremer was furious at having compromised herself by coming to the Verdurins' and had done so only upon the entreaties of her mother-in-law and husband, in the hope of renewing the lease. But, being less well-bred than they, she made no secret of the ulterior motive and for the last fortnight had been making fun of this dinner party to her women friends. "You know we are going to dine with our tenants." That will be well worth an increased rent. As a matter of fact, I am rather curious to see what they have done to our poor old La Raspelière" (as though she had been born in the house, and would find there all her old family associations). "Our old keeper told me only yesterday that you wouldn't know the place. I can't bear to think of all that must be going on there. I am sure we shall have to have the whole place disinfected before we move in again." She arrived haughty and morose, with the air of a great lady whose castle, owing to a state of war, is occupied by the enemy, but who nevertheless feels herself at home and makes a point of showing the conquerors that they are intruding. Mme. de Cambremer could not see me at first for I was in a bay at the side of the room with M. de Charlus, who was telling me that he had heard from Morel that Morel's father had been an 'agent' in my family, and that he, Charlus, credited me with sufficient intelligence and magnanimity (a term common to himself and Swann) to forego the mean and ignoble pleasure which vulgar little idiots (I was warned) would not have failed, in my place, to give themselves by revealing to our hosts details which they might regard as derogatory. "The mere fact that I take an interest in him and extend my protection over him, gives him a pre-eminence and wipes out the past;" the Baron concluded. As I listened to him and promised the silence which I would have kept even without any hope of being considered in return intelligent and magnanimous, I was looking at Mme de Cambremer. And I had difficulty in recognising the melting, savoury morsel which I had had beside me the other afternoon at teatime, on the terrace at Balbec, in the Norman rock-cake that I now saw, hard as a rock, in which the faithful would in vain have tried to set their teeth. Irritated in anticipation by the knowledge that her husband inherited his mother's simple kindliness, which would make him assume a flattered expression whenever one of the faithful was presented to him, anxious however to perform her duty as a leader of society, when Brichot had been named to her she decided to make him and her husband acquainted, as she had seen her more fashionable friends do, but, anger or pride prevailing over the desire to show her knowledge of the world, she said not, as she ought to have said: "Allow me to introduce my husband," but "I introduce you to my husband," holding, aloft thus the banner of the Cambremers, without avail, for her husband bowed as low before Brichot as she had expected. But all Mme. de Cambremer's ill humour vanished in an instant when her eye fell on M. de Charlus, whom she knew by sight. Never had she succeeded in obtaining an introduction, even at the time of her intimacy with Swann. For as M. de Charlus always sided with the woman, with his sister-in-law against M. de Guermantes's mistresses, with Odette, at that-time still unmarried, but an old flame of Swann's, against the new, he had, as a stern defender of morals and. faithful protector of homes, given Odette—and kept—the promise that he would never allow himself to be presented to Mme. de Cambremer. ''She had certainly never guessed that it was at the Verdurins' that she was at length to meet this unapproachable this unapproachable person. M. de Cambremer knew that this was a great joy to her, so great that he himself was moved by it and looked at his wife with an air that implied: "You are glad now you decided to come, aren't you?"

Mme. Verdurin whispered in her husband's ear "Shall I offer my arm to the Baron de Charlus? As you will have Mme. de Cambremer on your right, we might divide the honours." "No," said M. Verdurin, "since the other is higher in rank" (meaning that M. de Cambremer was a Marquis), "M. de Charlus is, strictly speaking, his inferior." "Very well, I shall put him beside the Princess." And Mme. Verdurin introduced Mme. Sherbatoff to M. de Charlus; each of them bowed in silence, with an air of knowing all about the other and of promising a mutual secrecy. M. Verdurin introduced me to M. de Cambremer. Before he had even begun to speak in his loud and slightly stammering voice, his tall figure and high complexion displayed in their oscillation the martial hesitation of a commanding officer who tries to put you at your ease and says: "I have heard about you, I shall see what can be done; your punishment shall be remitted; we don't thirst for blood here; it will be all right." Then, as he shook my hand: "I think you know my mother," he said to me. The word 'think' seemed to him appropriate to the discretion of a first meeting, but not to imply any uncertainty, for he went on: "I have a note for you from her." M. de Cambremer took a childish pleasure in revisiting a place where he had lived for so long. "I am at home again," he said to Mme. Verdurin, while his eyes marvelled at recognising the flowers painted on panels over the doors, and the marble busts on their high pedestals, he might all the same have felt himself at sea, for Mme. Verdurin had brought with her a quantity of fine old things of her own. In this respect, Mme. Verdurin, while regarded by the Cambremers as having turned everything upside down, was not revolutionary but intelligently conservative in sense which they did not understand. They were thus wrong in accusing her of hating the old house and of degrading it by hanging plain cloth curtains instead of their rich plush, like an ignorant parish priest reproaching a diocesan architect with putting back in its place the old carved wood which the cleric had thrown on the rubbish heap, and had seen fit to replace with ornaments purchased in the Place Saint-Sulpice. Furthermore, a herb garden was beginning to take the place in front of the mansions of the borders that were the pride not merely of the Cambremers but of their gardener. The latter, who regarded the Cambremers as his sole masters, and groaned beneath the yoke of the Verdurins, as though the place were under occupation for the moment by an invading army, went in secret to unburden his griefs to its dispossessed mistress, grew irate at the scorn that was heaped upon his araucarias, begonias, house-leeks, double dahlias, and at anyone's daring in so grand a place to grow such common plants as camomile and maidenhair. Mme. Verdurin felt this silent opposition and had made up her mind, if she took a long lease of La Raspelière or even bought the place, to make one of her conditions the dismissal of the gardener, by whom his mistress, on the contrary, set great store. He had worked for her without payment when times were bad, he adored her; but by that odd multiformity of opinion which we find in the lower orders, among whom the most profound moral scorn is embedded in the most passionate admiration, which in turn overlaps old and undying grudge; he used often to say of Mme. de Cambremer who, in '70, in a house that she owned in the East of France, surprised by the invasion, had been obliged to endure for a month the contact of the

Germans: "What many people can't forgive Mme. la Marquise is that during the war she took the side of the Prussians and even had them to stay in her house. At any other time, I could understand it; but in war time, she ought not to have done it. It is not right." So that he was faithful to her unto death, venerated her for her goodness, and firmly believed that she had been guilty of treason. Mme. Verdurin was annoyed that M. de Cambremer should pretend to feel so much at home at La Raspelière. "You must notice a good many changes, all the same," she replied. "For one thing there were those big bronze Barbedienne devils and some horrid little plush chairs which I packed off at once to the attic, though even that is too good a place for them." After this bitter retort to M. de Cambremer, she offered him her arm to go into dinner. He hesitated for a moment, saying to himself: "I can't really go in before M. de Charlus." But supposing the other to be an old friend of the house, seeing that he was not set in the post of honour, he decided to take the arm that was offered him and told Mme. Verdurin how proud he felt to be admitted into the symposium (so it was that he styled the little nucleus, not without a smile of satisfaction at his knowledge of the term). Cottard, who was seated next to M. de Charlus, beamed at him through his glass, to make his acquaintance and to break the ice, with a series of winks far more insistent than they would have been in the old days, and not interrupted by fits of shyness. And these engaging glances, enhanced by the smile that accompanied them, were no longer dammed by the glass but overflowed on all sides. The Baron, who readily imagined people of his own kind everywhere, had no doubt that Cottard was one, and was making eyes at him. At once he turned on the Professor the cold shoulder of the invert, as contemptuous of those whom he attracts as he is ardent in pursuit of such as attract him. M. de Charlus's error was brief. His divine discernment showed him after the first minute that Cottard was not of his kind, and that he need not fear his advances either for himself, which would merely have annoyed him, or for Morel, which would have seemed to him a more serious matter. He recovered his calm, and as he was still beneath the influence of the transit of Venus Androgyne, now and again he smiled a faint smile at the Verdurins without taking the trouble to open his mouth, merely curving his lips at one corner and for an instant kindled a coquettish light in his eyes, exactly as his sister-in-law the Duchesse de Guermantes might have done.

As for Cottard, blocked up on one side by M.de Charlus's silence, and driven to seek an outlet elsewhere, he turned to me with one of those questions which so impressed his patients when it hit the mark and showed them that he could put himself so to speak inside their bodies; if on the other hand it missed the mark, it enabled him to check certain theories, to widen his previous point of view. "When you come to a relatively high altitude, such as this where we now are, do you find that the change increases your tendency to choking fits?" he asked me with the certainty of either arousing admiration or enlarging his own knowledge. M. de Cambremer heard the question and smiled. "I can't tell you how amused I am to hear that you have choking fits," he flung at me across the table. He did not mean that it made him happy, though as a matter of fact it did. For this worthy man could not hear any reference to another person's sufferings without a feeling of satisfaction and a spasm of hilarity which speedily gave place to the instinctive pity of a kind heart. But his words had another meaning which was indicated more precisely by the clause that followed: "It amuses me," he explained, "because my sister has them too." And indeed it did amuse him, as it would have amused him to hear me mention, as one of my friends, a person who was constantly coming to their house. "How small the world is", was the reflection which he formed mentally and which I saw written upon his smiling face when Cottard spoke to me of my choking fits. And these began to establish themselves from the evening of this dinner-party, as a sort of interest in common, after which M. de Cambremer never failed to inquire, if only to hand on a report to his sister. As I answered the questions with which his wife kept plying me about Morel, my thoughts returned to a conversation I had had with my mother that afternoon. Having, without any attempt to dissuade me from going to the Verdurins' if there was a chance of my being amused there, suggested that it was a house of which my grandfather would not have approved, which would have made him exclaim: "On guard!" my mother had gone on to say: "Listen, Judge Toureuil and his wife told me they had been to luncheon with Mme. Bontemps. They asked me no questions. But I seemed to gather from what was said that your marriage to Albertine would be the joy of her aunt's life. I think the real reason is that they are all extremely fond of you. At the same time the style in which they suppose that you would be able to keep her, the sort of friends they more or less know that we have, all that is not, I fancy, left out of account, although it may be a minor consideration. I should not have mentioned it to you myself, because I attach no importance to it, but as I imagine that people will mention it to you, I prefer to get a word in first." "But you yourself, what do you think of her?" I asked my mother. "Well, it's not I that am going to marry her. You might certainly do a thousand times better. But

I feel that your grandmother would not have liked me to influence you. As a matter of fact, I cannot tell you what I think of Albertine; I don't think of her. I shall say to you, like Madame de Sévigne 'She has good qualities', at least I suppose so. But at this first stage I can praise her only by negatives. One thing she is not, she has not the Rennes accent. In time, I shall perhaps say, she is something else. And I shall always think well of her if she can make you happy." But by these very words which left it to myself to decide my own happiness, my mother had plunged me in that state of doubt in which I had been plunged long ago when, my father having allowed me to go to *Phèdre* and, what was more, to take to writing, I had suddenly felt myself burdened with too great a responsibility, the fear of distressing him, and that melancholy which we feel when we cease to obey orders which, from one day to another, keep the future hidden, and realise that we have at last begun to live in real earnest, as a grown-up person, the life, the only life that any of us has at his disposal.

Perhaps the best thing would be to wait a little longer, to begin by regarding Albertine as in the past, so as to find out whether I really loved her. I might take her, as a distraction, to see the Verdurins, and this thought reminded me that I had come there myself that evening only to learn whether Mme. Putbus was staying there or was expected. In any case, she was not dining with them; turning to Cottard I asked "Is Madame Putbus here?" "No, thank heaven," replied Mme. Verdurin, who had overheard my question) "I have managed to turn her thoughts in the direction of Venice, we are rid of her for this year."

"I have more or less taken a little house between Saint-Martin-du-Chêne and Saint-Pierre des Ifs," said M.de Charlus, "But that is quite close to here, I hope that you will come over often with Charlie Morel. You have only to come to an arrangement with our little group about the trains, you are only a step from Doncières," said Mme. Verdurin, who hated people's not coming by the same train and not arriving at the hours when she sent carriages to meet them. She knew how stiff the climb was to La Raspelière, even if you took the zigzag path, behind Féterne, which was half-an-hour longer; she was afraid that those of her guests who kept to themselves might not find carriages to take them, or even, having in reality stayed away, might plead the excuse that they had not found a carriage at Douville Féterne, and had not felt strong enough to make so stiff a climb on foot. To this invitation M. de Charlus responded with a silent bow.

I asked Brichot if he knew what the word Balbec meant. "Balbec is probably a corruption of Dalbec" he told me. "Bec in Norman is a stream; the river that has given its name to Balbec is by the way, charming. Seen from a *falaise* (*fels* in German, you have indeed, not far from here, standing on a height, the picturesque town of Falaise), it runs close under the spires of the church, which is actually a long way from it, and seems to be reflecting them." "I should think so," said I, "that is an effect that Elstir admires greatly. I have seen several sketches of it in his studio." "Elstir! You know Tiche?" cried Mme. Verdurin. "But do you know that we used to be the dearest friends. Thank heaven, I never see him now. No, but ask Cottard, Brichot, he used to have his place laid at my table, he came every day. Now, there's a man of whom you can say that it has done him no good to leave our little nucleus. I shall show you presently some flowers he painted for me; you shall see the difference from the things he is doing now, which I don't care for at all, not at all! I don't know whether you call it painting, all those huge she-devils of composition, those vast structures he exhibits now that he has given up coming to me. For my part, I call it daubing, it's all so hackneyed, and besides, it lacks relief, personality. It's anybody's work."

"Look, I shall be able to show you his flowers now," she said to me, seeing that her husband was making signals to her to rise. And she took M. de Cambremer's arm again. M. Verdurin tried to apologise for this to M. de Charlus, as soon as he had got rid of Mme. de Cambremer, and to give him his reasons, chiefly for the pleasure of discussing these social refinements with a gentleman of title, momentarily the inferior of those who assigned to him the place to which they considered him entitled. But first of all he was anxious to make it clear to M. de Charlus that intellectually he esteemed him too highly to suppose that he could pay any attention to these trivialities. "Excuse my mentioning so small a point," he began, "for I can understand how little such things mean to you. Middle-class minds pay attention to them, but the others, the artists; the people who are really of our sort, don't give a rap for them. Now, from the first words we exchanged, I realised that you were one of us!" M. de Charlus, who gave a widely different meaning to this expression, drew himself erect. After the doctor's oglings, he found his host's insulting frankness suffocating. "Don't protest, my dear Sir, you are one of us, it is plain as daylight," replied M. Verdurin.. "Observe that I have no idea whether you practise any of the arts, but that is not necessary. It is not always sufficient. Dechambre, who has just died, played exquisitely, with the most vigorous execution, but he was not one of us, you felt at once that he was not one of us. Brichot is not one of us; Morel is, my wife is, I can feel that you are......" " What were you going to tell me?" interrupted M. de Charlus, who was beginning to feel reassured as to M. Verdurin's meaning, but preferred that he should not utter these misleading remarks quite so loud. "Only that we put you on the left," replied M. Verdurin. M. de Charlus, with a comprehending, genial, insolent smile, replied: "Why! That is not of the slightest importance, *here!*" And he gave a little laugh that was all his own—a laugh that came to him probably from some Bavarian or Lorraine grandmother, who herself had inherited it, in identical form, from an ancestress, so that it had been sounding now, without change, for not a few centuries in little old-fashioned European courts, and one could relish its precious quality like that of certain old musical instruments that have now grown rare.. "But," M. Verdurin explained, stung by his laugh, "we did it on purpose. I attach no importance whatever to titles of nobility," he went on, with that contemptuous smile which I have seen so many people whom I have known, unlike my grandmother and my mother, assume when they spoke of anything that they did not possess, before others who thus, they supposed, would be prevented from using that particular advantage to crow over them. "But, don't you see, since we happened to have M. de Cambremer here and he is a Marquis, while you are only a Baron......" "Pardon me," M. de Charlus replied with an arrogant air to the astonished Verdurin, "I am also Duc de Brabant, Damoiseau de Montargis, Prince d'Oléron, de Carency, de Viareggio and des Dunes. However, it is not of the slightest importance. Please do not distress yourself," he concluded, resuming his subtle smile which spread itself over these final words: "I could see at a glance that you were not accustomed to society."

Mme. Verdurin came across to me to show me Elstir's flowers. If this action, to which I had grown so indifferent, of going out to dinner, had on the contrary, taking the form that made it entirely novel, of a journey along the coast, followed by an ascent in a carriage to a point six hundred feet above the sea, produced in me a sort of intoxication, this feeling had not been dispelled at La Raspelière. "Just look at this, now," said the Mistress, showing me some huge and splendid roses by Elstir, whose unctuous scarlet and rich white stood out, however, with almost too creamy a relief from the flower-stand upon which they were arranged. "Do you suppose he would still have the touch to get that. Don't you call that striking? And besides, it's fine as matter, it would be amusing to handle. I can't tell you how amusing it was to watch him painting them. One could feel that he was interested in trying to get just that effect." And the Mistress's gaze rested musingly on this present from the artist in which were combined not merely his great talent but their long friendship which survived only in these mementoes of it which he had bequeathed to her; behind the flowers which long ago he had picked for her, she seemed to see the shapely hand that had painted them, in the course of a morning, in their freshness, so that, they on the table, it leaning against the back of a chair had been able to meet face to face at the Mistress's luncheon party, the roses still, alive and their almost lifelike portrait. Almost only, for Elstir was unable to look at a flower without first transplanting it to that inner garden in which we are obliged always to remain. He had shown in this watercolour the appearance of the roses which he had seen, and which, but for him, no one would ever have known; so that one might say that they were a new variety with which this painter, like a skilful gardener, had enriched the family of the Roses.

"From the day he left the little nucleus, he was finished. It seems, my dinners made him waste his time, that I hindered the development of his *genius,*" she said in a tone of irony. "As if the society of a woman like myself could fail to be beneficial to an artist," she exclaimed with a burst of pride. Close beside us, M. de Cambremer, who was already seated, seeing that M. de Charlus was standing, made as though to rise and offer him his chair. This offer may have arisen, in the Marquis's mind, from nothing more than a vague wish to be polite. M. de Charlus preferred to attach to it the sense of a duty which the plain gentleman knew that he owed to a Prince, and felt that he could not establish his right to this precedence better than by declining it. And so he exclaimed: "What are you doing? I beg of you! The idea!" The astutely vehement tone of this protest had in itself something typically 'Guermantes' which became even more evident in the imperative, superfluous and familiar gesture with which he brought both his hands down, as though to force him to remain seated, upon the shoulders of M. de Cambremer who had not risen: "Come, come, my dear fellow," the Baron insisted, "this is too much. There is no reason for it! In these days we keep that for Princes of the Blood."

I made no more effect on the Cambremers than on Mme. Verdurin by my enthusiasm for their house. For I remained cold to the beauties which they pointed out to me and grew excited over confused reminiscences; at times I even confessed my disappointment at not finding something correspond to what its name had made me imagine. I enraged Mme. de Cambremer by telling her that I had supposed the place to be more in the country. On the other hand I broke off in an ecstasy to sniff the fragrance of a breeze that crept in through the chink of the door. "I see you like draughts," they said to me. My praise of the patch of green lining-cloth that had been pasted over a broken pane met with no greater success: "How frightful!" cried the Marquise. The climax came when I said: "My greatest joy was when I arrived. When I heard my step echoing along the gallery, I felt that I had come into some village council-office, with a map of the district on the wall." This time, Mme. de Cambremer resolutely turned her back on me. "'You don't think the arrangement too bad?" her husband asked her with the same compassionate anxiety with which he would have inquired how his wife had stood some painful ceremony. "They have some fine things." But, inasmuch as malice, when the hard and fast rules of sure taste do not confine it within fixed limits, finds fault with everything, in the persons or in the houses of the people who have supplanted the critic: "Yes, but they are not in the right places. Besides, are they really as fine as all that?" "You noticed," said M. de Cambremer, with a melancholy that was controlled by a note of firmness, "there are some Jouy hangings that are worn away, some quite threadbare things in this drawing-room!" "And that piece of stuff with its huge roses, like a peasant woman's quilt,'" said Mme. de Cambremer whose purely artificial culture was confined exclusively to idealist philosophy, impressionist painting and Debussy's music. And, so as not to criticise merely in the name of smartness but in that of good taste: "And they have put up windscreens! Such bad style! What can you expect of such people, they don't know, where could they have learned? They must be retired tradespeople. It's really not bad for them." "I thought the chandeliers good," said the Marquis, though it was not evident why he should make an exception of the chandeliers, just as inevitably, whenever anyone spoke of a church, whether it was the Cathedral of Chartres, or of Rheims, or of Amiens, or the church at Balbec, what he would always make a point of mentioning as admirable would be: "the organ-loft the pulpit and the misericords." "As for the garden, don't speak about it," said Mme. de Cambremer. "It's a massacre. Those paths running all crooked."

I seized the opportunity while Mme. Verdurin was pouring out coffee to go and glance over the letter which M. de Cambremer had brought me, and in which his mother invited me to dinner. With that faint trace of ink, the handwriting revealed an individuality which in the future I should be able to recognise among a thousand, without any more need to have recourse to the hypothesis of special pens, than to suppose that rare and mysteriously blended colours are necessary to enable a painter to express his original vision. Indeed a paralytic, stricken with agraphia after a seizure, and compelled to look at the script as at a drawing without being able to read it, would have gathered that Mme. de Cambremer belonged to an old family in which the zealous cultivation of literature and the arts had supplied a margin to its aristocratic traditions. He would have guessed also the period in which the Marquise had learned simultaneously to write and to play Chopin's music. It was the time when well-bred people observed the rule of affability and what was called the rule of the three adjectives. Mme. de Cambremer combined the two rules in one. A laudatory adjective was not enough for her, she followed it (after a little stroke of the pen) with a second, then (after another stroke) with a third. But, what was peculiar to herself was that, in defiance of the literary and social object at which she aimed, the sequence of the three epithets assumed in Mme. de Cambremer's notes the aspect not of a progression but of a diminuendo. Mme. de Cambremer told me in this first letter that she had seen Saint-Loup and had appreciated more than ever his "unique—rare—real" qualities, that he was coming to them again with one of his friends (the one who was in love with her daughter-in-law), and that if I cared to come, with or without them, to dine at Féterne she would be "delighted—happy—pleased." Perhaps it was because, her desire to be friendly outran the fertility of her imagination and the riches of her vocabulary that the lady, while determined to utter three exclamations, was incapable of making the second and third anything more than feeble echoes of the first. Add but a fourth adjective, and, of her initial friendliness, there would be nothing left. Moreover, with a certain refined simplicity which cannot have failed to produce a considerable impression upon her family and indeed in her circle of acquaintance, Mme. de Cambremer had acquired the habit of substituting for the word (which might in time begin to ring false) "sincere," the word "true." And to show that it was indeed by sincerity that she was impelled, she broke the conventional rule that would have placed the adjective "true" before its noun, and planted it boldly after. Her letter ended with: *"Croyez à ma mon amitié vraie." "Croyez à ma sympathie vraie."* Unfortunately, this had become so stereotyped a formula that the affectation of frankness was more suggestive of a polite fiction than the time-honoured formulas, of the meaning of which people have ceased to think.

Mme. Verdurin insisted upon a little violin music next. To the general astonishment, M. de Charlus, who never referred to his own considerable gifts, accompanied, in the purest style, the closing passage (uneasy, tormented, Schumannesque, but, for all that, earlier than

Franck's Sonata) of the Sonata for piano and violin by Fauré.

When the piece came to an end, I ventured to ask for some Franck, which appeared to cause Mme. de Cambremer such acute pain that I did not insist. "You can't admire that sort of thing," she said to me. Instead she asked for Debussy's *Fêtes*, which made her exclaim: "Ah! How sublime!" from the first note. But Morel discovered that he remembered the opening bars only, and in a spirit of mischief, without any intention to deceive, began a March by Meyerbeer. Unfortunately, as he left little interval and made no announcement, everybody supposed that he was still playing Debussy, and continued to exclaim "Sublime!" Morel, by revealing that the composer was that not of *Pelléas* but of *Robert le Diable* created a certain chill. Mme. de Cambremer had scarcely time to feel it, for she had just discovered a volume of Scarlatti, and had flung herself upon it with an hysterical impulse. "Oh! Play this, look this piece, it's divine," she cried. And yet, of this composer long despised, recently promoted to the highest honours, what she had selected in her feverish impatience was one of those infernal pieces which have so often kept us from sleeping, while a merciless pupil repeats them indefinitely on the next floor. But Morel had had enough music, and as he insisted upon cards, M. de Charlus, to be able to join in, proposed a game of whist. "He was telling the Master just now that he is a Prince," said Ski to Mme. Verdurin, "but it's not true, they're quite a humble family of architects."

I turned to Ski and assured him that he was entirely mistaken as to the family to which M. de Charlus belonged; he replied that he was certain of his facts, and added that I myself had said that his real name was Gandin, Le Gandin. "I told you," was my answer, "that Mme. de Cambremer was the sister of an engineer, M. Legrandin. I never said a word to you about M. de Charlus. 'There is about as much connection between him and Mme. de Cambremer as between the Great Condé and Racine." "Indeed! I thought there was," said Ski lightly with no more apology for his mistake than he had made a few hours earlier for the mistake that had nearly made his party miss the train.

"Do you intend to remain long on this coast?" Mme. Verdurin asked M. de Charlus in whom she foresaw an addition to the faithful and trembled lest he should be returning too soon to Paris. "Good Lord, one never knows" replied M. de Charlus in a nasal drawl. "I should like to stay here until the end of September." "You are quite right;" said Mme. Verdurin; "that is the time for fine storms at sea." "To tell you the truth, that is not what would influence me. I have for some time past unduly neglected the Archangel Saint Michael, my Patron, and I should like to make amends to him by staying for his feast, on the 29th of September, at the Abbey on the Mount." "You take an interest in all that sort of thing?" asked Mme. Verdurin, who might perhaps have succeeded in hushing the voice of her outraged anti-clericalism, had she not been afraid that so long an expedition might make the violinist and the Baron 'fail' her for forty-eight hours. "You are perhaps afflicted with intermittent deafness," M. de Charlus replied insolently. "I have told you that Saint Michael is one of my Glorious Patrons." Then, smiling with a benevolent ecstasy, his eyes gazing into the distance, his voice strengthened by an excitement which seemed now to be not merely aesthetic but religious. "It is so beautiful at the offertory when Michael stands erect by the altar, in a white robe, swinging a golden censer heaped so high with perfumes that the fragrance of them mounts up to God." "We might go there in a party," suggested Mme. Verdurin notwithstanding her horror of the clergy. "At that moment, when the offertory begins," went on M. de Charlus who, for other reasons but in the same manner as good speakers in Parliament, never replied to an interruption and would pretend not to have heard it, "it would be wonderful to see our young friend Palestrinising, and even performing an aria by Bach. The worthy Abbot, too would be wild with joy, and that is the greatest homage, at least the greatest public homage that I can pay to my Holy Patron. What an edification for the faithful! We must mention it presently to the young Angelico of music, himself a warrior like Saint Michael"

"We are so pleased to have met M. de Charlus," said Mme. de Cambremer to Mme. Verdurin. "Had you never met him before? He is quite nice, he is unusual, he is *of a period* "(she would have found it difficult to say which), replied Mme. Verdurin with the satisfied smile of a connoisseur, a judge and a hostess. Mme. de Cambremer asked me if I was coming to Féterne with Saint-Loup.

I could not suppress a cry of admiration when I saw the moon hanging like an orange lantern beneath the vault of oaks that led away from the house. "That's nothing, presently, when the moon has risen, higher and the valley is lighted up, it will be a thousand times better. I like the view of the valley even more than the sea view", Mme. Verdurin went on, "You are going to have a splendid night for your journey." "We ought really to find out whether the carriages are ready, if you are absolutely determined to go back to Balbec to-night," M. Verdurin said to me, "for I see no necessity for it myself. We could drive you over to-morrow morning. It is certain to be fine. The roads are excellent." I said that it was impossible. "But in any case it is not time yet," the Mistress protested, "Leave them alone, they have heaps of time. A lot of good it will do them to arrive at the station with an hour to wait. They are far happier here. And you, my young Mozart," she said to Morel, not venturing to address M. de Charlus directly, "won't you stay the night. We have some nice rooms facing the sea." "No, he can't," M. de Charlus replied on behalf of Morel, who had not heard. "He has a pass until midnight only. He must go back to bed like a good little boy, obedient, and well-behaved," he added in a complaisant, mannered, insistent voice, as though he derived some sad pleasure from the use of this chaste, comparison and also from letting his voice dwell, in passing, upon any reference to Morel, from touching him with (failing his fingers) words that seemed to explore his person.

Mme. Verdurin bore down upon me. "I heard Mme. de Cambremer invite you to dinner just now. It has nothing to do with me, you understand. But for your own sake, I do hope you won't go. For one thing, the place is infested with bores. Oh! If you like dining with provincial Counts and Marquises whom nobody knows, you will be supplied to your heart's content." "I think I shall be obliged to go there once or twice. I am not altogether free however, for I have a young cousin whom I cannot leave by herself." (I felt that this fictitious kinship made it easier for me to take Albertine about) . "Anyhow," she said to me, "before you dine with the Cambremers, why not bring her here, your cousin? Does she like conversation, and clever people? Is she pleasant? Yes, very well then. Bring her with you. The Cambremers aren't the only people in the world. I can understand their being glad to invite her, they must find it difficult to get anyone. Here she will have plenty of fresh air, and lots of clever men. In any case, I am counting on you not to fail me next Wednesday. I heard you were having a tea-party at Rivebelle with your cousin, and M. de Charlus, and I forget who else. You must arrange to bring the whole lot on here, it would be nice if you all came in a body. It's the easiest thing in the world to get here; the roads are charming; if you like I can send down for you. I can't imagine what you find attractive in Rivebelle, it's infested with mosquitoes. You are thinking perhaps of the reputation of the rockcakes. My cook makes them far better. I can let you have them here, Norman rock-cakes, the real article, and shortbread; I need say no more. Ah! If you like the filth they give you at Rivebelle, that I won't give you, I don't poison my guests Sir, and even if I wished to, my cook would refuse to make such abominations and would leave my service.

Those rock-cakes you get down there; you can't tell what they are made of, I knew a poor girl who got peritonitis from them, which carried her off in three days. She was only seventeen. It was sad for her poor mother," added Mme. Verdurin with a melancholy air beneath the spheres of her temples charged with experience and suffering. "However, go and have tea at Rivebelle, if you enjoy being fleeced and flinging money out of the window. But one thing I beg of you, it is a confidential mission I am charging you with; on the stroke of six, bring all your party here, don't allow them to go straggling away by themselves. You can bring whom you please. I wouldn't say that to everybody. But I am sure that your friends are nice, I can see at once that we understand one another. Apart from the little nucleus, there are some very pleasant people coming on Wednesday. You don't know little Madame de Longpont. She is charming, and so witty, not in the least a snob, you will find, you'll like her immensely. And she's going to bring a whole troop of friends too," Mme. Verdurin added to shew me that this was the right thing to do and encourage me by the other's example. "We shall see which has most influence and brings most people, Barbe de Longpont or you. And then I believe somebody's going to bring Bergotte," she added with a vague air, this meeting with a celebrity being rendered far from likely by a paragraph which had appeared in the papers that morning, to the effect that the great writer's health was causing grave anxiety. "Anyhow, you will see that it will be one of my most successful Wednesdays, I don't want to have any boring women. You mustn't judge by this evening, it has been a complete failure. Don't try to be polite, you can't have been more bored than I was, I thought myself it was deadly. It won't always be like tonight you know! You are coming again with your cousin, thats settled.....? You might bring your cousin to stay. She would get a change of air from Balbec. Anyhow, give your cousin my message. We shall put you in two nice rooms looking over the valley, you ought to see it in the morning with the sun shining on the mist! By the way, who is this Robert de Saint-Loup of whom you were speaking?" she said with a troubled air, for she had heard that I was to pay him a visit, at Doncières, and was afraid that he might make me fail her. "Why not bring him here instead, if he's not a bore. I have heard of him from Morel; I fancy he's one of his greatest friends," said Mme. Verdurin with entire want of truth, for Saint-Loup and Morel were not even aware of one another's existence. But having heard that Saint-Loup knew M. de Charlus, she supposed that it was through the violinist, and wished to appear to know all about them.

"Here come the carriages", said M.Verdurin and accompanied us to the door. "But you don't look to me as if you were properly wrapped up my boy;" said M. Verdurin, whose age allowed him to address me in this paternal tone. I declined the rug which, on subsequent evenings I was to accept when Albertine was with me, more to preserve the secrecy of my pleasure than to avoid the risk of cold. Then looking his watch, doubtless so as not to prolong the leave-taking in the damp night air, he warned the coachmen not to lose any time, but to be careful when going down the hill, and assured us that we should be in plenty of time for our train. This was to set down the faithful, beginning with the Cambremers, one at one station, another at another, ending with myself, for no one else was going as far as Balbec.

CHAPTER THREE

I was dropping with sleep. I was taken up to my floor not by the liftboy, but by the squinting page, who to make conversation informed me that his sister was still with the gentleman who was so rich, and that, on one occasion, when she had made up her mind to return home instead of sticking to her business, her gentleman friend had paid a visit to the mother of the squinting page and of the other more fortunate children, who had very soon made the silly creature return to her protector. "You know, Sir, she's a fine lady, my sister is. She plays the piano, she talks Spanish. And you would never take her for the sister of the humble employee who brings you up in the lift, she denies herself nothing; Madame has a maid to herself, I shouldn't be surprised if one day she keeps her carriage. She is very pretty, if you could see her, a little too high and mighty, but, good lord, you can understand that. She's full of fun. She never leaves a hotel without doing something first in a wardrobe or a drawer, just to leave a little keepsake with the chambermaid who will have to wipe it up. Sometimes she does it in a cab, and after she's paid her fare, she'll hide behind a tree, and she doesn't half laugh when the cabby finds he's got to clean his cab after her. My father had another stroke of luck when he found my young brother that Indian Prince he used to know long ago. It's not the same style of thing, of course. But it's a superb position. The travelling by itself would be a dream. I'm the only one still on the shelf. But you never know. We're a lucky family; perhaps one day I shall be President of the Republic. But I'm keeping you talking" (I had not uttered a single word and was beginning to fall asleep as I listened to that flow of his). "Good-night, Sir. Oh! Thank you, Sir. If everybody had as kind a heart as you, there wouldn't be any poor people left. But, as my sister say's, there will always have to be the poor so that now that I'm rich I can s— t on them. You'll pardon the expression. Good night; Sir."

Every day I went out with Albertine. She had decided to take up painting again and had chosen as the subject of her first attempts the church of Saint-Jean de la Haise which nobody ever visited and very few had even heard of, a spot difficult to describe, impossible to discover without a guide, slow of access in its isolation, more than half an hour from the Epreville station, after one had long left behind one of the last houses of the village of Quetteholme.

On our first visit we took a little train in the opposite direction from Féterne, that is to say towards Grattevast. But we were in the dog days and it had been a terrible strain simply to go out of doors immediately after luncheon. I should have preferred not to start so soon; the luminous and burning air provoked thoughts of indolence and cool retreats. It filled my mother's room and mine, according to their exposure, at varying temperatures, like rooms in a Turkish bath. Mamma's dressing-room, festooned by the sun with a dazzling, Moorish whiteness, appeared to be sunk at the bottom of a well, because of the four plastered walls on which it looked out, while far above, in the empty space, the sky, whose fleecy white waves one saw slip past, one behind another, seemed (because of the longing that one felt), whether built upon a terrace or seen reversed in a mirror hung above the window, a tank filled with blue water, reserved for bathers. Notwithstanding this scorching temperature, we had taken the one o'clock train. But Albertine had been very hot in the carriage, hotter still in the long walk, across country, and I was afraid of her catching cold when she proceeded to sit still in that damp hollow where the sun's rays did not penetrate. Having, on the other hand, as long ago as our first visits to Elstir, made up my mind that she would appreciate not merely luxury but even a certain degree of comfort of which her want of money deprived her, I had made arrangements with a Balbec jobmaster that a carriage was to be sent every day to take us out; to escape from the heat we took the road through the forest of Chantepie. The invisibility of the innumerable birds, some of them, almost seabirds that conversed with one another from the trees on either side of us, gave the same impression of repose that one has when one shuts one's eyes. By Albertine's side, enchained by her arms within the carriage, I listened to these Oceanides. And when by chance I caught sight of one of these musicians as he flitted from one leaf to the shelter of another, there was so little apparent connection between him and his songs that I could not believe that I beheld their cause in the little body, fluttering, humble, startled and unseeing. The carriage could not take us all the way to the church. I stopped it when we had passed through Quetteholme and bade Albertine good-bye. For she had alarmed me by saying to me of this church as of other buildings, of certain pictures: "What a pleasure it would be to see that with you!" This pleasure was one that I did not feel myself capable of giving her. I felt it myself in front of beautiful things only if I was alone or pretended to be alone and did not speak. But since she supposed that she might, thanks to me, feel sensations of art which are not communicated thus—I thought it more prudent to say that I must leave her, would come back to fetch her at the end of the day, but that in the mean time I must go back with the carriage to pay a call on Mme. Verdurin or on the Cambremers, or even spend an hour with Mamma at Balbec, but never farther afield. To begin with, that is to say. For Albertine having once said to me petulantly: "It's a bore that Nature has arranged things so badly and put Saint-Jean de la Haise in one direction, La Raspelière in another, so that you're imprisoned for the whole day in the part of the country you've chosen." As soon as the toque and veil had come, I ordered, to my eventual undoing, a motor-car from Saint-Fargeau *(Sanctus Ferreolus,* according to the curé's book). Albertine, whom I had kept in ignorance and who had come to call for me, was surprised when she heard in front of the hotel the purr of the engine, delighted when she learned that this motor was for ourselves. I made her come upstairs for a moment to my room. She jumped for joy. "We are going to pay a call on the Verdurins." "Yes, but you'd better not go dressed like that since you are going to have your motor. There, you will look better in these." And I brought out the toque and veil which I had hidden. "They're for me? Oh! You are an angel," she cried, throwing her arms round my neck. Aimé who met us on the stairs, proud of Albertine's smart attire and of our means of transport, for these vehicles were still comparatively rare at Balbec, gave himself the pleasure of coming downstairs behind us. Albertine, anxious to display herself in her new garments, asked me to have the car opened, as we could shut it later on when we wished to be more private.

    On this first occasion it was not I alone that was to go to La

Raspelière as I did on other days, while Albertine painted; she decided to go there with me. She did indeed think that we might stop here and there on our way, but supposed it to be impossible to start by going to Saint-Jean de la Haise. That is to say in another direction, and to make an excursion which seemed to be reserved for a different day. She learned on the contrary from the driver that nothing could be easier than to go to Saint-Jean; which he could do in twenty minutes, and that we might stay there if we chose for hours, or go on much farther, for from Quetteholme to La Raspelière would not take more than thirty-five minutes! We realised this as soon as the vehicle, starting off, covered in one bound twenty paces of an excellent horse. Distances are only the relation of space to time and vary with that relation. We express the difficulty that we have in getting to a place in a system of miles or kilometres which becomes false as soon as that difficulty decreases. Art is modified by it also, when a village which seemed to be in a different world from some other village becomes its neighbour in a landscape whose dimensions are altered. In any case the information that there may perhaps exist a universe in which two and two make five and the straight line is not the shortest way between two points would have astonished Albertine far less than to hear the driver say that it was easy to go in a single afternoon to Saint-Jean and La Raspelière, Douville and Quetteholme, Saint-Mars le Vieux and Saint-Mars le Vêtu, Gourville and Old Balbec, Tourville and Féterne, prisoners hitherto as hermetically confined in the cells of distinct days as long ago were Méséglise and Guermantes, upon which the same eyes could not gaze in the course of one afternoon, delivered now by the giant with the seven-league boots, came and clustered about our tea-time their towers and steeples, their old gardens which the encroaching wood sprang back to reveal. Coming to the foot of the cliff road, the car took it in its stride, with a continuous sound like that of a knife being ground, while the sea falling away grew broader beneath us. The old rustic houses of Montsurvent ran towards us, clasping to their bosoms vine or rose-bush; the firs of La Raspelière, more agitated than when the evening breeze was rising, ran in every direction to escape from us and a new servant whom I had never seen before came to open the door for us on the terrace, while the gardener's son, betraying a precocious bent, devoured the machine with his gaze. As it was not a Monday we did not know whether we should find Mme. Verdurin, for except upon that day, when she was at home, it was unsafe to call upon her without warning. The new and more swift-footed servant, who had already made himself familiar with these expressions, replied that "if

Madame has not gone out she must be at the 'view of Douville'," and that he would go and look for her, came back immediately to tell us that she was coming to welcome us. We found her slightly dishevelled for she came from the flower beds, farmyard and kitchen garden, where she had gone to feed her peacocks and poultry, to hunt for eggs, to gather fruit and flowers to "make her table-centre," which would suggest her park in miniature; but on the table it conferred the distinction of making it support the burden of only such things as were useful and good to eat; for round those other presents from the garden which were the pears, the whipped eggs, rose the tall stems of bugloss, carnations, roses and coreopsis, between which one saw, as between blossoming boundary posts, move from one to another beyond the glazed windows, the ships at sea. From the astonishment which M.and Mme. Verdurin, interrupted while arranging their flowers to receive the visitors that had been announced, showed upon finding that these visitors were merely Albertine and myself, it was easy to see that the new servant, full of zeal but not yet familiar with my name, had repeated it wrongly and that Mme. Verdurin, hearing the names of guests whom she did not know, had nevertheless bidden him let them in, in her need of seeing somebody, no matter whom. And the new servant stood contemplating this spectacle from the door in order to learn what part we played in the household. Then he made off at a run, taking long strides, for he had entered upon his duties only the day before.

When Albertine had quite finished displaying her toque and veil to the Verdurins, she gave me a warning look to remind me that we had not too much time left for what we meant to do. Mme. Verdurin begged us to stay to tea; but we refused.

I supposed that was out of favour with her, but she called us back at the door to urge us not to 'fail' on the following Wednesday, and not to come with that contraption, which was dangerous at night, but by the train with the little group, and she made me stop the car, which was moving down hill across the park, because the footman had forgotten to put in the hood the slice of tart and the shortbread which she had had made into a parcel for us. We started off, escorted for a moment by the little houses that came running to meet us with their flowers.

When Albertine thought it better to remain at Saint-Jean de la Haise and paint, I would take the car, and it was not merely to Gourville and Féterne, but to Saint Mars le Vêtu and as far as Criquetot that I was able to penetrate before returning to fetch her. While pretending to be occupied with anything rather than herself and to be obliged to forsake her for other pleasures, I thought only of her. On my return I left the car at Quetteholme, ran down the sunken path, crossed the brook by plank and found Albertine painting in front of the church all spires and crockets, thorny and red, blossoming like a rose bush. The lantern alone showed an unbroken front; and the smiling surface of the stone was abloom with angels who continued, before the twentieth century couple that we were, to celebrate, taper in hand, the ceremonies of the thirteenth. It was they that Albertine was endeavouring to portray on her prepared canvas, and, imitating Elstir, she was laying on the paint in sweeping strokes, trying to obey the noble rhythm set, the great master had told her, by those angels so different from any that he knew. Then she collected her things. Leaning upon one another we walked back up the sunken path, leaving the little church, as quiet as though it had never seen us, to listen to the perpetual sound of the brook. Presently the car started, taking us home by a different way. We passed Marcouville l'Orgueilleuse. Over its church, half new, half restored, the setting sun spread its patina as fine as that of centuries. Rising in a warm dust, the many modern statues reached, on their pillars, halfway up the golden webs of sunset. In front of the church a tall cypress seemed to be in a sort of consecrated enclosure. We left the car for a moment to look at it and strolled for a little. No less than of her limbs, Albertine was directly conscious of her toque of Leghorn straw and of the silken veil (which were for her the source of no less satisfaction), and derived from them, as we strolled round the church; a different sort of impetus, revealed by a contentment which was inert but in which I found a certain charm; veil and toque which were but a recent, adventitious part of my friend, but a part that was already dear to me, as I followed its trail with my eyes, past the cypress in the evening air. She herself could not see it, but guessed that the effect was pleasing, for she smiled at me, harmonising the poise of her head with the headgear that completed it: "I don't like it, it's restored," she said to me, pointing to the church and remembering what Elstir had said to her about the priceless, inimitable beauty of old stone. Albertine could tell a restoration at a glance. One could not help feeling surprised at the sureness of the taste she had already acquired in architecture, as contrasted with the deplorable taste she still retained in music. I cared no more than Elstir for this church, it was with no pleasure to myself that its sunlit front had come and posed before my eyes, and I had got out of the car to examine it only out of politeness to Albertine. I found, however, that the great impressionist had contradicted himself; why exalt this fetish of its objective architectural value, and not take into account the transfiguration of the church by the sunset? "No, certainly not," said Albertine, "I don't like it; I like its name *orgueilleuse*. But what I must remember to ask Brichot is why Saint-Mars is called *le Vêtu*. We shall be going there next, shan't we?" she said, gazing at me out of her black eyes over which her toque was pulled down, like her little polo cap long ago. Her veil floated behind her. I got back into the car with her, happy in the thought that we should be going next day to Saint-Mars, where, in this blazing weather when one could think only of the delights of a bath, the two ancient steeples, salmon-pink, with their lozenge-shaped tiles, gaping slightly as though for air, looked like a pair of old, sharp-snouted fish, coated in scales, moss-grown and red, which without seeming to move were rising in a blue, transparent water. On leaving Marcouville, to shorten the road, we turned aside at a crossroads where there is a farm. Sometimes Albertine made the car stop there and asked me to go alone to fetch, so that she might drink it in the car, a bottle of Calvados or cider, which the people assured me was not effervescent, and which proceeded to drench us from head to foot. We sat pressed close together. The people of the farm could scarcely see Albertine in the closed car, I handed them back their bottles; we moved on again, as though to continue that private life by ourselves, that lovers existence which they might suppose us to lead, and of which this halt for refreshment had been only an insignificant moment; a supposition that would have appeared even less far-fetched if they had seen us after Albertine had drunk her bottle of cider; she seemed then positively unable to endure the existence of an interval between herself and me which as a rule did not trouble her; beneath her linen skirt her legs were pressed against mine, she brought close against my cheeks her own cheeks which had turned pale, warm and red over the cheekbones, with something ardent and faded about them such as one sees in girls from the slums. At such moments, almost as quickly as her personality, her voice changed also, she forsook her own voice to adopt another, raucous, bold, almost dissolute. Night began to fall. What a pleasure to feel her leaning against me, with her toque and her veil, reminding me that it is always thus, seated side by side, that we find couples who are in love. I was perhaps in love with Albertine, but as I did not venture to let her see my love, although it existed in me, it could only be like an abstract truth, of no value until one has succeeded in checking it by experiment as it was, it seemed to me unrealisable and outside the plane of life. As for my jealousy, it urged me to leave Albertine as little as possible, although I knew that it would not be completely cured until I had parted from her for ever. I could even feel it in her presence, but would then take care that the circumstances should not be repeated which had aroused it.

I might have dispensed with seeing her every day; I was going to be happy when I left her, and I knew that the calming effect of that happiness might be prolonged over many days. But at that moment I heard Albertine as she left me say to her aunt or to a girl friend: "Then to-morrow at eight-thirty. We mustn't be late, the others will be ready at a quarter past." The conversation of a woman one loves is like the soil that covers a subterranean and dangerous water; one feels at every moment beneath the words the presence, the penetrating chill of an invisible pool; one perceives here and there its treacherous percolation, but the water itself remains hidden. The moment I heard these words of Albertine, my calm was destroyed. I wanted to ask her to let me see her the following morning, so as to prevent her from going to this mysterious rendezvous at half-past eight which had been mentioned in my presence only in covert terms. She would no doubt have begun by obeying me, while regretting that she had to give up her plans; in time she would have discovered my permanent need to upset them; I should have become the person from whom one hides everything. Besides, it is probable that these gatherings from which I was excluded amounted to very little, and, that it was perhaps from the fear that I might find one of the other girls there vulgar or boring that I was not invited to them. Unfortunately this life so closely involved with Albertine's had a reaction not only upon myself; to me it brought calm; to my mother it caused an anxiety, her confession of which destroyed my calm. As I entered the hotel happy in my own mind, determined to terminate, one day soon, an existence the end of which I imagined to depend upon my own volition my mother said to me, hearing me send a message to the chauffeur to go and fetch Albertine: "How you do waste your money." (Françoise in her simple and expressive language said with greater force: "That's the way the money goes.") "Try," Mamma went on, " not to become like Charles de Sévigne, of whom his mother said: 'His hand is a crucible in which gold melts.' Besides, I do really think you have gone about quite enough with Albertine. I assure you, you're overdoing it, even to her it may seem ridiculous. I was delighted to think that you found her a distraction, I am not asking you never to see her again, but simply that it may not be impossible to meet one of you without the other." My life with Albertine, a life devoid of keen pleasures—that is to say of keen pleasures that I could feel—that life which I intended to change at any moment, choosing a calm interval, became once again suddenly and for a time necessary to me when, by these words of Mamma's, it found itself threatened. I told my mother that what she had just said would delay for perhaps two months the decision for which she asked, which otherwise I would have reached before the end of that week.

After dinner, the car brought Albertine back; there was still a glimmer of daylight; the air was not so warm, but after a scorching day we both dreamed of strange and delicious coolness; then to our fevered eyes the narrow slip of moon appeared at first (as on the evening when I had gone to the Princesse de Guermantes's and Albertine had telephoned to me) like the slight, fine rind, then like the cool section of a fruit which an invisible knife was beginning to peel in the sky. Sometimes too, it was I that went in search of my mistress, a little later in that case; she would be waiting for me before the arcade of the market at Maineville. At first I could not make her out; I would begin to fear that she might not be coming, that she had misunderstood me. Then I saw her in her white blouse with blue spots spring into the car by my side with the light bound of a young animal rather than a girl. And it was like a dog too that she began to caress me interminably. When night had fallen and, as the manager of the hotel remarked to me; the sky was all 'studied' with stars; if we did not go for a drive in the forest with a bottle of champagne, then, without heeding the strangers who were still strolling upon the faintly lighted front, but who could not have seen anything a yard away on the dark sand, we would lie down in the shelter of the dunes; that same body in whose suppleness abode all the feminine, marine and sportive grace of the girls whom I had seen for the first time pass before a horizon of waves, I held pressed against my own, beneath the same rug, by the edge of the motionless sea divided by a tremulous path of light, and we listened to the sea without tiring and with the same pleasure, both when it held its breath, suspended for so long that one thought the reflux would never come, and when at last it gasped out at our feet the long awaited murmur. Finally I took Albertine back to Parville. When we reached her house, we were obliged to break off our kisses for fear lest some one should see us; not wishing to go to bed she returned with me to Balbec, from where I took her back for the last time to Parville; the chauffeurs of those early days of the motor-car were people who went to bed at all hours. And as a matter of fact I returned to Balbec only with the first dews of morning, alone this time; but still surrounded with the presence of my mistress, gorged with an inexhaustible provision of kisses. On my table I would find a telegram or a postcard. Albertine again! She had written them at Quetteholme when I had gone off by myself in the car to tell me that she was thinking of me. I got in to bed as I read them over. Then I caught sight, over the curtains, of the bright streak of daylight and said to myself that we must be in love with one another after all since we had spent the night in one another's arms. When next morning I caught sight of Albertine on the front, I was so afraid of her telling me that she was not free that day and could not accede to my request that we should go out together; that I delayed as long as possible making the request. And when at last I made up my mind, when with the most indifferent air that I could muster, I asked: "Are we to go out together now, and again this evening?"' and she replied: "With the greatest pleasure," then the sudden replacement, in the rosy face, of my long uneasiness by a delicious sense of ease made even more precious to me those outlines to which I was perpetually indebted for the comfort, the relief that we feel after a storm has broken. I repeated to myself: "How sweet she is, what an adorable creature!" in an excitement less fertile than that caused by intoxication, scarcely more profound than that of friendship, but far superior to the excitement of social life. We cancelled our order for the car only on the days when there was a dinner party at the Verdurins'.and on those when, Albertine not being free to go out with me, I took the opportunity to inform anybody who wished to see me that I should be remaining at Balbec. I gave Saint-Loup permission to come on these days, but on these days only. For on one occasion when he had arrived unexpectedly, I had preferred to forego the pleasure of seeing Albertine rather than run the risk of his meeting her, than endanger the state of happy calm in which I had been dwelling for some time and see my jealousy revive. And I had been at my ease only after Saint-Loup had gone. And so he pledged himself, with regret, but with scrupulous observance, never to come to Balbec unless summoned there by myself. In the past, when I thought with longing of the hours that Mme. de Guermantes passed in his company, how I valued the privilege of seeing him! Other people never cease to change places in relation to ourselves. In the imperceptible but eternal march of the world, we regard them as motionless in a moment of vision, too short for us to perceive the motion that is sweeping them on. But we have only to select in our memory two pictures taken of them at different moments, close enough together however for them not to have altered in themselves—perceptibly, that is to say—and the difference between the two pictures is a measure of the displacement that they have undergone in relation to us. He alarmed me dreadfully by talking to me of the Verdurins, I was afraid that he might ask me to take him there, which would have been quite enough, what with the jealousy that I should be feeling all the time, to spoil all the pleasure that I found in going there with Albertine. But fortunately Robert assured me that, on the contrary, the one thing he desired above all others was not to know them. "No," he said to me, "I find that sort of clerical atmosphere maddening." I did not at first understand the application of the adjective 'clerical' to the Verdurins, but the end of Saint-Loup's speech threw a light on his meaning, his concessions to those fashions in words which one is often astonished to see adopted by intelligent men. "I mean the houses," he said, "where people form a tribe, a religious order, a chapel. You aren't going to tell me that they're not a little sect; they're all butter and honey to the people who belong, no words bad enough for those who don't. The question is not, as for Hamlet, to be or not to be, but to belong or not to belong. You belong, my uncle Charlus belongs. I can't help it, I never have gone in for that sort of thing, it isn't my fault."

The faithful had succeeded in overcoming the qualms which they had all more or less felt at first, on finding themselves in the company of M. de Charlus. No doubt in his presence they were incessantly reminded of Ski's revelations, and conscious of the sexual abnormality embodied in their travelling companion. But this abnormality itself had a sort of attraction for them. It gave for them to the Baron's conversation, remarkable in itself but in ways which they could scarcely appreciate, a savour which made the most interesting conversation, that of Brichot himself, appear slightly insipid in comparison. From the very outset, moreover, they had been pleased to admit that he was intelligent. "The genius that is perhaps akin to madness," the Doctor declaimed, and albeit the Princess, athirst for knowledge insisted, said not another word, this axiom being all that he knew about genius and seeming to him less supported by proof than our knowledge of typhoid fever and arthritis. And as he had become proud and remained ill-bred: "No questions, Princess, do not interrogate me, I am at the seaside for a rest. Besides, you would not understand, you know nothing about medicine." And the Princess held her peace with apologies, deciding that Cottard was a charming man and realising that celebrities were not always approachable. In this initial period, then, they had ended by finding M. de Charlus an agreeable person notwithstanding his vice (or what is generally so named). Now it was, quite unconsciously, because of that vice, that they found him more intelligent than the rest. One might still venture, when he was not listening, upon a malicious witticism at his expense. "Oh!" whispered the sculptor, seeing a young railwayman with the sweeping eyelashes of a dancing girl at whom M.

de Charlus could not help staring, "if the Baron begins making eyes at the conductor, we shall never get there; the train will start going backwards: Just look at the way he's staring at him, this is not a steamtram we're on, it's a funicular." But when all was said, if M. de Charlus did not appear, it was almost a disappointment to be travelling only with people who were just like everybody else, and not to have by one's side this painted, paunchy, tightly-buttoned personage, reminding one of a box of exotic and dubious origin from which escapes the curious odour of fruits the mere thought of tasting which stirs the heart. From this point of view, the faithful of the masculine sex enjoyed a keener satisfaction in the short stage of the journey between Saint-Martin du Chêne, where M. de Charlus got in, and Doncières, the station at which Morel joined the party. For so long as the violinist was not there (and provided the ladies and Albertine, keeping to themselves so as not to disturb our conversation, were out of hearing), M. de Charlus made no attempt to appear to be avoiding certain subjects and did not hesitate to speak of 'what it is customary to call degenerate morals'. Albertine could not hamper him, for she was always with the ladies, like a well-bred girl who does not wish her presence to restrict the freedom of grown-up conversation. And I was quite resigned to not having her by my side, on condition however that she remained in the same carriage. For I, who no, longer felt any jealousy and scarcely any love for her, never thought of what she might be doing on the days when I did not see her; on the other hand, when I was there, a mere partition which might at a pinch be concealing a betrayal was intolerable to me, and if she retired with the ladies to the next compartment, a moment later, unable to remain in my seat any longer, at the risk of offending whoever might be talking, Brichot, Cottard or Charlus, to whom I could not explain the reason for my flight, I would rise, leave them without ceremony, and, to make certain that nothing abnormal was going on, walk down the corridor. And, till we came to Doncières, M. de Charlus, without any fear of shocking his audience, would speak sometimes in the plainest terms of morals which, he declared, for his own part he did not consider either good or evil. He did this from cunning, to show his breadth of mind, convinced as he was that his own morals aroused no suspicion in the minds of the faithful. How astonished M. de Charlus would have been, if, one day when Morel and he were delayed and had not come by the train, he had heard the Mistress say: "We're all here now except the young ladies." The Baron would have been all the more stupefied in that, going hardly anywhere save to La Raspelière, he played the part there of a family chaplain, like, the abbé in a stock company, and would sometimes (when Morel had 48 hours leave) sleep there for two nights in succession. Mme. Verdurin would then give them communicating rooms and, to put them at their ease, would say: "If you want to have a little music, don't worry about us, the walls are as thick as a fortress, you have nobody else on your floor, and my husband sleeps like lead." On such days M. de Charlus, would relieve the Princess of the duty of going to meet strangers at the station, apologise for Mme. Verdurin's absence on the grounds of a state of health which he described so vividly that the guests, entered the drawing-room with solemn faces, and uttered cries of astonishment on finding the Mistress up and doing and wearing what was almost a low dress.

For M. de Charlus had for the moment become for Mme. Verdurin the faithfullest of the faithful, a second Princess Sherbatoff. Of his position in society she was not nearly so certain as of that of the Princess, imagining that if the latter cared to see no one outside the little nucleus it was out of contempt for other people and preference for it. As this pretence was precisely the Verdurin's own, they treating as bores everyone to whose society they were not admitted, it is incredible that the Mistress can have believed the Princess to possess a heart of steel, detesting what was fashionable. But she stuck to her guns, and was convinced, that in the case of the great lady also it was in all sincerity and from a love of things intellectual that she avoided the company of bores. The latter were as it happened, diminishing in numbers from the Verdurins' point of view. Life by the seaside robbed an introduction of the ulterior consequences which might be feared in Paris. Brilliant men who had come down to Balbec without their wives (which made everything much easier) made overtures to La Raspelière and, from being bores, became too charming. This was the case with the Prince de Guermantes; whom the absence of his Princess would not, however, have decided to go 'as a bachelor' to the Verdurins', had not the lodestone of Dreyfusism been so powerful as to carry him in one stride up the steep ascent to La Raspelière, unfortunately upon a day when the Mistress was not at home. Mme. Verdurin as it happened was not certain that he and M. de Charlus moved in the same world. The Baron had indeed said that the Duc. de Guermantes was his brother, but this was perhaps the untruthful boast of an adventurer. 'Man of the world' as be had shown himself to be, so friendly, so 'faithful' to the Verdurins, the Mistress still almost hesitated to invite him to meet the Prince de Guermantes. She consulted Ski and Brichot: "The Baron and the Prince de Guermantes, will they be all right together?" "Good gracious, Madame, as to one of the two I think I can safely say." "What good is that to me?" Mme. Verdurin had retorted crossly. "I asked you whether they would mix well together." "Ah! Madame, that is one of the things that it is hard to tell." Mme. Verdurin had been impelled by no malice. She was certain of the Baron's morals, but when she expressed herself in these terms had not been thinking about them for a moment; but had merely wished to know whether she could invite the Prince and M. de Cbarlus on the same evening, without their clashing. She had no malevolent intention when she employed these ready-made expressions which are popular in artistic little clans. To make the most of M. de. Guermantes, she proposed to take him in the afternoon after her luncheon-party, to a charity entertainment at which sailors from the neighbourhood would give a representation of a ship setting sail. But, not having time to attend to everything, she delegated her duties to the faithfullest of the faithful, the Baron. "You understand, I don't want them to hang about like mussels on a rock, they must keep moving, we must see them weighing anchor, or whatever it's called. Now you are always going down to the harbour at Balbec-Plage, you can easily arrange a dress rehearsal without tiring yourself. You must know far more than I do, M. de Charlus, about getting hold of sailors. But after all, we're giving ourselves a great deal of trouble for M. de Guermantes. Perhaps he's only one of those idiots from the Jockey Club. Oh! Heavens, I'm running down the Jockey Club, and I seem to remember that you're one of them. Eh, Baron, you don't answer me, are you one of them? You don't care to come out with us? Look, here is a book that has just come, I think you'll find it interesting. It is by Roujon. The title is attractive: *Among men.*"

Already, as the summer drew to a close, on our journey from Balbec to Douville, when I saw in the distance the watering-place at Saint-Pierre desIfs where, for a moment in the evening, the crest of the cliffs glittered rosy pink as the snow upon a mountain glows at sunset, it no longer recalled to my mind the spectacle that in the morning, Elstir had told me, might be enjoyed from there, at the hour before sunrise, when all the colours of the rainbow are refracted from the rocks, and when he had so often wakened the little boy who had served him one year, as model, to paint him nude upon the sands.

The name Saint Pierre desIfs announced to me merely that there would presently appear a strange, intelligent, painted man of fifty with whom I should be able to talk about Chateaubriand and Balzac if I did not wish to dine at La Raspelière or to return to Balbec. So that it was not merely the placenames of this district that had lost their initial mystery, but the places themselves. The names, already half-stripped of a mystery which etymology had replaced by reason, had now come down a stage farther still. On our 'homeward' journeys, at Hermenonville, at Incarville, at Harambouville, as the train came to a standstill, we could make out shadowy forms which we did not at first identify, and which Brichot, who could see nothing at all, might perhaps have mistaken in the darkness for the phantoms of Herimund, Wiscar and Herimbald. But they came up to our carriage. It was merely M. de Cambremer, now completely out of touch with the Verdurins, who had come to see off his own guests and, as ambassador for his wife and mother, came to ask me whether I would not let him 'carry me off" to keep me for a few days at Féterne where I should find successively a lady of great musical talent, who would sing me the whole of Gluck, and a famous chess-player, with whom I could have some splendid games, which would not interfere with the fishing expeditions and yachting trips on the bay, nor even with the Verdurin dinner-parties, for which the Marquis gave me his word of honour that he would 'lend' me, sending me there and fetching me back again, for my greater convenience and also to make sure of my returning. At Incarville, it was the Marquis de Montpeyroux who, not having been able to go to Féterne, for he had been away shooting, had come to meet the train in top boots, with a pheasant's feather in his hat, to shake hands with the departing guests and at the same time with myself, bidding me expect, on the day of the week that would be most convenient to me, a visit from his son, whom he thanked me for inviting, adding that he would be very glad if I would make the boy read a little; or else M. de Crécy, come out to digest his dinner, he explained, smoking his pipe, accepting a cigar or indeed more than one, and saying to me: "Well, you haven't named a day for our next Lucullus evening? We have nothing to discuss? Allow me to remind you that we left unsettled the question of the two families of Montgomery. We really must settle it. I am relying upon you." Others had come simply to buy newspapers. And many others came and chatted with us who, I have often suspected, were to be found upon the platform of the station nearest to their little mansion simply because they had nothing better to do than to converse for a moment with people of their acquaintance. A scene of social existence like anyother in fact, these halts on the little railway. The train itself appeared conscious of the part that had devolved upon it, had contracted a sort of human kindliness; patient, of a docile nature; it waited as long as they pleased for the stragglers, and even after it had started would, stop to pick up those who signalled to it; they would then run after it panting, in which they resembled itself; but differed from it in that they were running to overtake it at full speed whereas it employed only a wise slowness. And so Hermenonville, Harambouville, Incarville no longer suggested to me even the rugged grandeurs of the Norman conquest, not content with having entirely rid themselves of the unaccountable melancholy in which I had seen them steeped long ago in the moist evening air. Doncières! To me, even after I had come to know it and had wakened from my dream, how much had long survived in that name of pleasantly glacial streets, lighted windows, succulent flesh of birds. Doncières! Now it was nothing more than the station at which Morel joined the train, Egleville *(Aquilae villa)* that at which we generally found waiting for us Princess Sherbatoff, Maineville, the station at which Albertine left the train on fine evenings, when, if she was not too tired, she felt inclined to enjoy a moment more of my company, having, if she took a footpath, little if any farther to walk than if she had alighted at Parville *(Paterni villa)* The same place-names, so disturbing to me in the past that the mere Country House Year Book, when I turned over the chapter devoted to the Department of the Manche, caused me as keen an emotion as the railway time-table, had become so familiar to me that, in the time-table itself, I could have consulted the page-headed: *Balbec to Douville via Doncières,* with the same happy tranquility as a directory of addresses. In this too social valley, along the sides of which I felt assembled, whether visible or not, a numerous company of friends, the poetical cry of the evening was no longer that of the owl or frog, but the "How goes it?" of M. de Criquetot or the *"Xaipe"* of Brichot. Its atmosphere no longer aroused any anguish, and charged with effluvia that were purely human, was easily breathable, indeed unduly soothing. The benefit that I did at least derive from it was that of looking at things only from a practical point of view. The idea of marrying Albertine appeared to me to be madness.

Chapter Four

I was only waiting for an opportunity for a final rupture. And one evening, as Mamma was starting next day for Combray, where she was to attend the deathbed of one of her mother's sisters, leaving me behind so that I might get the benefit, as my grandmother would have wished, of the sea air, I announced to her that I had irrevocably decided not to marry Albertine and would very soon stop seeing her. I was glad to have been able, by these words, to give some satisfaction to my mother on the eve of her departure and she had not concealed from me that this satisfaction was indeed extreme.

I had also to come to an understanding with Albertine. As I was on my way back with her from La Raspelière, the faithful having alighted, some at Saint-Mars le Vêtu, others at Saint-Pierre des Ifs, others again at Doncières, feeling particularly happy and detached from her, I had decided, now that there were only our two selves in the carriage, to embark at length upon this subject. As we were getting near Parville, I felt that we should not have time that evening and that it was better to put off until the morrow what was now irrevocably settled. I confined myself, therefore, to discussing with her our dinner that evening at the Verdurins'. I must remember to ask Mme. Verdurin to let me hear some things by a musician whose work she knows very well. I know one of his things myself, but it seems there are others and I should like to know if the rest of his work is printed, if it is different from what I know." "What musician?" "My dear child, when I have told you that his name is Vinteuil, will you be any the wiser?" "You can't think how you amuse me," replied Albertine as she rose, for the train was slowing down. "Not only does it mean a great deal more to me than you suppose, but even without Mme. Verdurin I can get you all the information that you require. You remember my telling you about a friend older than myself, who has been a mother, a sister to me, with whom I spent the happiest years of my life at Trieste, and whom for that matter I am expecting to join in a few weeks at Cherbourg, when we shall start on our travels together (it sounds a little odd, but you know how I love the sea), very well, this friend (oh! not at all the type of woman you might suppose!), isn't this extraordinary, she is the dearest and most intimate friend of your Vinteuil's daughter, and I know Vinteuil's daughter almost as well as I know her. I always call them my two big sisters. I am not sorry to let you see that your little Albertine can be of use to you in this question of music, about which you say, and quite rightly for that matter, that I know nothing at all."

This was a terrible terra incognita on which I had just landed, a fresh phase of undreamed of sufferings that was opening before me. The truth of what Cottard had said to me in the casino at Parville was now confirmed beyond a shadow of doubt. What I had long dreaded, vaguely suspected of Albertine, what my instinct deduced from her whole personality and my reason controlled by my desire had gradually made me deny, was true! Behind Albertine I no longer saw the blue mountains of the sea, but the room at Montjouvain, where she was falling into the arms of Mlle. Vinteuil with that laugh in which she gave utterance to the strange sound of her enjoyment. For with a girl as pretty as Albertine, was it possible that Mlle. Vinteuil, having the desires she had, had not asked her to gratify them? And the proof that Albertine had not been shocked by the request but had consented, was that they had not quarrelled, indeed their intimacy had steadily increased.

But I reflected that she would presently be leaving Balbec for Cherbourg, and from there going to Trieste with Mlle Vinteuil's friend. Her old habits would be reviving. What I wished above all things was to prevent Albertine from taking the boat, to make an attempt to carry her off to Paris. It was true that from Paris, more easily even than from Balbec, she might, if she wished, go to Trieste but at Paris we should see; perhaps I might ask Mme. de Guermantes to exert her influence indirectly upon Mlle. Vinteuil's friend so that she should not remain at Trieste, to make her accept a situation elsewhere, perhaps with the Prince de —. whom I had met at Mme. de Villeparisis's and, indeed at Mme. de Guermantes's. And he, even if Albertine wished to go to his house to see her friend, might, warned by Mme. de Guermantes, prevent them from meeting. Of course I might have reminded myself that in Paris, if Albertine had those tastes, she would find many other people with whom to gratify them. But every impulse of jealousy is individual and bears the imprint of the creature in this instance Mlle. Vinteuil's friend—who has aroused it. It was Mlle. Vinteuil's friend who remained my chief preoccupation.

The thought of letting Albertine start presently for Cherbourg and Trieste filled me with horror; as did even that of remaining at Balbec. For now that the revelation of my mistress's intimacy with Mlle. Vinteuil became almost a certainty, it seemed to me that at every moment when Albertine was not with me (and there were whole days on which, because of her aunt, I was unable to see her), she was giving herself to Bloch's sister and cousin, possibly to other girls as well. The thought that that very evening she might be seeing the Bloch girls drove me mad. And so, after she had told me that for the next few days, she would stay with me all the time, I replied: "But the fact is, I want to go back to Paris. Won't you come with me? And wouldn't you like to come and stay with us for a while in Paris?" At all costs I must prevent her from being by herself, for some days at any rate, I must keep her with me, so as to be certain that she could not meet Mlle. Vinteuil's friend. She would as a matter of fact be alone in the house with myself, for my mother, taking the opportunity of a tour of inspection which my father had to make, had taken it upon herself as a duty, in obedience to my grandmother's wishes, to go down to Combray and spend a few days there with one of my grandmother's sisters.

Albertine left me, in order to go and dress and my mother entered the room; "Mamma, listen, I'm afraid you'll think me very changeable. But first of all, yesterday I spoke to you not at all nicely about Albertine; what I said was unfair." "But come;" my mother replied, "you said nothing unpleasant about her, you told me that she bored you a little, that you were glad you had given up the idea of marrying her."

"It is not that." I said to my mother: "I know how what I am going to say will distress you. First of all, instead of remaining here as you wished, I want to leave by the same train as you. But that is nothing. I am not feeling well here, I would rather go home. But listen to me, don't make yourself too miserable. This is what I want to say. I was deceiving myself, I deceived you in good faith, yesterday, I have been thinking over it all night. It is absolutely necessary, and let us decide the matter at once, because I am quite clear about it now in my own mind, because I shall not change again, and I could not live without it, it is absolutely necessary that I marry Albertine."

THE CAPTIVE

CHAPTER I

LIFE WITH ALBERTINE

At daybreak, my face still turned to the wall, and before I had seen above the big inner curtains what tone the first streaks of light assumed, I could already tell what sort of day it was. The first sounds from the street had told me, according to whether they came to my ears dulled and distorted by the moisture of the atmosphere or quivering like arrows in the resonant and empty area of a spacious, crisply frozen, pure morning; as soon as I heard the rumble of the first tramcar, I could tell whether it was sodden with rain or setting forth into the blue. It was, moreover, principally from my bedroom in Paris that I took in the life of the outer world during this period.

Now that my mistress had come, on our return from Balbec, to live in Paris under the same roof as myself, that she had abandoned the idea of going on a cruise, that she was installed in a bedroom within twenty paces of my own, at the end of the corridor, in my father's tapestried study, and that late every night, before leaving me, she used to slide her tongue between my lips like a portion of daily bread, a nourishing food that had the almost sacred character of all flesh upon which the sufferings that we have endured on its account have come in time to confer a sort of spiritual grace, what I at once call to mind in comparison is not the night that Captain de Borodino allowed me to spend in barracks, a favour which cured what was after all only a passing distemper, but the night on which my father sent Mamma to sleep in the little bed by the side of my own.

When Albertine had heard from Françoise that, in the darkness of my still curtained room, I was not asleep, she had no scruple about making a noise as she took her bath, in her own dressing-room. Then, frequently, instead of waiting until later in the day, I would repair to a bathroom adjoining hers, which had a certain charm of its own For I could hear Albertine ceaselessly humming:

For melancholy, Is but folly, And he who heeds it is a fool.

I loved her so well that I could spare a joyous smile for her bad taste in music.

The partition that divided our two dressing-rooms (Albertine's, identical with my own, was a bathroom which Mamma, who had another at the other end of the flat, had never used for fear of disturbing my rest) was so slender that we could talk to each other as we washed in double privacy, carrying on a conversation that was interrupted only by the sound of the water, in that intimacy which, in hotels, is so often permitted by the smallness and proximity of the rooms, but which, in private houses in Paris, is so rare.

On other mornings, I would remain in bed, drowsing for as long as I chose, for orders had been given that no one was to enter my room until I had rung the bell, an act which, owing to the awkward position in which the electric bulb had been hung above my bed, took such a time that often, tired of feeling for it and glad to be left alone, I would lie back for some moments and almost fall asleep again. It was not that I was wholly indifferent to Albertine's presence in the house. Her separation from her girl friends had the effect of sparing my heart any fresh anguish. She kept it in a state of repose, in a semi-immobility which would help it to recover. But after all, this calm which my mistress was procuring for me was a release from suffering rather than a positive joy. Not that it did not permit me to taste many joys, from which too keen a grief had debarred me, but these joys, so far from my owing them to Albertine, in whom for that matter I could no longer see any beauty and who was beginning to bore me, with whom I was now clearly conscious that I was not in love, I tasted on the contrary when Albertine was not with me.

I rang for Françoise. I opened the *Figaro*. I scanned its columns and made sure that it did not contain an article, or so-called article which I had sent to the editor, and which was no more than a slightly revised version of the page that had recently come to light, written long ago in Dr. Percepied's carriage, as I gazed at the spires of Martinville. Then I read a letter from Mamma. She felt it to be odd, in fact shocking, that a girl should be staying in the house alone with me. On the first day, at the moment of leaving Balbec, when she saw how wretched I was, and was distressed by the prospect of leaving me by myself, my mother had perhaps been glad when she heard that Albertine was travelling with us, and saw that, side by side with our own boxes (those boxes among which I had passed a night in tears in the Balbec hotel), there had been hoisted into the "Twister" Albertine's boxes also, narrow and black, which had seemed to me to have the appearance of coffins, and as to which I knew not whether they were bringing to my house life or death. But I had never even asked myself the question, being all overjoyed, in the radiant morning, after the fear of having to remain at Balbec, that I was taking Albertine with me. But to this proposal, if at the start my mother had not been hostile (speaking kindly to my friend like a mother whose son has been seriously wounded and who is grateful to the young mistress who is nursing him with loving care), she had acquired hostility now that it had been too completely realised, and the girl was prolonging her sojourn in our house, and moreover in the absence of my parents. She regretted that she had been obliged to leave us together, by departing at that very time for Combray where she might have to remain (and did in fact remain) for months on end, during which my great-aunt required her incessant attention by day and night.

Albertine would never think of shutting a door and, on the other hand, would no more hesitate to enter a room if the door stood open than would a dog or a cat. Her somewhat disturbing charm was, in fact, that of taking the place in the household not so much of a girl as of a domestic animal which comes into a room, goes out, is to be found wherever one does not expect to find it and (in her case) would — bringing me a profound sense of repose — come and lie down on my bed by my side, make a place for herself from which she never stirred, without being in my way as a person would have been. She ended, however, by conforming to my hours of sleep, and not only never attempted to enter my room but would take care not to make a sound until I had rung my bell. It was Françoise who impressed these rules of conduct upon her.

As soon as she entered my room, she sprang upon my bed and sometimes would expatiate upon my type of intellect, would vow in a transport of sincerity that she would sooner die than leave me: this was on mornings when I had shaved before sending for her. She was one of those women who can never distinguish the cause of their sensations. The pleasure that they derive from a smooth cheek they explain to themselves by the moral qualities of the man who seems to offer them a possibility of future happiness, which is capable, however, of diminishing and becoming less necessary the longer he refrains from shaving.

I inquired where she was thinking of going. "I believe Andrée wants to take me to the Buttes-Chaumont; I have never been there."

Of course it was impossible for me to discern among so many other words whether beneath these a falsehood lay concealed. Besides, I could trust Andrée to tell me of all the places that she visited with Albertine.

And as I knew that Andrée would tell me everything that she and Albertine had done, I had asked her, and she had agreed, to come and call for Albertine almost every day. In this way I might without anxiety remain at home. Also, Andrée's privileged position as one of the girls of the little band gave me confidence that she would obtain everything that I might require from Albertine. Truly, I could have said to her now in all sincerity that she would be capable of setting my mind at rest. At the same time, my choice of Andrée (who happened to be staying in Paris, having given up her plan of returning to Balbec) as guide and companion to my mistress was prompted by what Albertine had told me of the affection that her friend had felt for me at Balbec, at a time when, on the contrary, I had supposed that I was boring her; indeed, if I had known this at the time, it is perhaps with Andrée that I would have fallen in love. Notwithstanding all this, in case there might have been some secret plan made behind my back, I advised Albertine to give up the Buttes-Chaumont for that day and to go instead to Saint-Cloud or somewhere else.

I had even allowed Albertine to stay away for three whole days by herself with the chauffeur and to go almost as far as Balbec, so great was her longing to travel at high speed in an open car. Three days during which my mind had been quite at rest, although the rain of postcards that she had showered upon me did not reach me, owing to the appalling state of the Breton postal system (good in summer, but disorganised, no doubt, in winter), until a week after the return of Albertine and the chauffeur, in such health and vigour that on the very morning of their return they resumed, as though nothing had happened, their daily outings.

Of Albertine, I had nothing more to learn. Every day, she seemed to me less attractive. It was certainly not, as I was well aware, because I was the least bit in love with Albertine. Love is nothing more perhaps than the stimulation of those eddies which, in the wake of an emotion, stir the soul. Certain such eddies had indeed stirred my soul through and through when Albertine spoke to me at Balbec about Mlle. Vinteuil, but these were now stilled. I was no longer in love wIth Albertine, for I no longer felt anything of the suffering, now healed, which I had felt in the tram at Balbec, upon learning how Albertine had spent her girlhood, with visits perhaps to Montjouvain. All this, I had too long taken for granted, was healed. In the meantime, I was employing a thousand circumstances, a thousand pleasures to procure for her in my society the illusion of that happiness which I did not feel myself capable of giving her. I should have liked, as soon as I was cured, to set off for Venice, but how was I to manage it, if I married Albertine, I, who was so jealous of her that even in Paris whenever I decided to stir from my room it was to go out with her? Even when I stayed in the house all the afternoon, my thoughts accompanied her on her drive, traced a remote, blue horizon, created round the centre that was myself a fluctuating zone of vague uncertainty. "How completely," I said to myself, "would Albertine spare me the anguish of separation if, in the course of one of these drives, seeing that I no longer say anything to her about marriage, she decided not to come back, and went off to her aunt's, without my having to bid her good-bye!"

Sometimes I met my landlady, Mme. de Guermantes, in the courtyard, going out for a walk, even if the weather was bad, in a close-fitting hat and furs. I knew quite well that, to many people of intelligence, she was merely a lady like any other, the name Duchesse de Guermantes signifying nothing, now that there are no longer any sovereign Duchies or Principalities. But upon most evenings, at this hour, I could count upon finding the Duchess at home. It sometimes happened that I met in the courtyard as I came away from her door M. de Charlus and Morel on their way to take tea at Jupien's, a supreme favour for the Baron. I did not encounter them every day but they went there every day. Morel had told M. de Charlus that he was in love with Jupien's niece, and wished to marry her, and the Baron liked to accompany his young friend upon visits in which he played the part of father-in-law to be, indulgent and discreet. Nothing pleased him better.

The patronage of M. de Charlus brought it about that many customers for whom she had worked received her as a friend, invited her to dinner, introduced her to their friends, though the girl accepted their invitations only with the Baron's permission and on the evenings that suited him. "A young seamstress received in society?" the reader will exclaim, "how improbable!"

The day may come when dressmakers—nor should I find it at all shocking--will move in society. Jupien's niece being an exception affords us no base for calculation, for one swallow does not make a summer. In any case, if the very modest advancement of Jupien's niece did scandalise some people, Morel was not among them, for, in certain respects, his stupidity was so intense that not only did he label "rather a fool" this girl a thousand times cleverer than himself, and foolish only perhaps in her love for himself, but he actually took to be adventuresses, dressmakers assistants in disguise playing at being ladies, the persons of rank and position who invited her to their houses and whose invitations she accepted without a trace of vanity. Naturally these were not Guermantes, nor even people who knew the Guermantes, but rich and smart women of the middle-class, broad-minded enough to feel that it is no disgrace to invite a dressmaker to your house and at the same time servile enough to derive some satisfaction from patronising a girl whom His Highness the Baron de Charlus was in the habit—without any suggestion, of course, of impropriety—of visiting daily.

Nothing could have pleased the Baron more than the idea of this marriage, for he felt that in this way Morel would not be taken from him. It appears that Jupien's niece had been, when scarcely more than a child, "in trouble." And M. de Charlus, while he sang her praises to Morel, would have had no hesitation in revealing this secret to his friend, who would be furious, and thus sowing the seeds of discord. For M. de Charlus, although terribly malicious, resembled a great many good people who sing the praises of some man or woman, as a proof of their own generosity, but would avoid like poison the soothing words, so rarely uttered, that would be capable of putting an end to strife. Notwithstanding this, the Baron refrained from making any insinuation, and for two reasons. "If I tell him," he said to himself, "that his ladylove is not spotless, his vanity will be hurt, he will be angry with me. Besides, how am I to know that he is not in love with her? If I say nothing, this fire of straw will burn itself out before long, I shall be able to control their relations as I choose, he will love her only to the extent that I shall allow."

M. de Charlus's love for Morel acquired a delicious novelty when he said to himself: "His wife too will be mine just as much as he is, they will always take care not to annoy me, they will obey my caprices, and thus she will be a sign (which hitherto I have failed to observe) of what I had almost forgotten, what is so very dear to my heart, that to all the world, to everyone who sees that I protect them, house them, to myself, Morel is mine." This testimony in the eyes of the world and in his own pleased M. de Charlus more than anything.

At the stage that our narrative has now reached, it appears, as I have since heard, that Jupien's niece had altered her opinion of Morel and M. de Charlus. Morel never ceased to complain to her of the despotic treatment that he received from M. de Charlus, which she ascribed to malevolence, never imagining that it could be due to love. She was moreover bound to acknowledge that M. de Charlus was tyrannically present at all their meetings. In corroboration of all this, she had heard women in society speak of the Baron's terrible spite. Now, quite recently, her judgment had been completely reversed. She had discovered in Morel (without ceasing for that reason to love him) depths of malevolence and perfidy, compensated it was true by frequent kindness and genuine feeling, and in M. de Charlus an unimaginable and immense generosity blended with asperities of which she knew nothing. And so she had been unable to arrive at any more definite judgment of what, each in himself, the violinist and his protector really were.

One evening, Albertine was obliged to mention a plan that she had in her mind; I gathered at once that she wished to go next day to pay a call on Mme. Verdurin, a call to which in itself I would have had no objection. But evidently her object was to meet some one there, to prepare some future pleasure. Otherwise she would not have attached so much importance to this call. That is to say, she would not have kept on assuring me that it was of no importance.

I said carelessly, so as to make her tremble, that I intended to go out the next day myself. and I set to work to suggest to Albertine other expeditions in directions which would have made this visit to the Verdurins impossible, in words stamped with a feigned indifference beneath which I strove to conceal my excitement. But she had detected it. It encountered in her the electric shock of a contrary will which violently repulsed it; I could see the sparks flash from her eyes.

Later when Albertine returned to my room, she was wearing a garment of black satin which had the effect of making her seem paler, of turning her into the pallid, ardent Parisian, etiolated by want of fresh air, by the atmosphere of crowds and perhaps by vicious habits, whose eyes seemed more restless because they were not brightened by any colour in her cheeks.

"Guess," I said to her, "to whom I've just been talking on the telephone. Andrée"

"And may one be allowed to know why you telephoned to Andrée?" "To ask whether she had any objection to my joining you to-morrow, so that I may pay the Verdurins the call I promised them at la Raspelière." "Just as you like. But I warn you, there is an appalling mist this evening, and it's sure to last over to-morrow. I mention it, because I shouldn't like you to make yourself ill. Personally, you can imagine I would far rather you came with us. However," she added with a thoughtful air: "I'm not at all sure that I shall go to the Verdurins. They've been so kind to me that I ought, really........ Next to yourself, they have been nicer to me than anybody, but there are some things about them that I don't quite like. I simply must go to the Bon Marché and the Trois-Quartiers and get a white scarf to wear with this dress which is really too black."

Albertine was lying when she told me that she probably would not go to the Verdurins, as I was lying when I said that I wished to go there. She was seeking merely to dissuade me from accompanying her, and I, by my abrupt announcement of this plan, which I had no intention of putting into practice, to touch what I felt to be her most sensitive spot, to track down the desire that she was concealing and to force her to admit that my company on the morrow would prevent her from gratifying it. She had virtually made this admission by ceasing at once to wish to go to see the Verdurins.

"If you don't want to go to the Verdurins," I told her, "there is a splendid charity show at the Trocadéro." She listened to my urging her to attend it with a sorrowful air.

On the morrow of that evening when Albertine had told me that she would perhaps be going, then that she would not be going to see the Verdurins, I awoke early, and, while I was still half asleep, my joy informed me that there was, interpolated in the winter, a day of spring.

Françoise brought in the *Figaro*. A glance was sufficient to show me that my article had not yet appeared. She told me that Albertine had asked whether she might come to my room and sent word that she had quite given up the idea of calling upon the Verdurins, and had decided to go, as I had advised her, to the special matinée at the Trocadéro— what nowadays would be called, though with considerably less significance, a 'gala' matinée—after a short ride which she had promised to take with Andrée. I was delighted that Albertine should be going to this matinée, but still more reassured that she would have a companion there in the shape of Andrée.

I was studying the newspaper, and my attention was caught by the following: "To the programme already announced for this afternoon in the great hail of the Trocadéro must be added the name of Mlle. Léa who has consented to appear in *Les Fourberies de Nérine*. She will of course sustain the part of Nérine, in which she is astounding in her display of spirit and bewitching gaiety." It was as though a hand had brutally torn from my heart the bandage beneath which its wound had begun since my return from Balbec to heal. The flood of my anguish escaped in torrents, Léa, that was the actress friend of the two girls at Balbec whom Albertine, without appearing to see them, had, one afternoon at the Casino, watched in the mirror. It was true that at Balbec, Albertine, at the name of Léa, had adopted a special tone of compunction in order to say to me, almost shocked that anyone could suspect such a pattern of virtue: "Oh no, she is not in the least that sort of woman, she is a very respectable person."

Of course, I was still at the first stage of enlightenment with regard to Léa. I was not even aware whether Albertine knew her. No matter, it all came to the same thing. I must at all costs prevent her from—at the Trocadéro, renewing this acquaintance or making the acquaintance of this stranger.

My belief, that Albertine would do nothing that was not harmless, this belief had vanished. I was living no longer in the fine sunny day, but in a day carved out of the other by my anxiety lest Albertine might renew her acquaintance with Léa and more easily still with the two girls, should they go, as seemed to me probable, to applaud the actress at the Trocadéro where it would not be difficult for them, in one of the intervals, to come upon Albertine. I no longer thought of Mlle. Vinteuil; the name of Léa had brought back to my mind, to make me jealous, the image of Albertine in the Casino watching the two girls. I thought only of how I was to prevent her from remaining at the Trocadéro.

I decided that I must set to work immediately, remembered that Françoise was ready to go out and that I was not, and as I rose and dressed, made her take a motor-car; she was to go to the Trocadéro, engage a seat, look high and low for Albertine and give her a note from myself. In this note I told her that I was greatly upset by a letter which I had just received from that same lady on whose account she would remember that I had been so wretched one night at Balbec. I reminded her that, on the following day, she had reproached me for not having sent for her. And so I was taking the liberty, I informed her, of asking her to sacrifice her matinée and to join me at home so that we might take a little fresh air together, which might help me to recover from the shock. But as I should be a long time in getting ready, she would oblige me, seeing that she had Françoise as an escort, by calling at the Trois-Quartiers (this shop, being smaller, seemed to me less dangerous than the Bon Marché) to buy the scarf of white tulle that she required. I urged Françoise, when she had got Albertine out of the hall, to let me know by telephone, and to bring her home, whether she was willing or not.

When I was ready, Françoise had not yet telephoned; I ought perhaps to go out without waiting for a message. But how could I tell that she would find Albertine, that the latter would not have gone behind the scenes, that even if Françoise did find her, she would allow herself to be taken away? Half an hour later the telephone bell began to tinkle and my heart throbbed tumultuously with hope and fear. There came, at the bidding of an operator, a flying squadron of sounds which with an instantaneous speed brought me the words of the telephonist, not those of Françoise whom an inherited timidity and melancholy, when she was brought face to face with any object unknown to her fathers, prevented from approaching a telephone receiver, although she would readily visit a person suffering from a contagious disease. She had found Albertine in the lobby by herself, and Albertine had simply gone to warn Andrée that she was not staying any longer and then had hurried back to Françoise. "She wasn't angry? Oh, I beg your pardon; will you please ask the person whether the young lady was angry?" "The lady asks me to say that she wasn't at all angry, quite the contrary, in fact; anyhow, if she wasn't pleased, she didn't show it. They are starting now for the Trois-Quartiers, and will be home by three o'clock."

Albertine would not be meeting Léa or her friends. Whereupon the danger of her renewing relations with them, having been averted, at once began to lose its importance in my eyes and I was amazed, seeing with what ease it had been averted, that I should have supposed that I would not succeed in averting it. I felt a keen impulse of gratitude to Albertine, who, I could see, had not gone to the Trocadéro to meet Léa's friends, and showed me, by leaving the performance and coming home at a word from myself, that she belonged to me more than I had imagined. My gratitude was even greater when a bicyclist brought me a line from her bidding me be patient, and full of the charming expressions that she was in the habit of using. "My darling, dear Marcel, I return less quickly than this cyclist, whose machine I would like to borrow in order to be with you sooner. How could you imagine that I might be angry or that I could enjoy anything better than to be with you? It will be nice to go out, just the two of us together; it would be nicer still if we never went out except together. The ideas you get into your head! What a Marcel! What a Marcel! Always and ever your Albertine."

The frocks that I bought for her, the yacht of which I had spoken to her, the wrappers from Fortuny's, all these things having in this obedience on Albertine's part not their recompense but their complement, appeared to me now as so many privileges that I was enjoying; for the duties and expenditure of a master are part of his dominion, and define it, prove it, fully as much as his rights. And these rights which she recognised in me were precisely what gave my expenditure its true character:

I had a woman of my own, who, at the first word that I sent to her unexpectedly, made my messenger telephone humbly that she was coming, that she was allowing herself to be brought home immediately. I was more of a master than I had supposed. More of a master, in other words more of a slave. I no longer felt the slightest impatience to see Albertine. The certainty that she was at this moment engaged in shopping with Françoise, or that she would return with her at an approaching moment which I would willingly have postponed, illuminated like a calm and radiant star a period of time which I would now have been far better pleased to spend alone.

Taking advantage of the fact that I still was alone, and drawing the curtains together so that the sun should not prevent me from reading the notes, I sat down at the piano, turned over the pages of Vinteuil's sonata which happened to be lying there, and began to play; seeing that Albertine's arrival was still a matter of some time but was on the other hand certain, I had at once time to spare and tranquillity of mind.

Rising from the piano, I went down to the courtyard to meet Albertine, who still did not appear. As I passed by Jupien's shop, in which Morel and the girl who, I supposed, was shortly to become his wife were by themselves, Morel was screaming at the top of his voice, thereby revealing an accent that I had never heard in his speech, a rustic tone, suppressed as a rule, and very strange indeed. His words were no less strange, faulty from the point of view of the French language, but his knowledge of everything was imperfect. "Will you get out of here, *grand pied de grue, grand pied de grue, grand pied de grue,*" he repeated to the poor girl who at first had certainly not understood what he meant, and, now, trembling and indignant, stood motionless before him. "Didn't I tell you to get out of here, *grand pied de grue, grand pied de grue;* go and fetch your uncle till I tell him what you are, you whore." Just at that moment the voice of Jupien who was coming home talking to one of his friends was heard in the courtyard, and as I knew that Morel was an utter coward, I decided that it was unnecessary to join my forces with those of Jupien and his friend, who in another moment would have entered the shop, and I retired upstairs again to escape Morel, who, for all his having pretended to be so anxious that Jupien should be fetched (probably in order to frighten and subjugate the girl, an act of blackmail which rested probably upon no foundation), made haste to depart as soon as he heard his voice in the courtyard. The words I have set down here are nothing, they would not explain why my heart throbbed so as I went upstairs. These scenes of which we are witnesses in real life find an incalculable element of strength in what soldiers call, in speaking of a military offensive, the advantage of surprise, and I still heard ringing in my ears the accent of

those words ten times repeated:
"*Grand pied de grue, grand pied de grue,*" which had so appalled me.

That afternoon , after my drive with Albertine, I learned that a death had occurred which distressed me greatly, that of Bergotte. It was known that he had been ill for a long time past. Not, of course, with the illness from which he had suffered originally and which was natural. Nature hardly seems capable of giving us any but quite short illnesses. But medicine has annexed to itself the art of prolonging them. Remedies, the respite that they procure, the relapses that a temporary cessation of them provokes, compose a sham illness to which the patient grows so accustomed that he ends by making it permanent, just as children continue to give way to fits of coughing long after they have been cured of the whooping cough. Then remedies begin to have less effect, the doses are increased, they cease to do any good, but they have begun to do harm thanks to that lasting indisposition. Nature would not have offered them so long a tenure. It is a great miracle that medicine can almost equal nature in forcing a man to remain in bed, to continue on pain of death the use of some drug. From that moment the illness artificially grafted has taken root, has become a secondary but a genuine illness, with this difference only that natural illnesses are cured, but never those which medicine creates, for it knows not the secret of their cure.

The circumstances of his death were as follows. An attack of uraemia, by no means serious, had led to his being ordered to rest. But one of the critics having written somewhere that in Vermeer's *Street in Delft* (lent by the Gallery at The Hague for an exhibition of Dutch painting), a picture which he adored and imagined that he knew by heart, a little patch of yellow wall (which he could not remember) was so well painted that it was, if one looked at it by itself, like some priceless specimen of Chinese art, of a beauty that was sufficient in itself, Bergotte ate a few potatoes, left the house, and went to the exhibition. At the first few steps that he had to climb he was overcome by giddiness. He passed in front of several pictures and was struck by the stiffness and futility of so artificial a school, nothing of which equalled the fresh air and sunshine of a Venetian palazzo, or of an ordinary house by the sea. At last he came to the Vermeer which he remembered as more striking, more different from anything else that he knew, but in which, thanks to the critic's article, he remarked for the first time some small figures in blue, that the ground was pink, and finally the precious substance of the tiny patch of yellow wall. His giddiness increased; he fixed his eyes, like a child upon a yellow butterfly which it is trying to catch, upon the precious little patch of wall. "That is how I ought to have written," he said. "My last books are too dry, I ought to have gone over them with several coats of paint, made my language exquisite in itself, like this little patch of yellow wall." Meanwhile he was not unconscious of the gravity of his condition; in a celestial balance there appeared to him, upon one of its scales, his own life, while the other contained the little patch of wall so beautifully painted in yellow. He felt that he had rashly surrendered the former for the latter. "All the same," he said to himself, "I have no wish to provide the 'feature' of this exhibition for the evening papers."

He repeated to himself: "Little patch of yellow wall; with a sloping roof, little patch of yellow wall." While doing so he sank down upon a circular divan; and then at once he ceased to think that his life was in jeopardy and, reverting to his natural optimism, told himself: "It is just an ordinary indigestion from those potatoes; they weren't properly cooked; it is nothing." A fresh attack beat him down; he rolled from the divan to the floor, as visitors and attendants came hurrying to his assistance. He was dead. Permanently dead? Who shall say? Certainly our experiments in spiritualism prove no more than the dogmas of religion that the soul survives death. All that we can say is that everything is arranged in this life as though we entered it carrying the burden of obligations contracted in a former life; there is no reason inherent in the conditions of life on this earth that can make us consider ourselves obliged to do good, to be fastidious, to be polite even, nor make the talented artist consider himself obliged to begin over again a score of times a piece of work the admiration aroused by which will matter little to his body devoured by worms, like the patch of yellow wall painted with so much knowledge and skill by an artist who must for ever remain unknown and is barely identified under the name Vermeer. All these obligations which have not their sanction in our present life seem to belong to a different world, founded upon kindness, scrupulosity, self-sacrifice, a world entirely different from this, which we leave in order to be born into this world, before perhaps returning to the other to live once again beneath the sway of those unknown laws which we have obeyed because we bore their precepts in our hearts, knowing not whose hand had traced them there—those laws to which every profound work of the intellect brings us nearer and which are invisible only—and still! —to fools. So that the idea that Bergotte was not wholly and permanently dead is by no means improbable.

Chapter II

After dinner, I told Albertine that, since I was out of bed, I might as well take the opportunity to go and see some of my friends, Mme. de Villeparisis, Mme. de Guermantes, the Cambremers, anyone in short whom I might find at home. I omitted to mention only the people whom I did intend to see, the Verdurins. I asked her if she would not come with me. She pleaded that she had no suitable clothes. "Besides, my hair is so awful. Do you really wish me to go on doing it like this?" And by way of farewell she held out her hand to me in that abrupt fashion, the arm outstretched, the shoulders thrust back, which she used to adopt on the beach at Balbec and had since then entirely abandoned. This forgotten gesture retransformed the body which it animated into that of the Albertine who as yet scarcely knew me. It restored to Albertine ceremonious beneath an air of rudeness, her first novelty, her strangeness, even her setting. I saw the sea behind this girl whom I had never seen shake hands with me in this fashion since I was at the seaside

I said to Albertine, who was not dressed, or so she told me, to accompany me to the Guermantes' or the Cambremers', that I could not be certain where I should go, and set off for the concert at the Verdurins' at which I expected to see Mlle. Vinteuil and her friend whom Albertine must at all costs be prevented from meeting. I was just going to hail a cab when I heard the sound of sobs which a man who was sitting upon a curbstone was endeavouring to stifle. I came nearer; the man, who had buried his face in his hands, appeared to be quite young, and I was surprised to see, from the gleam of white in the opening of his cloak, that he was wearing evening clothes and a white tie. As he heard my step he uncovered a face bathed in tears, but at once, having recognised me, turned away. It was Morel. He guessed that I had recognised him and, checking his tears with an effort, told me that he had stopped to rest for a moment, he was in such pain. "I have grossly insulted, only today," he said, "a person for whom I had the very highest regard. It was a cowardly thing to do, for she loves me." "She will forget perhaps, as time goes on," I replied, without realising that by speaking thus I made it apparent that I had overheard the scene that afternoon. But he was so much absorbed in his own grief that it never even occurred to him that I might know something about the affair. "She may forget, perhaps," he said. "But I myself can never forget. I am too conscious of my degradation, I am disgusted with myself! However, what I have said I have said, and nothing can unsay it. When people make me lose my temper, I don't know what I am doing. And it is so bad for me, my nerves are all on edge," for, like all neurasthenics, he was keenly interested in his own health. If, during the afternoon, I had witnessed the amorous rage of an infuriated animal, this evening, within a few hours, centuries had elapsed and a fresh sentiment, a sentiment of shame, regret, grief, showed that a great stage had been passed in the evolution of the beast destined to be transformed into a human being. Nevertheless, I still heard ringing in my ears his *"grand pied de grue"* and dreaded an imminent return to the savage state. I had only a very vague impression, however, of what had been happening, and this was but natural, for M. de Charlus himself was totally unaware that for some days past, and especially that day, even before the shameful episode which was not a direct consequence of the violinist's condition, Morel had been suffering from a recurrence of his neurasthenia. As a matter of fact, he had, in the previous month, proceeded as rapidly as he had been able, a great deal less rapidly than he would have liked, towards the seduction of Jupien's niece with whom he was at liberty, now that they were engaged, to go out whenever he chose. But whenever he had gone a trifle far in his attempts at violation, and especially when he suggested to his betrothed that she might make friends with other girls whom she would then procure for himself, he had met with a resistance that made him furious. All at once (whether she would have proved too chaste, or on the contrary would have surrendered herself) his desire had subsided. He had decided to break with her, but feeling that the Baron, vicious as he might be, was far more moral than himself, he was afraid lest, in the event of a rupture, M. de Charlus might turn him out of the house. And so he had decided, a fortnight ago, that he would not see the girl again, would leave M. de Charlus and Jupien to clean up the mess (he employed a more realistic term) by themselves, and, before announcing the rupture, to "b— off" to an unknown destination.

Now, on the contrary, actually to "b— off" for so small a matter seemed to him quite unnecessary. It meant leaving the Baron who would probably be furious, and forfeiting his own position. He would lose all the money that the Baron was now giving him. The thought that this was inevitable made his nerves give away altogether, he cried for hours on end, and in order not to think about it any more dosed himself cautiously with morphine. Then suddenly he hit upon an idea which no doubt had gradually been taking shape in his mind and gaining strength there for some time, and this was that a rupture with the girl would not inevitably mean a complete break with M. de Charlus. To lose all the Baron's money was a serious thing in itself. Morel in his uncertainty remained for some days a prey to dark thoughts. Then he decided that Jupien and his niece had been trying to set a trap for him, that they might consider themselves lucky to be rid of him so cheaply. He found in short that the girl had been in the wrong in being so clumsy, in not having managed to keep him attached to her by a sensual attraction. Not only did the sacrifice of his position with M. de Charlus seem to him absurd, he even regretted the expensive dinners he had given the girl since they became engaged, the exact cost of which he knew by heart, being a true son of the valet who used to bring his 'book' every month for my uncle's inspection. For the word book, in the singular, which means a printed volume to humanity in general, loses that meaning among Royal Princes and servants. To the latter it means their housekeeping book, to the former the register in which we inscribe our names. (At Balbec one day when the Princesse de Luxembourg told me that she had not brought a book with her, I was about to offer her *Le Pêcheur d'Islande* and *Tartarin de Tarascon,* when I realised that she had meant not that she would pass the time less agreeably, but that I should find it more difficult to pay a call upon her.)

Notwithstanding the change in Morel's point of view with regard to the consequences of his behaviour, albeit that behaviour would have seemed to him abominable two months earlier, when he was passionately in love with Jupien's niece, whereas during the last fortnight he had never ceased to assure himself that the same behaviour was natural, praiseworthy, it continued to intensify the state of nervous unrest in which, finally, he had announced the rupture that afternoon. And he was quite prepared to vent his anger, if not (save in a momentary outburst) upon the girl, for whom he still felt that lingering fear, the last trace of love, at any rate upon the Baron. He took care, however, not to say anything to him before dinner, for, valuing his own professional skill above everything, whenever he had any difficult music to play (as this evening at the Verdurins') he avoided (as far as possible, and the scene that afternoon was already more than ample) anything that might impair the flexibility of his wrists. Similarly a surgeon who is an enthusiastic motorist, does not drive when he has an operation to perform. This accounts to me for the fact that, while he was speaking to me, he kept bending his fingers gently one after another to see whether they had regained their suppleness. A slight frown seemed to indicate that there was still a trace of nervous stiffness. But, so as not to increase it, he relaxed his features, as we forbid ourself to grow irritated at not being able to sleep or to prevail upon a woman, for fear lest our rage itself may retard the moment of sleep or of satisfaction. And so, anxious to regain his serenity so that he might, as was his habit, absorb himself entirely in what he was going to play at the Verdurins', and anxious, so long as I was watching him, to let me see how unhappy he was, he decided that the simplest course was to beg me to leave him immediately.

As my cab, following the line of the embankment, was coming near the Verdurins' house, I made the driver pull up. I had just seen Brichot alighting from the tram at the foot of the Rue Bonaparte, after which he dusted his shoes with an old newspaper and put on a pair of pearl grey gloves. I went up to him on foot. Just as we were coming to Mme. Verdurin's doorstep, I caught sight of M. de Charlus, steering towards us the bulk of his huge body, drawing unwillingly in his wake one of those blackmailers or mendicants who nowadays, whenever he appeared, sprang up without fail even in what were to all appearance the most deserted corners, by whom this powerful monster was, evidently against his will, invariably escorted, although at a certain distance, as is the shark by its pilot, in short contrasting so markedly with the haughty stranger of my first visit to Balbec, with his stern aspect, his affectation of virility, that I seemed to be discovering, accompanied by its satellite, a planet at a wholly different period of its revolution, when one begins to see it full, or a sick man now devoured by the malady which a few years ago was but a tiny spot which was easily concealed and the gravity of which was never suspected. "And what,"Charlus went on, turning to myself, "has become of your young Hebrew friend, whom we met at Douville? "You must tell your young Israelite, since he writes verses, that he must really bring me some for Morel. For a composer, that is always the stumbling block, to find something decent to set to music. One might even consider a libretto. It would not be without interest, and would acquire a certain value from the distinction of the poet, from my patronage, from a whole chain of auxiliary circumstances, among which Morel's talent would take the chief place, for he is composing a lot just now, and writing too, and very pleasantly, I must talk to you about it. As for his talent as a performer (there, as you know, he's already a past-master), you shall see this evening how well the lad plays Vinteuil's music; he overwhelms me; at his age, to have such an understanding while he is still such a boy, such a kid! Oh, this evening is only to be a little rehearsal. The big affair is to come off in two or three days. But it will be much more distinguished this evening. And so we are delighted that you have come," he went on, employing the plural pronoun doubtless because a King says: "It is our wish." "The programme is so magnificent that I have advised Mme. Verdurin to give two parties. One in a few days time, at which she will have all her own friends, the other to-night at which the hostess is, to use a legal expression, 'disseized.' It is I who have issued the invitations, and I have collected a few people from another sphere, who may be useful to Charlie, and whom it will be nice for the Verdurins to meet."

But the Baron had proscribed several ladies of the aristocracy whose acquaintance Mme. Verdurin, on the occasion of some musical festivity or a collection for charity, had recently formed and who, whatever M. de Charlus might think of them, would have been, far more than himself, essential to the formation of a fresh nucleus at Mme. Verdurin's, this time aristocratic. Mme. Verdurin had indeed been reckoning upon this party, to which M. de Charlus would be bringing her women of the same set, to mix her new friends with them, and had been relishing in anticipation the surprise that the latter would feel upon meeting at Quai Conti their own friends or relatives invited there by the Baron. She was disappointed and furious at his veto. It remained to be seen whether the evening, in these conditions, would result in profit or loss to herself. The loss would not be too serious if only M. de Charlus's guests came with so friendly a feeling for Mme. Verdurin that they would become her friends in the future. In this case the mischief would be only half done, these two sections of the fashionable world, which the Baron had insisted upon keeping apart, would be united later on, he himself being excluded, of course, when the time came. And so Mme. Verdurin was awaiting the Baron's guests with a certain emotion. She would not be slow in discovering the state of mind in which they came, and the degree of intimacy to which she might hope to attain.

I could not refrain from alluding to Mlle. Vinteuil. "Isn't the composer's daughter to be here," I asked Mme. Verdurin, "with one of her friends?" "No, I have just had a telegram," Mme. Verdurin said evasively, "they have been obliged to remain in the country." I felt a momentary hope that there might never have been any question of their leaving it and that Mme. Verdurin had announced the presence of these representatives of the composer only in order to make a favourable impression upon the performers and their audience. "What, didn't they come, then, to the rehearsal this afternoon?" came with a feigned curiosity from the Baron who was anxious to let it appear that he had not seen Charlie. The latter came up to greet me. I whispered a question in his ear about Mlle. Vinteuil; he seemed to me to know little or nothing about her. I signalled to him not to let himself be heard and told him that we should discuss the question later on. He bowed, and assured me that he would be delighted to place himself entirely at my disposal. I observed that he was far more polite, more respectful, than he had been in the past. I spoke warmly of him who might perhaps be able to help me to clear up my suspicions—to M. de Charlus who replied: "He only does what is natural, there would be no point in his living among respectable people if he didn't learn good manners." These, according to M. de Charlus, were the old manners of France, untainted by any British bluntness. Thus when Charlie, returning from a tour in the provinces or abroad, arrived in his travelling suit at the Baron's, the latter, if there were not too many people present, would kiss him without ceremony upon both cheeks, perhaps a little in order to banish by so ostentatious a display of his affection any idea of its being criminal, perhaps because he could not deny himself a pleasure, but still more, doubtless, from a literary sense, as upholding and illustrating the traditional manners of France, and, just as he would have countered the Munich or modern style of furniture by keeping in his rooms old armchairs that had come to him from a great-grandmother, countering the British phlegm with the affection of a warmhearted father of the eighteenth century, unable to conceal his joy at beholding his son once more. Was there indeed a trace of incest in this paternal affection? It is more probable that the way in which M. de Charlus habitually appeased his vicious cravings, as to which we shall learn something in due course, was not sufficient for the need of affection, which had remained unsatisfied since the death of his wife; the fact remains that after having thought more than once of a second marriage, he was now devoured by a maniacal desire to adopt an heir. People said that he was going to adopt Morel, and there was nothing extraordinary in that. The invert who has been unable to feed his passion save on a literature written for women-loving men, who used to think of men when he read Musset's *Nuits* feels the need to partake, nevertheless, in all the social activities of the man who is not an invert, to keep a lover, as the old frequenter of the opera keeps ballet-girls, to settle down, to marry or form a permanent tie, to become a father.

M. de Charlus took Morel aside on the pretext of making him tell him what was going to be played, but above all finding a great consolation, while Charlie showed him his music, in displaying thus publicly their secret intimacy. In the mean time I myself felt a certain charm. For albeit the little clan included few girls, on the other hand girls were abundantly invited on the big evenings. There were a number present, and very pretty girls too, whom I knew. They wafted smiles of greeting to me across the room. The air was thus decorated at every moment with the charming smile of some girl. That is the manifold, occasional ornament of evening parties, as it is of days. We remember an atmosphere because girls were smiling in it.

"I feel that it is our duty to enlighten him," Mme. Verdurin said to Brichot. "Not that I have anything against Charlus, far from it. He is a pleasant fellow and as for his reputation, I don't mind saying that it is not of a sort that can do me any harm! As far as I'm concerned, in our little clan, in our table-talk, as I detest flirts, the men who talk nonsense to a woman in a corner instead of discussing interesting topics, I've never had any fear with Charlus of what happened to me with Swann, and Elstir, and lots of them. With him I was quite safe, he would come to my dinners, all the women in the world might be there, you could be certain that the general conversation would not be disturbed by flirtations and whisperings. Charlus is in a class of his own, one doesn't worry, he might be a priest. Only, he must not be allowed to take it upon himself to order about the young men who come to the house and make a nuisance of himself in our little nucleus, or he'll be worse than a man who runs after women." And Mme. Verdurin was sincere in thus proclaiming her indulgence towards Charlism. Like every ecclesiastical power she regarded human frailties as less dangerous than anything that might undermine the principle of authority, impair the orthodoxy, modify the ancient creed of her little Church. "If he does, then I shall bare my teeth. What do you say to a gentleman who tried to prevent Charlie from coming to a rehearsal because he himself was not invited? So he's going to be taught a lesson, I hope he'll profit by it, otherwise he can simply take his hat and go. He keeps the boy under lock and key, upon my word he does." And, using exactly the same expressions that almost anyone else might have used, for there are certain not in common currency which some particular subject, some given circumstance recalls almost inevitably to the mind of the speaker, who imagines that he is giving free expression to his thought when he is merely repeating mechanically the universal lesson, she went on: "It's impossible to see Morel nowadays without that great lout hanging round him, like an armed escort." M. Verdurin offered to take Charlie out of the room for a minute to explain things to him, on the pretext of asking him a question. Mme. Verdurin was afraid that this might upset him, and that he would play badly in consequence. It would be better to postpone this performance until after the other. Perhaps even until a later occasion. For however Mme. Verdurin might look forward to the delicious emotion that she would feel when she knew that her husband was engaged in enlightening Charlie in the next room, she was afraid, if the shot missed fire, that he would lose his temper and would fail to reappear on the sixteenth.

What ruined M. de Charlus that evening was the ill-breeding—so common in their class—of the people whom he had invited and who were now beginning to arrive. Having come there partly out of friendship for M. de Charlus and, also out of curiosity to explore these novel surroundings, each Duchess made straight for the Baron as though it were he who was giving the party and said, within a yard of the Verdurins, who could hear every word: "Show me which is mother Verdurin; do you think I really need speak to her? I do hope, at least, that she won't put my name in the paper tomorrow, nobody would ever speak to me again. What! That woman with the white hair, but she looks quite presentable."

M. de Charlus, while his guests fought their way towards him, to come and congratulate him, thank him, as though he were master of the house, never thought of asking them to say a few words to Mme. Verdurin. Only the Queen of Naples, in whom survived the same noble blood that had flowed in the veins of her sisters the Empress Elisabeth and the Duchesse d'Alencon, made a point of talking to Mme. Verdurin as though she had come for the pleasure of meeting her rather than for the music and for M. de Charlus, made endless pretty speeches to her hostess, could not cease from telling her for how long she had been wishing to make her acquaintance, expressed her admiration for the house and spoke to her of all manner of subjects as though she were paying a call. She expressed her regret that she would not be able to remain until the end, as she had, although she never went anywhere, to go on to another party, and begged that on no account, when she had to go, should any fuss be made for her, thus discharging Mme. Verdurin of the honours which the latter did not even know that she ought to render. One must, however, do M. de Charlus the justice of saying that, if he entirely forgot Mme. Verdurin and allowed her to be ignored, to a scandalous extent, by the people of his own world whom he had invited, he did, on the other hand, realise that he must not allow these people to display, during the 'symphonic recital' itself, the bad manners which they were exhibiting towards the Mistress. Morel had already mounted the platform, the musicians were assembling, and one could still hear conversations, not to say laughter, speeches such as "it appears, one has to be initiated to understand it." Immediately M. de Charlus, drawing himself erect, as though he had entered a different body from that which I had seen, not an hour ago, crawling towards Mme. Verdurin's door, assumed a prophetic expression and regarded the assembly with an earnestness which indicated that this was not the moment for laughter, whereupon one saw a rapid blush tinge the cheeks of more than one lady thus publicly rebuked, like a schoolgirl scolded by her teacher in front of the whole class.

The concert began, I did not know what they were playing, I found myself in a strange land. Where was I to locate it? Into what composer's country had I come? I should have been glad to know. I found myself, in the midst of this music that was novel to me, right in the heart of Vinteuil's sonata; and, more marvellous than any maiden, the little phrase, enveloped, harnessed in silver, glittering with brilliant effects of sound; as light and soft as silken scarves, came towards me, recognisable in this new guise. My joy at having found it again was enhanced by the accent, so friendlily familiar, which it adopted in addressing me, so persuasive, so simple, albeit without dimming the shimmering beauty with which it was resplendent. Its intention, however, was, this time, merely to show me the way, which was not the way of the sonata, for this was an unpublished work of Vinteuil in which he had merely amused himself by making the little phrase reappear for a moment. No sooner was it thus recalled than it vanished and I found myself in an unknown world. What was now before me made me feel as keen a joy as the sonata would have given me if I had not already known it, and consequently, while no less beautiful, was different. Whereas the sonata opened upon a dawn of lilied meadows, parting its slender whiteness to suspend itself over the frail and yet consistent mingling of a rustic bower of honeysuckle with white geraniums, it was upon continuous, level surfaces like those of the sea that, in the midst of a stormy morning beneath an already lurid sky, there began, in an eery silence, in an infinite void, this new masterpiece, and it was into a roseate dawn that, in order to construct itself progressively before me, this unknown universe was drawn from silence and from night. This so novel redness, so absent from the tender, rustic, pale sonata, tinged all the sky, as dawn does, with a mysterious hope. And a song already thrilled the air, a song on seven notes, but the strangest, the most different from any that I had ever imagined, from any that I could ever have been able to imagine, at once ineffable and piercing, no longer the cooing of a dove as in the sonata, but rending the air, as vivid as the scarlet tinge in which the opening bars had been bathed, something like the mystical crow of a cock, an ineffable but over-shrill appeal of the eternal morning. But very soon, the triumphant motive of the bells having been banished, dispersed by others, I succumbed once again to the music; and I began to realise that if, in the body of this septet, different elements presented themselves in turn, to combine at the close, so also Vinteuil's sonata, and, as I was to find later on, his other works as well, had been no more than timid essays, exquisite but very slight, towards the triumphant and complete masterpiece which was revealed to me at this moment. How did it come about that this revelation, the strangest that I had yet received, of an unknown type of joy, should have come to me from him, since, it was understood, when he died he left nothing behind him but his sonata, all the rest being non-existent in indecipherable scribblings. Indecipherable they may have been, but they had nevertheless been in the end deciphered, by dint of patience, intelligence and respect, by the only person who had lived sufficiently in Vinteuil's company to understand his method of working, to interpret his orchestral indications: Mlle. Vinteuil's friend. Even in the lifetime of the great composer, she had acquired from his daughter the reverence that the latter felt for her father. It was because of this reverence that, in those moments in which people run counter to their natural inclinations, the two girls had been able to find an insane pleasure in the profanations which have already been narrated. (Her adoration of her father was the primary condition of his daughter's sacrilege. And no doubt they ought to have foregone the delight of that sacrilege, but it did not express the whole of their natures.) And, what is more, the profanations had become rarefied until they disappeared altogether, in proportion as their morbid carnal relations, that troubled, smouldering fire, had given place to the flame of a pure and lofty friendship. Mlle. Vinteuil's friend was sometimes worried by the importunate thought that she had perhaps hastened the death of Vinteuil. At any rate, by spending years in poring over the cryptic scroll left by him, in establishing the correct reading of those illegible hieroglyphs, Mlle. Vinteuil's friend had the consolation of assuring the composer, whose grey hairs she had sent in sorrow to the grave, an immortal and compensating glory. What she had enabled us, thanks to her labour, to know of Vinteuil was, to tell the truth, the whole of Vinteuil's work. Compared with this septet, certain phrases from the sonata, which alone the public knew, appeared so commonplace that one failed to understand how they could have aroused so much admiration.

M. de Charlus repeated, when, the music at an end, his guests came to say good-bye to him, the same error that he had made when they arrived. He did not ask them to shake hands with their hostess, to include her and her husband in the gratitude that was being showered on himself. There was a long queue waiting, but a queue that led to the Baron alone, a fact of which he must have been conscious, for as he said to me a little later: "The form of the artistic celebration ended in a 'few-words-in-the-vestry' touch that was quite amusing." The guests even prolonged their expressions of gratitude with indiscriminate remarks which enabled them to remain for a moment longer in the Baron's presence, while those who had not yet congratulated him on the success of his party hung wearily in the rear. A stray husband or two may have announced his intention of going; but his wife, a snob as well as a Duchess, protested: "No, no, even if we are kept waiting an hour, we cannot go away without thanking Palamède, who has taken so much trouble. There is nobody else left now who can give entertainments like this." Nobody would have thought of asking to be introduced to Mme. Verdurin any more than to the attendant in a theatre to which some great lady has for one evening brought the whole aristocracy; they gave the credit to M. de Charlus, saying: "how clever Palamède is at arranging things; if he were to stage an opera in a stable or a bathroom, it would still be perfectly charming." Several of them engaged Charlie on the spot for different evenings on which he was to come and play them Vinteuil's septet, but it never occurred to any of them to invite Mme. Verdurin. This last was already blind with fury when M. de Charlus who, his head in the clouds, was incapable of perceiving her condition, decided that it would be only decent to invite the Mistress to share his joy. And it was perhaps yielding to his literary preciosity rather than to an overflow of pride that this specialist in artistic entertainments said to Mme. Verdurin: "Well, are you satisfied? I think you have reason to be; you see that when I set to work to give a party there are no half measures. I do not know whether your heraldic knowledge enables you to gauge the precise importance of the display, the weight that I have lifted, the volume of air that I have displaced for you. You have had the Queen of Naples, the brother of the King of Bavaria, the three premier peers. If Vinteuil is Mahomet, we may say that we have brought to him some of the least movable of mountains."

The Baron's volubility was in itself an irritation to Mme. Verdurin who did not like people to form independent groups within their little clan. How often, even at La Raspelière, hearing M. de Charlus talking incessantly to Charlie instead of being content with taking his part in the so harmonious chorus of the clan, she had pointed to him and exclaimed: "What a rattle he is! What a rattle! Oh, if it comes to rattles, he's a famous rattle!" But this time it was far worse. Inebriated with the sound of his own voice, M. de Charlus failed to realise that by cutting down the part assigned to Mme. Verdurin and confining it within narrow limits, he was calling forth that feeling of hatred which was in her only a special, social form of jealousy. Mme. Verdurin was genuinely fond of her regular visitors, the faithful of the little clan, but wished them to be entirely devoted to their Mistress. Willing to make some sacrifice, like those jealous lovers who will tolerate a betrayal, but only under their own roof and even before their eyes, that is to say when there is no betrayal, she would allow the men to have mistresses, lovers, on condition that the affair had no social consequence outside her own house, that the tie was formed and perpetuated in the shelter of her Wednesdays. In the old days, every furtive peal of laughter that came from Odette when she conversed with Swann had gnawed her heartstrings, and so of late had every aside exchanged by Morel and the Baron; she found one consolation alone for her griefs which was to destroy the happiness of other people. She had not been able to endure for long that of the Baron. And here was this rash person precipitating the catastrophe by appearing to be restricting the Mistress's place in her little clan. Already she could see Morel going into society, without her, under the Baron's aegis. There was but a single remedy, to make Morel choose between the Baron and herself, and, relying upon the ascendancy that she had acquired over Morel by the display that she made of an extraordinary perspicacity, thanks to reports which she collected, to falsehoods which she invented, all of which served to corroborate what he himself was led to believe, and what would in time be made plain to him, thanks to the pitfalls which she was preparing, into which her unsuspecting victims would fall, relying upon this ascendancy, to make him choose herself in preference to the Baron. As for the society ladies who had been present and had not even asked to be introduced to her, as soon as she grasped their hesitations or indifference, she had said: "Ah! I see what they are, the sort of old good-for-nothings that are not our style, it's the last time they shall set foot in this house." For she would have died rather than admit that anyone had been less friendly to her than she had hoped.

"Ah! My dear General," M. de Charlus suddenly exclaimed,

abandoning Mme. Verdurin, as he caught sight of General Deltour, Secretary to the President of the Republic, who might be of great value in securing Charlie his Cross, and who, after asking some question of Cottard, was rapidly withdrawing: "Good evening, my dear, delightful friend. So this is how you slip away without saying good-bye to me," said the Baron with a genial, self-satisfied smile, for he knew quite well that people were always glad to stay behind for a moment to talk to himself.

Taking advantage of the Baron's having withdrawn to speak to the general, Mme. Verdurin made a signal to Brichot. He, not knowing what Mme. Verdurin was going to say, sought to amuse her, and never suspecting the anguish that he was causing me, said to the Mistress: "The Baron is delighted that Mlle. Vinteuil and her friend did not come. They shock him terribly. He declares that their morals are appalling. You can't imagine how prudish and severe the Baron is on moral questions." Contrary to Brichot's expectation, Mme. Verdurin was not amused: "He is obscene," was her answer. "Take him out of the room to smoke a cigarette with you, so that my husband can get hold of his Dulcinea without his noticing it and warn him of the abyss that is yawning at his feet." Brichot seemed to hesitate. "Come along, get hold of Charlus, find some excuse, there's no time to lose," said Mme. Verdurin, "and whatever you do, don't let him come back here until I send for you. Oh! What an evening," Mme. Verdurin went on, revealing thus the true cause of her anger. "Performing a masterpiece in front of those wooden images. I don't include the Queen of Naples, she is intelligent, she is a nice woman" (which meant: "She has been kind to me"). "But the others. Oh! It's enough to drive anyone mad. What you can expect, I'm no longer a girl. When I was young, people told me that one must put up with boredom, I made an effort, but now, oh no, it's too much for me, I am old enough to please myself, life is too short; bore myself, listen to idiots, smile, pretend to think them intelligent. No, I can't do it. Get along, Brichot, there's no time to lose." "I am going, Madame, I am going," said Brichot, as General Deltour moved away. But first of all the Professor took me aside for a moment "I am not speaking evil of the Baron; but I am afraid that he is expending upon Morel rather more than a wholesome morality enjoins, and yet, in keeping the man occupied while Mme. Verdurin, for the sinner's good and indeed rightly tempted by such a cure of souls, proceeds—by speaking to the young fool without any concealment—to remove from him all that he loves, to deal him perhaps a fatal blow, it seems to me that I am leading him into what one might call a man-trap, and I recoil as though from a base action." This said, he did not hesitate to commit it, but, taking him by the arm, began: "Come Baron, let us go and make a cigarette, this young man has not yet seen all the marvels of the house." I made the excuse that I was obliged to go home. " Just wait a moment," said Brichot. "You remember, you are giving me a lift, and I have not forgotten your promise."

"Wouldn't you like me, really, to make them bring out their plate, nothing could be simpler," said M. de Charlus. "You promised me, remember, not a word about Morel's decoration. I mean to give him the surprise of announcing it presently when people have begun to leave, although he says that it is of no importance to an artist, but that his uncle would like him to have it" (I blushed, for I thought to myself, the Verdurins would know through my grandfather what Morel's uncle was). "Then you wouldn't like me to make them bring out the best pieces," said M. de Charlus. "Of course, you know them already, you have seen them a dozen times at La Raspelière "But you are not looking well, and you will catch cold in this damp room," he said, pushing a chair towards me. "Since you have not been well, you must take care of yourself, let me go and find you your coat. No, don't go for it yourself, you will lose your way and catch cold. How careless people are; you might be an infant in arms, you want an old nurse like me to look after you." "Don't trouble, Baron, let me go," said Brichot, and left us immediately; not being precisely aware perhaps of the very warm affection that M. de Charlus felt for me and of the charming lapses into simplicity and devotion that alternated with his delirious crises of grandeur and persecution, he was afraid that M. de Charlus, whom Mme. Verdurin had entrusted, like a prisoner, to his vigilance, might simply be seeking, under the pretext of asking for my greatcoat, to return to Morel and might thus upset the Mistress's plan. "But what on earth is he doing, that is my greatcoat he is bringing," the Baron said, on seeing that Brichot had made so long a search to no better result. "I would have done better to go for it myself. However, you can put it on now. Are you aware that it is highly compromising, my dear boy, it is like drinking out of the same glass, I shall be able to read your thoughts. No, not like that, come, let me do it," and as he put me into his greatcoat, he pressed it down on my shoulders, fastened it round my throat, and brushed my chin with his hand, making the apology: "At his age, he doesn't know how to put on a coat, one has to titivate him, I have missed my vocation, Brichot, I was born to be a nurserymaid."

As cowardly still as I had been long ago in my boyhood at Combray when I used to run away in order not to see my grandfather tempted with brandy and the vain efforts of my grandmother imploring him not to drink it, I had but one thought in my mind, which was to leave the Verdurins' house before the execution of M. de Charlus occurred.

"I simply must go," I said to Brichot. "I am coming with you," he replied, "but we cannot slip away, English fashion: Come and say good-bye to Mme. Verdurin," the Professor concluded, as he made his way to the drawing-room with the air of a man who, in a guessing game, goes to find out whether he may 'come back'.

While we conversed, M. Verdurin, at a signal from his wife, had taken Morel aside. The violinist had begun by deploring the departure of the Queen of Naples before he had had a chance of being presented to her. M. de Charlus had told him so often that she was the sister of the Empress Elizabeth and of the Duchesse d'Alençon that Her Majesty had assumed an extraordinary importance in his eyes. But the Master explained to him that it was not to talk about the Queen of Naples that they had withdrawn from the rest, and then went straight to the root of the matter. "Listen," he had concluded after a long explanation: "listen; if you like, we can go and ask my wife what she thinks. I give you my word of honour, I've said nothing to her about it. We shall see how she looks at it. My advice is perhaps not the best, but you know how sound her judgment is; besides, she is extremely attached to yourself, let us go and submit the case to her."

And while Mme. Verdurin, awaiting with impatience the emotions that she would presently be relishing as she talked to the musician, and again, after he had gone, when she made her husband give her a full report of their conversation, continued to repeat: "But what in the world can they be doing? I do hope that my husband, in keeping him all this time, has managed to give him his cue,"

M. Verdurin reappeared with Morel who seemed greatly moved. "He would like to ask your advice," M. Verdurin said to his wife, in the tone of a man who does not know whether his prayer will be heard. Instead of replying to M. Verdurin, it was to Morel that, in the heat of her passion, Mme. Verdurin addressed herself. "I agree entirely with my husband, I consider that you cannot tolerate this sort of thing for another instant," she exclaimed with violence, discarding as a useless fiction her agreement with her husband that she was supposed to know nothing of what he had been saying to the violinist. "How do you mean? Tolerate what?" stammered M. Verdurin, endeavouring to feign astonishment and seeking, with an awkwardness that was explained by his dismay, to defend his falsehood. "I guessed what you were saying to him," 'replied Mme. Verdurin, undisturbed by the improbability of this explanation, and caring little what, when he recalled this scene, the violinist might think of the Mistress's veracity. "No," Mme. Verdurin continued, "I feel that you ought not to endure any longer this degrading promiscuity with a tainted person whom nobody will have in her house," she went on, regardless of the fact that this was untrue and forgetting that she herself entertained him almost daily. "You are the talk of the Conservatoire," she added, feeling that this was the argument that carried most weight; "another month of this life, and your artistic future is shattered, whereas, without Charlus, you ought to be making at least a hundred thousand francs a year." "But I have never heard anyone utter a word, I am astounded, I am very grateful to you," Morel murmured, the tears starting to his eyes. But, being obliged at once to feign astonishment and to conceal his shame, he had turned redder and was perspiring more abundantly than if he had played all Beethoven's sonatas in succession, and tears welled from his eyes which the Bonn Master would certainly not have drawn from him.

"If you have never heard anything, you are unique in that respect. He is a gentleman with a vile reputation and the most shocking stories are told about him. I know that the police are watching him and that is perhaps the best thing for him if he is not to end like all those men, murdered by hooligans," she went on, for as she thought of Charlus, the memory of Mme. de Duras recurred to her, and in her frenzy of rage she sought to aggravate still further the wounds that she was inflicting on the unfortunate Charlie, and to avenge herself for those that she had received in the course of the evening. "Anyhow, even financially, he can be of no use to you, he is completely ruined since he has become the prey of people who are blackmailing him, and who can't even make him fork out the price of the tune they call, still less can he pay you for your playing, for it is all heavily mortgaged, town house, country house, everything." Morel was all the more ready to believe this lie since M. de Charlus liked to confide in him his relations with hooligans, a race for which the son of a valet, however debauched he may be, professes a feeling of horror as strong as his attachment to Bonapartist principles.

"I should never have suspected it," Morel groaned, in answer to Mme. Verdurin. "Naturally people do not say it to your face, that does not prevent your being the talk of the Conservatoire," Mme. Verdurin went on wickedly, seeking to make it plain to Morel that it was not only M. de Charlus that was being criticised, but himself also. "I can well believe that you know nothing about it; all the same, people are quite outspoken. Ask Ski what they were saying the other day at Chevillard's within a foot of us when you came into my box. I mean to say, people point you out. As far as I'm concerned, I don't pay the slightest attention, but what I do feel is that it makes a man supremely ridiculous and that he becomes a public laughing-stock for the rest of his life." "I don't know how to thank you," said Charlie in the tone we use to a dentist who has just caused us terrible pain while we tried not to let him see it, or to a too bloodthirsty second who has forced us into a duel on account of some casual remark of which he has said: "You can't swallow that." "I believe that you have plenty of character, that you are a man," replied Mme. Verdurin, "and that you will be capable of speaking out boldly, although he tells everybody that you would never dare, that he holds you fast." Charlie, seeking a borrowed dignity in which to cloak the tatters of his own, found in his memory something that he had read or, more probably, heard quoted, and at once proclaimed: "I was not brought up to eat that sort of bread. This very evening I will break with M. de Charlus. The Queen of Naples has gone, hasn't she? Otherwise, before breaking with him, I should like to ask him........" "It is not necessary to break with him altogether," said Mme. Verdurin, anxious to avoid a disruption of the little nucleus. "There is no harm in your seeing him here, among our little group, where you are appreciated, where no one speaks any evil of you. But insist upon your freedom, and do not let him drag you about among all those sheep who are friendly to your face; I wish you could have heard what they were saying behind your back. Anyhow, you need feel no regret, not only are you wiping off a stain which would have marked you for the rest of your life, from the artistic point of view, even if there had not been this scandalous presentation by Charlus, I don't mind telling you that wasting yourself like this in this sham society will make people suppose that you aren't serious, give you an amateur reputation, as a little drawing-room performer, which is a terrible thing at your age. I can understand that to all those fine ladies it is highly convenient to be able to return their friends' hospitality by making you come and play for nothing, but it is your future as an artist that would foot the bill. I don't say that you shouldn't go to one or two of them. You were speaking of the Queen of Naples—who has left, for she had to go on to another party—no, she is a splendid woman, and I don't mind saying that I think she has a poor opinion of Charlus and came here chiefly to please me. Yes, yes, I know she was longing to meet us, M. Verdurin and myself. That is a house in which you might play. And then I may tell you that if I take you—because the artists all know me, you understand, they have always been most obliging to me, and regard me almost as one of themselves, as their Mistress—that is a very different matter. But whatever you do, you must never go near Mme. de Duras! Don't go and make a stupid blunder like that! I know several artists who have come here and told me all about her. They know they can trust me," she said, in the sweet and simple tone which she knew how to adopt in an instant, imparting an appropriate air of modesty to her features, an appropriate charm to her eyes, "they come here, just like that, to tell me all their little troubles; the ones who are said to be most silent, go on chatting to me sometimes for hours on end and I can't tell you how interesting they are. Poor Chabrier used always to say: 'There's nobody like Mme. Verdurin for getting them to talk.' Very well, don't you know, all of them, without one exception, I have seen them in tears because they had gone to play for Mme. de Duras. It is not only the way she enjoys making her servants humiliate them, they could never get an engagement anywhere else again. The agents would say: 'Oh yes, the fellow who plays at Mme. de Duras's. That settled it. There is nothing like that for ruining a man's future. You know what society people are like, it's not taken seriously, you may have all the talent in the world, it's a dreadful thing to have to say, but one Mme. de Duras is enough to give you the reputation of an amateur. And among artists, don't you know, well, you can ask yourself whether I know them, when I have been moving among them for forty years, launching them, taking an interest in them; very well, when they say that somebody is an amateur, that finishes it. And people were beginning to say it of you. Indeed, at times I have been obliged to take up the cudgels, to assure them that you would not play in some absurd drawing-room! Do you know what the answer was: 'But he will be forced to go, Charlus won't even consult him, he never asks him for his opinion. Somebody thought he would pay him a compliment and said: 'We greatly admire your friend Morel.' Can you guess what answer he made, with that insolent air which you know? 'But what do you mean by calling him my friend, we are not of the same class, say rather that he is my creature, my protégé.' " At this moment there stirred beneath the convex brows, of the musical deity the one thing that certain people cannot keep to themselves, a saying which it is not merely abject but imprudent to repeat. But the need to repeat it is stronger than honour, than prudence. It was to this need that, after a few convulsive movements of her spherical and sorrowful brows, the Mistress succumbed: "Some one actually told my husband that he had said 'my servant,' but for that I cannot vouch," she added. It was a similar need that had compelled M. de Charlus, shortly after he had sworn to Morel that nobody should ever know the story of his birth, to say to Mme. Verdunn: "His father was a flunkey." A similar need again, now that the story had been started, would make it circulate from one person to another, each of whom would confide it under the seal of a secrecy which would be promised and not kept by the hearer, as by the informant himself. These stories would end, as in the game called hunt-the-thimble, by being traced back to Mme. Verdurin, bringing down upon her the wrath of the person concerned, who would at last have learned the truth. She knew this, but could not repress the words that were burning her tongue. Anyhow, the word 'servant' was bound to annoy Morel. She said 'servant' nevertheless, and if she added that she could not vouch for the word, this was so as at once to appear certain of the rest, thanks to this hint of uncertainty, and to show her impartiality. This impartiality that she showed, she herself found so touching that she began to speak affectionately to Charlie: "For, don't you see," she went on, "I am not blaming him, he is dragging you down into his abyss, it is true, but it is not his fault, since he wallows in it himself, since he wallows in it," she repeated in a louder tone, having been struck by the aptness of the image which had taken shape so quickly that her attention only now overtook it and was trying to give it prominence. "No, the fault that I do find with him," she said in a melting tone—like a woman drunken with her own success— "is a want of delicacy towards yourself. There are certain things which one does not say in public. Well, this evening, he was betting that he would make you blush with joy, by telling you (stuff and nonsense, of course, for his recommendation would be enough to prevent your getting it) that you were to have the Cross of the Legion of Honour. Even that I could overlook, although I have never quite liked," she went on with a delicate, dignified air, "hearing a person make a fool of his friends, but, don't you know, there are certain little things that one does resent such as when he told us, with screams of laughter, that if you want the Cross it's to please your uncle and that your uncle was a footman." "He told you that!" cried Charlie, believing, on the strength of this adroitly interpolated quotation, in the truth of everything that Mme. Verdurin had said! Mme. Verdurin was overwhelmed with the joy of an old mistress who, just as her young lover was on the point of deserting her, has succeeded in breaking off his marriage, and it is possible that she had not calculated her lie, that she was not even consciously lying. A sort of sentimental logic, something perhaps more elementary still, a sort of nervous reflex urging her, in order to brighten her life and preserve her happiness, to stir up trouble in the little clan, may have brought impulsively to her lips, without giving her time to check their veracity, these assertions diabolically effective if not rigorously exact. "If he had only repeated it to us, it wouldn't matter," the Mistress went on, "we know better than to listen to what he says, besides, what does a man's origin matter, you have your own value, you are what you make yourself, but that he should use it to make Mme. de Portefin, laugh" (Mme. Verdurin named this lady on purpose because she knew that Charlie admired her) "that is what vexes us: my husband said to me when he heard him: 'I would sooner he had struck me in the face.' For he is as fond of you as I am, don't you know, is Gustave" (from this we learn that M. Verdurin's name was Gustave). "He is really very sensitive." "But I never told you I was fond of him," muttered M. Verdurin, acting the kind-hearted curmudgeon. "It is Charlus that is fond of him." "Oh, no! Now I realise the difference, I was betrayed by a scoundrel and you, you are good," Charlie exclaimed in all sincerity. "No, no," murmured Mme. Verdurin, seeking to retain her victory, for she felt that her Wednesdays were safe, but not to abuse it, "scoundrel is too strong; he does harm, a great deal, of harm unconsciously; you know that tale about the Legion of Honour was the affair of a moment. And it would be painful to me to repeat all that he said about your family," said Mme. Verdurin, who would have been greatly embarrassed had she been asked to do so. "Oh, even if it only took a moment, it proves that he is a traitor," cried Morel.

It was at this moment that we returned to the drawing-room. "Ah!" exclaimed M. de Charlus when he saw that Morel was in the room, advancing upon him with the alacrity of the man who has skilfully organised a whole evening's entertainment with a view to an assignation with a woman, and in his excitement never imagines that he has with his own hands set the snare in which he will presently be caught and publicly thrashed by bravoes stationed in readiness by her husband. "Well, after all it is none too soon; are you satisfied, young glory, and presently young knight of the Legion of Honour? For very soon you will be able to sport your Cross," M. de Charlus said to Morel with a tender and triumphant air, but by the very mention of the decoration endorsed Mme. Verdurin's lies, which appeared to Morel to be indisputable truth. "Leave me alone, I forbid you to come near me," Morel shouted at the Baron. "You know what I mean, all right, I'm not the first young man you've tried to corrupt!"

My sole consolation lay in the thought that I was about to see Morel and the Verdurins pulverised by M. de Charlus. For a thousand times less an offence I had been visited with his furious rage, no one was safe from it, a king would not have intimidated him. Instead of which, an extraordinary thing happened. One saw M. de Charlus dumb, stupefied, measuring the depths of his misery without understanding its cause, finding not a word to utter, raising his eyes to stare at each of the company in turn, with a questioning, outraged, suppliant air, which seemed to be asking them not so much what had happened as what answer he ought to make. And yet M. de Charlus possessed all the resources, not merely of eloquence but of audacity, when, seized by a rage which had long been simmering against some one, he reduced him to desperation, with the most outrageous speeches, in front of a scandalised society which had never imagined that anyone could go so far.

The fact remains that, in this drawing-room which he despised, this great nobleman (in whom his sense of superiority to the middle classes was no less essentially inherent than it had been in any of his ancestors who had stood in the dock before the Revolutionary Tribunal) could do nothing, in a paralysis of all his members, including his tongue, but cast in every direction glances of terror, outraged by the violence that had been done to him, no less suppliant than questioning. In a situation so cruelly unforeseen, this great talker could do no more than stammer: "What does it all mean, what has happened?" His question was not even heard.

Thus to anticipate the days that followed this party, to which we shall presently return, M. de Charlus could see in Charlie's attitude one thing alone that was self-evident. Charlie, who had often threatened the Baron that he would tell people of the passion that he inspired in him, must have seized the opportunity to do so when he considered that he had now sufficiently 'arrived' to be able to fly unaided. And he must, out of sheer ingratitude, have told Mme. Verdurin everything. Flitting from one supposition to another, the Baron never arrived at the truth, which was that the blow had not come from Morel. It is true that he might have learned this by asking him for a few minutes conversation. But he felt that this would injure his dignity and would be against the interests of his love. He had been insulted, he awaited an explanation.

As for the social side of the incident, the rumour spread abroad that M. de Charlus had been turned out of the Verdurins' house at the moment when he was attempting to rape a young musician. The effect of this rumour was that nobody was surprised when M. de Charlus did not appear again at the Verdurins', and whenever he happened by chance to meet, anywhere else, one of the faithful whom he had suspected and insulted, as this person had a grudge against the Baron who himself abstained from greeting him, people were not surprised, realising that no member of the little clan would ever wish to speak to the Baron again. It might be supposed, in view of M. de Charlus's terrible nature, the persecutions with which he terrorised even his own family, that he would, after the events of this evening, let loose his fury and practise reprisals upon the Verdurins. We have seen why nothing of this sort occurred at first. Then the Baron, having caught cold shortly afterwards, and contracted the septic pneumonia which was very rife that winter, was for long regarded by his doctors, and regarded himself, as being at the point of death, and lay for many months suspended between it and life. Was there simply a physical change, and the substitution of a different malady for the neurosis that had previously made him lose all control of himself in his outbursts of rage? For it is too obvious to suppose that, having never taken the Verdurins seriously, from the social point of view, but having come at last to understand the part that they had played, he was unable to feel the resentment that he would have felt for any of his equals; too obvious also to remember that neurotics, irritated on the slightest provocation by imaginary and inoffensive enemies, become on the contrary inoffensive as soon as anyone takes the offensive again them, and that we can calm them more easily by flinging cold water in their faces than by attempting to prove to them the inanity of their grievances. It is probably not in a physical change that we ought to seek the explanation of this absence of rancour, but far more in the malady itself. It exhausted the Baron so completely that he had little leisure left in which to think about the Verdurins. He was almost dead.

Chapter III

"Guess where I have been; at the Verdurins'," I said on my return. I had barely had time to utter the words before Albertine, a look of utter consternation upon her face, answered me in words which seemed to explode of their own accord with a force which she was unable to contain "I thought as much."

"I didn't know that you would be annoyed by my going to see the

Verdurins." I replied. It is true that she did not tell me that she was annoyed, but that was obvious; it is true also that I had not said to myself that she would be annoyed. And yet in the face of the explosion of her wrath, as in the face of those events which a sort of retrospective second sight makes us imagine that we have already known in the past, it seemed to me that I could never have expected anything else. "Annoyed? What do you suppose I care, where you've been. It's all the same to me. Wasn't Mlle. Vinteuil there? "

Instead of telling her that I was sorry, I became malicious. There was then a moment in which I felt a sort of hatred of her which only intensified my need to keep her in captivity. "Besides," I said to her angrily, "there are plenty of things which you hide from me, even the most trivial, things, such as for instance when you went for three days to Balbec, I mention it in passing." Albertine, cutting me short, declared as a thing that was perfectly natural: "You mean to say that I never went to Balbec at all? Of course I didn't! And I have always wondered why you pretended to believe that I had. All the same, there was no harm in it. The driver had some business of his own for three days. He didn't like to mention it to you. And so, out of kindness to him (it was my doing! Besides it is always I that have to bear the brunt), I invented a trip to Balbec. He simply put me down at Auteuil, with my friend in the Rue de L'Assomption, where I spent the three days bored to tears. You see it is not a serious matter, there's nothing broken. I did indeed begin to suppose that you perhaps knew all about it, when I saw how you laughed when the postcards began to arrive, a week late. I quite see that it was absurd, and that it would have been better not to send any cards. But that wasn't my fault. I had bought the cards beforehand and given them to the driver before he dropped me at Auteuil, and then the fathead put them in his pocket and forgot about them instead of sending them on in an envelope to a friend of his near Balbec who was to forward them to you. I kept on supposing that they would turn up. He forgot all about them for five days, and instead of telling me the idiot sent them on at once to Balbec. When he did tell me, I fairly broke it over him, I can tell you! And you go and make a stupid fuss, when it's all the fault of that great fool, as a reward for my shutting myself up for three whole days, so that he might go and look after his family affairs. I didn't even venture to go out into Auteuil for fear of being seen. The only time that I did go out, I was dressed as a man, and that was a funny business. And it was just my luck, which follows me wherever I go, that the first person I came across was your Yid friend Bloch. But I don't believe it was from him that you learned that my trip to Balbec never existed except in my imagination, for he seemed not to recognise me."

I did not know what to say, not wishing to appear astonished, while I was appalled by all these lies. With a sense of horror, which gave me no desire to turn Albertine out of the house, far from it, was combined a strong inclination to burst into tears. This last was caused not by the lie itself and by the annihilation of everything that I had so stoutly believed to be true that I felt as though I were in a town that had been razed to the ground, where not a house remained standing, where the bare soil was merely heaped with rubble—but by the melancholy thought that, during those three days when she had been bored to tears in her friend's house at Auteuil, Albertine had never once felt any desire, the idea had perhaps never occurred to her to come and pay me a visit one day on the quiet, or to send a message asking me to go and see her at Auteuil.

Once again I had to be careful not to keep too long a silence which might have led her to suppose that I was surprised. I said to her tenderly: "But, my darling, I would gladly give you several hundred francs to let you go and play the fashionable lady wherever you please and invite M. and Mme. Verdurin to a grand dinner." Alas! Albertine was several persons in one. The most mysterious, most simple, most atrocious revealed herself in the answer which she made me with an air of disgust and the exact words to tell the truth I could not quite make out (even the opening words, for she did not finish her sentence). I succeeded in establishing them, only a little later when I had guessed what was in her mind. We hear things retrospectively when we have understood them. "Thank you for nothing! Fancy spending a cent upon those old frumps, I'd a great deal rather you left me alone for once in a way so that I can go and get some one decent to break my........"
****Casser le pot--- French slang for anal intercourse**** As she uttered the words, her face flushed crimson, a look of terror came to her eyes, she put her hand over her mouth as though she could have thrust back the words which she had just uttered and which I had completely failed to understand.

I continued to press her. "Anyhow, you might at least have the courage to finish what you were saying, you stopped short at *break.*" "No, leave me alone!" "But why?" "Because it is dreadfully vulgar, I should be ashamed to say such a thing in front of you. I don't know what I was thinking of, the words—I don't even know what they mean, I heard them used in the street one day by some very low people—just came to my lips without rhyme or reason. When Françoise told me that you had gone out (she enjoyed telling me that, I don't think), you might have knocked me down with a feather. I tried not to show any sign, but never in my life have I been so insulted."

"My little Albertine," I said to her in a gentle voice which was drowned in my first tears, "I might tell you that you are mistaken, that what I did this evening is nothing, but I should be lying; it is you that are right, you have realised the truth, my poor child, which is that six months ago, three months ago, when I was still so fond of you, never would I have done such a thing. It is a mere nothing, and it is enormous, because of the immense change in my heart of which it is the sign. And since you have detected this change which I hoped to conceal from you, that leads me on to tell you this: My little Albertine" (and here I addressed her with a profound gentleness and melancholy), "don't you see, the life that you are leading here is boring to you, it is better that we should part, and as the best partings are those that are ended at once, I ask you, to cut short the great sorrow that I am bound to feel, to bid me good-bye to-night and to leave in the morning without my seeing you again, while I am asleep." 'She appeared stupefied, still incredulous and already disconsolate: "To-morrow? You really mean it?" And notwithstanding the anguish that I felt in speaking of our parting as though it were already in the past—partly perhaps because of that very anguish—I began to give Albertine the most precise instructions as to certain things which she would have to do after she left the house. And passing from one request to another, I soon found myself entering into the minutest details. "Be so kind," I said, with infinite melancholy, "as to send me back that book of Bergotte's which is at your aunt's. There is no hurry about it, in three days, in a week, whenever you like, but remember that I don't want to have to write and ask you for it, that would be too painful. My Albertine, never see me again in this world. It would hurt me too much. For I was really fond of you, you know."

When I felt that my company was boring Gilberte, I had still enough strength left to give her up; I had no longer the same strength when I had made a similar discovery with regard to Albertine, and could think only of keeping her at any cost to myself. With the result that, whereas I wrote to Gilberte that I would not see her again, meaning quite sincerely not to see her, I said this to Albertine as a pure falsehood, and in the hope of bringing about a reconciliation.

"I don't know where I shall be going," she said, in a worried tone. "Perhaps I shall go to Touraine, to my aunt's." And this first plan that she suggested froze me as though it were beginning to make definitely effective our final separation. She looked round the room, at the pianola, the blue satin armchairs. "I still cannot make myself realise that I shall not see all this again, to-morrow, or the next day, or ever. Poor little room. It seems to me quite impossible; I cannot get it into my head." "It had to be; you were unhappy here." "No, indeed, I was not unhappy, it is now that I shall be unhappy." "No, I assure you, it is better for you." "For you, perhaps!" I began to stare fixedly into vacancy, as though, worried by an extreme hesitation, I was debating an idea which had occurred to my mind. Then, all of a sudden: "'Listen, Albertine, you say that you are happier here, that you are going to be unhappy." "Why, of course." "That appals me; would you like us to try to carry on for a few weeks? Who knows, week by week, we may perhaps go on for a long time; you know that there are temporary arrangements which end by becoming permanent." "Oh, how kind you are!" "Only in that case it is ridiculous of us to have made ourselves wretched like this over nothing for hours on end, it is like making all the preparations for a long journey and then staying at home. I am shattered with grief." I made her sit on my knee, I took Bergotte's manuscript which she so longed to have and wrote on the cover: "To my little Albertine, in memory of a new lease of life." "Now," I said to her, "go and sleep until to-morrow, my darling, for you must be worn out." "I am very glad, all the same." "Do you love me a little bit?" "A hundred times more than ever."

I should have been wrong in being delighted with this little piece of play-acting, had it not been that I had carried it to the pitch of a real scene on the stage.

At all costs I multiplied the favours that I was able to bestow upon her. I thought: "I must speak to Albertine about a yacht I mean to have built for her." As for the Fortuny gowns, we had at length decided upon one in blue and gold lined with pink which was just ready. And I had ordered, at the same time, the other five which she had relinquished with regret, out of preference for this last. Yet with the coming of spring, two months later, I allowed myself to be carried away by anger one evening. It was the very evening on which Albertine had put on for the first time the indoor gown in gold and blue by Fortuny which, by reminding me of Venice, made me feel all the more strongly what I was sacrificing for her, who felt no corresponding gratitude towards me. Now that life with Albertine had become possible once again, I felt that I could derive nothing from it but misery, since she did not love me; better to part from her in the pleasant moment of her consent which I should prolong in memory.

I should have to let her leave the house without my seeing her, then, rising from my bed, making all my preparations in haste, leave a note for her,—and, without seeing her again, leave for Venice.

I rang for Françoise to ask her to buy me a guide-book and a time-table, as I had done as a boy, when I wished to prepare in advance a journey to Venice, the realisation of a desire as violent as that which I felt at this moment; I forgot that, in the interval, there was a desire which I had attained, without any satisfaction, the desire for Balbec, and that Venice, being also a visible phenomenon was probably no more able than Balbec to realise an ineffable dream, that of the gothic age, made actual by a springtime sea, and coming at moments to stir my soul with an enchanted, caressing, unseizable, mysterious, confused image.

Françoise having heard my ring came into the room, in considerable uneasiness as to how I would receive what she had to say and what she had done. "It has been most awkward," she said to me, "that Monsieur is so late in ringing this morning. I didn't know what I ought to do. This morning at eight o'clock Mademoiselle Albertine asked me for her trunks, I dared not refuse her, I was afraid of Monsieur's scolding me if I came and waked him. It was no use my putting her through her catechism, telling her to wait an hour because I expected all the time that Monsieur would ring; she wouldn't have it, she left this letter with me for Monsieur, and at nine o'clock off she went." Then—so ignorant may we be of what we have within us, since I was convinced of my own indifference to Albertine—my breath was cut short, I gripped my heart in my hands suddenly moistened by a perspiration which I had not known since the revelation that my mistress had made on the little tram with regard to Mlle. Vinteuil's friend, without my being able to say anything else than: "Ah! Very good, you did quite right not to wake me, leave me now for a little, I shall ring for you presently."

THE SWEET CHEAT GONE

CHAPTER ONE

GRIEF AND OBLIVION

My hope was that Albertine had gone to Touraine, to her aunt's house, where after all, she would be fairly well guarded and could not do anything very serious in the interval before she came back. I forsook all pride with regard to Albertine, I sent her a despairing telegram begging her to return upon any conditions, telling her that she might do anything she liked, that I asked only to be allowed to take her in my arms for a minute three times a week, before she went to bed. And had she confined me to once a week, I would have accepted the restriction.

She did not, ever, return. My telegram had just gone to her when I myself received one. It was from Mme Bontemps. Alas! It was not a suppression of suffering that was wrought in me by the first two lines of the telegram:

"My poor friend, our little Albertine is no more; forgive me for breaking this terrible news to you who were so fond of her. She was thrown by her horse against a tree while she was out riding. All our efforts to restore her to life were unavailing. If only I were dead in her place!"

No, not the suppression of suffering, but a suffering until then unimagined, that of learning that she would not come back. And yet, had I not told myself, many times, that quite possibly, she would not come back? I had indeed told myself so, but now I saw that never for a moment had I believed it. As I needed her presence, her kisses, to enable me to endure the pain that my suspicions wrought in me. I had continued to do so since her departure for Touraine. I had less need of her fidelity than of her return. And if my reason might with impunity cast a doubt upon her now and again, my imagination never ceased for an instant to bring her before me. Instinctively I passed my hand over my throat, over my lips which felt themselves kissed by her lips still after she had gone away, and would never be kissed by them again; I passed my hands over them, as Mamma had caressed me at the time of my grandmother's death, when she said: "My poor boy, your grandmother, who was so fond of you, will never kiss you again." All my life to come seemed to have been wrenched from my heart. My life to come? I had not then thought at times of living it without Albertine? Why, no! All this time had I, then, been vowing to her service every minute of my life until my death? Why, of course! This future indissolubly blended with hers I had never had the vision to perceive, but now that it had just been shattered, I could feel the place that it occupied in my gaping heart.

Françoise was bound to rejoice at Albertine's death, and it should, in justice to her, be said that by a sort of tactful convention she made no pretence of sorrow. But the unwritten laws of her immemorial code and the tradition of the medieval peasant woman who weeps as in the romances of chivalry were older than her hatred of Albertine and even of Eulalie. And so, on one of these late afternoons, as I was not quick enough in concealing my distress, she caught sight of my tears, served by the instinct of a little old peasant woman which at one time had led her to catch and torture animals, to feel only amusement in wringing the necks of chickens and in boiling lobsters alive, and, when I was ill, in observing, as it might be the wounds that she had inflicted upon an owl, my suffering expression which she afterwards proclaimed in a sepulchral tone as a presage of coming disaster. But her Combray 'Customary' did not permit her to treat lightly tears, grief, things which in her judgment were as fatal as shedding one's flannels in spring or eating when one had no 'stomach'. "Oh, no, Monsieur, it doesn't do to cry like that, it isn't good for you." And in her attempt to stem my tears she showed as much uneasiness as though they had been torrents of blood. Unfortunately I adopted a chilly air that cut short the effusions in which she was hoping to indulge and which might quite well, for that matter, have been sincere. Her attitude towards Albertine had been, perhaps akin to her attitude towards Eulalie, and, now that my mistress could no longer derive any profit from me, Françoise had ceased to hate her. She felt bound, however, to let me see that she was perfectly well aware that I was crying, and that, following the deplorable example set by my family, I did not wish to 'let it be seen'. "You mustn't cry, Monsieur," she adjured me, in a calmer tone, this time, and intending to prove her own perspicacity rather than to show me any compassion. She went on: "It was bound to happen; she was too happy, poor creature, she never knew how happy she was."

Then a recollection which had not come to me for a long time—--for it had remained dissolved in the fluid and invisible expanse of my memory—suddenly crystalised. Many years ago, when somebody mentioned her bath-wrap, Albertine had blushed. At that time I was not jealous of her. But since then I had intended to ask her if she could remember that conversation, and why she had blushed. This had worried me all the more because I had been told that the two girls, Léa's friends, frequented the bathing establishment of the hotel, and, it was said, not merely for the purpose of taking baths. But, for fear of annoying Albertine, or else deciding to await some more opportune moment, I had always refrained from mentioning it to her and in time had ceased to think about it. And all of a sudden, some time after Albertine's death, I recalled this memory, stamped with the mark, at once irritating and solemn, of riddles left for ever insoluble by the death of the one person who could have interpreted them. Might I not at least try to make certain that Albertine had never done anything wrong in that bathing establishment. By sending some one to Balbec, I might perhaps succeed. While she was alive, I should doubtless have been unable to learn anything. But people's tongues become strangely loosened and they are ready to report a misdeed when they need no longer fear the culprit's resentment

I asked myself whom I could best send down to make inquiries on the spot, at Balbec. Aimé seemed to me to be a suitable person. Apart from his thorough knowledge of the place, he belonged to that category of plebeian folk who have a keen eye to their own advantage, are loyal to those whom they serve, indifferent to any thought of morality, and of whom—because, if we pay them well, in their obedience to our will, they suppress everything that might in one way or another go against it, showing themselves as incapable of indiscretion, weakness or dishonesty as they are devoid of scruples—we say: "They are good fellows," In such we can repose an absolute confidence. What the woman in the baths would have to say might perhaps put an end for ever to my doubts as to Albertine's morals. My doubts! Alas, I had supposed that it would, be immaterial to me, even pleasant, not to see Albertine again, until her departure revealed to me my error. Similarly her death had shown me how greatly I had been mistaken when I believed that I hoped at times for her death and supposed that it would be my deliverance. So it was that when I received Aimé's letter, I realised that, if I had not until then suffered too painfully from my doubts as to Albertine's virtue, it was because in reality they were not doubts at all. My happiness, my life required that Albertine should be virtuous, they had laid it down once and for all time that she was. Furnished with this preservative belief, I could without danger allow my mind to play sadly with suppositions to which it gave a form but added no faith., I said to myself, "She is perhaps a woman lover," as we say "I may die to-night"; we say it, but we do not believe it, we make plans for the morrow. This explains why, believing mistakenly that I was uncertain whether Albertine, did or did not love women, and believing in consequence that a proof of Albertine's guilt would not give me anything that I had not already taken into account, I was able to feel before the pictures, insignificant to anyone else, which Aimé's letter called up to me, an unexpected anguish, the most painful that I had ever yet felt, and one that formed with those pictures, with the picture alas, of Albertine herself, a sort of precipitate, as chemists say, in which the whole was invisible and of which the text of Aimé's letter, which I isolate in a purely conventional fashion, can give no idea whatsoever, since each of the words that compose it was immediately transformed, coloured for ever by the suffering that it had aroused.

"MONSIEUR,

"Monsieur will kindly forgive me for not having written sooner to Monsieur. The person whom Monsieur instructed me to see had gone away for a few days, and, anxious to justify the confidence which Monsieur had placed in me, I did not wish to return empty-handed. I have just spoken to this person who remembers (Mlle A.) quite well."

Aimé who possessed certain rudiments of culture meant to italicise *Mlle A* between inverted commas. But when he meant to write inverted commas, he wrote brackets, and when he meant to write something in brackets he put it between inverted commas. Thus it was that Françoise would say that someone *stayed* in my street meaning that he abode there, and that one could *abide* for a few minutes, meaning *stay*, the mistakes of popular speech consisting merely, as often as not, in interchanging—as for that matter the French language has done—terms which in the course of centuries have replaced one another.

"According to her, the thing that Monsieur supposed is absolutely certain. For one thing, it was she who looked after (Mlle A.) whenever she came to the baths. (Mlle A.) came very often to take her bath with a tall woman older than herself; always dressed in grey, whom the bath-woman without knowing her name recognised from having often seen her going after girls. But she took no notice of any of them after she met (Mlle A.). She and (Mlle A.) always shut themselves up in the dressing-box, remained there a very long time, and the lady in grey used to give at least 10 francs as a tip to the person to whom I spoke. As this person said to me, you can imagine that if they were just stringing beads, they wouldn't have given a tip of ten francs. (Mlle A.) used to come also sometimes with a woman with a very dark skin and long handled glasses. But (Mlle A.) came most often with girls younger than herself, especially one with a high complexion. Apart from the lady in grey, the people whom (Mlle A.) was in the habit of bringing were not from Balbec and must indeed often have come from quite a distance. They never came in together, but (Mlle A.) would come in, and ask for the door of her box to be left unlocked, as she was expecting a friend, and the person to whom I spoke knew what that meant. This person could not give me any other details, as she does not remember very well, which is easily understood after so long an interval. Besides, this person did not try to find out, because she is very discreet and it was to her advantage, for (Mlle A.) brought her in a lot of money. She was quite sincerely touched to hear that she was dead. It is true that so young, it is a great calamity for her and for her friends. I await Monsieur's orders to know whether I may leave Balbec where I do not think that I can learn anything more. I thank Monsieur again for the little holiday that he has procured me, and which has been very pleasant especially as the weather is as fine as could be. The season promises well for this year. We hope that Monsieur will come and put in a little appearance. I can think of nothing else to say that will interest Monsieur."

    At last I saw before my eyes, in that arrival of Albertine at the baths along the narrow lane with the lady in grey, a fragment of that past which seemed to me no less mysterious, no less alarming than I had feared when I imagined it as enclosed in the memory, in the facial expression of Albertine. No doubt it was because in that silent and deliberate arrival of Albertine with the woman in grey I read the assignation that they had made, that convention of going to make love in a dressing-box which implied an experience of corruption, the well concealed organisation of a double life, it was because these images brought me the terrible tidings of Albertine's guilt that they had immediately caused me a physical grief from which they would never in time to come be detached
    Then I asked myself whether I could be certain that the bath-woman's revelations were false. A good way of finding out the truth would be to send Aimé to Touraine, to spend a few days in the neighbourhood of Mme Bontemps's villa. If Albertine enjoyed the pleasures which one woman takes with others, if it was in order not to be deprived of them any longer that she had left me, she must, as soon as she was free, have sought to indulge in them and have succeeded, in a district which she knew and to which she would not have chosen to retire had she not expected to find greater facilities there than with me. No doubt there was nothing extraordinary in the fact that Albertine's

death had so little altered my preoccupations. When our mistress is alive, a great part of the thoughts which form what we call our loves come to us during the hours when she is not by our side. Thus we acquire the habit of having as the object of our meditation an absent person, and one who, even if she remains absent for a few hours only, during those hours is no more than a memory. And so death does not make any great difference. When Aimé returned, I asked him to go down to Chatellerault, and thus not only by my thoughts, my sorrows, the emotion caused me by a name connected, however remotely, with a certain person, but even more by all my actions, by the inquiries that I undertook, by the use that I made of my money, all of which was devoted to the discovery of Albertine's actions, I may say that throughout this year my life remained filled with love, with a true bond of affection.

And she who was its object was a corpse. Aimé established himself in quarters close to Mme Bontemps's villa; he made the acquaintance of a maidservant of a jobmaster from whom Albertine had often hired a carriage by the day. These people had noticed nothing. In a second letter, Aimé informed me that he had learned from a young laundress in the town that Albertine had a peculiar way of gripping her arm when she brought back the clean linen. "But," she said, "the young lady never did anything more." I sent Aimé the money that paid for his journey, that paid for the harm which he had done me by his letter, and at the same time I was making an effort to discount it by telling myself that this was a familiarity which gave no proof of any vicious desire when I received a telegram from Aimé: "Have learned most interesting things have abundant proofs letter follows." On the following day came a letter the envelope of which was enough to make me tremble; I had guessed that it came from Aimé, for everyone, even the humblest of us, has under his control those little familiar spirits at once living and couched in a sort of trance upon the paper, the characters of his handwriting which he alone possesses.

"At first the young laundress refused to tell me anything, she assured me that Mlle Albertine had never done anything more than pinch her arm. But to get her to talk, I took her out to dinner, I made her drink. Then she told me that Mlle Albertine used often to meet her on the bank of the Loire, when she went to bathe, that Mlle Albertine, who was in the habit of getting up very early to go and bathe was in the habit of meeting her by the water's edge, at a spot where the trees are so thick that nobody can see you, and besides there is nobody who can see you at that hour in the morning. Then the young laundress brought her friends and they bathed and afterwards, as it was already very hot down here and the sun scorched you even through the trees, they used to lie about on the grass getting dry and playing and caressing each other. The young laundress confessed to me that she loved to amuse herself with her young friends and that seeing Mlle Albertine was always wiggling against her in her wrapper she made her take it off and used to caress her with her tongue along the throat and arms, even on the soles of her feet which Mlle Albertine stretched out to her. The laundress undressed too, and they played at pushing each other into the water; after that she told me nothing more, but being entirely at your orders and ready to do anything in the world to please you, I took the young laundress to bed with me. She asked me if I would like her to do to me what she used to do to Mlle Albertine when she took off her bathing-dress. And she said to me: 'If you could have seen how she used to quiver, that young lady, she said to me (oh, it's just heavenly) and she got so excited that, she could not keep from biting me.' I could still see the marks on the girl's arms. And I can understand Mlle Albertine's pleasure, for the girl is really a very good performer."

I had indeed suffered at Balbec when Albertine told me of her friendship with Mlle Vinteuil. But Albertine was there to comfort me then and the Albertine whom I had loved had remained in my heart. Now, in her place—to punish me for having pushed farther a curiosity to which, contrary to what I had supposed, death had not put an end— what I found was a different girl, heaping up lies and deceits one upon another, in the place where the former had so sweetly reassured me by swearing, that she had never tasted those pleasures, which in the intoxication of her recaptured liberty, she had gone down to enjoy to the point of swooning, of biting that young laundress whom she used to meet at sunrise on the bank of the Loire, and to whom she used to say "Oh, it's just heavenly." A different Albertine, not only in the sense in which we understand the word different when it is used of other people. If people are different from what we have supposed, as this difference cannot affect us profoundly, as the pendulum of intuition cannot move outward with a greater oscillation than that of its inward movement, it is only in the superficial regions of the people themselves that we place these differences. Formerly, when I learned that a woman loved other women, she did not for that reason seem to me a different woman, of a peculiar essence. But when it is a question of a woman with whom we are in love, in order to rid ourself of the grief that we feel at the thought that such a thing is possible, we seek to find out not only what she has done, but what she felt while she was doing it, what idea she had in her mind of the thing that she was doing; then descending and advancing farther and farther, by the profundity of our grief we attain to the mystery, to the essence. I was pained internally, in my body, in my heart—far more than I should have been pained by the fear of losing my life—by this curiosity with which all the force of my intellect and of my subconscious self collaborated; and similarly it was into the core of Albertine's own being that I now projected everything that I learned about her. And the grief that had thus caused to penetrate to so great a depth in my own being the fact of Albertine's vice, was to render me later on a final service. Like the harm that I had done my grandmother, the harm that Albertine had done me was a last bond between her and myself which outlived memory even, for with the conservation of energy which belongs to everything that is physical, suffering has no need of the lessons of memory. Thus a man who has forgotten the charming night spent by moonlight in the woods, suffers still from the rheumatism which he then contracted. Those tastes which she had denied but which were hers, those tastes the discovery of which had come to me not by a cold process of reasoning but in the burning anguish that I had felt on reading the words: "Oh, it's just heavenly," a suffering which gave them a special quality of their own, those tastes were not merely added to the image of Albertine as is added to the hermitcrab the new shell which it drags after it but, rather like a salt which comes in contact with another salt, alters its colour, and what is more, its nature. When the young laundress must have said to her young friend: "Just fancy, I would never have believed it, well, the young lady is one too! "to me it was not merely a vice hitherto unsuspected by them that they added to Albertine's person, but the discovery that she was another person, a person like themselves, speaking the same language, which, by making her the compatriot of other women made her even more alien to myself, proved that what I had possessed of her, what I carried in my heart, was only quite a small part of her, and that the rest which was made so extensive by not being merely that thing so mysteriously important, an individual desire, but being shared with others, she had always concealed from me, she had kept me aloof from it, as a woman might have concealed from me that she was a native of an enemy country and a spy; and would indeed have been acting even more treacherously than a spy, for a spy deceives us only as to her nationality, whereas Albertine had deceived me as to her profoundest humanity, the fact that she did not belong to the ordinary human race, but to an alien race which moves among it; conceals itself among it and never blends with it.

I had as it happened seen two paintings by Elstir showing against a leafy background nude women. In one of them, one of the girls is raising her foot as Albertine must have raised hers when she offered it to the laundress. With her other foot she is pushing into the water the other girl, who gaily resists, her hip bent, her foot barely submerged in the blue water. I remembered now that the raising of the thigh made the same swan's neck curve with the angle of the knee that was made by the droop of Albertine's thigh when she was lying by my side on the bed, and I had often meant to tell her that she reminded me of those paintings. But I had refrained from doing so, in order not to awaken in her mind the image of nude female bodies. Now I saw her, side by side with the laundress and her friends, recomposing the group which I had so admired when I was seated among Albertine's friends at Balbec. And if I had been an enthusiast sensitive to absolute beauty, I should have recognised that Albertine recomposed it with a thousand times more beauty, now that its elements were the nude statues of goddesses like those which consummate sculptors scattered about the groves of Versailles or plunged in the fountains to be washed and polished by the caresses of their eddies. Now I saw her by the side of the laundress girls by the water's edge, in their two-fold nudity of marble maidens in the midst of a grove of vegetation and dipping into the water like bas-reliefs of Naiads. Remembering how Albertine looked as she lay upon my bed, I thought I could see her bent hip, I saw it, it was a swan's neck, it was seeking the hips of the other girl. Then I beheld no longer a leg, but the bold neck of a swan, like that which in a frenzied sketch seeks the lips of a Leda whom we see in all the palpitation peculiar to feminine pleasures, because there is nothing else but a swan, and she seems more alone, just as we discover upon the telephone the inflexions of a voice which we do not distinguish so long as it is not dissociated from a face in which we materialise its expression. In this sketch, the pleasure, instead of going to seek the face which inspires it and which is absent, replaced by a motionless swan, is concentrated in her who feels it. At certain moments the communication was cut between my heart and my memory. What Albertine had done with the laundress was indicated to me now only by almost algebraical abbreviations which no longer meant anything to me; but a hundred times in an hour the interrupted current was restored, and my heart was pitilessly scorched by a fire from hell, while I saw Albertine, raised to life by my jealousy, really alive, stiffen beneath the caresses of the young laundress, to whom she was saying: "Oh, it's just heavenly."

What came to my rescue against this image of the laundress, was—

certainly when it had endured for any while—the image itself, because we really know only what is novel, what suddenly introduces into our sensibility a change of tone which strikes us, the things for which habit has not yet substituted its colourless facsimiles. But it was, above all, this subdivision of Albertine in many fragments, in many Albertines, which was her sole mode of existence in me. Moments recurred in which she had merely been good, or intelligent, or serious, or even addicted to nothing but sport. And this subdivision, was it not after all proper that it should soothe me? For if it was not in itself anything real, if it depended upon the successive form of the hours in which it had appeared to me, a form which remained that of my memory as the curve of the projections of my magic lantern depended upon the curve of the coloured slides, did it not represent in its own manner a truth, a thoroughly objective truth too, to wit that each one of us is not a single person, but contains many persons who have not all the same moral value and that if a vicious Albertine had existed, it did not mean that there had not been others, she who enjoyed talking to me about Saint-Simon in her room, she who on the night when I had told her that we must part had said so sadly: " That pianola, this room, to think that I shall never see any of these things again" and, when she saw the emotion which my lie had finally communicated to myself; had exclaimed with a sincere pity: "Oh, no, anything rather than make you unhappy, I promise that I will never try to see you again." Then I was no longer alone. I felt the wall that separated us vanish. At the moment in which the good Albertine had returned, I had found again the one person from whom I could demand the antidote to the sufferings which Albertine was causing me. True, I still wanted to speak to her about the story of the laundress, but it was no longer by way of a cruel triumph, and to show her maliciously how much I knew. As I should have done had Albertine been alive, I asked her tenderly whether the tale about the laundress was true. She swore to me that it was not, that Aimé was not truthful and that, wishing to appear to have earned the money which I had given him, he had not liked to return with nothing to show, and had made the laundress tell him what he wished to hear. No doubt Albertine had been lying to me throughout. And yet, in the flux and reflux of her contradictions, I felt that there had been a certain progression due to myself. That she had not indeed made me, at the outset, admission (perhaps, it is true, involuntary in a phrase that escaped her lips) I would not have sworn. I no longer remembered. And besides she had such odd ways of naming certain things, that they might be interpreted in one sense or the other, but the feeling that she had had of my jealousy had led her afterwards to retract with horror what at first she had complacently admitted. Anyhow, Albertine had no need to tell me this. To be convinced of her innocence it was enough for me to embrace her, and I could do so now that the wall was down which parted us, like that impalpable and resisting wall which after a quarrel rises between two lovers and against which kisses would be shattered. No, she had no need to tell me anything. Whatever she might have done, whatever she might, have wished to do, the poor child, there were sentiments in which, over the barrier that divided us, we could be united. If the story was true, and if Albertine had concealed her tastes from me, it was in order not to make me unhappy. I had the pleasure of hearing this Albertine say so.   Besides, had I ever known any other? The two chief causes of error in our relations with another person are, having ourself a good heart; or else being in love with the other person. We fall in love for a smile, a glance, a bare shoulder. That is enough; then, in the long hours of hope or sorrow, we fabricate a person, we compose a character. And when later on we see much of the beloved person, we can no more, whatever the cruel reality that confronts us, strip off that good character, that nature of a woman who loves us, from the person who bestows that glance, bares that shoulder, than we can when she has grown old eliminate her youthful face from a person whom we have known since her girlhood. I called to mind the noble glance, kind and compassionate, of that Albertine, her plump cheeks, the coarse grain of her throat. It was the image of a dead woman, but, as this dead woman was alive, it was easy for me to do immediately what I should inevitably have done if she had been by my side in her living body (what I should do were I ever to meet her again in another life), I forgave her.

At times my jealousy revived in moments when I no longer remembered Albertine, albeit it was of her that I was jealous. I thought that I was jealous of Andrée, but Andrée was to me merely a substitute, a bypath, a conduit which brought me indirectly to Albertine. So it is that in our dreams we give a different face, a different name to a person as to whose underlying identity we are not mistaken.

Once, I was under the illusion that I beheld the unknown desires and pleasures that Albertine felt, when, some time after Albertine's death Andrée came to see me. For the first time she seemed to me beautiful, I said to myself that her almost woolly hair, her dark, shadowed eyes, were doubtless what Albertine had so dearly loved, the materialisation before my eyes of what she used to take with her in her amorous dreams, of what she beheld with the prophetic eyes of desire on the day when she had so suddenly decided to leave Balbec. Like a strange, dark flower that was brought to me from beyond the grave, from the innermost being of a person in whom I had been unable to discover it, I seemed to see before me, the unlooked for exhumation of a priceless relic, the incarnate desire of Albertine which Andrée was to me, as Venus was the desire of Jove. Andrée regretted Albertine, but I felt at once that she did not miss her. Forcibly removed from her friend by death, she seemed to have easily taken her part in a final separation which I would not have dared to ask of her while Albertine was alive, so afraid would I have been of not succeeding in obtaining Andrée's consent. She seemed on the contrary to accept without difficulty this renunciation, but precisely at the moment when it could no longer be of any advantage to me. Andrée abandoned Albertine to me, but dead, and when she had lost for me not only her life but retrospectively a little of her reality, since I saw that she was not indispensable, unique to Andrée who had been able to replace her with other girls.

While Albertine was alive, I would not have dared to ask Andrée to take me into her confidence as to the nature of their friendship both mutually and with Mlle Vinteuil's friend, since I was never absolutely certain that Andrée did not repeat to Albertine everything that I said to her. But now such an inquiry, even if it must prove fruitless, would at least be unattended by danger. I spoke to Andrée not in a questioning tone but as though I had known all the time, perhaps from Albertine, of the fondness that Andrée herself had for women and of her own relations with Mlle Vinteuil's friend. She admitted everything without the slightest reluctance, smiling as she spoke. From this avowal, I might derive the most painful consequences; first of all because Andrée, so affectionate and coquettish with many of the young men at Balbec, would never have been suspected by anyone of practices which she made no attempt to deny, so that by analogy, when I discovered this novel Andrée, I might think that Albertine would have confessed them with the same ease to anyone other than myself whom she felt to be jealous. But on the other hand, Andrée having been Albertine's dearest friend, and the friend for whose sake she had probably returned in haste from Balbec, now that Andrée was proved to have these tastes, the conclusion that was forced upon my mind was that Albertine and Andrée had always indulged them together.

I said casually to Andrée: "I have never mentioned the subject to you for fear of offending you, but now that we both find a pleasure in talking about her, I may as well tell you that I found out long ago all about the things of that sort that you used to do with Albertine. And I can tell you something that you will be glad to hear although you know it already: Albertine adored you." I told Andrée that it would be of great interest to me if she would allow me to see her, even if she simply confined herself to caresses which would not embarrass her unduly in my presence, performing such actions with those of Albertine's friends who shared her tastes, and I mentioned Rosemonde, Berthe; each of Albertine's friends, in the hope of finding out something. "Apart from the fact that not for anything in the world would I do the things you mention in your presence," Andrée replied, " I do not believe that any of the girls whom you have named have those tastes." Drawing closer in spite of myself to the monster that was attracting me, I answered: "What! You are not going to expect me to believe that, of all your band, Albertine was the only one with whom you did that sort of thing!" "But I have never done anything of the sort with Albertine. "Come now, my dear Andrée, why deny things which I have known for at least three years, I see no harm in them, far from it. Talking of such things, that evening when she was so anxious to go with you the next day to Mme Verdurin's, you may remember perhaps………".

Before I had completed my sentence, I saw in Andrée's eyes, which it sharpened to a pin-point like those stones which for that reason jewellers find it difficult to use, a fleeting, worried stare, like the heads of persons privileged to go behind the scenes who draw back the edge of the curtain before the play has begun and at once retire in order not to be seen. This uneasy stare vanished, everything had become quite normal, but I felt that anything which I might see hereafter would have been specially arranged for my benefit. At that moment I caught sight of myself in the mirror; I was struck by a certain resemblance between myself and Andrée. If I had not long since ceased to shave my upper lip and had had but the faintest shadow of a moustache, this resemblance would have been almost complete. It was perhaps when she saw, at Balbec, my moustache which had scarcely begun to grow, that Albertine had suddenly felt that impatient, furious desire to return to Paris. "But I cannot, all the same, say things that are not true, for the simple reason that you see no harm in them. I swear to you that I never did anything with Albertine, and I am convinced that she detested that sort of thing. The people who told you were lying to you, probably with some ulterior motive," she said with a questioning, defiant air. "Oh, very well then, since you won't tell me," I replied. I preferred to appear to be unwilling to furnish a proof which I did not possess. And yet I uttered vaguely and at random the name of the Buttes-Chaumont. "I may have gone to the Buttes-Chaumont with Albertine, but is it a place that has a particularly evil reputation?"

In short, if, albeit Andrée had those tastes to such an extent that she made no pretence of concealing them, and Albertine had felt for her that strong affection which she had undoubtedly felt, notwithstanding this Andrée had never had any carnal relations with Albertine and had never been aware that Albertine had those tastes, this meant that Albertine did not have them, and had never enjoyed with anyone those relations which, rather than with anyone else, she would have enjoyed with Andrée. And so when Andrée had left me, I realised that so definite a statement had brought me peace of mind.

But perhaps it had been dictated by a sense of the obligation, which Andrée felt that she owed to the dead girl whose memory still survived in her, not to let me believe what Albertine had doubtless, while she was alive, begged her to deny.

CHAPTER TWO

MADEMOISELLE DE FORCHEVILLE

With the coming of winter, on a fine Sunday, which was also All Saints' Day, I had ventured out of doors. I came towards the Bois, and as I followed the paths separated by undergrowth, carpeted with a grass that diminished daily, the memory of a drive during which Albertine had been by my side in the carriage, floated now round about me, in the vague mist of the darkening branches in the midst of which the setting sun caused to gleam, as though suspended in the empty air, a horizontal web embroidered with golden leaves. Moreover my heart kept fluttering at every moment, as happens to anyone in whose eyes a rooted idea gives to every woman who has halted at the end of a path, the appearance, the possible identity of the woman of whom he is thinking. "It is perhaps she!" We turn round, the carriage continues on its way and we do not return to the spot. These leaves, I did not merely behold them with the eyes of my memory, they interested me, touched me, like those purely descriptive pages into which an artist, to make them more complete, introduces a fiction, a whole romance; and this work of nature thus assumed the sole charm of melancholy which was capable of reaching my heart. The reason for this charm seemed to me to be that I was still as much in love with Albertine as ever, whereas the true reason was on the contrary that oblivion was continuing to make such headway in me that the memory of Albertine was no longer painful to me, that is to say, it had changed; but however clearly we may discern our impressions, as I then thought that I could discern the reason for my melancholy, we are unable to trace them back to their more remote meaning. Like those maladies the history of which the doctor hears his patient relate to him, by the help of which he works back to a more profound cause, of which the patient is unaware, similarly our impressions, our ideas, have only a symptomatic value. My jealousy being held aloof by the impression of charm and agreeable sadness which I was feeling, my senses reawakened.

A little farther on I saw a group of three girls, slightly older, young women perhaps, whose fashionable, energetic style corresponded so closely with what had attracted me on the day when I first saw Albertine and her friends, that I hastened in pursuit of these three new girls and, when they stopped a carriage, looked frantically in every direction for another. I found one, but it was too late. I did not overtake them. A few days later, however, as I was coming home, I saw, emerging from the portico of our house, the three girls whom I had followed in the Bois. They were absolutely, the two dark ones especially, save that they were slightly older, the type of those young ladies who so often, seen from my window or encountered in the street, had made me form a thousand plans, fall in love with life, and whom I had never been able to know. The fair one had a rather more delicate, almost an invalid air, which appealed to me less. It was she, nevertheless, that was responsible for my not contenting myself with glancing at them for a moment, but becoming rooted to the ground, staring at them with a scrutiny of the sort which, by their fixity which nothing can distract, their application as though to a problem, seem to be conscious that the true object is hidden far beyond what they behold. I should doubtless have allowed them to disappear as I had allowed so many others, had not (at the moment when they passed by me) the fair one—was it because I was scrutinising them so closely?—darted a stealthy glance at myself; then, having passed me and turning her head, a second glance which fired my blood. However, as she ceased to pay attention to myself and resumed her conversation with her friends, my ardour would doubtless have subsided, had it not been increased a hundredfold by the following incident. When I asked the porter who they were: "They asked for Mme la Duchesse," he informed me. "I think that only one of them knows her and that the others were simply seeing her to the door. Here's the name, I don't know whether I've taken it down properly." And I read: "Mlle Déporcheville," which it was easy to correct to 'd'Eporcheville,' that is to say the name, more or less, so far as I could remember, of the girl of excellent family, vaguely connected with the Guermantes, whom Robert had told me that he had met in a disorderly house, and with whom he had had relations. I now understood the meaning of her glance, why she had turned round, without letting her companions see. How often I had thought about her, imagining her in the light of the name that Robert had given me. And, lo and behold, I had seen her, in no way different from her friends, save for that concealed glance which established between me and herself a secret entry into the parts of her life which, evidently, were concealed from her friends, and which made her appear more accessible—almost half my own—more gentle than girls of noble birth generally are. In the mind of this girl, between me and herself, there was in advance the common ground of the hours that we might have spent together, had she been free to make an appointment with me. Was it not this that her glance had sought to express to me with an eloquence that was intelligible to myself alone. My heart throbbed until it almost burst, I could not have given an exact description of Mlle d'Eporcheville's appearance, I could picture vaguely a fair complexion viewed from the side, but I was madly in love with her. All of a sudden I became aware that I was reasoning as though, of the three girls, Mlle d'Eporcheville could be only the fair one who had turned round and had looked at me twice. But the porter had not told me this. I returned to his lodge, questioned him again, he told me that he could not enlighten me, but that he would ask his wife who had seen them once before. She was busy at the moment scrubbing the service stair. While the porter went in search of his wife, my chief anxiety—as I thought of Mlle d'Eporcheville, and since in those minutes spent in waiting, in which a name, a detail of information which we have, we know not why, fitted to a face, finds itself free for an instant, ready if it shall adhere to a new face to render, retrospectively, the original face as to which it had enlightened us strange, innocent, imperceptible—was that the porter's wife was perhaps going to inform me that Mlle d'Eporcheville was, on the contrary, one of the two dark girls. In that event, there would vanish the being in whose existence I believed, whom I already loved, whom I now thought only of possessing, that fair and sly Mlle d'Eporcheville whom the fatal answer must then separate into two distinct elements, which I had arbitrarily united after the fashion of a novelist who blends together diverse elements borrowed from reality in order to create an imaginary character, elements which, taken separately—the name failing to corroborate the supposed intention of the glance—lost all their meaning. In that case my arguments would be stultified, but how greatly they found themselves, on the contrary, strengthened when the porter returned to tell me that Mlle d'Eporcheville was indeed the fair girl.

From that moment I could no longer believe in a similarity of names. The coincidence was too remarkable that of these three girls one should be named Mlle d'Eporcheville, that she should be precisely (and this was the first convincing proof of my supposition) the one who had gazed at me in that way, almost smiling at me, and that it should not be she who frequented the disorderly houses.

Then began a day of wild excitement. Even before starting to buy all the bedizenments that I thought necessary in order to create a favourable impression when I went to call upon Mme de Guermantes two days later, when (the porter had informed me) the young lady would be coming again to see the Duchess, in whose house I should thus find a willing girl and make an appointment (for I should easily be able to take her into a corner for a moment), I began, so as to be on the safe side, by telegraphing to Robert to ask him for the girl's exact name and for a description of her, hoping to have his reply within forty-eight hours (I did not think for an instant of anything else, not even of Albertine), determined, whatever might happen to me in the interval, even if I had to be carried down in a chair were I too ill to walk, to pay a long call upon the Duchess. If I telegraphed to Saint-Loup, it was not that I had any lingering doubt as to the identity of the person, or that the girl whom I had seen and the girl of whom he had spoken were still distinct personalities in my mind. I had no doubt whatever that they were the same person. But in my impatience at the enforced interval of forty-eight hours, it was a pleasure, it gave me already a sort of secret power over her to receive a telegram concerning her, filled with detailed information. At the telegraph office, as I drafted my message with the animation of a man who is fired by hope, I remarked how much less disconcerted I was now than in my boyhood and in facing Mlle d'Eporcheville than I had been in facing Gilberte. From the moment in which I had merely taken the trouble to write out my telegram, the clerk had only to take it from me, the swiftest channels of electric communication to transmit it across the extent of France and the Mediterranean, and all Robert's sensual past would be set to work to identify the person whom I had seen in the street, would be placed at the service of the romance which I had sketched in outline, and to which I need no longer give a thought, for his answer would undertake to bring about a happy ending before twenty-four had passed.

Finally, on the following morning, after a night of happy sleeplessness I received Saint-Loup's telegram: "de l'Orgeville, *de* preposition, *orge* the grain barley, *ville* town, small, dark, plump, is at present in Switzerland." It was not she!

A moment before Françoise brought me the telegram, my mother had come into my room with my letters, had laid them carelessly on my bed, as though she were thinking of something else. And withdrawing at once to leave me by myself she had smiled as she left the room. And I, who was familiar with my dear mother's little subterfuges and knew that one could always read the truth in her face, without any fear of being mistaken, if one took as a key to the cipher, her desire to give pleasure to other people, I smiled and thought: "There must be something interesting for me in the post, and Mamma has assumed that indifferent air so that my surprise may be complete and so as not to be like the people who take away half your pleasure by telling you of it beforehand. And she has not stayed with me because she is afraid that in my pride I may conceal the pleasure that I shall feel and so feel it less keenly.

Mamma had left the post by my side, so that I might not overlook it. But I could see that there was nothing but newspapers. No doubt there was some article by a writer whom I admired, which, as he wrote seldom, would be a surprise to me. I went to the window, and drew back the curtains.

I opened the *Figaro.* What a bore! The very first article had the same title as the article which I had sent to the paper and which had not appeared, but not merely the same title . . . why, there were several words absolutely identical. This was really too bad. I must write and complain. But it was not merely a few words, there was the whole thing, there was my signature at the foot.

It was my article that had appeared at last!

What I am holding in my hand is not a particular copy of the newspaper, it is any one out of the ten thousand, it is not merely what has been written for me, it is what has been written for me and for everyone. To appreciate exactly the phenomenon which is occurring at this moment in the other houses, it is essential that I read this article not as its author but as one of the ordinary readers of the paper. For what I held in my hand was not merely what I had written, it was the symbol of its incarnation in countless minds. And so, in order to read it, it was essential that I should cease for a moment to be its author, that I should be simply one of the readers of the *Figaro*. But then came an initial anxiety. Would the reader who had not been forewarned catch sight of this article. I open the paper carelessly as would this not forewarned reader, even assuming an air of not knowing what there is this morning in my paper, of being in a hurry to look at the social paragraphs and the political news. But my article is so long that my eye which avoids it (to remain within the bounds of truth and not to put chance on my side, as a person who is waiting counts very slowly on purpose) catches a fragment of it in its survey. But many of those readers who notice the first article and even read it do not notice the signature; I myself would be quite incapable of saying who had written the first article of the day before. And I now promise myself that I will always read them, including the author's name.

After luncheon when I went down to Mme de Guermantes, it was less for the sake of Mlle d'Eporcheville who had been stripped, by Saint-Loup's telegram, of the better part of her personality, than in the hope of finding in the Duchess herself one of those readers of my article who would enable me to form an idea of the impression that it had made upon the public—subscribers and purchasers—of the *Figaro*.

When I entered the drawing-room, I saw the fair girl whom I had supposed for twenty-four hours to be the girl of whom Saint-Loup had spoken to me. It was she who asked the Duchess to 'reintroduce' me to her. And indeed, the moment I came into the room I had the impression that I knew her quite well, which the Duchess however dispelled by saying: "Oh! You have met Mlle de Forcheville before." I myself; on the contrary, was certain that I had never been introduced to any girl of that name, which would certainly have impressed me, so familiar was it in my memory ever since I had been given a retrospective account of Odette's love affairs and Swann's jealousy. In itself my twofold error as to the name, in having remembered de l'Orgeville as d'Eporcheville and in having reconstructed as d'Eporcheville what was in reality Forcheville, was in no way extraordinary. Our mistake lies in our supposing that things present themselves ordinarily as they are in reality, names as they are written, people as photography and psychology give an unalterable idea of them. As a matter of fact this is not at all what we ordinarily perceive. We see, we hear, we conceive the world quite topsy-turvy. We repeat a name as we have heard it spoken until experience has corrected our mistake, which does not always happen. I should therefore, have had no reason to be surprised when I heard the name Forcheville (and I was already asking myself whether she was related to the Forcheville of whom I had so often heard) had not the fair girl said to me at once, anxious no doubt to forestall, tactfully, questions which would have been unpleasant to her: "You don't remember that you knew me quite well long ago, you used to come to our house: your friend Gilberte. I could see that you didn't recognise me. I recognised you immediately." (She said this as if she had recognised me immediately in the drawing-room, but the truth is that she had recognised me in the street and had greeted me, and later Mme de Guermantes informed me that she had told her, as something very odd and extraordinary, that I had followed her and brushed against her, mistaking her for a prostitute). I did not learn until she had left the room why she was called Mlle de Forcheville. After Swann's death, Odette, who astonished everyone by her profound, prolonged and sincere grief; found herself an extremely rich widow. Forcheville married her, after making a long tour of various country houses and ascertaining that his family would acknowledge his wife. (The family raised certain objections, but yielded to the material advantage of not having to provide for the expenses of a needy relative who was about to pass from comparative penury to opulence.) Shortly after this, one of Swann's uncles, upon whose head the successive demise of many relatives had accumulated an enormous fortune, died, leaving the whole of his fortune to Gilberte who thus became one of the wealthiest heiresses in France. But this was the moment when from the effects of the Dreyfus case there had arisen an anti-semitic movement parallel to a more abundant movement towards the penetration of society by Israelites. The politicians had not been wrong in thinking that the discovery of the judicial error would deal a fatal-blow to anti-semitism. But provisionally, at least, a social anti-semitism was on the contrary, enhanced and exacerbated by it. Forcheville who, like every petty nobleman, had derived from conventions in the family circle the certainty that his name was more ancient than that of La Rochefoucauld, considered that, in marrying the widow of a Jew, he had performed the same act of charity as a millionaire who picks up a prostitute in the street and rescues her from poverty and mire; he was prepared to extend his bounty to Gilberte, whose prospects of marriage were assisted by all her millions but were hindered by that absurd name "Swann." He declared that he would adopt her.

Certain women who were old friends of Swann took a great interest in Gilberte. When the aristocracy learned of her latest inheritance, they began to remark how well bred she was and what a charming wife she would make. People said that a cousin of Mme de Guermantes, the

Princesse de Nièvre, was thinking of Gilberte for her son. Mme de Guermantes hated Mme de Nièvre. She announced that such a marriage would be a scandal. Mme de Nièvre took fright and swore that she had never thought of it. One day, after luncheon, as the sun was shining, and M. de Guermantes was going to take his wife out, Mme de Guermantes was arranging her hat in front of the mirror, her blue eyes gazing into their own reflection, and at her still golden hair, her maid holding in her hand various sunshades among which her mistress might choose. The sun came flooding in through the window and they had decided to take advantage of the fine weather to pay a call at Saint-Cloud, and M. de Guermantes, ready to set off, wearing pearl-grey gloves and a tall hat on his head said to to himself: "Oriane is really astounding still. I find her delicious," and went on, aloud, seeing that his wife seemed to be in a good humour: "By the way, I have a message for you from Mme de Virelef. She wanted to ask you to come on Monday to the opera, but as she's having the Swann girl, she did not dare and asked me to explore the ground. I don't express any opinion, I simply convey the message. But really, it seems to me that we might......" he added evasively, for their attitude towards anyone else being a collective attitude and taking an identical form in each of them, he knew from his own feelings that his wife's hostility to Mlle Swann had subsided and that she was anxious to meet her. Mme de Guermantes settled her veil to her liking and chose a sunshade. "But just as you like, what difference do you suppose it can make to me, I see no reason against our meeting the girl. I simply did not wish that we should appear to be countenancing the dubious establishments of our friends. That is all."

"And you were perfectly right," replied the Duke. "You are wisdom incarnate, Madame, and you are more ravishing than ever in that hat." "You are very kind," said Mme de Guermantes with a smile at her husband as she made her way to the door. But, before entering the carriage, she felt it her duty to give him a further explanation: "There are plenty of people now who call upon the mother, besides she has the sense to be ill for nine months of the year. . . . It seems that the child is quite charming. Everybody knows that we were greatly attached to Swann. People will think it quite natural," and they set off together for Saint-Cloud.

This friendly attitude on the part of the Duke and Duchess meant that, for the future, they might at the most let fall an occasional "your poor father" to Gilberte, which, for that matter was quite unnecessary, since it was just about this time that Forcheville adopted the girl. She addressed him as 'Father', charmed all the dowagers by her politeness and air of breeding and it was admitted that, if Forcheville had behaved with the utmost generosity towards her, the girl had a good heart and knew how to reward him for his pains. Doubtless because she was able, now and then, and desired to show herself quite at her ease, she had reintroduced herself to me and in conversation with me had spoken of her true father. But this was an exception and no one now dared utter the name Swann in her presence.

I had just caught sight, in the drawing-room, of two sketches by Elstir which formerly had been banished to a little room upstairs in which it was only by chance that I had seen them. Elstir was now in fashion. Mme de Guermantes could not forgive herself for having given so many of his pictures to her cousin, not because they were in fashion, but because she now appreciated them. Fashion is, indeed, composed of the appreciations of a number of people of whom the Guermantes are typical. But she could not dream of buying others of his pictures for they had long ago begun to fetch absurdly high prices. She was determined to have something, at least, by Elstir in her drawing-room and had brought down these two drawings which, she declared, she preferred to his paintings.

Gilberte recognised the drawings "One would say Elstir," she suggested. "Why, yes," replied the Duchess without thinking, "it was, as a matter of fact, your fa . . . some friends of ours who made us buy them. They are admirable. To my mind, they are superior to his paintings." I who had not heard this conversation went closer to the drawings to examine them. "Why, this is the Elstir that. . . ." I saw Mme de Guermantes's signals of despair. "Ah, yes! The Elstir that I admired upstairs. It shows far better here than in that passage. Talking of Elstir, I mentioned him yesterday in an article in the *Figaro*. Did you happen to read it?" "You have written an article in the *Figaro?*" exclaimed M. de Guermantes with the same violence as if he had exclaimed: "Why, she is my cousin." "Yes, yesterday." "In the *Figaro*, you are certain? That is a great surprise. For we each of us get our *Figaro*, and if one of us had missed it, the other would certainly have noticed it. That is, so, ain't it, Oriane, there was nothing in the paper." The Duke sent for the *Figaro* and accepted the facts, as though, previously, the probability had been that I had made a mistake as to the newspaper for which I had written. "What's that, I don't understand, do you mean to say, you have written an article in the *Figaro?*" said the Duchess, making an effort in order to speak of a matter which did not interest her. "Come, Basin, you can read it afterwards." "No, the Duke looks so nice like that with his big beard sweeping over the paper," said Gilberte. "I shall read it as soon as I am at home." "Yes, he wears a beard now that everybody is clean-shaven," said the Duchess, "he never does anything like other people. When we were first married, he shaved not only his beard but his moustaches as well. The peasants who didn't know him by sight thought that he couldn't be French. He was called at that time the Prince des Laumes." "Is there still a Prince des Laumes?" asked Gilberte, who was interested in everything that concerned the people who had refused to bow to her during all those years. "Why, no!" the Duchess replied with a melancholy, caressing gaze. "Such a charming title! One of the finest titles in France! "said Gilberte, a certain sort of banality emerging inevitably, as a clock strikes, the hour, from the lips of certain quite intelligent persons. "Yes, indeed, I regret it too. Basin would have liked his sister's son to take, it, but it is not the same thing; after all it is possible, since it is not necessarily the eldest son, the title may pass to a younger brother. I was telling you that in those days Basin was clean-shaven; one day, at a pilgrimage—you remember, my dear," she turned to her husband, "that pilgrimage at Paray-le-Monial—my brother-in-law Charlus who always enjoys talking to peasants, was saying to one after another: 'where do you come from?' and as he is extremely generous, he would give them something, take them off to have a drink. For nobody was ever at the same time simpler and more haughty than Mémé. You'll see him refuse to bow to a Duchess whom he doesn't think duchessy enough, and shower compliments upon a kennelman. And so, I said to Basin: 'Come, Basin, say something to them too.' My husband, who is not always very inventive—" "Thank you, Oriane," said the Duke, without interrupting his reading of my article in which he was immersed— "approached one of the peasants and repeated his brother's question in so many words: 'Where do you come from?'

'I am from Les Laumes.' 'You are from Les Laumes. Why, I am your Prince.' Then the peasant looked at Basin's smooth face and replied: ' 's not true. You're an English'.

When M. de Guermantes had finished reading my article, he paid me compliments which however he took care to qualify. He regretted the slightly hackneyed form of a style in which there were "emphasis, metaphors as in the antiquated prose of Chateaubriand"; on the other hand he congratulated me without reserve upon my 'occupying myself': "I like a man to do something with his ten fingers. I do not like the useless creatures who are always self-important or agitators. A fatuous breed!"

Gilbert; who was acquiring with extreme rapidity the ways of the world of fashion, announced how proud she would be to say that she was the friend of an author. "You can imagine that I shall tell people that I have the pleasure, the honour of your acquaintance."

"You wouldn't care to come with us, to-morrow, to the Opéra-Comique?" the Duchess asked me; and I thought that it would be doubtless in that same box in which I had first beheld her, and which had seemed to me then as inaccessible as the submarine realm of the Nereids. But I replied in a melancholy tone: "No, I am not going to the theatre just now; I have lost a friend to whom I was greatly attached." The tears almost came to my eyes as I said this, and yet, for the first time, I felt a sort of pleasure in speaking of my bereavement. It was from this moment that I began to write to all my friends that I had just experienced a great sorrow, and to cease to feel it.

Another person in whom the process of oblivion, so far as concerned Albertine, was probably more rapid at this time, and enabled me in return to realise a little later a fresh advance which that process had made in myself (and this is my memory of a second stage before the final oblivion), was Andrée. I can scarcely, indeed, refrain from citing this oblivion of Albertine as, if not the sole cause, if not even the principal cause, at any rate a conditioning and necessary cause of a conversation between Andrée and myself about six months after the conversation which I have already reported, when her words were so different from those that she had used on the former occasion. I remember that it was in my room because at that moment I found a pleasure in having semi-carnal, relations with her, because of the collective form originally assumed and now being resumed by my love for the girls of the little band, a love that had long been undivided among them, and for a while associated exclusively with Albertine's person during the months that had preceded and followed her death.

We were in my room for another reason as well which enables me to date this conversation quite accurately. This was that I had been banished from the rest of the apartment because it was Mamma's day. Notwithstanding its being her day, and after some hesitation, Mamma had gone to luncheon with Mme Sazerat thinking that as Mme Sazerat always contrived to invite one to meet boring people, she would be able, without sacrificing any pleasure, to return home in good time. And she had indeed returned in time and without regret, Mme Sazerat having had nobody but the most deadly people who were frozen from the start by the special voice that she adopted when she had company, what Mamma called her Wednesday voice. My mother was nevertheless, extremely fond of her, was sorry for her poverty—the result of the extravagance of her father who had been ruined by the Duchesse de X…… a poverty which compelled her to live all the year round at Combray, with a few weeks at her cousin's house in Paris and a great 'pleasure-trip' every ten years.

I remember that the day before this, at my request repeated for months past, and because the Princess was always begging her to come, Mamma had gone to call upon the Princesse de Parme, who, herself, paid no calls, and at whose house people as a rule contented themselves with writing their names, but who had insisted upon my mother coming to see her, since the rules and regulations prevented Her from coming to us. My mother had come home thoroughly cross: "You have sent me on a fool's errand," she told me, "the Princesse de Parme barely greeted me, she turned back to the ladies to whom she was talking without paying me any attention, and after ten minutes, as she hadn't uttered a word to me, I came away without her even offering me her hand. I was extremely annoyed however, on the doorstep, as I was leaving, I met the Duchesse de Guermantes who was very kind and spoke to me a great deal about you. What a strange idea that was to tell her about Albertine. She told me that you had said to her that her death had been such a grief to you. I shall never go near the Princesse de Parme again. You have made me make a fool of myself."

Well, the next day, which was my mother's at-home day, as I have said, Andrée came to see me. 'She had not much time, for she had to go and call for Gisèle with whom she was very anxious to dine. "I know her faults, but she is after all my best friend and the person for whom I feel most affection," she told me. And she even appeared to feel some alarm at the thought that I might ask her to let me dine with them. She was hungry for people, and a third person who knew her too well, such as myself, would, by preventing her from letting herself go, at once prevent her from enjoying complete satisfaction in their company.

The memory of Albertine had become so fragmentary in me that it no longer caused me any sorrow and was no more now than a transition to fresh desires, like a chord which announced a change of key. And indeed the idea of a momentary sensual caprice being ruled out, in so far as I was still faithful to Albertine's memory, I was happier at having Andrée in my company than I would have been at having an Albertine miraculously restored to life. For Andrée could tell me more things about Albertine than Albertine herself had ever told me. Now the problems concerning Albertine still remained in my mind when my affection for her, both physical and moral, had already vanished. And my desire to know about her life, because it had diminished less, was now relatively greater than my need of her presence. On the other hand, the thought that a woman had perhaps had relations with Albertine no longer provoked in me anything save the desire to have relations myself also with that woman. I told Andrée this, caressing her as I spoke. Then, without making the slightest effort to harmonise her speech with what she had said a few months earlier, Andrée said to me with a lurking smile: "Ah! yes; but you are a man. And so we can't do quite the same things as I used to do with Albertine." And whether it was that she considered that this increased my desire (in the hope of extracting confidences, I had told her that I would like to have relations with a woman who had had them with Albertine) or my grief, or perhaps destroyed a sense of superiority to herself which she might suppose me to feel at being the only person who had had relations with Albertine: "Ah! we spent many happy hours together, she was so caressing, so passionate. Besides, it was not only with me that she liked to enjoy herself. She had met a nice boy at Mme Verdurin's, Morel. They understood each other at once. He undertook (with her permission to enjoy himself with them too, for he liked virgins), to procure little girls for her. As soon as he had set their feet on the path, he left them. And so he made himself responsible for attracting young fisher-girls in some quiet watering-place, young laundresses, who would fall in love with a boy, but would not have listened to a girl's advances. As soon as the girl was well under his control, he would bring her to a safe place, where he handed her over to Albertine. For fear of losing Morel, who took part in it all too, the girl always obeyed, and yet she lost him all the same, for, as he was afraid of what might happen and also as once or twice was enough for him, he would slip away leaving a false address. Once he had the nerve to bring one of these girls, with Albertine, to a brothel, at Corliville, where four or five of the women had her at once, or in turn. That was his passion, and Albertine's also. But Albertine suffered terrible remorse afterwards. I believe that when she was with you she had conquered her passion and put off indulging it from day to day. Then her affection for yourself was so strong that she felt scruples. But it was quite certain that, if she ever left you, she would begin again. She hoped that you would rescue her, that you would marry her. She felt in her heart that it was a sort of criminal lunacy, and I have often asked myself whether it was not after an incident of that sort, which had led to a suicide in a family, that she killed herself on purpose.

When Andrée left me, it was dinner-time. "You will never guess who has been to see me and stayed at least three hours," said my mother. "I call it three hours, it was perhaps longer, she arrived almost on the heels of my first visitor, who was Mme Cottard, sat still and watched everybody come and go—and I had more than thirty callers— and left me only a quarter of an hour ago. If you hadn't had your friend Andrée with you, I should have sent for you." "Why, who was it?" "A person who never pays calls." "The Princesse de Parme?" "Why, I have a cleverer son than I thought I had. There is no fun in making you guess a name, for you hit on it at once." "Did she come to apologise for her rudeness yesterday?" "No, that would have been stupid, the fact of her calling was an apology. Your poor grandmother would have thought it admirable. It seems that about two o'clock she had sent a footman to ask whether I had an at-home day. She was told that this was the day and so up she came." My first thought, which I did not dare mention to Mamma, was that the Princesse de Parme, surrounded, the day before, by people of rank and fashion with whom she was on intimate terms and enjoyed conversing, had when she saw my mother come into the room felt an annoyance which she had made no attempt to conceal. And it was quite in the style of the great ladies of Germany, which for that matter the Guermantes had largely adopted, this stiffness, for which they thought to atone by a scrupulous affability. But my mother believed, and I came in time to share her opinion, that all that had happened was that the Princesse de Parme, having failed to recognise her, had not felt herself bound to pay her any attention, that she had learned after my mother's departure who she was, either from the Duchesse de Guermantes whom my mother had met as she was leaving the house, or from the list of her visitors, whose names, before they entered her presence, the servants recorded in a book. She had thought it impolite to send word or to say to my mother "I did not recognise you," but—and this was no less in harmony with the good manners of the German courts and with the Guermantes' code of behaviour than my original theory—had thought that a call, an exceptional action on the part of a royal personage, and what was more a call of several hours duration, would convey the explanation to my mother in an indirect but no less convincing form, which is just what did happen.

As for the last occasion on which I remember that I was conscious of approaching an absolute indifference with regard to Albertine (and on this occasion I felt that I had entirely arrived at it), it was one day at Venice, a long time after Andrée's last visit.

CHAPTER THREE

VENICE

My mother had brought me for a few weeks to Venice and—as there may be beauty in the most precious as well as in the humblest things—I was receiving there impressions analogous to those which I had felt so often in the past at Combray, but transposed into a wholly different and far richer key. When at ten o'clock in the morning my shutters were thrown open, I saw ablaze in the sunlight, instead of the black marble into which the slates of Saint Hilaire used to turn, the Golden Angel on the Campanile of San Marco. In its dazzling glitter, which made it almost impossible to fix it in space, it promised me with its outstretched arms, for the moment, half an hour later, when I was to appear on the Piazzetta, a joy more certain than any that it could ever in the past have been bidden to announce to men of good will. I could see nothing but itself, so long as I remained in bed, but as the whole world is merely a vast sun-dial, a single lighted segment of which enables us to tell what o'clock it is, on the very first morning I was reminded of the shops in the Place de l'Eglise at Combray, which, on Sunday mornings, were always on the point of shutting when I arrived for mass, while the straw in the market place smelt strongly in the already hot sunlight. But on the second morning, what I saw, when I awoke, what made me get out of bed (because they had taken the place in my consciousness and in my desire of my memories of Combray), were the impressions of my first morning stroll in Venice, Venice whose daily life was no less real than that of Combray, where as at Combray on Sunday mornings one had the delight of emerging upon a festive street, but where that street was paved with water of a sapphire blue, refreshed by little ripples of cooler air, and of so solid a colour that my tired eyes might, in quest of relaxation and without fear of its giving way, rest their gaze upon it. Like, at Combray, the worthy folk of the Rue de l'Oiseau, so in this strange town also, the inhabitants did indeed emerge from houses drawn up in line, side by side, along the principal street, but the part played there by houses that cast a patch of shade before them was in Venice entrusted to palaces of porphyry and jasper, over the arched door of which the head of a bearded god (projecting from its alignment, like the knocker on a door at Combray) had the effect of darkening with its shadow, not the brownness of the soil but the splendid blue of the water. On the piazza, the shadow that would have been cast. at Combray by the linen-draper's awning and the barber's pole, turned into the tiny blue flowers scattered at its feet upon the desert of sun-scorched tiles by the silhouette of a Renaissance façade, which is not to say that, when the sun was hot, we were not obliged, in Venice as at Combray, to pull down the blinds between ourselves and the Canal, but they hung behind the quatrefoils and foliage of gothic windows. Of this sort was the window in our hotel behind the pillars of which my mother sat waiting for me, gazing at the Canal with a patience which she would not have displayed in the old days at Combray, at that time when, reposing in myself hopes which had never been realised, she was unwilling to let me see how much she loved me. Nowadays she was well aware that an apparent coldness on her part would alter nothing, and the affection that she lavished upon me was like those forbidden foods which are no longer withheld from invalids, when it is certain that they are past recovery.

Several of the palaces on the Grand Canal had been converted into hotels, and, feeling the need of a change, or wishing to be hospitable to Mme Sazerat whom we had encountered—the unexpected and inopportune acquaintance whom we invariably meet when we travel abroad—and whom Mamma had invited to dine with us, we decided one evening to try an hotel which was not our own, and in which we had been told that the food was better. While my mother was paying the gondolier and taking Mme Sazerat to the room which she had engaged, I slipped away to inspect the great hall of the restaurant with its fine marble pillars and walls and ceiling that were once entirely covered with frescoes, recently and badly restored. Two waiters were conversing in an Italian which I translate: "Are the old people going to dine in their room? They never let us know. It's the devil, I never know whether I am to reserve their table *(non so se bisogna conservargli la loro tavola)*. And then, suppose they come down and find their table taken! I don't understand how they can take in *forestieri* like that in such a smart hotel. They're not our style."

Notwithstanding his contempt, the waiter was anxious to know what action he was to take with regard to the table, and was going to get the lift-boy sent upstairs to inquire, when, before he had had time to do so, he received his answer: he had just caught sight of the old lady who was entering the room. I had no difficulty, despite the air of melancholy and weariness that comes with the burden of years, and despite a sort of eczema, a red leprosy that covered her face, in recognising beneath her bonnet, in her black jacket, made by W—, but to the untutored eye exactly like that of an old charwoman, the Marquise de Villeparisis. As luck would have it, the spot upon which I was standing, engaged in studying the remains of a fresco, between two of the beautiful marble panels, was directly behind the table at which Mme de Villeparisis had just sat down.

"Then M. de Villeparisis won't be long. They've been here a month now, and it's only once that they didn't have a meal together," said the waiter. I was asking myself who the relative could be with whom she was travelling, and who was named M. de Villeparisis, when I saw, a few moments later, advance towards the table and sit down by her side, her old lover, M. de Norpois. His great age had weakened the resonance of his voice, but had in compensation given to his language, formerly so reserved, a positive intemperance. The cause of this was to be sought, perhaps, in certain ambitions for the realisation of which, little time, he felt, remained to him and which filled him all the more with vehemence and ardour; perhaps in the fact that, having been discarded from a world of politics to which he longed to return, he imagined, in the simplicity of his desire, that he could turn out of office, by the pungent criticisms which he launched at them, the men whose places he was anxious to fill. Thus we see politicians convinced that the Cabinet of which they are not members cannot hold out for three days. It would, however, be an exaggeration to suppose that M. de Norpois had entirely lost the traditions of diplomatic speech. Whenever important matters were involved, he at once became, as we shall see, the man whom we remember in the past, but at all other times he would inveigh against this man and that with the senile violence of certain octogenarians which hurls them into the arms of women to whom they are no longer capable of doing any serious damage.

Mme de Villeparisis preserved, for some minutes, the silence of an old woman who in the exhaustion of age finds it difficult to rise from memories of the past to consideration of the present. Then, turning to one of those eminently practical questions that indicate the survival of a mutual affection: "Did you call at Salviati's?" "Yes" "Will they send it to-morrow?" "I brought the bowl back myself. You shall see it after dinner. Let us look what there is to eat." "Did you send instructions about my Suez shares?" "No; at the present moment the market is entirely taken up with oil shares. But there is no hurry, they are still fetching an excellent price. Here is the bill of fare. First of all, there are red mullets. Shall we try them?" "For me, yes, but you are not allowed them. Ask for a risotto instead. But they don't know how to cook it." "That doesn't matter. Waiter, some mullets for Madame and a risotto for me." A fresh and prolonged silence. "Why, I brought you the papers, the *Corriere della Sera*, the *Gazzetta del Popolo*, and all the rest of them. Do you know, there is a great deal of talk about a diplomatic change, the first scapegoat in which is to be Paléologue, who is notoriously inadequate in Serbia. He will perhaps be succeeded by Lozé, and there will be a vacancy at Constantinople. But," M. de Norpois hastened to add in a bitter tone, "for an Embassy of such scope, in a capital where it is obvious that Great Britain must always, whatever may happen, occupy the chief place at the council-table, it would be prudent to turn to men of experience better armed to resist the ambushes of the enemies of our British ally than are diplomats of the modern school who would walk blindfold into the trap." The angry volubility with which M. de Norpois uttered the last words was due principally to the fact that the newspapers, instead of suggesting his name, as he had requested them to do, named as a 'hot favourite' a young official of the Foreign Ministry. "Heaven knows that the men of years and experience may well hesitate, as a result of all manner of tortuous manoeuvres, to put themselves forward in the place of more or less incapable recruits. I have known many of these self-styled diplomats of the empirical method who centred all their hopes in a soap bubble which it did not take me long to burst. There can be no question about it, if the Government is so lacking in wisdom as to entrust the reins of state to turbulent hands, at the call of duty an old conscript will always answer 'Present!' But who knows" (and here M. de Norpois appeared to know perfectly well to whom he was referring) "whether it would not be the same on the day when they came in search of some veteran full of wisdom and skill. To my mind, for everyone has a right to his own opinion, the post at Constantinople should not be accepted until we have settled our existing difficulties with Germany. We owe no man anything, and it is intolerable that every six months they should come and demand from us, by fraudulent machinations, and extort, by force and fear, the payment of some debt or other, always hastily offered by a venal press. This must cease, and naturally a man of high distinction who has proved his merit, a man who would have, if I may say so, the Emperor's ear, would wield greater authority than any ordinary person in bringing the conflict to an end."

A gentleman who was finishing his dinner bowed to M. de Norpois.

"Why, there is Prince Foggi," said the Marquis. "Ah, I'm not sure that I know whom you mean," muttered Mme. de Villeparisis. "Why, of course you do. It is Prince Odone. The brother-in-law of your cousin Doudeauville. You cannot have forgotten that I went shooting with him at Bonnétable?" "Ah! Odone, that is the one who went in for painting?" "Not at all, he's the one who married the Grand Duke N's sister." M. de Norpois uttered these remarks in the cross tone a schoolmaster who is dissatisfied with his pupil, and stared fixedly at Mme de Villeparisis out of his blue eyes. When the Prince had drunk his coffee and was leaving his table, M. de Norpois rose, hastened towards him and with a majestic wave of his arm, himself retiring into the background, presented him to Mme de Villeparisis. And during the next few minutes while the Prince was standing beside their table, M. de Norpois never ceased for an instant to keep his azure pupils trained on Mme de Villeparisis, from the weakness or severity of an old lover, principally from fear of her making one of those mistakes in Italian which he had relished but which he dreaded. Whenever she said anything to the Prince that was not quite accurate he corrected her mistake and stared into the eyes of the abashed and docile Marquise with the steady intensity of a hypnotist.

    A waiter came to tell me that my mother was waiting for me, I went to her and made my apologies to Mme Sazerat, saying that I had been interested to see Mme de Villeparisis. At the sound of this name, Mme Sazerat turned pale and seemed about to faint. Controlling herself with an effort: "Mme de Villeparisis; who was Mlle de Bouillon?" she inquired. "Yes." "Couldn't I just get a glimpse of her for a moment? It has been the desire of my life." "Then there is no time to lose, Madame, for she will soon have finished her dinner. But how do you come to take such an interest in her?" "Because Mme de Villeparisis was, before her second marriage, the Duchesse d'Havré, beautiful as an angel, wicked as a demon, who drove my father out of his senses, ruined him and then forsook him immediately. Well, she may have behaved to him like any girl out of the gutter, she may have been the cause of our having to live, my family and myself, in a humble position at Combray; now that my father is dead, my consolation is to think that he was in love with the most beautiful woman of his generation, and as I have never set eyes on her, it will, after all, be a pleasure.

    I escorted Mme Sazerat, trembling with emotion, to the restaurant and pointed out Mme de Villeparisis. But, like a blind person who turns his face in the wrong direction, so Mme Sazerat did not bring her gaze to rest upon the table at which Mme de Villeparisis was dining, but, looking towards another part of the room, said: "But she must have gone, I don't see her in the place you're pointing to." And she continued to gaze round the room, in quest of the loathed, adored vision that had haunted her imagination for so long. "Yes, there she is, at the second table." "Then we can't be counting from the same point. At what I call the second table there are only two people, an old gentleman and a little hunchbacked, red-faced woman, quite hideous." "That is she!"

One evening a letter from my stockbroker reopened for me for an instant the gates of the prison in which Albertine abode within me alive, but so remote, so profoundly buried that she remained inaccessible to me. Since her death I had ceased to take any interest in the speculations that I had made in order to have more money for her. But time had passed; the wisest judgments of the previous generation had been proved unwise by this generation, as had occurred in the past to M. Thiers who had said that railways could never prove successful. The stocks of which M. de Norpois had said to us: "even if your income from them is nothing very great, you may be certain of never losing any of your capital," were, more often than not, those which had declined most in value. Calls had been made upon me for considerable sums and in a rash moment I decided to sell out everything and found that I now possessed barely a fifth of the fortune that I had had when Albertine was alive. This became known at Combray among the survivors of our family circle and their friends, and, as they knew that I went about with the Marquis de Saint-Loup and the Guermantes family, they said to themselves: "Pride goes before a fall!" They would have been greatly astonished to learn that it was for a girl of Albertine's humble position that I had made these speculations. Besides, in that Combray world in which everyone is classified for ever according to the income that he is known to enjoy, as in an Indian caste, it would have been impossible for anyone to form any idea of the great freedom that prevailed in the world of the Guermantes where people attached no importance to wealth, and where poverty was regarded as being as disagreeable, but no more degrading, as having no more effect on a person's social position than would a stomach-ache. Doubtless they imagined, on the contrary, at Combray that Saint-Loup and M. de Guermantes must be ruined aristocrats, whose estates were mortgaged, to whom I had been lending money, whereas if I had been ruined they would have been the first to offer in all sincerity to come to my assistance. As for my comparative penury, it was all the more awkward at the moment, inasmuch as my Venetian interests had been concentrated for some little time past on a rosy-cheeked young glass-vendor who offered to the delighted eye a whole range of orange tones and filled me with such a longing to see her again daily that, feeling that my mother and I would soon be leaving Venice, I had made up my mind that I would try to create some sort of position for her in Paris which would save me the distress of parting from her. The beauty of her seventeen summers was so noble, so radiant, that it was like acquiring a genuine Titian before leaving the place. And would the scant remains of my fortune be sufficient temptation to her to make her leave her native land and come to live in Paris for my sole convenience?

One evening, an incident occurred of such a nature that it seemed as though my love must revive. No sooner had our gondola stopped at the hotel steps than the porter handed me a telegram which the messenger had already brought three times to the hotel, for owing to the inaccurate rendering of the recipient's name (which I recognised nevertheless, through the corruptions introduced by Italian clerks, as my own) the post-office required a signed receipt certifying that the telegram was addressed to myself. I opened it as soon as I was in my own room, and, as I cast my eye over the sheet covered with inaccurately transmitted words, managed, nevertheless, to make out: "My dear, you think me dead, forgive me, I am quite alive, should like to see you, talk about marriage, when do you return? Love. Albertine." Then there occurred in me in inverse order a process parallel to that which had occurred in the case of my grandmother: when I had learned the fact of my grandmother's death, I had not at first felt any grief. And I had been really grieved by her death only when spontaneous memories had made her seem to me to be once again alive. Now that Albertine was no longer alive for me in my mind, the news that she was alive did not cause me the joy that I might have expected. Albertine had been nothing more to me than a bundle of thoughts, she had survived her bodily death so long as those thoughts were alive in me; on the other hand, now that those thoughts were dead, Albertine did not in anyway revive for me, in her bodily form. And when I realised that I felt no joy at the thought of her being alive, that I no longer loved her, I ought to have been more astounded than a person who, looking at his reflection in the glass, after months of travel, or of sickness, discovers that he has white hair and a different face, that of a middleaged or an old man. This appals us because its message is: "the man that I was, the fair young man no longer exists, I am another person".

The night passed. In the morning I gave the telegram back to the hotel porter explaining that it had been brought to me by mistake and that it was not addressed to me. He told me that now that it had been opened he might get into trouble, that it would be better if I kept it; I put it back in my pocket, but determined that I would act as though I had never received it. I had definitely ceased to love Albertine. So that this love after departing so widely from the course that I had anticipated, when I remembered my love for Gilberte, after obliging me to make so long and painful a detour, itself too ended, after furnishing an exception, by merging itself, just like my love for Gilberte, in the general rule of oblivion.

When I heard, on the very day upon which we were due to start for Paris, that Mme Putbus, and consequently her maid, had just arrived in Venice, I asked my mother to put off our departure for a few days; her air of not taking my request into consideration, of not even listening to it seriously, reawakened in my nerves, excited by the Venetian springtime, that old desire to rebel against an imaginary plot woven against me by my parents (who imagined that I would be forced to obey them), that fighting spirit, that desire which drove me in the past to enforce my wishes upon the people whom I loved best in the world, prepared to conform to their wishes after I had succeeded in making them yield. I told my mother that I would not leave Venice, but she, thinking it more to her purpose not to appear to believe that I was saying this seriously, did not even answer. I went on to say that she would soon see whether I was serious or not. And when the hour came at which accompanied by all my luggage, she set off for the station, I ordered a cool drink to be brought out to me on the terrace overlooking the canal, and installed myself there, watching the sunset, while from a boat that had stopped in front of the hotel a musician sang "sole mio."

The sun continued to sink. My mother must be nearing the station. Presently, she would be gone, I should be left alone in Venice, alone with the misery of knowing that I had distressed her, and without her presence to comfort me. The hour of the train approached. My irrevocable solitude was so near at hand that it seemed to me to have begun already and to be complete. For I felt myself to be alone.

This Venice without attraction for myself in which I was going to be left alone, seemed to me no less isolated, no less unreal, and it was my distress which the sound of "sole mio," rising like a dirge for the Venice that I had known, seemed to be calling to witness. No doubt I ought to have ceased to listen to it if I wished to be able to overtake my mother and to join her on the train, I ought to have made up my mind without wasting another instant that I was going, but this is just what I was powerless to do; I remained motionless, incapable not merely of rising, but even of deciding that I would rise from my chair.

But at length, from caverns darker than that from which flashes the comet which we can predict,—thanks to the unimaginable defensive force of inveterate habit, thanks to the hidden reserves which by a sudden impulse habit hurls at the last moment into the fray—my activity was roused at length; I set out in hot haste and arrived, when the carriage doors were already shut, but in time to find my mother flushed with emotion, overcome by the effort to restrain her tears, for she thought that I was not coming. Then the train started and we saw Padua and Verona come to meet us, to speed us on our way, almost on to the platforms of their stations, and, when we had drawn away from them, return—they who were not travelling and were about to resume their normal life—one to its plain the other to its hill.

The hours went by. My mother was in no hurry to read two letters which she had in her hand and had merely opened, and tried to prevent me from pulling out my pocket-book at once so as to take from it the letter which the hotel porter had given me. My mother was always afraid of my finding journeys too long, too tiring, and put off as long as possible, so as to keep me occupied during the final hours, the moment at which she would seek fresh distractions for me; bring out the hard-boiled eggs, hand me newspapers, untie the parcel of books which she had brought without telling me. We had long passed Milan when she decided to read the first of her two letters. I began by watching my mother who sat reading it with an air of astonishment, then raised her head, and her eyes seemed to come to rest upon a succession of distinct, incompatible memories, which she could not succeed in bringing together. Meanwhile I had recognised Gilberte's hand on the envelope which I had just taken from my pocket-book. I opened it. Gilberte wrote to inform me that she was marrying Robert de Saint-Loup. She told me that she had sent me a telegram about it to Venice but had had no reply. I remembered that I had been told that the telegraphic service there was inefficient, I had never received her telegram. Perhaps she would refuse to believe this. All of a sudden, I felt in my brain a fact which had installed itself there in the guise of a memory, leave its place which it surrendered to another fact. The telegram that I had received a few days earlier, and had supposed to be from Albertine, was from Gilberte. As the somewhat laboured originality of Gilberte's handwriting consisted chiefly, when she wrote one line, in introducing into the line above the strokes of her t's which appeared to be underlining the words, or the dots over her i's which appeared to be punctuating the sentence above them, and on the other hand in interspersing the line below with the tails and flourishes of the words immediately above it, it was quite natural that the clerk who dispatched the telegram should have read the tail of an *s* or *z* in the line above as an "—*in*e" attached to the word "Gilberte." 'The dot over the *i* of Gilberte had risen above the word to mark the end of the message." As for her capital G, it resembled a gothic '*A*'. Add that, apart from this, two or three words had been misread, dovetailed into one another (some of them as it happened had seemed to me incomprehensible and this was quite enough to explain the details of my error and was not even necessary.

CHAPTER FOUR

A FRESH LIGHT UPON ROBERT DE SAINT-LOUP

"Oh, it is unheard of," said my mother. "Listen, at my age, one has ceased to be astonished at anything; but I assure you that there could be nothing more unexpected than what I find in this letter." "Listen, first to me;" I replied; "I don't know what it is, but however astonishing it may be, it cannot be quite so astonishing as what I have found in my letter. It is a marriage. It is Robert de Saint-Loup who is marrying Gilberte Swann."

"Ah!" said my mother, "then that is no doubt what is in the other letter, which I have not yet opened for I recognised your friend's hand." "Was I right in telling you that you would find nothing more astonishing?" I asked her. "On the contrary! " she replied in a gentle tone, "it is I who can impart the most extraordinary news." "This letter is to announce the marriage of the Cambremer boy" "Oh!" I remarked with indifference, "to whom? But in any case the personality of the bridegroom robs this marriage of any sensational element." "Unless the bride's personality supplies it."   "And who is the bride in question?" "Ah, if I tell you straight away, that will spoil everything; see if you can guess," said my mother who, seeing that we had not yet reached Turin, wished to keep something in reserve for me as meat and drink for the rest of the journey. "But how do you expect me to know? Is it anyone brilliant? If Legrandin and his sister are satisfied, we may be sure that it is a brilliant marriage." "As for Legrandin, I cannot say, but the person who informs me of the marriage says that Mme de Cambremer is delighted. I don't know whether you will call it a brilliant marriage. To my mind, it suggests the days when kings used to marry shepherdesses, though in this case the shepherdess is even humbler than a shepherdess, charming as she is. It would have stupefied your grandmother, but would, not have shocked her." "But who in the world is this bride?" "It is Mlle d'Oloron." "That sounds to me tremendous and not in the least shepherdessy, but I don't quite gather who she can be. It is a title that used to be in the Guermantes family." "Precisely, and M. de Charlus conferred it, when he adopted her, upon Jupien's niece." "Jupien's niece! It isn't possible!" " It is the reward of virtue. It is a marriage from the last chapter of one of Mme Sand's novels," said my mother. "It is the reward of vice, it is a marriage from the end of a Balzac novel," thought I. "After all," I said to my mother, "when you come to think of it, it is quite natural. Here are the Cambremers established in that Guermantes clan among which they never hoped to pitch their tent; what is more, the girl, adopted by M. de Charlus, will have plenty of money, which was indispensable now that the Cambremers have lost theirs; and after all she is the adopted daughter, and, in the Cambremer's eyes, probably the real daughter—the natural daughter—of a person whom they regard as a Prince of the Blood Royal. A bastard of a semi-royal house has always been regarded as a flattering alliance by the nobility of France and other countries." My mother, without abandoning the caste system of Combray which meant that my grandmother would have been scandalised by such a marriage, being principally anxious to echo her mother's judgment, added: "Anyhow, the girl is worth her weight in gold, and your dear grandmother would not have had to draw upon her immense goodness, her unbounded indulgence, to keep her from condemning young Cambremer's choice. Do you remember how distinguished she thought the girl, years ago, one day when she went into the shop to have a stitch put in her skirt? She was only a child then. And now, even if she has rather run to seed, and become an old-maid; she is a different woman, a thousand-times more perfect. But your grandmother saw all that at a glance. She found the little niece of a jobbing tailor more 'noble' than the Duc de Guermantes." But even more necessary than to extol my grandmother was it for my mother to decide that it was 'better' for her that she had not lived to see the day. This was the supreme triumph of her filial devotion, as though she were sparing my grandmother a final grief. "And yet, can you imagine for a moment," my mother said to me, "what old father Swann—not that you ever knew him, of course—would have felt if he could have known that he would one day have a great-grandchild in whose veins the blood of mother Moser who used to say: 'Ponchour Mezieurs', would mingle with the blood of the Duc de Guise!" "But, listen, Mamma, it is a great deal more surprising than that. For the Swanns were very respectable people; and, given the position that their son occupied, his daughter, if he himself had made a decent marriage, might have married very well indeed. But all her chances were ruined by his marrying a courtesan." "Oh, a courtesan, you know, people were perhaps rather hard on her, I never quite believed............" "Yes, a courtesan, indeed I can let you have some startling revelations one of these days." Lost in meditation, my mother said: "The daughter of a woman to whom your father would never allow me to bow, marrying the nephew of Mme de Villeparisis, upon whom your father wouldn't allow me to call at first because he thought her too grand for me!" Then: "The son of Mme. de Cambremer to whom Legrandin was so afraid of having to give us a letter of introduction because he didn't think us smart enough, marrying the niece of a man who would never dare to come to our flat except by the service stairs!"

What I was to learn later on—for I had been unable to keep in touch with all this affair from Venice—was that Mlle de Forcheville's hand had been sought first of all by the Prince de Silistrie, while Saint-Loup was seeking to marry Mlle d'Entragues, the Duc de Luxembourg's daughter. This is what had occurred. Mlle de Forcheville possessing a hundred million francs, Mme de Marsantes had decided that she would be an excellent match for her son. She made the mistake of saying that the girl was charming, that she herself had not the slightest idea whether she was rich or poor, that she did not wish to know, but that even without a penny it would be a piece of good luck for the most exacting of young men to find such a wife. This was going rather too far for a woman who was tempted only by the hundred millions, which blinded her eyes to everything else. At once it was understood that she was thinking of the girl for her own son. The Princesse de Silistrie went about uttering loud cries, expatiated upon the social importance of Saint-Loup, and proclaimed that if he should marry Odette's daughter by a Jew then there was no longer a Faubourg Saint-Germain. Mme de Marsantes, sure of herself as she was, dared not advance farther and retreated before the cries of the Princesse de Silistrie; who immediately made a proposal in the name of her own son. She had protested only in order to keep Gilberte for herself. Meanwhile Mme de Marsantes, refusing to own herself defeated, had turned at once to Mlle d'Entragues, the Duc de Luxembourg's daughter. Having no more than twenty millions, she suited her purpose less, but Mme de Marsantes told everyone that a Saint-Loup, could not marry a Mlle Swann (there was no longer any mention of Forcheville) Some time later, somebody having carelessly observed that the Duc de Châtellerault was thinking of marrying Mlle d'Entragues, Mme de Marsantes, who was the most captious woman in the world mounted her high horse, changed her tactics, returned to Gilberte, made a formal offer of marriage on Saint-Loup's behalf and the engagement was immediately announced.

Very soon the drawing-room of the new Marquise de Saint-Loup assumed its permanent aspect, from the social point of view at least, for we shall see what troubles were brewing in it in another connection; well, this aspect was surprising for the following reason: people still remembered that the most formal, the most exclusive parties in Paris, as brilliant as those given by the Marquise de Guermantes, were those of Mme de Marsantes, Saint-Loup's mother. On the other hand, in recent years, Odette's drawing-room, infinitely lower in the social scale, had been no less dazzling in its elegance and splendour. Saint-Loup, however, delighted to have, thanks to his wife's vast fortune, everything that he could desire in the way of comfort, wished only to rest quietly in his armchair after a good dinner with a musical entertainment by good performers. And this young man who had seemed at one time so proud, so ambitious, invited to share his luxury old friends whom his mother would not have admitted to her house. Gilberte, on her side, put into effect Swann's saying: "Quality doesn't matter, what I dread is quantity." And Saint-Loup, always on his knees before his wife, because he loved her, and because it was to her that he owed these extremes of comfort, took care not to interfere with tastes that were so similar to his own. With the result that the great receptions given by Mme de Marsantes and Mme de Forcheville, given year after year with an eye chiefly to the establishment, upon a brilliant footing, of their children, gave rise to no reception by M. and Mme de Saint-Loup. They had the best of saddle-horses on which to go out riding together, the finest of yachts in which to cruise—but they never took more than a couple of guests with them. In Paris, every evening, they would invite three or four friends to dine, never more; with the result, that by an unforeseen but at the same time quite natural retrogression, the two vast maternal aviaries had been replaced by a silent nest.

The person who profited least by these two marriages was the young Mademoiselle d'Oloron who, already suffering from typhoid fever on the day of the religious ceremony, was barely able to crawl to the church and died a few weeks later. The letter of intimation that was sent out some time after her death blended with names such as Jupien's those of almost all the greatest families in Europe, such as the Vicomte and Vicomtesse de Montmorency, H.R.H. the Comtesse de Bourbon-Soissons, the Prince of Modena Este, the Vicomtesse d'Edumea, Lady Essex, and so forth. No doubt even to a person who knew that the deceased was Jupien's niece, this plethora of grand connections would not cause any surprise. The great thing, after all, is to have grand connections. Then, the *casus foederis* coming into play, the death of a simple little shop-girl plunges all the princely families of Europe in mourning.

TIME REGAINED

CHAPTER ONE
TANSONVILLE

About this time I used to see a good deal of Gilberte with whom I had renewed my old intimacy: for our life, in the long run, is not calculated according to the duration of our friendships. Let a certain period of time elapse and you will see reappear (just as former Ministers reappear in politics, as old plays are revived on the stage) friendly relations that have been revived between the same persons as before, after long years of interruption, and revived with pleasure. After ten years, the reasons which made one party love too passionately, the other unable to endure a too exacting despotism, no longer exist. Convention alone survives, and everything that Gilberte would have refused me in the past, that had seemed to her intolerable, impossible, she granted me quite readily—doubtless because I no longer desired it. Although neither of us avowed to themselves the reason for this change, if she was always ready to come to me, never in a hurry to leave me, it was because the obstacle had vanished: my love.

I had heard that Gilberte was unhappy, betrayed by Robert, but not in the fashion which everyone supposed; Robert, a true nephew of M. de Charlus, went about openly with women whom he compromised, whom the world believed and whom Gilberte supposed more or less to be his mistresses. It was even thought in society that he was too barefaced, never stirring, at a party, from the side of some woman whom he afterwards accompanied home, leaving Mme de Saint-Loup to return as best she might. Anyone who had said that the other woman whom he compromised thus was not really his mistress would have been regarded as a fool, incapable of seeing what was staring him in the face, but I had been pointed, alas, in the direction of the truth, a truth which caused me infinite distress, by a few words let fall by Jupien.

What had been my amazement, when, having gone, a few months before my visit to Tansonville to enquire about M. de Charlus, in whom certain cardiac symptoms had been causing his friends great anxiety and having mentioned to Jupien, whom I found by himself, some love letters addressed to Robert and signed Bobette which Mme de Saint-Loup had discovered, I learned from the Baron's former factotum that the person who used the signature Bobette was none other than the violinist who had played so important a part in the life of M. de

Charlus. Jupien could not speak of him without indignation:

"The boy was free to do what he chose. But if there was one direction in which he ought never to have looked, that was the Baron's nephew. All the more so as the Baron, loved his nephew like his own son. He has tried to separate the young couple, it is scandalous. And he must have gone about it with the most devilish cunning, for no one was ever more opposed to that sort of thing than the Marquis de Saint-Loup. To think of all the mad things he has done for his mistress! No, that wretched musician may have deserted the Baron, as he did, by a mean trick, I don't mind saying; still, that was his business. But to take up with the nephew, there are certain things that are not done."

If Jupien traced back to a quite recent origin the fresh orientation, so divergent from their original course, that Robert's carnal desires had assumed, a conversation which I had with Aimé and which made me very miserable, showed me that the headwaiter at Balbec traced this divergence, this inversion, to a far earlier date. He was speaking to me of a far earlier time when I had made Saint-Loup's acquaintance, through Mme de Villeparisis, at this same Balbec. "Why, surely, sir," he said to me, "it is common knowledge, I have known it for ever so long. The year when Monsieur came first to Balbec, M. le Marquis shut himself up with my lift-boy, on the excuse of developing some photographs of Monsieur's grandmother. The boy made a complaint, we had the greatest difficulty in hushing the matter up. I am convinced that, if Aimé was not lying consciously, he was entirely mistaken; either the lift-boy had lied, or it was Aimé who was lying. Had it not been that the thought distressed me, I should have found a refreshing irony in the fact that, whereas to me sending the lift-boy to Saint-Loup had been the most convenient way of conveying a letter to him and receiving his answer, to him it had meant making the acquaintance of a person who had taken his fancy. Everything, indeed, is at least twofold. Upon the most insignificant action that we perform, another man will graft a series of entirely different actions; it is certain that Saint-Loup's adventure with the lift-boy, if it occurred, no more seemed to me to be involved in the commonplace dispatch of my letter than a man, who knew nothing of Wagner save the duet in *Lohengrin,* would be able to foresee the prelude to *Tristan.*

I was convinced that Saint-Loup's physical evolution had not begun at that period and that he then had been still exclusively a lover of women. More than by any other sign, I could tell this retrospectively by the friendship that Saint-Loup had shewn for myself at Balbec. It was only while he was in love with women that he was really capable of friendship. Afterwards, for some time at least, to the men who did not attract him physically he dispayed an indifference which was to some extent, I believe, sincere--for he had become very curt—and which he exaggerated as well in order to make people think that he was only interested in women. But I remember all the same that one day at Doncières as I was on my way to dine with the Verdurins, and after he had been gazing rather markedly at Morel, he had said to me; "Curious, that fellow, he reminds me in some ways of Rachel. Don't you see the likeness? To my mind, they are identical in certain respects. Not that it can make any difference to me." But if Robert found certain traces of Rachel in Charlie, Gilberte, for her part, sought to present some similarity to Rachel, so as to attract her husband, wore like her bows of scarlet or pink or yellow ribbon in her hair, which she dressed in a similar style, for she believed that her husband was still in love with Rachel, and so was jealous of her. That Robert's love may have hovered at times over the boundary which divides the love of a man for a woman from the love of a man for a man was quite possible. He remained no less attached to Rachel than before and paid her scrupulously but without any pleasure the enormous allowance that he had promised her, not that this prevented her from treating him in the most abominable fashion later on. This generosity towards Rachel would not have distressed Gilberte if she had known that it was merely the resigned fulfilment of a promise which no longer bore any trace of love. But love was, on the contrary, precisely what he pretended to feel for Rachel. Homosexuals would be the best husbands in the world if they did not make a show of being in love with other women.

    Mme de Forcheville would have preferred a more brilliant, perhaps a princely marriage for Gilberte (there were royal families that were impoverished and would have accepted the dowry) and a son-in-law less depreciated in social value by a life spent in comparative seclusion. She had not been able to prevail over Gilberte's determination, had complained bitterly to all and sundry, denouncing her son-in-law. One fine day she had changed her tune, her son-in-law had become an angel, nothing was ever said against him except in private. The fact was that age had left unimpaired in Mme Swann, (become Mme de Forcheville) the need that she had always felt of financial support, but, by the desertion of her admirers, had deprived her of the means. She longed every day for another necklace, a new dress stuidded with brilliants, a more sumptuous motor-car, but she had only a small income, Forcheville having made away with most of it, and—what Israelite strain controlled Gilberte in this?—she had an adorable, but fearfully avaricious daughter who counted every penny she gave her husband, not to mention her mother. Well, all of a sudden Odette discerned, and then found her natural protector in Robert. That she was no longer in her first youth mattered little to a son-in-law who was not a lover of women. All he asked of his mother-in-law was to smooth down some little difficulty that had arisen beteen Gilberte and himself, to obtain his wife's consent to his going for a holiday with Morel. Odette had lent her services and was at once rewarded with a magnificent ruby. To pay for this, it was necessary that Gilberte should treat her husband more generously. Odette preached this doctrine to her with all the more fervour in that it was she herself would benefit from her daughter's generosity. Thus thanks to Robert, she was enabled, on the threshold of her fifties (some people said, of her sixties) to dazzle every table at which she dined, every party at which she appeared, with an unparalleled splendour without needing to have, as in the past, a "friend" who now would no longer have stood for it, in other words have paid the piper. And so she had entered finally, it appeared, into a period of ultimate chastity, and yet she had never been so smart.

It was not merely the malice, the rancour of the once poor boy against the master who has enriched him and has moreover made him feel the difference of their positions, that had made Charlie turn to Saint-Loup in order to add to the Baron's sorrows. He may also have had an eye to his own profit. I formed the impression that Robert must be giving him a great deal of money.

Tears came to my eyes when I reflected that I had felt in the past for a different Saint-Loup an affection which had been so great and which I could see quite well from the cold and evasive manner which he now adopted, that he no longer felt for me, since men, now that they were capable of arousing his desires, could no longer inspire his friendship. How could these tastes have come to birth in a young man who had been so passionate a lover of a woman that I had seen him brought to a state of almost suicidal frenzy because "Rachel, when from the Lord" had threatened to leave him? Had the resemblance between Charlie and Rachel—invisible to me—been the plank which had enabled Robert to pass from his father's tastes to those of his uncle, to complete the physiological evolution which even in his uncle had occurred quite late in life?

I recalled his affection for myself, his tender, sentimental way of expressing it, and told myself that this also, which might have deceived anyone else, meant at the time something quite different, indeed the direct opposite of what I had just learned about him. But from when did the change date? If it had occurred before my return to Balbec, how was it that he had never once come to see the lift- boy, had never once mentioned him to me? And as for the first year, how could he have paid any attentionto the boy, passionately enamoured as he then was of Rachel? The first year I had found Saint-Loup peculiar, as was every true Guermantes. Now he was even more individual than I had supposed. The doubt that Aimé's word had left in my mind tarnished all our friendship at Balbec and Doncières.

   I went to spend a few days at Tansonville where we dined now at an hour at which in the past I had long been asleep at Combray. And this on account of the heat of the sun. And also because, as Gilberte spent the afternoon painting in the chapel attached to the house, we did not take our walks until about two hours before dinner.

   What struck me most forcibly was how little, during this visit, I lived over again my childish years, how little I desired to see Combray, how meagre and ugly I thought the Vivonne. But where Gilberte made some of the things come true that I had imagined about the Méséglise way was during one or those walks which, after all, were nocturnal even if we took them before dinner—for she dined so late. I said to her: "You were speaking the other day of the little footpath; how I loved you then!" She replied: "Why didn't you tell me? I had no idea of it. I was in love with you. Indeed, I flung myself twice at your head." "When?" "The first time at Tansonville, you were taking a walk with your family, I was on my way home, I had never seen such a dear little boy. I was in the habit;" she went on with a vague air of modesty, "of going out to play with little boys I knew in the ruins of the keep of Roussainville. And you will tell me that I was a very naughty girl, for there were girls and boys there of all sorts who took advantage of the darkness. The altar-boy from Combray church, Theodore, who, I am bound to confess, was very nice indeed (Heavens, how charming he was!) and who has become quite ugly (he is the chemist now at Méséglise), used to amuse himself with all the peasant girls of the district. As they let me go out by myself, whenever I was able to get away, I used to fly there. I can't tell you how I longed for you to come there too; I remember quite well that, as I had only a moment in which to make you understand what I wanted, at the risk of being seen by your people and mine, I signalled to you so vulgarly that I am ashamed of it to this day. But you stared at me so crossly that I saw that you didn't want it." And, all of a sudden, I said to myself that the true Gilberte—the true Albertine—were perhaps those who had at the first moment yielded themselves in their facial expression, one behind the hedge of pink hawthorn, the other upon the beach. And it was I who, having been incapable of understanding this, having failed to recapture the impression until much later in my memory after an interval in which, as a result of our conversations, a dividing hedge of sentiment had made them afraid to be as frank as in the first moments—had ruined everything by my clumsiness. I had lost them more completely— albeit, to tell the truth, the comparative failure with them was less absurd—for the same reasons that had made Saint-Loup lose Rachel.

"And the second time," Gilberte went on, "was years later when I passed you in the doorway of your house, a couple of days before I met you again at my aunt Oriane's, I didn't recognise you at first, or rather I did unconsciously recognise you because I felt the same longing that I had felt at Tansonville." "But between these two occasions there were, after all, in the Champs—Elysées." "Yes, but there you were too fond of me, I felt that you were spying upon me all the time." I did not ask her at the moment who the young man was with whom she had been walking along the Avenue des Champs-Elysées, on the day on which I had started out to call upon her, on which I would have been reconciled with her while there was still time, that day which would perhaps have changed the whole course of my life, if I had not caught sight of those two shadowy forms advancing towards me side by side in the dusk.

Long after the time of this conversation, I asked Gilberte with whom she had been walking along the Avenue des Champs-Elysées on the evening on which I had sold the bowl: it was Léa in male attire. Gilberte knew that she was acquainted with Albertine, but could not tell me any more. Thus it is that certain persons always reappear in our life to herald our pleasures or our griefs.

CHAPTER TWO

M. de CHARLUS
During the war, his opinions, his pleasures

On one of the first evenings after I had returned to Paris in 1916, as I wished to hear people talk about the war, the only subject that was of interest to me, I went to see Mme Verdurin after dinner because she had become one of the queens of wartime Paris as if it were the Directoire of 1795. The ladies of that time had a queen who was young and beautiful and was called Mme Tallien. Now there were two who were old and ugly and were called Mme Verdurin and Mme Bontemps.

The duchesses who were to be found nowadays at Mme Verdurin's came, although they were not aware of it, for the same thing that the 'Dreyfusards' had sought, namely the pleasure of satisfying their political curiosity and meeting their need to talk among themselves about the stories they had read in the newspapers. Mme Verdurin would say "Come at five o'clock to talk about the war" in the same way as she used to say "talk about things" and "in the interval, you will listen to Morel." However Morel had no right to be there as he had not been discharged from military service. He had simply not rejoined his unit and was a deserter but no-one knew this.

Whenever I was at Mme Verdurin's, she would try to introduce me to Andrée, not wanting to recognize that I had known her for a long time. However Andrée came rarely with her husband but she was still a very good and sincere friend. Following her husband's aesthetic taste which rejected the Ballets Russes, she said of the Marquise de Polignac "he had his house decorated by Bakst; how can he manage to sleep there! I much prefer Dubuffe." However the Verdurins, in the fatal process of fashion which ends by finishing back where it started, said that they couldn't abide the modern style, particularly as it came from Munich, nor the white walls and only liked antique French furniture with dark walls.

It was very surprising at this time when Mme Verdurin was able to attract anyone she chose to come to her house, to see her make indirect advances to someone with whom she had completely lost contact, Odette. It did not seem possible that she could add anything to the brilliant society that the 'little group' had become. A long separation, as well as easing old grievances, sometimes revives friendship. And then the phenomenon which not only leads the dying to speak only of long familiar names but also brings the elderly to dwell in their childhood memories has a parallel in social affairs. In order to succeed in the attempt to get Odette to visit her again, Mme Verdurin didn't use her most faithful supporters but the less faithful who had also kept in touch with other salons. She said "I don't know why I never see her here, perhaps she is annoyed with me, I have no quarrel with her. What have I ever done to her. She has met both her husbands at my house. If she wants to come back, she knows the door is open" These words which would have wounded the 'Mistress' if they hadn't been dictated by her own imagination, were passed on but without success. Mme. Verdurin waited in vain for Odette to come until other events, which we will hear of later, brought her for quite other reasons.

The Verdurin salon, whilst it kept the same spirit, had moved for the time being to one of the largest hotels of Paris, as the shortage of heat and light had made it too difficult to hold receptions in their old home, the former Venetian Embassy, which was dripping with damp. The new salon lacked for nothing in comfort, the narrow dining room, which Mme. Verdurin used at the hotel, was an irregular shape with startling white walls, like a screen against which, every Wednesday and nearly every other day, all the most interesting, the most varied, the most elegant women of Paris delighted to benefit from the wealth of the Verdurins, which thanks to good luck, was increasing at a time when the richest were cutting back as they couldn't get at their income. The form taken by the receptions had changed, without ceasing to enchant Brichot, who as the Verdurins' influence grew, found new and increasing pleasures in the confined space, like the surprises in a Christmas stocking. On some days there were so many for dinner that the private dining room was not large enough and dinner was served in the large dining room on the floor below, where the faithful, hypocritically bemoaning the loss of the intimacy of the upstairs room, were in fact delighted----by making a privileged group as they used to when they travelled on the little railway----to be the object of envy for all the tables around. Without doubt, in normal peacetime, an item of gossip sent privately to the Figaro or the Gaulois would have told all the world, which could not get into the dining room at the Majestic, that M. Brichot had dined with the Duchess of Duras. Since the war, the gossip columnists had supressed that sort of information (they filled their space with funerals, citations and Franco-American banquets), publicity was only possible by childish and limited methods as in the Middle Ages before the invention of printing, by being seen at the Verdurin's table. After dinner, everyone went up to the 'Mistress's salon and the telephoning started. Most of the grand hotels at this time were full of spies who took note of the news telephoned by M. Bontemps with an indiscretion whose lack of security about his information was fortunately balanced by its inaccuracy.

The restaurants were full for dinner in the evenings and if I saw, passing by in the street, a poor chap on leave from the front, released for six days from the continuous threat of death and due to return to the trenches, glance for a moment at the brightly lit windows, I suffered as at the hotel at Balbec where the fishermen used to watch us dine, but I suffered more because I knew that the misery of the soldiers was greater than that of the poor, uniting them all, more touching still and more noble; it was with a philosophic nod of the head, without resentment, that he who was about to return to the war, looking at the bustle of those hunting for tables, said "You wouldn't know there was a war on here would you?"

Then at nine thirty, although no-one had had time to finish their dinner, all the lights were turned off by order of the police and in this restaurant where I had dined with Saint-Loup one evening during his leave, by nine thirtyfive there was another rush to gather up overcoats from the cloakroom attendants which took place in a mysterious gloom like that of a room where magic lantern slides are being shown or like that of the cinemas to which all the diners were rushing. But after that hour, for those who, like me on the evening of which I speak, had dined at home before going out to visit friends, Paris was even darker, at least in some quarters, than it had been in the Combray of my childhood. The visits that I made were like visits made to neighbours in the countryside such as when Swann used to visit us after dinner, without meeting anyone in the darkness of Tansonville on the little rural lane leading to the rue St Esprit and now I met no-one in the streets from rue de la Clotilde to the rue Bonaparte.

I had visited Paris in 1914 for a medical consultation and I had then returned very soon to my nursing home. Although my doctor's treatment was based on isolation, I had been given a letter from Gilberte. Gilberte had written to me (this was about September 1914) that although she had wished to stay in Paris in order to get news of Robert more easily, the regular raids around Paris had worried her so much, particularly about her daughter that she had left Paris on the last train which went to Combray; it did not even reach Combray and it was only thanks to a farmers cart on which she had made a terrible journey of ten hours that she had been able to reach Tansonville. "And here, think what awaited your old friend" Gilberte's letter to me ended "I had left Paris in order to escape the German planes, thinking that at Tansonville I should be safe. I hadn't been there more than two days, when, you wouldn't believe it, but the Gernans arrived who had invaded the area after defeating our troops near to La Fere, and a German Staff Officer followed by a regiment appeared at the gates of Tansonville which I was obliged to accommodate with no chance of escaping, not by train or anyhow."

Was the German officer so well behaved or was it possible to see in Gilberte's letter something connected to the spirit of the Guermantes who were of Bavarian stock and connected to the highest German aristocracy? Gilberte emphasised the good behaviour of the officers and even that of the soldiers who had only "asked for permission to gather forget-me-nots from the side of the lake"; good behaviour which she contrasted to the violent disorder of the French refugees who had invaded the estate destroying everything before the arrival of the main German army.

Now on my second return to Paris, on the day after my arrival, I had received another letter from Gilberte who had obviously forgotten the letter I have just referred to or at least had forgotten what she said in it, for her departure from Paris at the end of 1914 was now described in hindsight in a very different way. "You perhaps do not know, my dear friend" she wrote to me "that it will soon be two years that I have been at Tansonville. I got there at the same time as the Germans. Everyone had tried to stop me leaving. They thought I was mad. Look, they said, you are safe in Paris and you are thinking of leaving for the battleground, just at the moment when everyone else is trying to escape. I didn't think that this criticism was at all fair. Never mind, if I have only one good point, I am not a coward, or if you prefer, I am loyal and when I know that my dear Tansonville was threatened, I couldn't bear to leave our old steward to defend it on his own. I thought it was my place to be at his side. It is thanks to this determination that I have been able to save the chateau to some extent-- when all the others in the neighbourhood , abandoned by their frantic owners have nearly all been razed to the ground---and not only the chateau but the precious collection which my darling father held so dear." In short, Gilberte was now convinced that she had not gone to Tansonville, as she had written to me in 1914, to flee from the Germans and to get to a place of refuge but on the contrary to defend her chateau from them. They were not still at Tansonville but she hadn't ceased to have a regular coming and going of soldiers at her home which was much greater than that in the streets of Combray which brought tears to Françoise's eyes, and to lead as she said, this time with truth, the life of the front. There were reports in the newspapers describing her conduct in glowing terms and suggesting that she should get a medal. The end of her letter was absolutely correct. "You haven't any idea of what this war is like, my dear, and the importance which gets attached to a road, a bridge, a piece of high ground. Sometimes I have thought of you on the walks which you made so pleasant and which we took together in the countryside, which has now been devastated by the immense battles for that road, for that place you loved where we went together so often. Probably you would be the same as I, you wouldn't think that the obscure Rousainville and the boring Méséglise from where our letters came and where we went to find the doctor when you were ill, would ever become famous places. Indeed my dear, they haven't achieved fame of the same order as Austerlitz or Valmy. The battle of Méséglise lasted more than eight months, the German casualties were more than a hundred thousand men, they destroyed Méséglise but they never took it. The little road that you loved so much, that we called the hawthorn rise and where you pretended to have fallen in love with me in your childhood, even though as I have told you, it was I who had fallen in love with you, I cannot tell you how important it became. The great field of corn which it ran beside is the famous 'Hill 307' which you have heard of so often in the official bulletins. The French blew up the little bridge over the Vivonne which you said didn't remind you of your childhood as much as you would have wished, the Germans replaced it, for a year and a half, they held half of Combray and the French, the other."

 The evening of the day when I received this letter, while pondering about these memories, Saint-Loup fresh from the front and on the point of returning there, came to see me for just a few moments; the news that he was coming to see me had moved me strongly. When he came into my room, I had approached him with some sense of nervousness; he had that stamp of the supernatural which marked all those on leave from the front which we experience when we meet someone struck with a fatal illness, who however still gets up, dresses himself and goes out for a walk. It seemed that there was something almost cruel in the short leaves given to the fighting soldiers. To start with, one thought "They won't want to go back, they will desert" And indeed they didn't just come from places which seemed unreal to us because we had only read about them in the newspapers and that we could not imagine that they had been taking part in these titanic combats and had returned with only a bruised shoulder; they had come among us for an instant from the shores of death to which they would return, impossible for us to understand, filling us with a feeling of mystery, like the dead we summon, who appear for a moment, who we do not dare to interrogate and who would at most be able to reply "You would not be able to imagine."

I worked out that Robert had found alternatives in the army which had gradually made him forget that Morel had behaved as badly to him as he had to his uncle. However he had preserved a great friendship for him and felt a great desire to see him again which he kept on putting off. I thought it kinder to Gilberte not to tell Robert that if he wanted to meet Morel, he had only to go to Mme Verdurin's house.

All the time I had been remembering Saint-Loup's visit I had kept on walking and then in order to go to Mme. Verdurin's house had made a long detour; I was nearly at the Pont des Invalides. Once I had left the bridge behind me, there was no more day in the sky and there was hardly any light in the town; stumbling here and there into the dustbins, mistaking one road for another, I followed a network of little streets and then surprised myself by arriving on the boulevards. There an impression of 1815 took over from the Directoire. Just as in 1815, it was a very mixed procession in the uniforms of the troops from all the allies, among them the Africans in baggy red trousers, of Hindus in white turbans which were enough for me to create from the Paris where I was walking, an exotic imaginary city, in an Orient with no precise detail of dress and skin colour, but arbitrarily imaginary in setting, just as the town where Carpaccio lived became a Jerusalem or a Constantinople when he assembled there a marvellously mixed throng which wasn't more coloured than the one before me. Walking behind two Zouaves, who didn't seem to be taking any notice of him, I observed a large fat man in a soft felt hat, a long overcoat and a purple complexion to which I wondered if I should give the name of an actor or of a painter equally known for many homosexual scandals. In any case I was certain that I did not know the promenader, so I was very surprised when our glances met to see that he had an uncomfortable air and made a show of stopping and coming up to me like someone who wanted to demonstrate that you have not surprised them in doing something they would have preferred to have kept secret. For a moment I wondered who was saying 'hello' to me: it was M. de Charlus. In his case, the evolution of his illness or the revolution of his vice had reach the extreme point where the little original self, his inherited qualities, had been entirely overtaken by the defects or genetic evil which accompanied them. M. de Charlus had gone as far as it was possible to go from himself, or perhaps he had so completely taken on the mask of what he had become, which was a mask worn not just by him but by many other inverts as well, that I had mistaken him for another of that type, following the Zouaves on the open street, for another of them who was not M. de Charlus, not a grand lord, not a man of culture and imagination, whose only resemblance to the Baron was this mask common to them all, which now belonged to him as well and, until I looked more closely, covered him completely.

It was thus that, intending to visit Mme. Verdurin, I had met M. de Charlus. Certainly I should not have found him at her house as in the past; their quarrel had only become worse and Mme. Verdurin made use of current events to discredit him even more. Having said for a long time that she found him common, finished, more unfashionable in his assumed insolence than the most pompous, she now combined this condemnation and disgust for him by saying he was 'pre-war'. The war had put a gulf between him and the present according to the 'little clan' which put him into a completely dead past. On the other hand,---and this was addressed to the political world which was less well informed---she described him as a complete outsider both from social and intellectual society. "He sees no-one, no-one receives him" she said to M. Bontemps whom she easily persuaded. There was some truth in these words. M. de Charlus' situation had changed. Being less and less about the world, being quarrelsome by crotchety nature and having , by awareness of his social status, disdained to be reconciled with most of those who were the cream of society, he lived in an isolation, which was not caused , as that in which Mme. de Villeparisis died, by aristocratic ostracism, but by what was worse to the eyes of the public, for two reasons. It was now well known that M. de Charlus had a bad reputation which made those not well informed think that that was the reason for people not meeting him, but it was his own choice not to circulate; so the effect of his own bilious nature appeared to be that of the contempt of those on whom he exercised it.

In brief, people in society were disenchanted with M. de Charlus not because they understood him too well but because they had never understood his rare intellectual quality. They found 'pre-war' unfashionable because those who were the most incapable of judging its merits were those most ready to accept the dictates of fashion; they had not probed the depths of, not even touched the surface of, the men of quality of the previous generation and now they were condemning them en bloc because this was now the fashion of a new generation that they will not understand any better. As for the further accusation, that of being a German sympathiser, the middle of the road tendency of the fashionable world made them reject it, but it found a cruel and determined interpreter in Morel who having been able to protect the position in the press and in society which M.de Charlus had established for him by taking twice as much effort to set it up as it would take later to destroy it, pursued the Baron with an implacable hatred; it was not just cruel on Morel's part but doubly reprehensible, as whatever his precise relationship with the Baron had been, he had experienced the Baron's deep kindness which he normally hid from everyone.

Even if M.de Charlus and Mme. Verdurin never met now, both---with some small differences of no great importance---continued as if nothing had changed; Mme. Verdurin to receive her guests, M.de Charlus to pursue his pleasures; for example at Mme. Verdurin's, Cottard now appeared at the receptions in the uniform of a Colonel from a production of 'l'Ile du Rêve' which was similar to that of an Haitian Admiral and wearing a large sky blue sash recalling those of 'The Children of Mary'; as for M.de Charlus, he found himself in a city from which all the older men, who up to now had been his preference, had disappeared and he had imitated those Frenchmen, who had been lovers of women in France, but when they moved to the colonies had been forced by necessity to take up, first the habit and then a taste for, little boys.

The first of these characteristics of the Verdurin salon disappeared very quickly when Cottard died 'facing the enemy' according to the newspapers, even though he had never left Paris, but he was indeed very overworked for his age; he was followed soon after by M. Verdurin, whose death caused grief to only one person who was, would you believe it, Elstir!

So the Verdurins held their dinners (Mme.Verdurin carried on by herself after M. Verdurin's death) and M.de Charlus followed his pleasures, without any concern that the Germans---held back by a bloody barrier that was continually being renewed---were only an hours drive from Paris. One might think that Mme.Verdurin thought of them when she held her political salons, when they discussed every evening the situation of both the armies and of the fleets. They thought in fact of the hecatombs of the destroyed regiments, of the drowned passengers, but by an inverse operation, those things that concern our own wellbeing are magnified many times and those that do not affect us directly, are greatly diminished so that the death of millions of unknowns disturbs us only a little and is almost less worrying than a cold draught. Mme. Verdurin who suffered from migrains because she wasn't able to find croissants to dip in her morning coffee, had obtained from Cottard a permit which allowed her to have some made in the restaurant to which we have referred earlier. This had been almost as difficult to procure from the authorities as the appointment of a general. She collected her first croissant on the same morning as the sinking of the Lusitania. Whilst dipping her croissant in the coffee and folding her newspaper so that would prop itself open leaving her other hand free to dip her croissant she exclaimed, "How shocking! This is far worse than the most horrifying plays" But the drowning of all these people must have seemed minimised a thousandfold because with these grievous thoughts on her mind and at the same time filling her mouth, the look which passed over her face, probably produced by the croissant which was so effective against the migraine, was on balance, one of a gentle satisfaction.

After the air-raid last night, when the sky had been more disturbed than the earth, it was as calm as the sea after a storm. But like the sea after a storm, it had not returned to absolute peace. Aeroplanes still climbed like rockets towards the stars and searchlights marched slowly across the sky divided by a blade of stardust, like an errant milky way. The aeroplanes seemed to become part of the constellations and one might almost have been transported to another hemisphere seeing all these new stars. M.de Charlus told me of his admiration for these pilots but as he did so, he couldn't prevent himself giving vent to his pro-German feelings nor conceal his other tendencies both of which he denied. He said "I also admire the German pilots who fly the Gothas and the Zeppelins, think of the courage it takes. They are just heroes. Perhaps they do drop their bombs on civilians but then our anti-aircraft batteries fire at them. Aren't you afraid of the Gothas and the bombing? The Parisians don't seem to be worried about them. Someone told me that Mme.Verdurin gives parties every day, I only know that because someone mentioned it to me, I know absolutely nothing about them, I have broken off with them completely," he added. "These parties will seem , if the Germans continue to advance, to be the last days of our Pompei. I think we might share tomorrow the fate of the towns of Vesuvius whose women thought they were threatened with the fate of the cursed cities of the plains in the Bible. They have found an inscription on the walls of one of the villas of Pompei saying Sodom and Gomorra."

I don't know if it was the name of Sodom or the bombing which made M.deCharlus lift his eyes for a moment to the sky but he soon looked down to earth again. "I admire all the heroes of this war" he said "Look here, my dear chap, these English soldiers of whom I thought nothing at the beginning of the war, just simple football players who presumed to compare themselves with the professionals---and what professionals---well now they are aesthetically like Greek athletes, I really mean the ancient Greeks, my dear, they are like Plato's young men or perhaps rather the Spartans. I have a friend who has been to their camp at Rouen. He has seen prodigies, yes real prodigies, you have no idea. Its not Rouen any more, its quite another place, obviously there is still the old Rouen with its emaciated saints on the cathedral, its still beautiful but quite another thing. And then our French 'poilus', I can't tell you what excitement I find in our 'poilus', the little boys from Paris, look, like that one passing now, with his sharp air, his smart and funny manner. I often fancy stopping them to have a chat, what tact, what good sense; and how amusing and polite the lads from the provinces are, with their rolling rr's and their regional slang.... I have always spent a lot of time in the countryside myself, sleeping in farms, I know how to get on with them; but our admiration for the French musn't make us undervalue our enemies, that would diminish us as well. You don't know what sort of soldiers the Germans are, if you haven't seen them as I have, goosestepping down the 'Unter den Linden'.

"Now", he said "I must leave you". He stopped for an instant to say goodbye and taking me by the hand, squeezed it hard which is a habit common to Germans of the Baron's tendency, and he continued to crush it for a little while, as Cottard would have said, as if M.de Charlus had wished to revive a suppleness in my joints that they had never lost.

When the Baron left me, I began to get the feeling of an oriental evening as in 'A Thousand and One Nights' which I used to like so much and, as I got lost in the network of dark streets, I thought of Caliph al Raschid in search of adventures in the unknown quarters of Baghdad. The warm weather and the effort of walking had made me thirsty but all the bars had been closed for some time and because of the fuel shortage, the few taxis that I saw, driven by Asians or Negroes, wouldn't even bother to respond to my signals. My only hope of finding a drink to give me enough strength to get home, would be a hotel but in this street so far from the centre that I had now reached, all the hotels had closed due to the bombing. So had nearly all the shops, whose owners, without staff or driven by fear to flee to the country had left a handwritten notice to say they would reopen at some distant and doubtful date. Those businesses still open had similar notices to say that they would only be open twice a week. I felt that misery, surrender and fear had taken over the quarter. I couldn't have been more surprised to see among these deserted houses, that there was still one where life seemed to have defeated fright and bankruptcy, bringing activity and prosperity. Behind shuttered windows, lights, covered to comply with the blackout regulations, were turned on with no regard for economy. Every minute the door opened to let some new visitor in or out. This was a hotel which must rouse the envy of all the neighbouring businesses because of the money its owners would be earning.

My attention was caught when I saw an officer leaving it, about twenty yards in front of me, although it was too dark for me to be able to recognise him. Something about him struck me even though I could not see his face, nor his uniform, which was hidden under a greatcoat. It was the extraordinary contrast between the great number of points which his body passed and the tiny number of seconds which his exit took; he gave the appearance of someone attempting flight during a siege. Even if I couldn't identify him properly, perhaps it was the shape, the slimness, the bearing or the speed, or some quality special to him, that made me think it must be Saint-Loup. This officer, capable of occupying so many different points in space in so little time, disappeared up a side street without noticing me and I was left asking myself whether or not to enter this hotel, whose modest appearance made me very doubtful whether it could have been Saint-Loup whom I had seen leaving it. Then I remembered that Saint-Loup had been unjustly mixed up in a spy scandal because his name had been found in some letters taken from a German officer. The authorities had treated him fairly at the time but in spite of myself, I made a connection between that and what I had just seen. Perhaps this hotel was a rendevous for spies! The officer had only just gone when I saw a group of privates from various units enter the hotel which added weight to my suspicions. On the other hand, I was extremely thirsty. I said to myself "I might be able to get a drink here" which gave me a reason to satisfy my curiosity in spite of the anxiety which was mixed with it. I do not think it was curiosity about the encounter which made me decide to climb the stairs as far as the door of a small room which stood open, no doubt because it was so warm. I thought at first that I wouldn't be able to satisfy my curiosity because I saw a number of people asking for a room who were told that there were none left but I soon realised that this must be because they didn't belong to the spy ring as a moment or two later an ordinary seaman came up and was immediately offered No 28. I was able, thanks to the darkness, to watch unobserved, some soldiers and two workmen who were chatting quietly in a small stuffy room, covered with coloured pin-ups of women cut from magazines and illustrated reviews; these chaps were exchanging patriotic ideas: "we don't really have any choice, we will have to do the same as all the rest" one of them said; another, responding to a good luck wish that I had not heard, said "that's OK, I don't think I'm going to be killed"(I gathered he would be returning to a dangerous posting next day) "after all, I am only twenty two years old, and I haven't done six months yet, it wouldn't be fair"; his tone showed even more than the wish to live for a long time, his confidence that natural justice and the fact that he was only twenty two years old, gave him a better chance of not being killed and that it ought to be impossible for him to be killed. "Its amazing in Paris" said another, "one wouldn't know there was a war on. Are you still going to join up, Julot?" "Of course I will. I want to go and knock some sense into the dirty Boches." "Now Joffre, there's a man who sleeps with Ministers' wives, he's not a man who has achieved anything". "Its dreadful to hear people talking like that" said a pilot, who was a little older turning towards the workmen who had been making these comments; "You had better not talk like that when you get to the front, if the 'poilus' hear you, you will be for it!"

The banality of this talk didn't make me want to hear any more of it and I was just going to go on in or back downstairs when I was shaken out of my indifference by hearing these phrases which made me shudder. "I'm surprised the manager hasn't got back yet, damn me, at this hour of night I can't think where he will find chains" "After all, the chap is already chained up;" "He's chained up all right, but he is and he isn't; if I had been chained up like that I could easily get out of it." "But the clasp is closed" "I know it's closed but it can be forced open. The trouble is the chains aren't long enough" "Don't try and tell me what's going on, I have been beating him up all last night until my hands were bleeding; it's your turn to beat him up tonight" "No, it's not me, it's Maurice" "But, tomorrow is my Sunday, I've been promised that."

I understood now why they needed the sailors strong arms. When they had sent away the peaceful folk, it wasn't that there was a nest of spies in this hotel. A horrible crime would be committed if something wasn't done soon to expose it and arrest the guilty ones. All this was happening on this night which was both peaceful and threatening, which was taking on the character of a dream or a fable; I now entered the hotel with deliberation intending to see justice done with the pleasure of a poet.

I touched my hat to everyone in the room and they all acknowledged my salute with varying degrees of politeness without disturbing themselves too much. "Can you tell me, whom I need to see? I would like to take a room and for someone to bring me a drink there." "You must wait a minute, the manager has just gone out"; "The boss is upstairs" interrupted another of the group, "you know very well, he mustn't be disturbed"; "Do you think there might be a room for me?" "I think so, No 43 should be free" said the young man who was sure he would not be killed because he was only twenty two years old, as he moved up on the sofa to make room for me. "We could open the window a bit, it's very smoky in here" said the pilot, and indeed everyone had either his pipe or a cigarette. "OK but close the shutters first, we mustn't show a light because of the Zeppelins."

Just then the manager came in, dripping with sweat and loaded with yards of heavy chain, enough to hold down a crowd of convicts; I've got a load here, if all you lot weren't so lazy, I wouldn't have to get it myself." I told him I was looking for a room for just a few hours, that I couldn't find a cab and that as I was a little sick, could someone bring me a drink to the room.

"Pierrot, go to the cellar and find some cassis, then go and get No43 ready. There's No 7 ringing; they say they are ill, ill my foot, they've been taking cocaine and they look half cut, they should be thrown out. Have you changed the sheets in 22? Good. There's No7 again, run and see what they want. Now then Maurice, what are you doing there, you know very well that someone is waiting for you; get on up to 14a and look sharp about it!"

Maurice hurried out after the manager, who seemed somewhat annoyed that I had seen the chains and he disappeared carrying them with him.

Soon I was shown up to No43 but the air was so unpleasant and my curiosity was so great that when I had drunk my cassis, I went downstairs again, then I had another idea and went back up to the floor above my room. All at once I heard muffled cries from a room at the end of the corridor, I ran quickly to it and put my ear to the door. "Please, please, I implore you, have pity, let me go, don't beat me so hard" came a voice, I will kiss your feet, I beg you, I won't do it again, have pity!" "No, you scoundrel" replied someone else, "and as you are making such a row and throwing yourself about on your knees, I shall have to tie you down to the bed; no pity for you." Then I heard the crack of a cat-of-nine-tails probably barbed with nails as it was followed by cries of anguish.

Then I saw that this room had an ox-eye window high up giving onto the corridor and that its curtain had not been drawn; I crept up to this window and there chained to bed like Prometheus to his rock, being beaten by Maurice with a nailed cat-of-nine-tails, already bleeding and covered with scars which showed that this wasn't the first time he had been tortured, in front of me was M.de Charlus. All of a sudden the door opened and someone entered who fortunately didn't see me, it was Jupien. He went to the Baron with an air of respect and a knowing smile. "Well, well; and can I help?" The Baron told Jupien to send Maurice out for a moment. Jupien dismissed him with a easy air. "Can we be heard?" asked the Baron and was reassured by Jupien. "I didn't want to talk in front of that little fellow, who is very polite and does his best, but I don't find him brutal enough. He looks the part, but he calls me scoundrel as if it were a word he had learned by rote." "Oh, no-one has told him what to say" replied Jupien, without realising how improbable this was. "He has just been involved in the murder of the porter at La Villette." "Ah, that's very interesting," said the Baron with a smile. "And I have, just downstairs a butcher, a man from the abattoir, who looks like him, he was passing by chance, would you like to try him?" "Oh yes, willingly"

I saw the butcher come in; indeed he did look a little like Maurice, but more strangely, both were of a type which I had not previously classified, but which also included Morel. Perhaps not in the features of Morel's face with which I was familiar, but in the face that loving eyes seeing Morel in a different way than I, would be able to identify.

Now that I had put together in my mind from bits of my memories of Morel, a model of how he might seem to someone else, I realised that these two young men, one of whom was an apprentice jeweller and the other an employee in a hotel, were in some sense Morel's successors. It seemed that M.de Charlus, at least in this sort of love, was always faithful to the same type, and the desire which had lead him to choose these two young men one after another, was the same as that which had led him to stop Morel on the station platform at Doncières.

I got down and went downstairs to the little room where Maurice, uncertain whether he would be recalled and whom Jupien had told to wait in any case, was in the middle of a game of cards with his friends. One of them was very worried about a Croix de Guerre which had been found on the floor and no-one knew who had lost it or where to send it, without causing embarrassment to the holder. Then they talked about the goodness of an officer who had sacrificed himself in order to save his orderly. "There are some good folk even among the rich. I would be pleased to die for someone like that" said Maurice, who had obviously only beaten the Baron so fiercely from an automatic habit, or because the effect of a poor education, or from the need for money and an inclination to earn it in a way which would cause less trouble than hard work and possibly give a better return. Perhaps as M.de Charlus had feared, he was very kindhearted and it seemed, brave as well. He had had tears in his eyes when he talked about the death of the officer and the young twenty two year old had been equally moved.

The manager hadn't yet come back when Jupien came in complaining that they were talking too loudly and that the neighbours were complaining. He was absolutely amazed to see me. "All of you get out on the landing!" They all got up to go, but I said "It would be easier if all these young men stayed here and I came outside with you for a moment." He followed me with great concern and I explained to him how I came to be there.

We heard some steps on the stairs. With that lack of discretion which was second nature to him, Jupien couldn't help telling me that it was the Baron coming down who must not see me at any cost, but that if I would like to go into a little room next to where the young men were, he would open the shutters, a dodge that he had worked out so that the Baron could see and hear without being seen, and now, he said, I could do the same to him. "But sit very still!"

Soon the Baron came in, walking with some difficulty because of the wounds which he must be used to receiving. Although he had taken his pleasure and was only coming in to settle up with Maurice, he looked round at all the young men with a tender and enquiring look, expecting to have the pleasure of a few loving but platonic words with each of them. They all appeared to know him and M.de Charlus stopped with each one for a while. Speaking in what he thought was their language, affecting the local slang in order to get more involved in the low life for some sadistic enjoyment.

He went up to Maurice to give him his fifty francs but first put his arm around him, "You never told me that you had stabbed an old dame at Belleville," and M.de Charlus gurgled with ecstasy putting his face up to Maurice's, "Oh, M'sieu le Baron" protested the gigolo, who hadn't been warned, "How can you believe that!" Whether in fact it was false, or if true, that the culprit found it so horrible that he wanted to deny it, he went on: "I would never hurt one of our people, a Boche, yes, because we are at war, but a woman and an old woman at that...." This declaration of virtue had the effect of a cold shower on the Baron who moved quickly away from Maurice, giving him his money, but with the look of someone who has been tricked but doesn't want to make a fuss, who pays up but is not at all pleased. The bad impression made on the Baron was aggravated by the way that he was thanked, "I will send this to my old parents, keeping back just a bit for my chum who is at the front" These touching sentiments disappointed M.de Charlus almost as much as the common conventional words irritated him.

"How ordinary he is; one would never guess he was a prince" the regulars said, when M.de Charlus had left, led downstairs by Jupien, to whom the Baron never stopped complaining about the good nature of the young man.

Jupien came to find me in the dark cave , from which I had been too scared to make a move, and took me downstairs. "I don't want you to think badly of me" he said, "this hotel doesn't make as much money as you think, I have to take some honest tenants and with only them I wouldn't be able to make ends meet. Here it is the opposite of the Carmelite teaching, it's thanks to the evil that the good survives. I run this hotel , or rather as you have seen, I have a manager to run it for me, only to be of service to the Baron and to divert him in his old age. It is mainly to prevent him getting bored because the Baron is a big baby you know. Even though he has everything here that he can possibly want, he still goes off on dangerous adventures and generous though he is, that will lead to trouble sooner or later. I must confess too, I have no grand scruples about making money out of this sort of thing. What goes on here is very much to my taste. Is it forbidden to get paid for doing things that I don't think are wrong!" And giving me a casual wave, as his aristocratic clientele and the team of young men that he led like a pirate king, had given him a rather cavalier manner, he took his leave.

He had hardly left me than the air-raid siren sounded the alert, followed immediately by a violent barrage of firing. I had the feeling that there was a German plane very close overhead, which was confirmed by a sudden explosion as bombs dropped nearby. I had left Jupien's hotel at the beginning of the alert; the streets had become completely black except occasionally a low flying enemy plane dropped flares where it it intended to drop a bomb. I couldn't find my way, I thought of the day when as I was going to Raspelière, I met an aeroplane which seemed like a god and made my horse rear up. I thought that my meeting now would be different and that an evil god would kill me. I rushed on to escape like a traveller pursued by a tornado; I went in circles around dark squares from which I couldn't find the way out.

At last, the flames from a fire lit my way and I was able to find my way again even though the gunfire continues to rumble. My thoughts were returning to another subject; I was thinking of Jupien's hotel, perhaps reduced to ashes by now, by the bomb which had fallen very close to me as I left it, the hotel on whose walls M.de Charlus could prophetically have written Sodom as had been done by the unknown inhabitant of Pompei, with no less prescience, at the beginning of the volcanic eruption. But what did the sirens and the planes matter to those who had come looking for pleasure!

At last the all clear sounded as I arrived home. I met Françoise coming up from the basement with the butler. She had thought that I must have been killed. She told me that Saint-Loup had looked in without being able to stop, to see if he had dropped his Croix de Guerre when he had visited me that morning. He had just noticed that he had lost it and before rejoining his regiment tomorrow morning, had wanted to find out, if by some chance it was at my home. He had searched everywhere with Françoise, but hadn't found it. Françoise thought he must have lost it before coming to see me, because, she said, she remembered very clearly and could swear that he didn't have it when she had seen him. In this she was mistaken, which shows the value of sworn statements and of memory. I had no doubt where the cross had been lost. However, even if Saint-Loup had been amusing himself this evening at Jupien's hotel, that was only while he was filling in time, for wanting to see Morel again, he had used all his connections to find out which regiment Morel was in, believing that he had enlisted, so that he could go and see him, but up to now, he had only received contradictory reports.

My departure from Paris was delayed by news which caused such sadness that I was quite unable to make any preparations to leave. I had been told of the death of Robert Saint-Loup, who had been killed whilst protecting the retreat of his men, the day after his return to the front. For several days, I shut myself away in my room thinking of him. I remembered his arrival, that first day I met him at Balbec, when, dressed in his whiteish woolen suit, with his flashing green eyes rolling like the sea, he had crossed the hall next to the dining room, whose windows looked out on the sea. I remembered him as someone so special, who had seemed to me to be the one person whom I had a great wish to make my friend. This wish had been realised beyond my greatest dreams without bringing the pleasure for which I had hoped. Afterwards I understood all his great merits and other qualities as well which were concealed under his elegant exterior. All these, the good and the bad, he had given without reserve, every day, and at the end in going out to attack a trench by his selflessness, by offering all that he possessed, as he had when he ran along the ledge at the back of the seats in the restaurant, so as not to inconvenience me. I had seen him for so short a time in total but in places so varied and in such different circumstances and at such long intervals: in the hall at Balbec, in the Rivebelle, in the barracks, at military dinners at Doncières, at the theatre, at the home of the Princesse de Guermantes; this only made me see his life in brighter, sharper pictures and feel a sharper regret for his death than we often feel for the people we love better, but whom we have seen so often that the image we have of them is only of a diffuse average made up of an infinite number of images all slightly different.

Saint-Loup was the cause of regret, not just by his death, but because of what he had done in the weeks before he died; Saint-Loup's efforts to find Morel had resulted in the general, under whose command Morel should have been, listing him as a deserter, and having him arrested. Because Saint-Loup had shown interest in the case, the general wrote to him to advise him of what was happening. Morel had no doubt that his arrest had been caused by the spite of M.de Charlus and insisted on making a statement saying: "there is no doubt that I am a deserter but I have been led astray and am not wholly responsible."He provided information about M.de Charlus and M.de Argencourt, with whom he had also quarrelled, about matters in which he had had no direct involvement but which both had told him in the double confidence of lovers and of inverts. This resulted in the arrest of both gentlemen. The arrest caused less grief to both of them than learning that the other had been a rival and the case revealed that there had been many other unknown rivals that Morel had picked up every day on the street. Both were soon released however, as was Morel, because the letter which the general had written to Saint-Loup had been returned, endorsed 'deceased; killed in action with honour'. The general in consideration of his death, arranged that Morel should simply be returned to the front; there he acted with bravery, escaping all danger and returned at the end of the war with the cross which M.de Charlus had previously sought in vain for him and which he owed indirectly to the death of Saint-Loup.

CHAPTER THREE

An afternoon party
at the house of the Princesse de Guermantes

The nursing home to which I went next didn't restore me to health any better than the first and it was a long time before I left it. During the journey by train as I returned to Paris, I was struck with even greater force by my awareness of my lack of literary skill. I recall that the train stopped in open country. The sun shone on an avenue of trees running alongside the railway track lighting just half of their trunks. "Trees" I thought, "you have nothing more to say to me, my frozen heart doesn't listen to you any longer. I may be here in the open air but it is with frigidity and boredom that I am unable to distinguish between the glowing front of your trunks and the shaded rear. If I had ever thought of myself as a poet, I now know that I am not. Perhaps in this new barren part of my life which opens before me, I may be able to find an inspiration among humanity which I can no longer find in nature. The time when I might perhaps have been able to praise the glories of nature will never return."

My long absence from Paris had not prevented old friends, on whose lists my name still remained, from continuing faithfully to send me invitations; on my return I found one for a reception given by Berma in honour of her daughter and son-in-law and another for an afternoon party the next afternoon at the house of the Prince de Guermantes, my sad thoughts on the train journey weren't the least of my motives in deciding to accept. It seemed it was not worth depriving myself of the life of a man of the world for that famous 'work' that I had for so long hoped to start tomorrow but which perhaps had never had a basis in the real world.

As Mama was going at the same time to a small tea party with Mme Sazerat, I had no worries about going to the Princesse de Guermantes' party. I took a carriage to go there because the Prince de Guermantes no longer lived in the old house but in a magnificent new one which he had had built in the Avenue du Bois. At least the fact that the prince had moved had some benefit for me for the carriage which had come to collect me went by way of the Champs-Elysées The streets were very badly paved at that time but as soon as I arrived there, my thoughts were taken up by a feeling of great calmness, one would have thought that all of a sudden the carriage was travelling so easily, so smoothly and without noise in the way that when the gates of the park are opened, one glides on drives covered with fine sand or dead leaves; there was nothing real about this but I immediately felt that all the barriers had been removed as if I no longer had to make any effort to adapt or to pay attention which we do unconsciously when we are faced with something new. The streets which we were passing at that moment were those, forgotten for such a long time, which I used to take with Françoise to go to the Champs-Elysées. The earth itself knew where it had to go, its resistance was vanquished. Like a pilot who has painfully run along the runway, abruptly takes off, I rose slowly to the heights of memory. For me, these Parisian streets will always have a different character than the others.

When I arrived at the Champs-Elysées, as I wasn't interested in hearing all the concert which was going to be given at the Guermantes, I stopped the carriage intending to walk a little way on foot and noticed another carriage which was stopping as well. A man was seated in it with glazed eyes and an arched figure, perched rather than seated in its depth, looking like a child on its best behaviour. His straw hat didn't conceal a wild forest of white hair and a snow white beard hung from his chin like that which the snow leaves on the statues in a public park. It was M. de Charlus, seated beside an attentive Jupien, recovering from a stroke, of which I had not been told (I had only been told that he had lost his sight, which had been a temporary problem, because now he could see perfectly well) and whose hair, unless he had always tinted it until now and had been forbidden to continue doing so because it would tire him, was rather sprouting forth locks of hair like brilliant geysers of silver which gave the ageing and decaying prince the majesty of Shakespeare's King Lear. When Jupien had helped the baron to descend and after I had greeted him, the baron talked to me in such a low and rapid whisper that I couldn't understand what he was saying and when I asked him to repeat something for the third time, his annoyance caused a grimace of impatience which surprised me as his face had been so impassive due no doubt to the traces of his stroke. When I was able to understand his whispered words, I could tell that his illness had not affected his intellect. There had always been at least two M. de Charluses without counting the others. The intellectual one spent his time complaining that he was losing his memory which made him confuse one word or a letter for another; but when he was indeed about to do that, the other M. de Charlus, the subconscious one, who looked for envy when the other looked for pity, immediately took control, like the conductor of an orchestra whose musicians have made a mistake in a passage and who with great skill makes it appear that what comes afterwards is what was originally intended. Even his memory was intact; he went out of his way to show that he could recall some ancient memories of me of little importance which showed me that he had kept or had recovered all his clarity of mind. Without turning his head, shifting his glance or changing his inflection he said "Here is a pillar with the same advertisement as the one I was standing in front of the first time I met you at Avranches, no, I'm wrong, it was at Balbec." And it was indeed an advertisement for the same product. He went on talking to me about the past, no doubt to convince me even more that he had not lost his memory; he spoke as if in a funeral oration but without the sadness. He went on listing all the people in his family or his social circle who were no more, less it appeared with regret that they had died, than with satisfaction that he had survived them. It seemed that remembering their death made him more aware of his own recovery. With a triumphal harshness, he repeated in monotonous, sepulchral tones and with a slight stammer, Hannibal de Bréauté, dead! Antoine de Mouchy, dead! Charles Swann, dead! Adalbert de Montmorency, dead! Baron de Talleyrand, dead! Sosthene de Doudeauville, dead! And each time the word 'dead' seemed to fall on the deceased like a heavy clod of earth thrown by a gravedigger wanting to bury them even deeper.

M.de Charlus asked to sit down on a chair for a rest while Jupien and I took a short walk and he painfully took from his pocket what appeared to be a prayerbook. I was not sorry to have a chance to hear from Jupien some details about the baron's state of health. "I am pleased to talk to you , sir" said Jupien "but we mustn't go further than the Rond Point. God be thanked, the baron is doing well now but I daren't leave him alone; its always the same, he is too kind hearted, he would give away everything he has, and thats not all, he still chases after men as if he were young himself and I have to keep an eye on him" "All the more since he has recovered his own" I replied, "I was very sad when I heard that he had lost his sight" "His stroke did have that effect, he could see absolutely nothing. For several months during his treatment, which has turned out well, he lost his sight as completely as if he had been born blind." "That would at least have made your supervision less necessary" "Not in the least. The moment we arrived at a hotel, he wanted to know what this or that waiter looked like. I told him they were all horrors, but he knew very well that that couldn't be true and that I must be lying about some of them. You see what a little rascal he is. He would get a special feeling, perhaps from a voice, I don't know. Then he would arrange to send me on an urgent errand. One day, you must excuse me for bothering you with all this, but after all, you did turn up by chance at the 'Temple of Immodesty', I've nothing to hide from you,(he always took an unpleasant satisfaction in revealing the secrets that he knew) I returned from one of these so called 'urgent errands' sooner than he expected because I was sure that it had been arranged on purpose and when I got to the baron's door I heard a voice say "What?" "Really" replied the baron "Is it your first time" I went in without knocking and was horrified by what I found. The baron, deceived by a voice which was deeper than is usual at that age, (this was when he was completely blind) was with a child of less than ten years.

"My god" exclaimed Jupien, "I was right to think we should not go far away, look there, he has already found a way of getting into conversation with a young gardener. Goodbye sir, I had better leave you now and not have my invalid by himself for a moment longer because he is no better than a big baby."

I got down again from my carriage a little before arriving at the Prince de Guermantes house and began to think again of the weariness and boredom with which I had tried the day before to identify the point which separated light and shadow on the trunks of the trees.

While I was thinking these sad thoughts, I entered the courtyard of the Guermantes house and in my distraction I didn't see a carriage which was approaching and the warning shout of the driver just gave me time to jump aside and I pulled back enough to stumble unwittingly against some badly laid paving stones in front of the coach house. At the moment when I recovered my balance, I put my foot on a stone which was a little higher than the one before it, all my discouragement evaporated before the same glow of happiness which I had experienced at various times of my life such as when I had seen the trees which I had recognised on a journey near Balbec, or the bell towers of Martinville, savoured a madeleine dipped in an infusion and of so many other sensations of which I have spoken and which the later works of Vinteuil had seemed to encompass.

As at the moment when I had tasted the madeleine, all worry about the future, all intellectual doubts were dispersed. Those which had just been worrying me about the reality of my gifts for literature and even of the reality of literature were lifted as if by magic. This time I promised myself not to be content to ignore why without any new reasoning or having found any decisive argument, the indissoluble difficulties had suddenly lost their importance as I had done on the day when I had tasted the madeleine dipped in an infusion. The happiness that I had experienced was indeed the same that I had experienced in eating the madeleine and which I had then put on one side to seek for profound causes. There was a simple material difference in the images invoked. A deep azure intoxicated my eyes, an impression of freshness, a dazzling light swirled around me and in my wish to grasp it without daring to move as when I tasted the madeleine in seeking to recreate for myself what it was that it was recalling to me, I remained, ignoring the laughter of the crowd of chauffeurs, staggering as I had just done, one foot on the higher paving stone, one on the lower; but repeating exactly the same movement did not reproduce the effect; if, forgetting the Guermantes party, I succeeded in rediscovering what I had felt when I placed my feet like that, the dazzling and vague vision brushed past me again as if it had said "Grasp me as I pass if you have the strength and solve the riddle of happiness that I am setting you." Then suddenly I recognised it; it was that Venice which my efforts to describe and the so-called snapshots of my memory had never brought back to me; the sensation which I had had so long ago from two uneven paving stones in the Baptistery of St Mark, had been restored to me this very day together with all the other associated feelings which I had felt on that day in the past, which had lain in wait in their proper place for all the series of forgotten days and from which a chance shock had imperiously summoned them. In the same way, the taste of the little madeleine had reminded me of Combray. But why should the visions of Combray and Venice, each at their different moments, give an ecstatic joy, equivalent to a certainty without the need of further evidence, to make me unconcerned about death.

I was absolutely determined to find an answer this very day, but nevertheless I entered Guermantes' mansion because we always give priority to following the external role we are playing over our internal needs and today my role was that of a guest. When I arrived on the first floor, the butler asked me to wait for a moment in a small library next to the main reception room just until the piece of music that was being played had finished, the princess had forbidden the doors to be opened until the end of the piece. At this very moment another reminder came to reinforce that which the uneven paving stones had given me and to encourage me to continue with my task. A waiter ineffectively trying to do his job without making any noise, clinked a spoon against a plate.

The same feeling of happiness overcame me as had been caused by the uneven paving stones. The feeling was of great warmth again but quite different, with a smoky smell blended with the fresh fragrance of a cedar forest and I realised that what now seemed to be so attractive was the same row of trees that I had found so annoying to see and describe whilst we were stopped in front of the little wood. Just before that, while opening a bottle of beer that I had in the compartment, I had heard the noise of a workman working with a hammer on the wheel of the train. The identical noise of the spoon striking the plate had made me believe for a moment in a sort of stupefaction before I had time to adjust that I was again in the railway compartment. One might say that the signs which were that day contradicting my lack of faith in my literary abilities, had the strength to multiply themselves because one of the Prince de Guermantes' staff had recognised me and had brought to me in the little library a selection of petits fours and a glass of orangeade, I dried my mouth with the napkin he had given me and instantly, as for the character in 'A Thousand and One Nights' who unknowingly performed exactly the rite which made the obedient Genie appear, visible only to him and ready to carry him wherever he desired, a new azure vision passed in front of my eyes but this time it was clear and salty, it grew into bluish breasts and the impression was so strong that I seemed to be reliving the moment when I had experienced it before, I thought that the servant had just come to open the window onto the beach and that everything was encouraging me to go down and walk along the sea wall; the napkin that I had taken to dry my mouth had exactly the same feeling of stiffness and starchiness as that with which I had had so much trouble to dry myself in front of the window on the first day I had arrived at Balbec, and now in the Guermantes' library, the napkin displayed in its folds and creases, the blue and green ocean colours of a peacock's tail. It was not only the colours that I enjoyed but the whole moment of my life that they brought back to me, which had been a longing for life which feelings of tiredness or sadness had prevented me from enjoying at Balbec and which now, freed from the imperfections of external perception, pure and disembodied, filled me with joy.

The piece of music that was being played might finish at any moment and I would have to go into the salon, so I forced myself to understand clearly as quickly as possible that nature of the identical pleasures that I had experienced three times in a few minutes and then to learn the lesson that I could draw from them. I began by comparing these various happy experiences which had in common that I had felt them both in the present time and at a moment in the past and that the noise of the spoon on the plate, the unevenness of the paving stones, the taste of the madeleine, had made the past invade the present and left me uncertain as to which of them was real, the reality was the part of me which experienced the sensation of taste which the past and the present had in common, knew that it had an existence independent of time and that it only appeared when there was this coincidence between the present and the past; then it was able to find the only place in which it could exist and enjoy its being, which is outside of time. That explained why my worries about my death had ceased from the moment when I had recognised, subconsciously, the taste of the little madeleine, because part of me was existing out of time and therefore not concerned with the problems of the future. It was only when I was able to be quite still and free from immediate pleasures that this part of me was able to come to the fore and be released from the present by the miracle of these coincidences. This was the only way in which I would be able to recover properly all my previous experience, the remembrance of time past which all the efforts of my conscious memory and my intelligence had been unable to achieve. It needed only a noise or a smell, heard or breathed at some time in the past and experienced again now, for the sense, real if not actual, of the present and the past being united, to be able to release the actual truth of memory which is usually hidden and then our real self which had appeared to be dead perhaps for many years, although not so in fact, awakes, rouses itself and receives the nourishment from the gods which has been provided for it.

The information that the rational brain perceives directly from the world around it is sometimes more superficial and less essential than that which life has given us, despite ourselves, by an impression, physical because we have received it through our senses, but from which we can distil its essence. Whether I was dealing with memories such as the view of the steeples of Martinville, or the unevenness of the paving stones or the taste of the madeleine, it was important to interpret the sensations as the signs of more than outward things and to try to think of their spiritual equivalent by getting away from the shadow of what I had actually known. It seemed to me that the only way I could do this was by creating a work of art. I was already feeling the implication of this for me because whether my memories arose from the sound of the spoon or the taste of the madeleine or from those truths whose forms I tried to make sense of in my head or belltowers, or wild herbs, which made up a complex and unintelligible mixture, their primary characteristic was that I was not able to choose them, they were of themselves. I felt that that must be a test of their authenticity. I had not been searching for the two paving stones that I had stumbled against in the courtyard. It was precisely that lucky chance, inevitable because the sensation having been encountered, controlled the truth of the past which it revived, the images which it released, since we feel its efforts to reach the light as we feel the joy of reality refound. It controls the accuracy of all the images of the time it brings with it, with the exact mixture of light and shade, the highlights and the gaps of recollection and forgetfulness which memory or conscious effort always loses.

There is a book within us which is the most difficult of all to decipher; it is the only one which has been printed into us by life itself. Whatever ideas have been left in us by life, the actual image, the trace of the impressions that life has made on us is still the proof of its essential truth. Ideas shaped by simple intelligence have only logical truth, a possible truth and the selection is arbitrary. This inner book is made up of images which have not been constructed by ourselves. It is not that the ideas that we have cannot be justified logically, but we do not know if they are true. Only the impression, however slender it seems, however unlikely its mark, is an indicator of truth and because of that is alone worth embracing by the mind because it alone is able, if it knows how, to release this truth, of leading the mind to an absolute perfection and giving it unalloyed pleasure. The impression is for an author the same as experimentation is for the scientist except the scientist must do the intellectual work before and the author must do it afterwards. Things that we haven't had to decipher and make clear by our own efforts, or which were clear before we worked at them, don't belong to us. Only the things we draw from our own obscure depths and which no one else knows, belong to us.

As I was coming into the library, I had remembered what the Goncourts said about the beautiful first editions that it held and I had promised myself that I would look at some of them while I was being made to wait there. Following this line of thought, I glanced at these precious volumes without paying too much attention to any them until the moment when I casually opened *Francois le Champi* by George Sand, when I was disturbed by some feeling quite out of keeping with my actual thoughts, until with an emotion that almost brought tears to my eyes I realised the connection between the feeling and my thoughts.

This was the book that my mother had read aloud to me at Combray almost until morning had come and it still held for me all the delight of that night. Of course the 'pen' of George Sand , to use Brichot's

633

expression who always liked to say of a book that it was written by 'a lively pen', didn't seem to me now to have been written by the same magic pen as it had seemed to my mother so long ago before she had slowly modelled her literary tastes on my own. But it was a pen which I had unconsciously magnetised in the way that schoolboys often do and here were a thousand fragments of Combray that I hadn't thought of for many years dancing of their own accord, to hang head to tail in an endless chain, shimmering with memories.

I had seen this *Francois le Champi* for the first time in my little room at Combray during the night which was the sweetest and the saddest of my life, where I had also(at a time when the mysterious Guermantes seemed quite inaccessible to me) obtained from my parents that first surrender from which I was able to date the start of the decline of my health and my determination, my daily avoidance of a difficult work which grew worse every day, and which I was now restarting this very day in this library of the very same Guermantes, this most wonderful day which illuminated not only my early tentative thoughts but also the object of my life and perhaps of art itself.

Then a new light dawned on me, less startling than that which had made me see that a work of art would be the only way of recovering lost time and I understood that my whole life could be the material for this work of literature; I understood that this material had come from frivolous pleasures, the idleness, the tenderness and in the sadness that I had stored up without understanding their purpose or even their survival in the same way as the seed puts in reserve everything that will supply the plant. Like the seed, I might die when the plant had grown, I might find that I had lived for it without realising it, without my life ever appearing to be in contact with the books I wanted to write and for which when I used to make myself sit at a table, I had been unable to find a subject. So all my life up to now could, and could not, be described under the title 'A Vocation'. It could not be, in the sense that writing had played little part in my life. It could be, in that this life with its recollections of sadnesses and joys formed a reserve similar to the starch in the ovules of plants which provides the nourishment to enable them to produce seed; even at the time when it is not certain that the plant will come to fruition, the hidden chemical and respiration processes are at their most active stage. In the same way my life had been supported by the things that would lead it to mature. Those who might later get nourishment from it, would not know how it had been provided any more than those who eat the bread know what healthy things it contains, even though they had sown the seed and harvested the grain.

I now understood that the most insignificant episodes of my life had come together to give me a lesson in idealism that would be of help to me now. My meetings with M. de Charlus for example, had convinced me, even before his love of Germany gave me the same lesson, and even better than my love for Mme. de Guermantes or for Albertine, or St.Loup's for Rachel, that what actually happens is unimportant, what really matters is what happens in the mind; that the phenomenon of sexual inversion, so little understood and so uselessly condemned, is stronger than that other power of love, love which shows us beauty deserting a woman who we no longer love and coming to rest in a face which others find ugly and which one day may displease us and still more surprising to see beauty receiving all the attentions of a great gentleman which he used to devote to a beautiful princess when it has migrated beneath the cap of a bus conductor. Doesn't the surprise that I felt every time I later saw the faces of Gilberte, Mme. de Guermantes or Albertine on the Champs-Elysées, in the street or on the beach, show how much memory only survives in a way that changes more and more from that in which it is first found?

An author must not be offended if his heroines are given a masculine face by a homosexual, this slightly aberrant characteristic is the only way the homosexual can fully understand what he is reading. If M. de Charlus had not given Morel's face to the traitress over whom Musset shed tears in his *Nuits d'Octobre* or in his *Souvenir* then he would not have been able either to cry or to understand because it was by that narrow and devious route that he was able to gain access to the truths of love. An author only refers to 'his reader' by a convention used in prefaces and dedications. In fact every reader when he reads, is reading about himself. The work of an author is only a sort of optical instrument which he offers to the reader so that he can see himself in a way that he would perhaps not have been able to do without the book. The recognition by the reader is a proof of its truth and to some extent vice versa the difference between the two texts can often be due to the reader not the author. A book can also be too learned, too obscure for the naive reader and only offer him a cloudy glass through which he cannot read. But other characteristics such as homosexuality may oblige the reader to read in a particular way to get a proper understanding. The author must not be offended but on the contrary must give the reader the maximum freedom and tell him to find out whether he sees better through this glass or that or the other.

I had realised that it was a gross misconception to rely completely on the actual object when it is the mind which is important; I had lost my grandmother in fact many months after I had lost contact with her, I had seen people change their appearance according to the preconception that I or others had of them, one person appearing in many guises according to who is looking at them (such as Swann for instance at the beginning of this story, according to whom he met) even for one person as the years go by (the variation in the name of Guermantes and the different Swanns for me). I had seen love give to someone a quality which was only in the eye of the lover. I had understood this all the more because I had stretched the gap between objective reality and love to its extreme limit (Rachel for Saint-Loup and for me, Albertine for me and Saint-Loup, Morel or the bus conductor for Charlus and other people)

It seemed to me when I thought about it that the substance of my experience came to me in connection with Swann, not only because of the link between him and Gilberte but because it was at Combray that he had given me the wish to visit Balbec and without his suggestion my parents would never have had the idea to send me there and then I would not have met Albertine. It was her face certainly which when I saw it for the first time on the beach had given me some thoughts which I would no doubt be able to use in my writing. I was right to connect those ideas to her because unless I had gone out on the sea wall that day, if I had never met her, none of those ideas would have developed for me (unless they had been given me by some other girl). On the other hand, I was wrong as well because the source of pleasure that in hindsight we like to find in the face of a beautiful woman comes from our own senses and I am quite sure that Albertine, and certainly the Albertine of that time, would not have understood what I was going to write. But it was precisely because of that (it is an indication that it is better to avoid being too intellectual), and because she was so different to me, that she had been able to give me inspiration through my suffering and through the effort of thinking about things which were not the same as myself. If Albertine had been able to understand these pages, she would have been unable to inspire them.

Without Swann, I would not have made the aquaintance of the Guermantes, because my grandmother would not have met Mme. de Villeparisis again, I would not have got to know Saint-Loup or M. de Charlus, who introduced me to the Duchess de Guermantes and she to her cousin and indeed everything linked back to Swann right up to my presence at this moment at the house of the Princess de Guermantes where I had suddenly discovered the idea of my book (This meant that

I owed Swann not just the material but also the decision to use it.) This was a very slender prop to support the understanding of my life. (This made 'Guermantes' Way' appear to derive from 'Swann's Way') However someone may influence our life who is a very mediocre person, much inferior to Swann. Possibly I might have gone to Balbec if some friend or other had pointed out a pretty girl that I might enjoy there, even though I would probably never have got to know her.

At this moment, the butler came to tell me that the first piece of music had finished and that I could leave the library and go to the main reception rooms. This reminded me where I was. It did not shake me from my line of reasoning that my new start in life, which I had been unable to find in solitude, was going to be made by returning to society at a fashionable gathering. I felt that the energy released in my spiritual life was so strong that it could survive just as well in the salons with all the guests just as well as in the library; it seemed to me that even in the midst of so many people, I would be able to preserve my solitude.

When I climbed the staircase which led from the library, I found myself directly in the large reception room and in the middle of a party which appeared very different to those I had attended in past years and which would take on a special aspect for me. Indeed from the moment I entered the room, even though I held firmly to the project I had set for myself, I was shaken by a theatrical surprise which raised the greatest barrier to my intentions. A barrier which no doubt I would overcome but which even while I continued to ponder on the conditions for my work of art, interrupted my thoughts by something repeated a hundred times and well calculated to give me pause for thought. From the first moment, I couldn't understand why I couldn't recognise my host or his guests, because everyone seemed to be wearing a white powdered wig which disguised them completely. The prince, while receiving his guests, still had the same goodnatured air of a king of the fairies, which I had noticed when I first met, but this time, following the dress code which he had imposed on his guests, he was dressed up in a white beard and dragged his feet as if they were weighted down with lead. He seemed to be acting the role of one of the 'Ages of man' His moustaches were as white as if the hoar frost of 'petit Poucet's' forest clung to it. It seemed to be very inconvenient for his mouth and once he had made the effect he should have taken it off. In truth, I could only work out who he was by identifying certain personal characteristics.

While some had become completely white and some had only white moustaches, I couldn't think what little Lezensac had put on his face; without bothering about tinting his hair, he had found a way of covering his face with wrinkles and his eyebrows with bristles, none of which suited him; his complexion had hardened, bronzed and become solemn, this gave him such an appearance of age that one could no longer call him a young man. Then I was surprised to hear someone address a little old man with the silvery moustaches of an ambassador as Duc de Chattelleraut who only had a slight resemblance to the youth I had met once while visiting Mme. de Villeparisis. I was eventually able to identify someone by discarding the elements of his disguise and substituting his natural features by an effort of memory, my first thought ought to have been and for a moment nearly was, to congratulate him on being so well made up; I had had the same hesitation before I recognised him as that shown by an audience, who, even when they had been warned by the programme, when a great actor comes on stage in a role where his appearance has been completely changed from his own, hesitates for a breathless moment before breaking into applause.

The difficulty which I was having in putting the appropriate name to the faces around me, was shared by everyone who noticed mine for they took no more notice of me than they would if they had never seen me before or were trying to extract the memory of someone else from what they actually saw.

A young woman who I used to know, now white and shrunk into a little old witch, seemed to show that in the last act of a play, the characters should be made up beyond recognition. But her brother still stood so upright and so like himself that it was surprising on such a youthful face to see that his moustache was turning white. The human landscape at this party was given a melancholy tone by the patches of snow white on beards which used to be jet black in the same way as the first yellow leaves on the trees show that autumn has already arrived when one is still hoping to enjoy a long summer which seems hardly to have begun. Ever since my childhood I had been accustomed to living from day to day; having seen everyone's reaction to myself and from what I had seen of everyone else, I realised for the first time, which shook me greatly, that having seen the changes that time had made in the others, time had passed for me as well. Although I did not mind that they had got old, I was desolated by the warning that gave me of the approach of my own old age. This was confirmed to me by one remark after another, each one striking me like a blast from the trumpets of the 'Last Judgement'. The first came from the Duchesse de Guermantes. I saw her walking between a double line of curious onlookers who, without understanding how the superb details of her make up and its aesthetics affected them, were moved by her reddish hair, her pink flesh rising from wings of black lace, strangled by her necklaces and saw in the inherited grace of her lines, the likeness of some sacred and ancient fish covered in jewels which was the incarnation of the presiding genius of the Guermantes family. "Ah!" she said to me "What a pleasure it is to see you, my very oldest friend." In my self esteem as a young man from Combray, I had never expected that I might be counted as one of her real friends, sharing the mysterious life which went on among the Guermantes such as M. de Bréauté, M. de Forestille or even like Swann all of whom were now dead; I should have been flattered but instead I was mortified. "Her oldest friend," I said to myself, she's exaggerating, perhaps one of the oldest, but am I really---------."

Almost immediately afterwards someone spoke of Bloch; I asked if they meant the young Bloch or his father (I didn't know that the father had died during the war from the shock, it was said of hearing that France had been invaded) the Duchess replied "I didn't know that he had children or even that he was married, but it is obviously the father we are talking about as he is certainly not a young man;" she added with a smile "He could even have sons who would already be grown men." So I understood that they were talking about my old friend. He happened to come in to the room at just that moment; I could hardly recognise him. Among other changes he was now called Jaques de Rozier, not just as a nom de plume but as his proper name under which it would have taken the instinct of my grandfather to detect the trace of the gentle valley of Hebron and the chains of Israel which my friend had clearly broken. A fashionable English style had completely changed his appearance and he had shed every Jewish trait that he could. His hair naturally curly, was parted in the middle and combed flat with brilliantine. His nose was still large and red but somewhat blocked by a permanent cold which perhaps explained the nasal accent in which he lazily pronounced his words because he had found , as well as a hair style to suit him, a manner of speaking in which his old nasal tones took on a disdainful air which went with his swollen nostrils. Thanks to the hair style, to removing his moustache, to the smart style and the strength of his will, his Jewish nose had disappeared in the same way that a humpback can be made to look straight if properly managed. Above all the biggest change in Bloch's appearance had been achieved by adopting an impressive monocle. The mechanical part which this monocle took in Bloch's face replaced all the difficult tasks which the human face has to perform, to be handsome, to express wit, benevolence and endeavour. Just the presence of this monocle on Bloch's face meant that there was no real need to ask whether it was handsome or not just as when one looks at English things in a shop and the assistant tells you that they are the height of fashion, there is no further need to wonder if you actually like them. Bloch sat there behind his eyeglass with a haughty air, distant and relaxed as if it magnified eight times and in keeping with his flat hair and his monocle, his features were quite expressionless. I saw superimposed on Bloch's face that weak and opinionated look, the feeble wagging head which quickly coming to rest in which I would have identified the weary pontifications of an amiable old man if I had not realised that it was my old friend and if my memories had not enlivened him with the spirit of youthfulness which he seemed to have lost. I had known him at the threshold of life, he had been my close friend, a young man whose youth I was equating to that with which I was unconsciously crediting myself since I didn't believe that I had lived for that long. I heard someone say that he looked his age and I was astonished to see on his face some of the most characteristic signs of an old man. I realised that that was because he was indeed just that and that it was from those young men who survive for long enough that life produces its old men.

    I could only be helped, as far as the material for my book was concerned, by the cruel discovery which I had just made about the passage of Time. As I had decided that my book could not be made up only of the truly perfect impressions which are outside of Time, among the important in which I intended to set them were those which related to Time, to the Time in which men, societies and nations exist and grow. I should not only deal with the alteration to which our external appearance is subject of which I was getting new examples every minute because at the same time as I was thinking about my work, now decisively under way and from which I must not be distracted, I was continuing to greet people that I had known and to chat with them. Age had not marked them all in the same way, I met someone who asked my name and told me that he was M. de Cambremer and then to show me that he knew who I was, he asked me "Do you still suffer from choking fits" and when I said yes, he replied" You see that hasn't prevented a long life" as if I were already a centenarian. While I was talking to him, I kept my eyes fixed on two or three features which I was trying to reconcile with my previous memories of him. Then he half turned for a minute and I saw that he had been completely changed by the addition of enormous red pouches on each cheek which prevented him from properly opening either his mouth or his eyes, so much that I was stunned, not wanting to stare at this kind of anthrax which I thought it better that he should mention first. Like a courageous invalid he didn't refer to it and went on laughing; I was afraid to appear lacking in kindness if I didn't ask him about it and tactless if I did. "Don't they come more rarely as you get older" he asked me, continuing to talk about my choking fits. I told him that they didn't. "Ah! My sister has many fewer than she used to have" he said in a contradictory tone as if it could not be any different for me than for his sister and as though, if age were a cure which had worked for his sister, then he could not admit that it would not make me healthy too.

A stout lady greeted me while I was taken up with the various problems which were weighing it down. I paused for a minute before I replied thinking that perhaps she couldn't recognise people any better than I could and that she had taken me for someone else, then her confidence convinced me otherwise, then in case this was someone with whom I had had a relationship, increased the warmth of my smile while I still searched her featured to find the name that I had lost. Just as an exam candidate at a viva, uncertain how to answer seeks in the face of the examiner the answer for which he would do better to search his own memory, so I smiled and searched the face of this stout lady. I began to see a resemblance to Mme. de Forchville and so my smile began to be mingled with respect and my indecision started to diminish. Then a second later, "You were mistaking me for my mother; I am getting to look like her." And I recognised Gilberte.

When I met Mme. de Forcheville, she seemed to have been injected with a liquid, some sort of paraffin oil which swells up the skin and protects it from change, she had the appearance of a courtesan of earlier years who had been preserved for ever. I had started by thinking that everyone would have stayed the same as before and then I discovered that everyone had become old but once I had accepted that everyone had become old, I didn't find them so bad. In Odette's case it wasn't just that, I knew her age and knew that I was visiting an old woman; there seemed to have been a more miraculous defiance of the laws of time than the conservation of radium has to the laws of nature. If I didn't recognise her when I first re-met her it was not because she had, but because she hadn't changed. In the last hour I had worked out what addition time can make to people and how much needs to be subtracted in order to discover the people I used to know, I now made a rapid estimate and adjusted the Odette I used to know by the tariff of years which had passed over her with the result that I found myself looking for someone who could not be the person in front of my eyes because she looked exactly the same as years before. How much had been achieved by paint or by dyes? Her golden hair was drawn quite flat and into a ruffled chignon like a large mechanical doll with a face with a fixed doll-like air of surprise above which was a straw hat, also flat; she might have been coming to play her part in a New Year's Eve review representing 'The Exhibition of 1878', (which she had certainly attended, and if she had had then, the age that she had today, she would have been its most fantastic exhibit). The way that Mme. de Forcheville looked was so miraculous that one couldn't say that she regained her youth but that rather with her carmine and her rouge she was coming into flower again. In the same fashion as being the incarnation of the Exhibition of 1878 she could now be the prize exhibit of a horticultural show. To me in particular, she didn't seem to be saying "I am the Exhibition of 1878" but rather "I am the Garden of Acacias of 1892" as she seemed as if she might still be there. Because she had not changed, it almost seemed as if she were not alive, she was like a dried rose. I said good day to her and she tried vainly for a little while to read my name on my face. I told her who I was and thanks to the spell it cast, I was freed of the appearance of an Arbutus tree or a Kangaroo which age had given me and she recognised me and started to talk to me in that very special voice which people, who had applauded when they heard it in a little theatre, had been astonished to find when they were invited to lunch with her, went on through all her conversation for as long as they wanted to listen. Her voice had retained the same insincere and cloying warmth with the trace of an English accent. Even while her eyes seemed to be looking at me from a distant shore, her voice sounded sad, almost beseeching, like those of the dead in *The Odyssey* which Odette would still have been able to perform. I complimented her on her youth. "You are very polite, my dear" she replied and as she found it very difficult to make any remark, even if she meant it, without adding some elaboration that she thought stylish, she repeated several times "Thank you so much, thank you so much"

Once upon a time, I used to take long walks to see her in the Bois and the first time I had visited her in her house, words seemed to fall from her mouth like precious treasure; the minutes I spent with her now seemed interminable because I couldn't think of anything to say to her and so I left.

Bloch asked questions of me in the same way as I used to do when I first went into society and as I still did about people I used to know but who were now as distant as the people from Combray whom I used to want to 'place'. Bloch's eye gleamed as he pondered on what might be the conversations of these wonderful people; I thought that I had perhaps exaggerated the pleasure I had found with them, which I had never felt when I was alone and could sort them out in my mind. Bloch may have realised this "Perhaps you have put them in too good a light" he said, "for instance, our hostess here, the Princesse de Guermantes; I know very well that she is no longer young but it wasn't so long ago that you were telling me of her incomparable charm and marvellous beauty. I can see she has a grand manner and I agree about her extraordinary eyes that you mentioned but I don't see that she is so very special as you said. Obviously she is very well bred, but really......" I was obliged to explain to Bloch that we had not been talking about the same woman. The real Princesse de Guermantes had died and the prince, ruined by the defeat of Germany, had married the ex Mme. Verdurin who Bloch had not recognised. "You must be wrong" said Bloch "I've looked her up in the current Gotha and found that the Prince de Guermantes of this address married someone with a most impressive list of titles, give me a minute and I will remember them all,---- married to Sidonie, Duchesse de Duras, née de Beaux." Indeed, Mme. Verdurin, shortly after the death of her first husband had married the old ruined Duc de Duras which had made her a cousin of the Prince de Guermantes and the Duc had died two years later. That had been a very useful stepping stone for Mme. Verdurin and now by her third marriage, she had become the Princess de Guermantes and held a great position in the Faubourg St Germain which would have much surprised those ladies of the rue de l'Oiseau in Combray, the daughters of Mme. Goupil and the daughter-in-law of Mme. de Sazerat who before Mme. Verdurin had become Princesse de Guermantes had said scornfully "The Duchesse de Duras" as if it were a role that Mme. Verdurin had taken on the stage. Their caste principle dictated that she would be known as Mme. Verdurin until she died, this new title would not give her any more status and had rather a negative effect by getting her 'talked about', which elsewhere meant that a woman had a lover, in the Faubourg St Germain was used of someone who published books and among the bourgeois of Combray described those who made unsuitable marriages. When she married the Prince de Guermantes they could only say he must be a fake Guermantes and an impostor. I had to reconcile myself to the continuity of the title, that there was still a Princesse de Guermantes who had no connection to the princess who had so charmed me, who was no more, defenceless in death, who had been robbed; it was also distressing to see all Princess Hedwige's possessions, all her house and everything she owned being enjoyed by another woman.

The succession of a name is sad as are all successions, as are all usurpations of property; without a break, an unending torrent of new Princesses de Guermantes would come on until the millennium, one woman after another would be the Princess de Guermantes regardless of death, heedless of everything that might change or wound our hearts and like a sea, the name would submerge those who bore it from time to time in an infinite and enduring calm.

I sat down beside Gilberte de Saint-Loup. "How do you come to be at a a crowded party like this?" she asked me "I wouldn't have thought you would be mixed up in a great massacre like this, I would have expected to see you almost anywhere else than at one of these great singsongs my aunt runs; she is my aunt you know" she added with a little bit of edge in her tone, as having been Mme. de Saint-Loup well before Mme. Verdurin had joined the family, she thought of herself as having been a Guermantes for ever and damaged by her uncle's unfortunate marriage to Mme. Verdurin which she had often heard the family make jokes about, though naturally it was only when she wasn't present that they had laughed about the poor marriage that Saint-Loup had made when he married her. She showed more dislike for her ill-favoured aunt because the Princesse de Guermantes, from the sort of contrariness which inclines intelligent people to break with conventions, from the need of the elderly to keep a link with their past and to give a background to her elegant present, liked to refer to Gilberte saying "I can tell you that I have known her for ages, I knew her mother very well, she was a great friend of my cousin Marsantes. It was at my home that she met Gilberte's father. As for poor Saint-Loup I used to know all his family, his uncle often used to come to La Raspelière."

"You see the Verdurins weren't Bohemians at all" people told me who had heard the Princesse de Guermantes talking like this. "They were friends all the time with Mme. de Saint-Loup's family. I was perhaps the only one who knew from what my grandfather had told me that the Verdurins were indeed not Bohemians but that was not proved by the fact that they knew Odette! It is as easy to tell tales of the past, which no one knows about, as it is to tell travellers tales about countries which no one has visited.

"Now," concluded Gilberte "as you sometimes leave your ivory tower, wouldn't you find a little intimate party with me would suit you better, where I could invite a few kindred spirits. Grand dos like this aren't much use to you. I saw you talking to my aunt Oriane who has all sorts of good qualities but it wouldn't be unfair if we were to say that she wasn't a member of the intellectual elite." I didn't feel able to tell Gilberte all about my thoughts of the last hour but I thought she might be of use to me as a simple distraction, which I wouldn't find if I had to talk about literature with the Duchesse de Guermantes any more than with Mme. de Saint-Loup. Tomorrow I was going to return to my solitary life but this time with a real goal in mind. I would not let anyone interrupt me in my work at home because the duty to get on with my work must come before mere politeness or even kindness. No doubt there would be some people who hadn't seen me for a long time who would insist on visiting me to see for themselves that I had recovered. They would insist on coming when their day's work or life's work was finished or interrupted and were feeling the same need to see me as I used to have to see Saint-Loup; that is because, as I had observed at Combray when my parents would reproach me at a time when unknown to them I had already made the most praiseworthy resolutions, we all have internal timekeepers which are at different times, one person is ready to rest when another is about to start work, the judge is ready to pass sentence when the guilty one has repented and changed his ways long since. I must have the strength to tell everyone who wanted to see me or get me to go to them, that I had a very urgent and important matter that I had to deal with, without delay, that I had a most urgent appointment that I must keep, with myself. Yet because there is not a lot in common between our real internal self and our external appearance, as they share the same name and body, the self denial which makes us sacrifice simple duties or even pleasures, may seem to everyone else like egotism.

Sometimes I would need to have periods of rest and to meet people but instead of these intellectual conversations which would be thought appropriate for a writer, I thought I should restrict myself to a diet of a little flirtation with some young woman in the flower of life, like the famous horse which was fed only on roses. This immediately reminded me again that that was what I had dreamt of at Balbec, when before I had met them properly, I had seen Albertine, Andrée and their friends on the beach. Alas, although I wanted them so much at this moment I could not expect to find them again. The passage of time which had transformed everyone I had seen today including Gilberte, would certainly have turned them into very different women than those that I treasured in my memory as it would also have changed Albertine if she had not died. I was hurt that I had to look within myself to find them because time which changes the real people doesn't have the power to change the picture of them that we hold in our memory.

When I looked at Gilberte, I didn't say to myself "I want to see you again," but what I said to her was that I would very much like it if she invited me to meet some young girls of whom I would ask nothing more than to revive in me the dreams and sorrows of our past and the remote possibility of a chaste kiss. She listened to my request with a smile and then appeared to be giving the matter some serious consideration. I was happy about this as it distracted her from noticing a group near to us which would certainly not have pleased her. It consisted of the Duchesse de Guermantes in deep conversation with a frightful old woman who I couldn't for the life of me think who it was. Bloch, who was just passing by, whispered in my ear "Isn't it strange to see Rachel here." The magic name broke the spell which had laid on Saint-Loup's mistress the disguise of a dirty old woman and I knew exactly who she was. Things had gone well for her, she had become a famous actress and later on in the event she was going to recite some verses from Musset and La Fontaine that the Duchess de Guermantes, Gilberte's aunt, was discussing with her at this very moment. The sight of Rachel could never be pleasant for Gilberte and I was very annoyed to learn that she was going to give a recitation and to demonstrate her friendship with the Duchess. For a long time the Duchess had thought of herself as having a leading role in Paris society and hadn't allowed for the fact that this position only exists in the minds of those who believe in it and that there were many newcomers who as they never saw her and never read her name in the reports of fashionable parties didn't think she had any place in society at all. She never bothered with the Faubourg St Germain set except for very rare and occasional visits because as she said "they bored her to death" and pleased herself by dining with one or another actress whom she found enchanting. The next generation had come to the conclusion that the Duchesse de Guermantes, in spite of her name, must be some impostor who had never been in the best society. It was true that she still went to the bother of entertaining several royalties whose friendship was disputed among other grand hostesses but they only came rarely as they had a very select circle and the duchess using the old protocol which other people were ignoring wrote "Her Majesty has commanded the Duchess de Guermantes....." or "has deigned....", so the newcomers thought that the duchess's position was therefore much lower.

The discussion from which I was trying to distract Gilberte's attention was broken up by our hostess coming to look for Rachel as it was time for her to start her recitation and soon after she left the duchess, Rachel appeared on the stage. My conversation with Gilberte was interrupted by the sound of Rachel's voice. Her acting was well thought out because it was based on the conception that the poem that the actress was going to recite had an existence of its own before being heard and that we would only hear a part of it as if the artist, walking by us on a road, was only within earshot for a short while. Nevertheless, the audience was astonished to see this woman, before she had said a single word, bend her knees, open her arms to embrace someone invisible, become knock-kneed and then, just in order to deliver some very well known lines, adopt a very entreating tone. Everyone had been pleased when a very familiar poem had been announced but when they had seen Rachel, before she started, stare around her with wild eyes, raise her hands in entreaty and groan with each word, everyone was uneasy, almost shocked, at this exhibition of emotion.

I noticed, without any gratification to my vanity as she had become so old and ugly, that Rachel was flashing her eyes at me in a discreet way. Throughout the recital an alluring smile fluttered in her glance which seemed to be inviting an acceptance she wanted to draw from me. When the poem was over, as we were close to Rachel, I heard her thank Mme. de Guermantes and at the same time, as I was standing next to the Duchess, she turned to me with a friendly greeting. Then I realised that what I had taken to be a look of desire was only intended to get me to recognise and greet her. I responded warmly. "I was sure that he hadn't recognised me" she simpered to the duchess. "But of course" I said with assurance "I knew who you were immediately."

The life of the duchess had become very unhappy for a reason which also had the effect of lowering the society in which M. de Guermantes moved. For some time now, although he was still fit, advancing years had calmed his desires and he had ceased his infidelities but now he had fallen in love with Mme. de Forcheville without anyone quite knowing how it had started. The liaison had taken on such proportions that the old man, following in this last love the pattern of his earlier affairs, isolated his mistress to the extent that if my love for Albertine had, with big differences, repeated Swann's love for Odette, M. de Guermantes' love recalled that which I had had for Albertine. He made her have lunch and dinner with him, he spent all his time at her house; she showed off to her friends who without her would never have had any contact with the Duc de Guermantes and came to meet him in the same way as people visit a king's mistress in order to meet the king.

Certainly, Mme. de Forcheville had been in society for many years but returning to being a kept woman again and kept by such an excessively proud old man who was nevertheless the most important man in her house, she lowered herself to make sure that she only wore the gowns that pleased him, served the food that he liked, and flattered her friends by telling them that she had talked to him about them in the same way that she had told my great uncle that she had talked about him to the Grand Duke, who had sent him cigarettes; in a word, by force of circumstances and in spite of the position in society that she had won, she had become again what she had been in my childhood, the lady in pink.

This liaison with Mme. de Forcheville, which was only an imitation of his old liaisons, lost the Duc de Guermantes his second chance of becoming President of the Jockey Club and also of taking a seat as an Honorary Member of the Academy of Fine Arts, just as when M. de Charlus had been publicly linked with Jupien and so had lost the Presidency of the Union Club and also of the Society of Friends of Old Paris. The two brothers with such different tastes had fallen into disgrace because of their own laziness, from a sort of loss of will, one from his natural inclination and the other from what is seen as not being a natural inclination, and both had lost their places in society.

The old duke went nowhere now as he spent all his days and evenings with Odette, but today as she herself was attending Princesse de Guermantes' party, he had come for a moment to see her, despite the nuisance of having to meet his wife. I might not have recognised him if the duchess had not pointed him out to me a few moments before. He was no more than a ruin but superb, even more than a ruin, a beautiful romantic thing, perhaps a rocky cliff in a storm. His face was like a crumbling block of stone, beaten on all sides by waves of suffering; angered at the pain, by the rising tide which surrounded it, it had kept the style and hauteur that I had always admired and his head was like a fine classical bust, badly damaged, but which we would still be proud to have as an ornament in our study.

The duke only stayed for a few minutes, but long enough for me to see that Odette made fun of him to her younger admirers. It was strange that although he had been somewhat ridiculous when he used to behave like a theatrical king, he had now taken on a really grand appearance, rather like his brother whom old age had made him resemble by stripping him of all his fripperies. He was quite unable to tear himself away from Odette and spent all his time installed in the same armchair at her house which old age and gout made it difficult for him to leave. M. de Guermantes allowed her to receive her friends who were delighted to be presented to the duke and to let him talk to them about high society in the past and about the Marquise de Villeparisis and the Duc de Chartres. He also permitted her to invite some friends to have dinner with him. Following a habit he had kept up with his previous mistresses which didn't surprise Odette who had had to put up with the same from Swann and which reminded me of my time with Albertine, he insisted that everyone left early so that he could be the last to say goodnight to Odette. Needless to say, that hardly had he left but she was off to rejoin the others. The duke had no idea that this was happening or liked to give the feeling that he knew nothing about it; old men get shortsighted, become hard of hearing, their perception is dulled and fatigue makes them relax their vigilance. Odette deceived M. de Guermantes and treated him without charm or respect. She was mediocre in this role as she had been in all the rest. It wasn't that she hadn't had good parts but that she didn't know how to play them. Now she was playing the part of a recluse. This meant that every time I wished to visit her, I was unable to do so because M. de Guermantes wanted to combine the requirements of his health and his jealousy and only permitted her to entertain during the daytime and specifically forbade any dancing.

Odette thought, even though I had only written a few articles and published some essays, that I had become a well known author and this led her to remark naively about the times when I used to wait to see her in the Avenues des Acacias and later to visit her at her home: "Oh! If only I had known that that little boy would one day become a great author". She had heard that authors like to hear love stories from women to use as material and she went on "You must come and take tea with me some day and I will tell you how I met M. de Forcheville. Actually" she said with a melancholy air, "I have led a very cloistered life because my great loves have been for men who have been dreadfully jealous. I don't include M. de Forcheville because he was really rather dull and I have only been able to love very clever men. M. Swann now, he was just as jealous as the poor duke; I give up everything for him because I know he has such a dreadful time at home. I loved M. Swann passionately and I found I could sacrifice dancing, society and everything else to do what pleased the man I loved or even what would keep him from worrying about me. Poor Charles, he was so clever, so fascinating, exactly the kind of man I loved."

Perhaps this was true. There had been a time when Swann had

pleased her, at precisely the time when she wasn't 'his kind of woman', yet he had loved her for so long and so unhappily. This contradiction surprised him when he eventually realised it, but it should not be a surprise for anyone when we realise how much suffering 'women who are not their type' inflict on men in general.

As she told me her stories, bit by bit, I realised with horror just how much Swann did not know and how much he would have suffered if he had known, because he had pinned his hopes on this woman; he was practically certain that she was attracted to this man or that woman from the way in which she looked at them. And she was telling me this, just to give me material for writing novels. She was mistaken, not because she didn't have plenty of interesting things to tell me but because I could only use things that came from her without her knowing and under my control and which could draw from her the principles which governed her life.

M. de Guermantes fulminated against the duchess because of the unconventional company she kept, about which Mme. de Forcheville made sure that the duke was well informed. The duchess herself was very unhappy. When I talked to M. de Charlus about this he claimed that the first fault was not on his brother's side and that the duchess' reputation for chastity was nothing more than an uncounted number of cleverly concealed sexual adventures. I had never heard any gossip suggesting that. Nearly everybody thought of her as someone special and that her reputation was irreproachable. I couldn't decide which of these two perceptions was true because truth is nearly always hidden from three quarters of the world. I remembered very well some roving glances that the duchess had cast around the nave at Combray but this did not disprove either idea as they could be taken to support both equally well. In my childish imaginings, I had taken these glances for a moment as invitations to love which were meant for me. Later on, I had realised that they were only the benevolent glances that Ladies of the Manor, like the one in the church's stained glass window, bestowed on their tenants. Should I now think that my first idea had been correct after all and that if the duchess had never talked to me of love, that was because she was more afraid of being compromised with a nephew of her aunt's friend than with an unknown lad, met by chance at the church of St. Hilaire at Combray.

Gilberte certainly had some of her mother's characteristics and it was indeed that skill that I had unconsciously counted on when I had asked her to introduce me to very young girls. After thinking about the request that I had made and wishing to keep any benefit within the family, she came back to me with a more daring suggestion than I would have expected; "If you would like it, I will go and look for my daughter so that I can introduce you to her. She is over there chattering with young Mortemart and some other unimportant young people. I sure she would be a pleasant young girl friend for you." I asked if Robert had been pleased to have a daughter. "Oh! He was very proud of her. Of course, with his tastes" she added naively, "he would have preferred a boy." This daughter, whose name and fortune could have given her mother good reason to hope she would marry royalty and crown the social climb of Swann and his wife, ended up by marrying an obscure author because she wasn't in the least snobbish and brought the family even lower than the level where it had started. Later generations wouldn't believe that the parents of this humble household had had a high social position.

Gilberte's words gave me surprise and pleasure which were rapidly replaced as soon as Mme. de Saint-Loup went into the other room by the idea of Time Past which Mlle de Saint-Loup had brought to me before I had even seen her. Like everyone else, she was like a cross roads on which roads converged from many different directions. There were many which met in Mlle de Saint-Loup from my point of view. First of all there were the two important 'Ways' where I had walked and dreamed so often; on her father, Robert de Saint-Loup's side, the 'Guermantes Way'; on her mother's side, the Méséglise way, which was 'Swann's Way'. The latter, by the young girls mother and the Champs-Elysées, led me directly to Swann, to my evenings at Combray, near to Méséglise. The former, by her father, led to my afternoons at Balbec where I saw him beside the sunlit sea. Already links were forming between these two main roads. Swann was very largely responsible for my visit to Balbec, where I had met Saint-Loup, because of what he had told me about the churches and particularly the persian one which I had so much wanted to see. On the other hand, through Robert de Saint-Loup, nephew to the Duchesse de Guermantes, I was led again at Combray to the Guermantes Way. Mlle de Saint-Loup connected me to many other parts of my life, to the 'lady in pink' who was her grandmother and whom I had seen at my great uncle's house. There was another cross link here because my great uncle's valet, who had announced me that day, and whose gift of a photograph allowed me to identify the 'lady in pink', was the uncle of a young man who not only M. de Charlus but also Mlle. de Saint-Loup's father had loved which had made her mother so unhappy. Wasn't it Mlle. de Saint-Loup's grandfather Swann who had first mentioned Vinteuil's music to me and wasn't it Gilberte who had told me about Albertine and then it was when I discussed Vinteuil's music with Albertine that I discovered her great love for a woman and began my life with her, which had led to her death and had caused me so much sorrow. It was Mlle de Saint-Loup's father who had tried to find Albertine and bring her back to me. This reminded me of my whole life in society, whether in Paris at the Swanns' or the Guermantes' salons or on the other hand at the Verdurins' house which made a link between the two Combray 'Ways', the Champs-Elysées and the beautiful terrace at La Raspelière. In order to be able to recall our friendship for those people we have known in the past, we have to be able to connect them to the places where we have spent our life. If I were to sketch Saint-Loup's life, it would involve all the places and interests of my own life, even those parts in which he was not directly involved such as with my grandmother or with Albertine. By contrast the Verdurins were linked both to Odette's past and to Robert de Saint-Loup through Charlie, and as well, the music of Vinteuil had played a most important part in what happened at their house. Life weaves between people and events a complex web of threads so that between any single point of our past and another there are so many connections that one is spoilt for choice.

Now, here at the home of Mme. Verdurin, who had become the Princesse de Guermantes, I was going to be introduced to Mlle. de Saint-Loup whom I was going to ask to be Albertine's successor; what wonderful memories I had of all the times we had together, of our trips in the little tram, to Douville to visit Mme. Verdurin, the same Mme. Verdurin who, long before my love for Albertine, had first made and then broken the love between Mlle. de Saint-Loup's grandfather and grandmother. All around us were pictures painted by Elstir who had himself introduced me to Albertine and to complete this interweaving of the threads of my past, just like Gilberte, Mme. Verdurin had married a Guermantes.

I could see Gilberte coming back to me. Her marriage to Saint-Loup and all the worries it had given me at the time, still seemed so fresh in my mind as they had indeed this very morning, that I was astonished to see beside Gilberte a young girl of about sixteen years old, whose height brought home to me just how long ago that had been, which I had been so unwilling to recognise.

Here was Mlle. de Saint-Loup in front of me; she had deep set, clear and piercing eyes. I was struck by her nose which was modelled on that of her mother and grandmother and cut off by a horizontal line at its base, beautiful but rather too short. This was so characteristic that I would have known it out of a thousand others and was filled with wonder that nature could like a great sculptor, give the daughter, like her mother, this powerful and decisive feature. This charming nose, slightly protruding like a curved beak, not like Swann's but like Saint-Loup's. The soul of that Guermantes had vanished but his charming head with the piercing eyes of a soaring bird had been placed on the shoulders of Mlle. de Saint-Loup, which roused old memories among those who had known her father. I found her truly beautiful, full of hope for the future. She was created by the years I had lost; smiling happily, she seemed like my own youth.

This idea of time that I had just constructed told me that it was time for me to make a start. It was high time, which confirmed the worry which had gripped me from the moment when I had entered the drawing room and the made up faces had given me the feeling of Lost Time; was there still enough time? Our minds have a landscape which we are only allowed to study for a little while. I had been like a painter climbing a path beside a lake hidden behind a curtain of rocks and trees, he reaches a gap, the whole view opens up in front of him and he takes up his brushes but night is already falling, he can no longer see to paint and daybreak will never come for him.

In order to carry out the work as I had just conceived it in the library, I would have to search deeply into the images which I would have to recreate in my memory. But my memory was already worn out, so I might well be worried that although I was young enough to expect to have some years ahead of me, my time might come at any minute. If I had the strength to finish my work, I knew that the circumstances, which today at this party in the Princesse de Guermantes' house had given me both the idea for the work and the fear that I might not finish it, had dictated the structure I should use, of which I had had an inkling long ago in the church at Combray, at a time which had so much effect on my life; it would be the structure of Time which is usually invisible to us. I would try to make this Time dimension obvious in my description of the world which would differ greatly from the way it is perceived through our deceiving senses.

I often asked myself not just whether I had enough time but was I in a fit state to finish my work. Illness which had obliged me like a harsh director of conscience to die to the world, had done me a good turn (like a seed which if it does not die when it is sown, will remain sterile, but if it dies, will bear a good harvest), after idleness had protected me from facility, illness would perhaps protect me against idleness; illness had sapped my physical power and, as I had noticed long ago at the time when I had ceased to love Albertine, the power of my memory. If only I still had the power of memory that I had on the evening which had been evoked when I picked up *Francois le Champi*. It was on that evening that my mother had surrendered and from which dated the slow death of my grandmother, the decline of my will and of my health. Everything was fixed from the moment when unable to wait for the morning to put my lips to my mother's face, I had summoned up my courage, jumped from my bed and had gone in my nightgown to wait in the moonlight at the window until I heard M. Swann leaving. My parents had seen him to the door, I had heard the opening gate make the bell ring and then close again. At this very moment in the Prince de Guermantes house, I heard again my parents footsteps leading M. Swann, the tinny endless clamour of the little bell ringing to tell me that M. Swann had left and that mama would be coming upstairs, I could hear it all vividly now although it was so far away in the past. As I pondered about everything that had happened between the moment when I had heard those sounds and this party at the Guermantes, I was frightened to think that that bell was still ringing within me and that I was unable to stop its clanging noise until I could remember how it stopped, in order to be able to relearn this, I had to shut my ears to the conversations of all the masks around me. In order to hear the bell better I had to descend deep into myself. So the ringing must always have been there and with it everything that had happened between then and now, all that undefined past which I had been unaware that I carried within myself. I already existed when it had rung and as I could still hear it ringing, it could never have stopped, I could never have had a moments rest, or have stopped existing, thinking or being conscious because that ancient moment was still there within me and I could still recover it, return to it even if I had to descend to my deepest levels of memory to find it. It was this concept of Time incorporated within us, of the years past being inseparable from us that I was determined to make the theme of my work.

If I was allowed enough time to finish my work. I would not fail to stamp it with the idea of Time which had come to me so strongly today and in it I would describe all men, even though it makes them seem like monsters, as occupying a much larger place in Time than the very limited one allowed them in space, a place in contrast, extended without limit, because, like giants immersed in time, they exist simultaneously in all the epochs, separated by so many days, that they have lived in.